Vengeful Flames

Vengeful Flames

Children of The Ancients

Brittany Mendes

Vengeful Flames is a nonstop adventure fantasy from numerous points of view. These elements are meant to showcase the unfortunate reality of worst-case scenario situations and are not meant to glorify any actions listed below. Reality for some can be too much for others. It should not be taken for granted or idolized. These elements include:

War crimes, graphic language, graphic sexual activities, sexual violence including rape, domestic violence, graphic violence including torture, abusive relationships, cannibalism, religious cult activity, religious sacrifices, child abuse, off page childhood sexual trauma, suicidal ideations, eating disorders, self-harm, pregnancy, PTSD, death.

Vengeful Flames

Text Copyright © 2025 by Brittany Mendes

No part of this publication may be reproduced, stored in or introduced into a retrieval system, or transmitted, in any form, or by any means, electronic, mechanical, photocopying, recording, or otherwise, without prior written permission of the copyright owner. To request permission, please contact: saharagal7@yahoo.com.

This is a work of fiction set in an alternate world than our own. Any names or characters, businesses or places, events or incidents, are fictitious and a product of this author's imagination. Any resemblance to actual persons, living or dead, or actual events is purely coincidental.

Published by Kindle Direct Publishing

ISBN: 979-8-218-72301-9 (paperback)

Library of Congress Control Number: 2025913861

Subjects: Fantasy-Medieval

Interior design, layout by Kindle Direct Publishing

Front and Rear Cover Design by;
https://www.fiverr.com/orders/FO71F535C6803/activities

Illustration design by:

Risa Waddell at Risa's Arts and Prints;
https://www.facebook.com/profile.php?id=61563781965619

Set in Garamond

Printed in the U.S.A

Acknowledgments

For my family,

Without you, I would not have made it as far as I have, I am forever grateful for your love and support, as well as your patience. You gave me a second chance at life, giving me the support system I needed to heal and grow.

For my husband,

You have always accepted me with my flaws and pushed me to go forward with my dreams. You helped teach me to have an internal strength that boosted me further than I ever thought possible. Without you, I would never have strived to go as far as I have, and for that I am forever thankful.

For the survivors,

Your trauma does not dictate who you are, keep on fighting. You are not alone even though some days might make it feel that way. Don't give up, don't ever let the bastards win.

Part One

Oich: Kingdom of the Moon God

Prologue

Across the Hollow Sea, tendrils of fog dragged themselves across the churning black water. The fishermen stood atop their rickety wooden boats, too thoroughly absorbed with their nets to see the thick mist creeping their direction. The icy cold waves beat against their boats in a consistent rhythm, the fishermen wrapped themselves up tightly against the bitter chill of the winter winds. An unnatural wall of fog swallowed up the vessels like a hungry sea creature doing its best to conceal the morning sun completely. Darkness quickly fell over the bay as the sun's rays were snuffed out, to anyone standing on the shore it looked as if night had come early. The men swore as the cold took hold, chilling them to their very bones, the fishermen all stopped with their tasks and looked at the shore as the fog overcame them. Never had the men been more thankful to be on the water, sending a prayer to those left on shore.

The dark fog billowed its way closer to the shore, devouring everything it touched as if it was starved. Children of all ages played on the shoreline, oblivious to the nightmare approaching as they chased each other through the sand. Men and women worked in the shallows, bracing against the freezing water that lapped against their knees, dutifully untangling the fish from the nets. A woman looked up at the sudden disappearance of light and cried out in warning, dropping the net she was unraveling as the fog overtook the shore.

Other women began to scream as they saw death approaching, alerting all to what was coming their way. Men and women dropped what they were doing, scooping up their children and sprinting to their homes. Chaos erupted as villagers began to see the incoming fog, abandoning their tasks and making a run for safety. Someone had begun ringing a bell in the village center, sounding the alarm for everyone to take cover. The inhabitants of the village who had managed to make it to their homes barred their doors and windows, putting out any source of light inside.

Darkness consumed the town whole, light and sound no longer present within; the town appeared to be frozen in time. Only a few poor souls remained on the streets, scrambling frantically to get to any shelter, knowing that if they didn't they were as good as dead. The village waited in terror, silently holding their breath as the mists held them captive.

Several minutes went by with nothing but eerie silence. One. Two. Three. The wind picked up and changed directions, pushing out towards the ocean instead of coming from it. Four. Five. The distant sounds of growls and teeth clicking came closer to the village. Six. Seven. Thunderous footsteps echoed between the wooden houses as the horde hunted. The energy surrounding the village braced itself, waiting for these apex predators to find their prey. Eight. Nine. Ten.

An aggregation of twisted and misshapen bodies moved lethally together en masse, carrying themselves with animal-like swiftness. The horde pushed its way through the streets as if it were of one mind, further showing how deadly the hunt for prey was. These bodies were all washed of color, their individual faces all gaunt as if they had been starved for some time. All the teeth these creatures had were elongated and sharp, perfect for shredding apart flesh. Lengthened fingers curved into what looked like talons. If you looked hard enough you could see these creatures once had human characteristics. Different heights, different skin tones, some even still wore clothes that remained mostly intact; but these were no longer people, these were something feral, more wild, more dangerous.

The horde prowled down the dirt-covered streets, spreading out like a pack of wolves scenting down prey with their snake-like noses, two inverted nostrils flaring as they sniffed the cold morning air. Moving as one, these creatures spilled into the village like high tide, they entered every available space they could get into. A sound came from inside one of the houses, a child let loose an audible cry, barely perceptible to the villagers but loud enough for the creatures to hear. All the beings stopped, then in unison they all turned to the house. The creature nearest let loose an unearthly screech. Together as one, the horde charged and began throwing their bodies against the walls, tearing into the wooden doors and windows with their claws.

The family inside screamed as the creatures climbed on top of the roof, tearing at the wooden beams. The horde threw themselves against the house until the doors and walls began to splinter and give way. A man stood on the other side of the door pushing a torch through an opening and striking the nearest creature in the face. The creature went down immediately, squealing as the fire touched its flesh, only for it to be replaced by another. The monsters squeezed their way through any opening they could find, pouring into the house like an infestation. The family inside stood no chance as the horde reached them. All that existed now was teeth, claws, and blood. The family didn't even have time to scream before their throats were ripped from their bodies.

Chapter One

Catriona

Catriona sharpened a new set of daggers as she stood by the edge of the forge as her two brothers worked. She enjoyed cold winter days like this where she could be close to the warm fire. During the summer it was miserable inside the shop. With the heat of the day, and the fire going day and night, the heat of the forge could melt practically anything. Her twin brother Clyous fed the flames as her older brother Markous hammered away at the metal. Their mother Anita was busy talking with customers asking about their newer wares. Catriona rolled her eyes as the man and woman asked to see what jewelry they had in stock, the man insisted on a sturdy but elegant ring for his wife. They dressed like they had money, as an old-blooded family they had to have something, but if they were coming here, they were not rich by any means. Clyous was the only one in the family patient enough to work the metal into intricate designs, and given enough time and compensation, he could create beautiful pieces, but he was not a jeweler. They did not have precious stones to add to rings and necklaces. His pieces, being more sturdy than flashy, meant this couple did not have a mountain of gold to spend on jewelry.

This had been their family's blacksmith shop since they were children. A large stone building with the forge right outside the front door with stands for their wares, it was arguably one of the largest houses on the human side of the capital city. They were not fancy by any means, just efficient. Although, it did not compare to the blooded side of town. The family spent most of their days working the forge or selling out of the shop stall, pouring their blood, sweat, and tears into this place. Each one of them contributed to the shop in their own way. It was their livelihood, it's what kept them above the wretched poverty of Oich. It was all they had left after their father disappeared all those years ago.

Markous hammered away on the anvil; his light brown hair cut short so it wouldn't fall in his face as he hammered. Markous was only a few years older than the twins, but he acted as if he were nearly an old man. Having to take on the role his father had left open, Markous had an interesting blend of being mature for his age combined with acting like a spoiled child. Markous ran the forge, he had taken on the tasks of the head of the family to relieve some of the pressure on their mother. He liked to think he was truly the head

11

of the family, making decisions for everyone without consulting anyone else. A fact which Catriona fought him over every step of the way. Markous was tall but sturdy, years of working the forge had made him strong. As he worked, he wore a blacksmith's apron but no shirt, his logic for the lack of modesty was that there was no point getting a shirt dirty. Catriona didn't believe that for a single moment, Markous enjoyed showing off his muscles to any women that might be walking by their shop. He considered himself a bit of a ladies' man, Catriona considered him insufferable.

Clyous helped his older brother by rotating the metal between strikes. More modest than either of his siblings, Clyous wore a tunic underneath his blacksmith's apron. He was not as obsessed with himself as Markous was. Clyous enjoyed talking with customers as much as his mother did and loved nothing more than to learn from others, to hear about the goings-on of the capital. He would talk merchants' ears off if they let him. Clyous's personable nature was why the family put him in charge of purchasing and trades. If anyone was going to talk any of these rich, blooded merchants down in price, it would be him. Markous and Catriona had a habit of picking fights with the blooded merchants because they spoke to and treated them as slaves. Clyous had saved them both from beatings so often in the past that their mother had forbidden them from continuing to try and do business with others at all. That was when she appointed Clyous to his new position.

Clyous's face was remarkably similar to his twin's, with the exception of the beard he was growing on his handsome face. Where he looked very obviously a man, and she a woman, their faces very obviously mirrored each other. His dirty blonde hair fell just above his ears. They shared similar coloring, their skin tone identical, but Clyous had baby blue eyes that were always watching and evaluating what was going on around him. In truth, Clyous was more the ladies' man than Markous, the girls practically melted where they stood whenever her twin flashed them a smile. Any woman Clyous set his eyes on stood no chance; Catriona almost pitied them. To his credit, her twin did not appear to be like many men in that regard. He had had his lovers, that was certain, but he did not chase skirts the way their brother did. He cared more about the woman herself, whoever she might be at the time, Catriona constantly teased him for being a romantic.

Catriona, on the other hand, did not enjoy the company of others, the men of the city especially. She was not good at talking to customers and had no friends outside of her family. She simply did not care to. Her brothers and mother had given up trying to get Catriona out long enough to forge friendships years ago. Catriona had been involved in more street brawls than both of her brothers combined. Because of this, Markous had deemed her destined for spinsterhood early on and thankfully had not pushed the issue. Catriona was grateful for this fact, as most women her age had been married off already and were having children. Her mother, on the other hand, tried for years to temper her, wanting nothing more than for Catriona to find companionship with someone other than their family. Catriona flat out refused, she preferred to stay within the safety of their home rather than visit the taverns. She had seen the type of men who frequented those drinking halls, Markous being one of them. If she wanted companionship, she wanted something more than what those men had to offer, assuming there was anyone who could handle her temper. Catriona knew the issue wasn't with how she looked. She knew she was beautiful; many men had attempted to approach her before. However, Catriona wasn't like other women, she didn't wear dresses, she wore breeches.

Women didn't fight in Oich, it was forbidden, considered the ultimate act of defiance, but that didn't stop Catriona from training. Women were meant for two very distinct things in the eyes of society here, marriage and breeding. Although their mother raised her sons to be different in their thinking, their father had instilled in her that she needed to protect herself from men. Once he had disappeared from their lives, most likely killed by Oich guards on the way home from the merchant shops, she found comfort in keeping up with their old training routine. Her brothers hadn't stuck to the regimen, finding it unnecessary. Of course they would, they were men, they didn't have to worry about the same things she did. She had seen the women of the city who weren't so lucky.

Catriona had smaller features than her brothers, but not by much. She was as tall as they were, but maybe an inch shorter than Markous and less muscular. She did not spend hours a day beating on an anvil, although she could. Her physique was slender and feminine, she did have some curves, but her defining feature was her hair. It was so blonde it appeared almost white. Unbraided, her hair fell just past her hips, but she regularly wore it in a single braid tied at the end with leather twine. Unlike Clyous's baby blue, her eyes were steel grey. Where Markous looked more like their mother, Catriona and Clyous took on their father's likeness. Catriona was the only child that shared their father's hair color and his temper, according to their mother. This had always given Catriona a sense of pride.

The Kingdom of Oich was the southernmost kingdom in Stone Basin. It mostly consisted of farmlands and fishing harbors. The Kingdom of Gaelach, right above them was mostly wild forests. Airgid, above Gaelach was known for being the kingdom of minerals and gemstones. Oich was the main source of food for Stone Basin, making their kingdom overall better fed than the others. Airgid was a kingdom of riches and luxury but they had little to no natural resources to pull from the land to feed their people. Most of the steel and ore they purchased for their shop had been imported from Airgid, a costly endeavor lately. The prices of imported goods had gone up due to constant raids occurring on the road. Some up-and-coming rebellion had decided to terrorize the blooded.

"You're staring at those daggers like you're going to stick them in someone's back," Markous called, dipping his freshly hammered sword into the bucket of water beside his anvil.

"Maybe it's you." Clyous laughed at their brother before he took a swig from his waterskin.

Catriona smirked at them as their mother said goodbye to a customer and walked in their direction, undoubtedly sensing her children were up to no good.

"You're unusually quiet today, Cat," Anita said, eying her daughter suspiciously.

"Are you really upset about that?" Markous teased.

"I'm not," Clyous teased her.

"Are you two really starting this early?" Catriona looked up from her daggers, eyes blazing their direction.

"I'm always starting." Markous smiled back, promising to match her energy if she chose to act.

"Not with customers!" Anita hissed, turning to wave at the couple leaving with one of Clyous's forged rings.

"It's been a while since you and I have thrown down, little sister." Markous puffed out his chest playfully. "Think you can handle it?"

"Can you?" Catriona finally cracked a smile, sizing her brother up. "Last time I wiped the floor with you, and that was at least a year ago."

"Only because I let you." Markous turned a slight shade of pink.

"She beat the shit out of you." Clyous laughed.

"She did not," Markous argued, his voice defensive.

"Maybe if you actually trained with me you could keep up." Catriona couldn't help but push his buttons, it was the sisterly thing to do after all.

"Enough!" Anita hissed again, attempting desperately to rein her adult children in. "Really now?! A woman of twenty-two years should not be picking fights with her brothers. It is unbecoming and shows a lack of maturity. And shame on you, Markous, for goading her that way. She did win last time."

Clyous snickered as Markous had the decency to look embarrassed at his mother's berating. Catriona laughed too, Markous needed that ego checked occasionally, and their mother was the absolute best at it. Markous shoved Clyous playfully as they all laughed together.

Their mother glanced up to the sky, narrowing her eyes at the clouds. "I sense a shift. Best be on our guard."

Their mother had this habit of being able to guess events before they happened. They had joked with her for years that she possessed some sort of magical ability to see the future considering she was right most of the time. Anita waved off their jokes, calling it a mother's intuition. Catriona thought it could be something more, especially after the winter she had somehow predicted the forge would catch fire. If they hadn't been prepared, they could have lost everything to the flames. Ever since then, Catriona paid attention to their mother's vague predictions, she knew Clyous did too. Markous remained frustratingly naive to them, of course. As a whole, the family kept their jokes about it quiet though. Magic was a dangerous thing, anyone in Oich caught using magic was killed, even the rumor of possessing magic could get someone a death sentence.

Off in the distance, about a quarter of a mile away at the fishing village, they could hear the alarm bell ring. Everyone in the busy street stopped what they were doing to look towards the shoreline, confusion taking over. Catriona rushed to their stone house, quickly climbing up the side to get to the roof. They were on the southern edge of the capital city, but still some way in from the shore. Atop the roof, Catriona could see a wall of dark fog moving their direction at a rapid pace, it had already consumed most of the harbor and the village. From her vantage point she could hear screams echoing in the distance. Fear struck her, this could only mean one thing.

"Scourge!" Catriona bellowed down to individuals walking on nearby streets. "Take shelter!"

There was rapid movement, people began running around seeking shelter. Humans and blooded alike fled from the oncoming scourge. Catriona scrambled down off the roof, sheathing the daggers she had been polishing inside her boots and running to her mother, escorting her inside their house. Clyous and Markous were right behind them, barricading the heavy wooden door with iron rods their father had forged some years ago. The rods slid through the doorframe into the stone securing them in. It would be a matter of minutes now before they were overrun with those creatures, and Catriona doubted the capital guards would come to aid them. This part of town was mostly human after all, they were far enough away from the blooded side of the city to not matter. It was true that there were a few lower class blooded in the streets, but their abilities would get them back to their side before the slaughter started. Gods knew none of them would extend a hand to help any of the humans.

Catriona and her mother went to work on the windows, securing the wooden shutters and locking them to a set of iron bars. There were several that they needed to secure before the scourge hit their street. Catriona dashed to the final window; she reached through the iron bars to pull the last of the wooden shutters closed. As she did, she glanced outside and watched as the mist came over their house like a blanket of night.

Catriona quickly pulled the shutters into place and quietly backed away from the iron bars. She palmed one of the daggers, taking it from her boot and looking at her two brothers standing by the door. They too held weapons in their hands, preparing for a breach. Catriona watched their mother who stood frozen in fear near the barred window. Silence and shelter were their best chance of survival from the scourge. As long as the creatures didn't figure out that they were hiding inside the house, they would just pass by. These monsters rarely ventured this far into the city. Scourge were creatures of the night, these once human now grotesque monsters walked the earth with a nearly immortal lifespan to hunt and infect others with their blight. Catriona had heard that it is possible to kill scourge, but they were as tough skinned as blooded were. If you could get them into the light, it weakened them greatly, otherwise they were predators with no memories from their previous lives. They worked in packs, typically of three to ten. It was exceedingly rare for there to be more scourge than that working in unison. This fog provided them with the darkness they needed to penetrate the city and hunt new prey. Something about the fog itself seemed unnatural, magical even. No wonder the crown made a point of executing those who held magic. Controlling the fog to use creatures like this, now that was power.

Catriona took deep silent breaths in an attempt to calm her racing heart. She could hear the scourge, the sounds of sniffing and bare feet and hands of the scourge slapping against the dirt. The clicking sounds that the monsters used to hunt with each other became audible, meaning they were searching out prey. Catriona's pulse quickened at the scraping sound that suddenly came from their front door. Catriona could picture their long claws scraping against the wood as they passed, she willed her thunderous heart to quiet. She watched her brothers raise their weapons at the noise; she could tell they felt the same way she did. After a moment, the scraping stopped, signaling that the creature had moved on. Everyone in the house visibly released a silent breath of relief.

Screams echoed off in the distance, followed by the unnatural shriek in unison of the scourge. The sounds of the creatures around their home changed from searching for prey, to chasing down a helpless victim. They could hear bodies bouncing off the walls outside their home as the scourge were falling over each other to join the hunt. They had passed on, thank the gods.

Catriona glanced at her mother who let out an audible sigh. All at once her children turned to look at her in horror just as the wooden shutters exploded inward. Two mangled arms reached through the shattered wood grabbing their mother and pulling her against the iron bars. Anita screamed as the claws dug into her flesh. Catriona was in motion, sprinting across the room while simultaneously throwing a dagger in the direction of the attacking scourge. Catriona watched the dagger sink itself into the black eye of what looked to be a former young woman, knocking the creature backwards and forcing it to release her mother.

Catriona whipped her other arm forward again as she continued to advance toward the window, freeing a second dagger from her hand with equal deadly accuracy. For a second time her aim proved true, lodging the steel dagger into the monster's second eye, killing it as it fell back. She may have killed one, but Catriona knew now that the rest of the horde knew they were in there. Catriona pulled their mother into the center of the home, choking back her panic at the sight of blood on their mother's forearm. Oh gods, she'd been bitten.

"Back-to-back!" Markous yelled, taking a fighting stance next to Catriona. His face paled at the sight of their mother's injury, but he said nothing.

"Here!" Clyous handed Catriona a short sword.

The siblings stood with their backs to each other, weapons raised, and with their mother tucked away in the center of them. Catriona could feel the horde hit the walls of their home, shaking the structure as if there was an earthquake. She could hear their claws scraping against the stone.

They made it in, the first body threw itself through the splintered window, cutting through the iron bars with its claws and crawling its pale flesh and gnashing its teeth in their direction. The lower half of its body was still hanging out of the window into the street, back legs pushed the creature forward through the window. Before any of them could react, the creature was ripped backwards onto the street. Howling began to echo throughout the village; the unsettling noises of the scourge were drowned out by a new predator.

Through the broken window Catriona could see a flash of fur and teeth tearing through the line of scourge surrounding their home. The wolves had come! Another flash of fur, this time black, came streaking by their door. Then another, this one was red brown. The blooded wolves had arrived to take care of the invading predator. Catriona was genuinely surprised, if not relieved, to see them, believing that the royal guards wouldn't have bothered.

With chaos erupting out in the streets and no imminent threat coming for them, the siblings turned to their mother to visually examine her as she stood there clutching her arm. Blood trickled down her forearm where the scourge had sunk its teeth into her flesh. The wound wasn't deep, but the fact that it had punctured her skin meant the poisonous curse of the scourge was now in her bloodstream.

"Show me!" Catriona demanded, gently taking hold of their mother's trembling hand.

"So stupid of me," she muttered.

Catriona shared a look with her brothers, fear for their mother's life shining in all their eyes. The wound itself was not life threatening. If it were made by an animal or a knife it probably wouldn't even leave a scar, but a wound made by a scourge meant death. Death by turning into one themselves, losing their humanity, or being discovered by a blooded and then purged which was a nasty form of execution by fire that the crown believed could completely kill the scourge.

"We will hide it," Catriona said as convincingly as she could, moving across the room to rummage through a drawer for bandages. "We'll sneak her to a healer, maybe they can—"

"They can't!" she protested. "I will turn."

"No!" Catriona argued, this wasn't one of her visions, it couldn't be.

Clyous argued too, not wanting to lose their mother without a fight. "There is a healer here, one with the gift. She would be willing to help. There is a chance—"

18

"Don't be foolish!" his mother snapped, choking back tears. "If you are caught hiding me, they will burn you too!"

"We won't be caught," Markous cut in, handing a clean dress to their mother. "Let Catriona wrap it and change. We're going to find this healer as soon as you do."

The siblings shared a look; the decision had been made. They would risk it all, including their very lives, in order to try and save their mother. She was worth it to them, but if they were caught by the royal guards, they would all die, the risk of turning after being injured by a scourge was too great. Hiding something like this was a capital offense. Citizens were expected to turn their loved ones over immediately. Catriona had watched dozens of people burn for it. She had always hated the royal family for not trying harder to save those who were going to change, the true victims. There had to be enough magic left in the world, a healer out there somewhere who had figured out how to save people from changing regardless of it being outlawed.

But no, humans were just slaves to them. They were able to be used and discarded by any and all blooded on a whim, Catriona's mind raced as she finished bandaging her mother's wound. They were truthfully no better than animals. Her family stood there for a moment, sharing a look with each other that no single emotion could even begin to explain. Clyous was the first to move, making it to the front door and unlocking it, their choice now in motion. There were no sounds of scourge in the streets, no wolves and no more screams. Catriona could hear people starting to move around outside as if everything had gone back to normal. No doubt, they were inspecting the carnage. Now was the time to move, before any of the royal guards noticed the damage to their home and came looking.

Clyous opened the door the rest of the way, and as one unit with their mother again tucked between them, they took to the streets. It had begun to rain as they stepped out into the city, the cold rain washed away the still-warm carnage. Catriona held her mother's arm in the crook of her own, putting on a face she hoped to made it look like she was comforting her 'frightened' mother. Other villagers were wandering the streets in shock, while others began to clean up around the damaged buildings. The dirt streets quickly turned to mud, mixing with blood from the scourge's most recent victims.

They continued to walk towards the city square where a lot of the merchant shops and stores were located. Not many humans ventured this far into the city unless they were required to for work. Mostly, the blooded lived here or owned shops. Humans owning anything was a rare enough feat of its own, reminding Catriona that her family was at least lucky in that regard. She glanced up at the houses and shops as they went, they were definitely on the fancier side of the city now. The houses had changed from wooden one-bedroom hovels to multi-story rock homes. Even the streets changed from dirt to cobblestone, eliminating a lot of the mess. The blooded of Oich lived a comfortable and safe life, there was no doubt in Catriona's mind that the new-blooded royal guard had come just in time to eliminate the scourge before they made it to the blooded side of town. It was very possible that the blooded wouldn't have risked themselves if the scourge stayed in the poor district, what's a few more dead humans to them. Then again, if all of them had turned, Oich and the royal family wouldn't have stood a chance against that many uncontrollable scourge.

"You, over there—" a new-blooded guard stood on top of an overturned wagon, pointing at a group of humans, "Drag the bodies to the square and pile them up for burning," he commanded.

Catriona aided her mother in stepping over what remained of a small group of scourge. Limbs and torsos littered the muddy road, leaving pools of black blood to soak into the ground. Catriona swallowed hard at the gore, the carnage that even the new-blooded guards could leave behind was unfathomable. It proved to her just how low on the food chain humans were, and why they were so easily turned into slaves.

They continued walking, passing more human slaves and blooded guards working to collect and pile dead bodies up for burning. One particularly foul-tempered blooded had taken to beating a slave because he was not moving fast enough collecting body parts. Markous quickly ushered his family past the guard as he took a cane to the young man's back. Anger flared inside Catriona's heart, oh how she wanted to step in and stop it. She wanted to take the guard on herself and make him pay for how he treated her people. However, she knew better than to act, she might train regularly, but she wasn't willing to risk her family. The likelihood of her winning against one blooded was low, but they never fought alone. Blooded moved in packs, it wouldn't be long before more guards came to help him.

There had been no carnage for several minutes now, no more piles of bodies to be burned. The cold winter rain would make it hard for a fire, but they would at least be collected and taken to the edge of town where they would be covered in sap and fire powder to burn. The humans that lived on the other side of the city, their side, wore basic clothing like simple tunics and pants or skirts, nothing flashy and nothing fancy. Most humans hardly had any money to purchase jewelry or clothing with any designs. You might see a human with a tartan skirt or hood but that was as fancy as they got.

The blooded side of town was vibrant with colors and designs. Women walked around with colored dresses and scarves; jewelry was quite common. Still, nothing the blooded wore was made of the precious metal silver. Silver contained a magic that nullified the power of the blooded, making them easier to hurt and sometimes preventing their shift. Even as blacksmiths who occasionally dabbled in metalworking for jewelry, it was outlawed for anyone to work with silver.

The blooded elite walked around the streets talking to each other, laughing and joking. They checked out shops and bought things they wanted, not just things to survive. They were completely oblivious to what had happened on the edge of the city, wandering around without a care in the world. To them, they were never in any danger, Catriona had to remind herself. These finely dressed, posh-looking upper-class citizens were arguably more dangerous than scourge.

"Remember we're here for trade," Clyous said in an exhale, smiling at a couple of blooded women passing by.

"We need more ore and tools," Markous confirmed, playing along.

Even though they were technically unblooded, Catriona and her family were not poor by any means. Their family was well known as operating one of the better blacksmithing forges. Each one of them had their own niche. Markous was great with swords and axes, Clyous was excellent at the finer details and focused on accent pieces and jewelry, while Catriona's talent was honing a blade. Clyous knew this part of town better due to his talent of striking deals, but each one of them spent plenty of time arguing with merchants over the prices of one thing or another.

Clyous led them past the shops and towards one of the back alleys leading behind the shops. Now that the family had escaped the unbothered gaze of the elite townsfolk, their pace quickened, they knew their time was running out. Catriona pulled their mother along behind her down the narrow pathway, Clyous taking the lead, and Markous at their backs. They moved as a unit, they always had, it's how their father had trained them. Before their father had disappeared, he had made sure his children knew how to fight and how to protect each other. This was like slipping back into a good habit, like they had never stopped.

Finally, Clyous began to slow, coming up to the back entrance of a two-story home, it was very luxurious in design. Whichever blooded lived here was richer than most. Clyous shared a look with his siblings before knocking against the polished wood. About a minute passed before they heard soft footsteps, then the door opened. Standing in the doorway stood a

21

beautiful woman with striking emerald-green eyes and fiery red hair. She was beautiful, Catriona thought, as she spotted the freckles that covered her pale cheeks. Catriona watched her twin take a step back, smiling at this blooded woman. Now she knew exactly how he had learned about this healer.

"Hello," the woman greeted them warmly, observing the family as they stood in the alley.

"Bridget," Clyous greeted, "we need your help."

Bridget nodded in understanding, stepping back and allowing them to enter. "I can smell the wound, come in."

Catriona pulled their mother inside, walking past the beautiful female. Bridget's red hair cascaded down to her hips in ringlets. She wore an elegant forest-green gown with gold stitching on the hem. Red and gold gemstones were set in the delicate embroidery of her collar. She was extremely rich, Catriona looked at the woman's attire enviously. She might not wear dresses but that didn't mean she couldn't admire them. The woman had a kind face; compassion was shining through her deep-green eyes. A trait that was severely lacking in most blooded.

The group entered a large room with many glass windows. Glass, especially this colored glass, was exceedingly rare and expensive. Luckily, the windows had curtains to help conceal their presence while still letting in natural light. Bridget was the last to enter the room, shutting the door behind her.

"Let me see." Bridget made her way over to their mother carrying a bowl of medical supplies.

To her credit, without grimacing, Anita rolled up the sleeve of her dress to show the already soaked through bandages. The blood, where it should have been a dark red, was black and had an odor of rot due to infection from the scourge. Catriona watched as Bridget began to unwrap the bandages, her hands were gentle but sure of their movements. Her kind words comforted their mother as she worked.

"A scourge did this." Bridget finished unwrapping the bandages, walking them over to the fireplace and feeding the flames with them. "How long ago?"

"About an hour," Catriona answered, still watching the healer like a hawk. She might seem kind, but Catriona was not a trusting person.

There was no point in lying to this woman. Not only could she smell the rot better than they could, but why else would four humans be sneaking around on the blooded side of the city looking for a healer. By now, Bridget would be just as guilty as the rest of them for not having killed them when they first knocked on her door. Now the woman was even providing medical treatment to their mother to protect her from meeting a terrible fate.

"You are aware that there is no known cure." Bridget looked around at them sympathetically. "I can't guarantee that there's anything I can do to stop the change. At the very least, I can clean it up and help with the pain."

"But you can try?" Clyous pleaded, "Please."

Bridget's eyes grew sad as she looked at him, but she nodded just the same.

"Thank you," Catriona choked out, holding back tears.

Bridget went to a nearby table and started mixing herbs in a bowl. Markous stationed himself by the door as Catriona and Clyous stood by with their mother, trying to comfort her the best they could. Bridget continued to work, mixing her ingredients together. Before applying the medicine, Bridget placed her hands on their mother's wounded flesh. Catriona gasped when a golden light emanated from Bridget's palms, radiating a sunlight-like aura. Catriona had never seen anything like it. It was no wonder then why Bridget was risking herself helping a bunch of humans. If the royal family knew one of their blooded possessed magic, Bridget's life would be over.

Chapter Two

Danny

Danny slowed as he neared the top of the hill, carefully picking his footing so that the thick mud covering the ground didn't force him to slide back down. He closed his eyes and breathed in deeply, savoring the smell of the fresh, rain-covered forest. He swore he could smell the ocean from here; they weren't that far from the shore. Danny missed the ocean more than anything. Having spent the last few years of his life moving around Oich to avoid the royal guards, he didn't have a lot of time to come back and visit. Truthfully, the fishing village he was born in was in the other direction, and he had no desire to return there anytime soon, it was the ocean he missed. The salty air, the constant breeze, the water. Danny missed being out on the water and swimming in it. He never felt more at peace than when he was in or on the water. Danny's brothers always joked that he must be the offspring of the ancient and elusive race of sirens with how much he obsessed over being around the sea. But Danny was able to prove that he could not in fact breathe underwater and he could not sing for shit. Yet, he never denied his love for the sea. Being restricted to caves and forests burdened his soul, but he knew it was for a good cause.

The two men he traveled with came to stand beside him, having finally made it up the sloppy, mud-covered hill. Rama and Menolayous took a second to catch their breaths, not being as fast as he was. Danny glanced at his two adopted brothers with a smirk, he may not be as large and strong as Rama or as deadly with a blade as Menolayous, but he was better built for long and strenuous stretches of movement. A fact which he was delighted to point out to them whenever the opportunity arose.

"Finally made it, I see," Danny chided, glancing at the incredibly large man beside him. "Is your big-ass heart able to handle a small enough hill without exploding?"

Rama's laughter filled the air around them. "One of these days, little brother, I am going to enjoy watching someone run you into the ground."

"That's unlikely." Danny winked at him. "You'd think with those long-ass legs of yours, and all that muscle, that you'd be able to take bigger steps."

24

"He weighs too much; the mud had him slipping the whole way up." Menolayous fought back a smile as Rama turned to him threateningly.

"Fuck both of you." Rama extended his middle fingers at the two of them.

"At least it's stopped raining," Danny teased them. "Wouldn't want you two melting."

"*We're* not part fish." Rama straightened up, adjusting his cloak. "And it's the end of fucking winter. The rain is freezing. It's not conducive to anyone's health to stay out in weather like this."

"Actually, the rain would help us move about in the city more discreetly," Menolayous chimed in, evaluating the city walls they could just barely make out in the dark.

"Why do we have to sneak?" Rama countered. "We can just walk in. Humans are common there; all we have to say is that we're traveling with a trading wagon."

"What trading wagon?" Danny mused. "We've sacked the last few trying to return to the city."

"Pick one," Rama said, getting frustrated. "Let's just get out of this weather and get what we came here for."

"Which is?" Danny asked sarcastically.

"Supplies," Menolayous answered, still staring towards the city. "Recruits."

"A hot meal and some ale wouldn't be unwelcome either." Rama began walking to the main road. "Again, it's not like we must do a lot to blend in. We're bound to hear the local goings-on at one of the taverns."

"If we go to a tavern, you're going to get tore up drunk and start a fight, and Danny is going to start chasing skirts." Menolayous caught up to him. "We don't want to draw unwanted attention. At least until we're on our way out."

"Why do you assume I'm going to start the fight?" Rama asked, stepping around a puddle.

"And that I'm going to be chasing women around?" Danny asked, mocking that he had taken offense.

"Because that's what always happens with you two." Menolayous rolled his eyes at them.

"Nu-uh," Rama disagreed, "last time Danny started the tavern fight."

"Because he got caught sleeping with another man's wife," Menolayous countered.

"In my defense I didn't know she was married," Danny attempted to defend himself, but he couldn't hold back his smile. "No husband in their right mind would allow their young and beautiful wife to bar wench in his tavern. I'm the real victim here."

"Right." Menolayous veered to the left to avoid tripping on a branch.

Danny, however, couldn't see in the dark as well as his brother and did in fact trip over that same branch. "Shit!"

Menolayous snickered. The three of them continued walking towards the city's main gate. It was about a mile away. Walking around in rain-soaked fields and forests at night could be a dangerous endeavor, but once they reached the road, they were spared from encountering any more naturally formed obstacles.

As the three brothers neared the front gate, it was obvious something was wrong. Danny watched as Menolayous pulled his cloak closer around him to conceal the twin battle axes he wore at his waist. Danny did the same, thankfully he had the forethought to leave his longsword behind and instead opted for two short swords for better concealment. Rama had left all his weapons behind, not a fan of fighting with anything but his coveted battle axe. The three men kept their heads down as they passed through the gate, which was surprisingly unguarded. The black and red Oich banner stood guard over the gate like a sentinel, the longsword with a crescent moon at the hilt glared down at them with a promise. But no guards stood by it, nobody was guarding the gate except for that ominous banner. That was warning sign number one. Warning sign number two was the fact that there was so much movement on the streets at this late of an hour. Danny glanced up at the night sky, finding the moon almost at the center of it. It was nearly midnight and there were humans and blooded alike moving around as if it was the middle of the day.

It did not take long for Danny to figure out why there were so many of them awake. Just inside the gate were three large piles of bodies stacked on top of each other unceremoniously. Upon further inspection, Danny noticed that the bodies were a mix of everyday Oich citizens and what looked like scourge. By the gods, there were a lot of bodies and body parts in those piles. One of them was nearly as tall as Rama who was well over six feet tall. The brothers kept moving but continued to watch as the blooded guards ordered a group of human slaves to stack the piles up even higher. Horse drawn carts were still being brought in carrying even more dead.

"What the fuck happened here?" Rama whispered to them as they moved off to the side and out of the way of an oncoming horse.

"Looks like a scourge horde," Menolayous said, examining the situation with his sharp eyes. "I see dozens of scourge bodies mixed in with their victims."

"Scourge don't move in groups that large," Danny countered, his eyes fixed on a blooded guard who had just struck one of the humans for tripping and dropping a body.

"Apparently they did, and sometime recently at that." Menolayous's eyes also fixed on the beating that was occurring before them, anger flaring at the sight of the older man's mistreatment. "These men are exhausted. They must have been going at this for hours. My guess is the scourge attacked sometime earlier in the day."

"But scourge don't attack during the day." Rama tightened his fist in anger as the old man was finally allowed to return to his duties.

"No, they don't," Menolayous agreed. "Something strange happened to allow this."

After another moment of observing the slow progression of work happening before them, the three brothers did their best to blend into the shadows, avoiding catching the eye of any of the blooded guards. Watching the mistreatment of these humans angered them all. These men were exhausted and overworked. They had obviously just survived some sort of scourge attack hours ago and most likely lost a family member or friend to the beasts. There was no compassion in the guards' eyes, no caring. They would push their workers until they collapsed, Danny had seen it before. The guards of Oich were ruthless and cruel. Danny understood the need to burn the bodies, being bit by a scourge was a guaranteed way of becoming one of them, the curse did not differentiate between blooded or human. Burning the bodies was the only guaranteed way to make sure they would not rise again to feast on the living.

"Fuck it," Rama said, removing his cloak from his back and storing it in the alleyway beside them.

"What are you doing?" Danny asked, glancing around. "There are too many guards for us to fight."

27

"No shit." Rama finished securing his traveling pack on top of the cloak. "They need help. They're exhausted."

"We're not going to find recruits among these men." Menolayous observed them, also starting to remove his cloak and weapons. "There's no fight in them."

"It's not always about recruits." Rama glared at his brother. "I can't stop the guards from beating them, but if I can help them get the work done faster it will spare them from collapsing in exhaustion."

Danny saw the wisdom in his eldest brother's words and began shrugging off his weapons and cloak as well. The three of them jumped in to help two men unload a cart. Danny and Menolayous grabbed the corpse of a scourge, dragging it from the top of the pile down to the muddy street. Danny looked at it, repulsed, its clammy white skin felt almost slimy to the touch. Together they were able to drag it to the nearest pile and toss the creature into the mix.

"I hate these things." Menolayous scrunched his nose at the next corpse they began to drag. "Reminds me of running into their hives as a child."

"Hives?" Danny asked, surprised to hear Menolayous mention anything about his childhood.

"Yeah, that's what we called them." Menolayous huffed as they swung the dead weight up onto another pile, this time the body landing about halfway up. "They sleep in groups underground, almost like a beehive with how they're stacked on top of each other. If you're not careful moving through one of the cave systems, you'll end up walking in on one of these hives. If one of them wakes up they all wake up."

Danny stared at him incredulously. "Cave systems?"

Menolayous froze for a moment, realizing he had just opened himself up without knowing that he had done it. Danny loved his adopted brothers more than anything, they'd been together for nearly ten years now. During that time, they had grown up together, learned to fight, started a rebellion, you know the usual things lost boys did. They had grown to know each other very well, having been through a tremendous amount together, but a lot about the middle brother remains a mystery to them. Menolayous rarely shared anything about his time before he met them that day in the forest. At times he even flat out refused to speak regardless of how hard Danny or Rama pushed. Their brother was quiet and calculating, he never drank or chased women, and he was a damn fine warrior. He hated being around people he did not know, especially in large groups. Above all else, he absolutely hated being touched. He was the exact opposite of Danny and Rama, and they respected that, but it was times like this that reminded Danny just how closed off their brother was.

"Thanks for the help," a young man about their age said as he came towards them carrying body parts from a shredded scourge in his arms. "You're not from around here I see."

"What gave it away?" Rama asked as he picked up a corpse easily without assistance.

"Besides the fact that you're a giant?" the exhausted man said, looking up at him. "You look like you haven't been collecting dead bodies all day. Which means you must have just got to town."

"We did," Danny said pleasantly enough, Menolayous had gone silent. "What happened here?"

"About mid-morning the city was overtaken by a very large and dark fog bank. It blotted out the sun. Next thing we knew, alarm bells were going off and people were screaming. Then the horde of scourge invaded."

"Fog?" Rama asked, looking at his brothers. "That doesn't sound right."

"Not thick enough to black out the sun and cover a whole city." Danny stared back.

"We've been listening to guards talking, they think it's someone with magic in the city striking back at them for hunting down those with the gift," the man suggested, traces of excitement breaking through the exhaustion in his voice.

"That's rather unlikely," Rama was thinking out loud now. "Someone with that much magic would be openly hunted by the crown."

"Maybe the rebels have a witch at their disposal," the man suggested, thinking he was being helpful.

The three brothers shared a look before Danny said, "the rebels would never endanger the lives of the innocent."

Before the man could ask any more questions, Rama jumped in to change the subject. "Listen friend, we're here to trade. Are there any local merchants willing to do business with human traders?"

The man thought about it for a second. "You might find a few shops at the city center who will trade with you, but they will jack up the prices. I believe there is a blacksmithing shop close to the southern wall. It's run by a human family; they would happily do business with you."

"Humans running their own shop?" Danny asked, surprised. In Oich that wasn't a common occurrence.

"Yeah, it's run by a family. One of the best smitheries in the entire city. The eldest brother Markous runs it while his brother and sister help. You won't find sturdier steel for a better price around here. Be careful though, Markous has no patience, you'll want to talk to the younger brother if you want to bargain with them."

"If we want to bargain, maybe we should send Danny to bargain with the sister." Rama laughed.

The man stared at him like he'd never seen him before. "Only if you have a death wish."

"Overprotective brothers then?" Danny mused, seeing the possibility of a challenge.

"No." The man shook his head. "She's fucking crazy. She's more likely to cut your throat than listen to you mince words with her."

Ramas's laughter boomed while he glanced down at Danny. "I like the sound of this family already."

"It's your hide," the man said, getting back to work. "I'd rather work the rest of the night with these guards than try to go talk to them."

The three brothers watched as the man disappeared into the crowd, the remaining slaves were finishing up emptying the carts of bodies. One of the guards began to pour fire powder and sap over each pile while another followed up behind him with a torch. The flames ignited immediately, moving quickly over the bodies and engulfing the stack completely with the flames. After a minute or so, Danny could smell the rotten flesh begin to burn, he gagged and stepped back from them. Scourge could smell so nasty when they burned.

"What do you guys think about checking out the smithery in the morning?" Menolayous asked, eyes focused on the fire.

"Worth a shot." Rama too was focused on the burning. "If they're as volatile as they sound, they could be interested in supplying us in the future. They might even be willing to fight with us."

The sound of cries and begging broke through the crackling of the flames. The brothers turned to look, a dozen blooded guards or so were marching down one of the side streets. They were dragging, male and female slaves behind them. Danny made to move forward but Rama shot an arm out to stop him. There were far too many of them to fight, if any of them tried to save those people they would all be dead. So, they were forced to watch as the people were dragged towards the flames. Danny observed that each of these humans was injured in some way or another. The flames helped illuminate what looked like bite marks on their arms and legs, one man even had a chunk of his cheek missing. These people were infected by scourge, he realized. Even if they were able to save them from the guards, they could not save them from turning.

Danny watched in horror as a blooded guard lifted a screaming woman up and tossed her into the flames. The shackles she wore weighed her down into the pile, preventing any chance of escape. Danny watched as the flames overtook her, devouring her body whole. The rest of the infected were dealt with in a similarly gruesome fashion. Their screams for help echoed off the walls, drowning out the roaring of the fire. Tossing them straight into the fire was cruel. If the guards wanted to be merciful, they could have given them a quick death. All the guards did was laugh.

Chapter Three

Bridget

Bridget hummed to herself softly as she dressed for the day. She picked out a relatively plain ensemble, humbled by the girl's envious stare and plain clothing from the day before. Bridget tended to forget how unfortunate others were and silently chastised herself for her expensive attire. The human family she had helped yesterday, Clyous's family, had left before sundown to return to their side of the city. She had done all she could for their mother, cleaning and dressing the wound, she had risked using her magic to clean out the curse of the scourge. She hoped her magic would treat it as an infection.

Her magic seemed to be limited to healing infections, a helpful trait but an inconvenience for someone who had dedicated their life to being a healer. If she could do more, like heal wounds or cure diseases, then she could be even more helpful to others. Truth be told, Bridget was not positive that her magic would prevent the poor woman from changing into a scourge, but when they left, she could no longer smell the rot that came from the monsters. She had high hopes that she had saved the woman, which would mean she had found a cure for something that has plagued Stone Basin for the better part of a century. If there was a cure, they would no longer have to burn those who had been bitten. She could *actually* save people. There was only one way to know for sure, Bridget practically skipped down the stairs and aimed for the front door.

Bridget stepped onto the cobblestone street, pulling her tartan blue shawl over her head like a hood. She made her way to the city marketplace, intending to work her way towards the human side to check in on Clyous and his family at their shop. She was curious to see how their mother was doing. Truthfully, seeing Clyous again was a good enough reason as any to put a smile on her face. The very thought of seeing Clyous again made her smile. She had first met Clyous when he had come into the blooded side of Oich, he had been purchasing supplies for his family's shop. He was brave for a human; he approached her first and introduced himself. She had bumped into him several more times in the last several weeks, each and every time he seemed to seek her out for conversation. She believed this to be intentional on his part and not as coincidental as he played it off. It was very brazen for a human to pursue a blooded woman, let alone one of noble birth, but it was a nice change considering her lack of suitors in general.

Bridget passed a small pack of blooded children running past, they were passing back and forth a sewn leather ball. Her heart warmed at the sight of them playing together, she easily stepped around them and continued down the road. As she neared the marketplace, her wolven hearing picked up screams and the sound of people running. Her heart stopped, the wolf inside her began to thrash against its mortal cage at the potential threat. Bridget sped up, running towards the sounds. Maybe the guards had missed someone who had been infected, and a scourge was now among them.

It wasn't until Bridget passed the marketplace and shot down a side street that she finally saw the horror of it. It was not a scourge running loose and tearing into people, it wasn't as gory as all that; but the scene before her made her heart drop, she would have preferred to see a scourge. Six royal guards were separating a small group of humans from each other, and a crowd had begun to gather around to watch. To everyone's disbelief, the humans were fighting back with everything they had, a valiant effort, but a vain one. Humans did not fight back against any blooded, it was a death sentence. The blooded guards were cruel and vindictive. If a human failed to submit to them, they were typically turned into an example to discourage any others. Bridget recognized one of the men right away, Clyous was attempting to grapple with a guard that was standing between him and his mother.

"By the gods," Bridget murmured under her breath, frozen in place.

Clyous's mother was being dragged away from her family by a guard who had a firm grip on her hair. Clyous was fighting like a mad man to get to her, but another guard had grabbed him from behind which stopped his advance. Markous, the older brother, was raining punches down on a younger-blooded guard who he had somehow managed to knock down onto his back. But it was the girl, Catriona, who was at the center of the altercation, she created the most chaos out of all of them, her white braid billowing behind her. Catriona was ducking and weaving between the guards, successfully eluding capture and making ground towards her mother. If Bridget hadn't known better, she could mistake Catriona's unnatural speed as being a wolf's, she was so fast.

One of the guards swung a staff at her to push her back. She not only managed to dodge the blow by ducking underneath it, but she also swept the guard's feet out from under him. The crowd around began to gasp and scream as the guard hit the ground. Bridget sent out a silent prayer for the girl, unless she could escape, she was doomed. She had embarrassed a guard, and struck him, if they got their hands on her they would make a very public and painful example out of her. The closer Catriona managed to get to her mother, who was now tied to a post, the more driven to catch her the guards became. The girl's skills were impressive, Bridget would give her that, she had never seen anyone able to move like that before. Bridget suspected that if the girl had a blade in hand, this would be a very bloody event. There was one guard left between Catriona and her mother, the fire in the girl's eyes was enough to make even Bridget stall.

"Let her go!" Catriona spat. "She's not infected!"

"She was injured by a scourge." The guard began unraveling a whip that had been attached to his belt. "She will burn, so will you."

In probably the most reckless move Bridget had seen any person ever make, she watched Catriona pull a dagger from each boot and take a fighting stance. It was apparent to anyone with eyes that Catriona was not an ordinary human woman. Catriona moved with an unnatural grace and carried herself like a seasoned warrior. There were trained blooded guards with less grace than she had. She was beautiful for a human. With white silvery blonde hair, she stood out like a beacon. Her grey eyes shone as she fought, something about her eyes reminded Bridget of liquid silver, the bane of any wolf. She couldn't be older than twenty years of age, twenty-two at most? She looked young but carried herself as if she had walked this land for several decades.

Bridget observed that the girl was wearing a fitted tunic and pants as she had the day before. Yesterday, Bridget thought that odd for a woman, but now it made sense. Catriona needed to be able to move, which would be nearly impossible in a dress. Bridget knew that Catriona worked in her family's shop, but she suspected this wardrobe choice was less about labor. Catriona had one other surprising quality, one that Bridget admired as equally as she condemned. The girl was unafraid of the guards, an admirable trait for a warrior. However, it was a death sentence for a human to face blooded in any manner except for subservience. The blooded citizens of Oich followed the wolf hierarchy where submission to your superiors was a way of life. Blooded wolves of any status believed themselves to be above any human and expected absolute subordination. Catriona's lack of fear was defiance, a refusal to bow down. This was taken as a direct challenge, one that no blooded could dismiss. Catriona knew this but continued to fight, as did her family, even as they cried out in shock and anguish at the sight of her holding bladed weapons against a wolf.

"She knows not what she does!" Catriona's mother cried out. "Catriona you will stop! Now!"

"No!" Markous yelled, trying to break the grip of a guard who held onto him. He continued trying to get to his little sister.

"Let my mother go," Catriona warned, standing eerily still, her eyes scanning around them.

"This means death, little girl," the guard snarled. His canines elongated as he accepted her challenge.

"For you, maybe." Catriona moved fast, propelling herself towards the guard.

The guard snapped his arm back, sending the whip towards Catriona's hand, knocking one of her daggers to the ground. With her other hand Catriona thrust her hand forward, letting her last dagger sail through the air, it embedded itself hilt deep into the guard's shoulder. The guard let loose a howl, in the distance Bridget could hear other howls respond. With that, she knew that Catriona's stand was coming to an end against the blooded.

Catriona rolled forward, aiming for the guard's legs. The guard stepped away just in time to avoid Catriona's body, but as she shot past him, she managed to grab hold of the sword strapped to his hip. Before Catriona could free it completely from his belt, the guard grabbed the hilt with both hands securing it to himself. Then, with strength only a blooded could possess, the guard lifted Catriona off the ground and threw her about ten feet away from him. Catriona hit the ground so hard, Bridget could swear she heard Catriona's ribs crack at the moment of impact. Catriona recovered quickly, faster than any human should, and got back on her feet to prepare herself for the next attack.

Bridget heard them arrive, the reinforcements that the guard's howl had summoned were here. Bridget could hear padded feet and claws slapping against the cobblestone street as the wolves came bounding towards them from every direction. Catriona and her brothers froze in place at the presence of wolves in their natural form, the guard squaring off with Catriona smiled wickedly at her, knowing he had finally won.

Six wolves, each the size of a small horse, descended on the town square from various street entrances. The guards who held onto Clyous and Markous were still in human form, forcing the two of them to their knees before the new arrivals. A smaller pack of three wolves emerged from a side street led by a large black wolf; it was double the size of the others. Bridget recognized him immediately, if her heart could drop any lower than it already had it would be burrowing into the ground at the sight of him. The wolf shifted as he made his way slowly towards Catriona, his long legs allowing him powerful strides in her direction. She prayed he would not see her in the crowd, she recognized this was an incredibly self-centered thought considering the situation, but she wished for nothing more than to disappear

35

into the crowd. It had been years since she had seen him, let alone spoken to him. The surrounding crowd dropped to their knees at the sight of their prince, his powers of dominance rippling through the crowd, forcing her down to her knees as well. The power of an old blooded from a dominant bloodline could not be ignored unless someone directly challenged them, and Bridget most certainly would not. Catriona maneuvered herself towards the oncoming danger, recognizing the true and immediate threat instantly.

"You will stop," the prince growled at Catriona as he neared her.

The strongest wolf's command reverberated through the town square, tendrils of power now causing the already frozen crowd to tremble. All the surrounding blooded felt the command in their very bones, unable to stop themselves from obeying. Bridget felt her wolf fighting against the command, wanting nothing more than to growl and snarl at his approach. Ultimately, the power the prince commanded had made her wolf submit to him, like it had so many times before.

"Until my mother is released, I will not stop." Catriona was looking around now, undoubtedly realizing that not only was she completely surrounded, but she was also outmatched.

The prince stopped a few feet away from her, he stood with the self-righteous arrogance that only an old-blooded royal could possess. He eyed Catriona up and down, sizing up his prey. His eyes then turned to Catriona's mother who was weeping, still securely tied to the burning post. The prince's calculating eyes fell to the blooded guards that had failed to contain a human girl. He narrowed his eyes at them, releasing a low growl of disappointment in their direction. The new-blooded guards lowered themselves to the ground and bowed their heads in submission.

"The mother was infected by the scourge attack from yesterday," the old-blooded guard commander explained. "We were in the middle of seizing the woman for cleansing when her children interfered."

"If you wouldn't do the same for your mother you should be ashamed of the childbirth you put her through," Catriona spat at the guard.

"It's not a cleansing! You're trying to burn her alive!" Clyous shouted, fighting against his restraints.

"She's not infected!" Markous joined in. "Look at her arm! There's no rot, it's been over a day. If she was infected, she would have turned by now."

Finally, someone was speaking sense. The prince looked at the brother and then turned to look at the mother. Bridget closed her eyes and sent a prayer up to the gods. What Markous said was true, Anita should have turned by now. Which means it had worked, healing the human woman had worked! She had to do something. Speaking with him again be damned, if it spared them, she would deal with the consequences. As much as she hated it, his arrival was the only chance she had of helping them, he might actually listen to her.

"Your highness!" Bridget choked out, surprising herself and everyone else present. "I cannot smell the rot from here."

The prince moved to stand directly in front of her, she focused on her breathing, trying not to hyperventilate. It would be fine. She would be fine. She could make herself face him. The prince reached down, gently grabbing her chin and raising her face to look up at his. Bridget stared into the eyes of Prince Liam, brown eyes with golden flecks around the irises. The years he had spent working for his father had taken out any kindness she had seen in them as a child. The once kind look in his eyes had now been replaced with a cold and calculating stare, the look seemed to tell her he could devour her very soul. She shuddered slightly at the stark change.

"Ah, my dear Bridget, I thought that was you." Liam smirked at her. "With your keen, old-blooded senses and an affinity for healing, I am intrigued by this... situation."

Like nothing had changed, even though it had been years, Liam took Bridget by the hand and escorted her to Anita who was still bound to the burning post. This touch was familiar to her only for a moment, or at least it should be familiar. She had no idea who the real Prince Liam was now. She hadn't seen or heard from him in the last several years. Of course, she had heard all the rumors of the cruelty he inflicted on his enemies and his slaves. This couldn't be the same man she knew, could it? They stopped right in front of the sobbing woman. The prince began sniffing the air around her, searching for any sign of the rot. Anita was too afraid to look at either of them so instead she opted to close her eyes and turned her head to face away from them. Good, he would see that as submission.

Prince Liam seized the sleeve that partially hid the wound and ripped it free from the dress. "Take a look, dear one, and give me your honest healer's assessment."

Bridget nodded, then began to examine the wound she had spent hours trying to heal the day before. It was openly bleeding again, probably due to the tussle she was in minutes ago. Still, Bridget did not see any of the dark rot that usually accompanied a scourge infection. She sniffed the air above the wound, all she could smell was the metallic scent of blood, maybe a touch of earthiness. That was probably the street, muddy from yesterday's rainfall. She was clean, there was no infection within this woman.

"She smells clean, Your Highness." Bridget bowed to the prince as she stepped back. "I sense no infection within the human woman."

The prince nodded, then took her by the hand again, this time gently guiding her in front of Catriona. Both women stared at each other with wide eyes as they were forced face to face. The prince stood to the side but facing them, a very clear sign that neither woman was to look away.

"What's your assessment of this one?" The prince was eyeing Catriona up and down again. "How can a mortal woman evade capture and injure a handful of my new-blooded guards?"

Catriona stood a little straighter, visibly bracing herself for what might come. Bridget began to pick apart the woman's features, nothing seemed out of the ordinary. What stood before her was a mortal's body. No obvious signs of magic, no fangs hidden behind her lips, she looked like a perfectly normal human. Bridget sniffed the air around Catriona for anything that even resembled the smell of a wolf, nothing.

"I see and smell nothing that indicates anything other than human, My Prince." Bridget bowed her head one more time.

The prince stared into Catriona's eyes, to Bridget's horror she glared right back at him. No! He would take that as a challenge. So fast that even Bridget's reflexes missed it, Prince Liam grabbed Catriona by the throat with one hand and slammed her down, pinning her to the ground by her neck. Shouting sounded through the crowd as Clyous and Markous were dragged to another burning post and secured to it, much in the same fashion as their mother. Anita wailed as she watched her boys struggle against their captors. Catriona struck out at the prince but was unable to make contact. The prince had caught her hand with his, then growled down at her, his canines just inches away from her face.

"Burn the mother," the prince ordered as he grabbed Catriona by her hair and dragging her to yet another burning post.

Catriona fought with everything she had, but the old-blooded prince was too strong for her. One after the other, her hands were secured at the top of the post. She earned a world rocking punch to the face during the process. While temporarily stunned, Prince Liam grabbed the back of Catriona's tunic and ripped it open revealing her bare back. Bridget smelled something then, the blood trickling down Catriona's face smelled different. Something old and earthy, and interestingly similar to Catriona's mother's blood. It was not a human scent. The violence happening right in front of her snapped Bridget's thoughts back into focus. Fear and anger boiled inside her, fighting to see which emotion would take hold of her as she stood witness to this cruelty.

Bridget could feel the wolf raging against the walls of her body. It could not handle the stress of what was happening, desperately wanting to jump out and save the human family before her. Bridget fell back, clutching at her chest trying to will the beast back down, a nasty snarl emanating from her mouth in the process. The prince stopped, turning his attention to the girl he had known since childhood, what looked like compassion shone briefly in his eyes. Bridget was weeping now, thrashing as she fell to the ground, wrestling with the wolf inside. The blooded in the audience began to whisper about her as they always had, enraging the monster further. The prince took a step towards her cautiously, she bared her teeth at him and growled in warning.

"You will get ahold of your wolf," the prince commanded. Then more softly said, "Bridget, if you can't handle the stress you need to leave."

The wolf inside of her couldn't take it anymore, the wolf came out, gnashing its fangs at the prince.

Chapter Four

Catriona

Catriona watched in horror as the healer, Bridget, transformed into a very large auburn-colored wolf. The wolf matched the size of the prince, who had also shifted into his wolf form in response to hers. Bridget's wolf, however, looked half-starved and lacking in confidence. Catriona was stunned watching the creature struggle with itself, not responding to the shift well. Catriona waited and watched to see what the prince would do; the sudden shift could easily be taken as a challenge. But the prince just stood there, watching her, waiting to see what Bridget would do. Catriona was disappointed to see that almost immediately after recovering from the shift, Bridget's wolf bowed down to the dominant wolf standing before her.

There was a small spark of hope that had ignited when Bridget had spoken up, and it grew when she had transformed. Maybe they stood a chance if an old blooded backed them, but that spark of hope extinguished quickly once Catriona saw how easily the auburn wolf submitted. Catriona watched in shock as the healer transformed back and forth from human to wolf several times before finally remaining in human form. Bridget lay there exhausted from the rapid transformation, tears pouring down her face.

Catriona could hear muttering through the crowd about what was happening. "Weak," "Pathetic," "Runt," they said. Bridget's inability to control when she shifted only happened to the new-blooded, this trait in an old-blooded noblewoman was viewed as a weakness. It was no wonder why Bridget seemed to understand and have compassion for humans. In her pack, Bridget was the runt, the weakest link, the outcast. In their world that meant she was lowest of the low, she held no respect from the other wolves. Most of them anyway, the prince showed an unexpected amount of patience with her, which was surprising.

"Escort her back to her father's house," the prince ordered a few of the guards. "She is to make it there unharmed."

Catriona watched as two of the guards helped a shaking Bridget to her feet, guiding her down one of the side streets away from the crowd. For a moment Catriona thought she saw worry in the prince's eyes, but he turned them back towards her and they were full of rage. Catriona began to pull at the ropes that bound her wrists, trying to shake off the dizziness she felt from the blow the prince had delivered earlier. She was most likely concussed from that blow; she was lucky he hadn't broken her nose.

She fucking hated this, every gods damned second of it; she hated them touching her, hated that she couldn't move, and hated the fact that she knew exactly what was coming to her. It triggered memories inside of her, sending her fear spiraling as her fate seemed to be set in stone. She knew what she was risking fighting for her mother's life. She did not regret it for one second, but she had failed to save her. She had failed to save all of them, and now she would suffer the consequences. She had seen how humans were tortured, publicly beaten and humiliated by a bunch of guards were not high on her list of things to do today.

"Light it," the prince commanded, never taking his eyes off Catriona.

Catriona watched as the guards began to add bundles of wood around her mother's feet. Catriona screamed, fighting with the ropes that held her as she tried to get to her mother. She could see Clyous and Markous struggle against their bonds as well, but it was Anita's face that made Catriona's heart stop. Her mother was no longer crying, no longer pleading, instead she was looking at her daughter with the most loving expression Catriona had seen.

"I love you!" Anita called out to her as the guards lit the wood on fire. "You will survive this, all of this! I've seen it! Never stop fighting!"

"No!" Catriona screamed, tears falling from her eyes onto her bare shoulders.

Out of the corner of her eye Catriona could see that the prince had taken the whip from a guard's hand and was uncoiling it right behind her. Catriona's eyes snapped back to her mother as she began to cough from the smoke. Then she heard it, the crack of the whip immediately followed by what felt like a horse kicking her in the back. At first it was the dull pain of the impact, knocking the wind from her lungs; not half a second later, Catriona felt the sharp searing pain of her flesh being ripped apart.

Catriona couldn't inhale before the next crack of the whip. This time the leather crossed over her ribcage. Catriona fought to breathe, finally filling up her lungs. But instead of with air, she inhaled smoke, smoke from her mother's flesh burning not even ten feet from her. Sound came back to her all at once, like a crashing wave. Her mother's screams pierced her senses just as a third lashing came down on her. Catriona lost strength in her legs, collapsing but still forced to remain upright due to her bindings. She could hear her brothers yelling somewhere behind her, but she couldn't take her eyes off their mother.

Catriona watched as her mother's screams died out and her charred body slumped forward in the flames. Another lashing, she could feel the hot streams of blood running down her back, pooling in the dirt below. The tears had stopped; Catriona knew within her heart that her mother was dead. At least she wasn't suffering in the flames anymore. *Crack!* Catriona felt the pain of that strike, but it was almost as if it wasn't her pain anymore. Another lashing, more blood. Another. She couldn't breathe. Another, the edges of her vision began to black out. Another. Catriona did her best not to focus on what was happening, reality now too painful for her to bear. Only the pain of the leather on her flesh brought her back from the edge. She could feel her body weakening, she couldn't keep this up much longer. Another searingly painful crack of the whip came. Finally, Catriona stopped fighting and let the darkness take her.

Chapter Five

Menolayous

Menolayous watched as the last of the crowd left the city street. The crown prince had left shortly after the girl had lost consciousness. He had ordered a guard to stand by for the remainder of the night before he left, he wanted the girl to be left there as an example. It was so other humans would see what awaited them if they fought back. It had been several hours now and the only two souls still awake were the guard and himself.

Covered in a dark cloak, his slender and tall build was easily concealed against the stone wall he was leaning on. Menolayous favored dark clothing, he blended in with the darkness better. His long black hair was braided down his back, within the twists were silver beads. Real silver, in case he needed to melt it down for a weapon and he could carry these with him at all times, he liked to be prepared.

Menolayous had seen it all, from the moment the guards had grabbed the mother to now. He was not surprised when her children tried to save her, some families did try from time to time. They were always met with a similar fate, but it was a shock to see how hard the girl had fought. She was like wildfire tearing through the guards, her skills were impressive, but her speed wasn't natural. She was stopped by an old blooded, but only one as powerful as the Crown Prince of Oich; and even then, her fire didn't go out. There was something about her eyes, when the guards were able to hold her down. It reminded him of a trapped animal. She snarled, she clawed, and fought against their touch, desperate to be rid of it. A notion he recognized all too well, something he and the girl had in common. Only after her mother had died, and the blood loss took over did she finally give out.

Danny had been with him when this incident started. Menolayous had to hold his brother back when he had seen the girl fight so hard, and he had reminded his brother that if their rebellion was to succeed, they needed to lie low. Danny had taken off in search of their other brother just as the burning had begun. They were here for recruits and after seeing what the girl could do, they knew they needed her talents. Never mind the fact that they both felt for the girl and the situation that unfolded today, cruelty wasn't even the right word for how they were treated.

He looked back at the burning posts, the post that had held the mother just a few hours ago was no longer in existence. All that was left was a large pile of ash and embers. The girl was still tied to the center post, dangling from the ropes unconscious and bleeding. Her two brothers were still tied to the third post, but they were awake and alerted to the sound of the owl. The guard remained completely unaware of what was happening around him.

Menolayous raised the hood of his cloak to shield his face as he stepped into the town square. The guard saw him and stepped towards him, ordering him to halt. Menolayous did not listen, he continued his slow progression to the girl. The brothers were watching intently now. The older one scanning the alleyways for movement. The night was still and silent, the guard hadn't yet raised the alarm. Menolayous stopped when he saw the guard put his hand on the sword attached to his hip and watched as a large but silent shadow came up behind the guard whose focus was entirely on him. Just as the guard inhaled to shout out, the tip of a silver short sword burst through the front of his throat, spraying hot, life's blood over the cobblestones.

Menolayous moved swiftly, rushing forward with a type of grace he had been perfecting for over a decade on the battlefield. With his silver imbued battle axe, he swung deep into the guard's chest. Menolayous looked at the man standing behind the guard. Blonde curly hair pulled back and out of his face, blue eyes locking with his own. Danny removed the tip of the short sword from the throat of the guard then quietly lowered his body to the ground while Menolayous ripped the axe from his chest.

Another figure came from the shadows, this one making its way towards the girl's two brothers still tied to the post. They startled as he approached, staring up at the man who towered over them by at least a foot. With a shaved head save for a strip down the center, piercing green and gold eyes, and arms as thick as a man's waist, Rama cut a rather imposing figure. With a quick swipe from the blade of an axe, the two brothers stumbled forward, free from the post.

Rama looked at the two men and lifted a finger to his lips signaling silence. The two brothers nodded in understanding. Menolayous and Danny moved like a shadow across the cobblestones to the girl. As they approached, Menolayous heard Danny choke back a cry at the sight of her back. The lacerations were incredibly severe, every single one of them had ripped her open to show the meat underneath. He swore the one across her ribs was showing bone. Blood drenched her back and lower half of her body, and it still trickled from the open wounds. She was lucky these were the only wounds she carried, having seen the guards do much worse to others.

Menolayous shared a look with his brother, they both knew it was a miracle this girl was still alive. Something like rage and sorrow passed over Danny's face as he brought his dagger to the ropes that bound her wrists. Menolayous thought his eyes were playing tricks on him, the ropes looked singed around the edges. She wasn't that close to the fire. With a snap the unconscious girl fell backwards. Danny managed to catch her in his arms. Menolayous shrugged off his cloak as Danny checked on her breathing, peering into her face. She must be several years younger than they were. Dried blood and soot caked her hair on the side of her face closest to the fire that took her mother's life.

"Here," Menolayous whispered, handing over his cloak.

Danny wrapped the cloak around the girl as gently as he could, her brothers rushed to her side. Menolayous reminded them to stay silent. The younger brother reached up and cupped her face, not even trying to hide his tears. He was her twin, Menolayous realized.

Danny lifted her up easily enough as Rama pointed to the forest with his axe. As a group, the men moved silently through the alleyways, trying not to draw attention. They were dead men fleeing. Not only had they killed a blooded guard, helped prisoners of the crown escape, but they had also carried silver edged weapons. If they were caught, they would all be dead, experiencing a worse sort of fate than what had happened here earlier. They all seemed to know it, the brothers who followed them remained silent as they moved, their eyes scanning each alleyway they passed. The group had succeeded in making it outside the city walls and into the tree line before they heard a chorus of howls announcing the escaped prisoners.

Chapter Six

Danny

Danny could not believe the torture this woman had been through in the last few hours. He held the woman to his chest gently as their group made it to one of their less used campsites, one just outside the city in a hidden cavern. Rama was the last one to follow, making sure to cover any traces of them as they went in case the wolves came sniffing this far. Danny could feel the warmth of her blood reach his skin as it finally soaked through the cloak and his tunic. Thank the gods, he could still feel her breathing. Truthfully, he was terrified that she would bleed out before they could get her to safety. There was so much of it, her skin was losing its warmth the longer they moved. The cold rain that had begun to pour down on them wouldn't help keep her warm either, but it would at least help wash away the scent of her blood.

Danny glanced at his brothers as he ran, they too seemed to share the same concerns he did. They wanted the girl to live, she had to. They were willing to risk their lives to get her out alive, she had to make it. Rebellion be damned. It killed each of them to watch the horrors that regularly happened to the men and women of Oich at the hands of the corrupt and cruel leadership. They weren't able to step in; the odds were too great. Danny had wanted to step in the second he saw the girl fighting. If Menolayous hadn't stopped him, he might have, and as a result they all would have been killed. Danny was willing to risk himself, but not his brothers. He was glad this opportunity had presented itself, that they were able to do something to help this family. They were lucky, so damn lucky.

As they kept pace with Danny, the girl's brothers seemed to know it too. The girl's twin kept glancing in her direction like he wanted to take her from Danny's arms. Danny wouldn't give him the chance. He could understand the protectiveness, but Danny had better endurance to keep their pace fast. They looked strong, but he couldn't risk it. They needed to get somewhere safe before they tended to her wounds, and they really needed to get the bleeding under control.

Rage and fear consumed him wholly as he continued to push. He had never met these people before in his life, didn't know their names, he wasn't even from the same city. He came from one of the smaller fishing villages on the coast, he wouldn't have even been associated with a family from the inner city. All of that was behind him though, it was before he lost his family, before he joined this rebellion where it didn't matter where you came from. Now he mostly saw the atrocities that happened to others, just like he witnessed tonight. Watching this injustice, watching this young woman fight, not only for her life, but for the life of her mother, proved to him that deep down people were still good. Seeing her lose to the very monsters he was in the city to fight against, seeing the aftermath of what they had done to her, it filled him with rage. His rage fueled him on, to keep going even though he carried something heavy for miles. It was worth it to keep going, to keep fighting. She was worth it, she had shown the world that even she could keep fighting, so why not fight for her?

The group slowed as they approached the cavern entrance. They carefully stepped inside, walking single file through a few of the tightly fitted openings until they made it to a large open cavern. There was a small fire in the center of the cave where the redheaded woman waited. The two brothers slowed when they spotted her. She smiled cautiously at them. Danny did not wait for their introductions. He pushed himself forward still carrying the girl. It shouldn't surprise him that Bridget was already here and waiting for them. She knew of their hideout and knew that they were in the city. He had seen her there after the fight had stopped. He liked the healer well enough; she had helped them out on many occasions. She was one of the few blooded from Oich that gave a damn about anyone other than themselves.

"Bridget?" the twin brother spoke to the healer as if he knew her.

"Bring her here. I brought supplies." Bridget rummaged through a bag and began to pull out bottles of herbal tinctures and fresh bandages.

Danny brought the girl over and gently set her down on a freshly lain blanket by the fire. Her brothers were by her side in an instant, grief stricken, it appeared. Danny helped the healer gently roll her onto her stomach and remove the cloak, revealing the mess of her back. The eldest brother reached out as if to stop him, earning a glare promising pain if he stopped Danny from helping the girl.

"I've got it." The man matched Danny's intensity.

"Can we not do this, Markous?" The twin brother chastised his brother's protectiveness, then spoke to Bridget, "Please help her."

Bridget nodded, then went to work cleaning out the wounds before she began stitching the flesh back together. The twin brother, Clyous, was his name. Danny had picked it up while he and his brother bickered back and forth. He held onto his sister's hand as the healer worked. At that moment, Danny was thankful they had found Bridget all those months ago. She was unlike other blooded, she genuinely cared for human life. She did not see them as slaves to be treated in whatever way pleased their superiors; she hated how the blooded treated humans. That's why it wasn't a stretch when they had asked her to help them, to supply them with medicine and information. Bridget had been feeding them information for months now about incoming and outgoing trading wagons. Her knowledge of the merchants and how they operated was invaluable. At some point they had befriended the healer, and more times than he could count she had saved their asses.

Danny walked over to Rama who sat by the fire sharpening the blade of his axe. Markous came over and sat across from them. Rage flickered between the three of them, now that they were no longer on the run, they were able to slow down and process what had happened. Like Markous, Danny could understand the rage, he himself shared it even though he held no connection to this young woman. Truthfully, this reminded him of what happened with his mother before she died. Women shouldn't be mistreated, they should not be stripped publicly and lashed, and they should not be beaten. He knew Rama felt the same and was probably being reminded of the mistreatment of his own mother. Unfortunately, with how bad Oich had become over the years, this was an increasingly common occurrence. The world was unkind to women, and Danny strongly believed that they needed to change that.

"I don't know how to even begin to thank you," Markous started, as he stared at Rama.

"There's no thanks needed, a family that fought as hard as yours to protect each other should be able to understand why we couldn't leave you there," Rama answered sympathetically.

Markous nodded. Silence filled the space save for the crackling of the logs on the fire. Danny looked over at the still unconscious girl, Bridget continued sewing her wounds. Menolayous was nowhere to be seen. He was likely outside making sure they were not followed. Menolayous did not do well with strangers. Several more minutes had passed before Markous spoke again.

"You are part of the resistance, aren't you?" Markous dared to ask the question. In the wrong setting that type of question could mean death for everyone involved, but Danny figured they were past that point.

"Yes." Rama stopped sharpening his axe to look Markous in the eyes, his brother feared nothing.

"I heard rumors," Markous said quietly, "of rebels fighting back against the blooded to end the slavery of humans. I thought it was just wishful thinking."

"We're real." Rama continued with his work.

"It's not just us. There are about seventy or so rebels that have banded together against the crown. We're done being slaves to such cruel masters," Danny spoke out, casting a quick glance toward Bridget. "No offense."

Bridget looked up at him for a moment then continued her task. "None taken."

"We've been disrupting the trading routes by attacking the traveling merchants and caravans of supplies," Danny added, taking his eyes off the healer. "We've successfully liberated dozens of slaves now. Those who don't want to fight have left for Airgid."

"And Airgid accepts the escaped refugees of Oich?" Clyous didn't seem to believe them.

"We have a safe haven just north of the Gaelach border. We don't make it obvious that we're all a bunch of refugees from Oich, and the crown doesn't exactly come looking in another kingdom. The wild tribesmen of Gaelach don't care for politics making passage through relatively easy."

Markous continued to watch them, thinking over their words. Danny stood and walked towards Catriona, he stopped himself and instead decided to lean against the cave wall. He didn't need to be hovering around her so obviously right now, her brothers might take issue with it. Leaving her alone was becoming increasingly hard for him, and he could not figure out why exactly, except that maybe he just felt protective of the injured woman. Bridget had finished stitching the torn skin back together and was now cleaning off the blood and soot from the girl's back and face. Danny stared at her while her face was being wiped clean, he remembered seeing her for the first time earlier today. She was so beautiful it took his breath away, and when she started fighting, he found himself wanting to help her. He would have too, if Menolayous hadn't stopped him.

Catriona was her name. Guilt overwhelmed him as his eyes ran over the wounds on her back. He had left to go get Rama before they had started on her. Menolayous had been the one to send him, undoubtedly aware that Danny would have stepped in if he was there. Still, the regret for not helping her was eating him from the inside. His attraction to the young woman aside, this was why he and his brothers fought against the crown, to save people from horrors like this. To protect them from men, guards, people who preyed on the weak to feel powerful.

"I want to join."

Everyone's faces snapped in the direction of Markous who just sat there looking at them all.

"I want to fight with you against them. I want to stop them from hurting my family or others ever again."

Rama smiled.

Chapter Seven

Catriona

For a time… complete darkness was all there was. Pain did not exist. Suffering did not exist. She did not exist. Out of the black came sound, booming and vibrant, a change from the silent darkness. Then the memories flooded in like a river, emotional pain crashing upon her like a swift current. Once it felt like she was overflowing like a lake full to the brim, physical pain struck. It was a harsh winter storm enveloping her entirely, freezing everything over. The noises cracked like thunder; the pain struck her back like lightning and sent waves through her once calm lake. With a scream Catriona awoke, the elements crashing down on her harder now that she had returned to reality.

Catriona opened her eyes as she cried out, her eyes scanning and trying to assess for threats. She was in a cave; a dying fire glowed not many feet away from her. She craned her neck to look around and immediately regretted the movement, pain seared down her back as if the whip was freshly cracking against her skin. Dirt sprayed upwards into her face from her harsh exhale. She couldn't stand being face down in the dirt, panic began to creep in and her grip on reality started to slip into a once forgotten darkness. Her wrists and arms felt like they had been burned and blistered, she was afraid to try moving her legs.

"Cat?!"

She heard footsteps rushing towards her. Clyous came into her line of sight, she cried out in relief this time. Her brothers were here; she was safe. Nobody was going to hurt her with them around. The tears openly flowed as full realization came to light. Their mother was gone, dead. Her back was in tatters from the lashing the crown prince had given her. Yet somehow, she and Clyous had escaped. Fear struck her instantly; she was missing someone.

"Markous?" she cried out.

"Right here." Markous was beside her in an instant.

Clyous took her by the hand gently, lowering himself onto his stomach so they were face to face. It was something they used to do as children if the other was sick or upset. Her twin shared this connection with her; it was their way of grounding each other. Catriona let out an audible sob, all the pain she felt poured out with her tears. Her brothers wept with her. Clyous held onto her hand and Markous placed his hand gently on her head. Catriona lost track of time as they remained there together. They could have been there for a few minutes or several hours. Catriona clung to her brothers as she cried herself to sleep.

Catriona awoke sometime later, and her brothers nowhere in sight. She was still face down on the ground, with no comforting safety net nearby. She clenched her teeth and forced her arms underneath her, determined to get herself into a less compromising position. With teeth gritted and moving at a snail's pace, Catriona managed to lift herself high enough off the ground to throw a knee forward and hold herself up. She groaned from exertion. Her muscles were not only weak, but they screamed as she moved. The pain was nearly blinding, her body felt as heavy as a boulder. She made it into a sitting position, breathing heavily at this small victory. The world was spinning around her violently. She realized then that she definitely had a concussion.

The sound of movement to her right caught her attention. Catriona whipped her head towards the sound and spotted a man, maybe a year or two older than her, slowly rising to his feet as he stared at her with wide eyes. Catriona quickly assessed him, his stance indicated he was more likely to flee than attack her. She did not sense that he was a threat to her. He was handsome, she had to admit to herself. He had blonde curly hair that was hanging loose to his shoulders. He wore hunter's leathers with daggers strapped to his boots. His white tunic hung loose and open, showing off a well-muscled chest. His piercing blue eyes were staring at her, wide with surprise. He had to have known she was there; he couldn't have missed the unconscious person lying in the middle of the cave with their back ripped to pieces. Catriona couldn't understand why he looked so surprised until she looked down and realized her top half was completely uncovered. With speed she immediately regretted she covered her breasts with her arms, crying out in pain as the flesh of her back pulled sharply.

"Sorry. Sorry." He turned to face away from her, shielding his eyes. "I wasn't trying to startle you."

"Who the fuck are you?" she bit out, looking around for anything to cover herself. There was nothing except the blanket she was laying on, so she grabbed it out from under herself.

"I'm Danny," the man said, still facing the wall. "My brothers and I brought you here."

Catriona glanced around the cave. There was scattered gear and bedrolls lying around everywhere, but they were the only ones in the cave. She saw the embers of the campfire and a small pile of wood to her right. Her brothers had been here with her; they wouldn't have left her alone with this man if he was a threat to her. They knew him.

Seeming to sense her train of thought, Danny answered, "Rama took them hunting. The plan is to stay here for a few more days to give you time to recover, and we need food."

"Are there no supplies? Extra gear or clothes?"

"I believe Menolayous is sneaking back into the city to grab some things from your shop." Danny chanced a glance in her direction. "Here."

Danny, still facing away from her, tugged off his tunic. Catriona's face began to redden as she noticed just how fit this man was. With his eyes closed he turned to hand her the shirt. Catriona's face grew warm as her eyes locked onto the muscles of his back. Slightly embarrassed that she just ogled this man, she snatched the shirt from his hand, averting her eyes. She slipped it on carefully, wincing as the fabric brushed her wounds.

"Thank you," she muttered, looking back at him.

Danny gave her a small smile as he stood, walking over to a bedroll and rifling through it. He pulled out a jacket of sewn pelts and put it on, sparing Catriona from staring at his half-naked body.

"Where are we?" She half crawled onto a flat rock a few feet away, embarrassed at her lack of coordination.

Danny moved as if he were coming to help her. Catriona put her hand up, stopping him in his tracks. She was not broken; she could do this. She heaved herself onto the rock with more effort than she was willing to admit, but she moved slowly enough that she didn't think she pulled anything. Okay, maybe she was a little broken. She winced as she took a deep breath, her ribs were definitely broken. She must look like absolute shit.

"We're a few miles north of the city. We're inside a cave system that leads into the forests that border Gaelach."

"Have the blooded come looking for us?" Her fear began to peak at the thought of seeing the crown prince again after her escape.

"The first two nights Bridget reported an increase of guards around the city but after that, nothing. We think the crown is trying to stay tight lipped about a blooded guard being killed and three mortals escaping."

"They probably think it was those rebels that have been causing them problems on the trade routes," Catriona bit out, trying to roll her shoulders as carefully as possible.

Danny smiled at that. "It kind of was."

Catriona stared at him. "You're the rebels?"

"Oh, most definitely." There was a mischievous twinkle in his eye. "We live and breathe to terrorize the crown."

Catriona rolled her eyes at him but flashed him a half smile. She had heard rumors of these rebels targeting lazy old-blooded merchants as they traveled to the other capital cities around Stone Basin. They were causing such a stir that the merchants had begun hiring guards for protection during transport. Miraculously, these rebels had never been caught, but word of humans overpowering blooded was getting back to all the citizens of Oich.

"How are you feeling?" Danny asked her seriously.

She took a second before answering, "My head is spinning. I'm pretty sure I have a concussion. It feels like I've been drinking for days, and I'm nearly positive my ribs are cracked, if not broken."

Concern flooded his features. Danny looked like he desperately wanted to do something to help her but wasn't sure what exactly that would be.

"How bad is it?" She locked eyes with him, daring him to lie to her.

"Your face is pretty bruised up. You've been asleep for a few days, so the swelling has gone down. Your back was shredded pretty good. Bridget had to put in a lot of stitches to keep you together. She said that everything is going to heal over time, but you will most likely have scars."

Catriona nodded, at least he didn't lie. She bit back tears at hearing there would be scars. She never considered herself a particularly vain person, but men did not like scars on their women. It wasn't as if she were looking for a man, but she would be seen as damaged by anyone who sees the scars, that was a direct shot to her heart. She should be happy to have escaped alive with her brothers. She shouldn't be ungrateful for that gift.

"So why would a ragtag crew like yours risk yourselves to help us?" She found herself teasing him, desperate to change the conversation.

"I—" he paused "— we couldn't leave you like that."

They locked eyes for a moment, sharing this unnamed emotion between them. His eyes were pleading, like he was desperate to convey a message. The intensity of it was shocking to her. They heard footsteps coming from the mouth of the cave which gave Catriona a reason to look away.

An intimidatingly large man walked into the cave with a battle axe resting on his shoulders, with his other arm he carried the corpse of a large boar. He smiled when he saw her sitting up as if he knew her. Once his gigantic figure moved to the side, Catriona saw Clyous and Markous carrying firewood right behind him.

Clyous and Markous saw her as they approached, they dropped their handfuls of wood and rushed over to her. She opened her arms out wide and accepted the impact of the double hug. She grunted in pain at first contact, but they were surprisingly gentle with her.

"Isn't that your shirt?" she heard the giant ask Danny.

Danny smiled and shrugged his shoulders. In a brotherly way, the giant smacked Danny on the back of his head as he walked by. She peered over Clyous's shoulder at the two men who were smiling at each other. Danny looked over at her, Catriona looked away.

"How are you feeling?" Markous asked, pulling away.

"I'm okay," she answered, wincing at the movement. "I need clothes."

"Menolayous should be back sometime tonight," the giant said as he shoved a sharpened branch through the boar's body. "My name is Rama. I see you've already met my brother Danny." His eyebrows raised at her playfully.

"You don't look alike," she pointed out, matching his sarcasm.

"We're adopted, sort of," Danny answered and shrugged with a grin.

"Ah." She cracked a smile.

She continued to sit there as the boys got busy around the campfire. Rama set the boar up to be spit roasted as the others stacked wood or set up bedrolls. Catriona felt relatively useless, every time she moved her back screamed in protest. Or worse, one of the boys tried to come over and check on her. Ultimately, she was entirely too exhausted to do much of anything.

About an hour had passed and the boar was still roasting. The cave smelled absolutely wonderful. Catriona's stomach growled loudly at the presence of food. It had been several days since she'd eaten. Rama struck up most of the conversation, his boisterous attitude and love for jokes made the hour pass by relatively quickly. Regardless of the circumstances that brought them all together, Catriona felt comfortable with all of them there.

"Well look who finally decided to come to dinner," Rama boomed as Menolayous strode into the cave.

Menolayous carried a plethora of supplies with him. Behind him followed the redheaded healer that tried to save her mother. Catriona's heartbeat accelerated, her mind suddenly going back to the scenes in the city square. How Bridget had healed her mother, how she had tried and failed to stop the crown prince from burning her; and lastly, how she had shifted back and forth uncontrollably from wolf to human. Catriona shifted uncomfortably at her appearance, Bridget seemed unaware of it.

"I bring vegetables and bread." She smiled at them, holding up a bag. "I'll get started on some soup."

The boys cheered at that. Clyous went over to help Bridget with the food, Catriona noticed how his hand brushed hers as he took the bag. Danny and Markous began to help Menolayous with his supplies, going through each bag and sorting out the items. Catriona's face grew hot and her breathing shallowed. Regardless of all the activity around her, she could not stop the memories from taking over. She tried to focus on her breathing and fought back the tears that threatened to spill out. The smell of the boar suddenly turned to the smell of flesh. Suddenly, her stomach turned, and she dry heaved, gasping at how the movement affected her back and ribs.

Rama had been watching her silently, she realized, but he made no announcement about what was happening. She was thankful for that until Bridget's obnoxiously good hearing caught on.

"Catriona!" Bridget rushed forward, reaching a hand out to touch her shoulder.

Catriona violently jerked back, slapping Bridget's hand away forcefully. "Don't touch me!" she yelled.

Everyone stopped what they were doing to look their way. Tears were flowing freely down her face now. She was positive she had pulled a stitch, but she didn't care. Rama, who had still been watching her quietly, started to stand. Clyous made a step in her direction but froze when she glared at him.

Catriona looked at the healer again. "Don't fucking touch me like I'm some sort of weak wolf pup. Not from you."

Her words had stung the woman; Catriona could see the sadness in her eyes. She didn't care, not right now. Undoubtedly, this woman had saved her life, but she hadn't been strong enough to save their mother. If she had any control over the wolf within her she could have stopped the crown prince. She was the same size as him, clearly from an old blooded and dominant bloodline, and she seemed to know him. Yet, she was too weak to control her shift. With that, her mother's only chance of survival had been gone in an instant. Catriona's emotions and thoughts began to spiral out of her control, sending her deeper into the memories bubbling to the surface.

"Catriona," Clyous tried to sound sympathetic, but it came out more like a scold.

"I don't want to hear it!" she bit out, slowly rising to her feet.

All eyes were on her as she moved. She knew she should probably feel ashamed by her outburst. But truthfully, she didn't give a shit. Her mother was dead and the memories of how she died were still trying to claw their way back in. Bridget took a few steps away from her, bowing her head. In defeat or in sorrow, Catriona didn't care which. All she cared about was getting out of that cave.

Catriona began to move, or rather stumble her way towards the cave entrance, the sound of that whip began to overcome her with every step she took. She could no longer hear the sound of her footsteps or the voices behind her. All she could hear was the cracking of the fire and her mother's screams. Another crack. Catriona dry heaved again. She had made it outside, the cold winter air jarring her back to reality.

Finally, her senses started coming back to her as she inhaled deeply. No more smoke. She took a second to look around. They were indeed deep within the forest. Catriona glanced at pieces of the night sky through the pine needles way up above. She breathed in the earthy smell, grounding herself.

"What set you off more, the smoke or Bridget?" Rama approached from the mouth of the cave.

"Both." She stood there breathing in more cold air. "Seeing the blooded walk in was what started it."

Rama stopped and stood by her and she became very aware of how big he was. Even though he stood a foot and a half taller than her his presence was oddly comforting.

"Unfortunately, you're going to have those flashbacks for the rest of your life. There will be different triggers that will pop up, but the good news is you'll get better at keeping those memories at bay."

"You seem to know a lot about this."

"It's because I've seen a lot." Rama glanced at her. "All of us have. So, trust me when I say we get what you're going through."

There was a long pause where neither of them spoke. Catriona weighed his words carefully, using this time to continue to center herself. She finally chanced a look at Rama. He was looking down at her, assessing her, she realized. Watching and reading people, this is what he does.

"When I was thirteen, I watched my father drink himself to death. A very rich, blooded family, one of the few that owned personal slaves, had sold my mother off to another family like she was cattle. She was caught trying to escape and to return to us, so they killed her. My father hit the bottle hard while I had to take over the stables. After he passed, I started to realize that they treated their horses better than their slaves."

"Danny had it harder than I did. He was the second son of a fisherman. He had an older brother. His father had a temper and would beat Danny's mother with a weighted rope. One night it got so bad that Danny, along with his brother, tried to stop it but the noise of the fight attracted the wrong attention. The guards came to their house and ended up killing Danny's brother and father. Danny's mother died the next day from her injuries."

A tear slid down her cheek, they had suffered unimaginable childhoods.

"I'm sorry that happened to you," Catriona whispered.

"It is what it is." Rama shrugged. "I'm telling you these stories not because we want your sympathy. I'm telling you about us in the hopes that you might learn to trust us, and to understand that you're not alone."

"What about the quiet one? Menolayous?"

"He's never talked about his life and what it was like before he met us, but all the signs are there. I honestly believe he's seen more than all of us combined."

"How'd you find each other?"

"We were all hunting and tracking the same deer." Rama laughed heartily. "Never caught the fucking thing."

58

Catriona cracked a smile before speaking up, "I asked Danny, but he couldn't give me a straight answer. Why did you three risk yourselves for us?"

"Danny was going to intervene once he saw them tie you to that post. He saw his mother being beaten again in his mind. He wasn't going to let them do that to you."

"They would have killed him."

"Yes, picking a fight with an old-blooded crown prince would have guaranteed it. Even for another blooded." Rama raised an eyebrow at her; her face warmed at how she had treated Bridget. "Danny wouldn't have cared. He's wild, that one. No sense of self-preservation."

"I didn't—" she started.

"I understand why you did it. It's natural to want to place blame, but Bridget isn't responsible for what happened to you. I would encourage you to place the blame where it belongs."

She heard him and understood the logic behind the words, but the beast inside her still wanted to rage. She wanted someone easy to blame.

"The only way Menolayous could get Danny to stop was to send him to find me. It was an effort to save our brother's life, or so I thought when Danny came and got me. After we got you all out of the city Menolayous told us what happened. He told us you single-handedly took on three blooded guards and won. I won't lie to you; we need someone who can fight like that."

"So, you want to recruit us?" she snorted as she asked, not exactly sure how to feel about this information.

"Yes." He winked at her. "But that's not all. Even after we helped you all escape, the normal plan of action would be to make sure you were back on your feet again, then recruit you or send you to our stronghold. No, it was the fact that Danny would not put you down. He wouldn't even hand you over to one of us."

She really did not know how to process that information.

"I have a feeling we're going to be sticking around for a while. Besides, I apparently missed all the fun. I want to see what you can do." The grin completely consumed his face at this point, throwing out the challenge.

"You're on." She laughed then winced. "After Bridget takes out my stitches."

"Come on, killer." Rama nudged her with his shoulder gently.

Together they turned and walked back into the cave. Rama helped slowly guide her inside when she began to falter. The smoke hit her in the face, and she started to hyperventilate. She willed her heart to stop racing and pushed on, Rama's large hand on her shoulder was as comforting as her brothers'. They made it to the large cavern. Markous and Menolayous were tending to the boar which was no longer on the spit. Clyous was sitting with Bridget next to the large pot of soup. Danny was standing near the entrance of the cave trying hard not to look like he was waiting for them to come back in.

Everyone glanced at their approach but continued with their tasks. Catriona sat down on a bedroll, glancing around at the others. Clyous looked at her from across the cavern, flashing her a grin. He was not mad at her then, good. Rama made his way over to the boar, his loud laugh echoing throughout the cave.

He began to carve up the meat as everyone gathered around. Catriona just sat there, averting her eyes from the boar's leg dripping juices into the fire. Her stomach lurched but she held it down. Taking a deep breath, she concentrated on breathing as normally as possible.

She felt someone come sit beside her. She looked up and was staring into Danny's blue eyes. He handed her a bowl of soup, smiling at her kindly. She thanked him and took the bowl. It was just broth and vegetables. She sent a prayer of thanks up to the gods. She hadn't been sure she would be able to eat the meat after watching it cook over the fire. She looked up at him again and noticed he had a bowl of soup instead of meat. She wondered if that was his preference or if he was being considerate. Rama's words echoed through her head just then. Yes, she also had a feeling that him and his brothers would be sticking around for a while.

Chapter Eight

Danny

It had been several weeks now since they had managed to escape the capital city. Their luck had held so far, no guards had tracked them this deep into the forest. Rama had been spending a lot of time talking with Clyous and Markous about the finer points of the rebellion. Where their strongholds were, how they chose to attack, the different ways they personally had been wreaking havoc against the crown. It was good for everyone, having these conversations. It really opened the blacksmiths' eyes to what was really going on outside the city, how bad it actually was. Danny had seen Clyous turn pale when Rama described the living conditions of some of the far away villages and how the human citizens were treated. It made how they were dealt with seem like a day at the beach. All it did for Markous was feed his anger towards the blooded.

Danny noticed Menolayous was slowly getting used to everyone. He had barely spoken the first few nights while everyone stayed in the cave. It was obvious the quiet warrior was uncomfortable with their new companions; he was very guarded and mistrusting at first. Only now was he engaging in conversation with any of the blacksmith siblings. He was finally coming back into the cave at night to sleep. During their first week there it was as if he had disappeared. Danny assumed he was braving the winter weather and sleeping outside.

Bridget came and went every few days, not able to keep up her appearance as an Oich citizen while living out in the woods with a small band of rebels. Every time she returned, she managed to bring supplies with her. Bridget made a point to keep checking on Catriona with each visit to make sure she was healing properly and wasn't doing anything too active. Everyone could tell Catriona was thankful for the healer, especially now that Bridget had finally given her permission to move around with the caveat that she did nothing strenuous enough to pull out the last of her stitches. Catriona couldn't be more thrilled at this revelation, days and weeks of being trapped inside a cave was visibly driving the woman mad. Danny suspected the poor woman was out of her mind keeping true to her limitations.

Danny stepped out into the cold, brisk morning air, inhaling deeply as he stretched in the pale sunlight. Glancing around he spotted Menolayous nearby working on binding feathers to new arrow shafts. It wasn't a surprise that his brother was awake before everyone else, he always seemed to be first awake and last asleep. He supposed this was a better alternative than his brother sleeping outside in the winter frost. Although, he most likely wasn't sleeping enough on this schedule.

"Morning," Danny greeted him sleepily.

Menolayous nodded to him before diving back into his work. His hands worked expertly, wrapping the twine around the arrow and securing the shaped feathers.

"Don't you think we have enough arrows?" Danny asked, observing his progress. "You're the only one who uses them."

"They're not for me." Menolayous used his teeth to bite through a loose piece of twine hanging from the arrow shaft.

Danny spotted what looked like a brand-new bow resting at Menolayous's feet. By the looks of it Menolayous had just carved it, the bark freshly stripped from it and its curve had been sanded down. It was quality work for being out in the middle of the forest with the bare minimum of tools. It had probably taken him several days to make it. Danny noticed one distinct feature about it, the bow looked small compared to his usual hunting bow, it was more compact in size as if built for someone of smaller stature.

"You made it for her?" Danny realized, understanding why he was making so many arrows. "You're going to teach her to shoot?"

"She knows how to shoot." Menolayous sighed, stopping what he was doing to stare up at Danny. "I'm going to teach her to hunt and make her a better shot."

"That's uncharacteristically kind of you." Danny felt a lick of jealousy flicker inside him.

"She's getting restless." Menolayous raised his eyebrows at him as if sensing his jealousy. "And she isn't familiar with weapons."

"She's a blacksmith." Danny was utterly confused by his comment. "We've seen her fight, she's incredible."

"She's fast but she wasn't able to deal much damage with weapons. She can evade better than even I can, but once a blade is introduced, she falters. That's how she lost. That, and being taken to the ground. She has a talent, that's for sure, but she's never trained with true warriors before. Her technique needs honing. Imagine what she could do with some training and a blade in her hand that she isn't trying to throw." Menolayous picked up another arrow shaft for feathering. "You can help with that. She needs to regain her strength without hurting herself."

"Why not teach her yourself? A pretty girl like that's got to turn even your head." Danny held his breath waiting for his brother's response, he had no idea why he decided to push this. He supposed it was because he had to know if his brother was interested in her or not.

"That's all you, brother. I'll stick to teaching her how to hunt." Menolayous nodded his head north. "She's over there."

Danny stared in the direction his brother had just indicated. Menolayous had a puzzling personality, any man in his right mind would be interested in her. Still, he believed that, just like any beautiful woman that had come along before Catriona, he was simply uninterested. It was a relief Danny realized. He didn't need to worry about either of his brothers chasing after her, considering that's all he'd wanted to do these last few weeks.

"That's why you're up so early isn't it? To see her?" Menolayous gave him a sideways smirk. "You've got it bad."

"I have no idea what you're talking about," Danny answered, slightly defensive.

"She's going to chew you up and spit you out." Menolayous laughed. "She's not some bar wench you can smile at and have her swooning."

"About time someone did." Rama slowly emerged from the cave, taking a seat across from Menolayous. "Try not to let her pull her stitches while you're at it. Bridget won't be back to check on her for another couple of days. Unless of course you don't mind the thought of one of us putting our hands on her bare back so we can—"

"Fuck off already," Danny interrupted, not wanting to envision Rama's little scenario. He stalked off towards the tree line. "I hope you cut your hand open on those arrows you assholes."

He could hear them laughing behind him as he went. He loved his brothers dearly, but it was times like this when he hated them. They were completely right. Normally, Danny had no issues with pursuing a woman, he'd done it quite regularly if he was being honest. However, Catriona did more than just pique his interest, he loved everything about her. She was quick-witted and could talk shit like nobody's business. The girl was tougher than any man he'd ever met, and she was as stubborn as a mule. She wasn't like other women; she wasn't a delicate little flower he had to worry about picking.

Danny maneuvered his way through the forest for several minutes before he could hear her. He slowed his approach, creeping up to a small clearing. Catriona was standing at the edge of the clearing nearest to him. Her back was to him as she faced a wide tree. She seemed to be concentrating hard on the tree, taking deep and controlled breaths. He watched her intently, soaking up her intensity like it was warmth from the sun. She shot her arm forward; a dagger flew from her open palm shortly before it embedded into the tree. An impressive throw he had to admit, but he heard her slight gasp and wince at the movement.

"I thought Bridget said not to do anything too strenuous," Danny teased as he stepped into the clearing.

She glanced at him as he neared, face twisted into a slightly pained expression. "Throwing daggers isn't strenuous."

Danny clicked his tongue feigning disappointment. "It is with thirty something stitches still in your back."

She glared at him. "I can't hide out in that cave any longer. I'm losing my mind."

"It's a rough thing, surviving torture and imminent death." Danny smirked. "Gods be merciful and spare you from boredom."

"You're annoying." She gave him a look that confirmed her statement. "I'm used to working at the forge every day, or training. I can't exactly do either now."

"What exactly did your training entail?" He was genuinely curious about what this girl had managed to do on her own, it was obvious her brothers did not share her tenacity.

She thought for a moment before answering, "Stretching, cardio, rolls, and practicing with daggers."

"Have you sparred with anyone other than your brothers?" He raised an eyebrow in question.

"A few fist fights and tavern brawls, that's about it." She shrugged. "I didn't exactly have a ton of people lining up to train with me."

"And why is that?" he teased but was curious all the same. "You seem like such a delight to be around."

"Nobody could keep up," she answered flatly, a hint of irritation lacing her words.

That wasn't particularly surprising, most humans did not train as warriors. "What about a blooded? You can't tell me you never caught the eye of an up-and-coming young warrior?"

He watched her expression darken, her eyes boring into his as she answered simply, "No."

"Why do you train?" Danny surprised himself by asking. He wasn't worried about scaring her off with his direct approach, Catriona was stronger than most, and she herself was direct. "Women typically don't engage in any sort of warfare, not in Oich. Your brothers don't at all, so it's not a family affair."

"It used to be. When we were little our father had us drill almost daily. He said the only people in the world you could truly count on were your family, so we needed to learn how to protect each other. After he was gone my brothers stopped, focusing their energy on the shop."

"But you didn't?" This seemed important somehow, like her answer would unlock something between them, an understanding he craved.

"I did for a few years." She shrugged her shoulders. "I tried to be the daughter my mother wanted, but I quickly realized that being that girl, being human, meant I was an easy target. I train because I refuse to be easy prey."

"I can get behind that." And he truly meant it, that was a fairly logical thing to think. Catriona was not shielded from the evil of the world just because she had brothers, she likely saw tragic things happen to other women and refused to sit around and let it happen to her. "Would you like to train with someone? Learn how to perfect the use of more weapons than just a dagger?"

"What's the catch?" she asked suspiciously, eyeing him up and down as if he was about to spring something on her she wanted nothing to do with. "You want me to join your rebellion?"

"No catch." Danny raised his hands in mock surrender. "My brothers and I get tired of training with each other. Your speed, after honing your sword play, would be a force to be reckoned with. We like to encourage anyone to make themselves a threat instead of a target."

She stared at him, her eyes sweeping up his body slowly as she evaluated him. His chest fluttered ever so slightly as he savored her gaze. He couldn't help himself; he liked those steely-grey eyes staring at him like that.

65

How he wanted her eyes to appreciate him, to be on him at all times, to show interest in him as more than a mere sparring partner.

"Okay," was all she said as she locked her eyes on his.

"Okay." He cracked a genuine smile, maybe by spending more time with her he could enjoy her eyes on him even more often. "In the meantime, you can't do anything that's going to pull your stitches. The longer it takes for you to heal, the longer it will be before I put a sword in your hand."

"You'll be training me?" she asked, a smile tugging on her lips. "Not your brothers? I may have agreed to this too soon."

He sensed her playfulness emerging with that smile. Good, he wanted her to play, to push back. They needed to bond if they were going to train together, there had to be some amount of trust between them. And, if her goading and teasing him built that relationship he would be happier for it.

With a satisfied smirk he answered, "We each have our own talents and we're willing to share with you. I'm assuming we'll need to ask your brothers' permission of course."

Her nostrils flared, he hit the nerve he had aimed for. She liked to challenge others just as much as he did. If she wanted to play, he would definitely oblige her.

"My brothers haven't had a say in my life since we were children," she growled, having fallen into his trap at the first sign of a challenge.

"Good, I would hate to have to ask them for every little thing in explicit detail." He winked. "It would be rather awkward if they walked in on us if I was trying to fix a stitch."

He was delighted by the fact that her face was beginning to turn red. Was she imagining him touching her?

"Why you?" She glared at him.

"Would you prefer one of my brothers?" He knew he had her at that. "Menolayous doesn't touch people unless he's trying to kill them, and Rama's hands are too big. I used to sew fishing nets, I have a gentle touch, I promise," he teased with a wink.

Her blush deepened, much to his delight. He wanted that image in her head, wanted her to imagine his hands on her. He wanted to imagine it too, and to make it into a reality. Offering to train her might have been a mistake.

"Figures," she mumbled, composing herself. "You'll find any excuse to see me without a shirt on again."

As soon as he processed her words, he laughed. Here he was thinking he had won, that he had cornered her, and she came back at him swinging. He shouldn't really be surprised; the girl was a fighter through and through. She winked at him before walking past him in the direction of the cavern. His brothers were right; he was in serious trouble.

Chapter Nine

Clyous

Bridget was humming to herself as she pulled the yellow flower heads free from their stems, placing them inside the leather bag she wore around her waist. Clyous was happy to accompany her on this outing even though he had to admit he did not understand a thing about gathering herbs. Markous had mocked him for going with her, claiming that Clyous was going soft, stooping so low as to collect flowers. Markous had grown angrier by the day; a lot of his anger directed at his siblings or Bridget. Clyous tried his best to not take these outbursts to heart, he suspected this was how his brother was coping with their loss. Truthfully, Clyous did not mind accompanying Bridget on these adventures, he enjoyed her company immensely. He had also learned a lot from her, she enjoyed teaching him about the different plants they came across, pointing out what was edible and what was not, telling him which plants were poisonous to the touch. He had never met a woman like her before. Her intelligence in regard to medicine was unparalleled. Her magic might not heal basic injuries as she would wish, but she was a powerful healer regardless. He admired her for it.

These moments alone together were precious; they spent a majority of their time together in the company of their little group. With everyone sleeping in the same cave, Clyous found himself feeling incredibly crowded at times, something he had never had an issue with before. Their family home was about as large as the cavern they all stayed in, but he only had to share it with three other people, not six. It's not that Clyous didn't enjoy being around everyone else, he enjoyed swapping stories with their new friends around the fire. Having lived outside the city for many years the three warriors were a wealth of knowledge. They had traveled places and seen many things, something Clyous was envious about but sometimes he just wanted Bridget to himself, away from all the chatter. Silence was a precious commodity, as was not being surrounded by people. Time spent with Bridget was important to him, even if all they did was gather herbs.

"What exactly are you doing with these flowers?" Clyous asked as he watched her.

"We can make tea with them, it helps with any sort of inflammation," she said to him as she picked another handful. "Now that your sister has decided to start training again, I have a feeling I'm going to have to keep you lot stocked with medical supplies when I'm not around."

Clyous smiled at that. It had almost been a month now since they had made their escape from the capital city. The first few days of their arrival had been the hardest days of Clyous's life. He had watched his mother burn alive in front of him, and he hadn't been strong enough to save her. Just as he hadn't been strong enough to stop them from hurting Catriona. He couldn't get the sound of the cracking of the whip out of his head, or Cat's screams. That day was supposed to be the worst day he'd ever experienced, it should have been considering it was the day their mother died, but when Menolayous, Danny, and Rama had rescued them from certain death and brought them to this cave for safety, it had given Clyous hope.

The bitter truth of it was Clyous spent the next few days watching his sister lie there unconscious, nearly dead. The possibility of her dying or not being able to recover after they were lucky enough to escape seemed like a cruel joke being played on them by the Goddess of Chaos. In those few days they would occasionally hear the sound of howls in the distance, setting them all on edge. Every rustle of a bush, every thud, every twig snapping had him fearing they had been found. He was absolutely terrified of the Oich guards finding them and finishing what they started, or scourge picking up on their scent and hunting them down while they were so vulnerable. That hope he had attained made the possibility of their deaths that much more real. It wasn't until Catriona awoke that the fear and terror began to subside.

Catriona had made an excellent recovery, with Bridget's constant tending and five incredibly stubborn men that wouldn't allow her to overly strain herself, she wasn't exactly given any other option. Bridget had removed Cat's last stitches about a week ago, giving her the okay to start building her strength back. Unsurprisingly, Danny had seemed eager to assist her with this. Clyous was no fool, and Danny did not hide it well. He knew the man had been enchanted by his sister. And Danny was enchanted; there was no other logical way any man would put up with the amount of trash talk and attitude Catriona hurtled his way unless he was under some sort of enchantment. What was equally entertaining was that she seemed to like him too, not that his sister would admit it. Oh, she threw everything she had at him, Clyous suspected it was to see if he could in fact handle the nightmare his twin could be if she wanted, but Danny was surviving it, not just surviving, he seemed to enjoy it. Catriona, who would normally threaten any man who wouldn't catch the hint, was actually allowing Danny to keep coming around her. They sought each other out, even though the other never seemed to fully notice.

It had started with exercises to work on her speed and endurance. Menolayous had also offered to teach Catriona to hunt, working on shooting

69

a bow. Cat had excelled quickly; Rama had made a remark that Catriona must be the daughter of the Goddess of War herself because she had such a natural talent. Today, Danny had announced that Catriona was ready to start sparring with weapons. Clyous knew this excited his sister. She hadn't really had anyone to train with since their father abandoned them. He and Markous had kept too busy, not caring enough to train. Now Catriona had several people willing to train with her, and all of them capable warriors.

"I just hope she doesn't hurt anyone too critically," Clyous joked, perhaps their new companions had bitten off more than they could chew when it came to her.

"She's in good hands," Bridget responded, still focused on her flowers. "Each of them has survived many battles and hardships. She'll learn a lot from them."

"I have no doubts." Clyous nudged a rock with his foot. "She's just going to be insufferable the better she gets. If you think Markous's ego is huge, just wait until you see how cocky Cat gets about fighting."

"I'd say it's a good thing for her to get her confidence back, but knowing Danny, he'll have her as cocky and as competent as the rest of them."

"What makes you say that?"

"It's how Danny is, he'll challenge her, he'll push her hard, but he'll also make her feel powerful. He's very supportive, he will be with her especially."

The taste of jealousy coated his tongue when he asked, "Are you and Danny close?"

Bridget glanced up from her work and smirked at him. "Not in the way you're worried about. They are my friends, true and trusted friends. None of us have ever entertained the idea of it being something different."

This was a great relief to Clyous, even though he could admit to himself he was slightly embarrassed at how transparent he was. Bridget continued to watch him for a moment, a warm smile on her beautiful face. After a moment of him just staring back awkwardly, she returned to her work. Taking a step forward, Bridget's foot came down on a fallen tree branch, the weight pushing down on the rotting wood and causing it to snap.

The sound of the branch breaking reverberated through his body as if the sound had been magnified to such a degree that everything else was drowned out. Clyous inhaled sharply as his muscles locked, painful memories began to tug at him. Panic overcame him as he froze in place, his eyes and ears barely able to sense anything going on around him. Bridget turned to him and spoke, but he was unable to hear her words. All he could hear was the crack of a whip and Catriona's screams.

The images changed from Catriona being whipped to something more foreign. Catriona in a field somewhere, a hunting dagger in hand as she single-handedly fought against several wolves. He could see the images clear as day, but he couldn't hear anything except the fire crackling and Catriona's screams.

Bridget's hand on his made him startle violently out of this bizarre experience, bringing his focus back to the present. "Clyous? Are you okay?"

"Yeah," he choked out as he continued to ground himself, surprised by the sound of his voice. "I'm okay."

She stared up into his face, hands gently grasping his. She was concerned about him, and truthfully, so was he. He had never experienced anything like that before in his life. He supposed there would be times when something could trigger him and force him to relive memories of that day, it seemed like a natural reaction for anyone who experienced trauma. But that other part where he watched his sister fighting in a field, that wasn't something he had ever seen. It was possible his mind was playing tricks on him, showing him images that fed the fear of his sister being hurt again.

"You stepped on the branch," he forced out. He should probably explain himself so she didn't think he was losing it. "I didn't hear wood snapping. It sounded like a whip. It was like everything else in the world stopped, then I could hear my sister's screams."

Sadness replaced the concern on Bridget's face as she gently wrapped her arms around his middle. The physical contact seemed to help anchor him, her slender arms gently squeezing him as if to remind him that he was in fact loved. He released his breath, relaxing as he embraced her back. It felt nice to hold her, a soft presence that he could embrace for another moment. The panic slowly drained from him as they stood there.

"I'm sorry," was all she said, she understood what he was going through.

"It's just a branch," he mumbled, not sure if he was more frustrated at a branch setting him off or if he needed to reassure her that he was okay. "None of it is your fault."

71

Bridget pulled away slightly so she could look up at him. "Part of me agrees with Catriona and what she said when she finally woke up. If I was able to control my shift maybe I could have done something."

"No." Clyous gazed down into those perfect emerald eyes. "One blooded wouldn't have made a difference. My sister spoke out of anger; I don't believe that she meant it."

"I know," Bridget spoke softly. "But do you believe that?"

He was confused by her question, had he said or done something to make Bridget believe he blamed her? "No, it was never your responsibility to step in, they would have killed you."

"I mean, do you believe any of us doing something differently would have stopped it? Because I know you, guilt is eating at you whether you realize it or not."

Damn, she was right. As much as he did believe what he had just told Bridget about one wolf not being enough to save them, deep down he still believed if he had tried harder, if he had fought more in the beginning, maybe he could have changed the outcome. It wasn't a belief based on logic. Honestly, he had replayed that day in his head hundreds of times trying to find a solution he could never reenact and provide a different outcome.

"It's natural to feel guilt after something that traumatic," Bridget said gently. "I'm sure everyone has revisited that day several times trying to make it right, trying to find a solution; but the truth is, you're just torturing yourselves. There is no solving this, it's already happened. And, until you can accept that fact and begin to heal, broken branches are just the beginning of what will torment you."

She was right, he knew that without a doubt. He was very lucky to have a friend like her, to have someone there for him. This was one of the many reasons he cherished spending time with her. He wouldn't have been able to talk to the others about this, there was an unspoken rule between men that you did not discuss your feelings. At least with Markous there was, but with Bridget he felt like he could show her who he truly was without ridicule.

"Thank you," he said, gently kissing her cheek.

Chapter Ten

Markous

Markous sat across the fire from Rama, who was turning the recently skinned and prepared rabbits that hung over the flames. This was what they were all reduced to, cooking meat while his little sister was away from the fire and trained with Danny. Rama and his brothers were overly generous with how they were treating his family, something Markous was not sure the twins appreciated the way they should.

These warriors had rescued them from Oich, risking their lives and their mission to save them. They aided in Catriona's recovery, never once seeking repayment. Danny had even offered to start training with his sister, most likely to placate her self-destructive tendencies. Menolayous even worked with her on how to hunt, improving her skill with a bow. And all of them were overly considerate about her pathetic eating habits. They cooked meat away from her, Danny even regularly made other food that wasn't meat for her. His sister ate meat; he had never seen her turn down food before. She needed to get over herself and see how she was affecting everyone else with her little game. At least she contributed by hunting game for them, it was more than Clyous was doing.

Clyous did very little to help out around camp. Whenever the blooded brat strolled into camp Clyous would shove his head so far up her ass he could barely function. Markous didn't like the woman. For one thing she was a rich and blooded noblewoman from Oich, their "masters" and enemy, but the brat had a way of looking down at them like they were all beneath her. Markous was ashamed that his brother was so obsessed with her. The only reason he tolerated her presence was because she aided Rama and his brothers with intelligence from the city and she patched his sister up.

Markous was getting restless. He was ready to leave here and join the rebels. Unlike his siblings, he was prepared to join the cause, willing to fight against the crown who had taken everything from them. They only had each other left, and the other two seemed content in chasing after love interests. Their decision showed their age, their selfishness. Like always, it left Markous to step up and do the adult thing. He just needed Catriona to stop milking all of Danny's attention so Rama would make the call that it was time for them to head out. Like him, Rama was the head of his family. What he says goes, and Rama was waiting on his brother Danny.

"Where will we be going first?" Markous couldn't contain himself; he was excited and wanted to leave.

"Not too sure," Rama answered as he turned the rabbits yet again.

"What is your fighting experience?" the quiet one, Menolayous, asked from Rama's side.

"I can fight," Markous answered defensively.

"I've seen you fight." Menolayous's eyes bored into his. "You need work."

"Have you trained with weapons?" Rama asked, breaking the tension.

"No, but I can make weapons," Markous answered. "I get how to use them."

"Working on weapons isn't quite the same." Rama smiled at him kindly. "But smithing has made you strong."

"Why don't you train with your sister?" Menolayous asked pointedly, Markous sensed that the quiet one did not like him much. "Even now, Danny is going over basic weapons."

"Have you met my sister? She's impossible to work with. We wouldn't be able to make it one session before trying to kill each other."

Markous watched as the two men shared a look. A silent communication clearly passing between them. This made Markous shift uncomfortably, had he said something wrong?

"We'll be taking you to the Harrada Pass for training," Rama said as he returned to the rabbit. "We have a stronghold in the mountains run by a seasoned war chief. He's very good at training our newer recruits. Our best warriors have trained with him."

"Excellent." Markous clapped his hands together excitedly. "When can we go?"

Rama and Menolayous shared another look before Rama said, "In another week or two."

"Why so long?" Markous's excitement turned to frustration. "Catriona is better now. She's good enough to play a warrior, she's good enough to travel."

Rama's eyes narrowed at him through the flames. "Play a warrior?"

Markous began to backpedal in his mind, clearly he had said something wrong. "I just meant a woman has no business acting like she's a real warrior. What Danny is doing for her is kind and all, but the girl has been catered to her whole life. The bigger her head gets the more she'll think she can fight. Whatever modified training Danny is putting her through to placate her has at least made her strong enough to travel. We don't need to wait around for her anymore."

There, he explained it much better. Maybe now they would see that he was on their side and ready to move. They seemed antsy enough, Markous assumed they too were placating their youngest sibling. By allowing Danny to keep "training" her, all they did was feed into her delusions. Women did not fight. Catriona had some talent with it, but she would never be accepted on the battlefield. If anything, she would make herself more of a target.

"Your sister is a warrior," Menolayous growled. "Danny isn't modifying any training. She's learning what any man would and she's excelling."

Markous was taken aback by the venom and distaste lacing Menolayous's words. Markous could not understand this reaction, what had he said wrong? If anything, he should be mad at them for indulging her. He had them to blame if she tried to enter any battle.

Just as he was about to open his mouth to argue, Rama cut in, "We will leave in a week or two. It will take several days to hunt and prepare food for the journey. Spring nears, it is safer to travel now that the ground has stopped freezing over at night."

Rama cast Menolayous a look as if to say, 'end of conversation'. He could respect the older brother's reasoning. He envied how easily Rama could issue commands and wished his younger siblings listened as easily. Menolayous got up and left, marching out of the cave in a huff. Good, let him throw a fit out there, Markous would remain where he was. He could show Rama that he was the bigger man in this scenario. Markous was happy he had the opportunity to do so. He was also thrilled that they would be on the road soon. He would finally escape Oich and leave behind all the ghosts of his past.

Chapter Eleven

Catriona

Nearly a month and a half later Catriona found herself deep within the woods following hoof imprints in the soggy dirt. She carried the hunting bow Menolayous had made for her and a quiver of arrows he had showed her how to make. She was several miles away from their cavern, having to go out even farther into the forest to track this particular prey. The deer had brought her south, closer to the capital city than she would have liked to be.

She and Menolayous had embarked on this final hunting excursion in a last-ditch effort to collect enough food for their journey. Catriona was partially responsible for their delayed departure, having to take a good portion of the last month recovering from her injuries. Her stitches had been removed, and she had been slowly working on regaining her strength for a few weeks now. Thanks to Danny's relentless regimen she was back up to fighting speed, mostly. Her ribs were still incredibly tender, but otherwise they had healed. Bridget was convinced they had broken, which is why they took the longest to heal. Catriona was back to training regularly, and with Danny as a sparring partner, her ribs just had to go along with it, soreness be damned.

It was about time their group hit the road anyway, everyone was getting antsy just hanging around. Markous especially, his temper grew shorter by the day, particularly whenever anything involved herself or Clyous. Markous couldn't stand the fact that Catriona still couldn't eat meat and absolutely hated the fact that everyone else in camp was kind enough to cook meat away from her. Markous genuinely believed that Catriona was playing some sort of game with it and blamed her for why it was taking everyone so long to leave. Clyous, on the other hand, was "weak and pathetic" for spending most of his free time with Bridget whenever she was visiting. Markous was fixating a lot of his rage and hatred towards the healer simply because she was blooded. Markous's main goal in life was to leave the Kingdom of Oich, he didn't care how or why. Catriona did her best not to take his outbursts personally. Danny had suggested that this was probably Markous's way of trying to deal with them losing their mother. Catriona supposed each one of them was dealing with it differently, she just hated that Markous was taking it out on them so hard.

Her focus shifted back to the hunt; the extra food would help in case prey was scarce as they traveled. Catriona was still trying to figure out how she was going to manage. Bridget was due back today, bringing with her some supplies and hopefully information that could aid them in their escape. Clyous was taking this plan the hardest, Catriona supposed he didn't want to be too far from the healer. They had grown close these last few weeks, Catriona could understand his hesitation, but they were wanted. Staying in Oich, returning to the capital, these were guaranteed death sentences.

At the moment, the official plan was to gather what supplies they could and head farther north. The end goal was to take Clyous and Catriona to the rebel stronghold in Airgid while dropping Markous off in the Harrada Pass for training. Markous had pledged himself to the rebellion, he was at least wanting to stay busy. As for her and her twin, they were at a loss with what they wanted to do with the rest of their lives. Catriona felt lost and conflicted, she didn't want to leave her home, but there was nothing there for her anymore. Truthfully, she wanted to stay with everyone hiding out in the forest away from the Oich guards. While they were here it was almost as if she was safe to not make decisions, leaving meant she was now forced to face a world without her mother and possibly her brothers. She wasn't sure she was ready to be alone.

She stepped over a small stream, careful not to slip on any of the wet rocks as she made her way towards a clearing. The deer tracks led this direction, a hoofprint was in the mud by the stream. She was closing in, good. She and Menolayous had split up an hour ago, each of them following two different sets of tracks, she wasn't sure where he was now. Catriona silently made her way towards the break in the trees, peering around the ferns into the clearing. She spotted the doe about twenty feet away picking gently at the grass, not a care in the world. She envied the kind of peace the doe held, but peace did not exist, she was about to prove it. Fate seemed to always come out of nowhere, bringing with it violence and chaos. She nocked an arrow and pulled back the string of her bow. She took a deep slow breath, and on the exhale she released the string. The deer dropped to its knees before completely collapsing onto the damp grass, the arrow piercing it through the side.

Catriona smiled at the shot, happy with her success. She shouldered the bow and stalked forward, no longer concerned about making noise. She pulled out her hunting knife and started cutting at the thin flesh of the abdomen. The rusty tang of blood filled her nostrils as she felt the warm liquid coat her hands. It was comforting to work with her hands again, to be useful. She was thankful that Menolayous had taught her to hunt, she appreciated her new friends immensely. Without their encouragement and support she would have likely gone mad, Menolayous's faith in her had given her something to do. Keeping busy was a luxury she valued deeply.

She allowed her thoughts to wander as she began to remove the innards of the doe. She watched as the warmth from the carcass hit the cold, brisk, morning air, creating spirals of steam that poured from the dead beast. There was something beautiful about how the mist spiraled upwards, an elegance to it. Voices suddenly caught her attention, the sound bounced off the trees making it hard to pinpoint a direction. Catriona wiped her hands on the wet grass, cleaning off a good portion of the blood. She knew she was closer to the city than she should be, but she should still be far enough away that she shouldn't run into anyone. Catriona was on high alert now, needing to see who was nearby without revealing that she was out here. If it were Oich guards, she would need to get away quickly.

"Let go of me!" she heard a familiar voice shout. It was Bridget's voice.

The sound of her friend in distress pushed Catriona into motion. No longer concerned about making a sneaky getaway, she barreled forward through the trees in the direction of her friend. As she ran, Catriona unshouldered her bow and notched an arrow. Bridget shouldn't be yelling at someone this far into the forest. The healer must have been followed out here Catriona realized, but by who?

She came up on them then, three blooded men were surrounding Bridget, laughing and taunting her as she tried to push past them. The men weren't Oich guards, lacking any armor and carrying the most basic of weapons. They were dressed like noblemen of all things, men from the same social class as Bridget. She knew them, Catriona realized, which meant that they knew her. They knew she couldn't control her shift, that she couldn't fight. They hunted her down, waiting for her to be alone and away from anyone who might help her. Rage coursed through Catriona at this realization, she knew what they were here for.

Catriona watched as the tallest man came up behind Bridget and wrapped his arms around her from behind, trapping her arms underneath his. Bridget screamed as she tried kicking out at the man, but her attempts were unsuccessful. The men laughed even harder as she struggled. Their leader, the one who wore more finery, began tugging up on Bridget's skirts. Catriona fought with herself to stay in the present; it would do no good for her to be tugged back into her dark memories. She needed to help her friend, she would not allow this to happen to her, but Bridget couldn't fight, and Catriona had no silver-edged weapons. The others were too far away to be of any help, at least a mile or two. There wasn't an outcome that Catriona could see where she could save both of them. The blooded were likely to turn their attention to her the second she acted. Rape of a blooded woman was forbidden in Oich, part of their belief system was that blooded women were meant to be treated with respect in order to breed acceptable offspring. But they were also meant to submit to their husbands. Nobody cared what happened to a slave girl, however only the purest of believers would still look at the assault as a taint on their own honor.

"Scream as loud as you want, girl. There's nobody out here to save you," their leader mocked as he began to tear through Bridget's underskirts.

"Unless you can shift and fight us off." All three of them laughed at that. Bridget was crying now, begging them to stop.

It wasn't a decision Catriona had to think about, she made her choice as she pulled back on the string, aimed, and let loose the arrow. It stuck itself into one of the men's sides, piercing him in his ribcage. He roared and fell back away from Bridget, the others snapping their heads to him as he recovered. Her arrows were not silver tipped so they were not likely to kill him unless the arrow pierced something vital because the wounds would heal at a rapid rate. Still, they would hurt him, she would make sure they hurt. Catriona stepped from the trees, aiming at the man who had yet to touch her friend, firing another arrow which struck him in the shoulder. Bridget, seeing Catriona emerge, was able to pull free from her captor as she ran towards Catriona.

"Gentlemen—" Catriona aimed another arrow at the closest man, stepping forward to shield Bridget with her body. "Ladies don't appreciate being manhandled. It's time you left."

The men looked at each other exchanging snarls as they stared at the arrow she had pointed their direction. She recognized that look, blooded men angry at having someone step in between them and their prey. They were not entitled to her friend; they were not entitled to any woman. She was there to remind them of that fact, even if she couldn't kill them at least she would cause them immense pain. They would not be getting away with this without paying a price.

"Look here boys, we've got some slave bitch protecting the runt," the fancy-dressed prick snarled, his eyes locked on to Catriona's every movement.

"Go," Catriona whispered to Bridget, refusing to take her eyes off the rapists. "Get the boys here."

"I won't leave you," Bridget said, Catriona glanced at a split on her lip.

"No offense, but you're not helpful in a fight. Our best bet is for you to make it to the cave and bring them back to me."

The men began to fan out and approach them, like wolves surrounding their prey. This was going to be extremely hard without silver tipped weapons, but she would make do. She prayed to the gods that Bridget listened to her and ran. She might be able to hold them off long enough for Bridget to get to the cave. The boys making it back to her in time, well, that was to be determined.

With a final glance at her friend, Catriona inhaled deeply to steady herself. It was now or never. The men were getting closer, Bridget's chances of making it out were shrinking with every step they took.

"You've got to let me know if this is good for you," she sneered as she released the arrow.

There was movement from every direction as the arrow flew through the air. The arrow shaft embedded in their leader's other shoulder, causing him to drop to his knees. Good, they were weak, she should be thankful they were not trained warriors. Bridget turned and fled into the woods, sprinting at an unnatural speed towards the cave, towards Catriona's best chance of survival. The three men lunged for her as she threw herself sideways, letting loose two more arrows, each one hitting their mark.

Chapter Twelve

Bridget

Bridget pushed herself to her very limit, racing for the cave. Even in her human form Bridget was fast, she hoped she was fast enough. Her arms pumped hard as she weaved through the trees, her long skirts catching and ripping in the brush as she barreled on. Fear, anger at herself, and leaving Catriona there alone were what pushed her so hard. She should not have left her friend, it wasn't right. Nothing about this situation was right. If Bridget was more in control of her wolf, if she could fight, she would have stayed to help. But Catriona was right, Bridget getting help was their best chance. Her presence would only distract Catriona. These men were not warriors, yes most blooded nobles walked around carrying weapons pretending to be something special, but only the royal guards received combat training. Catriona had a chance to take them, to survive. She had the skill that those men did not. Bridget prayed to the Goddess of War and Fate to protect her friend.

Bridget stumbled slightly as she pushed through some brush, seeing a stream approaching she vaulted over the water, landing relatively gracefully on the slick rocks on the other side. Bridget took off again, scrambling up the muddy bank as she moved. Stopping wasn't an option, neither was slipping and falling. Even though Bridget's lungs burned as she inhaled the cold morning air she pushed harder. She could do this; she would do this.

She had no idea the men had followed her into the forest, but she wasn't exactly surprised either. The men of Oich were an entitled lot, treating women in the worst ways possible. The higher up the hierarchy the man was, the more he got away with doing unspeakable things to others. It wasn't unheard of for a nobleman to rape one of his slaves, it was looked down on, their belief system being that it tainted the blooded and any offspring it might create. But the assault of a noblewoman was a crime punishable by death in Oich. Part of their belief was that women were to be married off and submit to their husbands.

She had been harassed and mistreated for years because she was a "runt," but never had anyone try to come after her like this before. Her father was the second wealthiest merchant in the capital, holding an immense amount of power most men feared. Her true protector over the years had been her childhood friend Liam, such a powerful shifter who would not allow anything to come for her in this way. Now she was alone though, her father regularly traveled for business and Liam was no longer in the picture, it was only a matter of time before jealous and envious men decided to come for the woman who could not defend herself. She was at the bottom of the pack, easy prey just like a slave. She had been stupid, wandering around the city alone and disappearing into the forest without company. She was predictable, too comfortable, she had believed she was still untouchable. This was of course a lie, now that she could see the consequences of her naivety.

The cave was about a mile away now; she recognized the pathway she had stumbled onto. It was no more than a deer trail they used to move about; they had been worried a larger path would make it easier for Oich guards to track them to their hideout. Bridget scented something nearby, two familiar scents off to the right. It was Danny and Rama! Thank the gods!

She veered their direction, not caring that her sleeve ripped on a passing branch. They were closer, that was good. That meant there was a chance for Cat. She didn't care much why they were so far away from their cave, she only cared that they were there.

"I swear if we have to stay one more week with that arrogant asshole, I'm going to break a few of his bones," she could hear Danny say. "I can't stand the way he talks about her, or his younger brother."

"He's processing things differently than the other two," Rama countered. "Besides, he's their brother, they get to pick how to deal with him, not you."

Bridget crashed through the brush towards them. She could see the startled expressions on their faces as they reached for their weapons. They realized who she was quickly enough, not raising them at her as she skidded to a halt in front of them. It only took half a second before their eyes took in her appearance, their expressions turning dark.

"Come!" She breathed hard, grabbing Danny by the arms and dragging him behind her. "Now!"

"What's going on?" Rama called as he reached towards her as if to stop her.

"It's Catriona!" she got out, dodging his grip as she started running back the direction she came. "Three blooded tried to—" inhale "— she saved me. She's fighting them alone."

She saw fear immediately pass over the men's faces as they quickly put together what had happened. She had never seen Danny so afraid before, the expression on his face as he ran past all of them was of complete terror. He was afraid for her, for Catriona. Unlike other men from Oich, her friends not only refused to engage in the behaviors of others, but they also actively sought to end the violence against others. Danny had seen firsthand with his mother what men could do, he refused to allow that to happen to anyone else. It's why he still fought in the rebellion after all these years. But that look, it revealed too much. He cared for Catriona so much so that panic had seized him, sending him shooting through the trees like an arrow. Common sense had apparently left him, he had no idea where he was going, he just went. Bridget and Rama took off after him, with Bridget catching up to Danny easily enough and leading the way. They would make it back to her in time, they had to. She sent another prayer up to the Goddess of War and Fate, please, bless the fiery girl with your skills just long enough until they could get there.

Chapter Thirteen

Rama

After hearing Menolayous describe how Danny had been when he first saw Catriona fighting for her mother's life, watching his little brother now after hearing she was fighting a couple of blooded alone, the same blooded who had tried to rape Bridget, he could see what Menolayous had meant. Danny moved like a wild animal, the only one of them able to keep up with Bridget and her blooded speed. Rama prayed the girl was holding her own. He hoped she could fight like he heard she could, he had yet to go watch her train with Danny.

They passed the corpse of a gutted deer in a clearing. Most likely Catriona's work since she was out hunting. It at least meant she had some weapons on her even though they weren't silver edged. A minute or so later he could hear the fighting. He saw it then, what his brothers were talking about when they described how quickly Catriona could move. Catriona moved like wildfire spreading through a dry field. Armed only with what looked like a hunter's knife, she slashed at the thigh of one blooded and on the upswing sliced the cheek of the one that came up behind her. The third man picked himself up and out of the dirt and ran for her. She turned to face him, not paying attention to the other who had come up behind her. He grabbed her, pinning her arms down as the other one charged. Rama watched Catriona throw herself backwards over the man that held her and deliver a kick to the charging man's face.

Danny, ahead of all of them, tackled the man who was still standing, taking him to the ground. Rama jumped into the fray swinging his battle axe at the blooded that Catriona had knocked down. The blooded rolled out of the way just in time. Catriona reengaged with the man farthest away from her, the momentum behind her when she hit him was impressive. Rama looked at her then, there was confidence in her movements, no hesitation. She had the skill of a warrior, reflexes of one who had spent years on the battlefield. Her hair was coming out of its braid and her cheeks red with exertion. She had a bloody lip and red marks on the side of her face like she'd been hit, but she smiled as she slashed her knife at the blooded noble's chest. It was as if he was watching the Goddess of War herself unleashed upon those who had displeased her.

Catriona finished slicing up the blooded she had trapped underneath her and glanced around the clearing. Rama then watched her hurdle herself over everyone to get to the man wrestling with Danny. His brother was a great fighter but in a strength contest he was no match for any blooded. Knowing this, Rama guessed this is exactly why Catriona vaulted over the man. Grabbing his head and using her momentum and body weight to throw the man a foot into the air before crashing back down. Catriona had scrambled out of the way before the man could recover, allowing Danny to pierce his chest with his silvered short sword.

Only one man remained, everyone turned to face him. The blooded seemed to realize the situation he was in. As a last-ditch effort, he charged at Catriona and transformed mid-step into a black and grey wolf. The wolf, now larger and faster than the human girl by far, sank its teeth around one of her thighs and shook her like a rabbit he just caught.

With a yelp of pain Catriona was tossed around like a rag doll, struggling to free herself from the creature's fangs. Rama started forward to engage with the beast when he spotted a large red shape coming from behind him. It was Bridget he realized quickly. She had let her wolf come out to play. Her red-brown wolf was almost double the size of the other, albeit skinnier. To his surprise, the non-confrontational and usually timid healer came at the black-grey wolf from underneath and gripped his throat with her fangs.

The nobleman's wolf dropped Catriona who was immediately dragged away to safety by Danny. Bridget's wolf pinned him to the ground while emitting the most terrifying growl Rama had ever heard. To his surprise, Rama watched as the grey wolf rolled over and whimpered in submission. Well, that's an interesting turn of events.

For a moment longer Rama watched the two wolves. He knew Bridget didn't have it in her to rip the other wolf's throat out. Yet, she would get there he realized, her engaging at all was the first step. He crossed the clearing over to them and raised his axe high and brought it down hard. The blade of his axe came down on the wolf's neck. He raised the axe again, hitting the same spot through the thick and mangled fur. One more strike and the wolf's head was finally separated from its thick neck.

"Let me see," he could hear Bridget say.

Rama turned to look, Bridget was back in her human form sitting above a wounded Catriona. Danny was still holding onto Catriona, acting as if he intended to shield her from an oncoming threat. Catriona seemed too preoccupied with her bleeding leg to notice the awkward embrace, but Rama did his best to suppress a laugh. His brother had it bad, that's for damn sure.

"Will I turn?" Catriona asked Bridget.

"In theory, yes." Bridget was pulling a wrapping out of a small bag she always wore. "Your wound overall isn't that serious."

"Can you stop being the one who always gets hurt? At this rate we need to put you in a padded suit," Rama teased in an attempt to lighten the mood.

"Fuck off!" Catriona hissed through her teeth as Bridget poked at a spot on her thigh. "I didn't see you fighting off a pack of wolves single-handedly."

"Can we address the more immediate issue here, what are we going to do about Catriona turning," Danny chimed in, unamused by their antics.

"I think the more impressive topic is how Bridget shifted at will and went straight for the throat." Rama winked at the healer playfully.

Rama watched Bridget's face turn as red as her hair. The two women locked eyes for a moment, ignoring everyone else.

"Thank you—" Bridget started "—I'm sorry I—"

"Thank you for running fast," Catriona said, "and for stopping me from being ripped apart. I take back every mean thing I've ever said to you, I was wrong."

Bridget smiled down at her. "You've already been forgiven."

"Right." Catriona gave her a small smile. "Looks like I'll be joining your pack now anyway. Markous is going to be thrilled."

"Not necessarily. I'm confident that I was able to cleanse the curse from the scourge out of your mother. I'm just as confident I can cleanse you."

"Being a wolf sounds like it could be advantageous," Rama jested, enjoying the irritated look on Danny's face.

"For old blooded, yes." Bridget narrowed her eyes at Rama. "New blooded won't be able to control their shift. And during the full moon you'd be spending your time wandering around in your fur suit. At least for the first few years."

"Yeah, I think I'm good," Catriona answered. "No offense."

"None taken. Full moons can be rough."

"Arguably, creating a rebel force made of new blooded has got to be a decent plan," Rama said just to argue, nothing about turning sounded pleasant.

"Can you just shut up," Danny said through gritted teeth, directing his frustration at Rama.

"Fine. Give me your arm and I'll make you one," Bridget challenged him, good there was still some fight in there. "Then you can spend the next five to ten years shifting into a wolf whenever you get mad, or scared, or hungry, or excited, or aroused…"

"Okay, okay, I get it," Rama pleaded, allowing the healer to win this round.

"And whenever a dominant wolf comes by your wolf will submit to anything that wolf wants you to do. It makes it hard to rebel against someone who can control your very instincts. New blooded are never dominant. There's a reason why you don't see many of them in the capital, they are incredibly hard to control. It's why the crown sends them to the outer villages."

Bridget held her hands over the bite wound on Catriona's leg. Rama watched as golden light began to radiate down into the open wounds. He was always greatly impressed by this magic. She had used it on him once too when he had a badly infected battle wound. Apparently, along with infections and poisons, her magic could lift curses. He'd added that onto his mental checklist.

Rama remembered the day they had met Bridget over a year ago. Rama and his two brothers had attempted a raid on a trading convoy that was headed to Oich. Two of their raiding party were killed, leaving just them. They foolishly tried to take on five blooded guards that were escorting an old blooded who was disguised as a trader. After getting their asses kicked, they had fled into the forest where they hid for about a week. Danny had sustained a pretty deep cut from a sword that had gotten badly infected. Bridget had been out in the woods collecting herbs but decided to follow their scent anyways. She had used her golden magic just like she was now, it was a true gift from the Goddess of Healers for sure.

"Are you alright?" Danny asked Bridget.

Rama looked at her and saw her face starting to contort in pain. Catriona's face was turning very red, her forehead breaking into a sweat.

"It burns a little," Bridget said through clenched teeth.

"Catriona?" Danny asked as he stared down at her.

"Bridget, can you turn down the temperature a little?" Catriona begged, pulling the collar of her tunic down.

"I'm not doing that!" The golden light changed colors to red and white hues. It danced like a small flame above Catriona's injured flesh. "Ow!"

Bridget fell back holding her hands away from her. Rama caught her before she hit the ground. At the same time, Catriona let out a shout of pain, lying back against Danny, breathing heavily. Rama looked back to Bridget and saw that her hands were starting to blister as if she had held them over an open flame.

"What in the fuck?" Danny asked, looking between the girls.

Bridget started to examine both sides of her hands, they were both red and blistering in some places but otherwise they seemed fine. Catriona sat up, making a noise that drew everyone's attention. The bite marks on her thigh had disappeared completely. The girls looked at each other again.

"That wasn't me," Bridget exclaimed, "it couldn't be."

Chapter Fourteen

Menolayous

Menolayous returned to the cave about an hour or so ago. They had taken off during the early hours of the morning so they could hunt and bring back enough food to prepare for their journey. It was about time they finally left the seclusion of the cave; Catriona was healed sufficiently enough and was able to travel again. Seriously, the woman was training again, working with Danny on building her strength and endurance as well as mastering the use of daggers in combat. The road was not a safe place for any of them as fleeing rebels hiding from the crown. They could encounter a number of dangers, from scourge hunting at night to blooded who spotted them and chose to take a few more human slaves for themselves. Catriona would be the primary target for both types of enemies, being the smallest in the group she would be sought after by any ill-intentioned males they might encounter, blooded or otherwise. It was important that she was back in fighting shape. Menolayous hadn't minded staying in one place for so long, not being on the road every day was a relief. However, they couldn't stay here forever. It was a matter of time before a blooded wandered out this far, or a scourge came hunting and they were discovered.

Out of all their worries, the most pressing issue that drove them back to the road was Markous. The bastard was getting on everyone's nerves. Menolayous was certain, Markous's sudden abrasive attitude towards his siblings was how he was dealing with the trauma he had endured, but it was wearing on everyone. None of them could stand how Markous belittled and chastised his younger siblings, especially Danny. Anytime Catriona showed signs of grieving their mother, which oddly came out in how she ate, Markous would ridicule her relentlessly. It took a lot out of all of them to not beat the shit out of the older brother, his siblings needed to mourn in peace the way they needed to. Trying to force them to have a "kill them all" mentality like his own wasn't helping.

Unsurprisingly, when Menolayous had strolled back into camp dragging a boar carcass on a makeshift sled, Markous came rushing to help, leaving his younger brother at the cave entrance looking as if they had just been arguing again. Menolayous had taken notice that Rama and Danny were nowhere to be seen. Menolayous remained mostly silent as Markous and

Clyous helped him skin and section off the meat. Menolayous knew if he started in on how much of an ass Markous was being he wouldn't stop, which could very well escalate things to violence. He didn't feel like wiping the floor with Markous today when they still had so much to do.

The sound of footsteps approaching caught his attention long before the other two noticed. Menolayous spotted his brothers making their way to the mouth of the cave. Menolayous noted that they looked disheveled, as if slightly battle worn. Following closely behind them were Bridget and Catriona. Bridget was smiling and laughing with Catriona as if they were long lost friends. This was a change in their relationship dynamic for sure, and a welcomed one at that. Even more puzzling, after his eyes fell on Catriona, he noticed that although the girl was smiling and laughing, she looked rough. Her braid was unkempt and messy; dirt and blood splattered across her face and arms. Her tunic and pants were dirty and ripped. She had been fighting, he realized. Her brothers froze as she came into view, panicked at the sight of her.

"Cat?!" Clyous dropped his skinning knife and rushed to his sister. Surprisingly, Markous did the same. "What happened?"

"I'm fine." She smiled at them. "Really."

"She was wonderful!" Bridget beamed. "She saved me from a few blooded that had followed me from the city. It was like watching the Goddess of War grace us with her very presence."

"Yes, quite impressive," Rama mused. "Until she got trapped in the jaws of a wolf and had to be rescued by our gentle healer."

"Fuck off." Catriona laughed and simultaneously flipped Rama the middle finger. "Bridget was a true warrior today."

"Hardly." Bridget blushed deeply.

"So, what happened?" Clyous asked, confused and still showing concern. "Are you both okay?"

"We're okay," Catriona answered flatly, clearly done with the repeated question.

"A few blooded followed me as I snuck out of the city. Catriona heard them… harassing me." Bridget was obviously skipping over a specific detail, Menolayous could guess what it was. "Catriona took them on by herself. I ran to get help and came upon these two. By the time we got back to her she was slicing them to pieces."

"Until one of them sunk its fangs into her leg and shook her like a rabbit!" Rama was having fun bringing that part up.

"But then Bridget shifted and put the rabid wolf down!" Catriona said excitedly, intentionally ignoring Rama's little add-ins. "And Bridget healed me, *completely*."

This was an unexpected piece of information, Bridget hadn't ever been able to heal wounds before, just infections. Menolayous watched both of the women's faces shine brightly as they interacted with the others. They were proud of what they had accomplished today, and they should be. Fending off three blooded single-handedly, Bridget controlling her shift, these were significantly positive accomplishments. Even Danny and Rama were smiling at them proudly. These women had shown their strength today and proven their warrior spirit. At the end of the day that's all any of them really wanted for the people of Stone Basin, for them to be able to protect themselves.

"And I have you and Danny to thank," Catriona said excitedly, bouncing in front of him, their eyes locking. "Because of your training with my bow, I was able to slow them down long enough for Bridget to get help. Each arrow hit its mark. So, thank you, Menolayous."

His heart warmed slightly at her genuine smile. Before he had time to react or even register what was going on, Catriona leaned forward and embraced him in a hug. Menolayous jumped backwards to get away from her, the feel of her arms around him made him feel suddenly trapped. Menolayous could then feel the darkness creeping into his mind as panic took over his movements. She had touched him! Menolayous shook away the memories that had begun to crowd in.

"She didn't mean anything by it," Danny's voice cut through the darkness, bringing Menolayous back to the present.

Menolayous saw that Danny now stood directly in front of Catriona, shielding her from his view. Rama moved to Danny's side, also blocking her from him. Menolayous's gaze shifted to Bridget who was being dragged off to the side by Clyous and away from the danger. Everyone was staring at him now as if expecting him to…

"Brother, everything is okay," Rama said in a soothing voice, his large hands raised in a manner to show he wasn't a threat. "Catriona was just excited; you can put the knife down."

Reality came into focus at his brother's words. Menolayous suddenly realized he was clutching his skinning knife with a death grip. His breathing was ragged, and he could feel his heart racing in his chest. He had reacted to her touch, unsurprising if he was honest with himself. He hated people touching him. What he wasn't alright with was how much of that had been an instinctual reaction. How quick he had been to resort to violence, and against a friend at that. Catriona meant nothing by it, he knew that, but he couldn't stop himself from reacting. If he had slashed the blade at her instead of retreating, he would never have forgiven himself.

"I'm sorry," Menolayous stammered, lowering the blade. "Catriona, forgive me."

"It's okay," her voice came from behind his brothers. "I'm sorry, I forgot. I shouldn't have touched you."

"I shouldn't have reacted like that." Menolayous felt his face flush with shame.

Menolayous glanced around at his little group, all eyes were still on him. Fear shone on the faces of Clyous and Markous as they beheld for the first time, Menolayous's underlying darkness. Catriona and Bridget looked upon him as if they could understand his darkness, something he was positive they couldn't even begin to comprehend. The looks on his brothers' faces were what broke him. Etched on their faces was an odd combination of pity mixed with a look that said they were trying to determine whether or not he was a threat, like he was a wild animal that couldn't be controlled.

"I'm going to go clean up those blooded corpses," Menolayous choked out. "Make sure they can't be found."

Menolayous didn't wait for an answer before he turned and took off into the forest. Getting rid of the bodies was as good an excuse as any to escape their stares. This was why he typically avoided connecting to people. Once they saw his dark side there was no unseeing it. Menolayous hated himself for that darkness, he wished more than anything that it would just disappear; but it would never disappear, that dark part of him would always try to drag him back. He thumbed the raised scars on his forearm as he moved.

Chapter Fifteen

Danny

The deer Catriona gutted was being smoked just outside while everyone was working on collecting their things in preparation for the morning. Menolayous had brought the carcass back after disappearing for several hours. His reaction to Catriona wasn't unexpected, if anything Danny was thankful his brother hadn't struck out at her like he had at him several times over the years. Danny could not stop himself from feeling protective over her, even from his brother. Menolayous had stopped himself from harming her, even if his reaction was instinctual. He had fled into the forest for several hours to properly dispose of and conceal the bodies of the blooded. He had returned with the carcass of Catriona's deer as well as a few other stashed away supplies he had found. Nobody spoke about the incident upon his return, Menolayous seamlessly slid in to assist with the travel preparations. First of which was him helping Danny set up this smoking pit for the deer.

Danny was alone as he sat outside by the smoking pit tending to the meat. His preference would have been to help inside, but it was more important that Menolayous force himself to be around the others right now than continue to hide. Danny didn't have many possessions to pack, so he had volunteered himself to look after the smoking process. Smoking this meat was important, not just for the group as a whole but to ensure that the process was outside so as not to affect Catriona. Catriona seemed to be having some sort of physical revulsion when anyone started cooking meat, she wouldn't eat it. They were lucky if she even stayed in the cave while they all cooked and ate. They had all talked amongst each other, concerned that she was not eating enough. They had no way to truly tell when she fled the cave during mealtimes, so they had all opted to cook outside to better keep an eye on her.

Danny needed a break from Rama who had spent the last several hours teasing him for being so protective of Catriona. Much to his embarrassment, Danny had to agree with his big brother. He was acting like a lovesick fool every time he was around her, and what was worse, he couldn't seem to stop himself from becoming increasingly protective of her. She was so beautiful it was hard not to look at her. In fact, she had caught him staring several times but had failed to tell him off. Sure, they talked and were even friendly with each other, but they never spent a lot of time alone together other than training; and worst yet, he kept reaching out to touch her. It felt so natural, so normal, that he never thought about it before he did it. She would always give him this look like she was asking, "what are you doing?" He would always pull back then, second guessing himself.

Truthfully, he was well known for chasing after women, especially among the various warbands he and his brothers frequently visited. The chase was his favorite part. It did not take much for the women he chased to fall for him, he was very persistent after all. He could sweet talk like his life depended on it, easily wooing them. He knew he was attractive, he knew he was a charmer. His tastes were on the rougher side, which left him never completely satisfied. Women were too fragile, too easily scared by his intensity. He wanted a woman to fight with him, to match his intensity, to be his equal. Catriona, on the other hand, was not so easily charmed. She was not fragile, even as she healed, she easily proved how strong she actually was, and she challenged him.

She was not like other women, and that had him very much intrigued. His main concern was how comfortable she would actually be with him being physically affectionate. They barely knew each other, yet despite her being as strong as she was, he could tell something wasn't right with her, she mimicked Menolayous in this way to an extent. She was still processing what had happened to her, something he completely understood and respected. She had been through so much, putting himself in her life right now, especially like that, was not beneficial to her healing. He had too much respect for her to push her. So, he held back as much as he could, and that translated very openly into him acting like a lovesick dog.

"You're not half as bad as you think you are." Clyous came and sat beside him, taking a drink from a waterskin.

Danny scooted over on the log to make room for him. Clyous handed him the waterskin and he took a swig. The taste of alcohol hit him. He coughed in surprise feeling the spirits as they burned their way down his throat. Clyous chuckled, taking another swig himself.

"What are you talking about?" Danny coughed again, handing over the alcohol filled waterskin with raised eyebrows.

"My sister has a unique personality." Clyous took another drink. "You're not embarrassing yourself as much as you think you are. Trust me."

Danny gave him a look. "I doubt that."

"No, really. The looks she's giving you are because she's waiting for you to make a decision, she's not looking at you like you're a lovesick puppy."

"Why——?"

"I overheard Rama slinging you shit," Clyous answered. "You looked like you were starting to overthink things."

Danny wasn't sure how to react at first, but fuck it, Clyous had opened the door. The one thing you could say about the twins is that they were brutally honest and could see things most didn't. He respected that, it reminded him of his brothers. Markous was the only one out of their group who didn't quite fit.

"What do you mean she's waiting for me to make a decision?" Danny asked again, then he sighed, audibly frustrated before saying, "I'm supposed to be good at this."

"Well… I'm not going to pretend that I know my twin sister's mind or anything, but one thing I can tell you is she would have threatened or maimed you a while ago if she didn't like the idea of you being interested in her."

Danny couldn't exactly argue that logic. Just like he wasn't going to try denying his attraction to her either.

"I guess I do still have my head." Danny laughed, taking another swig. "I've never been this cautious with a woman before."

"She has an intimidating personality, only the strong have a chance." Clyous laughed. "I'm not kidding."

"She doesn't scare me," Danny found himself saying, the alcohol clearly at work. "I can't stand 'fragile' honestly."

"She'll make you eat those words, just wait." Clyous threw his head back and laughed. "I've seen many a suitor run screaming from our house, much to our mother's dismay. They either couldn't handle her sharp tongue, or well… the nice way to put it is that they probably didn't appreciate a woman who could knock them on their ass."

Curiosity overtook him, or maybe it was the spirits. "Has she had many suitors?"

Clyous raised an eyebrow at him. "That's not for me to say, and honestly, I don't know, she keeps certain things to herself. You ask her, I dare you."

Danny chuckled, tossing another piece of wood onto the fire. He knew better than that. He was curious if she had any lovers before, if she had been in love, or if there was someone back home she cared about. Last thing

95

he wanted to do was overstep, or assume she was experienced if she wasn't. The two men were starting to feel the effect of the alcohol now. He found that he liked Catriona's twin brother, the twins reminded him of Rama and Menolayous.

"Has she always been like that?" Danny felt the world start to spin ever so slightly. "Has she always been a spitfire?"

"Oh yes! Always." Clyous laughed a little too loud. "As a child she was always the troublemaker. I have a very fond memory of her starting a brawl with some of the other village children because they wouldn't let her play a ball game with them."

"How old were they?" He laughed.

"She was eight, they were all about ten. She beat the snot out of them."

The two laughed together, sharing the waterskin a few more times.

"So, she learned how to fight because of your village kids?"

"No. Actually, our father made a point to teach us, 'training' he used to call it. When we weren't working at the shop or in the forge, he had us drilling. Catriona took to it easier than we did. We eventually had to pick up more hours in the forge. Catriona continued to train with our father until he disappeared. Around sixteen she started training on her own again, her attitude about the world had completely changed."

"What do you mean disappeared?"

"He just wasn't there one morning. We have no idea what happened to him. He could have just up and abandoned us, or he could have pissed off a blooded guard on the way home. We don't know." Clyous's demeanor changed to something more solemn.

"I'm sorry." Danny didn't have the best relationship with his father but maybe they had.

Clyous shrugged and took another drink. "It is what it is."

"What about you?" Danny teased. "I've seen you around Bridget. What's going on with you two?"

Clyous flashed him the most mischievous grin. "A gentleman never tells."

"Like brother, like sister I see," Danny couldn't help but pick at him.

Laughter came from the cave entrance as the rest of the party started filing out. Rama helped Bridget carry over a large pot used for smoking meat and set it in the embers. Her hands were still blistered from earlier but nothing too serious. Everyone else sat around in a semi-circle getting ready for dinner, eating outside had become their new routine. Clyous flashed Danny a smile and a wink, then got up and sat next to Bridget. When Catriona emerged from the mouth of the cave wearing a wine-red traveling dress, Danny forgot to breathe for a moment. It was a simple cotton dress with golden stitching along the collar and the hem. The skirts did not drag on the ground like most dresses did, and there seemed to be a hood sewn onto the back of the collar. A simple design made for women who intended to travel. On her it was simple and elegant. The wine color of the dress made the color of her eyes stand out like silver flames. The fabric accentuated her figure in ways that her typical tunic and trousers never did.

Bridget smiled at her as Catriona walked past, taking a seat just outside everyone else, she never sat close to the fire if she could help it. Choosing to sit there left plenty of space open beside her. Danny wasn't sure if it was the alcohol or the conversation he just had with her twin brother, but he found himself moving over to sit beside Catriona. Once he sat, she gave him the look she always did. Instead of second guessing himself this time, he decided to make himself comfortable by stretching out, tossing an arm across her back and gently pulling her closer to him. If anything, Clyous had reminded him that she is not fragile and is perfectly capable of setting boundaries. Danny wasn't sure if drinking had been the best idea, liquid courage is what Rama called it. Danny did not drink that often, Menolayous wouldn't even touch the stuff. Their brother on the other hand could drink his weight in alcohol before it began to affect him.

Danny reached over to her, wrapping his arm around her lower back and scooting her closer to him so he could hold onto her easily. Surprisingly, not only did she let him, but he felt her body press up against his side as she made herself more comfortable. He could feel the warmth of her body against his, a welcome feeling for sure. He watched as Catriona glanced up at him knowingly with those silvery eyes of hers shortly before she picked at her vegetable soup. He could swear that she leaned into him a bit more. He willed his racing heartbeat to slow down before she noticed.

"That's a beautiful dress," Danny said to her quietly, observing how everyone else was engaged in their own conversations, including the social recluse Menolayous.

"Thank you." He could see her cheeks redden slightly at the compliment. "It's Bridget's spare. She's letting me wear it so my clothes can dry. I had to stitch them up and wash them after today's fight."

"I take it you're not used to wearing dresses." He reached forward to grab a bowl of soup himself.

"Is it that obvious?" Her cheeks still burned slightly from embarrassment, if he had known a simple dress would be the thing that tempered her usually sharp tongue, he would have stolen and hidden her trousers weeks ago.

"Not so much from you." Danny smiled at the thought of stealing her trousers anyway, just so she could stay in this dress longer. "But your brothers, who never miss an opportunity to pick fun at you, are pretending they don't even see you wearing it."

He watched as Catriona glanced at her brothers, who were indeed trying not to stare in her direction. Danny noticed that his brothers were also making a point not to stare in her direction, although he believed their motivation more around the fact that they wanted to give them privacy. Meddling bastards.

"I haven't worn a dress since I was sixteen. It's been years since they've seen me in one. Mother and I used to fight about it all the time. She wanted me to dress like a proper lady." Catriona smiled to herself at the memory. "She eventually gave up when I burned all my dresses and kept stealing Clyous's clothes."

"Why does that story not surprise me?" Danny laughed quietly. "Stubborn until the end."

"Mother used to say there was never a mule that could match me." Catriona's sweet laugh rang out. "Markous even went out and bought me a mule once just to prove mother's point. The beast grew sick of me trying to train it long before I was willing to give up. We ended up using it to help carry supplies for us when we visited the market, it was fine as long as I wasn't the one holding the lead."

The two of them laughed together at the story. Danny watched her smile reach her eyes at the memories of her childhood. He allowed himself a quick glance down at her chest, the bodice was doing an excellent job at showing off the tops of her breasts. Again, something her tunic never would allow. Yes, those old clothes of hers were definitely getting dragged off by a wild animal tonight. She had gone quiet when he had chanced a quick glance, not because she had caught him staring, but because she had gotten lost in

98

her memories. With all traces of her smile now gone, sadness filled her eyes as she stared into the bowl of soup in her hand.

"Did you eat meat before?" he asked her quietly, hoping to bring her back from whatever darkness she was staring into.

She nodded. "The meat cooking is what I can't stand. Truth be told I haven't actually had any since—" she went quiet again, her eyes chasing ghosts of her past.

"How is it being out here with the smoke and the deer? Is it any better?" He was noticing how much she wasn't eating, and it bothered him.

She took a bite of carrot and thought for a moment. "I'm doing okay. I think it's because the flames aren't touching it."

Danny rubbed his thumb along her side in slow circles. Shocked again at how easily she accepted this contact. She not only allowed this, but she seemed to like it, it was more than just shocking, he was at a loss for words.

"I'm going to have to figure it out soon anyway. Can't afford to limit my already limited food options once we hit the road."

"Maybe this smoked venison will be a good place to start. You're not seeing it cooked over a fire, and it won't need to be cooked after this for you to be able to eat it."

"Maybe." She pushed a chunk of potato around with her wooden spoon.

They sat there together, both relaxed and listening to the conversations around them. Catriona didn't take long to interject during a heated conversation between her brothers. Apparently, there were three ways one could properly edge a weapon with silver, each sibling having their own preference. The argument quickly turned heated, words and techniques being nitpicked by the three of them, making it impossible for the others to give an opinion. Danny loved watching how she laughed and argued with her brothers and his, he appreciated how close all of them seemed to be after everything that happened.

After some time, Danny spotted Clyous and Bridget sneaking off together into the forest out of the corner of his eye, not surprising. Clyous was a braver man than he was, he doubted even with this newfound acceptance of his touch he would be able to convince Catriona to sneak off with him without it becoming a war of words. Danny glanced at his two brothers who were now engaging in conversation with Catriona and Markous.

Menolayous was the only one from the group who hadn't been drinking from Clyous's waterskin, he had never known his brother to touch alcohol before. But he was in surprisingly good spirits and actually engaged in conversation with everyone. Rama had taken over the conversation by now, steering Markous and Menolayous back into the cave as he began retelling some more recent war stories. Markous was stupid enough to be enchanted by them, following the men towards the mouth of the cave. Danny had a sneaking suspicion that they had so graciously led Catriona's older brother away for his benefit. Danny knew them well enough to catch the glances of approval they sent his way as they both noticed how Catriona had chosen to stay. Their glances in his direction were quick, but their expressions were saying "about damn time."

Chapter Sixteen

Catriona

Catriona had definitely drunk too much. Danny handed her a waterskin filled with spirits during their meal. Of course she had indulged, finding herself laughing and joking with everyone. She didn't get to drink often back at home. Slaves had a hard time acquiring any, save for the few brave souls desperate enough to try and make it. At some point everyone had gone back inside for the night. Catriona had stayed outside with Danny, both of them apparently wanting to talk and admire the beauty of the night sky. She was nervous, she realized, not only because she was now completely alone with Danny, but she lowered her guard around him.

The dress had completely been Bridget's idea. It was true that Catriona needed to sew up her clothes after the fight today, but she had an extra set of pants and a shirt. Bridget had apparently brought a traveling dress with her just for Catriona. At first Catriona could not understand why the healer would even think in that direction, but Bridget's unnatural observation skills had picked up on Catriona's fixation on her sparring partner. The woman had made it her mission to help Catriona catch his attention as a woman, not just as a warrior.

According to Bridget, every woman needed a well-fitted dress in her arsenal. After some bickering about it, Bridget had explained that the dress, worn properly, could be just as dangerous as a dagger. Catriona couldn't argue that one, as much as she wanted to. The dress had most assuredly worked, Bridget could hardly contain her triumph throughout dinner, catching every time Danny had touched Catriona and when he came to sit beside her. Catriona had rolled her eyes at her friend, willing their silent conversation to go unnoticed.

Catriona had spotted Bridget and her twin sneaking off into the forest, maybe the healer would be successful in getting her own male attention tonight. Catriona was no fool, there was something between Bridget and her brother. She was happy for them, and happy that Bridget was becoming such a friend to her in the process. She had a sneaking suspicion that Bridget had led Clyous away in the hope of giving Catriona and Danny more space. It seemed like Danny's brothers had a similar idea in mind, leading Markous back into the cave with promises of more wine and war stories. She felt slightly embarrassed if that were the case, had her attraction to Danny been that obvious? Or had they done it for him?

"And you would just dive for these shells?" Catriona asked, trying to focus on the conversation and not her wandering thoughts.

"Oysters," he corrected. "And yes. Some of the best ones can be found in deeper water on the seafloor. Most fishermen will just dig some up in the shallows, but I loved to swim down and collect them."

"Sounds like an awful lot of work for a small amount of food." She scoffed, taking a drink from a water filled waterskin.

"They're not just food, some of them have pearls inside." He raised his eyebrows at her. "You know the same type of pearls some of the noble ladies would wear in jewelry."

"I wouldn't know, I'm not one for jewelry." She smiled at him. "Give me a good piece of steel and a whetstone."

"You're quite talented. I've never met a woman who could sharpen a blade like you can. You know your blades." He winked. "Both in the forge and in battle."

"You act surprised. What did you expect? Cooking and taking care of children all day while my husband is working? No thank you." She scoffed. "I'm too wild to be domesticated."

"So, settling down isn't something you might consider for yourself anytime soon?" He seemed genuinely curious, but her fear of his judgment was making her heart race. Men didn't typically want a woman who wanted to go to war.

"Not anytime soon. I want to live my life first, the arrival of children tends to limit one's freedom," and she meant what she said, she wasn't fit or ready to start having children, probably ever.

"What about finding a man?" A smile played at the corner of Danny's mouth. "Or have you sworn them off as too boring for you?"

"Oh, men have their uses." Catriona surprised herself with her boldness, it must be the alcohol. "The man just has to be able to survive me. I'm a difficult person to be around if you haven't noticed, men tend to find themselves emasculated around me."

He laughed out loud then. "Oh, believe me I have. I don't think I've ever met a more sarcastic or strong-willed woman in my life."

"See what I mean?" She nudged him playfully. "Most men can't handle me."

"Good thing I'm not like most men." Danny was staring into her eyes with an intensity that made her suppress a shudder.

"Are you not?" she demanded, having the urge to challenge him. This was what they did with each other, they pushed each other's buttons, challenged each other. "You seem like any other cocky self-assured man I've met."

Danny's eyes seemed to grow brighter in the moonlight, as if loving this new presentation of a challenge. "I'm only cocky and self-assured because I know just how good I actually am."

"Plenty of experience then?" she asked, praying the flush of her cheeks was not as visible as it felt. It wasn't just her face that was beginning to heat up, that look he was giving her was stirring up all kinds of other feelings.

"Oh, most definitely." He now turned his body to directly face hers; he was radiating confidence now.

The jerk now sat a foot or so from her, leaning back against the fallen log. He was handsome, that's for sure, she caught herself taking in just how much larger he was compared to her. His eyes continued to stare into hers with such intensity that she found herself blushing even more. It was as if his eyes were promising to do exactly what he wanted with her, and what she was wanting him to do to her.

"I'm not interested in a man who apparently has such deep commitment issues." She tried to scoot away then, sitting so close to him was making her body heat up. She was allowing him to get close to her, with how much her body was beginning to react to him, it was beginning to scare her.

"Who says I have commitment issues?" he purred, watching her try to scoot farther away with a smile, as if this was providing him some small victory. "If anything, I've just been waiting for the right woman who can handle me. I've been fortunate enough to pick up some skills along the way that will make that woman very very happy with me."

Lost for words, Catriona tried to scoot away again but found herself blocked by a protruding tree root. She really couldn't find an answer as to why she was trying to put distance between them. It seemed like the last few days all she had been wanting was for him to finally reach out and touch her, it had made training with him difficult. Now with them being so close, she

103

could feel the physical effects that his charm was having on her. Intimacy wasn't something she was great at.

"So you say. I wonder what all your lovers would say, if they would boast about your talents as much as you do." She laughed, trying to hide her discomfort with sharply edged words.

"What about you? What would your lovers say?" He was enjoying this, seeing his effect on her. The jerk.

"None of your business," she answered with a slight slur, damn the alcohol. "I don't kiss and tell."

"Or you've never been kissed at all." Danny seemed very interested in her facial expressions now, his eyes burrowing into hers.

"I've been kissed before," she argued, great, she had reduced herself to arguing.

"Don't think so." He smirked at her; he could smell the victory of this battle looming. "You don't act like you have."

"What's that supposed to mean?" Slight irritation at her steadily declining wit was making room for her nerves to take over.

"Nothing wrong with it. For women, maintaining innocence is a lot more important to some." He laughed at the expression on her face. "I'm not judging you I promise, I'm just intrigued."

Catriona was not sure what exactly made her do it, it very well could have been her temper which on a normal day was explosive to say the least; or it could have been just how much she had drank already, which again was quite a bit; but the reality of it was the challenge, she had never been one to shy away from a direct and pointed challenge. She did not like to look weak, to hide from adversity. So, she did the only thing she could think of to shut him up and gain ground in their little battle.

Catriona found herself grabbing Danny by the front of his tunic and pulling him to her. She pressed her lips against his before she completely realized what she was doing. She could feel his lips smile as soon as they touched. Before she had time to stop or even pull away, his arm wrapped around her waist and he hoisted her onto his lap, her skirts riding up to her bare thighs. Catriona now sat facing Danny with his hands gripping her hips, securing her against him. She wouldn't be able to move if she wanted to, and she kind of didn't want to.

"I stand corrected." He smiled up at her. "Now you have been kissed."

Realization dawned on her as she fought through her alcohol induced haze, because that was what she was choosing to blame. "You baited me on purpose!"

"You just keep solidifying my argument, beautiful." He winked up at her. "I've got to say, this is probably my new favorite view, you on top."

She pinched him hard. He laughed, grabbing her face gently and pulling it down to his. He kissed her slowly but very passionately. She allowed it, not that her body was really going to allow her to stop now. The touch of his lips to hers felt good, his tongue finding its way into her mouth thrilled her even more. Her fingers found their way into his silky soft curls as she continued to kiss him. She felt his hands roam downward to cup her ass, sending shivers up her spine at the touch. She knew her arousal was starting to take over her logic. Her back arched at the touch of his hands, wanting more from him.

He broke away from their kiss then, smiling up at her. "Easy there, beautiful, you don't need to prove anything to me, I promise."

"I'm not proving anything to you!" she snapped, irritation taking over again at how he was the one stopping this.

He laughed. "Maybe I am then."

Danny now maneuvered her so she was cradled in his arms rather than sitting on top of him. It was a less provocative position, but with her head now against his chest it still felt intimate. As irritated as she was at the sudden stop, she could start to see the logic of not going further. Fucking this man in front of the only cave entrance where their families now slept inside was probably not the brightest idea.

"What are you trying to prove then? How annoying you can be?" she sassed, but snuggled down against him, nonetheless.

"That I'm not a one-time fuck." He kissed her forehead before settling himself back into a more comfortable position. "And that I'm not afraid of commitment."

This surprised her, was he really concerned about what she had said? Or was he wanting something more from her besides having a good time? Danny continued to hold her against his chest, she felt comfortable here. His breathing eventually slowed, signaling that he had fallen asleep. Her eyes were growing heavy, the world spinning a little less. She smiled as she shut her eyes, getting comfortable against him before letting sleep take over.

She woke up with her head still on his shoulder. She sat up, rubbing the sleep from her eyes. The full moon was at its highest place in the night sky, meaning it was after midnight. Catriona looked around, thankful her head was no longer spinning. The fire pit was still smoking, embers barely putting off heat. The air was cold, cold enough to have been the reason Catriona had woken up. Her main source of warmth was the man her body was still pressed up against. Danny was fast asleep, sitting upright with his head tilted back against the log. It was then that she noticed his hand was extended out with his fingertips grazing her hip. He had still been holding her, she realized, cheeks flushing.

A far off howl sounded off in the distance. Several more echoed through the forest. Danny jerked awake at the sound, reaching for the sword leaning against the cave wall. Catriona silently got to her feet, reaching for a dagger. Something wasn't right, it must be one of the patrols Bridget had warned them about. One of the howls turned to barking and growls, as if the wolf was fighting with something.

"Scourge," Danny mouthed, taking her by the hand and leading her silently into the cave, "and patrols."

The two of them made their way silently inside the cave, guided by some light shed by the full moon above them. Danny walked over to Rama's sleeping figure tapping him on the shoulder. The giant woke up going for his axe, pausing when he saw his brother. Catriona went to Markous doing the same, mouthing the word scourge. Menolayous was up and silently moving to his bow. Catriona looked around for Clyous, he wasn't there. Her heart stopped, searching the cave frantically, she realized Bridget wasn't there either.

"Shit!" she swore quietly. "My brother and Bridget aren't here."

"I saw them sneak off at dinner," Danny whispered, worry furrowing his features. They had been lucky to have had no encounters with any scourge up until now.

"Let's go then." Rama held his axe at the ready, nodding to the cave entrance.

Chapter Seventeen

Bridget

The night air was chilly against her skin, the last days of winter were still clinging to them before the spring rains came. Bridget was happy that Clyous had asked her to join him on a nighttime stroll for a variety of reasons. The full moon had been making her antsy all evening, having an outlet for her to move about was doing her wolf some good. She was already struggling enough being alone with Clyous, it's not as if they hadn't been alone before but the full moon had sway over her in other ways, her desire for him only increased. She had also hoped that their departure would give Catriona and Danny some needed alone time, preferably without daggers in hand as they usually did for training. Those two had been attracted to each other since the beginning, but both of them were too stubborn or too scared to pursue it any further. That was why Bridget had purchased a traveler's dress for Catriona. It was something she could wear on the road, but also something that would most definitely catch Danny's eye. Seeing his expression when she had sat down for dinner was proof enough that Bridget's meddling was helpful.

Now Bridget prayed to the gods that she could gain enough courage to meddle where her own love interest was concerned. They had spent limited time together before the incident with his family, time together that she secretly cherished. Clyous was very handsome, with his blonde hair and large physique. Years of working as a blacksmith had helped him build those muscles, a feature that Bridget liked to admire whenever the opportunity presented itself.

"The full moon is really beautiful this far away from the city," Clyous commented while looking up. "The stars even seem brighter out here."

"The stars shine brighter during the full moon, at least from my experience." She followed his gaze, appreciating the night sky.

"How is the full moon for you?" he asked curiously. "I know for new blooded it controls their shift, but you were born moon touched, it appears to affect you differently."

"The moon can make me restless. Usually, I can't sleep, or I have trouble focusing," she confessed. "But it holds no sway over my shift. Those born blooded can usually master their shift by three years of age. They stop involuntarily shifting on the full moon, but its power still likes to remind us that it's there. Like me, others feel restless. We can be stronger during a full moon, if we're easily excited or scared those with less control can shift more spontaneously. Some of them even get a little wild, but that is all really."

"And new blooded, those who were turned, they cannot control it?" He seemed genuinely curious.

"No. They have a much harder time controlling their wolf because they were not born with it. It can take some of the new blooded up to five years to begin grasping control over themselves. Every full moon they have no choice; their wolves will fight to come out. But they also can shift if they experience any intense emotion. It's why it's so dangerous to have new blooded not paired up with a more experienced wolf. The dominant wolf will keep the younger one in line."

"Isn't there only one dominant wolf?" He reached out his hand to help her stabilize herself as she stepped over a log.

"Yes. Only one that has the power of command. That would be the king. As the king ages and weakens, the power begins to pass on to the nearest, most powerful wolf, which would be the crown prince. Once the king passes, all of that power will go to him."

"Why does it begin to pass before the king dies?"

"Nature's way of trying to level the playing field in case one wanted to challenge and defeat the other." She smirked. "Wolves are hostile with each other; dominance is arguably the most important thing to them."

"Aren't you one of them? You're a wolf," he challenged.

"Yes, well I'm not interested in challenging others." She sighed as she stopped walking. "I don't think I have it in me to hurt someone, let alone kill them. I've spent too much time as a healer trying to fix people, I can't stomach the idea of causing anyone pain or injury."

"That's a very kind and honorable way to think." Clyous smiled at her as he came to stand before her. "Maybe I can help with some of that restlessness."

Her heart fluttered slightly as he approached, curious as to what he would do. His hands found themselves on her lower back. Suddenly, there was no space between them, she looked into his face seeing the longing there. She took a deep breath, grounding herself as he brought his lips down to hers. She was shocked at the sudden show of affection, and even more shocked at the fact that she now found herself kissing him back ever so slightly. The kiss was extremely gentle, nothing like she had experienced before.

She was afraid to move, afraid to wrap her arms around him, to reach out and touch him. She feared he would get mad at her for being so bold, so she contained herself as best she could. She remained frozen there purely out of fear of annoying him, subsequently ending their outing. She stood there awkwardly. Liam never allowed her to touch him without permission; he demanded her complete submission. Any act she attempted to do without his command was considered a fight for dominance, and she was met with the ending of whatever pleasure she was getting from their encounter. Liam would stop whatever they were doing and leave her unfinished as a form of manipulation. At the time, she believed he was just too angry to continue. After the last few years passed, she had enough time to realize this was a control tactic, that as a man he needed to be in charge.

"I'm sorry." He pulled back from her and breathlessly said, "I misread the situation. Forgive me."

"I don't understand." Suddenly aware that his body was against hers, had she done something wrong? She had remained still; she hadn't tried to take over.

"You seem tense, like you didn't want me kissing you," he answered shyly.

Her cheeks reddened with embarrassment. "I do, I just, I didn't know if you wanted me to touch you."

He smiled at her then. "I mean yeah, I kind of do. That's why I kissed you."

"I'm sorry!" She turned her back to him, hiding her face which was now a very deep red.

She felt him come up behind her and wrap his arms around her waist. She could feel the hardness of his chest against her back; he was much larger than her. It was very comforting being held by him in that moment. She allowed herself to lean back on him, just a little bit. Probably not enough for him to really notice. She needed his touch, craved it above all else at the moment. She was just too afraid.

"You can touch me. You can do whatever you want actually. You can kiss me back, you can wrap your arms around me, you can even kick me if you want to." He chuckled as if reading her mind. "Preferably not kick me, but you can. I don't require anything from you except that you tell me if I'm crossing a line. Okay?"

She nodded, turning around to face him again, allowing the moon and the wildness of her emotions to take over. "Will you kiss me again?"

With a smile, Clyous obliged her and once again pressed his lips to hers. This time she willed her body to relax against his. She could feel his heartbeat against her palms where they were placed on his chest as they continued to kiss. She could feel her wolf stirring inside, the wildness of the moon seemed to be affecting both of them. Bridget found herself very quickly wanting more contact, wanting to push the line just a little bit more.

Gently, she nipped his lower lip, an action so unlike her she surprised even herself. It seemed to surprise him too, but Clyous seemed to like it. She felt his arms tighten around her waist pulling her even tighter against him. She allowed her hands to travel upwards, wrapping them around his neck. She could feel the pull of the moon, encouraging her to keep going, to cut loose, to let out her wild side. Clyous, to his credit, also seemed to want this from her. She could feel her usual caution and self-control beginning to slip away, she wanted more.

In the distance, a series of howls began to echo throughout the forest. Both of them froze at the sound. Other wolves were nearby. Wolves shouldn't be this far away from the city; there were no nearby blooded villages. This had to be a patrol. Her wolf senses went on high alert as several shrieks began sounding in unison throughout the forest, drowning out the howls. A wolf somewhere nearby began to growl and snap at something; Bridget could hear the sounds of many footsteps hitting the forest floor with her heightened senses. The wolf was fighting against what was most certainly a group of scourge. They had made a mistake wandering this far out into the woods at night.

A large silver wolf came crashing through the brush, snarling and snapping at the pale and gaunt body of a scourge that was actively tearing at its side. Bridget felt Clyous pulling her down to the dew-soaked ground, tucking their bodies underneath some ferns and using his body to cover hers. Her heart was pounding uncontrollably, fear taking over. Through a gap in the ferns, she watched in horror as four more scourge crawled rapidly out of the trees towards the struggling wolf. Their unnatural clicks and shrieks rang through her body, setting off the wolf inside. The scourge managed to bring the wolf down, despite it fighting with everything it had. With a few yelps of pain, the scourge finally silenced the beast by ripping its throat out with their claws. She watched them tear the carcass apart.

Bridget suppressed a whimper, a tear rolling down her cheek and falling to the cold earth. Clyous gave her a gentle squeeze on her shoulder to reassure her. They had to stay quiet. The scourge were about fifty feet away from them devouring the dead wolf's body. She prayed they would not catch their scent. They didn't stand a chance against five of them. A blooded who couldn't control their shift and a human did not have great odds.

The scourge all stopped feasting on the wolf's flesh and began scenting the air. Panic seized her, the wolf inside started to thrash against its restraints. A couple of unearthly shrieks sounded off in the distance setting this group into their own shrieks. In a flash, they were gone and heading off towards the sound of a hunt.

After a minute or so Clyous slowly got up, taking her shaking hands and helping her to her feet. He embraced her briefly, kissing her forehead and running a hand through her hair. His touch allowed her to start calming down, fear slowly leaving her. They were fine, they were alive. They needed to get back to the cave.

"Come on," he whispered, pulling her along.

They made their way back towards the cave as silently as they could. Trudging through the trees they were careful not to step on any branches or brush against any fern bushes. They could hear the howls and shrieks in the distance. Those must be the patrols the crown had sent in search of her pack. She couldn't say she pitied the ones that met their fate tonight. It meant one less enemy coming after her friends. However, she did not like watching the violence and feeling the pain of another wolf meeting their end.

She might not be part of their pack, but every wolf could sense each other when there was danger present. It was a wolf survival instinct that happened when a different predator was nearby. She should have been able to sense the danger and the other blooded when they got within a mile of her. Admittedly, she had been wholly absorbed in Clyous and what they were doing. It was entirely possible that's why she hadn't picked up on anything. She was fiercely angry at herself, not only for missing the approach of a predator, but also for how her lack of control over her shift would have been the death of them should they have had to fight.

"What the—?" Clyous whispered as they came up a small hill.

At the top of the hill lay several burned bodies in the center of what looked like a burn pile. At least three bodies of scourge lay charred and still smoking on the ground. Heat still radiated from the center but there were no more flames. Clyous knelt to touch the edge of the ashy ring, the embers

111

fighting against the cold dampness of the night air. Bridget walked around the pile, visually examining the pattern. It was almost as if these scourge were burned and laid out in some sort of ritual.

Bridget's ears picked up clicking sounds from approaching scourge, she could sense the predators homing in on them. She grabbed Clyous by the shirt, quickly standing him up. As she started moving, she then immediately froze in place. Three scourge crawled towards them on all fours moving in a truly unnatural way. Clyous unstrapped the only weapon he had, a war hammer, placing himself between her and those monsters.

The wolf inside thrashed violently, begging to be released. Clyous shouldn't be the one to face them, he was just a human. She should face the predators, after all she was one too. She took a few steps away from him, digging deep into herself. Deep enough to get to her wolf. It was time to let the wolf out to play.

The pain that rippled through her entire body as the beast fought its way to the surface was unimaginable, she did not shift often enough for this to be an easy task, but the pain seemed to spur the beast on, driving it harder. She could feel her flesh stretching as her bones and muscles shifted into something much larger than herself, her teeth and fangs growing into sharp points, her fingers turning into sharpened claws. She raised her head to the sky, letting loose a howl so loud that it echoed through the trees.

She felt them then, the creatures in front of her had locked onto them as a potential threat. She felt an internal tug towards three other wolves in the area and numerous other scourge. *Not today* she growled and lowered her head at the oncoming scourge. She broke before they did, pushing past Clyous and going for the closest creature. The scourge shot up to meet her, trying to sink its claws into her muzzle. She easily danced around it, taking its head into her jaws and ripping.

The other two charged before the body of the first hit the ground. She reached back, grabbing one by the thigh effectively pulling it off herself before it could sink its teeth into her. Clyous came up behind the other, bringing down his hammer onto its pale skull. When the three creatures lay there dismembered, Bridget turned her head to Clyous nosing his shoulder.

"I'm not hurt." He scratched her ears. "Promise."

Bridget glanced around the forest. She could sense a few less scourge roaming around, there were no more wolves. Thankfully, none of the scourge were remotely close to them. She did sense something approaching from the west, the cold wind blowing their scent in her direction. Her ears perked up.

She sniffed the air again. It was her pack approaching. She nudged Clyous in that direction. Clyous complied easily enough, tensing for a moment when he heard his family approaching. There they were, cresting the ridge coming in their direction. Bridget bounded up to them, startling them until they recognized her.

"Are you guys, okay?" Catriona whispered, glancing around.

Bridget nuzzled her face in response. Catriona smiled at her, scratching her ears. By the gods did that feel good, she let her tongue hang out the side of her mouth while Catriona continued to scratch. She saw Catriona throw her brother a glare, his response was to shrug.

"You really couldn't have picked a better time?" Rama teased.

Before Clyous could answer, Bridget growled lowly at the giant man. Rama raised his hands in submission and backed up a few steps. A smile spread across his face at the challenge.

"Alright. All I'm saying is pick a better time for a 'walk'." He laughed. "No need to bite my head off."

Still not entirely satisfied with his answer but not interested in going toe to toe with the only human that could look her in the eyes when she was in wolf form, Bridget decided to start back in the direction of the cave.

"We should go back to camp. We don't know how many more are out here," Menolayous suggested in a low voice.

The group silently agreed, all of them quietly walking back towards the cave. Bridget, feeling oddly satisfied with herself, trotted around the group in large circles. That's twice now she had controlled her shift, twice that she had saved someone she cared about, and twice now that she had won.

Chapter Eighteen

Morrigan

Morrigan watched the wolf girl from her hiding place in the trees. The girl was a surprise to her, that's for sure. She had come this way because of the golden glow the girl's spirit emitted, another with magic in their blood. Morrigan was eager to meet her, there weren't many of them left. She had watched this girl kissing the boy in the woods and decided it was best to stay out of sight. She wasn't going to interrupt, that would be rude. Something about this interaction brought warm memories to Morrigan's heart, how she too had enjoyed love as a youth.

Due to how absorbed the two were with each other Morrigan was unsurprised at how easily they were caught off guard when the creatures approached. She thought she would have to step in to save the girl from the scourge, but to her shock the girl had transformed into a large red wolf. Now that was something, magical blood mixed with a moon touched curse, this girl could really be something powerful. In all the centuries Morrigan had walked these lands, she had never seen a child of the moon and a child of the ancient ones share blood in one form.

As Morrigan continued to watch, she was surprised yet again. The group that the girl met up with had another with ancient blood. The white-hot light coming from her was practically blinding. She saw the two auras side by side. Both were probably the brightest she had seen in a very long time. A daughter of war and a daughter of healing as companions, this was an unusual pairing for sure. It intrigued the woman. Just as she thought how unlikely their companionship to be, she saw a flash of silver in one of the others. As the group disappeared through the trees Morrigan had to focus on the color. The boy, the one with the golden wolf girl, carried with him a shimmer of silver.

"Interesting," she said to the black raven resting on her shoulder. "Have you ever seen war and healing befriend each other?"

The raven looked at her, ruffling its feathers. *"An unusual pairing. I don't like it, a moon touched daughter of healing with a daughter of fate and war. I smell trouble brewing."*

"Me too," Morrigan responded, stroking the beast's feathers back into place. "Never have I seen any other child of the ancients willing to mix with a moon touched. One usually dominates the other."

After the group was good and gone, she climbed back down to the ground. She strolled over to the bodies of the creatures the girl had killed. She clicked her tongue in disappointment. Naive girl, they should have burned them. Morrigan brushed the raven from her shoulder, gently watching it fly off into the night. It was about time she returned to her hunt in the cave system where these creatures crawled out of. She extended her hand letting the magic rush out of her. Flames erupted from her fingerprints catching the corpses on fire. Good, now they'll remain dead.

Chapter Nineteen

Bridget

After the incident in the woods her pack decided to hit the road instead of waiting for sunrise. It took about an hour for them to pack up their gear and set out. Bridget had decided a while ago that she would remain in Oich to help gather information for the resistance. Her pack insisted on walking her back to the edge of the capital city. Considering what happened the last few days, she was genuinely thankful. The sudden appearance of the blooded patrols and the scourge meant it was time for everyone to move on. With the ground beginning to thaw out and the promise of rain to come, there was no better time for her group to hit the road before the trade routes became heavily traveled for summer trade.

The sun was starting to rise when they made it to the tree line, gold and pink rays of light were dancing across the sky. Bridget said her goodbyes to everyone, Catriona giving her a short embrace before allowing her brother to interrupt. Catriona had changed back into her regular pants and shirt for travel, which was probably for the best. Blending in while on the road was safer. She had never had the chance to ask how well the dress had actually worked for her last night. The two women had grown close over the last month, as close as they could, considering the circumstances. Having another female around was a nice change of pace, regardless of the stark differences in their personalities. Bridget would miss Catriona dearly and made a mental note to find out where she would end up so she could visit or at least write. Clyous took Bridget by the hand and walked her to the edge of the road, looking for some level of privacy no doubt. Everyone else suddenly found something interesting on the horizon, giving them a small moment of privacy.

"I'm kind of regretting my decision to stay," she whispered, wrapping her arms around his waist.

He dropped his arms over her shoulders, kissing her forehead. "Me too. I regret that our night was cut short."

Her cheeks reddened. "Have you decided what your plan is when you reach the stronghold?"

"I haven't yet." He pulled her away so he could look into her face. "But I can promise you that I won't be too far away. I'm finding there's a pretty good reason to stick around Oich, even if I can't enter the city again."

She smiled at that. Clyous bent down and pressed his lips against hers. Her heart raced as she felt his warmth, his desire for her. She took a step back, redder than ever, and smiled up at him. Oh gods was she in trouble.

"If you need anything at all just send word, okay?" He looked into her eyes. "Promise me."

"I promise," she whispered, she meant it.

"Good. I'll see you soon." It was his turn to promise.

She flashed him a smile before separating from his embrace. The longer she held him the more she wanted to stay. She waved to everybody as she walked away, leaving them in the shadows of the trees.

Bridget made her way to the main road, following it back into the city. She trudged her way through the cobblestone streets to her home, passing only a few shopkeepers who were beginning to open up for the day. Bridget was thankful most did not pay her any mind. Bridget had made it through the market and back into the blooded residential section of town, her large two-story home coming into view. Her father's voice echoed from her memories as she approached the unnecessarily large and elegant home. She should feel privileged to live in a place such as this. After all, they were the second richest family that resided in the capital, not that it meant anything to her. The house might be big, but it was always empty to her. She found more comfort sharing a crowded cave with people she cared for than sleeping on a luxurious feather bed in an empty house.

She managed to silently open her front door and slip in. Her father should still be away on a trading journey to Gaelach, so the silence was more out of habit than necessity. As soon as the door clicked behind her, she tensed. A familiar scent filled her nostrils, sending her inner wolf into whines of submission. She closed her eyes for a moment, willing her heart rate to slow.

"Your Majesty," she called out to what should have been an empty foyer.

A shadowy figure emerged from a doorway to her left. The man stood almost a foot taller than her with broad shoulders and an imposing physique. His posture, though meant to be casual, looked like a wolf about to spring out at any moment. Bridget had never known a man taller than him before meeting Rama, only Liam would be a close contender in size to the giant. Bridget admired his dark hair and how it shined in the morning's first rays of light, and that face, chiseled into his flesh like a marble statue, she would be a fool to deny how attractive this man was. His eyes danced at the sight of her as he stepped forward, offering a hint of a smile.

The Crown Prince of Oich stepped into the light revealing himself. He wore a black jacket with beautiful silver colored embroidery around the collar and buttons; emerald stones were stitched into the design. With matching black pants, he also carried an intricately designed bearded axe that hung from his belt. The man, in all his finery and lack of any snarls this morning, looked to be in better temperament today than the last time she had seen him, when he was ripping the flesh off Catriona's back. He had done a great job proving those rumors she had heard of his cruelty true. He had become his father's son.

"You've been gone for several days now. I was starting to get worried," Liam continued, advancing towards her with a predator's grace. He stopped then as his eyes caught on her bandaged hands. "What happened?"

Oh no! She resisted the urge to hide her hands behind her. Instead, as if obeying a silent order, she lifted them up for Liam to inspect, which he was already beginning to do. His large soft hands took hers for inspection, turning them over to see the extent of the damage. She looked at him, trying to hold back her overwhelming desire to pull away from him and from that darkness that surrounded him. Instead, she searched his face, swearing she saw concern growing in his eyes like a small flame being ignited.

"I went to the forest to collect some herbs," she said as pathetically as she could, might as well play on his concern if she could manage it. Keeping her ties to the rebellion a secret from him was her only chance of survival. "Some blooded men had followed me, I didn't know they were there until—" she let the tears flow then, not having allowed herself before. The experience had frightened her significantly, she realized.

Fear took over Liam's features as his eyes searched for signs of injury, his gaze catching the rips in her skirt. "Did they hurt you?"

"They tried." Tears were flowing freely now, not all of it was an act, she used to find comfort with him. Why not now, if it helped hide her friends? "They're dead now."

"Oh Bridget." Liam pulled her into a warm yet protective embrace, this was exactly how Bridget remembered him. She allowed herself to wrap her arms around his waist, burying her face in his shoulder as she savored the

118

gentleness of it. Memories began to flood back in, dampening the anger she was currently feeling towards him. This was Liam, her friend and her first love; not the Crown Prince of Oich, the dominant wolf who was responsible for the torture and deaths of so many families. He was still buried deep within the darkness.

"I was able to control it." She sniffed, finally pulling away from him. "I shifted, and I killed them."

He wiped away the tears with his thumb, smiling at her with pride. "They deserved it Bridget, don't for one second feel sorry for them. I'm so proud of you. You acted as someone with your bloodline should."

"I got turned around after that and started wandering the woods. I was asleep when a small group of scourge sniffed me out. A blooded guard was out there, I assumed you had sent him to look for me, he saved my life, but there were too many of them. They killed him, but I was able to shift and finish off the last of them. I've never been more scared in my life." She would not tell him about Clyous or her friends, she would not let him near them, whether Liam was still in there or not, she would never risk her new pack.

"Oh sweetheart." Liam gently cupped her face with his hands. "I'm so sorry for what you've been through these last few days. I was so worried about how long you'd been gone; I sent some trusted guards after you. If I had known, had I thought for one second you were in danger I would have come for you myself."

A lie? Or had he actually sent them out for her? It was hard to tell with him, they had so much history. He might have fallen into the role of crown prince a little too well, but she could not deny the fact that they had a genuine connection and that he cared for her or had at one point.

"I'm sorry I made you worry. When I went out there, I had no idea how dangerous it was." She took a step back out of his inviting embrace; it was best she continue to play the foolish damsel.

"You're home safe now, that's what's important. I'm so very proud of you for being able to shift. I know that has always been a struggle for you."

Unsure of how to proceed with this conversation, she made her way towards the room where she kept her healing supplies. Liam followed her, there was nothing awkward or uncomfortable about his presence there. As children he had spent a great deal of time in her home. Albeit, he had not been here in years since his royal duties had not only taken away his free time but had also changed him into someone she no longer recognized. They had grown up, choices had been made by both of them, and things had changed.

119

She could never love the man who tortured and killed humans for fighting to protect themselves. She couldn't forgive the deeds he has done in the name of a royal decree. She had always known he was capable of great violence; he had shown it numerous times while defending her from blooded, but back then he never hurt anyone who couldn't defend themselves.

"What would your father say to your trips out into the woods?" Liam asked while inspecting vials of herbs. "Would he even care?"

"It's hard to say." she began unpacking her bag. "If he bothered to be here long enough to notice, he might lecture me on how unbecoming it was for a woman of my status to be wandering around outside unaccompanied. Worried about my marriage prospects no doubt."

"Have you had any suitors?" Liam eyed her suspiciously, as if expecting to hear her say she had a line of suitors waiting for him to leave the house. He should not be asking her questions like that, he had forfeited that right years ago.

Bridget laughed nonchalantly as she pulled a jar off the shelf for her hands. "Nobody wants a 'runt' regardless of how rich her father is. I'm not a virgin as you well know, so my prospects are practically nonexistent."

"Hey." Liam took her by the hands, his eyes staring into hers with so much emotion. "There's not a single man in this city worthy of your hand."

She stared at him in disbelief, remembering the last time they had seen each other. He looked at her expression and his face dropped. As it should, he was the one who took away any good standing she had towards marriage.

"I don't think I will ever be able to express just how sorry I am for how things ended between us. I said some very cruel and untrue things. I hope one day you can find it in your gentle heart to forgive me."

She wasn't sure she could, but this was Liam. Her Liam, not the prince. A tear slid down her cheek. She tensed up, she would not allow herself to cry right now, she did not want him to see how much he affected her. Most likely seeing this, Liam took the jar from her and opened it, he then began to apply the medicine to her burnt palms. His hands were warm and surprisingly tender. He looked up at her, searching her eyes as he worked. The look he gave her stirred something deep inside, a familiar longing for his hands to be on her. Was this longing she felt just desire from the past, was this the dominant wolf stirring up her wolf, or had her misadventure with Clyous left her wanting. This was incredibly complicated, and dangerous.

120

"Regardless, nobody wants to marry me." She winced a little as his thumb passed over a broken blister.

"They are fools then." Liam finished applying the ointment then began to wrap her hands with clean bandages. "You can always marry me, if you'll have me. I am the one who mated you first, I will make this right."

Her heart skipped a beat, she had suddenly forgotten to breathe. "What?"

"Just think about it." He smirked, tying off the last bandage. "You're from an old dominant bloodline. Our children would be unstoppable, and it's not like we're complete strangers. I would protect you. We would be what we used to be. I would make up for everything I ruined all those years ago."

She stood quickly, face reddening instantly. "We haven't been together in years. And you just waltz back into my life under the pretext that you want to make everything right?"

"I've thought of you every day, regretted every moment away from you." Liam wrapped his arms around her waist and pulled her against him.

"Then why did you leave? Why did you make me leave?" she demanded, turning to face him, if he opened the door for this conversation, she was damn sure going to slam it in his face.

"I had to." He looked pained. "I couldn't take you where I was headed."

"I've heard rumors, whispers of the things you have done. I don't think I could have followed you there, I wouldn't have been okay with any of it."

He looked into her eyes sadly. "That's why, sweetheart, that's exactly why I had to end it."

She allowed him to continue holding her as she thought, knowing that if she pushed him away right now it would only make matters worse. Liam loved the chase, loved the challenge. Truthfully, a small part of her felt good to be around him again. It was equally unsettling being this close to a man she used to love, a man who had spent the last few years turning into a monster. She had seen him commit such monstrous acts not a month ago, but right now, it was like they used to be. Was he still in there?

"Why are you coming to me now? Why did you have to wait years to tell me this?" Irritation at him and the situation reared its ugly head once again.

"I had to do what I had to do. I did not enjoy it. Now I'm older, stronger and closer to inheriting the kingdom from my aging father. I can protect you now." He stared back at her. "I'm not afraid anymore. After seeing you the other day it reminded me how much I love you, how much I need you in my life. I miss us."

With her thoughts spinning, she pulled away, staring off towards the wall. This was not an ideal situation, she thought, trying to decide what to say. This wasn't something she had ever expected to hear from him, regardless of the fact her younger self dreamed of hearing those words. But, what about Clyous? Another man had found his way into her life, a man who didn't torture people or kill them over nothing. It was a newer relationship, if that's what you wanted to call it, but there were definitely feelings there. No, she couldn't stand what the crown was doing. She was here to spy for the rebellion, not to rekindle an old relationship. She took a deep breath to clear her mind.

"I don't need you to say anything. Just know that when you are ready, I will be here ready for you." Liam kissed her, his lips not as gentle as Clyous, but more commanding. "I do love you, Bridget. I always have."

And with that, the Crown Prince of Oich turned on his heel and walked out of the room. Bridget was frozen in shock until she heard her front door close. What had just happened?

Chapter Twenty

Menolayous

Menolayous scouted ahead of their group as they slowly made their way northeast, passing the capital city completely and making their way towards the lower half of the Kingdom of Gaelach. They were still deep within Oich territory, but the closer they made it to the other kingdom's borders the safer they were from the crown. They were not safer from the Gaelach silverbacks, who were arguably more dangerous than the crown prince and his cronies.

The Kingdom of Gaelach didn't operate with the same hierarchy and laws as the Kingdom of Oich. The blooded of Gaelach were obsessed with religion, spending most of their free time worshipping the Moon God. Like their counterparts in Oich, the silverbacks treated all humans like slaves, they also sacrificed humans in cult-like rituals and were rumored to dabble in dark magic. They were significantly less organized than Oich, not having harbors and farms, or even a standing royal guard. Instead, they harvested their forests for trade goods, scattering themselves out into various tribes rather than cities. Their capital was a temple to the Moon God, not a castle city. They were wild, and ruled not by a king, but by three siblings that called themselves priests.

Even though the Kingdom of Gaelach was several days away on foot, the thought of running into the black magic tribesmen had him on high alert. The others did not seem to notice the change in him, or even how much danger they would potentially be in if they continued north. Menolayous had past experiences that the others did not, his distrust of the Kingdom of Gaelach ran deeper than any cavern in Stone Basin, but he knew they would not be entering that kingdom just yet.

They had been traveling for several days now, trying to slip past the different Oich outposts unseen. They might not be in the capital anymore, but they were still wanted, and unfortunately, Catriona and her hair stood out. They had been traveling in constant downpours, the spring rains finally beginning to show themselves as the group trudged through the muddy roads. They had to put a halt to Catriona and Danny's training while they traveled, not having enough time in the day for it, but it also made unwanted noise and drew attention. Menolayous could see within Catriona the dimming of her usual fire. Her energy was starting to fade fast.

She was physically fit enough that the road itself wasn't to blame, it was her lack of eating. Where she used to be able to eat soups and vegetables for energy, they were lacking those essential things needed to thrive. Menolayous and his brothers had hoped she would be able to manage the smoked meat, but the very first night Markous had made such a big deal out of her eating habits she had refused to eat entirely and had fled into the woods to avoid his criticism. That was the first time Danny had verbally laid into the jackass, irritated at how Markous was treating his sister. Rama had to step in to save Markous's life, at that point everyone wanted to kill him.

Menolayous silently stalked through the trees towards the main road, avoiding the large puddles beginning to collect upon the forest floor. He had volunteered to scout ahead while everyone had stopped for a lunch break. This was not something they did when it was the three of them traveling together. They ate as they moved, only sitting down once they made camp for the night, but everyone was becoming increasingly concerned for Catriona, who seemed oblivious to the danger she was putting herself in. Her once fitted clothes were beginning to hang off of her and her pace was beginning to slow. So, they made a point of stopping and resting, doing what they could to encourage her to eat. They needed to do something soon; this was going too far.

The sound of horses caught his attention as he stalked closer to the tree line. Not long after he could hear men's voices as they talked amongst themselves. He could see a couple wagons being pulled by a small team of horses. Four blooded walked with the heavily laden wagon, it looked as if they were headed into Gaelach with produce and salted meats. The food was what caught his attention more than anything, it was food Catriona might be able to eat. By the gods did she need to eat something.

This would also be an excellent chance to test out their strength, really see what Markous and his brother and sister did when given a target. Markous had continually expressed his desire to join them in fighting back against the crown. Catriona and Clyous didn't seem to know what they wanted to do yet. They had no plans for their future aside from living day to day, and Catriona's will had seemed to begin shaking even at that. Menolayous suspected Clyous's lack of decision making had to do with Bridget. Maybe a small raid would push them into finally deciding what they truly wanted.

Menolayous allowed himself another moment of visually examining the wagon and the blooded that guarded it. With trees and brush as his camouflage, he silently crept back away from the road where he doubled back towards the group. He finally caught up with them about ten minutes back, they were noisily trudging through the rolling hills and thick fog. This was exactly why he scouted ahead; they were so damn loud.

"There's a heavily weighed down wagon up ahead." Menolayous approached them. "Four blooded total. They look like they're headed to Gaelach."

Rama smiled at him. "Just how I like my prey. Slow and fat."

Danny came up to them, nodding his head in agreement. The three of them looked back to their traveling companions who seemed confused at the exchange. Menolayous did a double take at Catriona, she was looking exceptionally worn out. She must not have eaten much when the group had stopped.

"You wanted to see what the rebellion has been doing besides saving damsels in distress, well, today's the day." Rama dropped his pack and began feeling around his belt for his weapons.

"What exactly is the point of attacking traveling merchants?" Catriona asked, not seeming overly enthused.

"Not only does it disrupt the flow of gold filtering back to Oich, but it helps us gather supplies for the cause," Danny explained as he was tying his hair back.

"A couple of wagons aren't going to cripple the crown," Catriona argued, a small spark returning to her eyes. "They're still going to drain those merchant families dry."

"Not our problem." Rama scoffed. "They're blooded."

"So is Bridget," Clyous joined the argument. "What if that was her father you killed?"

Menolayous watched as the oldest brother dropped his gear and started preparing, anger coursing through him. Markous wanted to fight blooded and was willing to blindly follow them into a scuffle just for the opportunity. This was how he had chosen to deal with the darkness he had lived through. Menolayous guessed it was better than not eating, like his sister. Hopefully it wouldn't get him killed. At least he seemed like he was prepared to fight with them instead of running off by himself. The twins, however, stood still where they were, still wearing their packs, their expressions sour. Interesting, he thought to himself, they seemed to prefer logic over blind loyalty. He admired them for that or was disturbed by the lack of fire inside them, maybe both.

"It's not Bridget, lover boy," Rama growled. "This has been a way of survival for us for years. Your sister has got to eat; this might be the only way we can get her something for a while."

Clyous stepped up to the giant in challenge. "If you're willing to kill over wagons or supplies and claim it's for the cause, then you're no better than they are."

Ballsy, Menolayous thought, and not entirely wrong either. There was some of that fire, the will to keep going. Clyous had it, Markous definitely had it. But Catriona? Danny stepped between the two men before it came to blows, Menolayous was not concerned if it did, the boy might be larger than him, but Menolayous was a far better warrior.

"We do not kill unless we have to," Danny said calmly. "It's not our way."

"Guess you've never been the merchant getting robbed," Clyous spat angrily. "Those supplies are their livelihoods."

"We've grown up around a lot of them. Most of them were kind to us, they treated us fairly. It doesn't feel right robbing them when we understand how hard they work for their supplies," Catriona explained, she sounded exhausted.

"Look, we're not asking you to follow us on some murder mission of your family friends," Rama called over his shoulder as he started off toward the main road. "You can hang out here until we've finished."

Menolayous watched as Markous followed Rama through the trees. Danny looked back at Catriona, shrugged his shoulders, then took off after his brother. The twins looked at each other for a moment before sighing in frustration.

"Come on, let's make sure they don't get themselves killed." Catriona dropped her pack and took off after Danny.

Clyous followed after her. Menolayous watched all of this for a moment before taking up the rear. She would at least still fight for others, that was a good thing. He watched her as they tried to catch up to the others. Her lack of speed was concerning, was this from not eating or the long hours of nightmares that plagued her at night? She had been fine for the most part during her healing process. In the last week or so, it's like the armor she was putting on for everyone was starting to crumble. Her pain was beginning to shine through the cracks.

After a few minutes they had caught up to Rama and Danny just before the tree line. Everyone was silent and stuck close to the ground. Menolayous scanned the top of the hill towards the main road and in the direction of the wagon, which was bumping along slowly in their direction, maybe thirty feet away. Rama signaled Menolayous to flank the wagon, which he did. Sneaking between the trees with a bow in his hand, Menolayous managed to get behind the wagons and the blooded without them knowing. The light rain helped contain the sound of his footsteps and undoubtedly masked their scent. Menolayous pulled back his arrow in preparation, the arrowheads had been tipped with silver.

"Hello there!" Rama's massive figure called out, stepping onto the road from the trees. "Passage requires that you pay a toll to continue on safely."

With a rocky hill to the right of the wagons, Menolayous behind them, Rama blocking the path ahead, and the rest of the party emerging on the left side from the forest, the blooded realized they were surrounded and drew swords in preparation for a fight.

"Step aside, young one," the older man warned. "The crown will hear of this either way. No place will be safe from King Cathal when he decides to come for those plundering his trading routes."

"That old dog?" Danny smirked. "I doubt he could track down a rabbit before keeling over."

Ever the shit-stirrer Danny was. Whatever the desired effect was, the blooded all growled at him in anger at the insult to their king. Markous laughed at Danny's quip, enjoying the torment of the blooded before him. Menolayous caught sight of Catriona who started to walk around to the front next to Rama, one of Danny's short swords in her hand.

"Gaylen," she calmly greeted him.

"Catriona!" The old man wavered, letting his guard down slightly. "You're alive?"

"I'm alive," she confirmed.

"We heard what happened to your mother, and that you tried fighting back. When we went to the town square the next morning your bodies were gone. We assumed you were all dead."

"Hoped is more like it," one of the younger blooded muttered, catching the old man's eye before quieting back down.

127

"Might as well be," Markous snarled. "None of you had come to help us, to speak up for us. You all left us to die!"

The old man looked at the three siblings with sad eyes. "There was nothing that could have been done. The crown prince had made the command—"

"I see that our years of partnership meant so little to you." Catriona glared at him.

"My dear," the blooded sounded like he was pleading with her. "We cannot go against the dominant wolf. It is impossible."

"I never took your family for cowards." Markous shot at one of the younger blooded, in response the man flashed Markous his fangs.

"Catriona my dear, here take some food. You look like you haven't eaten in days." The old man tried to hand her some salted pork; Catriona took a step back like it was a poisonous snake. The old man watched her, obviously troubled. "Are you safe here with these men? Would you like to come with us?"

"So your sons can abuse me all the way back to Oich where you'll hand me over to the crown for some gold? I know that would not be your intent Gaylen, but the look about your sons says otherwise."

Gaylen looked back at his boys and sighed, turning back to her. "All you had to do was simply allow the guards to take your mother and not fight as you did—"

"Fuck you!" Clyous bellowed. "Would you have let them do that to your daughter?"

"Our sister is of superior breeding, slave," one of the younger blooded piped up. "She would never be foolish enough to think she could stand up to any male. Your sister deserved her whipping."

"Silence!" Gaylen commanded.

"Talk nicely, I'm warning you." Danny pointed his short sword directly at the oldest brother.

"If I was the crown prince I would have killed her brothers in front of her too, just to put her in her place!" The other younger blooded flashed a grin in Catriona's direction.

"I guess that brings an end to negotiations." Rama threw his hands up in frustration.

Danny was the first to break formation, charging towards the last blooded who spoke, swinging his sword at the wolf's chest. Rama tucked his head and charged, crashing into the older man like a bull. Unfortunately, he had decided to get up and fight with his sons. Menolayous started firing off his arrows, they penetrated the nearest blooded. One, two, three, four, five. Menolayous watched the man try to shift but couldn't because of the silver sticking into his chest. He turned towards Menolayous then, as if he was going to charge. Six. The arrow pierced his throat. The man fell to his knees into the rain-soaked grass, dead.

Menolayous spotted the twins working in unison, slashing their blades at a single blooded. The man, unsurprisingly, moved faster than they did. Catriona was a lot slower than she had been a week or so ago. Clyous carried their fight, without his sister's speed, it highlighted the fact that Clyous was actually quite decent with an axe. Markous had joined Danny in his assault against the man who had spoken last. Markous delivered an impressive slice to the man's calf, severing muscles and forcing him to take a knee. Danny followed through with a strike of his own, his sword slicing open his stomach, his intestines spilling out onto the ground.

Rama had taken it upon himself to fight the old man single-handedly; he had shifted into a large grey wolf. The wolf was snapping its teeth inches away from Rama's face as he held the beast's head at bay. With all the other blooded dead, the rest of the group turned toward the last wolf. Rama shouted at them, insisting he had everything under control. Menolayous, not willing to wait around for his brother to overpower the wolf, put an arrow through its eye.

"Hey!" Rama shouted. "That one was mine."

"Work faster." Menolayous shrugged.

"I never liked Gaylen's sons anyway," Markous said, cleaning off his weapon.

Clyous nodded in agreement. "I always liked Gaylen though, when he wasn't trying to cheat us out of a fair deal anyways."

"Gaylen deserved better," Catriona said sorrowfully.

"Doesn't sound like his sons had a high opinion of you," Danny chimed in.

"They wouldn't. I refused to sleep with them." She shrugged as if that was an everyday occurrence. Knowing how blooded men treated women in the capital, he wouldn't doubt that it happened regularly.

Menolayous moved to the wagon for a better look. There were tons of produce, salted pork, and some other tradable supplies. It was entirely all too much for them to use. Rama joined him in examining the carts, stopping briefly to give each of the horses an apple.

"What are we going to do with all of this?" Danny asked as he was untying the scabbard of a long sword from one of the dead blooded.

"Who's even close?" Rama asked his brothers, they could not keep all this for themselves.

"I think Flinn and his group are about a day away, maybe two pulling this beast of a wagon," Menolayous answered.

Rama nodded. "They could use the food. I believe some were injured in a raid right before we went into Oich."

"I'll take the wagon to Flinn and feel out how his crew is doing, see what information they've gathered," Menolayous suggested.

"I'll go with you," Markous offered, glancing over to his siblings. "If there's work to be had, I'm your man!"

Rama thumped him on the back with mock pride. "They will be happy to take you, friend."

"What's our plan then?" Catriona asked. "It's not like we're safe going back home."

"We can still escort you to our stronghold outside Airgid," Danny offered.

"I don't want to leave Oich," Clyous spoke up. "I don't want to be too far away from Bridget. She might need our help. Besides I'm sure we can find plenty more recruits in the fishing villages."

"Clyous?" Catriona started reaching for her twin, but she stopped herself. "I guess I get it."

"What do you want to do?" Clyous asked her.

"I don't know," she answered quietly.

Menolayous watched as panic flashed in her eyes, the armor she wore around herself starting to crack even more. For someone who had been so strong, fighting against blooded, watching her mother die, her injuries, it was only a matter of time before the darkness started to come out. There was only one other time before this that he had seen her start to break, her first night awake back at the cave. She seemed to pull herself together relatively quickly after that, but she still couldn't eat meat. She hardly ate at all anymore. He had been waiting for a blowout or a break for weeks now, something that would be completely normal for someone dealing with a tragedy. She had been through too much. Now he swore he could see the break happening as her brothers were making decisions that did not directly involve her. Rama and Danny seemed to see it too, her brothers, however, seemed oblivious.

"Markous, Clyous, help me secure these wagons really quick." Rama tactfully drew them away.

Menolayous acted as if he was securing something in the back of the nearest wagon while Danny approached Catriona. Catriona stood almost frozen, staring at the ground and fighting off tears. Danny cupped her face with his hand bringing her chin up to look at him. Menolayous could see the tears were streaming then.

"What's wrong?" Danny asked her gently.

"I don't know what to do?" She was struggling to keep her voice even. "They know what they want to do, I don't. They both are choosing paths I don't think I can follow."

"You don't have to follow them," Danny said, trying to soothe her.

"I don't want to be left behind." She buried her face in Danny's shoulder.

Menolayous watched his brother embrace her. "You'll never be left behind. I promise."

Aside from the fact that Catriona was openly seeking comfort from Danny, she was very much baring her emotions out there for him to see. At least they had grown close enough that she could do that with him, she needed to be able to trust someone. It was time to give them space. Menolayous walked forward to where the others were. Rama turned to him as he approached, giving him a questioning look.

"You two mind filling these buckets with water from that stream up ahead?" Rama asked Markous and Clyous. "We should water the horses before changing course." The two brothers nodded, grabbing the buckets out of the wagon and taking off down the road. Yep, completely oblivious to their sister having a breakdown behind them. Rama and Menolayous shared a knowing look.

"It was bound to happen sometime." Rama shrugged his shoulders.

"I don't think she's ready to be away from her brothers. Not so soon after the burning, anyway. I don't think she has it in her to tell them though," Menolayous said, glancing backwards.

"Why?" Rama asked, his eyes still following the brothers as they went towards the trees.

"She probably doesn't want them to change what they want to do just for her," Menolayous answered. "What should we do?"

"I'm assuming Danny's taking care of her?" Rama inquired, seeing Menolayous nod, he continued. "It's up to her to communicate with her family. She's the only one who can make the decision."

Menolayous risked a quick glance backward. "I don't think today is going to be that day. She hasn't been eating or sleeping much."

"We'll take the boys to Flinn's crew. If Markous still wants to fight, I can take him the rest of the way to the Harrada Mountain Pass for more in-depth training. Clyous will want to stay with Finn so he can be closer to Bridget."

"What about her?" Menolayous nodded in Catriona's direction.

"She'll need to choose. I've got no problem helping her get to what she wants, but I won't make the decision for her," Rama answered with all the authority his years of experience had given him.

Menolayous thought for a moment before speaking, "She and Danny could stay at the Emerald Falls campsite. They'll be safe enough there for her to sort some of her issues out. We can come back for them after dropping off her brothers."

"You think Danny would be okay—" Rama paused, then laughed. "That was a dumb question. Never mind."

Menolayous chuckled. Three to four days alone with a beautiful girl he'd been fawning over for over a month now, no, Danny would be absolutely miserable. Maybe a few days without a bunch of people around would help her let out some of the demons she was struggling with.

Danny made his way over to them then, just as Menolayous spotted Catriona's brothers approaching with the water. Rama ran over the plan with Danny, who seemed to agree that it made the most sense. He left them to go talk to Catriona and see how she felt about it. Rama walked over to her brothers to give them their update, leaving out how Catriona was handling their impending departure. They also seemed eager and agreed. Catriona and

Danny returned to the wagons carrying all the dumped gear from the tree line. Danny had filled up their bags with food from the carts before returning to the group.

"So as of right now everyone is good with this plan?" Menolayous wanted clarification from his traveling companions.

Everyone nodded in agreement. Menolayous glanced over at Catriona who was unusually quiet. She had stopped crying but still looked like she was fighting with herself internally. It was now or never if Catriona was going to say something. After several moments, it looked like it was going to be never. She had at least made one decision today; she wasn't going to be the reason her brothers would be held back. That took an internal strength most people didn't have.

"Guess this is it, Cat." Clyous embraced his twin.

"Try to keep yourself safe, would you?" She hugged him back. "Both of you."

Markous took his turn hugging his sister. "You're the one who always ends up in trouble."

"Ha ha." She smirked, pulling away and showing a hint of a smile on her lips, her armor snapping back into place.

Clyous clasped hands with Danny as a farewell before grabbing his gear and loading it into a wagon. Markous clasped Danny's hand next, pulling him into a short embrace.

"As the older brother, I should warn you to treat my little sister with respect and to look out for her." Markous smiled at his own poorly timed joke. "But she's scarier than I am."

"Will you get going already!" Catriona pushed her brother playfully.

Markous laughed heartily before loading his bedroll into the wagon. Rama embraced Danny before moving to Catriona, handing her a large sack filled with food she could eat. When Rama hugged her, all Menolayous could see left of her was her braid and the sack still clutched in her hand, it was like Rama had swallowed her whole. When his brother pulled away, Catriona was smiling up at his brotherly affection. Danny nodded farewell to Menolayous.

Catriona stood before him, staring shyly at the ground. "I've learned my lesson about trying to hug you."

Menolayous felt a flush of shame at her words. He knew she meant it more as a joke, but the fact that his friend was afraid to embrace him really

133

rubbed him the wrong way. Slowly, against his very nature, Menolayous extended a hand and gently patted her cheek affectionately.

"Take care of my brother would you." Menolayous quickly removed his hand at the sight of her smiling. "And yourself, please?"

"Keep yourselves out of trouble, yeah?" Rama teased, climbing up into a wagon, almost tipping it over in the process.

"We'll be back in a couple of days," Menolayous promised, climbing into the wagon next to Rama.

They all waved goodbye as the horses started forward. All Menolayous could hear was the sound of the horses' hooves on the muddy road and the creaking of the wagon. Clyous and Markous had found a place to sit in the very back next to some of the ale barrels. Clyous sat next to him being unusually quiet and glancing back down the road at his sister. Menolayous looked back as well. Catriona stood in the middle of the road watching the wagon go. Danny stood beside her, taking her hand and leading her away.

"Is this a mistake?" Clyous asked him, finally facing forward again.

"Is what a mistake?" Menolayous looked at him closely.

"Leaving her alone after everything that's happened?"

"Depends on why you're leaving."

Clyous sat there for a moment before answering, "I think she was using Markous and I to avoid facing what's eating her alive inside."

This surprised Menolayous, was Clyous not as oblivious as he had thought? "So you're saying you're doing this for her sake?"

"If I had stayed, she wouldn't face her nightmares head on. She couldn't make her own decision on what she wanted to do, not in this state of denial she's been in." Clyous shifted uncomfortably. "She'd be too focused on affecting us. I love her enough to leave, so she can work past this."

Menolayous nodded his approval. "That's very wise."

"I know her better than my own mind sometimes. I just hope I'm right." Clyous leaned back in the seat staring up into the sky.

Chapter Twenty-One

Danny

Watching her standing in the middle of the road, seeing her brothers ride off with his, couldn't be described as anything else but hard. She looked empty, her eyes were almost blank. He couldn't even begin to understand what was going on in her head at that moment. He could easily guess that she had never been without her family before, but he could also state with certainty that everything that's happened to her this last month had been buried deep inside. Not having her brothers there to lean on meant she was going to have to face down those haunting memories.

When Menolayous had approached him about this change of plan, he had already seen the cracks starting. This wasn't some special romantic three-day getaway, no, he knew she needed this. He would be there for her to stop her from shattering completely, just like his brothers had been there for him when he was able to stop surviving and when he chose to start living.

Danny gently took her by the hand, pulling her away from the road. She followed him silently without protest. He took off eastward towards one of their secret camps behind Emerald Falls. They continued on their journey for several more hours, trudging through the rain and mud. She did not speak the entire time, not a single word.

Finally, Danny had found the river and turned their course upstream. They walked along the river for about an hour before the mouth turned into a deep pool. Lush greenery surrounded this pool, giving the waterfall that cascaded from the rocky mountainside its name, Emerald Falls.

Danny took Catriona by the hand, leading her towards the waterfall itself. As they approached, Danny located the hidden pathway covered with some overgrown ferns. He pressed himself tightly against the rock, encouraging Catriona to do the same. He inched himself sideways into a small alcove that led behind the cascading water. The roaring of the falls was almost deafening, it was part of the reason this hideout worked out so well, no amount of noise made inside could be heard outside.

Careful not to slip on the wet stone, Danny pulled Catriona inside the entrance to the cavern. He heard her sharp intake of breath and smiled. The two-level cavern wasn't large, maybe big enough to hold four people comfortably on the floor above them, but it was beautiful. Light came from a small opening at the top of the cavern ceiling, illuminating the blue water in front of them. Stalagmites were everywhere forming natural barriers, white crystal quartz was embedded in the stone walls making the light reflecting off them create intricate patterns. The path they were currently on allowed them to reach it with little effort. In front of them, spanning from the base of the waterfall to the base of the upper level was a churning and bubbling spring. Most of the cavern was taken up by this beautiful blue body of water. A cool mist from the crashing water pelted the walkway and ceiling above, keeping the air moist but surprisingly warm.

"Beautiful, isn't it?" Danny asked her, smiling.

"Yeah." Catriona was staring into the water.

"My brothers and I use this cave often." Danny pulled her along with him up the pathway. "The waterfall acts as a natural barrier for sound, and it helps hide our scents too so blooded and scourge can't find us in here."

They made it up to the top level of the cavern. The ground was soft and covered in grass. The larger rocks that were nearby had been collected and organized into a fire ring. A small stack of old firewood sat near the ring. Danny set down his pack and began laying out his bedroll on a bed of clover. He watched as Catriona was staring at the quartz embedded in the cave wall. He walked up behind her, gently removing her pack and laying her bedroll out for her.

"It's warm in here," she commented, turning back to him as she still took in their surroundings.

"Even if it's snowing out it stays warm," he explained. "The waterfall can go from ice cold to refreshing, but that pool has warm water year-round."

"How does it stay warm?"

"The heated water comes up from the ground. It's too hot to touch but the cold water from the falls cools it down." Danny started adding wood to the fire ring.

Catriona sat down next to him, handing him pieces of wood. She was quiet again. Danny finished stacking the wood and sat back. He pulled out some smoked venison from his bag and started snacking. He offered her a piece, which she took hesitantly.

"You need to eat something."

Danny watched her hesitantly take a bite. The look of disgust came over her face as she forced herself to chew. She was up in a flash sprinting towards the cavern entrance. Danny chased after her, coming up on her just in time to see her retching her stomach contents into a nearby bush. He reached forward, pulling her braid out of the way. He had hoped that she would be able to stomach it, he could feel her ribs underneath the tunic she wore.

"Come on." He patted her back gently as she stood back up slowly. "Let's go back inside."

Together they returned to their campsite. She sat down next to him looking pale. He couldn't take it anymore; she wouldn't be able to go much longer without food. The fact that she had deliberately not been eating infuriated him beyond reason. He knew meat was going to be the challenge, but it had progressed in a direction it shouldn't have. If they were going to do this, they might as well start now.

"You haven't been eating enough," he pointed out. "You've been losing weight, and your energy is shot."

"You see me eat." She rolled her eyes, brushing him off.

"Broth, and some vegetables. Not protein."

He watched as her eyebrows furrowed, she was going to fight him on this. Fuck it then, they were going to fight. At least that fire inside her was still burning. He was deathly afraid it had gone out.

"I can't stomach meat," she argued.

"And why not, Catriona?" His voice rose. "That's a mental barrier you put up for yourself. Give me one good reason why you're starving yourself."

"I'm not—" she started.

"You are!" Danny pushed. "Why not meat? What's going through your head when you eat it?"

"I don't owe you an answer," she ground out, standing up as if to storm off.

Danny shot up to block her path. "Tell me!"

"Fuck off!" She tried to step around him.

"What do you think about when you see meat cooking over a fire?"

137

"Stop!" she shouted, trying to go around again.

Danny grabbed her to stop her from trying to leave. Catriona violently pulled away from him, preparing to strike him. He saw the fear in her eyes, like she was a wild animal backed into a corner. He moved quickly, dodging the arm she was pulling back to strike with and taking her to the ground. He took control of her arms easily enough, pinning them to the ground so she couldn't keep trying to hit him. He sat on top of her, effectively restraining her as she tried to thrash around. She was angrier than a hornet's nest, swearing at him at the top of her lungs; but she was weak, he could feel it in her resistance.

"Get off!" she spat.

"Not until you answer my question." He matched her intensity. "And not until I'm positive you aren't going to try hitting me again."

"Fuck off!"

"Answer me," his voice softened ever so slightly. "Your mother didn't die so you could starve yourself to death. She told you to keep fighting. So, fight!"

That had done it. A sob burst out of Catriona, tears rolled down her face and into her hair. Danny wanted nothing more than to stop, to comfort her, but she needed to answer. Not for him, but for herself. She had to face this; she had to eat. She had to want to keep going, to not give up, and if anger kept her going, so be it.

"It reminds me of her!" she forced out. "How I couldn't stop them, how I've never been able to stop them. How much I hid from her, how I couldn't hide her from them. She was caught that day because a city guard wouldn't stop staring at me, and when I decided to mouth off like I always do she stepped between us. They scented her wound. Every time I eat meat or watch it cook, I see her burning to death in front of me. I don't eat because I don't deserve to be here, she does. I wish the flames would have burned me instead, I'm a fucking inconvenience to everyone. She's dead because I failed."

There it was. The painful truth she had been hiding from everyone. The reason why she wasn't eating, and why she couldn't decide on a future. In her mind she should have been dead, so why bother with the rest of it. His heart broke at this; he scooped her up into his arms and rolled sideways so he ended up on his back while holding her trembling body to his chest.

138

She continued to cry, gripping him tightly as he held onto her. Weeks and weeks' worth of this pent-up darkness was finally coming out. He felt he understood this better than anyone, what she was feeling now was what he felt after his mother died. Keeping those dark twisted thoughts inside was just as bad as letting poison fester. She had to get them out, he had to make sure she did. This was still just the start, Catriona had a long road to travel before she was healed. He just needed her to want to walk down it.

Danny held her gently, stroking her hair. After a while her tears began to slow, her body was no longer trembling. Danny could hear her soft breathing. He glanced down at the beautiful creature now asleep in his arms. She needed sleep almost as much as she needed food, he knew the nightmares had been keeping her up. He needed to get up and start on some sort of food she would eat, he would make sure she ate it. Her hand flexed for a moment in her sleep, leaving her palm on his chest. He smiled to himself before shutting his own eyes for a few moments. He could lay here just a little bit longer.

Chapter Twenty-Two

Morrigan

Drops of water rained down from the ceiling, condensation had been collecting for some time. The darkness inside the cave was all consuming, the ground was a combination of hard rock and a mixture of clay and mud, appearing as if it had been undisturbed for some weeks. The air was stagnant inside, unused yet old. There was no visible exit, instead it branched out into a series of endless underground tunnels.

Morrigan treaded carefully through one of those tunnels, spear in hand and poised for use. She did not dare risk light in this blackness, not while she hunted. She did not want her prey to know she was coming. Or worse yet, if she stumbled upon a hive of slumbering scourge, she might become the prey.

Months ago, Morrigan started noticing an increase of attacks from the scourge, especially in this area close to the Gaelach and Oich border. There was not just an increase in how many attacks were occurring but also how many scourge attacked at once. She noticed the bodies of the scourge were fresh, recently turned; instead of the withered, nearly translucent, older ones that hid within the dark caves. Reports of attacks started with small family compounds, advancing to smaller villages within weeks. More and more victims had fallen to the curse of the scourge.

It wasn't until the attack on a fishing village just outside the capital of Oich that she was sure of it. The unnatural fog had moved like a boat being steered towards the village, and for the scourge to just happen to use it to cover their hunt in a place that large? No, it wasn't natural, that fog was created with dark magic. That attack on Oich was a planned assault, most likely created to test the capital's defenses.

Magic was fading from this land. Less and less children were born with the blood of the ancients. The blooded were wary of such magic, and Oich had gone as far as outlawing its use. Anyone found using it was burned at the stake or worse. There was no safety for the children of the ancients in this kingdom, so the bloodlines dwindled. That's why seeing those girls weeks ago had been so shocking to her, those girls had survived in Oich all the way into adulthood without being discovered. The truth of the matter was that

140

they were probably not familiar with their magic, it was unlikely they understood its full potential. She did not see them with any markings, although that meant little from the top of a tree.

Morrigan set out on this mission months ago, pulling herself from her life of seclusion to discover who was responsible for this dark magic, and to uncover why they were weaponizing the scourge. Being an elemental blessed by the gods, it was in her blood to fight against and rid the world of dark magic. It was her duty, as was defending the children of the ancients. If she didn't stop this mysterious magic wielder and if history decided to repeat itself, then it was quite possible everyone in Stone Basin would die.

She reached out with her senses, mentally mapping the tunnel's wall as she pushed forward. She could sense, even through the darkness, the edge of the tunnel opening up into a tall alcove. She strained her ears hoping to pick up on any sounds that might not belong. All she could hear was the dripping of water and the wet sound her feet made as she traipsed through the claylike floor. Drip drip. Drip drip.

She turned into the alcove standing just inside the entrance. Drip drip. She reached out with her senses again feeling nothing but the darkness. Drip drip. Suddenly there was clicking echoing all around her. Thrusting her spear forward, she sent a wave of fire into the opening to strike the creature that remained within, lighting the alcove walls for just a moment. Within that moment she saw a scourge skewering itself against the spear in her hand as dozens of scourge started moving behind it.

She gathered what magic she could and clapped her hands together, forcing a concussive wave in their direction knocking the small horde back a few feet. As she pulled her hands apart, lightning bolts charged between them, lighting the area once more with dancing blue lights. She turned her palms in the direction of the threat, pushing the electrical coils out at the creatures as they rallied against her once more. The bolts took off, catching the first creature, then bouncing off it and splitting into even more springs of energy which began to search out other scourge, freezing them in place as the lightning burned them from the inside.

Morrigan ran back down the tunnel as fast as her feet could take her. She cast a flame ahead of her, illuminating the way like a bright ribbon. She could hear them chasing after her, the clicks and inhuman shrieks closing in. She threw her hands back sending a whip of flame backwards, striking a few of the nearest monsters. She punched a concussive wave upward, hitting the tunnel's roof. She had successfully struck a few loosened rocks causing a cave in right behind her as she ran. The ground shook beneath her feet as the rocks piled up, blocking the creatures from getting through.

She continued to run until she could no longer hear their infernal screams, then slowed down glancing behind her, nothing. She had managed to escape. She stopped then, leaning against the tunnel wall gasping for breath. Great, now she needed to find a new way out of this cave system without stumbling on another hive. She was thankful she had at least killed some of the bastards, maybe she was lucky enough to have trapped them in there. She held up a palm of flame, lighting the tunnel around her. No use hiding now.

She began walking down the tunnel then slowed when she saw the markings on the rocky surface. She began to study it, then gasped. Painted on this wall in dark blood was the shape of a beast created by intricate loops, twists, and knotwork.

"By the gods!" Fear overtook her at the sight of this curse; it was one she had not seen in over a century. "No! It can't be!"

She knew now what she was up against, this old enemy had risen from the dead. She stood no chance against this evil, not alone. She needed help from those descended from the ancient bloodline, magic would be the only way to defeat this evil, and if they didn't succeed, they would all die. Reluctantly, she placed her hands against the symbol, projecting her magic out through the tunnels and into the night sky. It shone like a beacon calling for aid. The survival of Stone Basin now depended on them answering her call for help.

*   *   *

Bridget woke suddenly, thrashing around in her bed, her legs tangled in her linen sheets. Her dreams that night had been fitful, filled with visions of the scourge overrunning the city. A sentence of death and destruction that seemed like a promise if something was not done. She could feel it then, the call for help, the energy had ignited her from within. The light had burst through the darkness, like a silvery flame engulfing the creatures where they stood, destroying the source of their darkness. There was evil lurking out there in the woods she realized, she could sense it creeping upon the boundaries of Oich, trying to find a way in. A raven-haired woman with electric blue tattoos all over her body stood there projecting this beacon. It was stronger than the howl of a dominant wolf, she could not look away from the images crashing into her mind. Bridget did not know what to make of this dream, but without a doubt in her mind she knew that this was real.

*   *   *

Clyous jolted awake, the others around him fast asleep next to the smoldering coals of the campfire. Images pulled on his mind, forcing him to look deep into the tunnel. The creatures moved through the tunnel like insects, pouring out of an opening into the land; a woman in black stood there staring at a blood-soaked cavern wall. There was an image there, an intricate painting of a beast drawn in blood. A full moon above the beast, a wolf. The woman was begging for help. This was a message, not just a dream he happened to have. This sorceress had reached out to him, and others. Suddenly, he could sense the darkness lurking in the trees north of him. There was truly a great evil hidden out there. He could also sense the others, they were like him he realized yet spread throughout the continent, some closer than others. The brightest light he could sense was familiar, not a day's travel from where he lay now. Without question he knew immediately that this was his sister. Farther to the south he sensed a golden light. His heart soared as he reached out for this light, Bridget.

Images of Bridget suddenly flashed through his mind, the scourge surrounding her, images of blooded hunting her and dragging her off into the forest. Flashes of tribesmen from Gaelach who performed some ritual under the night sky. Blood and bodies everywhere. Catriona stood in the middle of the ritual, completely engulfed in flames. Clyous shook the images from his mind as best he could, but they had taken hold. These were visions of what was to come, a plethora of outcomes that had not yet come to pass. Clyous could feel his neck and scalp burning as he let the magic take over. This was a warning, he knew it to be true. These were promised outcomes if nobody was able to stop this darkness. That woman in black had sent this warning to him, it ignited something deep down that he did not know was there. He knew if he didn't help her, help stop this darkness, he knew they would all be dead.

Chapter Twenty-Three

Catriona

"Catriona, wake up!" she could hear his voice in the distance.

Flames were all she could see, flames devouring her mother, her brothers, Danny and her friends. She was underground somewhere, in a tunnel system maybe. There were dead bodies covering the tunnel floor, pale and deformed. Designs were drawn onto the stone in blood, swirls and twisted knots created ornate designs. A sketch of a cruel and terrifying beast took up most of the space on the damp cavern wall. A woman stood next to it. She had raven-black hair that fell to her hips, pin straight and thick. Her olive skin made her golden-brown eyes shine brightly. She wore a dark leather hide dress with plated armor on her shoulders, forearms, and hips. Black feathers and animal bones were her chosen accessories, giving her a feral appearance.

"Who are you?" Catriona asked the woman cautiously, glancing around at the surrounding carnage.

"I am Morrigan, Guardian of the Ancients, protector of the old ways," she answered, eyeing her up and down with great interest. "I need your help, Firebird."

"It's just a dream. Catriona! Wake up," she heard his voice say in the distance.

"There is evil spreading across the land. If we do not stop it, no one will survive."

"Why do you want my help?" Catriona asked.

The woman looked at her confused. "You don't know, do you?"

"Know what?"

The woman stretched out her hands to Catriona, those same hands suddenly crackled to life with tiny dancing flames. "You are just like me."

Before Catriona could respond to the sorceress, she felt as if she were being dragged out of the tunnel and back into herself. She opened her eyes gasping for air, her surroundings waking her from the odd dream. Danny was beside her, concern written all over his face at the sight of her panic. She was back at the Emerald Falls campsite. She and Danny were the only ones there, no strange woman, no creepy blood art on the walls, no dead bodies.

"Hey, it's just me," Danny said. "You were having another nightmare."

Catriona blinked away the memories of the dark tunnel. "Sorry if I woke you."

"No need to be sorry." He smiled gently. "Just worried about you. That one seemed really bad, you were convulsing."

"It wasn't like the others. This one... I don't know. It wasn't anywhere I recognized, I didn't know the woman."

"So, you're dreaming about women now, huh?" Danny teased, trying to lighten the mood.

"Very funny." She smirked, reaching for the waterskin. "She had magic. She was asking for help. She told me I was just like her."

"Dreaming about some sorceress, that's got to be a good change of pace from your usual nightmares."

"Yeah," she answered quietly, still shaken up. "But there was still fire, she held it in her palm. I can never seem to escape the flames, no matter what I'm dreaming about."

"Well, since we're up we might as well eat." Danny, who had avidly been pushing food onto her the last four days, got up and started trying to revive the fire. Catriona stretched before joining him, pulling the last of the bread and hard cheese from her bag. She handed Danny half before taking a bite from the cheese block. She caught Danny watching her out of the corner of his eye until he saw her swallow it. As soon as she did Danny took a bite out of his.

That had been the last four days in a nutshell, Catriona ate, and Danny made sure she kept it down. The first day of eating was a little rough, her body hadn't been used to food. But Danny kept insisting she eat a little every other hour or so in an attempt to prevent her from getting sick and also to make sure that she was replenishing what she lost. Ever the mother hen, though Catriona supposed she needed it. The last few weeks she had been eating less and less every day, too focused on containing her grief so her brothers didn't see. She hadn't paid much attention to how the lack of food had affected her until it had gotten bad, but by then the change was drastic. She had found she didn't really care that she was starting to wither away. If it hadn't been for Danny making her face the truth, she probably wouldn't be functioning at all anymore. She very well could have let herself starve to death, deep down she knew she would have.

Thankfully their relationship had not been ruined by her lack of eating or trying to hit him. Danny seemed to have forgiven her quickly enough under the condition she start eating again and work out her demons with him while they were there. She had forgiven him, mostly, for making her talk about her feelings and what was on her mind. She supposed it was a good thing to have a friend care about her so much, especially since she wasn't that into caring about herself. Catriona had now settled with the fact that she was grieving, probably in the unhealthiest way she could, and grieving her mother and dealing with the trauma of the incident was pretty much taking up everything Catriona had.

Although Danny never directly brought up again how she had admitted to him she wished she had died, he very much wanted to help her move past that particular thought. He was there every time she awoke from a nightmare. The first night she had woken up in tears he held her until she calmed down. Afterwards, he had helped her dissect the nightmares, categorizing what was real and what wasn't. As painful as this process was, it helped quite a bit. His main priority seemed to be making sure she was healing, that she wasn't giving up.

She was thankful he was the one here with her and that she wasn't alone. Had Danny become one of her closest… friends? Could she call him a friend? Somehow "friend" didn't feel special enough of a label for him. There were times when he reached out and touched her, hugged her, pulled her to him and when she felt like they could be more than just that touch. There was no denying that his touch excited her, it made her wish he touched her more, but they hadn't crossed that line. Yet, she found herself wishing they would. She had overheard conversations amongst his brothers, it appeared as if Danny was quite experienced with this sort of thing, definitely more experienced than her. She had expected, based on those stories, that Danny would be the one pursuing her, but he seemed like he was waiting for something, her probably. It was like he was worried their timing wasn't right, and it would affect how much he was helping her. These had been a long and exhausting few days of talking and emotions.

"What do you want to do today?" she asked, taking another bite. "Another fun filled day of tearing into my deepest darkest secrets?"

He looked thoughtful for a moment then said, "I think we need to go look for food. That's the last of the cheese."

Catriona scrunched her nose. "You mean game, that needs to be cooked."

"I mean food. If we can successfully hunt something down, great. Foraging will need to be a priority too."

Catriona finished off her cheese, then stood. "All right, might as well get started."

"It's still dark," Danny pointed out with a mouthful of cheese.

"It's almost morning. Maybe we'll get lucky." She started towards the only bow they had, the bow and quiver of arrows Menolayous had gifted her, getting out of this cave might be good for her.

"Wait wait wait." Danny shot up towards the bow himself. "Who says you're the one who gets to go hunting?"

Catriona turned to face him, hiding the bow behind her back playfully. "I'm the better shot."

"I strongly disagree." Danny reached for the bow in her hand, but Catriona moved out of the way. "Hey!"

She smiled at him, taking a few steps back, goading him into her little game. "Disagree all you want, but you're not going to get this from me without a fight."

She was teasing him, trying to get a rise out of him. They had been in this cave for days now, dealing with some pretty heavy stuff. She craved an activity, something fun for a break from all the emotional conversations. Oh, and how she enjoyed watching him stare at her like that, like a cat playing with a mouse. The real question was which one of them was the cat. She stared into his eyes, he seemed amused by her antics, cracking a smile at her. He just stood there, not moving to stop her, not saying anything. Well, this was no fun, hunting might be a little more fruitful.

She turned quickly, intending to make a quick getaway to the cave entrance. With her back to him she managed a step forward before she felt his hand grip the nape of her neck. He was not squeezing, but it was firm enough to make her stop dead in her tracks. She was spun around, her face now inches away from his. She inhaled sharply in surprise, this was the first time he had touched her like this, with such commanding force. With her body pressed up against his, she became extremely aware of his hand which was now cupping the side of her face. Gently, he walked her back a few paces until her back was pressed against the cave wall.

Suddenly, his lips were on hers. Catriona's heart was racing at the surprise of it. His kisses were demanding but still gentle. The hand that had been cupping her face was now tangled in her hair at the nape of her neck, the other hand had trailed down her ribs and now rested on her lower back, pulling her closer to him. With their bodies pressed so close she could feel his desire growing. In response, her own desire had started to take over pretty much every logical thought she had.

She dropped the bow and quiver she was somehow still holding onto, barely acknowledging the sound of them hitting the ground. Her hands shot up, tangling themselves in his hair, pulling him even closer as she kissed him back. They hadn't kissed since their last night back at the cavern. He had stopped it, for whatever noble reason he wanted to profess at the time; but now with nobody else around and how close they had gotten over the last few days, she would make him eat his noble reason. She wanted this to keep going, to feel his hands on her bare skin, to feel all of him. If she was going to bare her soul for him to see, she sure as shit deserved to see all of him too. She reached for the end of his tunic, pulling it free from the waistband of his trousers. He stopped kissing her, surprised at first with her boldness, but allowing her to continue. Good, no attempt at a well-intended excuse this time. Her hands grazed the muscles of his stomach, she could feel him shudder ever so slightly before kissing her again.

Gasping for breath, she broke away from their kisses just as Danny started kissing her neck. It was her turn to quiver. Both of his hands dropped to her hips pushing her firmly against the rock. He dropped to his knees then, still holding up her hips and back, staring up at her with the most mischievous grin. Nerves hit her suddenly, at what she assumed was the anticipation of his next move. She closed her eyes, willing her racing heart to slow even just a little. She was aching with arousal now, mentally preparing for what was going to happen next, for what she wanted to happen next, she was getting very close to begging him for it.

She felt the warmth of his hands leave her and heard him stand still. Confused, she opened her eyes to see him standing a few feet away holding the bow and quiver. He looked very pleased with himself, this infuriated her beyond reason.

"Seriously?!" she barked at him. "All that for the bow?"

"You wanted to play, sweetheart." He winked at her in the most maddening way. "Didn't realize you would be so responsive."

"Fuck off!" She picked up a rock and threw it at him, which he dodged with a laugh. "Go hunt your stupid game."

He smiled at her again, eyes shining. "I'll be back in a little bit, okay?"

"You could just stay," she muttered to herself angrily as soon as his back was turned.

"If I stay any longer, I will rip those clothes off of you in less than thirty seconds," he called back from the path. "We're going to need plenty of food if we're going to keep that kind of behavior going."

Her face heated at that. Was he serious? She watched as he disappeared through the cave entrance behind the waterfall. She took several calming breaths to ground herself. Disappointment lingered with her as he left, how she wished he had stayed. Irritation started to replace disappointment; he had left her… again! She could try to feed into her anger by convincing herself he had only distracted her to get the bow. Yet, he was definitely as aroused as she was, and if feeling his size through their clothes was any true indicator, she was in for quite a surprise. And was that a promise for when he came back? Or was it a cheeky brush off? She wasn't too sure. But, if he wanted to play games, she would introduce him to a few. Catriona played for keeps, and she wasn't sure Danny was prepared for what she was going to bring to the table.

Chapter Twenty-Four

Rama

The wagon had just peaked over a hill, coming up on the ruins of an old windmill. Cut stones and old rotten wood beams lay in a pile where the windmill had once stood. By the look of it, the windmill had caved in on itself long ago, flinging debris outward onto the road and into the forest. This was not a recent event, this pile of rubble had been here for at least a generation. Rama could see some of the old markings and runes carved into what he believed to be the front door frame. The language of the forgotten ones was lost on him, but he knew they were a superstitious lot. Back when magic freely roamed the earth, before the scourge and before the blooded took over, it was a time that he used to dream about as a child. Now, the old ways were like this old windmill, destroyed and abandoned. It was truly a sad thing.

The wagons bumped along the rocky dirt road, getting closer to this once mighty structure. Rama had known to come here, he knew that Flinn and his warband used the old mill as a marker for those they called friends. Rama helped Flinn find this spot and set up his initial campsite, which consisted of two wooden huts built from beams from the mill. Flinn had a smaller warband, the last time Rama had been here he only had six other warriors with him. A few escaped slaves from Oich, determined to get revenge against the blooded. His brothers had helped train this warband before leaving, they had become rather capable warriors. Flinn had kept correspondence with them over the last few years, reporting his progress and activities. From the sound of it, Flinn had at least doubled his numbers and had successfully rescued many escaped slaves from the eastern villages in Oich. If his memory served him right, there was usually a scout somewhere nearby, Rama ran his eyes through the tree line searching for anything that wasn't supposed to be there. There, he spotted rustling from a tree nearby.

"Hello there!" Rama called out from the wagon, pulling the horses' reins so they stopped.

Both wagons had stopped moving now, Menolayous remained seated staring into the tree line, appearing completely uninterested. Knowing his brother, he had spotted the scout a while ago. Markous and Clyous still searching for any sign of life, completely overlooked the spot Rama and Menolayous were focusing on. He sighed, growing up as blacksmiths in the middle of the city had done nothing for their observation skills. That's another thing they would need to work on.

"Rama?" Connor emerged from his hiding place. "Menolayous? What brings you to our neck of the woods?"

"We stumbled across these wagons filled with supplies and figured you boys could use some food," Rama's voice boomed through the trees.

"Only if you brought ale." Connor waved him over laughing. "I'll let Flinn know you're here, go ahead and pull around."

Connor, the young lad, disappeared back into the trees, undoubtedly fetching the old war chief. Rama sat back down, taking the reins and urging the horses forward. Turning onto a hidden side road, the wagons followed it for another few minutes before coming up on Flinn's camp. Rama was impressed by what he was seeing, Flinn really had been expanding. Several wooden huts camouflaged with bushes and tree branches stood around an open but walled clearing. Even the wall was hidden well with plant growth, blending into the forest for any outsider's eyes. There weren't as many huts as he expected, they looked more like they were for storage than anything else. Until he looked up. Several tall trees stood clustered together at the center of this clearing, their branches flared out enough to touch the branches of trees just outside of the stronghold. Towards the midsection of these trees were what looked like platforms and treehouses. Rope bridges and pulleys connected the many huts, he could see several men walking on these platforms. The nearest tree hut was maybe fifty feet above him. He stood there for a moment, his jaw dropping at the sight. It looked like they had been using stone and rock from the ruined windmill to help them build. This was a small village but in the trees!

"Looks like they've been keeping busy," Rama said to Menolayous as the horses pulled the wagon next to one of the huts.

"No kidding," his brother responded, staring up at the trees. "Flinn was a carpenter. I didn't realize he was meant to be an architect. We've really been wasting his talents, haven't we?"

The four men stood together as they watched the warriors start to emerge. About two dozen men greeted them merrily. A lot of axes and bows were worn casually here, all of them dressed in warrior's garb or hunter's leathers. The occasional sash or hood of tartan was present, but no other form of decoration.

A redheaded man with a braided red beard approached with his arms open in greeting. "Welcome Rama, Prince of Thieves, bringer of meat and hopefully good spirits!"

"I believe there is a cask or two I haven't drunk yet!" Rama embraced Flinn as he approached. "I also bring with me a few new recruits!"

"I knew you had to be worth something, young Prince." Flinn laughed. Menolayous approached the warrior, offering a smile and a head nod in greeting, Flinn knew Menolayous enough to not attempt a friendly embrace. Markous and Clyous also approached but stayed back until Flinn wrapped them up in the same greeting he had given Rama.

"This is Markous and Clyous, our newest recruits from Oich. They can both fight, but better yet, they are both blacksmiths," Rama introduced them to his old friend.

"Blacksmiths, eh? Well then boys, I think I can waive your initiation fee." Flinn barked a laugh at his own joke. "You are more than welcome."

"Thank you." Clyous smiled back at the war leader. "I'm happy to be able to help where I can."

"Clyous here has a lady love still in Oich," Rama teased. "Figured your warband was the closest he could be while still contributing to the cause."

"Of course. I'll make sure to send him on many supply runs." Flinn laughed again. "What about you, Markous?"

"I'm just here to help wage war against the blooded," Markous responded proudly.

Rama didn't miss the look Clyous gave his brother. Undoubtedly, Clyous's attachment to Bridget made his brother's thirst for revenge against the blooded distasteful. Maybe taking Markous to the Harrada Pass encampment was a smart move on their part. It might be the very thing to keep the brothers from killing each other. Grief had a funny way of coming out of people. In Catriona's case it seemed to be mostly internalized, almost self-harming with how she kept it inside. Markous wanted to fight, wanted to kill every blooded he could. Anger was how he dealt with his grief. Clyous had yet to show his hand, but it was there. Probably the most levelheaded out of his siblings, he very well could be the only one processing things in a healthy way. Only time would tell if they would all survive their grief.

"We don't do that here." Flinn narrowed his eyes at Markous, all traces of a smile disappearing behind his slightly greying beard. "We do not discriminate who our enemies are, or our friends. There are a few blooded who aid us in our endeavors, they are treated just as despicably as humans by their own kind because of their gender or social class."

The tension amongst the group was growing to an uncomfortable level. Markous stared back at the war chief as if prepared to argue.

"I'll be taking Markous to the Harrada Mountains for some additional training," Menolayous said to Flinn as if reading Rama's mind. "If you don't mind letting us stay here for a day or two before setting off."

"Of course not. We would be happy to give you the royal welcome!" Flinn answered, enjoying the old joke between the three of them.

"Why do you keep referring to them as royalty?" Clyous asked the war chief, eyeing Rama curiously.

Flinn stared at Clyous for a moment before bursting into laughter. The other warriors did as well. This had been a running joke for years, ever since Rama had begun uniting escaped slaves into a single rebellion. He was too young to be labeled king back then, even mockingly, so Flinn and the other war chief Farren had mockingly labeled him the Prince of the Rebellion, and his brothers of course "inherited" the title as well.

"My boy." Flinn patted Clyous on the shoulder. "They are too modest to tell you I take it, but you find yourself in the company of two of the three princes of the rebellion."

"Princes?" Clyous raised an eyebrow at him, not missing the mocking tone. "Really?"

Rama shrugged his shoulders. "Titles mean little to me, it's more of an annoyance anyway, I get my hands dirty just as much as any warrior here."

"Two of the three? I would assume then that Danny would be the third?"

"You've met young Daniel then?" Flinn started in. "Well with a royal family approval you are more than welcome here."

"Why do they call you royalty?" Clyous asked again, as relentless as his sister for answers.

"We started the rebellion," Menolayous answered simply. "We'd raid some traders, or save an occasional slave, who would then in turn join us on our mission of mayhem and distraction. Just like Flinn here, we rescued him from lifelong servitude carving out wooden chairs and tables for rich blooded."

"I rescued you is more like it, lad." Flinn chuckled. "Connor, why don't you show the lads where they'll be sleeping tonight."

Rama watched the lanky boy, Connor, take the two with him towards the tree huts. Rama had been there when Connor had been rescued by Flinn during a raid on a guard outpost six years ago. Connor was but eight years old then, being treated the worst as the guards' personal whipping boy. The young boy had spent most of his childhood within the capital surviving by being a thief, until he wandered to an outer village that was. They had rescued him, and Connor had chosen to remain with Flinn, viewing him as a father figure. Many of them viewed the older war chief as a father figure, it was hard not to. The man looked after his warriors like his children, but there was a special place in his heart for young Connor, who was now close to fifteen years old.

The other warriors had started unpacking the wagons, carrying off the supplies to one of the stone huts on the ground. Quietly, Flinn addressed them both, "I'm going to assume you three were responsible for all the chaos coming out of Oich's capital?"

Rama shrugged. "Naturally."

"What exactly did you hear?" Menolayous asked, eyeing a warrior who walked by a little too slowly, trying his hardest to eavesdrop until he caught Menolayous's look of warning.

"Rumor has it that three prisoners of the crown up and disappeared into the night, leaving several dead blooded guards in town and in the forest. Prisoners of the crown prince no less."

"Definitely us." Rama shrugged. "We brought you two of them. Not going to find anyone more motivated to fight against the crown than these brothers."

Flinn scowled at Rama, the war chief in the old man showing through his look of disapproval. "The older one looks wild with revenge. He's likely going to get himself killed, if not one of us. I won't stand for his obvious distain of blooded, I have no patience for it."

"That's why I'm taking him," Menolayous chimed in. "Better odds if he trains with Farren. Farren will help get his mind and body right before we put him anywhere near the front lines. Hopefully learning to fight side by side with the few blooded Farren has up there will teach the fool respect."

Flinn nodded at the wisdom of it. "And what about this girl? Are you hiding her in the woods or something?"

Rama and Menolayous glanced at each other nervously. "What of her?"

"I heard this lass took on several blooded at once and was ballsy enough to go for the crown prince himself. She's rumored to have escaped too, albeit probably not in one piece."

"Catriona is Clyous's twin sister, and the rumors are true. She fights like a demon from the underlands. They fought to protect their mother who was bitten by a scourge. When the crown prince finally arrived at the melee, he lashed the flesh from Catriona's back in front of her brothers. We took them that night, after the dust had settled enough."

Flinn scowled at the story, it was a harsh reminder of what the enemy was willing to do. "Is the lass alright?"

"She's healing, mostly from grief at this point, Danny is with her," Rama answered.

"Was that wise?" Flinn asked, eyebrows raised. "Young Daniel can be a bit... forward with the lasses."

Rama laughed quietly. "Not this time, I've never seen him so easily flustered. He's been prancing around like a lovesick pup this last month or so. Never seen him so taken before."

The older man raised his eyebrows at that. "Flustered? Prancing?"

"If ever there was a match for our brother, it would be her." Menolayous chuckled. "Trust me. She can handle him."

Flinn barked out another laugh. "Well, if her reputation truly precedes her and she ever wants to pick up a sword and shield, send her our way. We could use a good shield maiden. By the sound of it we might be getting young Daniel too."

"What news have you received?" Rama changed topics.

"Farren continues to work with new recruits from the east. The stronghold outside Airgid remains protected. Farroway is still trying to partner up with blooded from Airgid to create some half-cocked fleet. McKinlay, I haven't heard from him in some time. He was fighting with the Gaelach cultists a month back. Haven't heard from him since, I'm worried his warband might be dead."

This was concerning news. McKinlay was a cunning warrior, he never took unnecessary chances. His warband was second in size only to Flinn's, to lose that many warriors without news of how, no that couldn't be it. They had to be holed up somewhere regrouping after a battle or something more likely. Rama glanced at his brother, expressing his concern without speaking.

"I can go to Gaelach and check on McKinlay on the way back," Menolayous offered. Rama knew of his brother's abhorrence in visiting Gaelach but could see his concern for the war chief and his men was genuine.

Rama nodded. "Good, send word when you figure out what's going on. I'll head back to Emerald Falls and collect our brother."

It was Menolayous's turn to nod in agreement. "Is there anything we can do to help you out, Flinn?"

"No, I should be fine. We're working on expanding our hovel here for more recruits. The boys are talking about bringing their families to our treetop city. We're well protected here; it's about time we start living like free men instead of hiding like criminals. We've got the numbers; we can protect our families now. Pretty soon we'll have a force large enough to start striking out at the crown directly."

"With a blacksmith on board, making silvered weapons will be easier."

"That it will," Flinn said. "Come, let's throw a pig on the fire and drink until we piss ourselves."

Rama smiled at the prospect of hot food and drink. He and Menolayous followed Flinn back to the camp's cooking pit where they joined in helping with the preparations. They would eat and drink with their men tonight, in the morning Rama would head back to collect his brother and Catriona. Hopefully Danny made some progress with her eating. He had no doubt, however, with all that alone time that they had made headway in other areas of their relationship. He chuckled to himself. Danny so easily flustered and prancing around, if those two haven't fucked yet he'd die from shock.

Chapter Twenty-Five

Danny

Danny stomped his way through the brush following the tracks he had found outside the cave entrance. Tracking this stag was probably one of the most difficult things he'd had to do in some time. It wasn't because the tracks were particularly hard to follow, there were very clear imprints in the mud, and headed in a relatively easy to maneuver direction. Nope, the difficulty was of his own making. He could not get his mind to stop replaying what had happened just an hour ago. His mind was still in that cave, where he wanted to be right now more than anything, with Catriona still in his arms looking up at him the way she had earlier. He could still feel her lips on his, her hands on his stomach, he breathed in deeply trying to return his focus to the forest around him. He looked down, shit, he'd lost the tracks again. This was getting ridiculous. After several minutes of searching and walking back in the direction he had come, he found them again. He followed them, for a fifth time now, trying to walk quietly through the brush.

Walking out of that cave, leaving her there out of breath and practically begging him to keep going; it was probably the hardest thing he'd ever done. At least she looked like she was going to start begging, that could be wishful thinking on his part. He had no doubts that she had enjoyed the kiss they shared and what he implied he was thinking about doing. Truth be told, when he crouched down in front of her he had every intention of stripping her out of her breeches and putting his mouth to work. What had stopped him was doubt. He didn't know how experienced she was at this sort of thing, and didn't want to take advantage or push faster than she was ready. However, this was also Catriona, she had no issues telling him off or threatening him with violence if he was pushing for something she didn't want.

He smiled at the memory, how mad she had been when he left, how red she'd turned when he promised to come back and strip her naked. He had every intention of fulfilling his promise, he just needed this little adventure to clear his head, also in case she needed to clear hers. But he wouldn't hold back when he returned, he needed to stop second guessing himself. She was perfectly capable of making her own decisions, he didn't need to try and make them for her. Now he wished to hurry up and find some sort of game so he could follow through with his promise. He had lost the tracks again, fuck! It was time he gave up on the stag and tried for something else.

He came to the edge of a spring, water bubbling softly as it flowed through the rocks. Sunrise left the sky in beautiful gold and pink hues. The rain had stopped for the time being, making it a truly beautiful morning. It was springtime, so a little bit of sunshine without rain was a rare thing. As he soaked in his surroundings, he tried to stop his mind from wandering again. He spotted a hare lazily picking at some berries not long after. Danny nocked an arrow and released it. Now they had a little bit of protein at least, maybe making a stew would help Catriona keep the meat down.

He grabbed the hare after removing the arrow, gutted it and then dressed it. Looking around, he spotted some ramsons growing in small clusters underneath a few intertwined trees. He was careful when he collected them, pulling the bulbs as gently as he could from the soil. Stew was looking more and more like a possibility. As he brushed off the dirt he glanced up and spotted a plethora of brown capped mushrooms. Perfect! He went and stood in the center of them, grabbing a few handfuls. His mind was back on Catriona again, but not about sex. First and foremost, he was still concerned about how much she was eating. With what he was able to gather so far, they would be eating better than they had since camping here, and as a stew she very likely would be able to keep the protein down this time. The dried deer jerky was a bust, and he couldn't cook meat in front of her even if it was for him. Maybe he could shred the meat thinly enough in the stew so he could get her to eat it without noticing it too much. It was worth a shot.

Danny stuffed the small bag he had with handfuls of mushrooms, filling it almost completely. The hare carcass and the ramsons took up the bottom of the bag. There, he could go back to her now, victorious. As he straightened up, he glanced around again at the large clusters of mushrooms. They formed a perfect circle, leaving an empty space in the middle where he was currently standing. He jumped out of the circle and scrambled away from it quickly. These rings in the ground were usually created by forgotten ones, it was said that if you were caught up in one you would be trapped there by the forgotten ones' magic until they decided to release you. He realized it was a superstition, but he knew some magic still existed. He was not taking that chance.

A loud whinny echoed through the woods from behind him. Danny looked back to the spring, seeing an uncommonly large black horse standing not fifteen feet away. The horse wore no bridle and no saddle, so he didn't think he had to worry about a rider lurking about. He approached the horse slowly, raising his hand for the horse to sniff. The horse stomped its front feet down as he approached, whinnying loudly in warning. He stopped approaching, he did not feel like being trampled to death today. As he visually examined this great and angry beast, he noticed just how bright the eyes were. They were bright gold, like liquid fire was projecting through its eyes. Its mane was exceptionally long, flowing in the slight breeze. It was a beautiful creature, but something about it didn't feel right to him.

The horse hooved at the rocky ground, pushing towards him. He backed away quickly trying to get out of its way. The black beast became more aggressive, snorting and neighing at him like it wanted him to turn around and leave. Danny obliged it, backing away slowly. The horse did not seem to like the direction he was headed. It charged forward, forcing him to turn and flee upstream, back towards the direction he came from. He really didn't want to have to shoot this horse, he wasn't sure it would do any good anyway, the horse was huge. Fuck it, he had no reason to stay out here.

He turned back in the direction of the cave, keeping his eye on the creature as he moved. It watched him as he went, seeming to approve of the direction he was going, it no longer approached him. Once he thought he was far enough away he turned to walk another direction to look for more small game. The horse was there exactly where he planned to go. It charged at him, then stopped. Danny ran around it, making his way back to the spring. What was with this horse?

He started off back towards the cave again, stepping quickly to stay ahead of it. As he walked, he kept glancing back to see where the horse had gone. He couldn't see it anymore, thankfully. He stood beside the waterfall, staring at the small pathway that led back to their camp. Well, he thought to himself, this was where he had wanted to be since he had left this morning. He didn't need some unhinged horse to get him to return, although he probably would have tried foraging for another half hour or so. He had more than enough food so it was time.

He took a deep breath to steady his nerves, suddenly worried that Catriona might still be mad at how he had left her. Or worse yet, decided that he had crossed a line. He stopped his train of thought, he was not going to talk himself out of this, he wanted her too much, and for too long to just give up now. Well, there was one way to find out what exactly was waiting for him back at camp, he would go and find out. He maneuvered along the small pathway, doing his best to keep the foraging bag from touching the water. He found himself squeezing past the waterfall, back pressed up against the damp stone wall. As he came around the corner he froze, careful not to drop the bag into the water.

Still partially hidden around the corner, he could see clearly into the cave. Catriona was standing at the edge of the hot spring completely naked. He had caught a glimpse of her topless before, but this… it was like staring at some sort of goddess, she was breathtaking. Just the shape of her made him want to fall to his knees and worship her. She was turning away from him undoing her braid. He caught a glimpse of her from the side, she looked like she was starting to gain weight again. Her ribs were definitely not as visible as they had been a week ago. As she had her back completely to him, she pulled her braid forward to work out the weave, then he saw them. Still relatively fresh but healed, they stood out as dark purple welts that crisscrossed against her pale flesh. The scars did not subtract from her beauty, no, they were a part of her now. She had earned those like a warrior, facing down her enemies, she didn't stop fighting. She survived them. Those scars were a badge of honor. Others might look away from them, she might even feel ashamed of them, he wasn't sure. But to him, they just announced the existence of a sad story. They were part of her, but they did not define her.

He watched as her beautiful blonde hair cascaded down her back. He held his breath as she gently stepped into the water. The pool was shallow there only coming to her knees. She waded into the steaming water until she was chest deep. She submerged herself underwater for a few seconds before coming back to the surface and was facing him now. Her eyes were still closed as she pulled strands of hair from her face. Her breasts were now directly in his line of sight, he couldn't look away. He shifted ever so slightly; his cock had gotten so hard it was now uncomfortably pushing against his trousers. The movement caught her attention; she opened her eyes and looked at him. He could not discern the expression she wore, nerves starting to take hold of him again. What the fuck? This wasn't his first time.

"Are you going to join me or just stand there?" she called out to him.

Chapter Twenty-Six

Catriona

The words that came out of her mouth sounded strange. A ring of challenge was there, as it was in nearly everything they shared. Her voice sounded far more confident than she felt. Catriona watched him cautiously, afraid to let her nerves show. She wasn't exactly sure what it was that made her call to him, wanting sex at all felt... wrong, and like something was wrong with her for even considering it with a man she hadn't known for all that long. It wasn't something her mother would have approved of, that's for sure, she believed sex was between two people who loved each other, who trusted each other. Catriona couldn't speak on the love aspect, but she cared for him without a doubt.

He had been there for her in a way she never experienced before. Her body was reacting to him in ways that startled her, but she was done being afraid. Danny was the one man she could trust implicitly. From the first time they had met he had gone out of his way to be respectful of her, never once chasing after her like one of his former one-night conquests. He had done everything he could to protect her and taught her to better protect herself. They spent countless hours together, traveling or training, they built their relationship. She knew without a doubt that he cared for her deeply, and she cared for him. Part of her hesitation up until now was what sex with him would change in her, would she fall for him even harder?

She watched him drop the bow and foraging bag on the path before striding over to the edge of the spring. Her eyes remained fixed on him as he began to remove his clothing, his eyes locked on her face. With each item of clothing gone, a bare section of his body was exposed to her, stirring her into even more of a nervous frenzy. Her eyes traced down the shape of him, drinking in everything she could. His blue eyes were still locked onto hers as he finally removed the final pieces of his clothing. Confidence radiated off his annoyingly handsome face as he revealed his erect penis. Her face heated as she stared, she knew she shouldn't be outright gawking at him, but at this point she couldn't look away. He knew how to play this game, how to tease her, how to throw her off her guard. But she was never one to back down, even if this was newer territory.

"Happy to see me?" Catriona teased him as her eyes remained fixed on his erection.

"Oh sweetheart," Danny practically purred. "I'm always happy to see you, but seeing you naked, now that's like a dream come true."

Her face heated at his words. "Don't patronize me."

"I'm unfamiliar with that word," Danny smirked at her. "You're going to have to use smaller words when all my blood is flowing down—"

"I don't understand why I thought this would be a good idea." Catriona glared at him.

"I'm standing mere feet away from you, completely naked, and all your arrogant ass can do is try to make jokes. You're so unserious."

He flashed her a small mischievous smile as he stepped into the steaming water, making his way over to her. She noticed with slight irritation that as his body submerged into the water, she couldn't keep ogling him, but his sudden presence directly in front of her snapped her back to reality. Her heart fluttered as she realized just how close his body was to hers. She took a deep breath, looking up into his face hoping his eyes would calm her thunderous heart. Her lips parted slightly as he approached. His hand reached out, grabbing hers and pulling her to him. She inhaled sharply at the sudden skin-to-skin contact, this was very real and not helping her nerves in any way. With a smile on his face, he closed the distance between them. He ran his fingers down her spine before bending down to kiss her. Her lips met his eagerly, her arms wrapping around his neck.

"Serious enough for you now?" Danny asked, his breath warm against her skin.

"Yes," Catriona said, her voice barely a whisper.

She felt herself tense up; this was Danny. If she wanted to do this with anyone, it was him. She had never wanted anyone else, trusted anyone else like this. She took a steadying breath, willing herself to settle down. As if sensing her nerves, Danny gave her a comforting smile.

"I make jokes in order to give you time to change your mind," he explained.

"But don't for one second think I don't look at you and want to prove how serious I'm going to be about us."

"Can you stop trying give me a means to escape and just kiss me already." She took a deep breath, trying to calm her racing heart. "It's ruining the moment."

He threw his head back and laughed before his hand lightly traced her face, his thumb grazing over her cheek as he stared into her eyes. There was no way he could understand her hesitation, but the fact that he acknowledged it was there was enough. His hesitant touch showed her that this would go no further unless she wanted it to. His eyes kept searching hers as if looking for her to answer. She knew then that she could say no and he would honor her wishes. He would never realize just how much that meant to her, how it helped her relax enough to give him a subtle nod.

Slowly, Danny lowered his lips to hers. He was going out of his way to ease her into this; to go at her pace so she could trust him before giving herself to him. Still, this gentleness couldn't last, this wasn't what she wanted, she wanted to feel strong. She wasn't breakable and delicate; it was something she needed to remind him of.

Her lips met his eagerly, tongue swiping at his lower lip as she urged him on. He matched her intensity, one hand wrapping around her waist to pull her closer against him while the other found its way into her wet hair. She could feel his hard erection against her hip, and something stirred inside her lower abdomen. A slight ache began to build between her legs as his lips met hers, increasing steadily as his hands caressed her hips. She trapped his lower lip between her teeth, giving it a playful nip.

"That's not playing fair." His voice was breathy as they pulled apart.

"Who said I'm fighting fair?" She smiled up at him with a mischievous grin.

His arm moved and before she could process his actions, she felt his hand caress up her side. His hand moved to her breast, massaging it firmly, coaxing a subtle gasp from her. His thumb teased her hardened nipple, gently circling in. There was something about the feel of his hand against her skin and the way his fingers pressed against that sensitive flesh. The throbbing between her legs was growing with every swipe of his thumb.

He inhaled deeply as if to calm himself. "You're making it harder for me to keep being gentle."

"Good," she purred with his lip caught once again between her teeth, "I can't stand gentle."

Emboldened by the feeling of arousal taking over, she reached a hand between them. Her hand wrapped around his cock, causing him to jolt slightly. He seemed frozen in place as she held him, as if holding back to see what she would do. Gripping his cock firmly, she pumped him once, wringing a full body shudder from him with that one single motion. He stared at her hungrily, his hands sliding down her hips, fingertips grazing the back of her thighs. She gasped at that, his hands now so close to where she ached for him. He was teasing her, she realized, two could play that game.

"So, you like this huh?" she teased, pumping him again for emphasis. She was thrilled to hear a moan escape his lips.

She slid her hand up and down his length, daring him to do something about it. As a response, he grabbed her hair, twisting it so he had a good grip at the base of her neck. He pushed her back against the edge of the pool, it was her turn to moan as his hard cock pressed between her legs, the throbbing sensation at the apex of her thighs now pulsing to the beat of her heart. He stroked a strand of her silken hair then gripped a handful of it at the base of her neck and guided her back a few feet into the shallow end until she found herself pressed against the shallow edge. The water from the pool came up just above her hips, the edge of the rock an inch or so above that.

"Be a good girl and lie back for me." Danny let go of her hair, encouraging her to lie on her back, exposing her to him.

"I wonder if you've ever been kissed like this." He looked at her as she shook her head, admitting her lack of experience. "The honor is all mine then," he said.

She marveled at how comfortable she was being this exposed to him, how easily she listened to what he was telling her. He stared down at her again with a wickedly mischievous smile. Her face flushed as she realized he was planning to do what he had promised earlier. Nerves and anticipation took hold of her as she began to sit up, unsure of what to do, what to expect. He tucked his arms underneath her knees pulling her ass closer to the edge of the rock, her breasts exposed to the cool air as the warm water caressed her back.

"What are you doing?" she asked, frustrated he was not touching her now.

"Teasing you." He smiled at her wickedly.

She glared at him. "It's kind of annoying. Can you get on with it already?"

"So impatient," he mused, lowering his head towards her thigh once more. "You're supposed to lie back and enjoy it."

"You're an ass," she said breathlessly as she felt the tip of his tongue run across her inner thigh.

He lowered his head, pressing his lips against the trail he left with his tongue. A hand moved down to her breast, his thumb playfully circling her hard nipple. The ache between her legs was now building as his lips and hands continued to tease her. She was painfully aware of how much she wanted to feel him in that spot he seemed so keen to avoid.

He continued to kiss the soft skin of her thigh causing her to squirm involuntarily. He chuckled quietly at her discomfort, his eyes locking with hers as his mouth disappeared between her legs. She could feel his breath against her center, even that sensation was enough to make her start squirming again. She couldn't help the subtle movements, it was as if her body was moving on its own accord, as if she were bewitched by his touch.

"Danny!" she called out, unable to contain her arousal building anymore. "Please!?"

Then she felt it, the warmth of his tongue gently moving across her center. Greedy for this new sensation, Danny seemed more than happy to oblige her. With each swipe of his tongue the pleasure built up. Her arousal was dominating everything to the point where she could barely think. The ache was building faster and faster, becoming so intense she could barely keep from moving. Instinctually, her hand flew down as if trying to push his mouth away from her, just for a moment of relief. Danny grabbed her hands, bringing them both down to her sides where he trapped them with his own. With a wicked smile he dove back down between her legs continuing to please her. Unable to squirm away, Catriona lay there, her breathing suddenly becoming labored as the arousal hit an all-time high. Sounds began to escape her mouth before she clamped it shut, this lack of self-control was astonishing, she only hoped she would not make a fool of herself.

"Danny!" she shouted, her voice strained as his name tumbled over her lips.

"That's it, Cat, make as much noise as you want, it lets me know I'm doing it right." He smirked as he watched her struggle to remain quiet. "We're not going to be done until you're shaking and screaming my name."

He devoured her, using the flat of his tongue to lick that bundle of nerves between her legs. As he gently nibbled on her clit, she felt herself start to buck as the waves of release crashed through her. He plunged two fingers inside her, continuing to tease her with his tongue. Fuck, she couldn't believe how fast she felt the ache building again. He plunged his fingers in and out of her, curling his fingers ever so slightly as he did. A loud moan poured from her throat as his fingers curled again, she wasn't fighting to hide it now. Especially since every noise she made seemed to spur him on even more. She could feel her arousal peaking as she called out for him, her back arching off the stone.

"That's it, come for me," he breathed, keeping the same movement that was driving her over the edge.

She gasped as she felt her inner walls tighten over his fingers, her pleasure spilling over and relaxing her completely as the wave began to subside. He must have gotten the response he was waiting for because he didn't even give her a chance to catch her breath. He pulled his fingers out, quickly flipping her onto her stomach and pulling her back into the pool enough so her ass was hanging in the water. Already, he was showing her things, giving her pleasure she had never thought possible. She was all in, ready for whatever he would throw at her next.

One hand was splayed on her lower back reverently while the other reached around her front to massage between her legs. His cock nudged her entrance, she could feel how slick she was, she was more than ready for him. He slid inside; she gasped as he filled her. Her body took a moment to adjust to his welcomed intrusion. After a few gentle testing thrusts, she began to feel that sensation build up yet again. His fingers continued to stroke her, giving a firmer touch of pleasure than his tongue. It was just what she needed. She began to feel her arousal building, quicker this time, and stronger than before.

"You feel fucking amazing, Cat," Danny grunted as he thrust into her again slowly. "Do you like what I'm doing to you?"

"Yes," she breathed as he slowly thrust inside her again.

"You're not making a lot of noise, beautiful," Danny said, slowing down even more. "Tell me what's going to make you start screaming my name."

She didn't need to think before answering, "Harder."

"Are you sure?" She could hear the hesitation in his voice.

As an answer, she timed it so he was actively thrusting into her when she threw her hips back, forcing him inside her completely. She inhaled sharply as she felt him slide in all the way, smiling as she heard a moan escape his lips this time. Yes, harder and deeper was hitting that sweet spot inside her. She knew she had surprised him with that, but he asked for it.

"By the gods, Cat!" she heard him say as he shuddered and pulled out of her. "You want hard, that's fine. Better hang on then."

Both hands went to her hips, pulling her even tighter against him. It was like he had been holding back until she had asked. Now that she had, he was unleashing himself. He filled her completely, repeatedly entering her with such an achingly sweet amount of force she wasn't able or willing to hold back her moans. He seemed to have lost all control as well, the sound of his heavy breathing and grunting only added to her already sensitive and aroused state. She could tell she was nearing the edge, a final thrust and she felt herself climaxing all over again. Her legs began to tremble as she clenched around his cock in spasms. He remained inside her as her body shook from the strong release, the sounds of pleasure and ecstasy coming from him told her he had crashed over the edge as well.

They sat there panting for another minute before Danny pulled himself from her. She felt him pull her back to him where he cradled her against his chest as he sat down in the warm water. They sat there together, intertwined in each other's arms while catching their breath. Catriona never felt so relaxed in her life, and never so spent. She nuzzled into his chest, letting her heavy eyelids droop.

"Thank you," he murmured, kissing the side of her head gently, "for trusting me with something so precious as that."

She didn't have the energy to argue with him, to correct his words. He was right about how precious this was to her. He probably couldn't fathom how this had changed things for her.

As if he was able to read her mind he said, "You realize this means you're mine now, right?"

"Excuse me?" She looked up at him confused.

"I told you weeks ago, I'm in this for the long run." He smiled down at her, the playful glimmer in his eye back once again. "You are mine, and I am yours. There will be nobody else for either of us after this."

"Are you trying to say you ruined me?" She laughed, resting her head on his chest once again. "It takes a lot more to ruin me, Danny."

"No, I'm saying you've ruined me." She could feel his face pull into a smile as he pressed his mouth against the top of her head. "Get some sleep, you're going to need it."

Chapter Twenty-Seven

Liam

<u>Fifteen years ago</u>

"But I don't want to wear this stupid outfit, it's itchy," little Liam whined to his mother, pulling on the heavily decorated doublet.

"You're the crown prince. When attending court, you will dress as such," his mother answered, trying to comb his hair into submission. "We're already late because his royal highness decided to roll around in the mud with some other young nobles."

Little Liam tried to bat her hand away from combing his unruly mane. "We weren't rolling. I was rescuing a fair maiden from those buttholes."

"Liam!" Queen Mara chided. "Language!"

"But it's true," he said stubbornly. "They were throwing rocks at my friend, trying to get her to change."

"Well—" his mother sighed, giving up on his hair. "It was noble of you to come to her defense, but she's going to have to master her shift if she wants the other kids to leave her alone."

His mother took him by the hand and headed down the hall towards the throne room. Liam struggled to keep up with her pace.

"But I want to be a knight when I grow up. Aren't knights supposed to protect the fair maids?"

His mother stopped walking, bending down in front of him, she said, "Yes darling, knights are supposed to defend the weak from evil."

Liam looked into her eyes sadly before saying, "When I get bigger maybe I can save you."

A tear slid down his mother's cheek as she subconsciously pulled her dress sleeves down to cover her bruises. She wiped it away quickly before saying, "There will be no talking like that, do you understand me? Your father will get angry if he hears you talking like that."

"Yes mama," little Liam answered, accepting the forehead kiss his mother gave him before setting off again.

They made it to the throne room, sneaking inside while a meeting took place. His mother led him to one of the back corners just out of sight from his father. Liam glanced around the throne room, a dark, windowless room made of stone. The only light came from torches bracketed into the wall. The room was also absent of color or decoration, save for the Oich banner standing tall and proud behind the throne. Even that flag was dark, black with a deep red lower half and a longsword with a crescent moon behind the pommel. His father, King Cathal, sat on the throne at the back of the room. His nobles lined the walls all waiting for their turn to speak. Liam looked at his father, an extremely large man who seemed to wear a permanent scowl. The other nobles in the chamber were careful not to get too close or draw the king's attention. His father was a very powerful man, even the warriors and nobles of Oich bowed down to the dominant wolf in submission.

"What brings you in front of me, Lord of Spices," his father mocked the man who stepped onto the floor for his turn to speak.

"Your Majesty." The man bowed deeply. "I have come to ask for permission to establish a trading route to Airgid. My spices sell well in that kingdom; I personally guarantee to bring back precious gems and gold for his majesty's personal collection."

"If you can get those self-righteous mongrels to trade precious gems for some seasoning you are welcome to it." The nobles laughed with the king at the jest. "You have my blessing; I expect first pick from what finery you do manage to bring back."

"Thank you, Your Majesty." The nobleman bowed before turning and walking out of the hall.

Liam recognized the nobleman, he was Bridget's father. Liam didn't like the man, he was mean to his friend. She was always covered in bruises and was terrified of him. He hated it when Bridget was scared, it reminded him of how scared his mother was of his father.

A guard came up to stand beside the king, whispering something in his ear. The king nodded once before the royal guard stepped forward to usher everyone out of the hall. Liam and his mother were the only ones left in the chamber besides the King and his guards.

Liam felt his mother's hand tighten on his as they remained in the corner. More guards emerged from one of the side doors dragging a prisoner. The human slave was dragged into the center of the chamber; he was weighed

169

down by heavy chains and unable to walk unassisted. The guard secured the chains to metal connectors in the floor.

"Your Majesty." A captain of the guard bowed. "We captured this slave for suspected use of magic. During our arrest two new-blooded guards were moderately injured before the rest of us were able to take him into custody."

"Injured how?" the king asked, raising his eyebrows.

"They were burned, Your Majesty."

"Was this incident seen by anyone else?" the king inquired, he did not like to be made a fool of by anyone, let alone a human.

"No, Your Majesty."

"Bring my son to me," the king called out.

Reluctantly, Liam's mother walked him up the side stairs to the throne. His father reached out for his hand, taking it with uncharacteristic gentleness. He led his son down the platform until they stood only a few feet away from the prisoner. Liam finally got a good look at the human; he was a man about the same age as his parents. He had the most interesting steely grey eyes, like liquid silver, and his hair was so fair in color it was almost white. Unique tattoos spiraled up his forearms and neck, it almost looked like flames from a fire.

"You have been accused of using magic," the king spoke to the slave. "And injuring two of my guards. What do you have to say about this?"

"I'm a blacksmith. Your guards attacked me, and I defended myself," the man answered defiantly. "Your Majesty."

"Why do I not believe you?"

"You're paranoid?" The human offered a shrug.

"Deny it all you want. There is one way to tell if someone carries the ancient bloodline." King Cathal glared down at the man. "Prince Liam, do you know what that way is?"

Liam looked up at his father, shaking his head. Up until now he thought magic users were only in the bedtime stories chambermaids told children before bed. Witches, sorcerers, these were part of fairytales, not real life. Magic didn't exist, not like knights. Knights still existed, so did evil kings.

"You can smell it in their blood." With an unnatural swiftness the king struck the man, his claws had come out, slicing five deep cuts down the

170

man's forehead over the brow bone and ending at the cheek. "It usually comes off as an earthy smell. What do you think, Prince Liam?"

Little Liam sniffed the air as the man recovered from the blow. Blood began to trickle down his face, Liam could smell the iron of the blood, but as he continued to inhale the scents, he smelled something that reminded him of freshly dug soil.

"I smell dirt!" he answered his father proudly, having found what his father wanted him to sense.

The king barked a laugh. "Dirt because their blood is tainted. See how he stares back in defiance? Those who carry the blood of the ancients are wild creatures. As you heard the captain say, this single man, this human slave, injured two of our blooded guards."

The man straightened up as best he could, staring the king in the eye as he ground out, "Your rule in Oich is soon coming to an end, My King. Just as you have made it your mission in life to stomp us out, we are making it our life's pursuit to end yours. We are everywhere, and we are watching you. When you least expect it, we will come for you. What you do to me does not matter, for I am easily replaced by more."

The king stared at the man for a moment, weighing his words. It was not often that anyone spoke to his father in such a way. Liam braced himself, not knowing what would happen next. His father had a bad temper and was prone to lashing out. Liam had seen his mother caught up in those temper flares a few times.

"You will die, as will the rest of you." The king smiled at the man then turned to his son. "Tell me, Prince Liam, how should we punish this man? You're old enough to watch what happens to prisoners, now you can decide."

"He is too young to make such decisions." His mother was approaching them from across the room looking panicked. "He's only a boy!"

"He is the Crown Prince of Oich," the king snarled at her approach, angered by her lack of submission. "Because I was generous enough with you as a husband to mate no other, he is my only son and heir. He needs to learn!"

"No!" his mother argued, grabbing Liam away from the king. "Not yet—"

Liam watched as the king struck his mother with the back of his hand. She fell to the floor clutching her face where he struck her. A loud growl came from the king, a wolf threatening its lesser, warning them to submit. Liam found himself stepping between his parents, responding to his father's challenge and saw the fury in his father's eyes, but he would not back down. He was a knight. He would protect his mama.

"Liam, move!" His mother tried to grab him.

The king was faster, batting the boy away like a fly, Liam's body hit the ground several feet away. He cried out in pain just as he saw his mother and father both shift. His mother's wolf was a tawny brown, larger than most other wolves, but she was still smaller than his father. The king's wolf stood as tall as a man, with an all-black coat.

His mother placed herself between him and his father, snarling in warning. A mother protecting her pup. The king, however, would not allow a challenge from anyone, even his wife. The two wolves charged at each other; all teeth, fur, and claws. Liam had trouble making out what was happening, the two wolves were moving too fast. He could smell fresh blood. Finally, after a minute or two he saw his father's wolf pinning his mother's wolf down by the scruff of her neck. There was blood in her coat, so much blood. She was yipping in pain.

Liam's eyes snapped back to the chained man as an intense heat hit the side of his face. Clearly taking advantage of the distraction, the prisoner was now actively trying to escape. Liam watched as he inhaled deeply, and as he breathed out so came fire. White and gold flames poured from this man's mouth, heating up the chains just enough for him to pull the chain links apart.

Liam, frozen with fear, was only several feet away from the prisoner. His mother's tawny brown wolf launched herself at the man. Already injured and bleeding, she moved too slowly. The man pushed out a wall of flame, knocking her back and burning her coat, but the flame had struck Liam too, his overcoat sleeve catching fire.

Distracted by the flame and the burning of his flesh, Liam did not see what happened next. Once the flames went out, he looked back to his mother who was now lying on the ground dead. His father and the guards charged at the man, but he created a magical wall of flame and none of the wolves could make it through. The man escaped through one of the side doors to the servants' quarters.

Liam crawled towards his mama, burying his face in her fur. He sat there clutching her coat, sobbing uncontrollably. A chorus of howls echoed in the chamber, then throughout the castle. The queen was dead. His mama was gone.

<u>Seven years ago</u>

It was a beautiful summer day. The sun was shining, the flowers still in bloom. Liam watched couples of dragonflies dance together above the lake as they zoomed around in the sun. He sat back on the tartan blanket he had brought with them, basking in the sunlight. This last winter had been brutal; it was like the sun had hibernated with the wildlife. Now that spring had come and mostly gone, the sun seemed to decide it was time to return to them. He enjoyed days like this away from the court, especially from his father. He could find no company better than what he was keeping right now. He smiled as he watched her pick flowers a few feet away.

Bridget's beautiful red curls glowed in the sunlight as she foraged through the grass. She appeared to be collecting those yellow flowers that were springing up everywhere. This was her favorite thing to do, collecting herbs and flowers and researching how they could help her practice her healing techniques. She had a healer's touch, learning from one of the older women in the castle. She took to it quickly and craved to learn more. That desire, that drive, was one of the things that made her so beautiful. She had this internal light, a goodness that he wished he had. She glanced up at him smiling. So damn beautiful. He was sixteen now, she was a year behind him. They had been friends since they were children, and they still were, but lately he had been finding himself appreciating other things about her besides their friendship.

Her once stick-like figure was starting to resemble that of a woman's. She had breasts now, and her hips now gave her an hourglass shape. She was easily the prettiest girl in their age group. Truthfully, he was surprised other boys weren't chasing after her. Then again, he had effectively marked her as off limits. It was few and far between that anyone felt like challenging the crown prince. It was probably for the best, most of the noble boys their age were asshats and she deserved better.

"Look what I found!" Bridget said, plopping down beside him on the blanket.

"Plants?" he said sarcastically, looking at the handful of yellow flowers.

She smiled and held them out for him to see. "Dandelions. I can make tea out of these, and it can help with swelling."

"You're amazing, you know that?"

He watched her blush; he loved it when she did that. Feeling courageous, Liam leaned forward, kissing her on the lips. It was warm and sweet, just like she was. He pulled away smiling, she was a darker shade of red. For a first kiss it wasn't bad, he was almost positive it was hers too. They sat there for a few moments not speaking.

"Why did you do that?" she asked quietly.

He looked at her, confused. "Because I like you. And I wanted to. Is that okay with you?"

"Yes. I'm just surprised is all."

"Why are you surprised? I spend most of my free time with you."

"I don't know." She looked away, clearly embarrassed.

For such a beautiful and intelligent girl, she sure had little to no self-confidence, but he understood why. Ever since they were children, she has had trouble controlling her shift, and other blooded took that as a sign of weakness. They had taken to calling her a runt, a rather vicious insult. This was not allowed by him. In fact, just earlier this week he had shifted in order to put a grown blooded in his place. Being of a dominant bloodline allowed him the advantage of size, even compared to adult wolves. Fighting had come easily enough to him, and he was more than happy to put his lessers in check, especially when it came to her.

"Everyone else can fuck off." He turned towards her sitting cross legged, taking her hands in his. "You are beautiful. You are so extremely smart. You are the light of my life right now and you keep me from sinking into my father's politics," and he meant what he said.

His father was now requiring him to accompany him to various meetings with the nobles. The cruelty and dominance over his life was coming in like a high tide. He was expected to become just like his father but wasn't sure he could. He didn't think he would ever be able to treat Bridget the way his father had treated his mother, couldn't bear the thought of hurting her, of killing her. Still, he was trapped unless he learned to submit, otherwise his father would kill him too. Liam had dreamed of the day he could challenge his father, but he was not strong enough yet. Until then, he would learn what he could and try his best not to become his father.

The one thing he and his father did agree on was how they handled those they found with magic. The man who had been in the throne room was as equally responsible for his mother's death as his father was. He still carried the scars on his arm from that magical fire. Every magic wielder, witch, and sorceress he had seen brought before the king was as dangerous and wild as that man had been. He had seen incredible displays of magic such as earthquakes and windstorms, but he had also seen some weak magic. Truthfully, every single one of them scared him, the unknown depth of their magic and what each of them was capable of. They were a threat to the kingdom, and they all deserved death.

"You are not your father," she reassured him. "I am very thankful you are in my life."

She leaned forward kissing him again. As they pulled away from each other they both smiled. It was getting late in the day; they needed to start heading back. They stood, gathered their things, and started back towards the city walls. They laughed and joked as they walked, enjoying each other's company.

Bridget stopped along the path to collect more dandelions. As she collected herbs, Liam spotted a deep purple flower. He walked over and picked it. It was a beautiful flower; it looked like mini purple bells were hanging off the green stem. Sniffing it, it had a powerful aroma, but it was unique in color. He picked a few of them, walking over to her. She turned to look at him as he presented them to her, hoping to make her smile. On seeing the flowers her face dropped. She knocked them out of his hand. That was a surprisingly aggressive move from her, one he found his wolf responding to as a challenge.

"What are you doing?" she yelled. "That's monkshood! That's poisonous to touch!"

He felt his face pale at her words. "How poisonous?" The look of fear in her eyes was enough of an answer. "What can we do?"

She began wringing her hands and pacing, spouting off her knowledge of the flower. "Let me think. Monkshood, also known as wolfsbane. It acts within minutes. Deadly to the touch, if ingested everything happens faster. Wolfsbane is the only known poison that can kill a blooded. What cures monkshood poisoning?"

Liam held up his hands staring at them intently. He swore he could feel them start to tingle. Maybe it was in his mind, maybe it wasn't. Just from touching it? Bridget was pacing now, thinking hard. He began to feel dizzy. Definitely not just in his head then.

"Bridget?" Liam asked, trying not to sound panicked. "I'm starting to feel funny."

"Do you trust me?" she asked, staring into his eyes.

"Yes."

175

"Can I trust you?" She looked at him intently.

He nodded, confused at her request. Of course he could trust her, she was his after all. Or would be. She reached for his hands. He began to pull away, he still had poison on them. She shook her head, grabbing his hands forcefully. The dizziness was getting worse by the second. He stared at her for a moment about to speak, when a soft glow came from her palms. He tried to jerk his hands back, but she held on. The golden light grew, sending a tingling sensation down his arms. He could feel his breathing become easier, he was no longer dizzy. She was healing him!

After another minute the glowing stopped. She released him, taking a step back, bowing her head in submission. She had magic he realized. Bridget, the girl he had grown up with, the same girl who could not control her shift also had ancient blood in her. He looked at his hands again, he no longer felt sick. She healed him with magic. He sat down. She dropped to her knees before him, tears streaming down her face.

"I'm so sorry," she cried. "I couldn't let you die. I'm sorry I kept this from you for so long. I know it's outlawed, I never chose this I promise."

Still somewhat shocked but unable to handle her tears, he gathered her into his arms to comfort her. "Stop crying sweetheart, please? I'm okay."

She buried her face into his shoulder. He started stroking her hair as he processed what just happened. She was of the ancient bloodline, he should drag her to his father so she could be cleansed. He couldn't, he wouldn't. Not her. Bridget was good and kind. She was not like the others he had met. No, he would not let his father hurt her.

"Who else knows?" he asked, still stroking her hair.

"Nobody." Her voice was muffled in his shoulder. "You're the first one I've told."

He pulled her back gently so he could look at her face. "You have to keep it that way, okay? If they find out... if my father finds out... He'll kill you, and I'm not strong enough to save you from him yet." She nodded, wiping away the tears. He kissed her again. "Thank you for healing me."

"Thank you for trusting me." Her face was still buried in his chest.

"Of course." He smiled. "As long as you are mine, and you submit to me, I'll always trust you." She meant the world to him. He would always fight for her.

Three years ago

"Shhh," Liam whispered in her ear. "Don't want them to hear you, do you?"

Bridget shook her head, desperate to remain quiet. They were currently tucked inside a little alcove out in the gardens. The night provided them with an extra layer of concealment, just about as much as the corner they were tucked into. The only way a passerby would even notice them is if she couldn't keep from moaning.

He held her to him; her plump little ass pressed against his cock as he worked to pull up her skirts. As soon as there was an opening in the cloth, he slipped his hands between her legs. She was already slick for him, good girl. As his fingers began to stroke her, she inhaled sharply. His free hand flew to her mouth and covered it.

"You're not very good at staying quiet are you, sweetheart?" He continued to rub her. "Can you feel how hard you make me?"

With her mouth still covered, she nodded again. Good, he loved it when she submitted easily. His fingers worked their way towards her entrance. He felt her open her legs for him and rewarded her with plunging two fingers inside her, removing them again just as quickly. He felt her breathing speed up, he swore he could hear a very muffled moan. He thrust them in and out, creating a fast rhythm while his thumb grazed that sweet spot between her legs.

He felt her start to squirm against him, whether she meant to or not, her ass was now grinding against his breeches. He growled at the sensation; she was driving him over the edge before he could get inside her.

He let go of her and spun her around pinning her back against the stone wall. Her bright emerald eyes were shining as she looked at him, her face flushed from their activity. And those lips, he pressed his against them. He grabbed the hem of her skirts again, pulling them up with one hand while the other worked to free himself from his breeches. There! With both hands he lifted her up, dutifully she wrapped her legs around his waist as he finally pushed inside her. By the gods, having her surrounding him was probably the best feeling in the world.

She worked her hands into his hair as he rolled his hips into hers. Normally he did not like her to touch him without her begging first, he was in control, not her, but he was already fully seated inside her, not willing to pull out to punish her for it. Usually, he would deny her climax just to show her he was the one in charge, but hers was too close to his own for him to care right now. He continued to pound into her, again and again and again. A loud moan escaped her sweet lips; he silenced it with his mouth. He felt her back arch with her climax before he sped up to meet his. When they were done, they stood there for a moment catching their breath. Liam gently lowered her back to the ground, readjusting himself back into his garments.

"That's my girl," he purred, kissing her. "I have to go to a meeting now. Meet you back in my chambers?"

She nodded. "Yeah. Are you wanting me to stay the night?"

"I would love nothing more."

She smiled up at him, giving him another quick kiss. "I'll see you when you're done."

He watched her as she walked away, admiring how her hips swished when she did. He double-checked his clothes making sure he was presentable before stepping out into the garden. He made his way through the grounds towards the king's private chambers. A guard stood by, letting him in as he approached.

Liam stepped inside, the door shutting behind him. A large map table was positioned in the center of this first room; the king was standing beside it examining a few wooden markers he had around Oich.

"Your Majesty." Liam bowed before advancing to the table.

"You're late." The king didn't look up from his task.

"My apologies, I was detained—" Liam started.

Like a flash of lightning his father crossed the room, backhanding him. To his credit, Liam held his ground. Showing weakness meant a beating. Showing defiance meant death. He kept his eyes pointed to the ground as he righted himself. Now was not the time to let his anger out.

"Do not lie to me!" the old wolf growled. "I can smell her on you."

Shit! Liam forced his body not to react. No clenching of the jaw, no flexing of his fists. He had to remain the perfect example of submission. If not for himself, then for her.

"Yes sir," he answered.

The King sniffed him once before returning to the table. "Come and look at this."

Liam obliged, walking over to the map. He glanced down at the map of Stone Basin. Red wooden markers were placed over several of the eastern villages of Oich.

"These markers are for attacks on blooded by human slaves. A few trading convoys robbed, a few prisoners freed, the same human male seems to be present at each incident."

"I thought the royal guards had captured their little ringleader," Liam recalled. "The blonde man with the bad attitude. I saw him in the cages as I was passing through the outer villages."

"Apparently that was the younger brother, according to my generals who were involved." His father moved around the room. "There are three of them, the big one, the oldest, Rama. He's in charge. They move like shadows, and they managed to get into the fort undetected and got their brother out without a single guard noticing."

"Are they of the ancient bloodline?" Liam asked.

"No," the king growled. "They're smart, and they're very skilled. They are becoming a big problem. I'm receiving reports that their little rebellion is becoming well known amongst the other slaves. We're seeing some pushback."

Liam asked, "What's the plan then?"

"I'm sending you to deal with them." The king was staring at him now, almost daring him to refuse.

"Me?" Liam said, surprised but quickly correcting himself. "What can I do?"

"Rule," the king snarled. "You've been kept at the castle too long. You've been occupying your time following that runt around like a lovesick pup when you should be out there learning how to be a king!"

Liam opened his mouth to argue but closed it again. As much as it infuriated him it was the truth. He didn't want to rule, to be like his father. He spent most of his free time with Bridget because he loved her. He loved that she was the opposite of this dark world he lived in. Arguing now would put her in danger, would put him in danger. So, he remained silent.

"You are lucky I did not remarry after your mother. Instead of creating additional heirs for you to compete with I chose to keep you around," his father threatened. "Partially due to the lack of available females with a halfway decent bloodline, but it seems you have found one for yourself.

179

Make no mistake boy, you may be a prince, but you dishonor yourself every time you fuck her outside of wedlock. You have tainted her right along with yourself. Mark my words, if you continue to put her cunt above your duties, I will wed her and breed her until I can create an heir who doesn't share the same bleeding heart as your mother."

Fear and panic now raced through him. Liam knew his father meant this as a threat to get him to do as he ordered, but his father was cruel enough to do as he said. Bridget's gentleness, her inability to shift and protect herself, his father would literally rip her to pieces. He couldn't stop him; she couldn't stop him. He was a king. It would only take once, one drop of blood in front of his father, and he would know of her bloodline. She would be beaten, tortured repeatedly by the king, then by the guards when he was done, and finally if she refused to submit to him, she would be burned to death if there was anything left to burn.

He had to be smart with how he spoke now. "As you command My King. How would you have me handle this pushback?"

Seemingly satisfied with his son's response he moved on from the girl. "Those who fight back should be lashed publicly. Leaving them on display will strike fear into those who want to fight back. Punish the whole family, burn down their homes. Be the prince that all will be too afraid to rebel against. Make them bow down to you, to me. Make them afraid."

He swallowed hard, calming his racing heart. "It will be done, My King."

"I want those brothers brought to me alive. I will make such an example of them, no slave will be brave enough to even think of defying the crown for the next hundred years." The king now stood in front of his son, looking him in the eyes. "Any magic will be met with the same fate they do here. They will burn."

"I will leave first thing in the morning." He bowed, trying to end the conversation quickly.

"Take a squad with you." The king waved him off. "Fail me Liam, and I will take what you think is yours."

Liam bowed again, backing out of the chamber now that he was dismissed. He had to force himself to walk at a normal pace, if anyone reported to his father that he was sprinting towards his rooms then Bridget stood no chance. He had to get her out of the castle, away from his father. He had to protect her from her promised fate. He had to convince his father she was nobody to him, a nobody wouldn't matter enough to be used as a threat.

His mind raced as fast as he wanted to. She was everything to him. Her light, her goodness, it was what had kept the darkness away. She was there for him after his mother's death, she trusted him with her magic, her kindness kept him from drowning in all the evil he had been trying to survive. Now, he was being forced to become that evil, and he had to protect her from it, from him.

He paused before opening his own door. He could scent her from here due to their earlier encounter. By the gods, if he knew how this night was going to turn out he would have done everything differently, but now he had to do something he never thought he'd do, something he wasn't sure he was capable of doing in order to protect her.

He opened the door and stepped inside. Bridget was sitting in a chair reading by the candlelight, her red hair glowing in the flickering light. She looked up from the pages smiling at him. He did his best to appear as the cocky prince everyone thought he was. He needed to act like she didn't matter to him anymore. She had to believe it.

"I think it's time you went home." He casually removed his overcoat, tossing it on a chair beside her. "We had our fun for the day. I'll send for you again when I need a good fuck."

Her face dropped as her eyes took him in. "What do you mean?"

"I'm tired and I want you to go," he forced himself to say.

"What's wrong?" She got up, moving towards him. "What happened with your father?"

"We talked about me going to the outer villages to put down some minor quarrels. I am to bend them into submission by any means necessary."

"Oh Liam." She reached for him as if to comfort him. "I'm sorry."

Adjusting his technique, he said, "Why? They're just slaves."

"They're people, your people," she argued. "This isn't like you. I know you're not cruel."

"Humans mean nothing to me." This wasn't working. She knew him too well. "We also talked about me finding a wife worthy enough to one day become queen."

"Oh." She pulled back then, this route clearly affecting her.

As painful as it was for him to use her biggest insecurity, it was the only thing he could use that she would believe. Not believing a word that was about to come out of his mouth, he kept going.

"So that means we're going to have to put an end to… whatever this is," Liam sneered. "I've got more important things than a runt to think about."

Tears began to pour from her eyes, her worst fears suddenly realized. Liam's heart broke right then and there. He wanted to take it all back, hold her in his arms and tell her the truth, but he knew she wouldn't leave him. She would risk it, risk herself. He would not risk her.

"We had fun," he forced his voice to remain even, "but it's time I found someone better, strong enough to share the weight of the crown. A woman pure enough to marry, not some weakling who cant keep her legs closed or even control her shift."

Bridget moved then, grabbing her hanging cloak and running out the door. He could hear her sobs as she ran past. Once she was gone, he just stood there in silence. Tears began to fall freely as he locked his door. Partially in shock from what he had just said to her, what he had just done, he kept staring off into the darkness. He felt the demons creeping up on him from the shadows, his light gone. Without her, he knew with certainty that the darkness would finally claim him, that he would become his father, the one thing he feared more than anything. But he would accept his fate if it meant protecting her.

Two months ago

He was on his way out of the capital city to lead another sweep of the eastern villages, searching for any new uprisings amongst the farmlands. More rebel activity was being reported, groups of rebel warriors had periodically been attacking some of the guard outposts, stealing supplies and weapons. The only way to keep the rebellious slaves in check was to constantly maintain a presence, and to deal with them harshly when captured. He had been back home at the capital for about a week, allowing his men to relax and visit their families. He had spent time catching up with meetings and strategizing a new plan to attack this rebellion head on. He longed for the rebellion to finally be put down, for good. He was tired, no, exhausted. He took no pleasure in what he had to do, what he allowed his men to do to keep the humans in their place. Capturing those three brothers, the so-called

"Princes of the Rebellion," was becoming more and more of a priority. Without them, Liam was not sure the rebellion would ever truly die.

He and his men were on their way down the main road leading out of the city when they heard it. A howl from a blooded guard calling for aid. Without missing a beat, he and his men shifted, darting in the direction the guard's howl had come from. With his senses now connecting to all the blooded within a mile, he was practiced enough to separate the civilians from the guards. He reached out as he ran, finally picking up on what the danger was. A single energy, a powerful one, was rapidly moving about within a small cluster of guards; idiotic guards that had not bothered to shift in order to overcome the threat, a failure he would deal with later.

He picked up his pace, homing in on the challenger. As he neared, he braced himself, preparing for a scourge or another dangerous creature. Instead, he could see a woman, a human by the look of her, fighting with several of his blooded guards. She moved like a demon, rolling between the men to avoid the snap of a whip. She was so fast that his men were unable to get their hands on her. He watched her try to take a sword from a guard, a move that slowed her down just enough. The old-blooded guard she was trying to steal from had managed to grab hold of her before she could get the sword unsheathed, tossing her into the air. She hit the ground hard, hard enough that he could hear the cracking of her ribs, but she seemed to recover quickly. She had the heart and speed of a true warrior, but not necessarily the skill. She left herself open for attacks, and she did not seem as comfortable holding a blade as she should.

Human or not, he was ending this now. He could not allow this humiliation of his men to continue. He slowed his pace as he sauntered directly towards her. The fighting stopped at his appearance, two human males also fighting against his guards were seized. They shared none of her fire, they were easy enough to overlook. As he approached, everyone around him bowed, except for her. He looked at her closely then as she took a defensive stance. She was not a rebel he realized, they would not have sent an unarmed woman into the city to fight alone. She was a slave, a rich slave. She must be one of the few human merchants allowed to operate within the city who had no direct master. Regardless, she knew who he was, he could see it in her eyes, the fear. Her eyes caught his attention; they were a steely grey that almost looked like liquid silver. And her hair, a blonde color so light it was almost white. A beautiful girl to be sure, but wild and untamed. A memory triggered inside him as he stared, a familiarity about her that suddenly became apparent. She looked just like the man he had met as a child, the one who had burned him and helped kill his mother, she was the spitting image of him.

His daughter maybe? The look of defiance that now came across her face was proof enough.

He shifted as he approached, barking an order at her and throwing his powerful command behind it. "You will stop."

"Not until my mother is released, I will not stop!" He believed her, greatly admiring her courage yet surprised at how she resisted his power.

He looked to the men the guards held; they looked to be her older brothers. Their features were similar, but their hair and eyes were not like hers. He glanced at a sobbing woman currently tied to a wooden post; this was their mother. What was happening here? He looked at the guards he and his men had come to aid. They looked disheveled and angry. This girl, this human, had beaten the shit out of them, without weapons. How could a human girl have bested blooded? He growled his displeasure at the guards, laziness or overconfidence in their abilities is why they had failed. Their failure made the crown look weak. He would punish them later.

The guard captain stepped forward offering an explanation, "The mother was infected by the scourge attack from yesterday. We were in the middle of seizing the woman for cleansing when her children interfered."

"If you wouldn't do the same for your mother you should be ashamed of the childbirth you put her through," the girl hissed, words filled with venom.

"It's not cleansing! You're trying to burn her alive!" one of the brothers shouted, the younger one.

"She's not infected. Look at her arm! There's no rot, it's been over a day. If she was infected, she would have turned by now," the eldest yelled.

Liam felt a wave of respect for these siblings. He understood why they fought so hard, he would have done the same. He looked from the brothers to the mother, her wound only partially visible. He sniffed the air but did not smell the usual rot that went with an injury from a scourge. There was no way to heal an infection like that except... he scented the air again. Her scent finally caught his attention, filling his nostrils and sending him into an internal frenzy.

"Your Highness," her voice called out, "I cannot smell the rot from here."

His eyes shifted to *her*; she was bowing to him in the crowd. His heart skipped a beat at the sight of her. Her red hair cascaded down her back in curls, bouncing slightly as she moved. She glanced up at him, her emerald

184

eyes shining. He had not seen her in years; she was just as beautiful as the last time he saw her. She had never bowed to him before, this was not how they were. Thinking again, he had made sure things had changed by the way he ended it. He'd gone above and beyond creating the reputation of being a violent dominant wolf. His exploits in dealing with disobedience were well known as was his cruelty when dealing out punishments. He had been careful to keep his distance and to paint the picture that he was truly his father's son. Her reaction to him just confirmed that he had succeeded, as much as it hurt him to see it so.

He had missed her, missed the closeness they shared. Regardless of his reasons, he had changed and done terrible things. He learned how to be his father's son, and made peace with the darkness, allowing it to take over inside him. But looking at her again, he saw the light she carried still shining brightly. He knew he shouldn't, that he should stop himself, but he didn't. Walking over to her he reached down and grabbed her chin gently. She rose to her feet, staring into his eyes for the first time in years.

"Ah, my dear Bridget, I thought that was you." He smiled at how brightly her eyes shone in the sunlight. "With your keen senses and affinity for healing, I am intrigued by this… situation."

Meaning he knew she had stopped the rot, just as she had stopped the poison for him all those years ago. He gently took her by the hand and led her to the mother. Truthfully, he was certain Bridget had healed the woman, maybe with this charade he could find a way to save the poor woman. With enough blooded realizing there was no infection, he might be able to play it off as an injury, not from the scourge. He would try if he could find a way that didn't show him as weak. He respected this family for protecting their own, he did not want to punish them if he didn't have to.

He ripped the woman's sleeve off, revealing an ordinary wound. "Take a look, dear one, and give me your honest opinion."

He was thankful that his reputation as a cold and ruthless prince had grown, so had hers as a respected healer. The fact that she was still alive was proof enough that she hadn't revealed her secret to anyone else. Which was why she had spoken out, but also why she was acting like she had never met them before. Bridget made a show of it, scenting the air and examining the wound.

"She smells clean, your highness. I sense no infection within the human woman." She stepped away from him.

He hated to admit it but distancing herself from him, even though it was to be expected, it still hurt. He looked at her, willing her to see the pain in his eyes, but her eyes had flickered in the direction of the younger brother, just for a moment. He watched as her body language shifted into something familiar, something she used to only do when looking at him.

A silent rage began to fill him up. He grabbed her by the hand again, dragging her over to the human girl. Was she an ordinary human, or was this in fact the daughter of the sorcerer he had met all these years ago? She had the same fire he did, the same liquid fire look to her, and she moved with a speed humans didn't have. She had ancient blood, he was sure of it. In his anger at the sudden realization that Bridget might have moved on since being with him, he felt the need to prove the girl's traitorous blood to be tainted.

"What's your assessment of this one?" he asked, urging something, anything, from her. "How can a mortal woman best a handful of my guards?"

The girl looked poised to fight, but he cared more about Bridget's response. Was she still the same girl he remembered, gentle and kind? Was she going to protect this girl because of what was going on between her and that boy? Or did she not know? Too many questions were swirling around in his mind, making it hard for him to keep his anger in check. He wasn't sure what he planned to do now, he was desperate to make a decision.

"I see and smell nothing that indicates anything other than human, My Prince." She kept addressing him so properly, it was disturbing coming from her.

He stared into the girl's eyes, trying to decide what to do, but she glared back at him in challenge. His wolf rattled inside him at this insolence, his grip on his anger loosening by the second. Fuck it, he was convinced now. She was the spawn of his enemy from all those years ago and a perfect outlet to unleash his anger on. He wrapped his hand around the girl's slender throat, lifting her off her feet before slamming her into the ground. How dare this human challenge him. He bared his teeth at her, demanding her submission. She did not give it. Instead, she struck out at him, he caught it easily enough, but the defiance of that look, of that strike, would not stand.

The brothers had been tied to another post; they tried to fight back but his men controlled them easily enough. Rage filled him, how dare this family openly defy him. He was the crown prince. Hadn't he sacrificed the last few years building a reputation no human would want to challenge? He could not let this stand, would not let it. His work had to be worth something.

"Burn the mother!" he ordered.

186

Grabbing the girl by her braid, he dragged her to the only available post. She fought with everything she had, which compared to him wasn't much. She was fast but she had the strength of a human. He secured her hands to the top of the post so she was facing the wood. As she continued to fight him, he cocked a fist back, punching her hard in the face. He watched her head rock back from the impact. Blood began to pour from her nose and a new split on her eyebrow.

There it was, that earthy smell only found in the blood of the ancients. Satisfied at guessing right, he grabbed the collar of her tunic and pulled. Her bare back was now exposed. Now he could punish her for everyone to see. He clearly spent too much time in the villages proving his dominance and he had neglected his own city. Now was as good a time as any to show the citizens of the capital he was not the one they wanted to be challenging.

A snarl erupted from the crowd behind him, silencing the crowd. A new challenger? He stopped and turned, seeing that the snarl had come from Bridget. A moment of panic came and went at the sight of her. He wouldn't know what to do if she decided to formally challenge him, she too was from a dominant bloodline, her size once shifted was nearly as impressive as his. He wasn't sure he would be capable of harming her, even in a challenge for dominance, but as his eyes fell on her, he breathed a sigh of relief. Her emotions were getting the better of her, her ability to shift was still wild and uncontrollable. Even after all these years she had yet to gain control over her wolf. She swayed for a moment as he watched her internal struggle for control. He barely stopped himself from rushing forward to catch her as she fell backward.

He did step forward though, unable to leave her in this state of shifting back and forth. She snarled at his approach, the wolf inside taking him in as a threat. Did she hate him, truly? Didn't her wolf realize who he was and that he would never hurt her? Guess it didn't, not that he could blame the beast after what he had done years ago, how he had been so cruel. There wasn't much good left in him.

"You will get ahold of your wolf." The wolf inside him answered the challenge from hers, but softly he said, "Bridget, if you can't handle the stress you need to leave."

His words had sent her over the edge. She shifted into her auburn wolf completely, it was now growling at him in anger as it stood, preparing for an attack. He stood up to her, accepting her anger, but not the challenge. He would not hurt her, he could never hurt her; and apparently, she wouldn't

Brittany Mendes

hurt him even as they stood face to face. Bridget shifted back into her human form, collapsing onto the ground from the pain of it. She was in tears and trembling from lack of control.

"Escort her back to her father's house. She is to make it there unharmed." The order had been made, his men would follow.

They escorted her away. He watched as she went, suddenly thankful that she would not be present to see the darkness he was about to unleash. He snapped his attention back to the humans. If she was a sorceress, then it was likely they all were. There was no sense in dragging them away for further examination, it would only draw more attention. He had them now, he would deal with them in a way that would extinguish any hope from rebel sympathizers that might be watching.

"Light it," he ordered.

His men quickly added bundles of wood underneath the mother's feet, igniting it. The girl began to pull against her restraints, screaming and cursing at him as her mother's skirts caught fire. He took a whip from one of the guards and waited. She struggled, but there was no sign of magic, no lightning, no earthquakes, nothing. She had ancient blood running through her veins, but she was not using her magic to save her mother. Did she even know?

The mother was talking to her daughter then, saying her goodbyes. Her children kept fighting, kept defying the inevitable. There, the girl's hands! The rope that secured her hands to the post began to smoke, like touching her flesh was touching flame itself. This was the daughter, but apparently, she didn't know what she was capable of. He had no doubt, if she did, she would've burned him alive.

He struck out with the whip; it caught her across her spine. He watched the flesh slice open and blood trickle down. The brothers yelled curses at him. The mother started screaming as the flame melted away her flesh. The girl barely recovered before the whip struck her again. More ripping of flesh, more blood. He let his anger and hatred fuel his strikes. Anger at having to do this at all. Hatred for magic and the man from his childhood, and now hatred for his daughter. Anger at having to be this person, the one who has to taint his soul.

He drove all his strength into those strikes, letting his anger drive him. It's how he got through punishing people like this, at least in the beginning. For a human, magic aside, he was impressed with how long the

188

girl had remained conscious; but like all things he set out to dominate, her strength finally gave out in surrender to him.

He wiped the sweat away from his forehead, dropping the whip. A crowd had gathered to watch. Good, the girl hung there, bleeding but breathing. The mother's corpse, now lifeless, was still burning. The brothers stood there in shock. He had done his duty; he could leave now.

"Keep them here overnight, post a guard," he ordered the captain. "In the morning take them to the king. He'll want to see the girl especially."

He felt numb as he walked away, leaving all that blood and suffering behind him, only to walk into more death and destruction. Nothing was safe with him anymore, he would most assuredly bring about suffering.

One week ago

Liam stood before the commander of the outpost, listening to the old man attempt to explain how he had let a bunch of human rebels attack and injure his men. Liam was not interested in the commander's excuses, but he was interested in the details he had managed to obtain after the attack. This particular warband had initiated their attack from the sea. The humans had utilized two-man fishing boats to sneak up on the fort from the coast, where defenses were weakest. They had attacked at night, taking advantage of surprising most of the guards as they were sleeping. A few humans had snuck into the outpost, locking the guards inside their sleeping quarters before pressing the attack. A very tactful approach Liam had to admit, it had worked. Before the blooded guards were able to break free of their confines, the humans had escaped on their fishing vessels.

After the attack, the command had sent his men into the surrounding villages to gather information on the rebels. It was probably the wisest thing he could have done. It was discovered that the war chief in charge of the attack on the outpost was named Farroway, and he was from one of those local fishing villages. The commander had managed to locate the war chief's wife and daughter, dragging them back to the outpost as prisoners.

"And you still hold the mother and child?" Liam asked the commander, interrupting even more excuses spewing from the old man's mouth.

"We still hold the mother," the commander answered nervously. "The child was... mishandled by some of the men. She succumbed to her injuries about a day ago."

189

Liam snapped his eyes to the commander's. Anger replaced the boredom he had experienced in the last hour. "Mishandled?"

"Yes, Your Grace." The old fool stumbled over his words. "While some of the men were having their way with the mother, a few of them decided to take the child too. She did not survive the encounter."

Liam struck out then, his claws raking down the old man's face, drawing blood. The old man stumbled back from shock, but Liam was on him again. His fists rained down upon the commander as he spoke. "Since... when... does... the... crown... condone... the... rape... and... murder... of... a... child?"

The surrounding guards froze in place as they watched the assault on their commander unfold. All of them were too afraid to get between the Crown Prince of Oich and their commander. Liam's rage fueled him. How dare they? A child?! Not until the commander hit the ground, bloody and curled up in a protective position, did Liam finally cease his attack.

"You are the commander of this outpost; you allowed this to happen!" Liam spat upon the old man. "Seize him! Restrain the men responsible for the death of the child too."

Guards shot forward at their prince's command, dragging the former commander to his feet. Three other guards were dragged forward and forced to their knees before their crown prince. Liam's rage did not falter as he looked upon the faces of these disgusting mongrels.

"WE DO NOT HARM CHILDREN," Liam growled, baring his fangs. He turned his gaze to the surrounding men. "We do not mix our blood with those of lesser status. Is that understood?"

"Yes, Your Majesty," the voices of his guards echoed throughout the outpost.

"Rip them apart," he ordered, turning to the commander's second in command. "You're in charge now. Take me to the mother."

The newly promoted commander saluted before turning on his heel and guiding Liam towards the cells. Liam didn't bother to look back to ensure his command was being followed, he could hear the screams of the men as their comrades shifted. The sound of flesh tearing and blood splattering was almost as loud as their screams. They deserved every second of being ripped apart, Liam held no regrets for creatures as vile as that.

When the new commander stopped before a cell, the guard on duty unlocked it and opened the door for Liam to walk in. Once he did, he was overpowered with remorse at the sight of the woman. She was alive, but she bore the injuries of the crimes that were committed upon her. Liam's stomach twisted in disgust at the sight of it. He had never understood the appeal of such treatment of others. His father looked at the coupling, forced or not, with any blooded and a slave as an abomination. Something as abhorrent as trying to breed with sheep.

Rape was outlawed not because his father was merciful, but because women who were not married to a blooded were not worth a man's time. A married man could do what he wished with his wife, if she refused to submit to him, he was within his rights to do as he must, for breeding and dominance. But committing such crimes against a blooded woman who you were not married to was punishable by death. Female slaves were raped, and most guards turned a blind eye to their treatment. Those with the traditional values of Oich, those who believed in worshipping the Moon God looked down on those who raped slaves with disgust. It was a crime against their beliefs, again not because they cared for the women, but because the women were valued at the same level as livestock.

Liam crouched down a few feet away from the woman, staring into her broken and bruised face. Her eyes turned to his, and all he could see was heartache. A mother's heartache. Her largest wound was the loss of her daughter, not the ones her own body bore.

"You killed them?" she finally spoke, her voice cracking from the strain.

"They deserved worse." Liam nodded, staring back into her eyes. "I know it means very little to you, but I am sorry about what happened to you and your daughter."

The woman continued to stare at him, as if expecting this to be a joke at her expense, but her head turned in the direction of the former commander's final screams as he was silenced forever.

"What do you want?" she asked him, eyes returning to him.

"Truthfully," Liam sighed as he spoke, "I don't know anymore. Forgiveness seems too much to ask at this point. Evil doesn't get second chances."

The woman cracked a smile, a small chuckle coming from her lips. "Evil doesn't avenge the lives of little girls."

Her response shook him deeply. He was evil, he had let the darkness in and let it manifest within him. He had committed horrible crimes upon others, tortured and maimed humans and blooded alike. He was not a good person even in the slightest, but a small glimmer of hope sparked at her words, his father would not have avenged the child. His father was evil incarnate. Maybe he had a chance after all.

"They will want to keep you here, if anything to bait your husband out of hiding," Liam explained to her. "They will present you to him one final time before slitting your throat in front of him. Do you want to see him again, before they kill you? Remaining alive would mean remaining here with them until he comes back."

She stared at him. "He will come to avenge us no matter what happens to me at this point. I would rather be done with this world, spare him from seeing my death, and spare myself from seeing the guards' faces every night."

Liam unsheathed a dagger at his hip, eyes searching the woman's as he moved. "Any final prayers?"

"May the Goddess of Healing watch over you, Prince."

Before she could inhale, Liams drug the blade of his dagger across the soft flesh of her throat. He watched as the blood poured from the open wound. What little light was left in her eyes finally died out just before her head slumped forward. Liam cleaned his dagger off on the hay she slept on before sheathing it. He stood, staring down at the poor woman.

"Burn the mother and daughter together," Liam ordered the guard, "and spread the word that Farroway's wife and child were killed as retribution for his attack on this outpost. Let's see if we can get the sea rat to come back out into the daylight."

Chapter Twenty-Eight

Grace

Grace and her two companions sat around the campfire in silence. All they could hear was the occasional snap of a log or crackle of flame. This forest was unnatural; it seemed to lack any form of life. Even the trees seemed hollow with no fresh growth or leaves. There were no signs of animal tracks in the dirt, deer trails, or nests in the trees. The only sounds in this forest were the noises they made as they sat there. The man and woman who sat across from her kept themselves busy sharpening their blades. Grace did the same, occasionally allowing her eyes to scan the trees behind them for anything that could be approaching. She wasn't comfortable being this out in the open, not in this forest, they were easy prey for scourge or any wandering tribesmen from Gaelach. They were passing through their territory after all.

Grace had been traveling for weeks since she received that vision sent to her by the sorceress. She and her two traveling companions shared the same dream the night of the woman's call for aid. Visions of scourge tearing apart the land filled her memory. Someone out there was tapping into a forgotten form of dark magic and weaponizing those awful monsters against innocents. There were dozens of them back at home who held ancient blood, but the three of them had been the only ones to answer the call.

Ingrid and Darragh had also come from the castle. Ingrid was a warrior; she spent her days training and drilling with Airgid's army. At twenty years old she had honed herself into an impressive killing machine, combining her unique gift with blades, she was an asset to their cause. Darragh was a hunter for the kitchens. He spent a lot of time in the woods hunting game, his gift allowed him an advantage on prey, and now to keep them safe on the road. They all knew each other from the castle, but none of them anticipated they would be out here together on a mission with an unknown trajectory. The others had deemed them crazy for embarking on this quest with little more than a shared dream.

The night of the vision, all those with ancient blood had gathered in the courtyard, all fifty of them who lived within the capital of Airgid. There was a heated debate amongst them about whether they should respond to the call for aid. Grace led the argument to venture out and find the woman, to join forces and use their skills as a single force to locate and kill this dark magic wielder. At least half had been moved by her argument and were willing to follow her. Until the queen joined the argument. Queen Valeria put her foot down, stating the defense of Airgid was priority. Only three of them had been willing to defy the queen, and they were sitting around this campfire.

"Five minutes," Darragh said quietly, palming his bow and grabbing an arrow. "Silverbacks. At least six."

Darragh's power was incredibly powerful, it granted him greatly increased senses. He could see miles away if he wished, he could hear a pin drop from across a field. His gift is what made him such an ideal hunter. Grace nodded to him, giving the command. Darragh silently scampered up a tree for a better vantage point. This had all been planned, a trap for the tribesmen. After days of scouting, Grace had determined the dark magic wielder was in this area, giving the orders. They needed to capture one so they could interrogate it.

Ingrid looked at Grace giving her a wink, it was time. Grace shut her eyes and concentrated on the center of her power, pulling at it to weave her creations. She opened her eyes, sitting around the camp were now a dozen soldiers performing various tasks. They were illusions, hollow and untouchable. They were meant as a distraction for the approaching silverbacks.

Grace could hear them now, sounds of large wolven bodies crashing through the forest in their general direction. Her illusions suddenly stopped their menial tasks and picked up their weapons, preparing for an inevitable attack. She had them form a protective perimeter around the camp. Ingrid took up her axe and shield, standing in the center of the camp. Grace did the same with her whip in one hand and dagger in the other.

"*Remember, we need one alive,*" Grace ordered through her mind connection to the other two.

"*At your command, Princess,*" Ingrid responded down the bond. "*The others are fair game right?*"

"*Yes. No survivors.*" Grace stood at the ready. "*Darragh?*"

"*Understood,*" his deep voice echoed down the bond. "*Here they come.*"

Grace could see shadowy figures now cresting the hill. "*Engage.*"

At the order, Darragh began raining arrows down on the approaching wolves. In response to the attack, the creatures began to separate, leaving their formation. Ingrid stepped forward while stomping her foot into the earth. Ice shot out from where her foot made contact, shooting toward the wolf that had been in the lead. As soon as the wolf's paws hit the

194

ice it began to slide. With another stomp to the ground Ingrid had icicles the size of a person shoot out from her ice path, impaling the wolf through its stomach. With a painful howl the wolf called out to the others, its blood streaming down the shards of ice.

With a flick of her fingers Grace had her illusions charge the oncoming blooded. The wolves engaged with the imaginary soldiers, slashing at them with their claws or trying to bite onto a limb. With none of the attacking blooded able to make contact, the wolves began running around confused from the chaos. Darragh rained down more silver-tipped arrows, each finding their mark in the hide of a large grey and white wolf. The great beast howled in pain at the impact, dropping to the ground as it succumbed to its injuries. Ingrid rushed up to it and sliced its exposed throat with the blade of her axe. Two wolves down, three more to go.

There was no other way to describe the scene before them except chaos. Grace continued to weave her illusions, adding not just soldiers but scourge. The silverbacks were having trouble keeping track of what was real and what wasn't. Darragh must have expended all his arrows because he was now on the ground slashing at the wolves with his sword. Ingrid, ever the warrior, used an impressive combination of magic and muscle. She danced between targets, expertly slashing at the wolves' sensitive areas with her axe and with each footstep she sent out more and more deadly ice shards to impale her enemies.

A wolf seemed to have figured out what the illusions were and where they came from. The grey beast padded its way through several attacking soldiers, not even reacting to them. Grace readied her whip, taking several steps back. She was able to hold the illusions until the beast lunged for her.

She dove out of the way, ducking behind a tree before coming to her feet. Her concentration had broken; there were no more illusions. There were three wolves left, one for each of them. Grace looked at her attacker again as he tracked her from where she stood. She stepped out from behind the tree flicking her wrist, sending her whip toward the beast. The tail of her whip, the part with silver blades woven into it, came across the wolf's face. The beast howled in pain, blood streaming down its fur.

"Come on, you fucker," she called out to it. "Come and take a bite."

The wolf lunged again, Grace was ready for it and flicked the whip upwards and it wrapped around a tree branch. She allowed her magic to flow through her body, so she was able to increase her speed as she climbed her whip to avoid the impact. She was fast enough thankfully, the wolf stopping just below her. She took a deep breath and dropped. As she landed on the beast she turned her dagger downwards, driving it into the back of the beast's neck. The creature collapsed under the weight, never to get up again.

Grace reached up and grabbed her whip's hilt, shaking it free from the branch. She turned to see Ingrid weaponless, commanding her ice to surround the wolf she faced off with. Grace winced slightly at the sight of the creature impaled by at least a dozen ice shards. The sound was unsettling, but it was better for a wolf to cry out in pain and death than the cries be from one of them.

With one wolf left, the two women turned to Darragh who was still ducking and dodging around a wolf's teeth. Ingrid stomped her foot into the ground again. This time the ice surrounded the beast, trapping it. In a last ditch attempt the beast shifted back into its human form. A pale man covered with ritualistic scars wearing clothing made from animal hide stood before them. Ingrid adjusted the ice prison for the smaller monster it now held.

"Fuck you!" the man snarled at them with a heavy accent.

"Now now, is that really how you treat your guests?" Grace smirked at him. "Do you really have bones sticking out of your nose as jewelry? Do you realize how unsanitary that is?"

The wolfman snarled at her.

"They're so friendly here," Ingrid said sarcastically, squatting down to look him in the face. "So wild and uncivilized."

"Why did you attack us?" Grace asked. She already knew why, but she wanted to hear him say it.

"We don't like intruders." The tribesman spat, Ingrid dodged it.

"Wrong answer." Ingrid moved her hands, the ice around him tightened slightly.

"Let's try a different one." Grace began to pace. "Why are you capturing ancient blooded?"

The tribesman's head fell forward, chin resting against his chest for but a minute. When he raised it, his eyes had changed to a deep red, an eerie smile spread across his face. "I wanted to eat them."

"Why?" Grace stared into his eyes, she believed he meant it.

"We've been waiting for you." The man smiled, actually smiled at her, his voice an echo lost amongst an array of other voices.

"Movement!" Darragh called, looking at the trees.

"Where?" Ingrid had her shield and axe ready.

"Everywhere!" Darragh yelled.

Grace looked around at the wolves appearing from every direction, snapping and snarling at them, but they kept their distance. Grace's pulse quickened, they were surrounded by dozens of them. The tribesmen they had trapped in the ice began to laugh. Her eyes shot to him, fear setting in, something here was very wrong.

"I've been waiting for you, Princess," multiple voices trickled out of the tribesman's mouth. "How I've wanted to taste your flesh for a long time."

Chapter Twenty-Nine

Catriona

Catriona found herself awake but she wasn't sure why. Danny was fast asleep next to her, his arm draped over her hip. All she could hear was the roaring of the waterfall and the crackling of the fire. Looking around, she didn't see anything unusual. She guessed it was still a few hours before sunrise.

She sat up slowly to look around the cave. The hooting of a night owl came from the waterfall entrance. Danny was sitting up now, putting his hands to his mouth and mimicking the call back, a familiar but large figure emerged onto the pathway slowly making its way towards them.

"Rama!" Danny called out, getting to his feet. Catriona smiled at how happy Danny was to see his brother approaching.

She was too; it had been about two weeks since they had seen anyone. When Rama reached the campsite, he gave his brother a bone-crushing hug.

"Sorry to wake you so early. I couldn't sleep so I decided to walk the rest of the way here."

Rama reached over to an unsuspecting Catriona, scooping her up into an embrace as well.

"It's good to see you, brother." Danny gestured for him to take a seat. "Are you hungry? We've got some smoked rabbit."

"Famished," Rama answered, sliding his pack off his shoulders and setting it down. "I would love some."

Danny made towards their stash of food while Catriona fed the fire. Rama sat down across from her, eyeing her with a toothy smile.

"What?" she asked, frowning at him.

"You look good." He gave her a wink. "It looks like you've been eating."

She furrowed her brows at his comment, feeling some embarrassment that she had not been taking care of herself. "You haven't even been back five minutes and you're already annoying me."

"What are big brothers for if not to annoy their little sister?"

"I'm not your sister," she shot at him, confused by his comment.

Rama nodded over to hers and Danny's sleeping rolls. They had been laid out next to each other, basically touching. Ever since that wonderful groundbreaking night they had been sleeping in each other's arms. Actually, that's kind of all they had been doing, sleeping together afterwards seemed so normal. Now that they were no longer alone, it must have been a little too obvious. Her cheeks reddened slightly at how perceptive Rama was.

"He's my brother. Seems like you two have gotten closer. Would you like me to call you something other than sister?"

Her cheeks continued to heat at his comment, the asshole didn't have to go and spell it out. She busied herself with the fire as Rama's laugh echoed through the cave. Danny had returned, handing both Rama and Catriona pieces of smoked rabbit. Catriona carefully took a bite; it was just the other day she had been able to eat these without being part of a stew. Danny had started her on a rabbit stew, now he was pushing her on the smoked meat.

"Why are you staring at her?" Danny asked his brother.

"She's eating meat." Rama was in fact staring at her, she flipped him off.

"It's a work in progress that would be helped if you stopped making such a big deal out of it," Danny lectured.

"Sorry!" Rama threw his hands up in surrender. "Just seems like a lot has changed in the last two weeks."

Danny glared at him, Rama wisely took a bite of rabbit before saying, "Again, my apologies for being here so early. Every time I tried to set up camp somewhere I kept coming across this crazy black horse. Fucker wouldn't let me stop anywhere so I just kept going."

"Ha!" Danny laughed loudly. "I ran into that same horse. The one with golden eyes, right?"

"Yes," Rama answered. "Fucker was huge. Very aggressive. Every time I tried to lay down to sleep it would come out of nowhere until I started moving again."

"I saw him a few days ago, it was the first day I was able to get some rabbits. Every time I kept trying to change directions to hunt down more game that great beast put himself in the way."

"It's not normal for a wild horse to be all the way out here, is it?" Catriona asked, mouth full of food.

199

"No, not one of that breed." Rama took a bite of rabbit. "You know it could be from one of those ancient legends."

"What legends?" Catriona asked.

"Oh no, don't get him started." Danny rolled his eyes. "He's obsessed with legends and anything to do with the ancient ones. He fancies himself a storyteller."

"Historian, if you don't mind," Rama corrected. "These stories used to be fact."

"Whatever." Danny took a bite of rabbit.

"As I was saying." Rama glared at his brother. "There was an ancient story, born from *fact*, that the Goddess of War and Fate would travel on a great black horse with golden eyes. Whenever she would stray from the path her horse would guide her back to the right one. Sounds like this horse really wanted us to stay on a specific path."

"I wasn't lost," Danny argued.

"Met-a-phorically!" Rama ground out, clearly irritated. "It doesn't have to be literal."

Catriona laughed at them. "How is a goddess supposed to help someone decide which way they want to go about something, couldn't she just tell them?"

"The horse isn't the Goddess, it belongs to her!" Rama growled in frustration.

"Sorry, how is a pet supposed to help?" Catriona corrected with a smile, oh she was enjoying this, he was the one who decided to call her sister after all.

"Well, it appeared when I was trying to decide whether or not I wanted to rest for a day or two before coming to find you. Every time I tried to make camp the beast would run up on me and try to chase me off. It could have been telling me to keep going towards you guys."

"That's interesting." Catriona turned to Danny. "Were you trying to decide something when you saw the horse?"

Danny, who was drinking from the waterskin, started to choke. "I have no idea what you mean."

"You said you were trying to decide if you were going to stalk more game. Maybe the horse was warning you that something bad would happen if you kept going," Rama suggested.

Danny's face turned red. "Yeah, that's probably it."

Realization dawned on Catriona as her face turned red too, he had been deciding whether or not to come back to her. By the gods this was a nightmare, Rama was essentially pulling them completely apart for all to see. Traveling with them both was going to be a pain in the ass.

Rama attempted to change the subject, "Anyways, ancient factual stories aside, Menolayous and I dropped Clyous off at Flinn's camp before Menolayous and Markous headed to the Harrada Pass."

"How is the old bear?" Danny asked, clearly thankful for the change of topic.

"Believe it or not, that bastard is building an entire village," Rama was animatedly talking with his hands now, "in the trees!"

"Seriously?" Danny looked skeptical.

"I'm not exaggerating. It's very impressive," Rama explained. "You two ought to see it sometime."

Catriona thought it sounded neat to see. Danny glanced over at her for a moment before returning to the conversation.

"There is some rather concerning news. McKinlay's warband is missing."

"What do you mean missing?" Catriona asked.

"Flinn hasn't heard anything from him in months. Menolayous is going to stop by after dropping Markous off to see what he can find. I'm hoping they're holed up somewhere after fighting with some tribesmen or something simple."

"What are you going to do?" Catriona asked him.

Rama shared a look with Danny before answering, "Truthfully, I'm here to ask you that."

Danny looked at her too. "I'll go with you, whatever you decide."

She glanced between the two of them for a moment. She should have guessed this was coming. She couldn't stay in this cave with Danny forever, as tempting as that sounded.

"What do you truly want?" Rama asked, not a hint of a smile on his face. "You can't give any wrong answers."

"And what, you're waiting for me to tell you so you can make my dreams come true?" Catriona was snotty with this question, but she didn't care. Her answer was wrong, it was selfish and wicked.

"Within reason." Rama was fighting a smile at her anger, like he knew what she wanted. "You deserve the future you want. You've been through enough."

"What I want is impossible." She stared him down. "You wouldn't want to help me."

"Try me," Rama was challenging her now, maybe he was like an older brother after all.

She glanced at Danny before saying, "I want to kill the Crown Prince of Oich."

Silence was what greeted her confession, but she was not ashamed. In fact, she kept going, "I want to make him suffer. I want to stare into his eyes as his life slips away. I want to feel his blood on my hands. I want to destroy everything about him."

Rama was smiling now, which surprised her. "Good."

She looked to Danny who gave her a slight nod. "I'm more than happy with this plan."

"Why do you both seem so happy about this? What I want is selfish and evil. Killing him is going to be next to impossible." She had expected them to tell her it was a bad idea, talk her out of it, or say she was a bad person for even thinking this way.

"We're fighting a rebellion against him and his father." Rama rolled his eyes at her. "It's kind of our end goal."

"You might find this surprising, Cat, but vengeance is kind of our thing. You wanting to kill the man who murdered your mother, the same one who whipped you nearly to death, *I* consider that a normal reaction." Danny had used her family's name for her, breaking down any defenses she was trying to throw up.

"One we would be more than happy to help you fulfill." Rama smiled, overly excited. "I'm here for the violence."

202

"Rama's just happy he's going to recruit you into his army." Danny rolled his eyes.

"Damn right I am. She can fight well."

The two started bickering back and forth over nonsense related to their rebellion. Catriona couldn't help but laugh at them, brothers indeed. It reminded her of the family dinners she used to have back home. Watching them made her feel almost whole again for a moment.

"I'll officially join your rebellion under one condition." The boys stopped arguing and looked at her.

"The prince is mine. I'm the one who gets to kill him."

"Deal," Rama answered her with a smile.

Chapter Thirty

Bridget

Bridget hummed to herself as she filled up a basket with different tonics and bandages. Once she had filled the basket, walking over to the merchant she dropped a few coins into his hand before leaving. She was a regular here, constantly picking up supplies for herself or Flinn's camp. It was not uncommon for the merchant and her to not exchange words unless she was asking about something specific. Most blooded tried not to interact with her much, a fact she has had to live with all her life. It used to bother her, but now she took from it a sense of peace. Being left alone was a gift at times.

She stepped onto the cobblestone street making her way towards the edge of the elite city center. Just outside the human section was where she occasionally met up with one of Flinn's men. It made the most sense to meet there, human presence was not as questionable here as meeting on the elite side, and if the messenger changed every time, she could easily pass off their meeting as providing medical supplies to a client. She might not be respected as a wolf, but she was respected as a healer. She was also well known for her "bleeding heart," or a more accurate representation would be that she simply provided services for humans. No other blooded healer did. It sickened her to see how little humans were valued and how poorly they were treated by her "people."

Bridget maneuvered through the crowd within the town square. Usually this would be an ordeal in itself, but today she found that some of the blooded moved aside at her approach. She watched a group of young women about her age move so she could walk by easily, nodding a greeting as she passed. This was certainly strange. Blooded only moved like that for a more dominant wolf, which she was not. She could feel pride coming from her wolf inside, as if it were standing tall and proud. That damn wolf was having her do all kinds of things lately, like standing up for herself and fighting back. Maybe the other wolves sensed it too.

Finally making it through the crowded square, she took a shortcut through one of the side streets. After a few minutes the cobblestone streets turned to dirt, and the people she passed no longer wore fancy, colorful, delicately woven clothes. Now everyone she passed wore mostly neutral colors and all clothes appeared roughly sewn together for heavy use. The drastic difference between classes in this city was enough to give anyone whiplash.

Bridget spotted the young man then; Connor she believed his name to be. She had only met him twice before. He stood just outside a small tavern that was frequented by a lot of the working-class humans. It was still about midday so there weren't as many tavern goers, but just enough that the meeting wasn't out of place.

"Such a beautiful day for a stroll." Connor smiled at her as she approached, showing his youth.

She smiled back. "It's always a beautiful day if the rains are held back."

"It's good to see you again, Miss Bridget." His eyes twinkled in the sunlight.

"It's good to see you too." She handed him the heavy basket of supplies. "Here, this should get you by for another couple of weeks."

Connor accepted the basket then lowered his voice, "Anything to pass on?"

"There's going to be an increase of nightly patrols around the fishing docks. There have been some minor squabbles between the humans and the regular guards about mistreatment. The crown," she swallowed, careful not to say Liam's name out loud, "plans to make an example of them. It sounds like the crown wants to put a stop to any and all resistance."

"Any names mentioned as the instigators?" Connor whispered, eyeing the crowd.

"Not that I've heard," she answered.

"Are you okay?" Connor asked with genuine concern. "We've heard that the crown prince has been seen knocking on your door. If you're in any danger, we can get you out of the city safely."

"Oh no, I'm fine really." She sighed. "He was a childhood friend. We hadn't seen each other in years. He was just stopping by."

"He's an incredibly dangerous man, Miss Bridget." Connor's youthful face showed genuine concern.

"I know what he is," she answered flatly. "I'm not in danger. Nobody suspects our connection."

He didn't look like he believed her. "If that changes at all, just send word. We'll come for you if you need us."

"Thank you." She knew they would try if she asked, but humans fighting against a city full of blooded didn't have the best odds.

"What an in though, if you could get close to the crown prince." Connor began to speculate, his age showing.

Wanting to end this conversation quickly she gently patted his arm. "Until next time, Connor."

And just like that they went their separate ways. It was never safe to stay for too long; it drew too much attention. Besides, she didn't want to talk about Liam to a boy she barely knew, Liam was a man she wasn't sure she really knew anymore. This single interaction alone proved to her just how complicated her life could be the more Liam was in it. On one hand Connor was completely right, getting close to the crown prince could be a gold mine of information she could gather for the cause. Not that she owed Liam a scrap of loyalty, but Connor was also right in the fact that Liam was an incredibly dangerous man. She had witnessed his cruelty firsthand; she had treated the wounds of his victims.

On the other hand, Bridget was confident that Liam, in general, wouldn't harm her. He had spent most of their lives protecting her, but he had spent the last few years devoting himself to tracking down and destroying the very rebellion she was aiding. Those last few years had changed him into something dark and cruel. If he were to find out she was aiding them, she was not sure how he would react.

Bridget fought with these thoughts as she made it all the way across town, finally coming to her front door. As she stepped inside, she noticed several wooden crates stacked in her foyer. She sniffed the air out of habit, not that she needed to, catching the strong odor of alcohol. Her father was back from one of his trading envoys to Airgid.

Cautiously, she hung her cloak on the coat peg by the door. She could hear him in the kitchen, rustling around in the pantry, probably looking for more spirits. Great. She hated it when he drank. Knowing she had better go check on him, she reluctantly entered the kitchen. Her father was as she figured, clumsily rummaging around the shelves for more alcohol. She watched him for a moment before he turned toward her. Yes, he was very intoxicated, eyes glassy and hair unkempt.

"Father." She acknowledged him politely, as she was expected to do.

He frowned at her. "And where have you been? No daughter to greet me upon my return?"

"I was seeing to a few patients this morning," Bridget lied easily enough. "Forgive me father, I was unaware of your return."

Her father snagged a bottle off the shelf and stumbled past her. "A woman of your birthright shouldn't be wandering around alone, healer or not. I'm going to assume since they didn't meet you here, that your clients were slaves."

Bridget remained silent, her father despised the fact that she helped slaves. She wished she had a relationship with her father that could convince her that his irritation was for her benefit. The truth was, she knew her father hated her. He blamed her for her mother's death. Her father was too weak to have gotten rid of her as a child, so he resented every breath she took growing up. Her parents had tried for years to conceive children before her but were ultimately unsuccessful. Her mother had become pregnant while he was away on a trading mission, causing her father to believe his young and beautiful wife had slept with another male, even though she denied it until her last breath. The pregnancy was hard on her, or so Bridget was told, and her mother passed away giving birth to her "miracle" child. Her father began to drink heavily after her mother's death, and at a very young age she discovered he was a violent drunk. Now that Bridget had reached adulthood, she knew she looked just like her mother. He always found a way to bring it up as a carefully layered insult. His one and only hope to rid himself of her was to marry her off, a task in which he was failing miserably.

"I've heard your trips to the forest haven't stopped either." He stared down at her, his body swaying slightly from the drink.

"It's the only place I can gather certain herbs," Bridget tried to explain.

"You don't seem to understand, or maybe you just don't care," he began to raise his voice. "You are the last descendant of our bloodline. You come from a powerful pack, dominant wolves that could rival those who wear the crown today. You should be the most desired woman in Oich, but you risk your already tainted honor by wandering around alone where anyone could take your virtue, completely ruining any decent marriage prospects."

"Tainted honor?" Irritation flared within her. "Because of my shift?"

"You are weak. And worse yet you've made it publicly known," her father snarled, taking a swig from the bottle. "You are a disappointment."

"And you're too old," she shot back. "Honor isn't what you think it is anymore. Being a virgin doesn't mean anything."

"Then why does nobody want you?" he sneered. "Tell me Bridget, explain to your very old father why a pretty girl with more riches than most nobles could dream of has yet to be married. Virgin or not, your weakness is a disease no man wants to touch for fear of it passing on."

His words stung as if he had slapped her. He always got like this when he drank, he became mean and spiteful. Unfortunately, he wasn't wrong. Her inability to shift had tainted her honor. Nobody in the last twenty-two years had even bothered to consider her for marriage, no one except Liam. He had been everything to her for so long that she had never questioned giving him her maidenhead. She had always believed they would get married someday, she had hoped anyway, but that dream had long since disappeared. There had been nobody else for years, and now she couldn't even say she was pure. For a noblewoman in Oich, that left her with no future.

Her father snorted as he pushed past her. "Your mother would be ashamed of what you've become."

Her wolf snarled as it rattled its internal cage at the insult. Bridget's hands balled up into fists, she allowed her anger to sweep over her.

Against her better judgment she snapped back at him, "And she would be proud of the pathetic drunk her husband has become?"

Like a flash his fist connected with her cheek, knocking her to the ground. She should have expected that. He now stood over her, fists clenched, face red with anger.

"How dare you!" he bellowed.

Usually, this was where Bridget curled up into a ball to protect her face and stomach from any further strikes. Showing her submission in hopes that he would stop. Usually she was terrified, too scared he would keep beating her, so she was happy to submit. But this time she wasn't afraid of him. She saw him for what he was, a sad old drunkard who hated his life, hated her. She had never had a strong attachment to her father; he had only made her life difficult. She would not be his victim anymore. So, she did the most defiant thing she could think of. Taking a chapter out of Catriona's book, she sat up and stared at him, looking into his hateful little eyes. And then she smiled, showing him the ultimate form of defiance. She would not bow down to him anymore.

He snarled and pounced, raining a hail of punches down on her. Bridget raised her arms to protect herself but still took several strikes on her face. She lashed out, managing to rake her nails down his face, drawing blood. He stumbled back reaching up to touch his wound, he pulled his hand back seeing the blood.

"You fucking bitch!" He rushed forward again, this time grabbing her by the hair then kicking her in the ribs. "How dare you defy me."

She screamed as he dragged her into the foyer, fist wrapped within her hair. She tried desperately to get her footing, but she couldn't. She did manage to claw the hand that had her hair wrapped up in it. Her father gave up on trying to drag her, returning to pummeling her with his fists. She felt the impact on her temple, then her cheek, and finally the edge of her eye. These blows were hard, harder than he'd ever hit her before. The last few punches to her head left her dazed.

Just when she could feel consciousness start to slip away from her, the blows stopped coming. She no longer felt her father hanging onto her. In a daze, she turned to look at where he was standing, except he wasn't there anymore. The sound of her father screaming drew her attention down the hall. Her father was now cowering on the floor in a near identical position she had been in moments ago. A larger figure stood over him.

"How dare you lay a hand on her!" Liam roared, striking her father repeatedly.

How had Liam got here? She looked at her front door, it had been forced wide open. She hadn't even heard it open. Her thoughts were slow to come, the world spinning slightly. Liam was here, and he was beating her father. She looked at them again, Liam was in fact doing that. Her father's face was now visibly bruised and bleeding. Liam was much stronger than her father, and more violent. Not that she cared he was beating her father, but Liam was undoubtedly going to kill him.

"Liam!" she called out, voice cracking. "Please stop."

He hadn't heard her, still too occupied with beating her father.

She tried again, this time louder, "Liam!"

Liam stopped, turning towards her. The look of rage on his face was just as shocking as his sudden appearance. She looked down at her father, who was now balled up on the floor sniveling. The pain from the assault was starting to fully hit her, her face now aching so bad she didn't want to speak.

Instead, she raised a shaky hand up to him, a silent request. The rage on his face turned to concern, he rushed to her, taking her hand gently.

"Bridget!" he choked out, his eyes examining her face. "I'm so sorry."

"Please don't kill him," she whispered, her eye felt like it was swelling closed.

"He deserves it," Liam ground out. "By the gods Bridget, your face."

"He does." She winced as Liam helped her sit up completely. "But please don't."

Liam nodded, after making sure she would not fall over he strode over to her father. Gripping her father by the throat, Liam lifted the old man's body off the ground and slammed him into the wall. Her father was terrified as the Crown Prince of Oich stared him in the face.

"You don't deserve any mercy," Liam snarled. "You are lucky your daughter has asked me to spare you."

Her father dared to glance in her direction, just for a moment. She sat up to her full height fighting against the pain and dizziness, showing her defiance once again.

"That will be the last time you lay a hand on her ever again. You will never speak to her with any disrespect, or show your unpleasant face to hers again," Liam snarled. "This is no longer your house. This is hers. I don't give a shit where you go, but it will not be here."

"Liam?" Bridget started to say.

Her father foolishly opened his mouth to argue. Not tolerating an ounce of defiance from this old man, Liam drew a dagger. With the deadly sharp blade, Liam severed her father's hand from his wrist. Bridget and her father's screams intermingled as the hand fell to the ground with a sickening plop.

"She is mine!" Liam dropped her father to the floor. "Not yours. Not anyone else's. Nobody touches her again. Leave! Now!"

In horror, Bridget watched her father drag himself upright and out of the house, cradling his stump. Liam stood there watching him as he ran, ensuring that he kept running. Liam bent down picking up the hand, chucking it out of the door like garbage before shutting it. Liam's attention shifted to her then, as it came back to her she stiffened slightly under his gaze.

Ever so gently, Liam scooped Bridget up into his arms and carried her up the stairs to her room. He softly set her down on her mattress. She could feel everything then, her ribs were undoubtedly bruised and her face ached fiercely. She looked down at her hands, they were covered in blood. A combination of hers and her father's. There was blood and skin under her fingernails. Her dress was ripped and also splattered with blood. The room was still spinning, she was most likely concussed, lovely.

"Bridget." Liam was kneeling before her with a wet cloth in his hands. "Let me see your face."

She relented, pulling her hair out of the way. With surprising tenderness, Liam pressed the cool cloth to her eyebrow, wiping up the blood. She flinched but remained still as he worked.

"How did you know?" she asked. "Why are you here?"

"I was coming to see you," he said, still concentrating on his work. "Then I heard you screaming."

"Oh!" She flinched as he began to clean up her split lip. "Ow."

"Sorry." Liam stopped, looking into her eyes. "Looks like you got him good. I saw the scratches on his face before I started in on him. I'm proud of you."

"I'm not," she answered truthfully. "I defied him. I've never done that before. He had to punish me."

"Don't," Liam warned her. "I don't know what's gotten into you lately, with fighting back and controlling your shift, but it's a great thing Bridget. Truly."

"Defiance gets you killed." She looked into his eyes. "Gets you lashed or body parts cut off."

"Sweetheart." Liam took her hands. "I want you to fight, to protect yourself."

She tried to pull her hands away, but he wouldn't let her.

"Bridget, I need you to understand that I would never hurt you," he pleaded with her. "I can only imagine how you must feel seeing me do those things. I must look like a monster to you. But I promise you, I will never hurt you."

"Why? Because I'm yours?" Bridget was feeling defiant again, her wolf raging against his touch.

"Because I love you!" Liam stood, irritated. "And yes, you are mine."

"I don't recall agreeing to that," she bit out against the pain in her face.

"Too bad." Liam began to pace out of frustration. "I claimed you. You're off limits to everyone except me now. You're safe."

"Safe, but not allowed to make a decision?"

"Seems like lately you've needed protection," Liam argued.

She was pushing him, she knew it but didn't care. "You just told me you wanted me to fight back, to hold my own. I want that for me too. I'd rather have a say in my life than be sheltered."

"You would rather be beaten than let me claim you?!" Liam shouted.

"I want to be able to choose for myself!" she shouted back. "You made a choice years ago that turned my world upside down. You at least owe me a choice now."

Liam stopped pacing and took a deep breath. "Fine!"

He turned to leave and she shouted after him, "Where are you going!"

"Giving you space to make a decision!" he shot back.

She could hear his footsteps go all the way down the stairs and out her front door. The house shook as he slammed it shut behind him. What has gotten into her lately? She sat there for a moment before the tears began to fall. Her body ached from the beating, but her heart hurt more. Liam had come for her as he always had, but she just shoved him away. She would no longer be a victim for anyone to control. No more.

Chapter Thirty-One

Menolayous

After several grueling days of traveling the steep mountain roads on horseback, Menolayous and Markous had finally made it to the Harrada Pass encampment. With their cloaks pulled over their heads to shield from the bitter wind, the two men made their way down the rocky path to the small castle erected at the top of the tallest mountain. Menolayous was impressed with the level of self-control he possessed, having stopped himself several times from pushing Markous down a ravine or deep crevice. If he were being totally honest, Markous wasn't as irritating without his siblings nearby to pick on. His traveling companion had grown more reserved with how he held himself, undoubtedly using this time away to reflect. Finally reaching the main gate, they were greeted by guards wearing several thick layers and heavy cloaks. Once the gate had been opened, they made their way inside the castle. Pulling up to the stables, Menolayous dismounted, Markous was right behind him.

"Welcome to the mountain encampment of Harrada Pass." Menolayous waved his hand at the mostly empty courtyard of a castle that predominantly lay in ruins. "At least it's not snowing."

"There's hardly anyone here," Markous called over the wind.

"Outside, no. Can you blame them?" Menolayous pointed to a door across the courtyard. "Come on. That's where we'll find Farren."

"Farren?" Markous followed Menolayous across what looked like an outdoor sparring pit.

Together they reached the heavy wooden door, managing to pull it open and step inside. As soon as the door shut behind them, they could feel the warmth from several fires inside the great hall. There were ten or so tables spaced out, all heavily laden with food and drink. There were so many men gathered around the tables that the great hall was nearly filled. They were all feasting and drinking together as if celebrating.

"Come on, let's go find someone in charge." Menolayous shrugged off his cloak.

"Did you say Farren? That's funny." Markous followed Menolayous's lead, shaking droplets of water from his cloak.

"Why is that funny?" Menolayous asked.

"That's my father's name," Markous answered.

"Do you have any idea where he could have gone all those years ago?" Menolayous knew Markous's father had disappeared some years ago, the three siblings varied in their beliefs on why he disappeared.

"I ended up here," a deep and familiar voice came from behind them.

Turning around, both men came face to face with an older male, a scar running down the side of his face, narrowly missing one of his steely grey eyes. "Markous, you look good."

Menolayous watched Markous's jaw drop. Looking back at the seasoned warrior he had known for years, he was now kicking himself for not seeing it before. Farren's hair, his eyes, they were the same as Catriona's. He had never seen eyes like that on anyone else. Why hadn't he put that together sooner? This man looked like an older version of Markous and Clyous, but with Catriona's hair and eyes.

"Father?" Markous rushed forward to embrace his father, both men wrapping their arms around each other.

Tears rolled down the old warrior's cheeks as he embraced his son. "Markous, my dear boy. I am so sorry for not being there."

Finally, after a minute or so Markous broke away from their embrace. "Where were you? What happened that you had to leave us?"

Tears slowed but still came. "The King of Oich had caught me using magic. I managed to escape, but I knew going home or simply sending you word about what had happened would have put you all in danger. He would have tracked us down."

"Magic?" Markous asked, confused. "What do you mean?"

As an answer, flames erupted out of Farren's hands like they were torches. "We're from an ancient bloodline, son. Magic is in our bones." Farren paused for a second. "Have none of you shown signs of magic?"

"No," Markous stammered, clearly surprised.

Farren stared at him for a moment, clearly working something over in his memory. "Did you ever replace the iron bars I built in the house?"

"What? No?" Markous blustered, obviously confused. "Why didn't you ever tell us you had magic? Why didn't Mother?"

"I didn't want any of you to know. It was safer for you that way." Farren extinguished the flames. "None of you inherited the gift?"

Markous began to shake his head, still clearly in shock at what was happening. Had Markous really not known, even after growing up with Catriona? To him, it was obvious the girl had magic with how she moved and how she fought. There was no way a normal human could take on blooded guards the way she had, not that easily. Even Rama couldn't move like she did, he was a mighty warrior. Markous and Clyous probably didn't see it because they watched her growing up. To them, her movements and speed might be considered normal.

"Catriona," Menolayous answered, both men now looked to him as if remembering he was there. "I'm suspecting anyway. She's incredibly fast, as fast as any blooded."

"Cat." Farren's eyes threatened to water again. "How is Cat? Clyous and your mother?"

Markous shifted awkwardly. "Mother's dead."

"Dead? How? When?" Farren's already choked up voice began to crack with the new revelation.

Menolayous answered, sparing Markous from the emotional outburst he was about to have if he opened his mouth, "About two months ago there was a scourge attack on Oich, it made it as far into the city as your shop. Your wife was injured by one. Your children found a healer with magic who managed to stop the infection. But the blooded found her anyways and made to burn her. Your children fought like seasoned warriors trying to free her. Catriona led the charge, fighting like a demon from the abyss, tearing into the guards like they were nothing, but once the crown prince entered the fray the fight was lost. Your wife was burned alive and Catriona... was whipped as she watched her mother burn. Catriona and her brothers were left as an example, but my brothers and I cut them loose and helped them escape."

Both Markous and Farren stood deathly still, grief washing over the both of them. Farren reached out, grabbing Markous's shoulder, and pulling him into another embrace.

"Where are your brother and sister now?"

"Clyous joined up with Flinn's warband. He wants to fight," Markous sobbed.

"And your sister?" Farren forced his son to look him in the face. "Where is Cat? Is she alright?"

"We left her outside of Oich. She's alive but—" Markous paused. "She's not right in the head. She's not eating."

So, Markous had seen it too, Menolayous thought to himself. Both of her brothers had seen it, acting as if they hadn't. Why? Clyous had made the decision to leave so Catriona could stop leaning on him and grieve, but why had Markous? Menolayous kept to himself just how Markous had been treating his sister. Menolayous knew Farren would not accept this behavior from his eldest son. Farren would work out exactly what happened soon enough.

"And you left her there alone? Why didn't you take her with you!?" Farren's voice began to rise. "That's your sister! You are supposed to take care of her."

"We didn't leave her alone," Menolayous answered for Markous, again. It was true the younger man deserved the ass beating he would surely get, but Menolayous needed to assure Farren the war chief that he and his brothers did not leave his daughter to die. "She's with Danny. Rama went back for them after dropping Clyous off."

"Why didn't she go with either of you?" Farren demanded, then turned his attention to Menolayous. "I helped train you and your brothers, watched you grow into men when I couldn't do that with my own children, don't you dare lie to me boy."

"She's broken, Farren," Menolayous tried to say as compassionately as possible. "Danny's the only one she would open up to. He was working on getting her to eat, to work out her grief. She's strong Farren, stronger than most, but with enough pressure even the strongest steel can start to crack. She just needs time."

"I'm so sorry!" Farren wept to his son. "I wasn't there to protect you, but I'm here now, for all of you."

"I'm headed into Gaelach before I meet up with my brothers and your daughter. I will tell her where you are," Menolayous offered. "I see it in your eyes, I would advise against going and finding her. Whatever work she's done towards healing could be undone by your sudden reappearance. She needs to choose when to see you."

Farren nodded to Menolayous in thanks. "Menolayous, please tell my children I love them, and that I'm here."

"I will," Menolayous promised.

Part Two

Gaelach: Kingdom of Ruin

Chapter Thirty-Two

Clyous

Clyous remained hidden in the alleyway as he watched the Crown Prince of Oich slam Bridget's front door closed and take off in the direction of the castle. The prince looked pissed, at what exactly, Clyous was not sure. Clyous contemplated for a moment how hard it would be to take him on in a fight, that idea quickly vanished. He didn't stand a chance. Besides, if he knew his sister, once she got back to fighting speed the crown prince would find himself at the top of Catriona's list, and nobody deserved that kill more than her, he wouldn't pretend like he would take it from her.

What the crown prince was doing at Bridget's family home was a mystery, and honestly it had him a bit concerned. Once the crown prince was out of sight, Clyous cautiously strolled forward trying not to look overly suspicious. Taking a few steps, he stopped, seeing a trail of blood leading from the street to the front of the house, not in the same direction the prince had gone.

Bending down over a decent sized puddle of it, he took a deep breath. He had noticed recently that after the initial dream with the sorceress, seeing things from the past or even the future had become more frequent. His dreams were regularly haunted by images of things fated to happen. He had gotten so good at deciphering these images that he could see what was going to happen the next day. If he touched an object and concentrated hard enough, images from the last person who possessed the item flooded into his mind, showing him what they had done to leave the item there. This gift was a shock to him, so he had kept it to himself. Oich had banned magic decades ago, the only person he knew would understand was inside that house right now.

He had yet to try his gift out on blood before, might as well give it a shot. He reached down with his hand, fingertips lightly brushing the pool of blood. Images flooded into his mind like a high tide. He saw a man drinking his weight in spirits. He could see images of Bridget then, staring at this drunk man directly. Then the images turned violent, he watched the man physically beat Bridget bloody. As panic began to seize him the images changed again. The prince had stopped the man and was now beating him. The last of the images were of the man fleeing from the house holding his wrist with no hand attached to it.

Clyous blinked away the images then bolted for the house. As he neared the front door, he spotted a severed hand lying on the ground. The front door was unlocked; he entered the house. The foyer was a disaster, broken crates and scattered drops of blood everywhere.

"Bridget!" Clyous shouted, looking around for any sign of where she could be.

"Clyous?" her quiet voice came from somewhere upstairs. "What are you doing here?"

Clyous bolted up the stairs and down the hallway, allowing his panic to control his movements. An open door revealed Bridget sitting awkwardly on the edge of a bed. Dropping down to his knees before her, Clyous inhaled sharply at the sight. Her face was in terrible shape. Her normally perfectly styled hair was in disarray like someone had tried to rip it out of her skull. Her lower lip was split and still bleeding. One of her eyebrows was also split and bleeding heavily over an eye that looked mostly swollen shut. The beginning darkness of bruises covered the left side of her face. He noticed her arms were gently cradling her ribcage.

"What the fuck happened?" he didn't bother trying to keep the panic out of his voice.

"My father gets a certain way when he drinks." She attempted a half smile but winced. "Ow."

"This isn't the first time?" Clyous asked, but he already knew the answer, women were severely mistreated in this patriarchal society, blooded or not.

"No, but this is the worst," there was no shame in her voice as she spoke, just an internal strength at the admission. Good, there shouldn't be shame.

"What was the crown prince doing here?" Clyous did not know, and his curiosity was as strong as his concern.

"Liam stopped it." Shame was layered in her voice at the mention of his mortal enemy, clearly upset by their connection. "He must have heard it from outside and came in to stop it."

As gently as possible, Clyous took her by the hands, staring up into her only good eye. "Bridget, why was the Crown Prince of Oich outside your

220

house? And why do you call him by his first name? Why would the man who murdered my mother and tortured my sister step in to stop a father from beating his daughter?"

A single tear trickled out of her good eye. "Liam and I grew up together. We were inseparable as children. He had always been very protective of me, but a few years ago, things ended between us, and I hadn't seen him since then. He turned into a monster. The first time I saw him again was the day he killed your mother."

"It's okay." Clyous embraced her gently, processing this new information. "I'm not mad. You don't need to feel bad. I'm just trying to understand."

"I had hoped that when I stepped in, he would spare your mother. I was wrong. He wasn't the same Liam I remembered." She was crying now. "He showed up a week or so later, visiting me here after I had left you guys in the forest. That Liam is the one I knew, he was kind, familiar… He asked me to marry him."

Clyous's heart beat a little louder, trying to keep his voice free from any jealousy, "And what happened?"

"I never gave him an answer. Not until today. I could never be with anyone who tortures others and feels nothing. He keeps acting as if he owns me. I made it very clear to him that I wasn't his, that I'm sick of everyone making choices for me, claiming me. Nobody owns me!"

"That would explain why I saw him leaving in a huff." Clyous felt the relief wash over him, as selfish as that was. "Should we be worried he's going to come back to hurt you?"

"No. That's the one thing about him that has stayed the same. Liam will never hurt me, physically anyway."

Clyous nodded in understanding. "He loves you."

Bridget nodded. "I loved Liam, but Liam was the crown prince's first victim, I don't believe there's much of Liam left anymore."

"I understand that." Clyous gave her a small smile. "So, what's the plan?"

"What do you mean?"

"You're sitting here in front of me looking like freshly tenderized steak. You're alone in a house surrounded by enemies; do you really want to stay here alone while you heal? Albeit you'll heal faster than I would."

"What's the alternative?" Bridget sniffed, dabbing at her bleeding eyebrow with a wet cloth.

"Come back with me," Clyous pleaded. "Please. Let's go to Flinn's treetop city away from all these assholes."

A smile slowly spread across her lips. "Okay. I'll come with you."

Clyous smiled back, feeling relief. "Okay! Let me help you pack."

Clyous stood up, looking around the room for her traveling pack. Bridget stood, bringing his attention back to her. She was not particularly steady on her feet; she swayed as she stood. She wrapped her arms around him as he carefully wrapped his hands around her waist and soaked in her warmth. He couldn't begin to understand how happy he was holding her, knowing she was coming with him. How touching her, even as simply as this, brought him peace.

She gently kissed him on the cheek. "Thank you."

Chapter Thirty-three

Menolayous

The forest in which Menolayous stood was eerily empty of life. With the animals gone and the sound of the wind lifeless, fear crept into his heart. Spring was new, but the rains had begun to thaw the ground, everywhere except this forest. The air was as cold as the winter snows. This place was wrong, unnatural, backwards to what the world should be. Menolayous had dreaded coming this far into Gaelach. Having been lucky enough to escape its grasp years ago he never thought he'd need to come back, but an old friend needed his help, he could not ignore their disappearance, not in a place like this.

After dropping Markous off with his father, Menolayous wasted no time in heading to McKinlay's camp to see what traces of the warband he could find. When he got there the camp had been abandoned for some time, which was very concerning. It looked like there had been a battle within the boundaries of the small war camp. A struggle had ensued between the warring parties leaving many odd tracks in the frozen dirt. What was left of their tents was ripped to shreds, their supplies had been knocked over and scattered. Nothing seemed to have been taken, he noted, so it wasn't thieves. Then again, what typical band of thieves would be brave enough to take on a warband of McKinlay's size.

Menolayous circled the camp, examining the footprints that danced around the main tent. What Menolayous found odd was that there were no bodies left at this camp, no dried blood stains or body parts left to the elements. It was almost as if nobody had been killed in the camp during the fight. The more likely scenario was that someone had taken the bodies. With no obvious graves around the camp, this was concerning. There was no way every single one of them had escaped, the overwhelming amount of enemy paw prints and footprints indicated otherwise. There! He spotted what looked like drag marks leading out of the camp.

Menolayous did his best to follow the trail, after several hours he came up on what looked like an abandoned campsite, this one small and only a few days old. He did his best to analyze the tracks here, there were three distinctly human footprints around the camp. One set was large, carrying its weight evenly as it moved. This set of prints belonged to a man, a hunter, it was noticeable how little of an imprint he left. The other two were noticeably smaller, women he guessed. Dozens of blooded wolf prints trampled over the human prints. There had been a fight here, and the man and two women were dragged away, leaving plenty of dried blood stains in the dirt. Unlike McKinlay's camp they had at least caused damage to their attackers. It was possible McKinlay's camp was surprised in the night. But these three, they were waiting for the attack to come.

"They were taken to the ruins of the Moon God," a woman's voice came from the trees, startling him.

Menolayous drew back an arrow, rapidly scanning the trees for the owner of the voice. All he could hear was laughter echoing through the space around him.

"If I had wanted to kill you, I would have done so already," the voice came again, the Gaelach accent heavy in their words.

"Who are you?" Menolayous demanded in his native tongue, frustrated with himself for letting someone sneak up on him without notice.

A woman suddenly appeared beside him, stabbing the pointed end of her spear into the dirt, a Gaelach custom to show him she meant no harm. He lowered his bow, looking her over. She was beautiful in a bold and striking way, with sharp features that were almost birdlike. She was older than him by at least a decade, but her age did not take away from her shocking appearance. Her raven black hair was braided behind her in intricate patterns, falling to her hips in several strands. She wore all black leather armor with silver vambraces and shoulder guards. She wore strange black leather breeches that seemed to have a braided leather skirt over them that fell almost to the ground in length. Blue tattoos covered her pale flesh in swirls and patterns. She wore black warpaint across her eyes, making the amber color shine. Black crow feathers covered what she wore like an outer layer.

"I am Morrigan," the woman greeted, "Guardian of the Ancients. You speak my language?"

Slightly taken aback by her fierce appearance and her old Gaelach accent, he slowly answered, "I am Menolayous, Seeker of Truths, and right now seeker of my missing friends. You are using the old dialect; I'm a bit out of practice."

"Were these children of old your friends?" The woman held her arm out to the camp, switching to the more commonly used tongue.

"No, I don't think so." Menolayous looked around. "My friends were part of a warband that went missing months ago. Their camp was back that way."

Morrigan looked in the direction he pointed.

"They were taken to the same place the children of old are. The ruins are where the dark worshippers practice their magic."

"Have you seen them? Are they still alive?" Hope began to take hold in him as he looked at this strange woman.

"I have not been able to get into the encampment alone," she answered simply, her accent thick. "I assumed you might be interested in working together."

"Why would you assume that? What if I was more interested in handing you off to these dark worshippers?" He wasn't, but he needed to judge where her allegiance lies.

The woman threw her head back and laughed. "You are friends with the healer, no?"

"How do you know Bridget?" Suspicion took hold of him, and he started to raise his bow again.

"I saw you all at the little cave, with the healer and the fiery girl." Morrigan raised an eyebrow. "You will help me, because it will help them. And I will help you find the warrior men you seek."

"You've been following us? Why?" He now pointed the bow directly at her heart.

Menolayous watched her raise her palms to him in surrender. One side of her mouth ticked up in a smile as she stared into his eyes. Menolayous felt the wind start to pick up around him. The push and pull of the wind grew stronger as if he was now standing in the middle of a wind tunnel. Morrigan stood there staring at him unphased, her braids whipping around wildly behind her. Lightning cracked across the grey sky, shaking the ground with its thunderous presence. Suddenly, Morrigan swiped her palms down, and everything stopped. No more wind, no more lightning. It was like… magic. Old magic.

"I am Morrigan, Guardian of the Ancients, I protect children of the old and all forms of magic. Your friends are like me, as are the victims whose camp we stand in. Dark forces are emerging, threatening all of us. Help me free those who were taken, and I will help save your friends."

Not entirely sure what to make of this sudden show of power, Menolayous was able to project his voice out, "Which way?"

Morrigan smiled, pulled her spear from the ground, and started walking. Menolayous followed quietly. After an hour, Morrigan's pace seemed to slow. Menolayous could hear the sounds of a distant camp coming from the bottom of the gulch. As quietly as they could, they inched close to the edge of the hill, trying to peer over.

"If you're not careful they're going to see you," a woman's voice called out from behind them.

Menolayous jumped once again, swearing quietly, there was no possible way he had missed another person sneaking up on him. "What the fuck is it with you women and sneaking up on people?"

A woman now stood behind them, dressed in leather armor. This woman was gorgeous, her features a lot softer than Morrigan's, a lot less tribal. Unlike Morrigan, she was clearly not from Gaelach. He noted the full lips, tanned skin, and light brown hair that fell to her shoulders in waves. Menolayous was drawn to her striking bright green eyes, around her pupils were gold flecks. Her leather armor was specially designed to fit her curves, arguably too well. It would be considered scandalous in the Kingdom of Oich. She wore dark leather breeches and a fitted corset top. A grey tunic lay underneath the corset, but a leather jacket covered all of it, spiked shoulder pads and reinforced forearms lined the jacket. Only the money from the richest kingdom could buy such a specially crafted suit. Menolayous finished assessing her as it dawned on him that he was staring at her unabashedly. The younger woman took notice of his gaze, seemingly aware of his attraction to her appearance. With a smirk, the woman returned the stare, eyeing him up and down. Finally, her eyes met his, it felt like she was peering directly into his soul with how deeply she stared.

"It's like he's never seen magic before." The woman looked to Morrigan as if suddenly annoyed by his attention.

"He had the same reaction with me." Morrigan shrugged.

"Do you two know each other?" Menolayous asked, looking between the two.

"Our familiarity goes back a century." Morrigan eyed the woman appraisingly.

"Officially no, but since she is here, I'm assuming you're here to rescue me," the woman answered. "My name is Grace, Crown Princess of Airgid, Master of Woven Illusions."

"I am impressed by your projection." Morrigan walked around the woman checking her out like one would when appraising a horse. "The hair moves to the rhythm of the wind, impressive."

"Thank you." Grace smiled as if Morrigan had just complimented her outfit. "It's rather tricky really. The only reason why this is working so well is because I can see you."

"Where are you?" Morrigan looked back down in the direction of the camp.

"Tied to a post about one hundred yards in," Grace said. "What are you doing?"

Overcome with curiosity and against his better judgement, Menolayous walked up to Grace and reached forward to touch her arm. His hand went through her as if she were made of a cool mist. She wasn't real, she was nothing but fog and light.

"What the fuck?!" Menolayous pulled his hand back quickly, shaking it as if he were trying to shake off a spider.

"Did you really have to bring a stupid one?" Grace asked Morrigan, rolling her eyes in irritation. "It's like he's never seen magic before."

"I haven't! Except Bridget!" Menolayous snapped. "Magic is outlawed in Oich."

"Who's Bridget?" Grace asked Morrigan.

"Another child of old," Morrigan answered. "She's got the touch for healing, and she's moon blooded."

"Really?" Grace was curious. "I didn't think it was possible to be both."

"Apparently it is." Morrigan shrugged again as the two carried on with their conversation like he wasn't there.

"What are you?" Menolayous demanded, running his hand through Grace's body again.

Sighing as if placating a child, Grace answered him, "This is an illusion I wove with my magic. I can talk to you guys because I've reached out

227

and touched your minds, I can see you, but I can't touch you. As long as I can concentrate, I can keep up this illusion."

Menolayous stared at the illusion open mouthed. Grace looked at Morrigan again. "Men, am I right?"

"Indeed," Morrigan answered.

"What exactly is the plan here?" Menolayous was getting frustrated. "I'm not even sure what's going on here."

"I thought you came with him," Grace said.

"Correction. I found him. I figured he might be more helpful than asking these ridiculously obvious questions." Morrigan rolled her eyes. "I saw him with a pack, with three ancient blooded, I assumed he was familiar with how we worked."

"Three?" Menolayous chimed in. "I only knew of Bridget for sure."

"The other two must not have manifested yet," Grace pondered out loud. "Who are you then?"

"I'm Menolayous. Since you both are so interested in titles, I am one of three princes of the rebellion in Oich. Brother of Two Assholes."

"So, you're one of the brothers," Grace said, finally directing her attention to him as if he were the most interesting person in the world. "We've heard so much about the three of you."

"I didn't realize we were that famous." Menolayous smiled at her, why exactly, he wasn't sure. "Princess? What would the Crown Princess of Airgid be doing all the way out here, captured by Gaelach tribesmen?"

"It's sort of a long story, but the short version is that it's her fault." Grace pointed at Morrigan. "She sent out a call for help to every magic user in Stone Basin. She has located a dark magic user who has been weaponizing scourge and kidnapping those with the ancient bloodline. If he's not stopped, everyone in Stone Basin will die."

"That is the shorter version," Morrigan acknowledged. "I had hoped more of you would come. Your queen is of the old ways is she not?"

"Yes, but my mother wants to ensure the safety of Airgid first and foremost. I came with two others like me but they were captured."

"Are they still with you?" Menolayous asked. Grace's features changed to be morose.

"I only sense your light down there," Morrigan answered. "What happened?"

"He ate them," Grace answered. Menolayous could tell she was almost in tears. "He's capturing those with magic and eating them. After he does, it's like he's absorbed their powers for himself."

"You've seen him?" Morrigan asked. "Is he still there? I don't sense anything."

"No." Grace stilled herself, that arrogant mask sliding back into place. "But he'll be back soon. He has made it clear he can't wait to eat me, and not in the fun way."

"I literally have no words." Menolayous was blown away by these two women and all the information being thrown his way at once, it was like he was living in his nightmares.

"We need to get her out of there," Morrigan said, looking to Menolayous. "Now."

"Do we have a plan?" Menolayous asked, glancing back towards the camp.

"There are about twelve blooded down here. The rest went with him to another temple. They're supposed to be back by nightfall," Grace said. "I've been throwing my illusions at them all day, but they've started to ignore them."

"I could throw fire down on them," Morrigan offered.

"I vote no fire," Grace countered. "I don't feel like getting burned to death."

"Can you make me look like one of them?" Menolayous asked. "I could walk in there and cut you loose."

"They can sense if you are one of theirs," Morrigan warned. "The scent. You wouldn't be able to get close to them."

"You said they're just ignoring your illusions now, right?" Menolayous asked, an idea sparking.

"Yes, that's what's so fucking annoying," Grace said, seething. "Are you keeping up at all?"

"Can you make ten more of me?" Menolayous did his best to ignore the sass pouring out of the royal.

229

"Yes, but they can't—" Grace finally got it. "Oh! That could work."

"Make ten more of me. I'll sneak down there to you. You can make one of your distracting illusions while I cut you free."

"Someone put on their thinking cap." Grace smirked at him. "Guess you're not just a pretty face."

"Are you always like this?" Menolayous glared at her, willing the redness of his face to be hidden underneath his beard. It wasn't often a woman gave him a compliment, especially one that looked like her.

"Perfect, charming, a joy to be around. Why yes, yes I am." Grace smiled at him like a fox before pouncing on its prey. "As soon as this illusion fades there will be ten of you. Move fast. They've got me by the altar."

At that, Grace's illusion disappeared into nothing. Menolayous moved down the embankment towards the camp. Everything inside him protested at this overly direct entrance. This very well could be how he died, trying to help two very bizarre and demanding sorceresses. Fuck it, he had to die sometime, right? He kept a fast pace, praying to the gods this was not some trick to get him trapped by the cannibalistic blooded. Then he saw, well… him. Many perfect replicas of himself were now scattered throughout the camp. He hated to admit it, but he was impressed at how much detail she had noticed about him.

Menolayous was now running beside three solid looking versions of himself. He continued off towards the altar, running by several blooded tribesmen who were sitting around a campfire, drinking and playing a game with carved bones. The tribesmen glanced up at him as he walked past, the beasts' eyes roamed to all the other illusions before returning to their conversation. He could see his illusions breaking off down different walkways, screaming nonsense at the tribesmen. Doing their best to ignore the illusions, some of the men couldn't stop themselves from throwing things at the illusions out of frustration. Grace was good, he'd give her that.

There, he spotted the altar just after the tribesmen's fire pits. Menolayous spotted Grace who was tied to a post in the center of the sacrificial altar. She looked like she was deep in concentration, her emerald eyes cast skyward. Menolayous snuck up behind the post, pulling out his dagger.

"*Make it quick,*" Grace's voice echoed in his head, and he jumped for the third time today. "*Oh please get over it and cut the damn rope.*"

230

"You're rather unpleasant when you don't get what you want right away," Menolayous said back in his head, finding it impossible not to argue with her.

"Remember that next time I demand something from you," Grace's voice had changed pitch ever so slightly, like she was teasing him.

Finally, he cut the rope, freeing Grace from the post, allowing her to crawl down from the raised altar. Slowly, Grace stepped towards a wooden table, grabbing a whip and dagger before securing them on her person. Menolayous followed, glancing down the pathway, he spotted a corpse lying in front of one of the stone columns. The head of a young blonde woman lay on its cheek facing him, blank eyes staring at him. The rest of her body lacked significant chunks of flesh and meat, some bones completely lacking tissue save for some sinew still connecting the bone. It reminded him of a carcass after wild animals had been feasting on it for a few days. He felt bile rise up from the back of his throat, he had seen death before, killed people and animals. But this, this was wrong.

"That was Ingrid," Grace's voice echoed in his head, all traces of her teasing now gone.

"What happened to her?"

"The Dark One ate her, right after he ate Darragh," her voice was sad, her emerald eyes losing some of their shine as she spoke about the deaths of her friends. *"They came here with me. We thought we were laying a trap for them. We were so very wrong."*

"The blooded ate them?" Menolayous gagged, this was something he was unfamiliar with the tribesman doing, it must be part of some new ritual to worship the Moon God.

"No," Grace said, as she turned down a path. *"The Dark One isn't blooded. He's different."*

"A mist approaches," Morrigan's voice echoed through both of their minds. *"He is here! Run!"*

Menolayous and Grace burst into a sprint, aiming for the edge of camp. Morrigan was right, a wall of dark fog was creeping their direction, clicking sounds and bone chilling shrieks came from within. Several tribesmen stepped out onto the path blocking their way, forcing them to slow. Glancing behind them Menolayous saw several more tribesmen standing in front of their only escape route.

"Fuck!" Grace cursed as she began untangling her whip.

The fog neared, not twenty feet away now. Menolayous could feel the wind around them pick up like a storm was hitting. Lightning streaked across the sky, columns of it coming down and striking the blooded tribesmen. Menolayous and Grace raced forward, vaulting over the charred corpses. They made for the uphill path out of the basin. Lightning continued to strike down the tribesmen as the two of them fled. Menolayous could see Morrigan standing ahead of them with her hands up to the sky twisting her magic in every direction.

Darkness passed over them as Menolayous and Grace fled upwards, the sound of scourge tearing into the remaining blooded behind them pushed them harder up the embankment. They were almost to the top, just a few yards until they reached the powerful sorceress. The ground they were running on suddenly turned to ice, Menolayous could only watch as Grace's feet slid out from underneath her.

"He is here!" Morrigan's voice echoed over the wind, they were now close enough to talk.

"This was Ingrid's gift!" Grace cried, more out of sorrow than of pain. She allowed Menolayous to help her up.

"Go! Faster!" Menolayous helped push Grace up the remainder of the path, unwilling to let her regain her balance before moving again.

Finally, they had made it out of the gulch, scrambling up the path and reaching Morrigan. The sky was now black around them; the mist was surrounding them like a shroud. Sounds of the scourge echoed up from the bottom of the gulch, they were tearing through what was left of the tribesmen. Apparently, the scourge had no loyalty to the other followers of the Dark One. Menolayous watched as their breath spewed into the darkness like steam, feeling the icy fingers of the storm scraping up against his flesh. Ice shards began to creep up on them from the center of the gulch, driving them backwards. He was afraid, he realized as he readied his axe, he had never faced such an opponent. Glancing sideways it appeared the women felt the same.

A man emerged from the pathway, walking so casually it was out of place. This man was tall, possibly as tall as Rama. His arms and legs were long and muscular, but he remained slender in frame. He wore a cloak of black furs that dragged on the ground behind him, a bear head acting as the cloak's hood. Aside from the cloak and a long black hide loincloth, this man was naked. No shoes, no tunic, just bare skin covered in scars and black tattoos. The top half of his face was painted black and white, almost as if the war paint was intended to look like the top half of a skull. There was something unsettlingly familiar about this man, something setting off deeply hidden memories he had managed to keep locked away. The man smiled at them as he approached, two rows of sharpened teeth stood out against the dark of the paint. What stood out the most to Menolayous was that this man's eyes were visible through the fog and through the darkness, like a candle in the dark. They were a piercing bright red, almost the color blood would make if a light shone behind it.

"Going so soon?" The man's voice was layered, like several different people spoke at once. "Did we not make you comfortable enough, Princess?"

For the first time since they had met, Grace fell silent. Menolayous glanced over at her, her hands had a slight tremble to them. She looked absolutely terrified of this man. Her grip tightened on the hilt of her whip, seeking comfort in the knowledge that she held a weapon. He could understand this fear, the security her whip gave her. He found himself clutching his axe, finding the leather grip provided some comfort, even though Menolayous doubted it would do much to a sorcerer this powerful. The air around them seemed as lifeless as the forest, like this man's very being was the presence of death itself. Unlike Menolayous, Grace had been here watching her friends get devoured, and who knows what had befallen her during her captivity. Against his better judgement, Menolayous stepped in front of Grace, shielding her from the man's sight.

"Menolayous," the layered voice spoke to him now, red eyes flicking to him as he moved. "It has been some time."

"Do I know you?" Menolayous asked, trying to keep his focus on the enemy before him rather than attempting to rack his memory.

"You used to." The sharpened teeth smiled at him.

They could hear dozens of bodies dragging up the dirt path came into focus. The audible clicking from the scourge now coming towards them from behind the Dark One. The pale creatures stayed behind the ice wall created by this powerful sorcerer as if waiting for the command to attack like well-trained hounds. It was like they were intelligent enough to understand what was expected of them.

"Are the voices in which you speak the voices of all your victims?" Morrigan chimed in, glaring up at this imposing creature, not an ounce of fear shown on her older face.

"I would love nothing more than to add your voice to the collection, Guardian of the Ancients. One so powerful as you would ring above all the others, a prize to be had."

"Nothing that is mine shall ever be yours." Morrigan seethed, stepping forward with her spear extended in front of her. "I will claim justice for all the children of old whose very essence you have taken."

The man smiled at her now, slowly lowering himself into a crouch. "You may try."

"*Grab my body and run!*" Morrigan's voice echoed through their heads. "*Do not let this abomination feast on me.*"

"*Wait what?*" Menolayous thought back, stepping to the side to draw attention away from Morrigan. "*What are you planning?*"

"*Girl!*" Morrigan snapped. "*Make it black as soon as I unleash my magic upon him. You both have to act fast. I will likely lose consciousness after releasing the amount of energy I am about to.*"

"How exactly do I know you?" Menolayous asked the man, who had now thankfully turned his eyes back to him as he moved.

"*Girl!*" Morrigan snapped.

"*Yes, I heard you!*" Finally, Grace responded, pulling herself out of her thoughts.

"*Do not let fear kill us now,*" Morrigan said. "*You know how to deal with burnout?*"

"*Yes, of course,*" Grace answered.

"Dig deep into your memories, and you'll find me." The Dark One smiled at him, sending shivers down his spine. "My appearance has changed since we last spoke."

"*Good,*" Morrigan said. "*Now!*"

Morrigan thrust her spear in the air, sending a ball of electricity into the sky. Menolayous stumbled back as the force from the magic hit like a wall. The lightning bolts struck out at the Dark One, knocking him over with such force he flew back several feet. As the scourge broke rank and lunged for them, Morrigan pushed a wave of red and orange flame out of her hands, knocking back the scourge that charged. Grace sprang forward, waving her hands in the air as she made for Morrigan who had now collapsed. Menolayous could not understand it. The scourge were now cowering on the ground, shrieking as if in pain. The Dark One also was not standing, instead clasping his ears against some magical entity.

"They can't see or hear!" Grace bit out, dragging Morrigan backwards. "All they can see is black and all they hear is high pitched screaming. Help me with her."

Shaking out of his stupor, Menolayous shot forward, scooping Morrigan's limp body up into his arms. Grace quickly wrapped her whip around her waist then picked up Morrigan's spear. Together they ran towards the woods, back in the direction of the old campsite. They needed to make distance; they needed to get away from the Dark One and his monsters. They ran as fast and hard as they could. Luckily, Morrigan's dead weight did not slow him down too much as he traipsed through the brush. Fear drove them on, Grace nearly as frantic as prey fleeing from a wild animal, desperate to get away. They would be lucky if they survived until nightfall, or to the next morning. Especially with these creatures hunting for them.

"Until next time," the Dark One's voices echoed in their heads, *"Princess."*

Chapter Thirty-Four

Catriona

Without the availability of horses, it had taken them almost four days of non-stop walking to finally reach the run-down windmill. Catriona was breathing heavily as she finally made it up the last grassy knoll. As far as she was concerned that road and the last four days of traveling could fuck off. Rama stood ahead of her, staring at the collapsed ruins of a windmill as if it were the most fascinating thing he could be looking at. Danny came up beside her, doing his best to hide a smile at how out of breath she was.

"What's so funny?" Catriona glared at him as she started removing her pack.

"Nothing." Danny threw his hands up in surrender.

"I have never been good at long distances, or hills," she argued, enjoying the weight of the pack off her shoulders.

"You'll need to work on that," Rama called back to her as he walked to the other side of the fallen turbine. "Your huffing and puffing will make anything requiring stealth impossible."

She flipped him off, finally able to slow down her breathing. Danny chuckled softly walking past her.

"I like it when you breathe heavily," he said to her quietly, giving her a wink.

Catriona was thankful for the fact that her face was already red from the exertion of walking up the hill. Danny grabbed her pack off the ground and shouldered it before going to stand next to Rama. Catriona reluctantly followed after sucking down a few deep breaths, she was trying to figure out what exactly they were looking for.

"How much farther is this camp?" Catriona asked, looking around at the forest.

"We're here," Danny answered simply, glancing down at her.

Rama put his hands to his mouth, mimicking a bird call in the direction of the forest. This was a similar bird call she had heard them use while on the road, she shouldn't be surprised that others may also be privy to this unique form of communication. The three of them stood there for a moment before an identical bird call echoed back to them. A teenage boy stepped out of the woods, waving to them happily in greeting.

"Hello Connor!" Rama called, walking towards him.

"Rama, Danny!" Connor greeted them warmly. "And your friend?"

"I'm Catriona." She smiled at him; he seemed friendly enough that she would at least try not to scare him away first thing.

"You're her!" Connor looked at her excitedly. "Clyous's sister?"

"Yeah," she answered awkwardly, glancing at Danny who shrugged.

"Is it true?" Connor was practically bouncing with excitement.

"Is what true?" she asked nervously.

"That you can take on blooded single-handedly?"

"I don't know about th—" she started.

"It's true." Rama laughed, enjoying the irritated look she shot in his direction.

"Did you really take on the city guards?" Connor asked.

Starting to get annoyed at being interrupted, she answered, "Yes but—"

"I heard the only one who was able to stop you was the crown prince himself!"

"Connor!" Danny shouted at the young man just enough to be heard above the young boy's excited questioning. "Enough, okay? We're all tired from traveling."

"Oh." Connor glanced from Danny to Catriona. "Sorry. Of course, follow me."

Catriona glanced at Danny, thankful for the intervention. The last thing she felt like doing right now was reliving that day with a complete stranger. Connor seemed nice enough, a very young man nearly out of boyhood. She was sure he meant no harm by his questions, she just didn't feel ready to talk about that with anyone other than Danny.

"So, Connor." Rama seamlessly slid into the awkward silence that now lay heavily between them all. "How has it been since I last stopped by?"

237

"Great!" Connor seemed happy enough for the change of topic. "Flinn has had us working on expanding the village. We just finished adding to the eastern wall. Having Clyous here has been a big help. He can fix our tools on site."

"Where is my brother?" Catriona asked as they walked, she had missed him terribly.

"He went into the capital city for some supplies. I heard he's got himself a woman there, so I expect he'll be gone for at least another day or so. I myself just came back with some medical supplies." Connor seemed proud of himself. "My first solo run."

Catriona, Rama, and Danny shared a knowing glance, Clyous had gone to see Bridget. Danny flashed her a mischievous smile, she had no doubt in her mind that Danny would be doing the same if she was still within the city. After another minute or so they found themselves underneath what appeared to be a treetop village.

"Whoa… you weren't kidding," Danny said, staring up at the walkways.

"Daniel," a voice called from the base of the trees. "It's about time you pulled yourself out of that dark wet cave and rejoined us here."

Rama snickered at the comment, earning an elbow in the stomach from Danny.

"Flinn!" Danny called out to a large slightly greying red-haired warrior, stretching his arms out wide at the approach of the older man.

Catriona watched as the two men embraced in greeting before Flinn embraced Rama. Men suddenly began to appear behind the trees, emerging from the huts or on the pathways above. They were all curious, she realized, all staring at the new arrivals. She noticed there were no women as she glanced around. Every man here was outfitted like a soldier, most wearing weapons and leather armor as they moved about. This wasn't just a hidden treetop city, this was a hidden fortress, and the rebel warband was coming out to greet them.

"And you must be Catriona." Without warning and completely caught off guard, Catriona found herself wrapped up in a smothering bear hug from the old war chief.

"Catriona, this is Flinn." Rama laughed as Flinn set her back down on the ground. "He's an old friend of ours and the chief of this warband."

"Pleased to meet you." Catriona flashed the man a smile.

"Pleasure is all mine, lass. Welcome to Collie, our hidden treetop paradise." Flinn gestured upward towards the tree houses. "You are all welcome here for as long as you wish."

"Actually, we were hoping to set up residence with you and your warband for a while," Rama spoke to the old warrior. "We figured you could use a few new swords."

Cheers of excitement rang throughout the warriors at Rama's words. Catriona watched in surprise at how happy the warriors were to hear they were staying. Flinn cracked a huge smile at the sight of his men in celebration, the old war chief refocusing his attention on Rama.

"Even if I wanted to object, it appears I would be outvoted on the matter." Flinn's laugh was contagious. "Just because you are the leader of this rebellion doesn't mean you're in charge of my camp, don't you be forgetting that."

"We're here to help, besides, I promised Catriona I would help her settle a debt between her and the crown prince. We may be here for a while."

Understanding seemed to hit the warrior as he glanced at her for a moment. "Of course. We're at your disposal, Your Highness. I'll find some accommodations for you boys. I'm sure I could find the lass her own private quarters."

She felt Danny's arm gently wrap around her waist, pulling her close to him. "Don't worry about it, I'll share with Catriona."

"Oh really?" Catriona whirled on him, irritation at the sudden declaration that she was his. "And you just decided this?"

Staring down at her, he answered as if leaving no room for argument, "Yes."

She squared up on him, not caring that everyone was starting to pay attention to their conversation. She did not know them, so she didn't care. Not sure if she was more irritated or shocked at his decision, it was a decision they had yet to discuss. She did not want to be owned, she had spent her entire life as a slave. She was not someone's property, no matter how many times they fucked. She could feel the desire to battle, the overwhelming urge to fight with him. After processing it for a moment, she realized not only was this Danny she was preparing to annihilate, but they were sort of a couple now. Rama had practically stated as much the moment he saw them in that cave. Ultimately, this sort of public declaration for each other would have

239

happened regardless of the fact they were standing in the middle of a rebel camp, so what did it truly matter that he announced it. Still, like every challenge she faced, especially with Danny, she refused to back down just because this was an inevitability.

"Is that so?" She straightened to her full height, looking him in the eye.

Flinn looked at Rama, both men holding back their laughter. The problem with Danny was that he didn't back down either. A smirk played at the corner of his mouth as he stared into her eyes, he was loving every minute of this, the jerk.

"You'd better sleep with one eye open Daniel or this honey badger might bite off your hand," Flinn joked, stepping towards him, effectively breaking the tension. "Come on, let's say hello to the lads. They've missed having you."

Flinn steered Danny towards a group of warriors who greeted him cheerfully. Everyone here seemed to know him, to like him. It wasn't that she was shocked or anything like that, Danny was very charismatic. It was more about the fact that there were so many of them that greeted him like a respected commander. To her, he wasn't old enough for this kind of reaction from older warriors. Then again, he had been doing this since he was very young. He had been involved in this rebellion for just over ten years.

"I told you." Rama came to stand next to her. "He's your problem now."

"I've gathered that," she said, sighing and looking up at him. "I just wish that was a discussion, not a demand."

"That was on purpose." Rama chuckled. "Most of the men here haven't seen their women in months or haven't been around anyone other than their brothers in arms. There's bound to be a few dumb enough or lonely enough to try chasing after you."

"I can handle myself," she argued.

"And now they've all seen it. Not only did they see your fire, but they saw his. He wanted to send a warning."

Catriona could understand that, and respect it to a degree, but she wasn't interested in any of them, he was it for her. Glancing around, she took note once again of the lack of women present, weighing the truth of Rama's words. She also caught a few of the men casting quick glances at her before returning to their tasks. Maybe Danny had a point to make this such a spectacle, this many men she did not know was making her uncomfortable.

"They all seem to love him," she changed topics, trying to focus on something else.

"He's a well-respected warrior. He has spent more time directly fighting with the different warbands than Menolayous or I. He has bled with most of them. He actually got captured many years ago trying to lead raids on some of the outer forts."

"Really?" Catriona looked at him, stunned.

"Really." Rama chuckled. "They threw him into one of the nearby forts' cages, thinking he was running the rebellion alone. Flinn sent word to us, Menolayous and I had to bust him out. He was so mad that we didn't let him figure it out on his own, he hardly spoke to us for a week, except for the occasional insult."

"It's hard to remember that you're all still young."

"We started this rebellion at too young of an age. It's taken its toll on each of us but in different ways. It's made us grow up too fast."

"I'm assuming that's why they keep calling you three by royal title?" She smirked. "Do they mean it as a joke or are they serious?"

"We mean it as a joke." Rama started walking towards Flinn and Danny. "They mean it."

"If Danny was busy doing the fighting, what did you and Menolayous do?"

"Staying with a warband for too long would start to affect Menolayous. So, he would go out and try to find more people interested in fighting or find people who needed help. I, on the other hand, have a way with words. I spent a lot of my time making friends and organizing the different warbands across Oich."

"How can Menolayous be with you and Danny if he can't stand to be around this many people for long? He can barely stand the group we had without finding reasons to run off."

"You're pretty observant." Rama chuckled.

"I've had to survive living in the capital. It wasn't an easy life, regardless of having money."

Rama sighed. "He can't stand staying with the warbands for long. He's very distrustful of people, especially this many men. If he does stay, he finds somewhere hidden outside camp."

"And you don't know why he's like that? Either of you?" Catriona asked.

"I have never asked, but I have my suspicions. You're one of the first to notice that there's a reason behind it. Most just look at him like he hates people or is an odd bird."

"It takes a woman's perspective sometimes," she mumbled, mostly due to watching the nearby men maneuver around them.

"What do you mean?" Rama asked, staring at her curiously.

She sighed, "Men don't usually have to worry about the same things women do. From a young age girls are taught to be careful around men, not to be alone with strangers and not drink too much in places where you could be easily taken advantage of. Those who aren't careful end up changed. They avoid groups of men especially, distrust all they don't know, hide, and especially don't like being touched. I see it all the time in the capital from neighboring girls. I've never heard it happening to a boy, but I imagine living with it afterward would be similar."

Rama froze as if he'd just been hit in the head by her words. Catriona stopped to watch him, had she gone too far? Had she crossed some sort of line? Rama looked as if he was now trapped inside his head working out a particularly hard problem. To Catriona it was an obvious assumption if one looked hard enough. Maybe she was right, that men wouldn't even begin to think that way, and maybe that meant she was right about why Menolayous acted that way, and more pieces of the puzzle began to fit together for Rama about his adopted brother.

"You look like you broke him," Danny said, coming up to them staring at Rama.

At the sound of Danny's voice, Rama seemed to come out of his thoughts, a mask of casual collectiveness now sliding into place. "Just trying to do some quick calculations on an empty stomach."

"Yeah, I'm pretty hungry myself." Catriona used those magic words to redirect Danny's attention back to her, away from his brother.

"Let's find some food then." Eager to accommodate Catriona's willingness to eat, he directed them forward.

Rama gave her a look that said, "thank you," she nodded. Together, the three of them went to an area that seemed to be designed for preparing large meals and for the warriors to sit together and eat it. There were at least six large tables strewn about next to a covered fire pit. Catriona was promptly handed a roll of bread, some cheese, and what smelled like pheasant. Aside from the smoked rabbit, she hadn't eaten cooked meat yet. She eyed it suspiciously as the others sat down with Flinn and Connor, engaging in conversation about the news from the capital city.

Danny kept glancing at her as she just sat there staring at the dead bird on the wooden plate. She had been eating meat, this was no different, she needed to take a bite so Danny could stop worrying. Her mouth dried up and her heart started pounding. She focused on her breathing just as Danny had taught her, slow and deep breaths through her nose. She could do this. She picked up a leg and took a small bite. She focused on chewing quickly. She had this.

"With how small she is, I'm surprised she's not tearing that bird to pieces," Flinn joked. "We've got plenty more for the lot of you. Eoin is the camp cook, the lad does a fine job with the food. You can really taste the flavor. His trick is he puts the birds on spikes and slowly roasts them over a fire. As the meat begins to cook and all the juices start to come out, he adds his seasoning. He cooks them to perfection. Of course, I ask him to keep mine on a little longer, I love the skin a little charred."

The smell of the fire rushed from her memories into reality. Burning flesh, the screams, the heat from the blaze that took her mother. She felt the world shattering blows from the whip slice into her back once again. She was up in a flash, moving past everyone to a nearby bush where she retched up what little amount of pheasant she had gotten down earlier.

"Is the lass alright?" she could hear Flinn ask from the table.

"It's complicated," she heard Rama say as she vomited again.

She felt Danny beside her, gently trapping the plait of her hair underneath his hand on her mid back. Tears streamed out of her eyes as she tried to concentrate on breathing. She hated this, this weakness. The cooking of meat should not send her running every time. Flinn was right, she was still on the smaller side, she should be eating more protein. She could feel that her tunic had ridden up, exposing her lower back, it was too big for her to fit properly. Although she was thankful she wasn't as small and frail as she had been when she stopped eating all together, there had been improvement, but not enough.

243

She knew everyone was watching her now, Flinn, Connor, the other warriors. Fighting with Danny right from the beginning and now this, yes, she was making great first impressions. Danny's hand gently circled her back trying to help soothe her, it was working. She felt the skin of his fingertips brush the flesh of her back, her stupidly oversized shirt, it had ridden up pretty far as she had bent over. She heard collective gasps from the men nearby. She froze in panic, Danny's hand stopped moving.

"Look at her back!" she heard Connor whisper loudly, then what sounded like someone hitting him across the back of the head. "Ow."

Shame and embarrassment flooded through her, they were seeing the scars. She stood quickly, tugging down her tunic and stuffing it into her breeches once again. Danny's hand dropped away but he still stood there next to her. He looked her in the eyes as she glanced at him. His emotions at this point were unreadable, but she knew he was giving her the space she needed to either run or stand strong. She loved him for that, as well as the fact that if she asked, he would step in.

"Go on!" she heard Flinn bark at the men. "You've all got jobs to do. Get to them."

The warriors all departed, giving Catriona another moment to right herself. When she turned back around all that remained at the table were Flinn and Rama. Connor had disappeared, as did the other men who had sat with them. She could see some of them in the background returning to their duties. Catriona sat back down, taking a drink of... ale? Someone had put a cup of ale down for her. She glanced up at the old warrior who gave her a look like he understood her.

"My apologies, lass," Flinn started. "Connor is still young and foolish. He meant no disrespect."

"It's fine," she hoped her voice came across as strong. "Thank you for the food. I'm sorry—"

"There's no need for apologies from you, lass." Flinn moved a pitcher of more ale closer to her. "Some of us, especially those of us who are older and have lived a little more, carry our own scars. Some fresher than others, and others as young as Connor who have yet to earn any."

"Earn?" Catriona looked at him, he spoke of her scars strangely.

"I might have been a slave in Oich like most of these men. If my accent hasn't betrayed me, I'm not from this land. I came from a different land at age ten, washed up on the shores of a fishing village some thirty years ago when my ship was capsized by a storm. Oich was strange to me for many reasons, but I was stuck here, never again able to return to my homeland." Flinn smiled at her warmly. "Back in my homeland, women fought side by side with the men. They were ferocious and skilled in war, and just like the men, our maidens earned their scars. They wore their scars proudly. It showed the world that they had faced great enemies and lived. Scars showed strength and were considered beautiful."

Catriona sat there for a moment, processing this gift the older man had just given her. He understood, and he was giving her a different way to look at herself. There was power behind this perspective, an inner strength. She reached forward, placing her hand on his and giving it a squeeze. The war chief squeezed back, lifting her hand to the bushiness of his moustache and kissing it gently.

"Come on. I think by now they've ought to have found you some lodging." Flinn stood, leading the three of them out of the eating area towards the trees.

Danny snagged the bread and cheese from her plate, handing them to her. Dutifully, she ate as they walked through the few huts that remained on the ground. Men were moving about and working on their daily tasks. She caught a few glances in her direction, and some whispers. Danny, seeing this, threw an arm over her shoulder as they walked. He glared at some of those men who whispered, sending them scurrying back to their chores.

They finally neared a group of four tall ash trees. Looking up through the branches and leaves, she could see small wooden houses built into each. There were rope bridges that spanned across the open space, connecting to each tree. There were also rope ladders that hung down from each tree, allowing entry into the homes through what looked like a door in the floor.

"Here you go." Flinn gestured upward. "Three of these are empty. That far one over there houses our mutual friend Clyous. There are no other homes that connect to this grove of trees so it will give you all some privacy."

"Thank you," Catriona, Danny, and Rama said at once.

Flinn laughed. "My pleasure. I've got to go check on the food smoking in the hut, so if you need me, I'll be working on the wooden frame."

They waved their farewells as the old war chief stalked off. Rama and Danny shared a look before glancing upward again.

"I've never lived in a treehouse," Rama said, examining each one. "I've always been too big for the branches to hold me."

"If Flinn built them I'm sure you'll be fine. He's a master carpenter." Danny smirked at him.

"It's not just that." Rama tugged on one of the rope ladders curiously. "I'm not sure I can fit through the opening in the floor."

Danny burst out laughing as Rama turned red. Rama stuck his middle finger out at his brother in irritation.

"How about this one?" Catriona called, standing underneath one of the rope ladders. "The hole in this one looks exceptionally large. Maybe Flinn designed it for your big head."

"Ha ha, so funny," Rama grumbled, walking over. "Although that idea isn't too far off. I'll try this one."

"Okay." Danny just stood there with crossed arms and a smile on his face. "I'll watch."

"Get fucked!" Rama snapped.

Catriona took Danny by the hand, trying to pull him away. "Come on, let's find which one we're going to stay in."

"In a minute. I want to see him get stuck." Danny laughed at Rama's expression.

Catriona stood on her toes, intentionally pressing her body against his as she whispered, "It's been a few days since we've had any time to ourselves."

The look of lust in Danny's eyes was enough to send subtle shivers of arousal between her thighs. It had been a few days since they hit the road with Rama. Catriona hadn't felt like facing the jokes and teasing that would ensue if she and Danny had snuck off together every night. It wouldn't be sneaking away anyway if two of the three travelers weren't at the camp. There had been one night when they thought Rama had fallen asleep early. Since they had been sleeping next to each other it didn't take long for Danny's hand to slip underneath her breeches and start to rub her between her legs. It took less than a minute after that before Rama loudly reminded them that he was a light sleeper, promptly ending any and all nighttime activities.

Danny, now ignoring his brother, took her by the hand and led her to the farthest treehouse of the four. He held onto the bottom of the rope ladder to stabilize it, gesturing for her to climb up and she did. As she made it to the top she paused, looking up into the hole in the floor. Reaching inside, she found a handle and began to pull herself in.

She had managed to get her upper torso through before she felt Danny's hand on her inner thigh, gently pushing her through faster and at the same time intentionally turning her on more. He had come up beside her so quickly she had jumped at his touch, now she sat on the floor of this treehouse with Danny quickly pulling himself through the opening. He tossed his pack off to the side before reaching down and undoing the straps to hers. She was now lying on her back, he wasn't even giving her the chance to move out of the way or sit up. As soon as he had freed her pack, he reached back to shut the door to the opening in the floor.

Then he was on her, eagerly opening her legs with his hands and pulling her to him as he pressed the hardness of his cock against her center. The ache down below struck the moment he put himself between her legs. Their lips met as his hands tangled in her hair pulling out her braid. She reached down, pulling his tunic up and over his head. He then did the same to her, exposing her breasts to him.

"You want to know something?" he asked, before taking one of her nipples into his mouth, swirling around it with his tongue.

"What?" she gasped, fighting off the desire to moan loudly as he now teased her nipple with his teeth.

She glanced around the room quickly, that's all it was, a room. She did not have high hopes the wooden walls would do anything to conceal sound. She just might die of embarrassment. Another graze of teeth against the sensitive tip of her breast brought her focus back onto Danny.

"Everything Flinn said was right." Danny switched over to her other nipple with his mouth while one of his hands took control, brushing the other in gentle circles.

"You're going to have to elaborate." Catriona breathed heavily. "I'm a little distracted."

"Distracted is good," he murmured against her skin, "but I'm being serious."

"Then you're going to seriously stop distracting me." She tried to wiggle away, but he grabbed both of her wrists with one hand, pinning them above her head. "That's not helping."

"Oh, I think it is." He gently bit her lip. "You're going to have to stop trying to seduce me and listen now."

"Really? I'm the one seducing you?" She tried to wiggle free again but couldn't.

"Every time you move like that it makes me want to jump straight to fucking you, so yeah you are." He growled as she did it again. "Stop for a second please."

"Fine." She stopped, he didn't let go of her at all.

"Flinn was right about your scars." Danny's face was serious. "You shouldn't be embarrassed about them. They're nothing to be ashamed of."

"I don't want to talk about them." She tried to move for real this time, he held her firmly. "Danny, I don't."

"You're going to, whether you want to or not." Danny stared down at her. "Unless you can actually get out of this, which I'm realizing now you can't, you're going to hear what I have to say about it before you hide in your own head."

"Fine." She squirmed again. "As fun as this started, I've got to say, you can be a major mood killer."

"If you like being pinned down or tied up I will happily accommodate afterward." That playful look returned to his eyes. "You are beautiful, even with your scars. They do nothing to change how beautiful you are. And they are nothing to be ashamed of. You survived something most people wouldn't have. You chose to keep fighting and you survived. You should be proud of yourself."

"I don't feel proud," she answered, finally giving up the struggle. "I didn't win. My mother is dead, and I let him hurt me."

"Surviving is winning, Cat," Danny said softly.

A single tear slid down her cheek towards the ground. Danny licked it up with his tongue, causing her to squeal and turn away from him.

"That is so gross!" She laughed, still not able to wiggle away from him completely.

"You don't think it's gross when I lick you down here." He popped the first button on her breeches. "You seriously can't get out of this?"

"No!" She sighed heavily in frustration. "I've never been good at ground fighting. I'm fast, I'm not strong. As long as I can keep moving I do fine, but if someone can get me to the ground, I'm done for."

"Hmm…" Danny popped the next button on her breeches. "Sounds like that's what we need to work on. Can't have other men being able to put you on your back."

"Someone almost sounds jealous."

"Incredibly possessive too." He kissed her throat, reaching his hand down to cup her underneath her hide breeches. "I'm the only one who gets you like this from now on."

He began to rub her, spreading around the wetness that had started flowing again. She inhaled sharply at the feeling, finally relaxing enough to open her legs further apart for him.

"What if another guy comes around with a bigger cock?" she teased.

Danny plunged his fingers inside her, immediately curling them in that way that made her arch her back with pleasure.

"I don't need a bigger cock to make you come," he whispered in her ear. "Want to see?"

She nodded her head yes, biting on her lip to try and keep from moaning loudly. There would never be another, she knew it and he knew it, but it was fun to challenge him nonetheless. Another wave of pleasure shot through her as his fingers worked.

She could vaguely hear the distant sound of birds outside. Danny stilled at the noise, like he was listening for more. Frustration set in as she stared at him, wanting him to keep going. Why had he stopped?

"Hey, love birds!" Rama's voice called from the ground beneath them. "Put your clothes on, we've got company."

Shit, they had made it obvious hadn't they, embarrassment took over. Danny pulled away from her, grabbing his tunic and handing hers to her. She reluctantly redressed herself, still irritated at the interruption.

"What's going on?" she complained.

"We don't use alarm bells here or have howls like the blooded guards. We communicate with animal calls. Bird calls mean there's a visitor approaching."

Chapter Thirty-Five

Grace

"So, the blonde's twin, who's sleeping with the redhead, is the other one with magic?" Grace stared at an increasingly frustrated Menolayous, she couldn't help herself, this was too much fun. "But the blonde doesn't know she has magic?"

"I believe an easier way to say that is the twins have magic," Morrigan said dryly, the older woman was also losing patience with her.

"The blonde's name is Catriona. Her brother is Clyous, and neither of them know." Menolayous grimaced, his patience starting to disappear.

"I don't get it. How can the redhead know but the twins not know? Regardless, even if it's outlawed, magic sparks whether you want it to or not. They had to have had some sort of incident, even as children that would have marked them as ancient blooded. Something has got to be hampering with their magic." Grace was being difficult on purpose, but she was genuinely curious at how two grown adults hadn't come into their magic yet.

They had been traipsing through the thick forests of Gaelach for several days, desperate to escape the reach of the tribesmen and this so-called Dark One. They barely stopped long enough to catch some sleep, let alone have enough time to make a proper meal. They had been harvesting berries and mushrooms on the move, eating as they pushed through the thick brush. Finally, as of earlier this morning, they crossed back into Oich territory. This was the first time they had actually stopped to make camp.

During their escape, she realized she had grown to like Menolayous. Within their few interactions anyway, he was not the talkative type. Out of everyone she had been surrounded by in Airgid, she didn't trust any of them to not have an ulterior motive when it came to how they interacted with her. Menolayous was different, he didn't seem to care what her status was in Airgid, the last few days all he cared about was getting both women to safety. He cared about Morrigan's survival about as much as her own, not treating them differently. Even after he had learned the men he was searching for had passed at the hands of this new enemy, he continued to protect them. He seemed driven more by honor than he did by the promises of success. In fact, when Menolayous had placed himself between her and the Dark One, she knew in that moment without a doubt he would lay down his life to make sure she was able to escape, and they didn't know each other. Truthfully, he seemed too good to be true, too real. There had to be something hidden within him that proved he was just as selfish as everyone else she had ever met. She was wary about forming a strong attachment to him until she could figure out what that was. So, she did what she always did when trying to figure someone out, she aggravated them. Only when someone was truly angry would they reveal who they were behind their mask.

"The King of Oich has been tracking down and burning ones of the ancient bloodline alive. It is outlawed to have magic in your blood there, the only person who could have helped the twins manifest anything wasn't there. The ability to touch and heal manifests through need, the blooded easily could have needed to use her magic," Morrigan cut in again, annoyingly so.

"And they don't know that their father is alive?" Grace narrowed her eyes at Menolayous.

"No," Menolayous said flatly, staring back at her unimpressed.

"And the blonde girl is fucking your brother who is also blonde. Or was it the giant?" Grace continued to push, wanting to see how far she could in fact push this quiet and reserved man.

"Giants have not walked this land for hundreds of years," Morrigan corrected, sharpening the blade of her spear. "Only the sons and daughters of the Mountain God remain."

"They're not together," Menolayous's voice began to rise. "Maybe they are now, I don't know. I've been stuck here with you the whole damn time."

"So, the giant isn't fucking anyone?" Grace smirked at him.

"Giants no longer live," Morrigan corrected.

"Yes, thank you," Grace brushed her off. "But seriously, how big is his—"

"Why do you enjoy being such a pain in the ass?!" Menolayous yelled at her from across the campfire, finally snapping.

"It's fun to make you mad." She laughed, finally satisfied at getting an outburst from him. Surprisingly, his face was still the same. There wasn't a flicker of anything from behind his mask, maybe there wasn't one after all. "Sorry, I'll stop. Please continue with all the group's backstories. Why am I joining up with them again?"

"In order to defeat the Dark One, we must join forces with more of the ancient bloodline. The fiery girl and the blooded healer have the brightest lights I have seen yet," Morrigan answered.

"Good for them." Grace rolled her eyes, jealousy prickling at her ever so slightly.

"If you tell Rama everything you know and have seen, he will help you," Menolayous explained, lowering the volume of his voice. "Rama wants to help people, not fight for a throne. The Dark One is capturing people with ancient blood and waging war against everyone in Stone Basin. He will redirect the rebellion to help."

"And you just know factually that this gentle giant is going to stop everything he's doing and go after the Dark One," Grace's voice was laced with sarcasm.

"He's my brother. I know him better than anyone." Menolayous furrowed his eyebrows. "If you don't like it, you are welcome to go back to Airgid, Princess. Use caution crossing back through Gaelach territory, I will not be coming to save you again."

Menolayous stared her in the eye with the challenge. She smiled at him with the most innocent expression she could muster. She knew that she could not go back home without help, she would not risk being trapped again, not by that monster. Still, all that bravado Menolayous was projecting out towards her was false. She knew that he would come for her again if she was captured, she could feel it in his energy. As irritating as she had been since he rescued her the first time, she had grown on him. She could sense this and also sense that he was a good man. He probably would try to stop her if she did try to turn around and go home. She was more surprised by this revelation as she read him from across the camp, she had never met anyone so genuine.

"I agree with this plan." Morrigan set down her spear. "With the Dark One gaining the powers of those he devours, he will be unstoppable soon. We will need allies."

"Alright, fine!" Grace threw her hands up in surrender. "How far away from their camp are we?"

"We'll make it there by midday tomorrow if we leave at first light," he answered, sounding somewhat defeated, she may have pushed him too far tonight. She could see the remorse coming off him in waves, he regretted his outburst.

She knew deep down that she could be a difficult person, and truthfully, she loved nothing more than to rattle people but she could tell when she pushed too far and right now, she could see the mental exhaustion had hit Menolayous like a blow to the head. She needed to stop, being bored wasn't an excuse to push someone past their limits. She had seen what she had needed to see. Even now, Menolayous was proving to be very kind and had been nothing but a gentleman.

She hated to admit it but the few hours of shut eye she managed to get these last few days had been riddled with nightmares. Ever since their escape from the ruins of the Moon God, every time she shut her eyes she relived her experiences there. How she, Ingrid, and Darragh had been dragged to the ruins and tied to a post like cattle. How the tribesmen had beaten them until the Dark One arrived. Darragh's and Ingrid's screams and that monster strapping them down to his altar, it all replayed in her mind over and over again. She could still feel his hands on her as he promised to fill her with his seed before feasting on her flesh. She was lucky that Morrigan and Menolayous came when they did, she was very lucky. Menolayous had been there for her every time the nightmare happened, gently waking her from the horrors of her memory. He even covered her with his cloak last night because she was shaking so badly.

She watched him as he settled into the silence, something he seemed thankful for. He and Morrigan weren't big talkers, but unlike Morrigan, who didn't seem to have a care in the world, Menolayous seemed at odds with sleeping in the same camp as them. Was it chivalrous behavior or a dislike of people that had him wanting to run away? Or, more realistically she was driving him mad. She mentally kicked herself, she should actually try to be nice to him if she wanted to keep being around him, which she realized that she did want. She was surprised to find that she actually liked him regardless of his serious and brooding personality.

Menolayous began to undo the braid behind his head, unraveling his long dark hair as it started to fall forward. He was very handsome when he started to relax, she thought to herself. She felt the sudden urge to run fingers through his hair, to reach out and touch him, to make a physical connection. She wanted to touch him, but also to get a better reading on his energy. Her powers worked best when she could make physical contact. Shaking that thought away, she continued to watch him. The silver beads he had braided into his hair looked like they were getting caught as he continued to unravel the braid. He hadn't had time the last several days to manage his long hair properly, being on the run like they were. The loose strands of hair were tangled around the beads quite badly, there was no way he would be able to do it himself. She got up and walked around the fire towards him.

"Here, let me help you," she said, reaching out gently and touching what was left of his braid.

Menolayous shot up and off the log so quickly that she gasped in surprise. He took several large strides away from her, spinning on her as if he was expecting her to attack him.

"I'm not going to bite you," she said, a little offended at the movement, she wasn't *that* unbearable to be around. "I was trying to help. Your beads looked tangled."

"Sorry. I—" He shook his head like he was trying to shake off a nightmare "—I'm not used to people touching me."

He looked embarrassed, she realized, at his reaction towards her. It was a bit extreme, but why had it been that way? She knew it wasn't her. His mask finally slipped, showing his carefully crafted mental barriers were not there, revealing what he had been hiding from them. His fear. His eyes were like windows; she could look inside them and see him battling his own demons inside his head. If simply trying to reach out and touch him had done this, she was amazed that he had stayed camping with them for so long. She was afraid to know what demons he faced to warrant such an intense reaction.

"I'm sorry for just jumping up and doing it," Grace said sincerely, wanting to ease his panic. "May I help you with your hair? It's tangled now, in the back."

After a moment of thinking, and reaching back to feel the knot of hair, Menolayous nodded and sat down in front of her. She could feel that this took a great amount of self-control on his part, forcing himself to sit there, allowing her to help him. Grace took the bone comb off his bedroll and began to gently untangle the knot from the silver bead. Menolayous sat as stiff as a board, very clearly not used to the gentleness of the contact. Her curiosity wandered as she worked. He was a warrior so he was used to violence and physical contact in that regard. He had carried Morrigan until Grace could help her with her burnout, he seemed to be fine with that. Was it because this touch was not a touch of necessity? Or was it because a woman was touching him?

"*Searching his memories without his permission will end poorly,*" Morrigan's voice echoed through her head down that permanent connection they had formed, not once did she look up from her spear.

254

"Wouldn't that apply to you too, seeing as you're now butting into mine?" she shot back.

"Talking is one thing. Feeling his emotions is another. But this man is not open, he shuts everything within. Do not break his trust by forcing yourself inside his head just because you are curious."

Morrigan was right and she knew it. Grace's gift of illusions also allowed her to enter someone's mind. She could sense emotions, read their thoughts, dig out specific memories, or literally drive them mad. Menolayous had been kind to her, had saved her life. She owed him too much to break down the barriers he held in place. Not only that but she did like him, she couldn't bring herself to enter his mind and dig through his memories. She was still concerned and curious as to why he was so secretive, so shut off. Maybe if they could build a trusting relationship she could eventually ask him. She had finally untangled the knot and began to comb through the rest of his hair. Having direct physical contact made it hard for her to shut out how he was feeling, not that she was trying particularly hard. She could sense he was reluctant to relax, and that he was stopping himself from enjoying the touch. Why would he do that with something so menial, especially if it brought him comfort?

Perhaps she could help with that. Closing her eyes as she continued to comb through his hair, she focused on feeling relaxed and comfortable, allowing this emotion to be carried down the connection between them and directly into him. She felt a noticeable slump of his shoulders as her emotions reached him. She smiled as she continued to work, happy that he was relaxed enough to have his back now gently leaning up against her body as she stood.

Morrigan finally finished with her spear, setting it on the ground beside her bedroll. She gave Grace a knowing and slightly irritated look. Grace shrugged her shoulders ever so slightly, feigning innocence, Morrigan was not convinced. She glanced at Grace, then to Menolayous, rolling her eyes. She got up and went to lay down on her bedroll for the night. Good, the old bat could mind her own business.

Grace continued to comb through his hair. Truthfully, she no longer needed to, but the craving for contact was seeping from him so strongly that she wanted to continue. She could sense happiness starting to sprout within him, an emotion she could tell wasn't as familiar to him as it should be.

Projecting and reading someone's emotions was tricky business. It required a balance and without that, their emotions could start to intermingle, making it impossible to tell whose was whose. It required a lot of concentration on her part. She was very intently focusing on not wanting to

255

dive deeper into his head, not wanting to invade his memories to find out why. She had succeeded in getting him to relax, maybe too much. She could feel that his guard was now completely down, something she did not believe he ever did. He was now completely open to her, completely raw to her magic. That's when the next emotion she felt from him took her completely off guard. This emotion was so strong, it seemed to grab her focus and pull her in.

Arousal now completely took over her senses. His arousal. Her breathing suddenly caught in her chest as nearly painful throbbing began at the apex of her thighs. She could feel her nipples start to harden and a dampness start between her legs. His need was powerful, overwhelmingly so. She stopped combing his hair then, placing her hands on his shoulders as she tried to center herself. She was feeling the female equivalent of what he was feeling. Her powers had taken away any self-control that he would regularly have over himself, so the intensity of it was definitely magnified. It was such a powerful pull that she found herself wondering how long it had been since he last laid with a woman.

She tried to backtrack out of his mind, but the strength of this unused emotion pulled her in even further. This emotion mimicked as if he was dying of thirst, the dryness of it was painful. Images began to flood her mind, images that he created. The two of them were tangled together naked and in the throes of passion, shared kisses, her naked body on display for him, her hands running through his hair, and her mouth around his cock. She inhaled sharply, finally able to break the hold his emotions had on her. No longer feeling the same arousal as him, she was able to refocus on reality.

The two of them remained motionless for another moment or two. He reached up with a hand gently laying it on one of hers, an action she knew he would not do, he did not touch people. She felt the calluses on his hands, the warmth and gentleness of his touch. Curious about what he would do next, she remained still. Surely with arousal that great he would need to act, this was something she honestly wouldn't mind helping him with. It had been a while for her too.

"Thank you," he said quietly as his walls snapped back into place, he began moving away from her.

She watched him as he laid down on his bedroll, facing away from her. With his arms crossed against his chest, he looked no different than he normally did. Really? That was all he was going to do about it? He wasn't going to engage with her that was obvious, but he wasn't going to go handle his sudden arousal himself? With how powerful and unused that emotion seemed to be for him, it was unbelievable to her that he chose to do nothing.

Pondering this, Grace went to her bedroll to lie down as well. She was very clearly the center of his fantasies at the moment; the scenes had pushed themselves into her head. He seemed to shove his barriers back up the second she broke the connection, maybe the intensity of it scared him. She had not created those emotions; she didn't even intensify them. That was all him after she had gotten him to let his barriers down. She wanted to believe that she had not caused this, and she knew she hadn't exactly. Breaking the connection just removed his ability to be relaxed, he threw the barriers up again probably mostly due to habit. She reached out her magic one more time, feeling for him. Her heart broke when she felt what was now radiating off of him, great sadness and shame.

Chapter Thirty-Six

Bridget

The sound of bird calls greeted them as Bridget and Clyous entered the camp from the windmill entrance. Clyous smiled at her kindly, leading her by the hand as they continued down the pathway. She recognized Connor emerging from his usual hiding place, waving in greeting excitedly. Cautiously, she raised her shawl up onto her head, hoping to conceal her face. It had only been two days but the bruises still covered her face in angry black and blue markings.

"Clyous, welcome back." Connor approached them happily. "Miss Bridget, is that you?"

"Hello Connor." She smiled sweetly at him.

He froze, finally catching sight of her injuries. "What happened? Did the prince do this to you?"

She caught Clyous's head swivel towards her in surprise. "No. An unforeseen circumstance. Maybe I should have left with you when you offered the other day."

"Connor, do you mind running ahead and getting Flinn?" Clyous asked, gently wrapping an arm around Bridget.

"Of course not," Connor said, turning and taking off at a run.

"You didn't have to make the poor boy run." Bridget winced as she started walking again. "What's so urgent that we need Flinn here?"

"It was mostly to get him away. Connor can be too easily excited." Clyous walked with her.

"Are you mad?" she asked hesitantly, glancing over at him.

"About what?" Clyous sounded surprised.

"That I know Connor, and that everyone seems to know about Liam," she answered with her head down, expecting the familiar possessiveness she always encountered with Liam.

"Why would I be mad about that?" Clyous stopped to look her in the face, giving her a small smile. "You are your own person. I have no stake in who you know or what you do. I'm just happy to be in your life."

Bridget had no words for that. Here she was used to being kept hidden and tightly controlled by the men in her life. It was something that, after being alone for the last few years, she had come to detest. She didn't know why she had assumed that being with Clyous would be the same, but she should have known that he was not Liam, or her father. Clyous supported her, he didn't want to control her, and she desperately wanted that.

"Are you ready for all of them to see you?" Clyous asked, gently tugging on her shawl.

She fingered the hem of her shawl nervously, pulling it down more. "Yes. As much as I don't want to be stared at, there's not really another alternative."

As they neared the smokehouse, they began to see the men moving about. She recognized many of them from earlier visits or having treated them in the past. Clyous was greeted warmly by the men. Once their eyes fell to Bridget, most of them stopped what they were doing at the sight of her face. She began to tremble slightly, stopping herself from completely covering up with her shawl. She could feel the gentle yet encouraging touch from Clyous as his hand rested on her lower back. She shouldn't need to hide from them.

Flinn emerged from the smokehouse brushing dirt off from his trousers. He spotted them, smiling at their approach. As soon as he caught sight of the bruises, his smile disappeared. The old warrior rushed forward, gently grabbing her hands as he took in the full extent of the bruises.

"Dear Bridget," Flinn's voice was laced with concern as he reached up, gently turning her head with his thumb. "Does the man who did this still breathe, lass?"

She nodded in answer, staring into his eyes. His eyebrows furrowed and his mouth disappeared behind his beard, but the war chief said no more. Instead, he gently embraced her much like a good father would. If only her father were more like this instead of being one that hurt her.

"Clyous! Bridget!" Catriona's voice called.

Bridget looked up, her eyes homing in on familiar white hair. Catriona was running to them, her undone hair billowing behind her. With a smile on her face, she launched herself into her twin brother. Bridget had forgotten that it had been weeks since the brother and sister had seen each other, and not necessarily when Catriona was doing her best. Bridget felt joy watching the reunion. Catriona looked happy, genuinely so, especially compared to the last time she had seen her. She also appeared better fed than she had been, though still not as well as the first time she had met her. Catriona's grief had been severe, but it looked as if she was starting to get a grip on it.

Finally breaking away from her brother's arms, Catriona went to embrace Bridget but stopped short. "What happened?"

By now Rama and Danny had joined them, both staring at Bridget's face in concern. Bridget pulled Catriona into a careful embrace, thankful she could stop the staring even for a moment. There was something different about an embrace from Catriona than the others. Even with Clyous, the others felt more protective of her. But with Catriona's embrace she could feel the other woman's strength calling to her own. They were truly friends. Catriona very prominently declared herself part of Bridget's pack, her family. A human would not understand how significant that was, especially to her. Bridget did not have a family growing up, she had her father and she had Liam. Compared to what she had now, Bridget realized that her father and Liam did not amount to much.

"I'm happy you're here." Bridget pulled away smiling.

Catriona smiled back. "Seriously, are you okay?"

"I'm fine," Bridget reassured her, then paused.

Catriona smelled different. Bridget leaned forward, sniffing her friend slightly, causing Catriona to look at her strangely. She then looked at Danny, understanding now what that change was. Their scents were intermingled now. Not just in the way two people's scents did when they were together all the time, or after just having sex. That was there too, but this scent was rarely observed even among blooded. This was love, love between a mated pair. They had picked to be with each other and nobody else, whether they knew it or not, the deed was done. They were now a part of each other.

Bridget leaned forward, whispering in Catriona's ear, "Not nearly as fine as you I see."

The two women smiled at each other knowingly. Catriona was practically beaming with happiness. Her smile was contagious, Bridget couldn't help but smile back. Catriona deserved happiness. Maybe having Catriona would now curb some of the wild that was buried within Danny, he needed something good and constant in his life. Bird calls began to sound throughout the camp again. Everyone began looking around expectantly.

"What is with all of these damn visitors," Flinn grumbled loudly. "This is supposed to be a hidden place."

"How can you still call it hidden when you've built an entire village in the trees," Menolayous called from up the road.

Everyone turned to look as Menolayous strode toward them flanked by two women. Bridget held onto Catriona's hand as they approached, nerves getting the better of her. One of the women she did not recognize, a beautiful woman with wavy brown hair that danced in the wind. She held herself well, she had a confidence about her that most women would crave. She wore fighting leathers with a spiked jacket, but no obvious signs of a weapon. A strange purple tattoo stemmed from behind her ear down the side of her neck, a series of intricate knots. The other woman Bridget did recognize, it was the sorceress from her dream. Her lightning shaped tattoos covering her arms and the exposed part of her chest, she carried a sharp spear in one hand. She wore an interesting combination of leather armor and silver plates. Feathers and bones acted like jewelry would for a normal lady, giving her an earthy, almost wild look to her.

"It's like we're being invaded by women," Flinn grumbled, his eyes lingering just a moment on the wilder of the two newcomers.

Bridget caught the twins glancing at each other quickly, then back to the sorceress. Had they recognized her as well? Before she could ask, Menolayous and his brothers greeted each other warmly with a quick embrace. Danny and Rama shared a strange look, and she knew why, Menolayous did not often allow anyone to touch him let alone initiate an embrace. Even with his brothers. The two strange women stood a few feet away, eyeing them curiously.

"I thought you said the redhead was bedding the male twin, not both," the woman with the spiked jacket asked Menolayous, pointing at the fact that Bridget was still holding Catriona's hand.

Menolayous sighed heavily, shaking his head at the woman's words. Bridget tried to let go of Catriona's hand, embarrassment taking hold. Catriona held onto her firmly before saying, "Too exotic for you?"

The woman smiled. "Nothing is too exotic for me."

"Who is this delightful creature?" Rama asked his brother sarcastically, sizing the woman up.

"This is Grace, heir to Airgid's throne." Menolayous gestured to the other woman. "This is Morrigan."

261

"Guardian of the Ancients," Morrigan's thick accent coated her speech, it caught Bridget off guard.

"Yes, sorry. Guardian of the Ancients." Menolayous took a breath to calm himself down. "They both are very into titles."

"What in the goddess's name is a guardian of the ancients?" Danny asked, amusement at his brother's discomfort written all over his face.

"My sole purpose of this life is to seek out and protect those with the ancient bloodline, and to keep the ancient traditions alive. I have come to train your children of old."

"You mean Bridget?" Danny asked.

"And your mate." Morrigan looked to Catriona now, then to Clyous. "And the twin brother."

"What do you mean?" Catriona glared at the woman.

"She means you and your brother have magic," Grace answered, almost bored.

"We don't have magic," Catriona argued, glancing at her brother. "Clyous?"

Clyous shifted then, away from everyone. Bridget followed him with her eyes as he walked toward Morrigan. The sorceress smiled at his approach, reaching out her hand for him to grasp. Clyous reached for it without hesitation. It was like a thunderclap came down from the sky, pushing air down on Morrigan and Clyous so their clothes and hair whipped around for a moment before the air settled again. Bridget held Catriona's hand tighter as she saw a silvery light run up and down Clyous's spine. Morrigan looked at him approvingly, as did Grace.

"You have realized the extent of your powers then," Morrigan stated. "Good."

"What is your gift?" Grace asked. "Show us your mark."

Dutifully Clyous pulled his jacket and tunic up and over his head, revealing the fine lines and cut of his muscular figure. Bridget only had a moment to greedily eye him up and down before seeing the glowing tattoo going down his spine. Intricate knotwork was now sketched down his spine in a thick column. The silvery glow seemed to come from underneath his hair line as well. Clyous brushed some of his hair to the side revealing the knotwork covered his skull as well, just concealed by his hair.

"I see things before they happen and I can see things that have happened if I touch a person or an object," Clyous answered before climbing back into his tunic. "The tattoo appeared after I figured out how to control it."

"The mark only appears once you have experienced the full extent of your power," Grace explained.

"We have not had a true seer in centuries." Morrigan smiled. "That is a powerful gift, boy."

Clyous looked at Bridget, then his sister. "I thought I was going mad. I didn't want to say anything."

"When?" Catriona bit out, hurt flashed across her face.

"Weeks ago. I had a dream that Morrigan was calling me for help. She told me what I was. After that the dreams started, then every time I touched something I could see the past."

"I had the same dream," Bridget said, looking back at the sorceress. "But I've known I have magic. I don't have a mark."

"You are gifted with the touch." Morrigan moved to her then. "An exceedingly rare gift, as rare as a seer, but you have no mark because you have not met your full potential."

"What can you do?" Grace asked, looking at her intently. "It can't be healing. Otherwise, you would have healed your face."

"I can—" Bridget stammered at the bluntness of what Grace had said. "I've only ever been able to heal infections or poisoning."

"You healed our mother from the curse of the scourge," Clyous said encouragingly. "And Catriona from the bite of a blooded."

"You're powerful enough to heal a curse but not your face?" Grace said incredulously.

"Grace," Menolayous tried to cut in.

"This girl has no self-preservation instincts." Frustration laced Grace's words, bringing shame to Bridget as she spoke.

Bridget felt Catriona's hand leave hers. Faster than her eyes could track, Catriona was now standing directly in front of Grace, almost chest to chest. Clyous and Danny moved to grab her, but Menolayous stopped them with a look. Apparently Menolayous felt that this was needed. The two women squared off with each other, sizing each other up.

"Watch how you talk to her," Catriona warned, her eyes now liquid silver.

"Does the wolf girl really need a bodyguard?" Grace smiled in challenge. "I see why they keep calling you the fiery one."

"You're new here so I'll fill you in. These are my people, my pack, Bridget is part of that. You fuck with my pack, I don't care what your magic is, I'll bury you."

Grace cocked her head, assessing the situation with amusement.

"Do not set her off," Morrigan warned. "She does not yet know her power. She could easily burn the forest down if you push her."

Grace glanced at the sorceress before taking a step back, creating distance. She kept her eyes trained on Catriona until Menolayous stepped between them with his hands raised.

"You have a fire inside you, one that you cannot control," Morrigan spoke to Catriona now. "You will need to master it."

"Everyone having magical gifts and what not seems really neat, but that doesn't explain why our brother brought you both here." Danny gently pulled Catriona back to him. "Menolayous would you be kind enough to explain? What happened with McKinlay's camp?"

"They are all dead," Menolayous answered sadly.

"Are you sure, lad?" Flinn asked, interjecting. "All of them?"

"Yes." Menolayous's eyes filled with sorrow. "I tracked them from the camp, finding myself in the heart of the Gaelach forest. Morrigan found me then, asking me to help her free Grace from some of the blooded tribesmen. McKinlay's warband had been taken to the same place so I agreed to help. When we got there—" Menolayous faltered.

Morrigan spoke up. "There is a dark one in Gaelach, one who practices dark forbidden magic. He has been stealing children of the old and absorbing their essence. As he grows more powerful, his reach expands. He is the one who is stirring up the scourge and attacking the cities. If we do not stop him, we will all die."

"The Dark One is in league with the cult leaders of Gaelach. The Moon Tribe has been giving him free reign in their kingdom to practice and develop his dark rituals," Grace finished. "He has the power of the tribesmen behind him as well as the scourge."

264

"So, you're telling me the attack on Oich, the scourge attack, was because this 'Dark One' sent them?" Catriona bit out.

"Yes," Morrigan answered.

"Why?" Clyous seemed enraged as well, as he should be. This attack is what started the chain of events that ultimately resulted in their mother's death.

"I do not know why he experiments with these creatures, only that he does," Morrigan answered.

"And you are here to what? Ask for help to start a war?" Rama asked Morrigan, assessing to see if she was a threat or a potential powerful ally.

"The war has already been started. We are behind in defending ourselves from it." Morrigan looked the tall man in the eye. "You have mountain blood in you."

Rama turned to Grace, obviously heated at the news. "And what is the Princess of Airgid doing with this sorceress? How did the Dark One get a hold of you?"

"So, you're the giant Menolayous spoke of." Grace smirked. "I would have assumed you would be smart enough to figure that out, but I guess your lack of oxygen up there makes it hard to think."

A smile spread across Rama's lips, loving the challenge this woman presented. "The princess has a bite."

She eyed him up and down, her attitude matching his. "I bet you taste good too. Want to find out how hard I can bite?"

"Can we all just stop for a moment!" Menolayous shouted, breaking the battle of wills. "Please."

Grace looked at Menolayous for a moment, then backed away from his brother. Rama did the same, eyeing his brother curiously before his gaze returned to Grace. Danny was eyeing Menolayous too, apparently the two brothers were seeing something different about him. Bridget hadn't figured out what was so interesting yet.

"We don't need to make any decisions right now." Menolayous looked at everyone in the group. "There is a lot of information that needs to be processed and worked through, and with this many aggressive personalities that is not going to happen any time within the next hour. So, my suggestion is we all take a day or so and reconvene this conversation into something more official."

"Agreed," Rama answered as the voice of the rebellion. "And you vouch for these women to stay here without causing issues?"

Menolayous looked to Grace, who promptly rolled her eyes but nodded. "Yes. They will not create problems."

"If Menolayous vouches for them then they are welcomed guests," Flinn said, his eyes casually glancing back to Morrigan. "Shall I call the other war chiefs for a council meeting?"

"Yes," Rama answered. "This will need to be a council meeting."

"Great," Flinn complained, "I'll have to make more lodging."

Bridget watched as the old war chief walked off, shouting orders to some of the men. Menolayous still stood next to Grace and Morrigan as Rama sized the women up. Grace was looking at Catriona and Danny with great interest.

"What can I do?" Bridget asked Morrigan, breaking the tension.

"You can heal all wounds with your touch," Morrigan answered. "But you can also cause great harm, even death if you wished."

She did not want to cause pain, that was the opposite of why she had become a healer. "How can I learn to heal all wounds?"

"Magic is driven by emotion," Grace explained, her voice softer than it had been as she evaluated her. "What do you think of when you heal an infection? What do you feel?"

"I feel like I'm cleaning something dirty. Like I'm making it pure again," Bridget answered.

Grace approached her, she felt everyone in the group tense. Grace ignored it, gently reaching up and lowering the shawl that covered Bridget's bruises. It was a kind gesture from someone who seemed so bent on pissing everyone off.

"May I?" Grace asked, holding out her hand.

Reluctantly, Bridget handed Grace her hand. Grace gently lifted Bridget's hand and placed the palm against her own face. With Grace's hand still there she grabbed Bridget's other hand as well, not moving it, just hanging onto it.

"If you want to heal, focus on something happy. Something alive and vivacious. This focus on life will help accelerate your healing." Grace smiled

266

kindly at her. "My power is of the mind. I'll help you intensify these feelings so you can see what you can do. Are you ready?"

Bridget nodded. She felt a presence in her mind, something foreign but gentle. She assumed that was Grace. Suddenly she could feel Grace's presence sifting through her mind, latching onto several newer memories. The happiness Bridget felt seeing Catriona so happy, the surprise and delight that Clyous stood by her no matter what. That he was there for her, not that he wanted to possess her. She could feel the golden light from within her pouring out of her hand, going into the tender tissues of her face. She began to feel the pain in her face lessen, her ribs began to tingle as well, then the pain disappeared. The glowing light ceased, Bridget opened her eyes to Grace's face, the faint traces of a purple glow coming from tattoos hidden behind her ears.

Grace let go of her hands, backing away from her slowly. Clyous gently reached out to touch Bridget's cheek. There was no more pain! She stretched slightly, no longer feeling the pull and sharpness in her ribs. She felt good, back to normal. She could see by the look in Clyous's eyes that her injuries were no longer visible. Everyone was looking at her in surprise now.

"I'd be careful of overexerting yourself for the rest of the day," Grace said. "Maybe go eat something. Using your powers, especially if you haven't mastered them yet, can lead to burnout."

"Will you teach me more?" Bridget asked both Morrigan and Grace.

Morrigan smiled at her as if she had won a great victory. "Why do you think I am here, child?"

Chapter Thirty-Seven

Menolayous

Menolayous glanced around the forest as he followed the tracks just outside of Collie. He honestly wasn't sure why he even bothered trying to follow her out here. She clearly was looking to be left alone, but just as much as he found her infuriating, he also couldn't seem to leave her alone. Menolayous did not have much experience around women, but he wasn't naive enough to pretend there wasn't an attraction there. She was very beautiful, that was as obvious as anything. Yes, she was extremely obnoxious most of the time, but that was the shield she chose to wear, he saw it for what it truly was.

She was very distrusting of people, a kindred spirit to him in that regard. She just went about it in a different way than he did. Instead of stepping back and watching others, she pushed them to their limit. She wanted to see the person for whom they were inside, not what they pretended to be. It's why she went for Catriona first thing upon meeting her this morning. He shouldn't have been surprised, both women were very strong willed. It was only natural that they butt heads, and he was under no false impressions that they were even remotely close to being done sizing each other up. On the other hand, Grace could see Bridget's warmth immediately upon pushing at her, she could see the healer's gentleness and responded to her the exact same. She had been extremely kind to Bridget after that.

It was shortly after Grace and Morrigan were shown to their treetop lodging that Grace had disappeared. She was so quick about it even Menolayous missed her sneaking off. So, he had followed her trail through Collie all the way to the forest. He followed her footprints to a nearby stream. There she sat on an old fallen log facing away from him. He approached cautiously, trying to figure out what she was doing. She was drawing. Grace had parchment resting in the flat of the stump and was sketching away with a piece of charcoal.

"You know it's not polite to approach a lady without announcing yourself," Grace called out to him, not once taking her eyes off her artwork.

"I'm impressed." Menolayous walked toward her, glancing at her parchment. He was shocked to see a very realistic charcoal drawing of a fox curled up inside a tree trunk. "Not many people could hear me approaching."

"I didn't." Grace paused long enough to glance up at him. "I can sense you though. I felt you coming once you entered the forest."

"That's a neat trick." Menolayous sat down across from her. "Being able to sense anyone who approaches."

"I can't do it with just anyone." Grace shrugged her shoulders at him. "We've formed a connection, a bond in my head. I can sense when anyone I have a direct connection with is near, feel their emotions. It's how I can talk to you inside your mind from a farther distance. With anyone else I just sense their life force."

"When exactly did you bond with me?" Menolayous asked, struggling to understand her words. Magic was a new concept for him.

Grace sighed as she set her artwork aside. "I owe you an apology. The other night when I was helping you with your braid, I could sense how uncomfortable you were with physical contact. So, I used my power to try and help relax you. I didn't intend to make you drop all your walls. I may have been sucked in by some of your emotions. At that point I inadvertently formed a connection between us."

Menolayous sat there for a moment, processing the horror she was admitting. He knew exactly what she was talking about, he had felt himself relax at her touch more than he had ever let himself with anyone before. If she had in fact entered his mind and felt his emotions... by the gods, that meant she knew everything that he was feeling. Everything he was thinking.

"So you read my mind?" Menolayous shot up, turning away from her so she could not see his embarrassment.

"No," Grace answered, her voice laced with guilt. "I would not allow myself to sink that far into you without your permission. I realize how far I went would probably be looked at like a violation."

Menolayous glanced at her, angry and embarrassed. Grace stared at him, guilt written all over her face.

"I want us to be friends and I can sense that you are a very private person. I respect that about you." Grace looked at the ground. "The only way I can see that happening is confessing this intrusion to you and promising you that it will not happen again without your permission."

Menolayous didn't know what to say to that. It was true he felt the violation of her intrusion, mostly his embarrassment of her reading his emotions especially in that specific moment. Her confessions to wanting to be his friend threw him for another loop, he wasn't entirely sure anyone had told him that before. He and his brothers had grown their relationship from the situations they survived. His friendships with Bridget and Catriona came more from a forced proximity to each other. Never before had someone he just met simply stated that they wanted to be friends with him. What's worse was he believed her, she appeared genuine in her remorse as well as her intentions, he could see that clearly enough.

"I will not enter your mind to dissect your emotions or your thoughts again," Grace started, "but because of that connection I can still feel some of you. I can tell you are embarrassed about what I felt from you that night. If it helps alleviate that embarrassment at all, or at least levels out the playing field a bit, I would like to confess that I also find you attractive, and I may have been slightly disappointed that you did not seem to want to act on those emotions."

Menolayous truly had nothing to say to that. He wasn't even sure he had heard the words come out of her mouth correctly. So, he did what he did best, he just stood there and stared, trying to wrap his mind around their current conversation. Grace seemed to accept this and returned to her artwork. Menolayous continued to watch as her slender hands moved over the parchments, using the charcoal to shade in the bark of the stump. She was very talented, he realized, she was probably the best artist he had met. The few artists he had known over the years typically stuck to knotwork designs, he had never seen anyone create such realistic work before.

"You are really good," Menolayous said, nodding to her art.

"Thank you." Grace smiled. "Back before I could project with my magic, this was how I used to show people what I could see."

"What do you mean?" he asked, puzzled by her statement.

Grace thought for a moment before answering, "When I was seventeen, I fell in love with a boy my age. I went to my parents to tell them I wanted to marry him, but my parents' advisor caught me before I could tell them. When I brushed up against him, I entered his mind, I could see his thoughts and feel his emotions. It was my first time actually using my power. I saw that the boy I was in love with was his nephew, the advisor had tasked him with wooing me. The advisor wanted his nephew next in line for my crown. When I went to my parents to tell them how their advisor had planned to put his nephew on their throne, my mother was angry at me for being foolish enough to fall in love, and for not thinking a boy was interested in me for my position."

Menolayous could see the emotional toll this confession had on her, he sympathized with her. "Not having the support of your parents seems like it would be incredibly hard."

"Yes, well," Grace sat up straighter before continuing her story, "it taught me the valuable lesson that I can't trust anyone. People always wear masks over who they really are. Since that particular incident, I have lived my life under the belief that people as a whole are not to be trusted, and to live my life as I see fit, not worrying about traditional values or what my parents think of my actions. Honestly, I've become a bit of a nightmare for them."

Menolayous finally sat back down, looking into her eyes. "I have a hard time trusting people too, as you've seen, but I have found my new family. They are the only people in this world that I do trust, and I trust them with my life."

Grace nodded her head at his words. "I can see that in them. I did not sense that any of them wore a mask, they were all incredibly genuine. Like you."

"Did you notice that before you started pushing, or after?" Menolayous felt a smile tug at the corner of his mouth.

"Bridget was clear as day." Grace rolled her eyes. "That girl is as gentle and innocent as they come. You can see that a mile away. The others did not try to hide from me when I reached out to sense them, but that blonde girl, Catriona, she's got something buried there. She is genuinely herself, but there is something dark buried beneath her angry demeanor. Until I know what that is, I find it unsettling."

"Maybe if you tried to be her friend like you try to be mine, she would share it with you," he suggested.

"I want to be a different kind of friend with you," she answered, staring back at him. "But you are right. I have never had true friends before. It would be nice to be accepted as Grace instead of as a princess for once."

Menolayous found himself blushing slightly at this comment. "You enjoy getting a rise out of me don't you?"

"It's become my favorite pastime." She smiled wickedly at him.

Menolayous stood then, smiling down at her. "Thank you for being honest with me, and for sharing. I would like to be your friend."

"I mean why wouldn't you, really?" That familiar cocky grin was now plastered across her beautiful face.

Menolayous laughed at how bold she was. When she wasn't directly trying to piss him off their interactions were quite pleasant. He could smell the faint traces of smoke in the air, turning his head back towards Collie.

"It's almost dinner time, are you planning on staying out here?" he asked her.

"I could go for some food." Grace uncrossed her legs and stood. "Lead the way, handsome."

Chapter Thirty-Eight

Morrigan

Morrigan stood outside her assigned home, peering down through the tree branches at the soldiers that moved below. In the one hundred and fifty years Morrigan had been walking this land, she had never once seen houses in the trees. In truth, the castles and stone buildings carved out of the mountains in Airgid were an impressive feat too. Nothing could compare to carvings as elegant as those and with that level of workmanship, but even with all the gems of the earth embedded in the most precious metals, there was something dreary about living under the mountains.

Morrigan much preferred the wilds of the forest. She craved the feeling of wind on her skin, the sun giving her warmth, and the cleansing that the rain and snow brought to her soul. These tree homes might be plain and basic in creation, but nothing could beat the beauty that was her view. Morrigan glanced over at the raven that flew down and perched atop the handrails beside her. She was surprised it took him so long to make an appearance.

"Humans never cease to amaze me," Storm said, he too kept his eyes trained on the men below.

"Thankfully," Morrigan drawled, "or these last hundred and fifty years would have been boring."

She watched as Storm's eyes locked in on the tall one, Rama. He was helping a few of the warriors carry a butchered hog towards the smokehouse.

"It's not often you see one with giant's blood," Storm said. *"As a child of the mountain, do you think it a disservice that he has no magic?"*

"Many who come from the mountain did not attain magic," Morrigan answered thoughtfully. "They were given size and strength that could rival other children of old. I would not call it a disservice at all."

"That may be." Storm ruffled his feathers. *"But the children of the moon have claws and teeth that can rip through all that muscle."*

"True," Morrigan acknowledged. "We have all the gods present here today; their descendants walk amongst us."

273

"The God of the Mountain is within the giant for sure, and the Goddess of War and Fate lies within the twins," Storm started listing off Morrigan's new companions. *"The God of the Moon and Goddess of Healing share a bloodline with the healer. That's an interesting mix for sure."*

"And we have a daughter of chaos amongst us as well. The princess is exceptionally gifted with the power of the mind," Morrigan explained. "She is quite powerful."

"We are missing two then." Storm hopped a few inches to the left, getting a better look at the movement below. *"Death and the sea."*

"I haven't seen a child of the Sea God for over fifty years. I fear they may have been wiped out completely." Morrigan stroked Storm's feathers gently. "As for death, that is our foe. A blooded who has been taken over by the God of Death. It has given him unnatural powers."

"The Moon God would not be happy with another god claiming one of his descendants." Storm leaned into her hand as she continued to stroke his wings.

"Unless he and the Death God are working together," Morrigan pondered. "That would complicate things."

"How long has it been since you faced the God of Death?" Storm asked, shaking off her affections.

"Fully, one hundred and fifty years, not since my creation. This is not the first dark one I have come across; it will be a matter of time before death completely takes over." Morrigan answered. "I look forward to paying back old debts."

After a moment of silence, Morrigan continued, "What have you learned, old friend? Seeing as you saw fit to abandon me in my time of need."

"I would hardly call it your time of need. You survived well enough." Storm clicked his beak at her. *"I was scouting the Kingdom of Oich. There is a rebellion going on there, it is led by these humans here. The young crown prince can't seem to beat them down enough to get a foothold. He is rash and foolish with his strategies. The crown is too occupied with them to notice what the rest of the continent is up to."*

"I do not know if the crown being distracted is a good thing or not," Morrigan wondered. "If the Moon God is truly working with the God of Death, then it is possible Oich may become an even bigger enemy than I first feared."

"As long as you see them as the enemy." Storm stretched out his wings preparing to take flight. *"I have seen what those soldiers do. I would love to peck out their eyes for it."*

"You will get your chance, little battle bird." Morrigan smiled as she watched him take off. "We will all get the chance."

Chapter Thirty-Nine

Rama

He watched as the tiny foal trotted to him easily, such an innocent and beautiful creature. It was so trusting, only having been born a day or so ago. Rama had been here in the stables to help the little fella into the world, an old routine he found comfort in doing. Rama had fond memories of working in the stables side by side with his father. It wasn't the memories of his lost family that he relished, it was the relationships he had with the horses themselves. Unlike his father, the horses not only valued his efforts, but they also appreciated his company. There was a working relationship between man and beast, a give and take that didn't exist outside the stables. Rama could admit his love for horses as well as for any other animal. There was an innocence to them that he admired, they weren't tainted like most people he knew. It was true they fought and could harm others, but there was always a reason behind it. It was unlike the senseless violence and pain humans and blooded alike chose to inflict upon others.

Rama stuck his thumbs into the core of an apple, effortlessly separating the fruit into several pieces. At the sound of the apple breaking apart, the mare moved from the hay pile she had been working on. Rama smiled at the new mother, holding a piece of apple out to her. She happily took it from his hand, her teeth crunching the apple as she savored the treat. Her foal nosed his empty hand playfully. Rama chuckled, scratching the young horse's chin gently at the contact.

"You'd think a great beast such as yourself would scare the poor animals away." Flinn chuckled as he strode into the stables. "But I am never surprised to see that you make friends with the beasts before you do the warriors."

"Animals are the only ones who can truly sense a person's intentions." Rama handed over the last of the apple to the hungry mare before standing. "Maybe they sense the beast in me is a kindred spirit."

The old war chief chuckled. "More like a giant kitten."

"What brings you to the stables, oh important one?" Rama teased. "I know for a fact you are afraid of horses."

"Only the ones taller than me." Flinn laughed, leaning against the stable door. "It's not my fault that happens to be all of them, *Prince.*"

Rama grimaced at the nickname, it had been years since Flinn first started using it, it would most likely be many more before he stopped. "How can I help you?"

"I was hoping to talk to you about your plans while you lot choose to remain in my city," Flinn answered.

"I wouldn't call this a city," Rama said, glancing around.

"But it will be soon. I have the resources and the manpower to really turn this place into something special."

"A fortress?" Rama asked seriously. "I can see the advantage of picking this location."

"No lad, a city." Flinn had that expression on his face Rama knew only too well, the old war chief had an idea. "It's about time we stopped hiding in the brush from our enemies, only to lash out like an injured dog when it best suits us. Many of my men haven't seen their families in over a year now. This isn't a life worth fighting for anymore, not without the people my men are fighting to share it with."

"That's a pretty tall order," Rama thought about it as he spoke, "there are many factors to consider in order to pull something like that off before the crown notices. Otherwise, you might find yourself in a city burned to ash before you could even raise the houses."

"Aye, that's where you come in," Flinn said excitedly. "If you truly mean to remain here with your family and choose to wage war on the crown, you could choose to wage war away from this city in the making. Keep the crown's attention on you and your brothers. You three have gotten very good at causing irritation where it's needed."

"Like a bad case of poison oak." Rama smiled at this plan. "We could do that, and as we're doing it we could reroute help and supplies back to Collie to speed up the process."

Flinn smiled wide at this. "I wouldn't be able to do this without you lads, and it's something that desperately needs to be done."

"You can count on us." Rama reached forward and patted the old war chief's shoulder affectionately. "It'll be just like old times."

Flinn bellowed a laugh. "Not quite like old times. I seriously doubt we'll have to rescue Danny as often now that he's decided to chase only one lass."

Rama laughed at that fact. "Thank the gods for that. I promised him last time if I had to break him out of one more jail cell I was going to leave him there until he learned his lesson."

Chapter Forty

Danny

"I swear to the gods, if you hit me with one of those, I will gut you like a squealing pig!" Catriona shouted, as another plank of wood came within feet of her head.

The man who was carrying it hadn't been paying attention to how far the wood was sticking out, he huffed and stalked off. Danny watched the man carefully, evaluating if he was needed to step in or not, but like always, Catriona pulled no punches with the men, her threat was heard and taken seriously. It wasn't as if Catriona needed protection, she was a wildcat wearing human clothing. She could more than handle herself with these men, but Danny was always trying to pay attention to her, and any potential threats or issues that might arise, he was ready to be by her side.

Danny glanced around at the edge of the camp, most of the Collie warriors were here to help with the beginnings of the wall. Flinn and Rama had agreed to work together to expand Collie from a war camp into an actual city, one where families could live together and be protected from their enemies. It seemed like a tall order if he was being honest, but even if all they did was better Collie's defenses with a wall, it was worth all their labor. Rama had told his brothers that as soon as a wall was built around the camp, they would be assisting Flinn in raids across Oich. Danny had led men before on missions like this, to draw the crown's attention away from what the rebellion was actually doing. Only this time, he wasn't going to be alone.

Catriona seemed eager to get out on the battlefield and test her skills. She had continued to train since their arrival in Collie. Eating regular meals again, she was getting better and faster by the day. He had gifted her his set of short swords to use, her fighting style more fitting for their size than his. He had kept the sword taken from the fallen blooded that had insulted Catriona on the road and had Clyous reshape the handle to fit his grip better. Catriona had sharpened the blade for him. Catriona had continued to work on her archery with Menolayous whenever she could get him away from Grace. Catriona had yet to expand her training with anyone else, something she kept mentioning. As much as Danny wanted to keep her all to himself, he recognized that she needed to test herself against other warriors. He didn't want to be the reason she was held back, he wanted her to excel.

279

"It's like they've been hit in the head too many times." Catriona's gaze followed the male warrior she had just snapped at, her eyes narrowing as she watched him carry a board towards the wagon, adding it to the pile.

"He might have been." Danny put down the adze he was using to shape the wood from chopped down trees into boards. "It's not nice to make fun of people who are slow in the head."

"I've never been accused of being nice before." Catriona winked, returning to the braided ropes she held in her hand.

"Are you two capable of not looking at each other like you're about to rip each other's clothes off?" Rama asked as he walked by, carrying three large boards on his shoulder.

Danny glanced over at Catriona who had turned a dark shade of red, swearing at her newly acclaimed brother. "Try not to trip, asshole."

"Maybe you should find yourself a woman," Danny teased as his brother paused before them. "Might help you relieve some of that frustration you've been hiding. You just need to find a woman you wouldn't accidentally crush."

Rama's laughter boomed throughout the work camp at Danny's comment. Rama, to his credit, had a great sense of humor, especially when directed at himself. Danny smiled up at his older brother, still impressed at how gentle the giant was. Where most warriors here could only carry one wooden board at a time, Rama was able to carry three effortlessly. If Rama was an ill-tempered man, Danny wouldn't want to find himself on the receiving end of Rama's strength.

"What about you, Bridget," Rama called out the healer who was about ten feet away helping Clyous as he worked on the forge. "Are you worried you'll break your lover?"

Catriona and Danny burst out laughing as the blooded woman's face turned as red as her hair. Leave it to Rama to drag others into his own personal joke. Clyous looked less than happy at the jibe, turning his attention back to beating his hammer against the metal he was working on the anvil.

"What about you, all powerful sorceress," Rama turned his attention to Morrigan who was sitting out of the way, stroking the feathers of a large black raven.

"Keep your sex talk to yourself, child," Morrigan responded, glancing in Rama's direction.

"Oh, I'm far from a child," Rama teased, walking towards the cart.

"I took my first lover before your great-great-grandfather was even conceived." Morrigan's bird squawked its agreement. "All I see before me is an overgrown child."

Rama's laughter boomed out over the camp yet again. Danny had to admit, this older woman had come to Collie with enough sarcasm and strong will to be divided between everyone here and still have some left over. Out of the two women who had arrived with Menolayous, she was the more tolerable of the two. Grace was rubbing everyone the wrong way. Her attitude and snarky remarks kept people on edge when she was around, especially Catriona. Danny knew it was a matter of time before the two women faced off; they were both incredibly strong-willed.

Danny had overheard many of the men commenting on Grace and her beauty, but when Danny looked at her, all he saw was a young woman dressed provocatively, seeking out male attention. The girl was a flirt as much as she was nasty. There were only three people in this camp that the Princess of Airgid seemed to get along with: the sorceress, Bridget, and his brother Menolayous, who was acting unusually social since his arrival at camp. Danny suspected a good part of his changed behavior was due to Grace. Danny supposed he shouldn't be surprised if his usually quiet and aloof brother found himself attracted to the woman, so many of the warriors seemed to have fallen ill with the same sickness. Danny watched as Rama dropped the boards into the wagon before turning towards Grace, who was sitting by the horses sketching something on a piece of parchment. Looks like both of his brothers were attracted to her, great.

"What are you working on over there, Princess?" Rama asked, now standing over the woman.

Grace looked up at him, an annoyed expression on her face. "I didn't ask for an eclipse."

Rama laughed as he looked down at the parchment. "Wow, that's impressive. Is that supposed to be Collie?"

"And here I was thinking you were just looking down my shirt," Grace teased, reluctantly handing him the parchment. "I was working on the most efficient design for your wall. Flinn asked if I could draw up what it would look like to help explain it better to everyone after you'd finished collecting supplies."

"How did Flinn know you could draw?" Rama asked teasingly. "Making your way around the camp already?"

"I told him." Menolayous's voice came from the other side of the wagon where he was helping a few warriors drag up freshly cut down trees for shaping.

Everyone was watching Menolayous with great interest now, Rama and Danny especially. Menolayous was talking more than he usually did, he even surprised them at their reunion by embracing them, something he had never done before. Their brother's focus seemed to be on Grace at that moment, and how close Rama was to her, but some things hadn't changed. The warriors he was working with falling trees were mostly shirtless from their exertions, while he was stripped down to just his tunic. Not something most people would look at and think was odd, but Danny knew that his brother's torso was nearly completely covered in scars. It was something he chose to keep from people. It was clear that even with his attention on Grace, he was still his cautious self.

"Are you sad I didn't start with you?" Grace quipped, snatching her sketch out of Rama's hands.

Danny watched as Catriona rolled her eyes at the other woman's flirting before saying something low enough so only he could hear, "By the gods she's going to end up sleeping with the entire camp isn't she?"

Danny caught Grace's movement then, her head whipping towards Catriona at her words. There was no way the princess had heard that, right? Suddenly Catriona clasped her hands to her ears as if trying to deafen a loud noise. Catriona's face scrunched up as if she was in pain, her eyes flicking back towards Grace. Danny watched as her normally grey eyes started to turn a molten silver color as they narrowed in on her opponent.

"Get out of my head you witch!" Catriona snapped so loudly everyone in the vicinity stopped what they were doing to look.

"If you want to talk shit, might as well say it loud enough to make a scene of it." Grace smirked at her.

Danny felt his anger rising as the two women locked eyes. Again, he wasn't concerned about Catriona being able to handle herself in a fight, but this woman had magic. Danny glanced at Catriona who was now standing, preparing herself for more of a confrontation.

"Unlike you, it's not necessary for me to get off by having everyone else watch." The venom in his lover's voice was practically dripping from her mouth.

282

"Pity." Grace too stood, showing she was unafraid of Catriona's aggressive display. "You must make all that noise while fucking for everyone to hear because it gets him off then. I figured a lowly girl like you from a capital city should have had enough practice by now you shouldn't need to resort to that to make sex exciting."

Catriona moved then, making her way towards Grace with the intent to bury her fist in the other woman's face. Luckily for everyone involved, Danny was faster, scooping Catriona up around the waist before she could make it far. Menolayous had done the same with Grace, who had also stepped up to meet Catriona's challenge.

"You are not making yourself friends, girl," Morrigan lectured Grace, looking between the two women.

"I can't be friends with someone who won't show who they really are," Grace snarled in Catriona's direction. "She's dangerous until she does."

"What the fuck is that supposed to mean?" Catriona seethed, trying to pull herself out of Danny's arms.

"Enough!" Menolayous barked, turning his attention to Grace. "Both of you are done for the day."

"I say just let them go at it," Rama joked. "Once they work out who is more dominant, they'll stop fighting."

"You're a pig," Grace snapped at him.

"I've been compared more to the size of a horse," Rama winked at her.

Morrigan's raven squawked loudly before taking off in flight. Danny watched as it circled above Rama for a moment before releasing bird excrement onto the giant man. As the shit hit his shoulder and began to roll down, the once cocky man suddenly became disgusted. Morrigan let loose a hearty laugh as Danny watched Rama take a cloth and wipe the mess from his flesh. Danny took this opportunity to toss Catriona over his shoulder and walk towards their home.

"You can put me down now," Catriona growled in irritation, but surprisingly she didn't put up too much physical resistance.

"Not a chance sweetheart." Danny smacked her behind once playfully. "I don't need you to rip her head off just yet."

"She's so fucking infuriating," Catriona answered. "She needs to get slapped around."

"I don't disagree," Danny answered as he made it to the outdoor kitchen, finally lowering her to her feet. "But I can't let you. At least not yet."

Catriona looked up into his face questioningly. "Is it because of Menolayous?"

"Partially." He grabbed two bowls of soup from the cook, handing one to her. "But she might be an important ally to the movement. If the Dark One is in fact as big of a threat as Menolayous was saying, we'll need as much help as we can get, and I doubt Airgid will come to our aid if you kill their only princess and heir."

Catriona grumped as they sat down at one of the wooden tables. "Has Menolayous ever brought women around?"

Danny took a spoonful of the rabbit stew while he thought of an answer. "No, I've never seen him with a woman, at least in that capacity. Even when we used to frequent taverns or parties, he was never interested. Even when they approached him."

"I'd ask if he even likes women." Catriona chewed on a piece of meat. "But I see the way he looks at her, in her stupid figure forming leather."

Danny chuckled. "Why do you always go back to what she's wearing when you're pissed at her?"

"She's dressed like a harlot playing warrior." Catriona gawked at him. "You have to have noticed."

"I don't think there's anyone in this camp who hasn't noticed, my love." Danny raised his eyebrows at her. "But why does it bother you? Are you jealous of all the male attention she's getting?"

"No." Catriona took another spoonful of soup, good, she was still eating. "It's just not fair."

"What's not fair?" Danny asked, staring into her eyes.

"She's got everything, doesn't she? A throne, money, allies, a family, and throw in her looks." Catriona's eyes were losing their liquid silver shine and going back to her usual steely grey.

"So, you're jealous not of the attention she's getting, but her looks?" Danny was beginning to realize this was in fact a deep-seated issue for Catriona. "I don't understand what you think is wrong with how you look."

"I'm skin and bones. Even back when eating wasn't a problem, I never had curves, not like hers anyways. I was never big enough for men to stare at, for you to stare at, and my skin has been shredded, it's not as soft looking and all in one piece like hers. I'm a nightmare to look at."

Danny could not believe what he was hearing. Did Catriona really think that about herself, that she was a nightmare to look at? And that he didn't enjoy looking at her? Both of those beliefs were very false. Danny hadn't been interested in looking at other women, especially not Grace. There was literally nothing about her that he found attractive. Catriona on the other hand, everything about her was intoxicating. Danny could see the sadness in Catriona's eyes, she really did believe this of herself.

Danny made the decision right then and there to break his rule about leaving Catriona alone while she ate. He reached for her, grabbing her hips and pulling her into a seated position on his lap. He wrapped his arms tightly around her waist and pulled her even closer. He buried his face into her neck, inhaling the floral scent of her hair. Since she was facing him, and trapped by his vice-like grip, she rested her chin on top of his head and set her arms on his shoulders.

"You are not a nightmare, Cat," Danny spoke while still nuzzling her. "There is not a single thing about you that is not attractive, nothing. You are a warrior not a princess. You are not a spoiled little girl; you are a strong woman. You are the most beautiful woman I've ever laid my eyes on."

"Danny—" Catriona started.

"No." Danny squeezed her tightly. "You don't get to argue with my perspective. To me you are absolutely perfect, a stunning and breathtaking creature. You have absolutely no reason to be jealous of someone like that."

He felt her lips gently caress his forehead. He looked up to see that her eyes were watering slightly at his confession. Good, that means she believes him. He meant every word of it, to him she was perfect. They had been at Collie for maybe a month now, they had officially been together for nearly two. In that short amount of time he had discovered an indisputable fact, that she was his, and he was hers. He had been with plenty of other women before and been in actual relationships with women. None of that could compare to how he felt about Catriona. Everything about her and how they were as a couple felt right. He knew that she was it for him, that twenty years down the road he would still want her by his side.

"Cat?" he asked, as he buried his face into her collarbone.

"Yes?" she answered, he could feel the muscles in her lower back tighten slightly in anticipation.

"We should get married."

"What?" Catriona tried to pull away, but he held onto her. "Are you crazy?"

"Just a little." Danny allowed her to pull back an inch or two so he could stare at her shocked face. "But I'm serious."

"We've only been sleeping together for a month." She tried to wiggle out of his grip.

"Nearly two," Danny corrected with a smile. "And so what? I know this feels right, that you're it for me."

"That's way too soon for a proposal," Catriona stammered, nerves obviously getting the better of her.

"This wasn't a proposal," Danny clarified. "This was a suggestion. I've got to get the idea in your head now so when I actually propose you won't have this panicked expression on your face."

"I'm not panicked," Catriona said. Panic was in fact laced in her tone.

"It's okay. I understand this was never a plan of yours. Nor was it mine, but you can't fight against fate, and sweetheart we're fated to be together if you haven't been able to tell." Danny stole a kiss from her then. "Just keep my suggestion in the back of your mind, okay?"

"Oh, there is no way I'm going to be able to forget this conversation." Catriona laughed. "Don't get upset if I start trying to run away from you if you keep bringing this up."

"Hmm, chasing my wild woman through the woods, only to catch her, wrestle her to the ground, and make love to her right then and there, don't tease me, love. I might just do that."

Danny laughed at how pink her cheeks were turning; oh she was suddenly interested in this idea too. He would save that one for a rainy day for sure.

"You're insatiable." She playfully pushed his mouth away from her exposed neck.

"And you're not complaining, you're bragging." Danny smiled at her as he felt all her muscles tense up with excitement. "You think we can make it back to work, or do I need to take you home and show you how good of an idea it is to marry me?"

Chapter Forty-One

Menolayous

Menolayous stood by his brothers as they watched the training below. Catriona had finally stepped into the ring with some Collie warriors to test herself against someone other than Danny. She had come a long way from being a back-alley scrapper to an actual warrior. She had perfected daggers quickly enough and had graduated to the art of twin short swords. Danny's old weapons suited her technique very well. She could still move around and evade while slicing out with the blades, keeping her from getting too close to her opponents. He was proud of how far she had come. He had only known her for about three months, but he felt comfortable calling her a friend. Friendship aside, she and Danny were now connected, possibly more than either was willing to admit. Rama and Menolayous had begun looking at her like a little sister, as Danny's other half. You could not have one without the other, and as a family unit they were all happy to welcome in another.

Menolayous could only hope that if one day he found someone of his own his brothers would welcome her to the family as they did Cat. Menolayous sighed as his thoughts wandered to his newest friend, a woman that he found great comfort in being around, but nobody else seemed to share the same sentiment. Ever since his arrival with Grace and Morrigan, tensions had been running high, or more accurately, Grace was managing to piss everyone off quite successfully. To her credit, Menolayous knew that she was actually trying to hold back, but that initial introduction to Catriona and even Rama had stuck in their minds.

That first night back Grace and Morrigan had stayed together in one of the huts Flinn had given them for lodging. The old war chief kept referring to the four circling tree homes as the royal palace, much to Rama's annoyance. Bridget and Catriona stayed together, wanting to catch up on things since they had last seen each other, much to Danny's frustration. Which left Clyous to himself and Menolayous with his brothers. They had spoken at length about what had happened in Gaelach, about what Menolayous had seen there. Menolayous did his best to conceal from his brothers the nightmares that had started again since coming face to face with that dark magic user, but he was sure they knew something was wrong. He had done his best to hide the nightmares while on the road, but his brothers knew him better than Grace or Morrigan by far. They were worried about him as usual, with the added factor of his sudden friendship with a woman he had dragged to camp with him.

Menolayous tried to talk about Grace as little as possible with his brothers, mostly to hide just how he felt about her. Ever since she had helped him with his hair that night in the woods, she was all he could think about. Embarrassment flooded back to him at the memory. Something so trivial, so normal for others, had completely knocked him off kilter. She was a righteous brat there was no doubt, but deep down she was a kind person. She had shown it when helping Bridget when she first arrived, and when she had helped him with his braid. She irritated everyone because she wanted to pull out who they really were, she wanted to see them "without a mask" as she called it. After her admission to him in the woods about her accidental intrusion and an explanation for why she was who she was, he felt a deeper connection with her. Magic aside, he felt that he could understand her desire to see people as they really were. He too had deep-seated trust issues, and when it came to who she was, he knew he was getting the real her.

He had agreed with her that he would like them to become friends, but what he was afraid to say that day was that he wanted to be something more. He could not understand her interest in him; women never seemed to be interested in him that way. Not that he could blame them, he didn't make it easy. He couldn't even allow women to reach out and touch him without having a complete panic attack, well, everyone except her. He couldn't remember the last time anyone had touched him like that, with such kindness. The feeling of her hands in his hair had relaxed him so deeply he not only found himself leaning against her but craving more. The need for human contact had quickly turned to desire for her. Not that what she was doing was anything particularly sexual in nature, but just that touch sent him spiraling down a path he very rarely found himself on. He would blame the magic she had admitted to using on him, but deep down he knew that magic had not conjured those feelings inside him. They already existed.

He hadn't spoken of this to his brothers, actually he had never spoken to his brothers about this sort of thing ever. There had never been a need to, because discussing this type of thing would mean he would have to tell them his most closed off secret, and he wasn't sure he ever could. It's why he had never been with a woman; he couldn't bring himself to face his past. He couldn't share it with them, but with eyes like a hawk and an over familiarity with how he was in general, his brothers recognized something was different about him now that Grace had come into his life.

"Remind me what we're watching here?" Menolayous asked, staring down into the sparring pit that the warband typically used for training.

"Perfection." Danny leaned forward against the rails as he watched Catriona shoot past a few of the warriors, delivering a nasty kick to the back of one of their legs.

Catriona was enjoying every opportunity to train with Flinn's men, she enjoyed testing out her skills with a blade. Flinn wanted to see what the girl was capable of, as did everyone else in camp, so she had many volunteers for sparring partners. Menolayous glanced over to the old war chief who stood there, mouth open, in what he assumed was a state of shock. Catriona had a way of doing that to people when they watched her fight. Menolayous tracked her as she slashed with her sparring dagger at another warrior's leg as she rolled by, coming up on another and slashing him up the front in what was most definitely a killing blow.

Rama whistled. "She's fast, I'll give her that. But there's always room for improvement."

"I actually just found out she can't ground fight," Danny mentioned, eyes still on his woman.

"That's a problem," Menolayous said, wincing as he watched one of the men hit the ground hard.

"I wonder how you found that out." Rama laughed, eyeing his brother.

Danny smirked at them but said nothing.

"And you haven't bothered to work with her on that?" Menolayous asked, surprised his overprotective brother hadn't tried to fix this issue.

"I'm really not the one who should be trying to teach her that," Danny laughed quietly. "We would never get anywhere."

Oh. Menolayous cleared his throat. That made sense. Menolayous considered offering to help, he could spar with people. He had to, it's how he learned. He was decent at fighting on the ground, but now that he thought about it, he probably shouldn't. He'd never fought with a woman before, and honestly, he would hold back if he thought he was hurting Catriona in any way. He was too messed up in the head, he didn't want to get triggered and end up hurting her.

"That's how the prince got ahold of her last time, right?" Rama asked Menolayous.

"Yeah, he choked her and slammed her to the ground then pinned her. It was the only thing that was able to stop her. She's exceptionally good at evading."

Menolayous saw Danny's hands tighten on the wooden railing, the memory of that day angered him. "Can one of you please train her? I don't want that to happen to her ever again."

"He's about my size, right?" Rama asked Menolayous again.

"A little shorter than you, but you're built like a tree, he's not," Menolayous answered.

"But he's blooded, a powerful one at that," Danny said. "If she's going to take him on one day, which she most undoubtedly will, she'll need to at least be able to get away from you going full speed."

"I agree," Rama said with a hint of a smile. "I've been wanting to see what she can do anyway."

And just like that, Rama easily vaulted over the railing into the sparring pit. Everyone had stopped fighting at the approach of their king, moving aside and out of the way so he could stand in the ring alone facing Catriona. She looked at him, catching her breath, a smile started to spread across her face.

"You really want to fight? Aren't you worried it will damage your royal pride?" Catriona taunted, joining in with the standard royal jokes that everyone in the camp was a party to.

"I'm just here out of brotherly concern. I heard you need some help with ground fighting," he said with a grin.

Catriona shot a look at Danny that made Menolayous take a step to the side. Danny smiled down at her as she flipped him off. Menolayous saw Bridget approaching the ring with a basket of supplies, she had come to tend to any injuries from the sparring pit. She watched the unfolding scene with interest, as did everyone else.

"You're going to have to catch me first." Catriona spun her daggers around in her hand, lowering herself into a fighting stance.

A warrior tried to hand Rama a training axe which he waved off. "Deal."

Suddenly, they both moved with surprising speed at the other, wanting to push the advantage of movement first. Catriona slashed at his forearm with her training dagger, to her obvious surprise he feinted left, missing the dull blade before grabbing her arm. She then rotated her arm in a large circle, slashing downward with her two daggers. Being forced to let go, Rama stepped back, evading that strike as well.

Catriona was after him again, slashing at his legs with her training blades. He dodged the blow, reaching down and snagging her by the neck and lifting her off the ground. She angled herself, delivering a powerful kick to his chest, forcing herself backwards and out of his grip. Rama straightened, smiling still as he watched her reposition herself.

"You're slippery, I'll give you that." He laughed, taking a step forward.

Catriona threw her arm back, launching the training dagger directly at his heart. With a gasp from the crowd, the dagger would have stuck Rama in the center of the chest had he not grabbed it. Flinging the dulled blade to the side, he went for her, no longer playing cat and mouse, and no longer holding back. Catriona ducked out of the way once, barely dodging a hefty blow directed at her face. She arced her blade upwards to slash across his ribs when Rama grabbed her hand, lifting her off her feet. Before she could react, he used his free hand to grab her around the throat and slammed her to the ground on her back. Menolayous winced at the sound of impact, but he understood what his brother was doing. Danny straightened as Rama then straddled her, knocking her last weapon far away.

"Do you know how to get out of this?" Rama asked her, still holding tight. "Stop panicking. It's only me, I'll walk you through it."

Catriona struggled but could not move. Rama held onto her firmly, but not in a way that would injure her. Menolayous could see the wild panic in her eyes, at that point she was reliving it all. Suddenly Grace was by his side, staring down into the sparring match.

"That's not a good idea," she told them as she watched Catriona. "You don't want that panic turning to anger."

"Since when did you start to care?" Danny glanced at her before returning his gaze to the sparring pit.

"I don't," Grace snapped. "I get the point of the training, but that girl is incredibly unstable right now. She has no control over her magic. She'll end up burning your entire camp down if you're not careful."

"Thanks for the input," Danny brushed her off.

"I'm trying to look out for you all," Grace argued.

291

"Then maybe you shouldn't preface it with saying that you don't care," Danny shot at her.

Grace looked to Menolayous, irritation apparent on her face. "*Why aren't they listening to me?*"

"*You didn't come off well in the beginning,*" he answered the voice in his head. "*It will take time for them to trust you.*"

"*And in the meantime, I'm supposed to let everyone die because they don't respect the amount of power that girl has?*"

"*We've never seen it. We've seen her fight, that's formidable in itself. But she needs to work on this, Rama is her best bet. Last time—*" his words died off inside his head.

Danny was now watching their silent exchange with genuine curiosity. Grace ignored him, holding out her hand to him in silent plea. He sighed, if she was going to be around them, she needed to know. He couldn't form the words, this was easier.

Menolayous nodded, closing his eyes as Grace gently rested her hand on the side of his face allowing the images to flash through his mind. First, it was when he had met Catriona after her fight with the prince. Then there were flashes of getting her to safety, how Danny wouldn't put her down. Scenes of Catriona losing weight, not sleeping, not being able to touch meat. He could feel Grace's presence inside his head, the shock and sadness she felt watching Catriona's story. His memories jumped backwards, to when he had first met his brothers in those woods so long ago. How kind they had been after finding him lost and roaming around in the woods. Years of their bond shining brightly against the darkness, how he learned to be comfortable around people again. Their backstories, their victories, their lives. His memories changed to the first time he had met Bridget, how she had come across them after a fight with some royal guards. They had been injured, and he had an infection from the wound. His memories jumped forward again to all of them at the cave, spending time together without worrying about the rebellion. It was one of the few times Menolayous could remember that he felt truly happy. They shifted again, this time to when he met Grace, to her hands brushing through his hair. His fantasies, what he wanted to do with her that night. Then came the shame, the fear. The secrets that he kept inside, why he couldn't act on those desires with her. He felt the need to explain why, so he opened himself up to her magic completely.

He now found himself back in Gaelach when he was ten years old. Standing in the middle of a corral built for cattle. Only it didn't hold cattle, it held the human victims the tribesmen planned to sacrifice to their god. Screams, blood, pain, death. So much killing, so many sacrifices. His mother's and sister's screams as they were violently raped by the silverbacks. Their pleas to stop, their begging. It wasn't just the girls that had to endure this pain. Panic seized him, his eyes opened wide, and he stepped backwards away from Grace. He centered himself quickly, rubbing his wrists and trying to stop the feel of the ropes that had held him so long ago.

"Menolayous?" Her voice rang clear in his head as he looked at her. *"I didn't mean to go that far back. I'm sorry."*

Breathing deeply through his nose, he stilled himself. *"I needed to show you; I couldn't find the words. I've never told anyone."*

Mostly out of reflex, he stepped away from her. Sadness filled her eyes as she looked at him, now she knew his darkest secret. He couldn't bear it, the sight of her pity, he needed to leave. He turned away from the sparring pit and took off. He raced down the pathway leading out of the village where he made for the forest. He needed to be alone; he needed to get away from everyone.

Chapter Forty-Two

Clyous

Clyous lay facing Bridget, enjoying every moment he was able to look into her smiling face. This was their first night sleeping side by side, even back at the cave outside the capital city they hadn't done anything more than share a few passionate kisses. Danny had outright refused to spend another night away from Catriona, giving Bridget only a few options for where she could stay the night. Rama and Menolayous shared one of the houses while Morrigan and Grace shared the other. Bridget had told him that she felt more comfortable with him than the others, a fact he was not going to take for granted or take advantage of. Truthfully, the admission brought him a sense of joy, he was happy that she was comfortable with him. Elated really.

"It's probably a good thing Flinn gave us houses this far away from everyone else." Bridget giggled as the subtle voices from the connected treehouse finally died down. "I honestly can't tell if they're fighting or having sex."

"Considering one of them is my twin sister, I'm choosing to believe that they're arguing over something." Clyous laughed. "Which is probably as likely as the later."

"I'm happy for them," Bridget said, turning onto her back and facing the ceiling. "They both deserve to be happy."

"What about you?" Clyous also turned over onto his back. "What would make you happy?" He watched her as she seemed to ponder this question.

"It's easier for me to answer with what I don't want."

"Okay, what don't you want?" He gently nudged her with his elbow.

"I don't want to live in Oich anymore, pretending to be a happy submissive citizen while playing spy. I don't want to be kept on the sidelines anymore." She sighed. "I don't want to be afraid. My whole life I've been playing this role where everyone treats me like I'm not important, or like they need to protect me. I just want to be my own person."

Clyous let the silence sit for a moment before saying, "Then don't do those things. Stay here. Having any actual healer here at camp would be more than welcome, I'm sure of it. Flinn absolutely loves you, he'd probably build you your own house if you asked him."

She rolled onto her side, looking at him again. "I guess I could. I could be free of my father and Liam, and of a society who treats me like I'm nothing because I don't value violence and dominance in the same ways they do."

"I think you would really like staying here." He brushed a strand of hair off her face. "Why do you seem hesitant?"

"It's against my wolf's nature to abandon the pack," she answered flatly. "Sometimes my wolf's very nature can be a hindrance. Getting away from all of them is the most logical choice for my well-being."

"But you wouldn't be leaving your pack," Clyous argued. "We're right here."

"Would you let me stay with you?" she asked nervously.

He smiled at that, leaning forward and gently kissing her on the forehead. "You can stay with me as long as you want. Forever, if that's what you pick."

She giggled again. "Thank you, that means the world to me."

They sat there for a few moments, staring into each other's eyes. Clyous was thankful that Bridget was in his life, that she wanted to stay with him. He found himself wanting to kiss her on the lips but resisted. He was too nervous; it might spoil the moment if she wasn't interested. He didn't want her to think that staying here with him came with any ulterior motives or any expectations. He meant it, regardless of what they were, he wanted her to feel safe here with him.

"Can I ask you some personal questions?" he asked, simply wanting to get to know her better.

"Sure." She smiled softly. "I'm an open book."

He paused, steeling himself for an answer that had the potential to create an uncomfortable situation. "Can we talk about Liam?"

Her smile dropped. "What would you like to know?"

"Everything. How did he come into your life? What happened to make you guys drift apart? What your feelings are for him."

295

"Liam and I grew up together. Truthfully, he was my only friend growing up. I was there for him when his mother was killed, and he was always there to protect me from everyone else."

"Who was he protecting you from? Your father?"

"As we got older, his presence often stayed my father's hand but he protected me from everyone else too. Part of being moon touched is the hierarchy. The strongest, like Liam, are always in charge, leaders of the pack. They are expected to rule, enforce laws, and put down anyone who challenges their dominance. Failure to do so means they are bumped down to the bottom."

"Where are you in this hierarchy?"

"I'm supposed to be at the top, right underneath Liam. My family has a strong, dominating bloodline. According to my father, our family and Liam's fought for dominance over a hundred years ago. My family obviously lost, leaving Liam's to rule Oich. Society forced me to the very bottom of the hierarchy. The expectation was that the pack would toughen me up or put an end to my weakness."

"I'm assuming that's where Liam came in."

She nodded. "He meant well. His mother taught him to be kind, to stand up for others, and he was always kind to me. We eventually fell in love. Young and naive love. We were too young to understand what we were doing, how our worlds influenced how we treated each other."

"He was your first then?"

"He's been my only," she answered.

This came to a bit of a shock to him. She'd never been with anyone else? "What happened to his mother?"

"Liam told me that his father had captured a sorcerer, and in his attempts to escape from them his mother was killed. Liam was never sure who dealt the killing blow, the sorcerer or his father. That's why Liam's hatred for anyone with magic made sense as he got older. I think he blames that incident on losing his mother and pours all of his hatred into dealing with anyone they find."

"You mean torturing and publicly executing magic users?" Clyous could not keep the bitterness from his voice. "Aside from what he did to Catriona and our mother, I have heard stories about him over the last few years. If there is any truth to them, we got off easy." His voice trailed off, he was willing himself to forget that train of thought with all his might.

"I honestly think that seeing me there stopped him," Bridget answered.

"Does he know about your magic?" He was genuinely curious now.

"Yes," she answered quietly. "Which means he knew that your mother was cured."

Clyous felt rage surge through him like a sudden fever. He willed his temper back into check, it would do him no good here. That bastard knew that his mother wasn't infected. Especially after Bridget spoke up. She had shown herself to the crown prince trying to save her, and he still did what he did.

"I wouldn't call that mercy," he seethed.

"No." She gently took one of his hands in hers. "I think he was afraid to show me what he really was. But it was already too late, I could see who he was when he ordered the fire lit. That alone is something I can never forget or forgive."

After several moments Clyous was finally able to steel himself against his anger. "What happened to you guys? What ended it?"

"His father did not like his son, the prince, spending so much time with a runt. The king started to force Liam to participate in various affairs of state, trying to change him into something cruel and wicked. He used Liam's hatred for magic to bring him into the darkness and slowly it began to take over. As far as our relationship went, Liam became very controlling with me, very jealous. He expected me to submit to him all the time, which I did, but he acted as if I was his prized possession and didn't want anyone else to look at me or speak to me. I never fully realized what that was until after we separated. Eventually, Liam ended things between us, claiming he needed to find a wife with more of a backbone. One who wasn't a runt, who wasn't weak, who hadn't whored herself out at the first chance she got."

"He actually said that to you?"

A tear slid down her cheek as she nodded. "Part of me believes he did it to keep his father away from me. He knew just what to say to completely shatter my heart, to make me run away from him."

"He's an asshole." Clyous wiped away the tear. "Letting you go like that was cowardly."

"I hadn't seen him in years, ever since he ended things between us. Not until that day with you and your family."

"I have no doubt in my mind that Catriona will one day repay that debt." Clyous knew it in his heart, had seen it with his gift several times in several different ways. Catriona would repay that debt in full.

"As is her right." Bridget nodded. "Since that day, Liam comes to find me whenever I am at the capital. Each time I've seen him he seems like the Liam I knew from all those years ago. He even asked for my hand in marriage, which I rejected."

"Is he likely to try and hurt you for turning him down?" Clyous felt legitimate concern.

"No," she answered. "The one thing I can say with certainty is that Liam would never hurt me."

"But he has hurt you," Clyous pointed out softly.

Bridget's expression changed into something sad as his words sunk in. The last thing he wanted to do was make her upset. But she needed to know, in order to better protect herself from a man like that. He had held her heart once, played with it, claimed it was his, then violently threw it to the side. The prince was a dangerous man, Clyous didn't believe that he wouldn't try to possess Bridget again. Clyous only hoped that she was right that he would not lay his hands on her at least.

Before either of them could speak, a loud crashing sound came from one of the other huts. That was not his sister's hut, this sounded louder and more violent. Then he heard shouts, Rama's voice booming into the night as if he were yelling at someone. Clyous and Bridget scrambled to their feet, rushing for one of the doors that led outside. As they got to the rope bridge Clyous could see they weren't the only ones responding to the shouting. Catriona and Danny were coming up right behind them, Clyous could see Grace and Morrigan also converging on the hut that lay between them. Being so late, everyone was in various stages of nightly undress, but the urgency of the sounds drove them forward.

"Menolayous, it's me! Put the fucking knife down!" they could hear Rama's voice booming from inside.

"What's happening?" Danny called, throwing open the door.

"Menolayous is having one of his bad nightmares!" Rama backed out through the open door toward his other brother, putting distance between himself and the knife. "I've never seen one so bad."

Clyous peered inside the hut, eyes focusing on the sole occupant. Menolayous stood in the center of the room holding a knife in one hand while slashing at invisible foes. Menolayous's appearance was shocking, not because he was shirtless, not because his long hair was down, but because his body was covered in scars.

Clyous heard Bridget gasp beside him as she beheld the intensity of marred flesh. The scars mostly appeared to be years old. Along the man's sides Clyous could see what looked like severe burn marks that traveled down past his belt line. As Menolayous slashed at an invisible opponent, his back revealed scars that matched Catriona's, but there were significantly more of them. Down his arms were fresher scars, tiny slashes as if made by a knife or dagger crisscrossed down his forearms. This man had been through the worst and back.

"Does he do this often?" Grace called from the other rope bridge.

"No." Rama cast her a suspicious glance. "They're not normally this bad. I couldn't seem to wake him up, then he pulled a knife on me."

"He battles with the darkness," Morrigan spoke with her eyes shut as if she were concentrating. "The Dark One has entered his mind through the shadows. He's feeding off the boy's past."

Everyone looked back to Menolayous who was still slashing wildly at the air. Wild wasn't even a good description, Menolayous was acting like a feral lynx with a foot caught in a hunter's trap. His eyes were open but unseeing, like there was nothing behind them.

"We need to wake him," Catriona announced to the group. "We need to break the connection between him and the Dark One before he hurts himself."

"Alright," Rama started to say, "Danny—"

"No!" Grace shouted out almost viciously. "If he's remembering the past, the approach of men will set him off, brothers don't matter here."

"What does that mean?" Danny began to challenge. "What makes you think you know our brother better than we do."

Catriona gently laid a hand on Danny's shoulder. "She's right."

Danny appeared very confused, as did Bridget and himself, but Rama looked between Grace and Catriona, nodding. They knew something the rest of them didn't but now was not the time to focus on that. Menolayous's thrashing was becoming more violent as he began looking towards the sounds of their voices.

"If I can lay my hands on him, I can pull him out," Grace called to Catriona.

"Be ready," was all his sister said before stepping inside the room.

As soon as her bare feet touched the floor, Menolayous swung his body around to face hers. A demonic voice now spilled from his mouth.

"The powerhouse has entered the arena," many voices echoed. "Your light is nearly blinding, little one. You've drawn me here, like a moth to the flame."

Bridget clung to Clyous at the sound. Menolayous spoke with voices that did not belong to him in perfect unison. His eyes observed his sister like they were assessing their next meal. This was the Dark One, Clyous realized, the monster he had seen in his visions. Before him, possessing the body of their friend, was the most dangerous dark force in all of Stone Basin. They were royally fucked.

"I don't believe we've met." Catriona walked in a slow circle around Menolayous, her voice steady as if she were completely unphased.

"Here I was thinking to myself, tonight was just another night to come visit Menolayous and reminisce over our lovely history, when suddenly a half-naked girl with wildfire steps forward." The knife changed hands. "How lucky am I? I never realized Menolayous had it in him to hide you from me. Then again, he's always been a tough nut to crack."

"I want you out of my friend," she called to the Dark One, still prowling in a semi-circle waiting for an opening.

"Oh, but I've been inside him many times. You'll never be able to erase those scars, in fact, many of what you see were caused by my hand."

"Get out," Catriona snapped.

"Let me inside you and I'll leave the poor boy alone," the Dark One teased. "No? Too proud? Or too scared of what the darkness will show you about yourself?"

With a taunting smile, the Dark One turned the knife onto Menolayous's arm, then began slashing at his flesh with the blade. Blood sprayed everywhere as the knife went to work on the already scarred flesh. Catriona launched herself, grabbing the hand with the knife with both her hands. With Menolayous's free arm, the Dark One dropped low, thrusting his

300

arm between Catriona's legs, and lifting. Catriona was raised into the air and then dropped onto the ground hard. Still holding onto the dagger with both hands, Catriona did not bother trying to evade the Dark One as he crawled on top of her in a predatory position.

"Where's the fire now?" the Dark One taunted, "Does this bring back memories for you?"

Before anyone could move in to help, Grace was there. Sneaking up behind Menolayous, she placed her hands on the sides of his head, concentrating. Within seconds Menolayous seemed to return to the scene in front of him, no more traces of the Dark One left in his eyes. Finding himself on top of Catriona, the real Menolayous threw himself off her, scampering to a corner.

"I'm sorry," he gasped, tears streaming down his face. "I'm sorry."

A collective sigh of relief went through the group. Danny rushed forward to check on Catriona, who thankfully wasn't hurt but was drenched in Menolayous's blood. Rama moved towards Menolayous, reaching out a hand. To everyone's surprise Menolayous stumbled back away from his brother, cowering at his approach.

"You're bleeding, brother," Rama's voice was laced with concern, but he stopped advancing. "Let us help you."

Despite the blood still flowing from his wounds, Menolayous shook his head. Now he was completely sitting in the corner. Menolayous wrapped his arms around his legs, burying his tear-soaked face into his knees to hide it from everyone. Clyous had never seen a man this broken before, had never expected it from someone so put together and stoic.

Bridget cautiously approached him, with a gentle voice she said, "Hold out your arm, Menolayous. That's it. Thank you."

Grace was by her side, the two women lowering themselves, so they sat at his height. A non-threatening approach he realized, as if they were approaching a baby deer or lost bear cub. Bridget slowly reached out, touching the bleeding wound gently. Menolayous flinched at the touch but allowed it. A golden glow emanated from her hands, flowing into the torn flesh. Clyous watched in awe as the wound began to heal right in front of them.

Once the cuts were healed, Bridget slowly backed away, returning to Clyous's side. She wrapped her arms around his waist, burying her face in his shoulder. Grace remained next to Menolayous, who was still curled up in a ball. She reached out, touching his arm gently. Menolayous looked up at her, recognition hitting him like a thunderclap.

Grace tried to pull Menolayous's arms from around his knees gently. Seeming almost thankful for the physical contact, Menolayous surprised everyone by wrapping his arms around Grace's waist and pulling her to him. Stunned, she now sat on her knees in between his legs facing him, and he held her in an embrace as if at that moment his life depended on it.

Grace embraced him back as he buried his face in her neck, trembling. Grace ran her fingers through his hair as he shook, this gesture alone seeming to help calm him slightly.

"You should leave them," Morrigan's voice echoed inside all their heads, Rama and Danny jumped. *"Your brother is safe now."*

"The Dark One won't come back?" Rama's voice asked.

"Not with Grace there. She will protect him, rebuild his defenses," Morrigan answered, starting to walk back towards her hut.

"I don't feel comfortable leaving her with him after all of that," Danny said, his voice hesitant.

"Have any of you ever been able to comfort him after a night terror?" Morrigan asked. *"You do not get to choose for others who they want to open up to."*

"Come on," Rama said, closing the door behind him, *"let's leave them be."*

The group left, scattering in different directions back to their own huts to process what had just happened. Bridget was still clinging to him as they headed back in the direction of their hut. As they left, Clyous could swear he heard quiet sobbing from Menolayous now that everyone had gone. He could also hear the gentle voice of Grace reassuring Menolayous that he was safe and that he was loved.

Chapter Forty-Three

Grace

Grace found him easily enough, easier than she should have with little to no hunting skills. For a tracker it should have been more difficult to find him after he had taken off in the early spring morning, seeing how he obviously wanted to get away from her and hide. She wasn't particularly surprised though and had even expected him to disappear at some point.

After Menolayous's brothers and the rest of them had left the treehouse last night, Grace had spent what was probably the better part of a few hours holding onto him or allowing him to hold onto her. Menolayous was in desperate need of comfort after being forced to relive his most terrible nightmares. For a reason unknown to her, he had picked her to share this with. She could tell by reading everyone else's emotions that this was a shocking sight for all of them. She was prepared to fight his brothers and even Catriona if they had tried to pull her away, but just as she had seen it, they knew he needed that comfort from her. So, she stayed the night with him. They hadn't spoken a single word to each other; they just sat or lay there in each other's presence. Grace was unsure who fell asleep first, but she did know that she had fallen asleep in his arms as he held her to his scarred chest. This was obviously a new coping mechanism for him, and she suspected that their closeness would make him uncomfortable to some degree. What she did not expect was to find Menolayous in the exact same spot he had found her less than a week ago, where she was sketching on her parchment with pieces of charcoal from the fire.

Last night was arguably one of the scariest events she'd ever experienced, the only night surpassing it was the night she had watched Ingrid be ritually torn apart and eaten. Both nights shared the same enemy, the Dark One, whatever he was. She could sense his presence the moment she laid eyes on Menolayous, she could sense their struggle over who possessed Menolayous's body. She was terrified when she came face to face with that monster, but not just for herself, she was actually more concerned about Menolayous. Grace had learned from an early age that the only person she could trust was herself. It's why she was always acting like a bitch, why she never formed attachments to her lovers, and why she never bothered to make friends. Now she felt herself putting this man before her own needs, she felt a deep protectiveness of him, and she was prepared to go down fighting if that's what it took to save her friend.

She was incredibly surprised and thankful that she was able to force the Dark One from Menolayous's mind. She hadn't been sure she was strong enough against such a powerful dark magic user, but she found that she was willing to risk her own life to protect his. She threw herself into the fray, entering Menolayous's mind to search out the parasite within. She saw that he was experiencing past memories, horrible images of his childhood surrounded her as she searched. She did her best to keep focused, knowing the sound of his pain was meant as a distraction for her as well as Menolayous himself. She finally found the dark lanky figure strolling around in Menolayous's memories. She forced him out, using up most of her magic to do so, but she had succeeded.

"If I didn't know any better," Grace said, as she maneuvered herself around the log to sit beside him, grimacing at the dampness of the morning dew. "I'd say you weren't hiding from me."

Menolayous glanced at her as she sat next to him. "I realize it probably appears that way considering how I left this morning, but it wasn't my intention. It's easier for me to think out here away from everybody."

Grace nodded in understanding; she lost herself in the wilderness as often as possible for that very reason. "If I made you feel uncomfortable at all—"

"You didn't." Menolayous gave her a half smile. "I was thankful you stayed. I found it very comforting, as you probably felt. You staying meant more to me than I know how to explain."

"If comfort makes you run, I'm not sure how to proceed with our relationship," Grace teased.

"Thank you, Grace," Menolayous said warmly. "Not just for saving me but staying with me.

"You're welcome," Grace answered. "I find that I'm willing to do just about anything for you, even face my greatest fears. Since we're in the habit of confessing personal information to each other I might as well add that in."

"Since we're making confessions... I'm embarrassed you saw me like that."

"Why?" she asked curiously, "It's not like most people would be able to stop the Dark One from entering their dreams. He's incredibly powerful."

304

Menolayous squirmed uncomfortably at her words. "It's not that. I've been plagued by nightmares for a long time. Sometimes I lose control of myself without even realizing it, I don't want anyone to see me like that."

"It's okay, it's what friends do, we see the bad sides of each other just as much as the good. It doesn't make me think less of you, if anything I got to see you with your shirt off." Grace gave him a teasing wink in an attempt to lighten the mood.

Menolayous's face dropped at her words, visibly affected. "You don't have to lie about that. I appreciate it, but I know how bad the scars are."

He was serious, she realized. He always wore a tunic during training, and even while helping build the wall. She couldn't blame him for wanting to hide the scars from people he didn't know, especially scars of that magnitude, but to hide them from friends? He didn't hide them from his adopted brothers, that wouldn't have been possible. She supposed she wasn't on that level, she shouldn't be. It was the fact that he thought she was lying about that, lying at all, that affected her in a way she didn't expect.

"You should know me well enough by now to know that I don't lie." Grace stared into his eyes. "I'm attracted to you, scars and all. They make up who you are. You shouldn't feel like you need to hide anything from me."

His cheeks reddened slightly at her words, but he recognized that they rang true and said, "My people have a centuries old tradition where they scar their bodies with inked images, tattoos that tell a person's story, something to be proud of."

"That's a Gaelach tradition, right?" After she saw the nod of his head she continued, "Why don't you have any?"

"If you haven't noticed." He laughed. "I have issues letting anyone touch me."

"You let me touch you, maybe I could tattoo you."

She watched Menolayous closely as he listened to her words. "I think I could handle that," he said.

"Great!" She clapped her hands together excitedly. "I only know how to draw. I don't actually know how to tattoo."

"I remember how, I'm just not artistic. I've been able to do simple designs since I was younger."

"Then you should be able to teach me." She winked. "More time to see you without a shirt on."

"Great, it'll take time for me to gather the correct supplies." He was smiling broadly at her now, accepting her teasing lightheartedly.

She beamed at how excited he was at this. He had a look about him, an ease she hadn't seen from him before. Good, he deserved to not walk around grumpy or on guard all the time. If she was able to do this for him, to give him something so he could look at himself and not want to hide, she didn't know a gift better than that.

"I have one condition." She stood before him, gently leaning forward and pressing her lips against his cheek. "If you ever find yourself in bed with me again, don't sneak out before I wake up."

Instead of the slight muscle tightening reaction at her touch she expected to see, instead, a gentle smile slowly spread across his face. She felt herself smile in response; she was growing on him.

"Consider it a deal." *He* winked at her, eliciting a giggle from her before hugging her around the waist. "Next time I won't."

Chapter Forty-Four

Rama

Rama watched them as they came back into Collie from the forest. Rama had suspected that Menolayous would take off into the forest at some point, it was something he'd done since they had met each other all those years ago. Whenever Menolayous took off, he and Danny knew that he needed space in order to work something out or ground himself. Every now and then they were able to corner Menolayous and possibly get some information out of him, usually it was information about what was bothering him. It was never why that information bothered him. He never told them what the nightmares were about, but he and Danny assumed it was from his childhood, whatever trauma their brother had endured before running into the forest to get away from it. Rama had always suspected Menolayous was from Gaelach, having run into him at its southernmost border. Through the years Menolayous had shown great resentment towards that kingdom, generally refusing to step foot inside of it, but he knew their traditions, their culture, he despised the blooded silverbacks more than anything. He would never talk about it, so Rama wasn't sure until now.

This woman, this entitled princess from Airgid, strolls into camp with Menolayous and suddenly everything about their brother began to change. Menolayous was confiding in her, telling her about his night terrors, telling her about his past, something he never did with Rama or Danny. Rama could admit it struck his jealousy bone, but it also concerned him. Nobody knew who this demon woman was. What they did know was that she had a bad attitude, directing most of it at Catriona. She claimed that his little sister was dangerously unstable, that she possessed a magic that could kill all of them if Catriona let it fly unchecked. Rama had never seen it, and honestly, he was reluctant to believe anything Grace said. *For all he knew, she was sinking her claws into Menolayous as a way to manipulate and control him.* Rama found himself trusting her less and less, subsequently the more he saw his brother get attached to her.

Rama watched as the two of them exited the trees, smiling at each other like lovestruck fools. Rama continued to watch as they pulled away from each other, their hands separating as if they had been intertwined. If Rama had feathers, they would be ruffled at the sight of this. Another example of how this woman was changing his brother; he was allowing someone to touch him. This was by far the most monumental change of them all, Danny and Rama had never been allowed to casually touch their brother. The occasional clap on the back or embrace after not having seen each other for some time should have been normal gesture between them, but with Menolayous the only time they were able to make physical contact with him and have it not turn into a shit fight, was ironically enough, during a fight. Whether it be for training or an actual battle, Menolayous did not balk at physical contact then, there was a purpose for it. The caveat being he did not like to be pinned down or have his movement limited.

When they were younger and dumber, Rama and Danny had taken this as a challenge, trying to overtake Menolayous just to prove they could. Menolayous was by far the better ground fighter, even if the two worked together Menolayous always ended up beating the ever living shit out of them. Once they got older and realized how their little game affected their brother they stopped playing it. It wasn't until Catriona's words a few days ago and the events from last night that proved how much of an ass both of them had been playing such a game. Something terrible had happened to their brother when he was younger, something that explained why he was so reclusive. Rama was afraid to ask him about it and felt more protective of him than ever before. Hence why the sudden appearance of a female in his brother's life had him on guard. *If he had proof that this harlot was using his brother for something nefarious, if she hurt his brother in any way, he would kill her.*

"Would you look at that." Danny had snuck up behind him, making himself comfortable while leaning up against one of the recently buried fence posts. "I've never seen him this happy before."

"You think he's happy?" Rama glanced over at Danny before returning his gaze to Grace, who was now headed back towards their tree homes. "Are you sure she's not manipulating him?"

"I'm not sure." Danny glanced at him with some level of concern in his words. "I don't like her, don't get me wrong. Her and Cat are like oil mixed with fire, but she doesn't strike me as conniving. She's brutally honest and has her own opinions. She doesn't seem like the type to play games like that."

"I've never seen our brother like this before, I just don't want him to get hurt," Rama admitted.

"Let's ask him about it," Danny suggested. "I for one don't want my suspicions to get in the way of his happiness. If you're that worried, we should talk to him."

308

"That's not likely to go well." Rama laughed. "You know how much he loves to talk."

Danny rolled his eyes as he pushed himself up and off the post. He nodded towards their brother, who had spotted them and began walking in their direction. Danny and Rama went to greet him, Menolayous was no longer smiling but he seemed in a good mood. Which was strange considering everything that happened last night. Anyone in their right mind would be terrified after being possessed by an evil sorcerer.

"How are you feeling?" Danny asked once Menolayous had neared them enough for conversation.

"Fine," Menolayous answered, glancing between the two of them. "As fine as I can be I guess."

"That was some scary shit, I don't know how I'd handle all that," Rama interjected honestly.

"The nightmares weren't anything too different from my normal. I didn't even feel the Dark One slip in. It wasn't until everyone showed up that I realized I wasn't in control of my body anymore." Menolayous gave over more information than Rama had expected.

"But Grace was able to get him out of your head, that's a good thing," Danny said encouragingly.

"Yeah," was all Menolayous said to that.

"Looks like you two are getting close," Danny suggested.

Menolayous did not answer. Instead, he gave the famous Menolayous reply, staring directly at Danny with no trace of emotion on his face. Now this was what Rama had expected from the beginning. It was something he did not understand. Why would he stop talking about her unless there was a reason to keep information from them? A woman in your life shouldn't be something to hide, especially from one's brothers. *Unless she was telling him to keep it from them, telling Menolayous he couldn't trust his brothers.*

"It just seems like you're happier now than you've ever been, and if Grace is the reason, then I'm happy she's in your life," Danny tried to explain. "I feel that way with Catriona. Having her in my life has made such a difference, in ways I never would have thought possible."

Rama's ears perked up at the sound of shouting and screams from a distance. All three of them stopped and swiveled their heads in the direction the sounds were coming from. Rama spotted what looked like a dark fog bank covering their tree homes. Fear overtook him as the clicking sounds and screams of the scourge began to intermingle with those of the warriors. Menolayous and Danny began racing in the direction of their homes. Rama quickly followed, shouting to the workers nearby to get their weapons and follow them. Quickly, the Collie craftsmen donned their fighting gear and became the warriors they were there to be, charging towards the oncoming enemy.

Rama caught up with his brothers easily as they rounded the hill, barreling headfirst into the fog. It was as if the sun had been completely covered, letting hardly any light inside the fog bank. Rama had a battle axe in hand as he charged forward to the sound of a woman screaming. The fog was so thick he could hardly see more than five feet in front of him. Danny and Menolayous stayed near enough as they searched, desperate to find their loved ones.

A woman's body hit the ground just within sight, a scourge going down with her as it tried to claw at her face and neck. Bridget was strong enough to hold the creature at bay, preventing it from sinking its claws into her flesh. Menolayous and Danny moved quickly, but not quick enough. Another figure had come to aid Bridget in the fog, driving a dagger through the back of the scourge's head as she ripped the beast from the healer. Grace stood there looking down at the blooded woman, coated in dark blood from the scourge.

"Are you okay?" Grace asked, reaching a hand down to Bridget and helping her to her feet.

"Yes! It didn't harm me." Bridget lifted her hand up into view, showing a superficial cut on her palm. "The creature was wearing a silver necklace. It cut me, I won't be able to shift."

"Grace!" Menolayous called to her as he ran up to her, embracing her quickly. "Are you hurt?"

"I'm fine." Grace turned her attention back to the healer. "Can you fight?"

"No." Bridget allowed the glow of her magic to quickly patch up the cut on her hand. "Not in this form."

"Stay beside me then," Grace ordered as she began unraveling a whip that was tied around her waist.

"Where is Catriona?" Danny asked Grace nervously, glancing around in the fog.

"I'm not sure. I was returning to the houses when the fog descended. I can't even tell how many there are, I've killed maybe three."

"I can smell her," Bridget said, looking to their left. "She and Morrigan are over there, it sounds like they're fighting."

"Let's go!" Danny charged in the direction Bridget had indicated, the rest of them followed.

The sound of warriors slashing away at these mindless monsters filled the air. Rama struck out at any of the scourge he came across as they moved, he successfully removed the head from one of the beasts as it tried to sink its teeth into one of the Collie warriors. Menolayous moved as quickly as Danny, letting his twin axe blades free as they cut into the flesh of their enemies. The brothers moved at an efficient pace, cutting down any scourge they came upon while Grace hovered around Bridget.

"Bridget!?" he could hear Clyous's voice cutting through the fog as they pushed toward the homes.

"Over here," Bridget called out to him as she dodged an oncoming scourge.

Grace was able to slide the tip of her dagger into the creature's eye socket, driving the beast to the dirt. Menolayous fell upon it then, severing the head from its shoulders, allowing Grace to pull her blade free and go back into position where she was protecting Bridget.

"Fucking die already!" they heard Catriona's voice cursing as if she were locked in a battle.

"Cat!?" Clyous's voice called. "Behind you!"

"Fuck—" Catriona's curse was cut off by the sounds of a struggle.

Rama could not see her or her twin brother. Panic began to set in at the realization that she was actively fighting off these beasts. Rama glanced over at Danny who was desperately trying to cut through a pair of scourge to go in the direction of his woman's voice. Menolayous joined Danny in his struggle, trying to get past the monsters. It almost seemed as if they were trying to delay Danny from getting to her, but these beasts were supposed to be mindless hunters.

"Stay with Bridget!" Grace shoved the healer into his arms as she turned to help Catriona.

"What are you doing?" Rama growled, righting the redhead as he glared at the princess. "It's too dangerous to take off alone."

311

"I can see her, you big idiot." Grace didn't bother pausing as she insulted him, vaulting over a skirmish between a warrior and a scourge.

Rama watched in utter shock and surprise as the princess took off, allowing herself to be swallowed up by the fog. Rama gripped Bridget's arms tightly, dragging her with him as he pushed forward. Danny and Menolayous having dispatched their foes, joined him as they pressed forward in a hurry. Rama could see figures just ahead through the thick veil of fog, it looked like three monsters dragging someone further back into the forest.

"Get... off... you... dickheads!" Catriona's voice emanated from the person being dragged back.

Danny and Menolayous charged forward with their weapons raised to aid her, but another figure got there first. With a loud crack, a whip lashed out, slicing across the face of one of the scourge, knocking it to the side. As the whip bounced off its first victim, the tip wrapped its way around the second scourge's neck. Grace threw herself to the side, pulling the monster with it as she threw her only dagger at the one remaining. The dagger buried itself hilt deep into the creature's gaunt face. Menolayous caught up with Grace, engaging with the scourge still attached to the end of Grace's whip. Danny and Bridget rushed to Catriona, who was lifting herself from the ground having been freed.

"Are you okay?" Danny asked her, holding her still so he could visually examine her. "Did they hurt you?"

"I'm fine," Catriona breathed heavily. "Fuckers seemed more interested in trying to drag me off than tear into me."

"Scourge don't drag people off," Bridget said, as she too eyed Catriona up and down. "They only care to devour."

"Not if they're controlled by the Dark One." Grace brushed herself off before retrieving her dagger from the dead scourge's skull. "He manipulates them to his will, uses the fog to move them during the day."

"Why would he do that?" Rama asked, looking around the fog as the battle continued on around them.

"He came for her," Grace said pointing at Catriona. "Probably me too if he could manage both. He wants her power."

"Thanks, by the way," Catriona said to Grace in the friendliest tone he heard them exchange to date.

"You're welcome." Grace gave her a half smile.

Suddenly the fog around them began to swirl, moving with a strong wind. The group huddled closer together preparing for an attack. After about a minute of this wind the fog began to clear, revealing a body ridden battleground all around them. Rama glanced around at a few fallen warriors, weapons still in hand. He was proud enough to say that he saw at least twice the number of dead scourge littering the earth. Morrigan began walking towards them, her hands raised to the sky as her blue magic danced in the wind. She was the one moving the fog from this place. As she continued, Rama watched a few remaining scourge begin to shriek as the sun's rays touched their skin, their flesh beginning to disintegrate. Lightning bolts shot through the air from Morrigan's hands, striking the remaining creatures and they fell to the ground lifeless.

"About time you showed up," Rama jested at the older sorceress, he had to admit he was thoroughly impressed by her magic.

Morrigan lowered her hands, allowing the wind to finally die down. "Someone had to clean up your mess, young one."

Rama laughed as he took her in and observed the whole scenario. All the more reason to have this wall built. It had been some time since Collie had experienced a scourge attack, let alone one of this magnitude. Scourge usually traveled in groups no larger than five, but as Grace pointed out they were sent here for a purpose. Rama could count about twenty from where he stood, and he knew he was not seeing them all. This attack meant several things, and none of them were good. The first was that the Dark One had real power, not just enough to enter his brother's mind and wreak havoc, but enough magic and control over the scourge to move a large group of them across the land during the day. The other problem was that the scourge were definitely going for Catriona. Apparently, seeing her last night was enough to spark his interest, and it also meant she did in fact have some sort of magic, something that the Dark One wanted for himself. If Grace and Catriona were of interest to him it did not bode well for his brothers or his newly acquired family. His personal issues aside, it was his job to protect them from this new enemy.

"Clyous!" Bridget broke Rama's train of thought, shouting to their only missing party member.

Clyous was helping Connor limp a man towards them, carrying him by the shoulders between them both. Rama recognized the warrior as having been with the camp for several years now. As they neared, Rama could see several bite marks on the warrior's forearm. Normally an injury from a scourge meant they would turn into one, but Bridget had healed Catriona and Clyous's mother, there was a good chance she could do it again.

"He's been bitten," Clyous huffed out, setting the warrior down on the ground.

Bridget knelt before him examining the wound. "Hold still, this will feel different."

Rama watched in awe as Bridget's hands began to emanate a golden glow as she gently grasped the warrior's forearm. In front of them all, the wounds began to heal and mend themselves at an unnatural speed. The warrior looked on, wide-eyed and clearly not quite believing what he was seeing.

"There," Bridget said, removing her hands from his completely uninjured arm. "You have nothing to fear now. You will not turn."

"Thank you, my lady." The warrior bowed his head to Bridget, showing his respect.

"Connor, bring all the wounded here so I can tend to them," Bridget ordered the younger male.

"Yes, Miss Bridget, right away." Connor took off, sprinting across the battlefield.

"Are you okay?" Clyous asked her after a quick embrace. "I went looking for you but couldn't find you."

"I'm okay, I got cut with silver so I couldn't shift. Luckily everyone found me quickly enough." Bridget smiled at him warmly.

"We need to talk about that," Grace and Catriona said at the same time, glancing at each other in surprise.

"You will need to learn to defend yourself, girl," Morrigan stated simply, eyeing Bridget up and down curiously. "You will not always be able to rely on your wolf. It would benefit you to learn."

"Yes, you should learn." Grace nodded her agreement. "You can't heal yourself forever."

Catriona glanced at Grace with an eyebrow raised. "I agree with them. This world is not friendly to women."

"I would like to learn," Bridget said. "I'm tired of being helpless,"

"We're all going to be helpless soon if we can't get this wall built," Rama stated the fact to everyone. "We're now looking at a direct assault from two separate and powerful enemies. Without defense around Collie we will be sitting ducks, easy to pick off."

"The Dark One has shown an interest in you, girl." Morrigan looked at Catriona now. "He wants your fire. He will not stop until he has it, you and Grace have targets on your back now. You two must work together and you must learn to control your magic."

Catriona glanced at Grace with a suspicious expression. "I've never experienced magic before. If I'm as dangerous as everyone seems to think I shouldn't be practicing here."

"We will test your skills outside of Collie," Morrigan declared. "We all need to work on training together, us women. There is much to learn and work on if we intend to survive this war."

"I'm game if you're game." Grace winked at Catriona, a small smile spread across her face.

"Only if I get a crack at you in the ring first." Catriona rose to meet the challenge. "You're more skilled than I thought."

"In more ways than one." Grace laughed. "It's on."

"By the gods, someone help us all," Danny made the joke to the group, causing everyone to laugh at the irony of the situation.

Chapter Forty-Five

Catriona

Catriona smiled as she watched Bridget approach. The healer had changed from one of her regular dresses to trousers and a man's tunic. Her long red hair was braided into two plaits behind her head. She looked extremely uncomfortable as she walked, most likely not used to menswear. It took everything in Catriona not to laugh out loud at the expression Bridget wore as she walked, laughing at her would not start off today's training lesson off well.

They were currently standing in an empty clearing, several minutes away from camp. When Bridget had come to her wanting to learn how to defend herself, Catriona knew right away that her shy friend needed privacy if she was going to do this. Not that any of the men back at camp had done anything wrong specifically, but they did like to hover around when Catriona entered the ring. Bridget being so new to this, Catriona was sure that all those eyes on her wouldn't do her any good.

"You've got this," Catriona tried to say encouragingly. "You'll get used to the trousers."

"I think I'm chafing already." Bridget winced. "Alright, what's first?"

"Well, have you ever been in a fight?" Catriona watched her shake her head. "Have you ever hit anyone?"

"No, I scratched my father last time he beat me."

"Well, at least we know you can take a hit." Catriona shrugged her shoulders awkwardly. "Rule number one, if you're getting hit, don't just let it happen. Fight back or run away. If you freeze, you'll just become a victim again."

"Okay, I can do that."

"As you've experienced with your father, their movements and strikes can be timed. The trick is to change your thinking from, 'I need to tense up' to 'move' or look for an opening and hit back."

"That I think I can do." Bridget seemed encouraged with this familiarity.

316

"Rule number two, also kind of a golden rule, movement is life. We are women, we are strong, we are powerful, but we won't be able to physically overpower a man. I'm able to do what I do because I utilize my speed. As long as I can move, I can fight."

"That actually makes a lot of sense."

"It's why Rama is insisting that I learn how to ground fight. I've been using my fighting style for years, there's always room for improvement. Luckily your wolf makes you stronger and faster in human form. That's an excellent thing. I believe if you can get these techniques down, human men shouldn't be too much of a challenge for you, but other blooded, males especially, will pose a larger threat. So that will be more of a challenge of skill than a feat of strength."

"I will need to be able to fight blooded," Bridget stated. "They are the only ones who have ever hurt me, and I suspect it will happen again."

Catriona nodded in understanding, after talking with Clyous, Catriona was also now concerned that the crown prince would be coming for Bridget at some point soon. "Rule number three, if you don't keep practicing, you'll either lose your skills or become complacent. Same with your fitness level, if you stop being active, you'll lose what strength you have worked to gain, so better not to lose it."

"Should I be writing these down?" Bridget asked, seeming mildly amused.

"No." Catriona laughed. "I was thinking about starting you with standing evasion and hand to hand. Once you get that down we'll progress to attack, and then maybe weapons."

"All today?" She looked concerned.

"Probably not," Catriona answered. "Now for the evasion techniques, I'm going to try and grab you in different ways, you get away from me by any means necessary."

"Okay?"

Catriona reached out, grabbing Bridget's wrist hard. Bridget tried to pull away, but Catriona held firm. With her free hand Bridget reached down trying to pry Catriona's hand from her wrist. It wasn't working. Catriona could see the frustration building behind Bridget's eyes.

"That's not going to work, especially if I were a man. Trying to pry my fingers off one by one will take too much time. Here, hang onto my wrist I'll show you."

The two women switched positions, Bridget now gripping Catriona's wrist tightly. In slow motion, Catriona locked her arm out, then rotated it in a large circle before successfully pulling away from Bridget's grip.

"That was a bit exaggerated but rotating my arm in a circle like that helps loosen the grip of all the fingers enough to pull away. Sometimes you can't do a full arm rotation and can do the circle with just your wrist." Catriona then demonstrated this. "See, your turn."

They practiced different variations of this move for several minutes until Catriona was sure Bridget had it down. The great thing was that Bridget seemed determined to master this. Having her engage in this would help her in the long run.

"Now that you have that down, try striking me as you break away. In a real-life scenario whoever is trying to grab you will reach for you again. Striking them as you make your escape gives you better odds of getting away."

"You mean actually hit you?" Bridget looked worried.

"Yes." Catriona raised her eyebrows. "It's part of training, just try not to break anything, okay?"

"Okay." Bridget looked nervous but adjusted her stance.

Catriona wanted to mix it up a little bit to see if Bridget could adjust what she had learned. Catriona rushed forward, grabbing Bridget's hair. Without missing a beat, and with incredible speed, Bridget's fist shot out and connected with Catriona's face. The blow was not only startling, but there was some strength behind it. Catriona released Bridget's hair, stumbling back a step.

"I'm sorry!" Bridget moved towards Catriona, stopping when Catriona held up her hand.

"Don't be." Catriona rubbed her cheek shaking off the hit. "Fuck, you hit hard."

"I'm sorry! I just reacted—"

"Good. I want you to react like that." Catriona flashed her a smile of approval. "Let's keep at it."

For the next several hours the women practiced the techniques. Bridget seemed to be a quick learner, so Catriona started to push harder. Eventually Bridget was able to escape any standing hold Catriona could put her in. She was also able to block and throw some strikes. For a first lesson, this was great progress. Both women, satisfied with the results and tired from the exertion now sat together in the field passing a waterskin back and forth.

"So, the wolf has some bite after all," Grace's voice called from the trees.

Catriona watched as Grace and Morrigan approached the center of the field. Catriona's eyes narrowed slightly at the princess as the two sauntered in their direction. Much to Catriona's irritation, the woman had proven to be a powerful and valuable member of their group. What the woman had done for Menolayous the other night was incredibly kindhearted, even saving Catriona from being dragged off by those beasts, but she had a venomous tongue. Catriona hoped it stayed behind the woman's teeth; she was too tired to deal with her appropriately.

"There was some improvement girl, you should be proud." Morrigan smiled at Bridget kindly. "You might not find yourself a better teacher. A man will only teach you how to fight like them, she will teach you how to live."

"Thanks." Bridget returned the smile.

"What brings you out here?" Catriona asked, not bothering to rise as they finally reached them. "Don't suppose either of you want a lesson."

"Quite the contrary," Morrigan said, then turned her attention to the blonde. "I was hoping to give you one since you so conveniently found yourself at a safe distance from the camp. We talked about it the other day, did we not?"

"Yeah, I think we should talk about this power you seem to think that I have," Catriona said, still seated. "What makes you think I have one at all, and why fire?"

"I see your light," Morrigan answered simply. "It is made of wildfire, a rare and powerful gift. Not quite as rare as healing or seeing events before they happen, but it is a powerful weapon."

After several moments of pause, and a confused look on Catriona's face, Grace interjected, "Morrigan's sole purpose in this world is to find and train anyone with magic in their blood. To better protect them. She can see the glimmers of magic they hold. Most of the time that's it, but according to her, your light is very bright and very unique. Something only those with wildfire apparently have."

"That is what I said," Morrigan argued.

"No, it's not." Grace rolled her eyes. "You're beginning to act your age, you're forgetting words."

"How old are you?" Bridget asked.

"Forty-eight years old in this body," Morrigan explained. "But my soul is as old as time."

"Right, you're acting old." Grace took a seat beside Bridget.

"In this body? How does that work?" Bridget inquired, holding the waterskin out to Grace, who silently shook her head.

"Every time my body perishes, I am reborn into another. This was a design by the gods to help me better protect their children who still walk on this land." Morrigan also took a seat. "My reincarnation has been overdue for some time now; I haven't survived a body this long before."

"Do you come back with all your memories? Do you come back the same?" Bridget asked.

"No. I am born into different bodies, and my memories remain hidden until I have learned the full extent of my powers. Once I have received my mark, the memories and my purpose are given back to me, and I begin my duties all over."

"That's incredible." Bridget genuinely seemed awed.

"An incredible pain in my ass," Grace mumbled. "It's like talking to my great-grandmother again. Extremely set in her ways and doesn't like change."

"I grew up with your great-grandmother, an incredibly powerful woman," Morrigan started on.

"I am aware, thank you." Grace rolled her eyes.

"How do you pick a body?" Catriona couldn't stop herself from asking. "Doesn't exactly seem fair to completely take over someone's life after your powers have been realized."

"Cat?" Bridget scolded.

"I'm being serious," Catriona continued, trying to find how this body swapping could be a good thing. "How is it fair for the families of these kids

320

to grow up with their son or daughter, then all of a sudden you show up and their child basically dies?"

Grace huffed a laugh as Morrigan looked at Catriona with an expression of frustration.

"They do not disappear," Morrigan said flatly. "I am still the person I was born to be of that lineage. I keep the same memories, I have the same personality, likes and dislikes, and as long as I'm not in a time of war I do not stray from the relationships I grew up with. The past knowledge returns to me as does my mission, but I do not replace the person that was, my spirit empowers them to be what this world needs. I was created as a protector, not a parasite."

"How were you created?" Bridget asked, amazed by this woman's story, Catriona rolled her eyes at the healer's excitement.

Catriona watched as a familiar black raven landed on Morrigan's shoulder. The sorceress stroked its feathers aimlessly, whispering to it so low Catriona couldn't hear what was being said.

"Like my old friend Storm here, we were created out of need," Morrigan finally answered. "Back in a time where the gods walked the land, they had relationships with each other as well as with mortals. The Gods of the Moon and the Mountain were always at odds with each other, causing great mischief amongst their people. The Goddess of Chaos enjoyed their turmoil and added in when she could, she enjoyed the conflict between them as did her followers. The God of the Sea kept mostly to himself as did his children, while the Goddess of Healing and Life tried to mend the rift between the battling gods. The Goddess of War and Fate ruled over all fairly, keeping them from utterly destroying each other. She saw the wisdom in having all of the gods, losing any would upset the balance of the world they were trying to create. But it was the God of Death, that everyone feared." Morrigan looked at everyone's faces.

"The God of Death was powerful within his abilities, but he hungered for more. He began to scheme against his counterparts, trying to find ways to take their power unto himself. When he made the Goddess of Life his first target, it angered all the gods. They banded together and banished the God of Death to the underlands, limiting his influence upon this world. There he remained for centuries, enduring the small sway he had on the other gods and mortals. Still, the influence he held was strong enough that a mortal who sought power through dark magic mistakenly allowed the God of Death to enter their body and take it over. Once again, the God of

Death walked the land, seeking to possess any power that wasn't his." Morrigan sighed deeply.

"When the gods discovered his return and realized they needed a child of their bloodline to walk amongst the mortals and other children of old, they created me. I was chosen by the Goddess of War and Fate to bear traces of magic from all the gods to better protect their descendants. I was tasked not only with protecting other descendants of their bloodlines from the God of Death, but also to seek him out whenever he returns and end him."

"So…" Catriona struggled to find the words, the severity of the threat they faced finally coming into perspective. "How many times have you faced the God of Death?"

"Once, but facing his dark creation, the count is twelve," Morrigan answered, her raven cawing in agreement.

"And there's no way to kill him, and stop him from coming back?" Catriona asked, determined to discover the solution to this riddle.

"Not that has ever been passed onto me," Morrigan replied. "I am forever bound to this reincarnation cycle alongside him."

Catriona sat there for a moment mulling over all this information. She glanced around at the other women who seemed to be doing the same thing. If what Morrigan was describing to them was true, that meant they would be facing down a god trapped in a human body, and here Catriona thought the blooded bastards of Oich were difficult enough, this was on a whole different level of difficulty.

"Just to be clear," Bridget began, "the children of the ancients are mortals with magic?"

"Yes," Morrigan answered, not elaborating any more.

Grace sighed with frustration. "The gods mated with the very mortals they created. Children of the ancients is the fancy way of saying we have gods' blood running in our veins. The amount we have determines how powerful we are. Whoever's blood we possess determines the type of abilities we have. As you can probably guess, wolf girl, you are a direct descendant of the Goddess of Healing. She does not procreate but instead blesses women who come to be with child. But you also share blood from the God of the Moon. Most other descendants from the gods would not allow a mix of bloodlines, one bloodline usually overpowers another, but the Goddess of

Healing is very kind and has always been known to work well with the other gods. So, it makes sense why your two bloodlines have merged."

"And I suppose it makes sense that Clyous and I are from the Goddess of War and Fate's bloodline," Catriona added in.

"Yes, but from both parents." Morrigan stared at her. "You and your twin are like two sides of a coin, but you both are incredibly powerful. There hasn't been a child of old as powerful as the two of you for a few centuries. The only way this would be possible is if both of your parents shared an ancestral bloodline."

Catriona shook her head. "That can't be. Neither of my parents had ever shown or spoken of having magic. I feel like that's something we would have noticed."

"Unless they hid it from you," Grace countered. "You and Clyous hadn't started manifesting until recently."

"Your father was one of the best blacksmiths in Oich, he had an affinity for being in the forge," Bridget offered Catriona kindly.

"Your father was a blacksmith?" Grace asked, surprised.

"Yeah, why?" Catriona eyed her suspiciously.

"Did he ever work with iron?" Morrigan asked, seeming concerned.

"Yeah, we all did." Catriona was glancing back and forth between the two women, clearly missing the issue. "We all worked iron. My father used iron to forge the bars we put on our windows and doors to defend against the scourge."

"At what age did he do this?" Morrigan asked.

"I was five years old. Why do you guys care about iron?"

Morrigan and Grace shared a look before Grace spoke up, "Iron is the one element that limits our powers. It's similar to the blooded and silver. If we're around too much of it, if we're wearing it, or if it cuts us, it will block our ability to use our magic."

"That's—" Catriona started to speak but couldn't finish her train of thought, why had her father surrounded them if he knew it dampened their powers. "Magic was outlawed. He did it to protect us from drawing attention from the Oich guards."

"That would make sense for why it has taken you this long to touch your fire," Morrigan agreed.

"And you've never left your home? Not to travel somewhere, stay a few nights free from your shop?" Grace asked, surprised.

"No," Catriona whispered, her mind wandering back to dark memories.

"What about your mother?" Bridget asked, pulling Catriona out of her thoughts. "Did she show an affinity for fire?"

"No." Catriona thought for a moment. "But she always seemed to know what was going to happen before it did."

"Both parents possessed gifts then." Morrigan nodded. "Creating twins with both powers, the Goddess works in miraculous ways."

"So if what you're saying is true, then Clyous and I are doubly powerful?" Catriona asked the older female. "Nothing could get in our way?"

"Every power has its limits, Firebird," Morrigan explained. "You must be careful not to let the fire take over. You can fuel it with your emotions, and that can be powerful. But if you are not careful, the fire can consume you from the inside until you are nothing. Grace has a similar limitation. She is incredibly powerful over the mind, but she can get lost inside someone else's head or trap herself in her own. She can drive herself just as mad as she can any foe. Magic is not meant to be let loose into the world unchecked."

"What about my power?" Bridget spoke up. "Can I over heal myself? How can my magic take over?"

"You, child, have the ability to drain the life from someone else." Morrigan stared at her. "Most born with your gift are also born with a compassionate and loving personality. You loath to cause harm to others, making your ability to kill as emotionally damaging as Catriona's fire or Grace's mind powers. But you are also a child of the moon. Your bloodlines create quick tempered and dominating personalities. As unique as the combination of your lineage is, it balances out. You are neither too wild nor too meek. I believe this was the gods' way of making you level enough to survive this world."

"What about my brother?" Catriona asked nervously. "He's the other half of the Goddess of War and Fate, he isn't as hot headed as I am, and he can't control fire."

"You are correct in saying that he is the other half of your bloodline. He is conditioned to see more than most and to use logic over emotions. His magic has the ability to drive him mad as well, not by his doing, but by how often futures can change. He has to ground himself in the present."

"How can one learn the extent of their power without crossing those lines?" Catriona asked quietly, magic wasn't sounding as exciting as it had in the beginning.

"Practice makes perfect." Grace smirked. "Typically, those with magic first learn of it at such a young age. It's surprising that you and Clyous had not. It seems that is the way your father designed it, whatever his reasons were."

"I am willing to take more lessons," Bridget piped up. "I want to learn everything I possibly can if you're willing to teach me."

"Happily, my child." Morrigan smiled. "But today needs to be about Catriona," she said as she turned to Catriona. "I can sense your power fighting against the cage you have it in. If you do not learn to free it, and in the right way, you could accidentally kill everything you hold precious."

"Fine," Catriona spat out, done with the theories. "Since everyone seems so worried about that, might as well."

"Let us discuss burnout first," Morrigan began.

"And that is?" Catriona asked, not hiding her frustration.

"Think of your power like a pitcher of water. You can only use so much of it at a time, only pour out so much water, before the pitcher is emptied," Morrigan explained. "Letting all the water out at one time is called burnout. It can be extremely dangerous for your body to experience that much of a drain on your magic all at once. Your power will refill over time, the more you practice the faster it can refill. Burnout makes everything more dangerous, and it takes twice as long to refill."

"How can you recover from burnout?" Bridget inquired, ever the dutiful student.

"That varies. Some might fall cold with a chill, their body no longer functioning properly. Others will heat up and catch a fever, nobody can withstand that for too long. You would treat these side effects like symptoms, warm them up or cool them down. If you can maintain their body's functions long enough, they can stabilize. But only ingesting yarrow root will guarantee a full recovery."

"Yarrow root is easy enough to find. It's the white flower you can find along the roadside, or deep in the forests. I've made poultices for people before." Bridget looked positively excited at learning this new information.

"You can make tea out of it. It's the easiest way to get someone back from burnout. I carry some dried yarrow root on me at all times. How much you need is dependent on how much power you express." Grace gently patted the small leather pouch dangling at her waist.

"You're going to go collect a bunch of it when we're done here, aren't you?" Catriona asked Bridget who was practically humming with excitement.

"Yes."

"Okay awesome. Don't use all your magic in one shot. Treat it like a cold. I'm ready to move on." Catriona stood, brushing off her trousers.

"You should have more respect for power." Grace looked up at her. "If you don't it will destroy you."

"Yeah, well it seems like everyone's been trying to destroy me lately. I might as well be the one to actually succeed." Catriona glanced around at everyone; their expressions were of great concern. "Kidding. Where do we start?"

The other three women stood, all facing each other. Morrigan spoke first. "Your power lies within your emotions. Anger, will, drive, arousal, fear. These emotions can control the flames, but rage, that is what will fuel it into an inferno. Harness your emotions and you can control and shift the flame."

"I'm angry all the time, I've never burned anyone before."

"Actually." Bridget glanced at her. "You burned me, remember? When I healed you, you burned my palms."

"But I wasn't angry then," Catriona argued.

"Your magic met her magic I'm guessing, they fed off each other for a few moments," Grace answered.

"That was the first time I was able to fully heal a wound." Bridget nodded. "It makes sense."

"So how am I going to use it now?" Catriona asked. "I'm angry all the time, I'm irritated right now. I don't see flames."

"You must experience rage in order to bring out the magic you have buried within," Morrigan answered. "After you bring it out the first time you will be able to draw on it whenever you desire."

326

"How exactly are you going to get her into a rage?" Bridget asked cautiously.

"Me," Grace answered with a smirk. "I'm exceptionally good at getting under people's skin."

"No shit." Catriona laughed.

Grace gave her a look. "Don't believe me?"

"Oh, on the contrary, Princess, all you've done since you got here is piss me off." Catriona glared back. "But I think I'm more likely to knock you on your pretty little ass before flames start flying everywhere."

"Catriona—" Bridget started but was shushed by Morrigan.

"Let them fight it out." Morrigan gently pulled Bridget away from the two women. "Afterwards they might coexist better."

"I'm worried Catriona might kill her," Bridget whispered.

Morrigan chuckled. "I wouldn't worry about that, but having you here helps their chances of survival."

Catriona stared Grace down as the other two walked away. "Going to use your emotional manipulation to piss me off?"

"I could, but I don't think that will be necessary." Grace shrugged off her jacket.

"Good. I don't want you in my head," Catriona spat out.

"Don't really want to be inside the head of a loose cannon." Grace took a casual fighting stance. "Peasants like you aren't really worth my time."

"Fuck you, Princess!" Catriona shouted. "While we're on the subject, how about you stay the fuck out of Menolayous's head too. He doesn't need some spoiled brat in there leading him on."

"Really? That's what you think I'm doing?" Grace cocked her head to the side. "You're a fucking idiot. I would never hurt him."

"And why is that? You spent a few weeks traveling on the road together and now you're so close?"

"Closer than you." Grace matched Catriona's temper blow for blow. "At least I know what's going on in his head. You couldn't even begin to imagine what others have been through beyond your own trauma."

"What the fuck do you know about my trauma?"

327

"Everything." Grace smirked, unraveling the braided belt around her waist. Only it wasn't a belt, it was a whip. "I know that it's going to be the very thing to send you over the edge, so let's visit that particular day."

"Fuck you!" Catriona felt herself start to tremble slightly at the sight of the whip snaking through the grass at Grace's command.

"Normally I would take you up on that, but I don't particularly like the idea of Danny joining in. He's really not my type." Grace winked at her before cracking the whip off to the side.

"You need to stop her!" Bridget turned to Morrigan desperately. "Not the whip!"

"Grace can handle herself," Morrigan answered, watching the two women face off.

"For someone who is allegedly such a challenge, you sure are acting like a scared bitch." Grace cracked the whip again, getting it closer to Catriona. "Do I need to beat your rage out of you?"

Catriona moved, lunging for Grace the moment the whip touched the ground. Catriona moved with incredible speed, going for the whip, but Grace was just as fast. Grace rolled away from Catriona creating distance. As she stood out of the roll, three more of Grace now stood in a semi-circle, all staring Catriona down with equal distaste. Catriona studied them, amazed at their sudden appearance. They were not mirrors of each other; they moved independently. It was impossible to tell which was the real Grace.

"Tell me Catriona, what does it feel like to be best friends with the ex-lover of your worst enemy?" the many Graces asked in unison as they circled her. "I'll wager the two of you have yet to talk about Prince Liam. How the same man that used to make her moan every night was the same man who made your mother scream until she couldn't anymore."

There was another crack from the whip. With balled up fists Catriona swung her head around, trying to identify the true Grace. Oh, how she wanted to break the woman's face right now. She could feel the anger starting to take over.

"How about the fact that your brother now covets her, this redheaded wolf girl. Do you think she compares the two, which male she prefers in bed?" The Grace that Catriona lunged for easily dodged her. "What about your mother, let's go back to her. Tell me, do you still hear her screams when you close your eyes? Do you still smell her flesh when you're cooking meat? Is that why you buried your fire?"

"Fuck you!" Catriona roared.

"When's the last time you were able to eat without getting sick? How much longer are you going to let this weakness take over you?" Grace asked, smirking at her from four different angles. "Hmm. Your mother seems to be more of a trigger. Let's go back to that night."

"Leave my mother out of this!"

"I don't think I will. I can sense your magic starting to boil over. It's okay to let it. Letting it boil over now will get me to stop," Grace offered with a snarky tone. "No? Okay then."

Another crack of the whip, this time Catriona felt the tail wrap itself around her wrist. With a sharp tug, Catriona was pulled sideways until she was on the ground. She felt the leather on her skin, the sound of the whip echoing through her head. Catriona started to smell the smoke again, to feel the hard blows across her back.

"Don't slip into it! Fight it!" Grace shouted, pulling the whip hard so Catriona was dragged forward again.

There it was, the rage that had been boiling up inside her. Catriona suddenly felt hot, like the flames were licking her inside, desperate to get out. With a scream of anger, she pushed the flames outward, igniting the air around her. Three of the four Graces disappeared into the inferno as the wall of flame burned from Catriona at the center pushing it on, the last one standing managed to roll out of the way. Bridget and Morrigan took several surprised steps backward, distancing themselves even more from the fire pouring out of her.

She could hear Grace's laugh above the flames. "You weren't kidding. She's raw power!"

"Stay back, young one. She can still stretch further at a moment's notice," Morrigan called back.

Catriona fought with her memories, closing off the sounds of her mother's screams. She forced an inhale of breath, she no longer smelled flesh burning, just the grass surrounding her. She opened her eyes to see her gold and orange flames surrounding her, the grass at her feet weeping its moisture before catching fire and shriveling to ash. This release of power felt good, like it was relieving pressure she had been keeping inside for so long. She pushed even further, emptying her pain and frustration into the flames. The flames shot out even farther, expanding at the base so she now stood in the center of a massive fire. Catriona had forgotten the women were there, missing them having to jump back another ten feet to avoid her flames. She was too busy feeling, feeling relief now that her flames were snapping and crackling around her.

"Catriona!" Grace's voice called from a distance. "You need to stop now."

"The girl is going to burn out if she keeps feeding her flames everything," Morrigan's voice came with the wind.

"Catriona!! Please stop!" Bridget's voice begged, but Catriona ignored her. "Why won't she stop?"

"She is giving herself over to the flames. Why did you not tell me she had a death wish, I would never have allowed this?" Morrigan snapped.

"What do you mean?" Bridget sounded upset.

"Catriona wants to die," Grace answered, staring through the flames. "She's feeding the flames with her pain; she's feeling relief for the first time. She needs to find a reason to stop before she lets them burn her up."

"I'll get Danny!" Bridget offered.

"We do not have time for that, I feel the burnout approaching," Morrigan answered.

"What drives her?" Grace's voice shouted over the roaring fire.

"Revenge," Bridget answered without hesitation.

Catriona took a deep breath, continuing to pour her pain into the flames. She felt lighter every second, like the fire was burning away all of her past. The memories of the night when she was pinned to the ground were fading, the feel of the whip across her flesh years later was gone, no more fear, no more anger. She just felt empty. She felt at peace. She felt so tired, tired from everything these last few months, tired of dealing with it all. She lowered herself to the ground, welcoming its support as her eyes grew heavy.

"So, you're a witch after all?" a voice called from the tree line. "I should have known."

Catriona looked up at the intruder. Standing there in his royal attire with an entitled expression plastered on his face, was the Crown Prince of Oich. Catriona stood at the sight of him, her attention now fully on him. She could feel her flames shift suddenly; she was surrounding herself with a cocoon of protection at the sight of him.

"Pretty little thing you are." Liam stepped forward, drawing a sword. "Can you go ahead and burn out already for me? I want to put my hands on you without getting burned."

With a shriek of rage, Catriona blasted all of her fire at the crown prince, engulfing his body with her wildfire. To her amazement he just stood there, seemingly unaffected by the flames she had spent to end him. The grass and trees around him burned away while he stood there completely unaffected. He wasn't real!

Catriona felt hands on either side of her face, Grace's hands. She felt Grace's presence force its way into her mind, feeling around in her memories. Suddenly the faces of her family began to flash before her, Clyous and Markous arguing in the forge, Rama flicking her on the nose while laughing, being curled up in Danny's arms, and even memories of today when she was training with Bridget. These were her reasons to stop feeding herself to the flames, she still had people she loved fighting for her every day. Catriona cut off the connection to her wildfire, feeling the exhaustion as her knees hit the ground.

"Catriona!" Bridget yelled as the other two women ran to her.

Catriona felt Grace holding her up gently, still pushing those fond memories through her. Reality started to come back to her. Catriona felt Bridget's body slam down in the ash next to her, taking her into her arms as Bridget cried in relief. Catriona didn't feel like she could move, her body suddenly felt like it weighed thousands of pounds. She felt cold then, her body suddenly became chilly. She glanced up at the three women looking down at her and smiled.

"Thank you," she said to Grace, "for bringing me back, but fuck you for getting into my head."

Grace laughed. "Believe it or not I actually want to be your friend."

"Show me yours since you've seen mine," Catriona said weakly.

Grace gently put her hand up to Catriona's face, sending her images. Grace as a child growing up in the palace, being taught how to be queen one day, her mother not allowing her to go play with other children, instead she was forced into different classes or lessons. Grace as a teenager, all the boys her age were too afraid to approach her. Except one, one she had shared her body with thinking it was love but it wasn't, the boy had thought he could become king one day. After it was made clear by her mother that he would not, the boy decided to share what they had done with everyone. Grace was older now, she was having trouble making friends who actually liked her for who she was, not what she was. Grace dressing for attention appeared, becoming mean and cruel, all because she resisted being forced into a role that kept her away from having anyone real. Then came Grace deciding to fight against the Dark One and then being captured. The horrors she had witnessed. Menolayous appearing to save her. The fact that he fought with her but still wanted to be around her. That night at camp when she accidentally went into his head. Meeting everyone here at the camp, seeing such strong personalities that refused to bow down. Her jealousy of Catriona, how everyone seemed to love her for who she truly was despite her constant bad attitude. How she wanted to belong to a group like that. The other day when Menolayous was willing to let her in, showing her what was truly inside him. That was what Grace truly wanted, to belong to something where she could be herself, for someone to love her for who she truly was.

"Now we're even," Grace said nervously. "Your secret is safe with me."

"I think we can be friends." Catriona smiled as she shut her eyes. "Just stop being such a bitch."

She could hear Grace's laugh as she drifted off into a deep sleep. "You first."

Chapter Forty-Six

Rama

Rama and his brothers were in the village discussing with Flinn an expansion for more houses when they spotted the smoke. Unsure what was happening, Flinn ordered the men to prepare for an attack. It did not take the brothers long to realize that their women were nowhere to be found. He could feel the panic radiating off both of them upon the realization that the girls were potentially out there past the walls and the men were preparing for battle. He also felt panic that their little family was not all together. Fear took hold over them all, fear of losing each other and their loved ones. It was no secret what could potentially happen to them if they were captured by enemy forces. Oich guards were not kind to women, especially those with magic. He knew that all of these scenarios began to play themselves out in his brothers' heads as well as his. Having to worry about others hadn't been a priority for any of them until now. It was amazing how much things had changed within the last six months.

Rama wasn't sure who took off first, Danny or Menolayous, but he followed his brothers toward the flames. Once they reached the edge of the clearing, they all stopped short, unable to continue forward. The clearing was on fire; the bushes and grass were completely engulfed in flames. He saw her then, her hair whipping wildly in the flames as if she had become a flame herself. A white glow radiated from magical markings that now covered her arms, legs, and sides. Her clothes and every blade of grass, bush, flower, and tree within twenty feet of her had been consumed by the flames. Her flesh did not appear to be burned, which was wholly surprising to him considering the destruction around her. But she wore her markings now as if they were armor, the scars on her back visible for all to see and tremble before. In fact, Rama was trembling, the power he could sense coming from this firestorm was immeasurable.

The heat from the flames kept them back, Rama could see Danny trying to push forward through the flames and raw power. Before he could grab his brother to stop him, he spotted a man crossing the field towards Catriona. It was the Crown Prince of Oich, maybe they were under attack after all. Catriona saw him now; it appeared they exchanged a few words before Catriona sent a blast of flame in his direction. With her power now concentrated on the prince, the flame surrounding her was redirected, giving the ground around her a temporary reprieve.

Then he spotted Grace coming up behind Catriona, putting her hands on Catriona's face just like she had done with Menolayous. Catriona collapsed, and the flames completely extinguished. Menolayous and Danny sprinted towards the women. Rama followed, taking in the destruction. Catriona's power was real, and worse yet, it wasn't just the power of flames. It was death, absolute destruction.

"What happened?" he heard his brother demand, scooping Catriona into his arms.

"She is fine," Morrigan answered Danny, realizing this wasn't an acceptable answer to him she added, "she has reached the limit of her powers. Now she knows what she is capable of before burning out."

Danny stripped off his tunic, using it to cover Catriona's naked body. Bridget helped him slip it over Catriona's head before Danny stood with her in his arms.

"Come on, I've got to get some yarrow root for her. Get her warm," Bridget ordered him, the healer inside of her taking control of the situation with ease. Danny nodded, taking off towards the village. "Morrigan, go with him."

"As you wish." Morrigan followed Danny with an expression that seemed to say she wasn't thrilled to be there. "You will need to collect quite a bit with how much power this girl just expended."

Menolayous was helping Grace to her feet, visually examining her for injury. Other than a few singe marks on her clothing, Grace appeared to be completely fine. Rama could almost sense the waves of relief washing over his brother. Rama had never seen him show this much emotion before, not until Grace had come into their lives. Normally, Rama would feel joy for his brother, but caring for someone like Grace was concerning. Not only were her powers of persuasion frightening to him, but her personality was too brash. She had a wickedly sharp tongue and had no issues with being as outspoken as she wanted, from years of being Airgid's princess he suspected. She acted as if she could get whatever she wanted, dressed for male attention, and butted heads with everyone around her. No, this wasn't who he had imagined for the brother that avoided people, who couldn't stand to be touched, who rarely opened up even to him. *He wondered if Grace was just toying with his brother, maybe she saw him as a challenge, someone to toss aside when she was done.* He wasn't sure Menolayous could handle that. He didn't trust her, not with his brother.

"Menolayous, can you help me collect some of the yarrow root for Catriona? I don't know how much she'll need, and I want to move quickly," Bridget called back as she worked her way towards the unburnt half of the clearing.

"Are you okay?" Menolayous gently tucked a strand of hair behind Grace's ear.

"I'm fine." She gave him a half smile. "Go on, go help them."

Menolayous nodded, taking off after Bridget. Grace watched them disappear before walking to the edge of the burn, picking something up off the ground. Rama watched in horror as Grace began wrapping a whip around her chest and waist like it was a belt. Realization began to dawn on him, *Grace used that whip on Catriona.* To set her off. *This woman was more dangerous than he gave her credit for, not a mistake he would make again.*

Rage filled him as the desire to protect his new sister pushed its way forward, *how dare she come for his family!* He rushed at her then, catching her completely off guard. She turned toward him and gasped just before his hands wrapped around her slender throat. With his momentum and long legs, he dragged her back several feet until they reached a tree. He pinned her by the throat to the tree with one hand, squeezing the air from her. Grace's eyes grew wide with real fear as she tried to claw his hand from her neck, but he was too strong. Rage drove him on, *she was dangerous, a threat to his family.* He knew he couldn't kill her, as much as he wanted to right then. Menolayous wouldn't understand it.

"What did you do?" he ground out, face inches away from hers.

She couldn't breathe; her face was beginning to change color. He relaxed his grip enough for her to suck in some air, not realizing exactly how hard he had been choking her. He wanted to kill her, but he needed to get better control over himself before he actually did just that. A small part of him couldn't believe what he was doing, it was almost as if he was losing control of himself and who he was. He had never wanted to harm or kill a woman before. He detested men who put their hands on their women, it was a cowardly thing to do, but Grace was not his woman, nor was she weak. She was a warrior, and he met her as a warrior, but he knew compared to him and his size she was small. He needed to remember that, needed to control whatever this rage was within him.

"Speak!" he ordered, still inches away from her face.

"What is it you think I did?" Grace coughed, still struggling against his grip.

"I think you got into her head and pushed her a little too far," Rama said, seething. "How dare you use a whip on her or summon the image of her worst nightmare. You don't even know what he did to her, what he will do to her if he ever finds her again."

"Are you going to let me explain or are you going to keep choking me?" she coughed out, still struggling for air.

"I think I'd rather just kill you at this point. Ever since you showed up, I've had to watch two members of my family get pushed over the edge."

Grace shot her hands forward, catching him around his throat. He felt her claw her way into the deep recesses of his mind. Memories began to flood through him, memories of his mother's death, his father drinking himself into an oblivion. Images of fights and battles he had been in flowed quickly behind his eyes. Voices of his enemies deafening him as they taunted him from the past. All the pain, every wound he's ever felt from battle, suddenly he felt all of it again. Fists struck him, swords and daggers sliced at his flesh. A wound from an arrow that had been completely healed for years suddenly felt as if the shaft was in him once more. Horses kicked him again in the legs and in the chest. All that pain struck him at once, crippling his grasp on reality. Then it stopped.

Rama's eyes cleared, he now realized he was on his knees before Grace. She was standing over him with her slender hand still barely covering his throat. *She had done this, she had used her magic against him, gotten into his head. She was able to do this because he allowed her time to concentrate, a mistake he would not make again. Is this what she did with Catriona, with Menolayous?*

"This is much better." Grace smirked at him. "I love it when men go down on their knees in front of me."

"Stay out of my head!" Rama growled as he yanked her to the ground by her arm.

As she fell, he maneuvered them both so he was on top, pinning her hands above her head. If she couldn't concentrate while touching him, she couldn't get inside his head again. That much about her power was clear. She struggled for a moment, but he was at least double her size. She wasn't going anywhere. He grunted as her pelvis bucked against his groin as she tried to move away from him. That caught his attention, redirecting some of that rage into the sexual tension he was now feeling. This was not the time to be thinking with his cock.

"I think I prefer being on top more than kneeling before you." He smiled down at her, mentally kicking himself for the flirtatious comment.

"Fuck off." She seethed, still wiggling against him trying to free herself. That was not helping where his mind was wandering. What the fuck was wrong with him, was she doing this?

"Explain yourself," he demanded, trying to ignore how her body felt underneath his. "Now!"

"Would you believe a word I say?" she spat, face contorted in fury. "Or would you just skip ahead to the part where you plan to kill me or threaten me. I don't have all day, asshole."

Irritation flooded through him once more; she had a natural talent for it. "Listen closely, Princess, because it will be the only time I warn you. If you hurt my family, I will fucking kill you."

"Consider me warned." She glared up at him.

Good girl, she knew when to shut her mouth and listen. Satisfied that she had taken his threat seriously, Rama released his grip on her hands. He stared down at her, beautiful and breathless. Everything about her was alluring to him, her face, her hair, her full lips. *She would be a good one to breed, she would give you strong offspring.* It was no surprise why most of the men watched her around camp, he himself did, but her barbed tongue kept the weaker ones away. He didn't mind her sharp tongue himself; in fact, it thrilled him. If only she wasn't a viper and currently setting sights on his brother. She remained unmoving except to glare up at him. It wasn't the usual way he chose to leave his women looking, but he was satisfied with her anger instead. He really needed to get his mind off the other thoughts.

Turning his back on her to walk away, he felt the sharp edge of a blade slice his flesh as a dagger was set against his throat. Only then did he feel her body weight as she placed her foot on his hip, hoisting herself onto his back, further securing the death blow she now had him in. He ground his teeth in frustration, otherwise unmoving. She had him; they both knew it. He willed his cock to behave, it wasn't every day someone got the better of him, especially a beautiful and feisty woman.

"Now, let me make myself perfectly clear, Prince of Thieves," she whispered into his ear, the very sound of her voice sending shivers of arousal through him. "I did nothing to hurt your family. Everything I have done has been to help them. It's not my fault you've been letting Menolayous walk around like an empty shell, and I don't want a lecture about pushing Catriona when you yourself pushed her the other day with training. I want her to

337

survive the next time she and the prince fight, and we both know that's only a matter of time. Don't judge the methods I use when you are the one who can't possibly understand what's going on in her head. Or his."

"And you do?" Rama grunted as Grace pushed the dagger into his neck, blood now trickled down from the cut.

"They let me in," she ground out. "Your brother let me in. He showed me things he could never talk about with you. That's why you hate me."

"Get out of my head!" he growled.

"You fucking moron, I don't have to be in your head to know that." She released some of the pressure. "I care about your brother."

The knife was removed from his flesh a moment before he felt her weight disappear. Slowly he turned to face her. She stood several feet away, dagger still in hand, standing as if prepared for him to charge at her again.

"Put your hands on me again and I will slit your throat," she promised him.

He looked at her then, willing himself to see her underneath her mask. Before him stood a strong woman, not afraid but cautious. She took him as the threat he himself was, he winced slightly at the sight of the red marks his hand had left on her throat. Reaching up to his cut, he pulled his hand back to see the blood, the pain grounding him back to reality. She had made it clear she was a threat too.

Did he truly believe that she meant no harm to his family? She wasn't wrong about him doing the same thing with Catriona. Doubt began to creep in, maybe he was wrong. If he was wrong about her, then he deeply regretted this encounter altogether. His eyes glanced down to her throat; it was already starting to bruise. His handprint was there reminding him of what he had just done. Shit. He wouldn't allow her to see the realization on his face, if only to keep her on her toes. He still meant every word; he just regretted his actions going as far as they did. He truly had no idea what had gotten into him, he was ashamed.

"Then we have an understanding." He flashed her a smile in response to the one slowly spreading across her beautiful face.

Grace spun the dagger around, sheathing it somewhere behind her back. She gave him a wink before turning around and taking off towards the trees. He watched her as she walked, hips swaying in that skin-tight leather.

She was a wildcard that's for sure, definitely someone more his type than he figured for Menolayous. Fuck, had he just screwed up?

"Grace," he called out, watching her pause, "please don't break my brother's heart."

She continued to walk away without looking back at him.

Chapter Forty-Seven

Bridget

"Thank you, guys, for helping me with this," Bridget said sincerely as she began pulling glass bottles out of a crate, setting them gently on the shelves. "It would take me at least a week to set up without your help."

"Don't mention it." Grace smiled at her as she wedged a knife between the lid and base of a new crate. "Really, if you think about it, we're helping ourselves. Having a healer's shop in the middle of Collie is going to benefit everyone."

"It will definitely help me." Catriona laughed, holding up a bandaged hand. She had survived another rough training session with Rama but had injured her wrist in the process.

"There's not enough help in the world for you," Grace teased Catriona, a smile spreading across both women's faces.

"See, isn't this nice," Bridget chimed in, observing the other two fondly. "Having friends."

Grace and Catriona glanced at each other for a moment before turning back to Bridget who was happy that everyone was starting to get along, she was happy that she had her own shop that Flinn and Clyous had built for her. She understood the admission probably made her seem strange to others, but she didn't care. She just wanted them all to be friends, she wanted to be a part of their lives.

"I've never had friends," Bridget explained unabashedly. "Nobody but Liam ever wanted to be around me growing up. It feels nice to have you guys in my life."

"I find that hard to believe. You're such a kind person, everyone wants to be around you," Grace said almost questioningly, adjusting the thick collar of her jacket around her throat.

"Oh, it's true. In a blooded and noble community, I was the laughingstock, the weak link. Kindness is considered a weakness where I grew up." Bridget unstopped a glass bottle, sniffing the contents. "Honestly, I was bullied a lot by the others. I was too weak and small to do anything about it."

"That's terrible." Grace finally worked to lift the lid off the crate. "I forget how different the blooded of Oich are compared to the blooded of Airgid."

"You have blooded in Airgid?" Catriona asked the princess.

"Oh, yes." Grace smiled. "They're some of our fiercest warriors, but they don't have a hierarchical society like Oich. They intermingle with humans just fine. As do the few children of the ancients we have. Airgid is more like a safe space for everyone, your race doesn't determine your social status, and the crown is passed down through lineage, not this dominant wolf bullshit."

"But hierarchies are our very nature, how do you get around that?" Bridget asked curiously.

"Usually, the most dominant lead part of our army. We give them command over enlisted blooded. It helps keep the group working together that way, but they still answer to the crown."

"That's wild." Bridget was staring at Grace wide eyed.

"I wouldn't say that bullying doesn't happen in Airgid, it does, but it's different. You wouldn't have been surrounded by blooded with sticks up their asses. You would still have been welcomed into the community, the humans and children of old would have had no issue with you. Although, in Airgid your kindness might have been taken advantage of more than you being bullied for it. Too many people want to climb the social ladder."

"I never had any friends either," Catriona admitted. "When I was really little, I had a few, but as I got older they couldn't handle my intensity. They expected me to grow up into some sort of soft-spoken lady. I figured real friends wouldn't ask me to change."

"Your intensity is something to get used to," Bridget teased, "but I wouldn't have you any other way."

"I think I'd try to teach you another word besides 'fuck'." Grace snickered and adjusted the collar of her jacket yet again. Maybe she was hiding a love bite from Menolayous?

"Hey!" Catriona looked mock offended. "Fuck is an acceptable multi-meaning word."

"Yes, but you only use it one way." Grace dodged a handful of packing hay Catriona threw in her direction. "When you get really mad the

341

only thing you know how to say is 'fuck you' or 'fuck off'. You need to get more creative with your insults."

Catriona laughed. "So, I'm a hot head, what else is new?"

"Real friends wouldn't have asked you to change." Grace brought the conversation back to its original track. "I was surrounded by people my entire life. A lot of them bent over backwards to be my 'friend' but they only wanted the label of friend, they would behave in ways they thought I would prefer. I could never trust any of them fully because they were never themselves around me."

"That sounds very lonely." Bridget looked sad at this.

"Speaking of bullies and assholes," Catriona looked to Bridget. "I can't say enough how sorry I am for that first night back in the cave. I was way over the line; I was looking for an easy outlet and you were standing right there."

"You've already apologized for that." Bridget looked at her friend curiously.

"I know, but you've become one of the most important people in my life, and I deeply regret anything I've done that upset you. You didn't deserve that, or anything else you've had to endure over the years. Honestly, I'm enraged at how many people think they can walk all over you."

Bridget blushed at her friend's confession, her words cutting straight to her heart. "It probably doesn't help that I've basically allowed it my entire life. People see me and see weakness; someone they can step on."

"Unfortunately, that was my first impression when meeting you," Grace said looking embarrassed. "I also am sorry for being such a bitch right out of the gate. I thought that maybe it was a façade, nobody could be that gentle and kind, especially after taking such a beating. But I realized quickly that you truly are that gentle at heart."

"You guys are going to make me cry." Bridget smiled, holding back tears of happiness.

Catriona looked to Grace with a mischievous smile, "I'm not apologizing to you, you're a bitch."

Grace smiled back at the challenge. "Same. You realize that you make terrible first impressions, and second impressions. It's a wonder anyone likes you at all."

"Better than everyone thinking I'm a whore or a parasite." Fire flickered in Catriona's eyes.

"Can we not fight, please?" Bridget begged.

The two women laughed at each other, their expressions changing to fondness. Bridget sighed in relief, happy that her new shop wasn't in danger of going up in flames.

"We're not fighting," Grace promised with a laugh. "Catriona and I are more similar than we wanted to admit early on. We've come to an... understanding of sorts. I respect her in more ways than I can express, I've seen what she's dealt with, I get why she is the way that she is."

"Makes the slave life look not so glorious doesn't it, Princess," Catriona mocked. "Although I'll admit, the politics you grew up with sound like a nightmare. Your parents seem pleasant."

"Yeah... well, no parent is perfect." Grace returned to her original task and began pulling out bottles of dried herbs from the crate sitting beside her. "I know my mother loves me, but she firmly believes in kingdom before family. I wish that she looked at me more like her daughter instead of the next queen."

"I can understand parental pressure," Bridget chimed in. "I swear that my father would have preferred I died along with my mother. Since my first breath I was a disappointment to him."

"Your father was a raging alcoholic, the only thing he wasn't disappointed in was a full bottle of liquor," Catriona seethed.

"Yeah... thanks to Liam he's roaming around with only one hand somewhere and no chances of regaining his social status. He probably believes dying would be easier."

"The one and only good thing I will give that bastard credit for." Catriona's demeanor completely changed when she began talking about her mortal enemy. "I still plan to end his life the first chance I get."

"I know," Bridget said quietly, afraid to meet her friend's eyes.

"Have you two talked about this at all?" Grace asked, taking a momentary break from emptying her crate. "I mean, there's a lot to this."

"We haven't," Catriona confirmed. "I think we've both been dancing around the topic."

343

"I understand why, I can't even fault you for wanting your revenge. If anyone deserves it, it would be the crown prince." Bridget felt the tears welling up again. "Liam was my childhood friend, my first love, but he died a long time ago and was replaced by his father's son. I will mourn Liam's death, but not the crown prince."

"I don't want to cause you pain," Catriona said, "but I can't let this go."

"You aren't causing me pain, the one responsible for that is marked." Bridget tried to hold back the tears but ultimately lost that battle. "Liam is gone; all that's left is his ghost."

"This got depressing really quick." Catriona stared down at a crate in front of her before reaching inside and pulling out what looked like a bottle of liquor. "But it just got more interesting."

"That's what I'm talking about!" Grace clapped her hands together excitedly, clearly happy for a change of mood.

Catriona uncorked the glass bottle, taking a long drink of the dark liquid inside. When she finally came up for air, Catriona made a face before handing the bottle over to Grace. Bridget watched as the other woman also took a large drink from the bottle; however, she hid her facial expressions a bit better than the former.

"It's like swallowing fire," Catriona coughed out.

"But in a good way." Grace echoed the same cough before offering the bottle to Bridget. "You carry some strong alcohol."

"The stronger the alcohol the better it is at cleaning my medical instruments." Bridget laughed as she took the bottle. "I'm really not much of a drinker, my father kind of ruined that for me."

"Take a drink," Catriona encouraged. "Setting up your shop will be a lot more fun if your world is spinning a bit."

"And if we're drinking this stuff, it won't be long." Grace laughed, returning to her crate.

Bridget pressed the edge of the bottle to her mouth, allowing the dark liquid to trickle past her lips. The second it touched her tongue it felt almost as if Bridget had stabbed herself with a fork. The sharpness of the flavor burned as she forced herself to swallow. As the liquid moved its way down her throat, she felt a burning sensation where the liquor passed by. She began coughing, trying to get cooler air into her lungs.

"You really don't drink, do you?" Catriona laughed as Bridget continued to cough against the fire now burning down her throat.

"No, I always left that to my father," Bridget was able to say when she finally caught her breath. "I don't understand why people enjoy drinking this stuff."

"It all tastes horrible. It's the effects people enjoy." Grace winked as she took the bottle and downed another mouthful before passing the bottle back to Bridget. "So, you're new to having friends and you're new to drinking, please tell me you've at least had sex before."

The question caught Bridget so off guard she choked a little on the alcohol that was already working its way down her throat.

"If we're going to be talking about my twin brother's sex life, I'm going to need more of this." Catriona plucked the bottle from Bridget's hands as she struggled to regain her breath.

"That's a private topic." Bridget's face began to burn; she was unsure if it was the current topic of conversation or the fact she inhaled the last mouthful of liquor.

"Isn't that what friends do?" Grace teased. "Aren't we supposed to talk about our hopes and dreams and good dick."

It was Catriona's turn to be caught off guard by Grace's boldness, spraying a mist of alcohol out of her mouth before collapsing in a fit of laughter.

"You are completely unhinged." Bridget giggled, watching as Catriona once again dared to take a drink from the bottle.

"I prefer the term direct." Grace laughed. "But unhinged isn't the worst thing I've been called."

"You still never answered her question." Catriona thrust the bottle into Bridget's open hands. "Have another drink."

"Not you too?!" Bridget sighed before steeling herself against another mouthful.

"What? I like dick, talking about it is probably fun. Besides, we're doing the friend thing aren't we? Just promise me you won't be too graphic about my brother; I still have to live with him after this."

"Lucky for you there's not much detail in that department," Bridget said in between drinks.

"Really?" Grace took the bottle from her. "That's surprising to be honest."

"Yeah," Catriona agreed, the liquor beginning to slow down her speech. "You guys have been dancing around each other for months now and haven't slept together?"

"Oh, we've slept together," Bridget answered, hearing that her own words were now laced with the alcohol. "But I mean that literally. I haven't had sex in years."

It was Grace's turn to choke on the alcohol. "Years?"

"Is there a reason why you haven't had sex with my brother?" Catriona asked, shocked.

"He hasn't really pushed for it," Bridget admitted shyly.

"Do you want to have sex with him?" Grace asked, staring at the healer with intense curiosity.

"Yes actually," Bridget exclaimed, frustrated over how slow Clyous had been taking things, "and I can't figure out why he doesn't."

"I'm sure that's not the case." Grace looked to Catriona. "Is your brother the shy type?"

"No," Catriona said and laughed. "No, he was quite the ladies' man back home."

"Maybe he's not interested in me like that." Bridget huffed a frustrated sigh.

"No." Grace handed her the bottle. "He's definitely interested in you. That's as clear as day."

"Maybe he's worried you don't want to?" Catriona offered. "Have you talked to him about it?"

"I don't think I'd be comfortable telling him I wanted to have sex." Bridget felt her cheeks burning yet again. "I might die of embarrassment."

"Great, they're both shy when it comes to each other." Grace rolled her eyes as she glanced at Catriona. "At least we're experienced enough to be past that awkward stage."

"Well—" Catriona started before pausing to take another drink "—I'm not so experienced myself. Danny was my first."

"Really?" Grace and Bridget asked in surprised unison.

"Yeah," Catriona slurred heavily, "but, he isn't shy about anything, so getting dick from him is easier than breathing air."

All three women burst out in hysterics. The alcohol bottle was now about halfway empty, their task of setting up the healer's shop lay forgotten.

"It's not like you two are quiet," Grace teased her, "and by the sounds of it he gives you some great orgasms."

"Best feeling in the world," Catriona agreed, a smile spread across her rosy cheeks. "I don't know if all sex is this good or if it's just him but I'm never stopping."

"As you shouldn't." Grace took a second to refocus on the conversation. "Not all sex is like that. Trust me. You got yourself a good one."

"How many people have you had sex with?" Bridget pointed at Grace very unceremoniously.

"Umm—" Grace took a minute to think. "Maybe twelve. Some of them at the same time."

"Twelve?" Bridget nearly dropped the bottle as it was handed to her.

"By the gods, Grace." Catriona laughed hard.

"I'm a bit of a free spirit; my tastes have been a little more exotic than most." Grace winked. "Mostly to piss off my parents. I did what I could to bring them shame, proving I wasn't a good little princess."

"And not all of the twelve were good?" Bridget couldn't stop herself before asking.

"By the gods, no." Grace laughed out loud. "A little more than half were responsible for pretty decent orgasms. The rest were just… there."

"I have a feeling you mean more by 'exotic' than just twelve sexual partners." Catriona swayed a little as she sat there.

"I'm not sure if you would consider both men and women exotic, or two at the same time in one instance." Grace raised an eyebrow, challenging the girl's propriety.

"Women too?" Bridget was absolutely shocked by Grace's words.

"Oh yes. Three," Grace spoke with pride, "I've been playing with my own pussy for years, playing with another woman's was easy enough."

Bridget blanched at Grace's obvious boldness, turning the deepest shade of red she surely had ever been in her life. Catriona took one look at Bridget's face and fell over in hysterics. Grace too began to laugh at just how innocent Bridget truly was.

"I'm a firm believer in don't knock it until you try it." Grace chuckled. "And I've tried just about everything."

"Since you're obviously the master," Catriona wiped away the tears from her eyes as she sat back up before continuing, "any suggestions for fun things I could do for him? I feel like he's always taking care of me."

"Have you sucked on his dick yet?" Grace asked, taking the bottle.

"You mean put it in my mouth?" Catriona asked, eyes widening.

"Come on—" Bridget took the bottle from Grace and took another deep drink "—even I knew that one."

The women burst out in hysterics once again.

"Yes." Grace snatched the bottle back from Bridget. "Imagine the neck of this bottle is his penis."

"It's a bit small but go ahead," Catriona said without emotion, creating another wave of hysterics among the women.

"As I was saying," Grace continued, hiding her smile, "this is his penis. You would essentially take your tongue and drag it around the outer rim of the glass here. Drives them absolutely crazy, they have a lot of feeling there at the tip."

"That doesn't sound like sucking to me." Catriona snickered.

"That's another thing you could do. The more of him you can fit in your mouth or down your throat the better it is for him."

"Just be careful not to choke on it." Bridget giggled as she gave advice.

"While he's in your mouth you can suck on it, keep licking it, all sorts of different things. Men are usually really good at telling you exactly what they like once you've got your mouth around them." Grace took another drink. "I've never met a man who doesn't like his dick being sucked, and you can completely get them off while doing that."

"Does Menolayous let you do that to him?" Bridget asked Grace, she was definitely feeling her world start to spin now.

348

"Menolayous and I haven't done anything," Grace answered. "We haven't even kissed."

"What? You don't want to make him lucky number thirteen?" Bridget teased.

"Oh, more than anything," Grace responded, "but he would be my last. I know for a fact that once I actually get together with him, he's going to ruin me for everyone else."

"I'm not sure he's that experienced." Catriona looked at the bottle, it was mostly empty by now.

"It's not the experience I want, it's him," Grace answered simply. "I've never met anyone so comfortable with who they really are, never met anyone okay with who I am. There is no way getting together with him would be casual. That's why I'm not pushing him and am letting him go at his own speed. I want him to be comfortable with me, to trust me."

"That's probably the sweetest thing I've heard come out of your mouth," Catriona half teased, half meant her words. "Menolayous is a great guy. I sincerely hope you two get the chance to be together."

"Me too!" Bridget chimed in, finishing off the bottle. "I hope Clyous finally decides to fuck me, and I hope you and Danny keep fucking forever."

"By the gods, Bridget." Grace laughed hysterically. "You need to get laid and build up your alcohol tolerance."

"No arguments from me." Bridget raised the empty bottle in the air like she was about to make a toast.

The women all fell to the ground in hysterics at that. There was a knock on the door before it opened up. Menolayous, Danny, and Clyous all walked in carrying more crates filled with supplies for the healer's shop. Rama had disappeared the last day or two, otherwise he probably would have walked in as well. They all stopped at the sight of their women rolling around on the wood floor laughing, the empty alcohol bottle lying between them all.

"Oh no," Danny said with a smile, "what nonsense do we have going on here?"

"This definitely looks like they've been working hard," Clyous said to Danny, a smile on his face. "I thought the alcohol wasn't for drinking."

"What can I say," Bridget wiped the tears from her eyes as she sat up to look at him. "I was thirsty."

The three women looked at each other before laughter once again escaped from them. The three men standing there missed their little joke, opting to set their crates down off to the side.

"Hey." Catriona chucked the empty bottle lightly at her brother. "You're in charge now. You need to make sure you whet her whistle."

Clyous just stared at them after he caught the bottle, the sound of their laughter now echoing throughout the small building. The three men seemed very amused at the women's antics, but the women were still too busy having fun.

"I'm glad to see you all getting along." Even Menolayous was smiling down at them.

"We're practically sisters now," Grace agreed, she then pointed to Danny. "And as your newest sister, I make you a peace offering."

"I'm terrified to know." Danny rolled his eyes at her with a smile on his face.

"I can't tell you," Grace attempted to stand with the help of Menolayous, "but you'll thank me for it later."

"What are you talking about?" Danny asked, helping a very drunk Catriona to her feet. "What is she talking about?"

"Nothing, dear," Catriona slurred, "but you can take me home. I need to lay down."

"Someone's going to get laid," Grace singsonged as Menolayous stopped her from toppling over.

It was Bridget's turn to laugh, falling into Clyous's open arms. "Oh, we definitely drank too much."

"Did you drink the whole bottle amongst yourselves?" Menolayous examined it, sniffing the empty bottle trying to identify the previous contents.

"Yes," Catriona held up a finger in Menolayous's direction, as if confirming what he was asking with her nonsensical hand gestures, "but we bonded, so sacrificing a bottle is no big issue."

"I'm happy you guys are finally getting along." Danny laughed, catching a wobbling Catriona. "But you probably shouldn't drink again unsupervised. You three obviously don't understand moderation."

"Who needs moderation when Catriona has such a big bottle to drink from?" Grace tried to say without laughing but ultimately failed.

The three women once again began howling with laughter as their men helped them out of the healer's shop. At least the menfolk seemed to be enjoying their antics as much as the women were. They were not quiet as they were escorted back towards their houses. Bridget watched as Menolayous and Grace made their way up the newly carved wooden stairs into their treetop home, followed by Catriona and Danny. Bridget may be so drunk the world was spinning, but she was with it enough to realize the girls would not have made it up that staircase without the help of their men.

With two hands firmly grasping her hips, Clyous helped guide Bridget up the wooden staircase. He walked behind her, not once lessening his grip. With each step she took the world spun faster and faster. Only when she made it to the very top and Clyous could wrap his arms around her waist did it remotely begin to slow. With some effort on his part, Clyous managed to get Bridget through their front door, helping her to the newly acquired feathered mattress they had gotten for their home.

"Are you finally taking me to bed?" she teased as she fell back onto the mattress, her limbs suddenly feeling extremely heavy to move.

"Technically yes," Clyous said, she could feel him start to untie one of her boots.

"I mean sex." Bridget laughed, her body now immobilized as the full extent of the alcohol took over her body.

She could feel Clyous pause as he worked the laces on her remaining boot. "Is that what you want?"

"I've only wanted it for weeks now," Bridget found herself confessing against her better judgement, "but apparently it takes nearly a third of a bottle of spirits to work up the courage to tell you."

Silence greeted her. She could feel her last remaining boot being pulled off, freeing her foot completely. The conscious part of her mind was worried maybe she had crossed a line by saying this to him, why else would he be so silent. But the drunk part of her did not seem to care, the other two were right, someone in this relationship needed to not be shy.

"I would be lying if I said I hadn't been thinking the same thing," Clyous said as he sat on the bed next to her, "but this isn't the best time for that conversation."

"Why not?" Bridget pouted, forcing herself to roll over and look at him.

"Because you are incredibly drunk." Clyous smiled down at her. "I'm not even sure you'll remember having this conversation tomorrow, and if I'm going to have sex with you for the first time, I want to make sure you won't ever forget."

Bridget felt the familiar heat return to her cheeks as she took in the look he had on his face. There was lust there, she could see it in his eyes. She sat up so she could be sitting face to face with him, she wanted to bask in the look he was giving her. She could more than respect his logic for not having sex with her tonight, not only was it the gentlemanly thing to do but it was also incredibly… sexy. He wanted their first time to mean something. Her eyes focused on his lips, and she caught herself leaning forward to steal a kiss.

Off in the distance in one of the nearby homes that occupied their friends, Bridget's keen hearing could pick up the sounds of passionate kisses. This made her pause for a moment as the kisses turned to something else that made a great deal more noise, Clyous rolled his eyes at the sound. By the sound of the heavy breathing Bridget was able to tell it was once again Danny and Catriona having sex. They really needed to work on soundproofing these homes if any of them were ever going to get any sleep. Bridget could hear what sounded like a belt buckle hitting the wood floor. Bridget stifled a giggle as Clyous did his best to hide a smile.

Not a minute or so later Danny's voice echoed through their small group of tree homes, "Grace!"

Grace's laugh broke the silence from the opposite direction, causing Bridget to burst into hysterics as well. It sounded like Catriona had wanted to try Grace's advice on Danny tonight.

"I'm guessing I don't want to know," Clyous teased, with a smile on his face.

"Nope, not right now anyway." Bridget lay back, pulling the covers over herself. "Ask me again when I'm sober and maybe I'll show you."

Chapter Forty-Eight

Liam

"Up ahead," the guard said in a low voice as he examined the tracks in the dirt.

Liam nodded, silently unsheathing his sword. The group of guards he traveled with did the same. They had been tracking this band of rebels all the way from the coast to the southern border of Gaelach. These rebels belonged to the war chief Farroway. After the demise of his wife and daughter, Farroway's efforts to strike back at the crown had tripled.

Liam did what he could for the woman, ending her life as gently as he could. He couldn't blame Farroway for his violent response, he would have done the same if he was in the same position, Liam could not allow these attacks to continue. Tracking down Farroway and his warband had become his priority these last few weeks.

Liam advanced forward slowly, willing his footsteps to be as silent as possible. They had stepped into Gaelach territory a few miles back. It was ill advised that anyone from a neighboring kingdom enter Gaelach uninvited, the tribesmen did not take kindly to intruders. These religious zealots weren't just formidable warriors, they used their prisoners as sacrifices to the Moon God. It was better to die in battle than to be captured by one of these cultists.

There was an odd silence that surrounded them just as low-lying fog began to creep through the trees, the guards were on high alert now. There was rumor that these tribesmen possessed traces of magic stolen from the forbidden rituals they practiced. It wasn't often that the guards of Oich had to face off against other blooded, but adding magic into the mix, that terrified his men. Liam stretched his senses outward, hoping to identify anyone approaching their direction. He couldn't pick up anything, literally anything. Including the men that he was surrounded by. There was definitely magic here if it was able to block his senses, his connection to the other wolves. He felt positively blind. Whatever vile magic these cultists wielded would be met with steel.

"Move up," Liam ordered his men, pointing in the direction the tracks led.

Liam's ears homed in on the sound of several objects whizzing quickly through the brush. Seconds later, before his eyes had time to try and catch up with the movement, he heard a sickening impact meeting flesh. Liam watched as each one of his men was struck with a crude looking arrow. Liam felt the impact of an arrow knock into his shoulder, missing his joint. The sharpness of the arrowhead dug into his flesh and muscle, shooting searing pain through his arm and torso.

Liam roared in fury as he ripped the arrow free from his flesh. At a quick glance Liam was able to discern that the only well-made part of the arrow was the arrowhead. Based on the uneven balance of the arrow's shaft and the mismatch of the feathers, Liam was surprised to see a silver-tipped point secured on the arrow. Silver, and made well enough to puncture, but not large enough to kill. These arrows were made to keep blooded from being able to shift. Meaning their attackers not only knew who they were but wanted them alive.

"Let's go!" Liam roared in the direction the arrows had flown from, sword raised and ready.

The sound of crunching footsteps on the frosted ground could be heard, emerging from behind a cluster of trees stood a tall tattoo-covered tribesman. Liam could see plenty of scarred flesh visible from underneath the man's furs and animal hide clothing. The tribesman's black stained mouth opened wide for a smile, revealing teeth sharpened into sharp points. There was movement all around Liam and his men as a dozen wolves charged from the trees aimed straight for them.

The large wolves met steel as they crashed into Liam's men, the sounds of yipping and shouting ringing out through the trees. For not being able to shift, Liam's men held their own fairly well against the pack of descending wolves. There were casualties on both sides as the melee began.

Two wolves simultaneously charged for Liam as the leader of the tribesmen stood and watched from the top of the knoll. Liam dove underneath an auburn wolf, thrusting his sword upward into the beast's belly, spilling out the creature's hot innards before its body hit the ground. Liam continued to move, not taking even a moment to recover before taking a swipe at the second wolf. The beast dodged him easily enough, sinking his teeth into Liam's leg before ripping him upward, toppling him onto his back. Liam hit the ground not a moment before the wolf pounced. Liam had enough time to unsheathe his dagger, thrusting it into the creature's silver mane. One, two, three, by the fourth stab Liam was able to pull his dagger from the creature's throat then redirected the point into the beast's eye. The wolf emitted its final howl of pain before dropping to the side lifeless.

Liam got to his feet, quickly glancing around him. His men were winning, their superior steel and training allowed them to best these creatures regardless of their inability to shift. Liam felt a flicker of pride at how skilled they had become under his training. Liam's gaze snapped to the leader who was still standing on the knoll observing him.

"Come down here and fight me you useless cur!" Liam roared, retrieving his abandoned sword on the ground.

The leader smiled down at him before shedding his cloak, pulling free a war spear tipped with a barbed silver tip. The silverback leaped from where he stood, angling his spear down upon Liam as gravity took his body back to the ground. Liam rolled out of the way just in time, recovering just fast enough to dodge a second attack as the leader jabbed his spear at Liam's chest. Liam knocked the spear to the side and slashed at the man's exposed torso, narrowly missing his flesh with the tip of his blade. The leader reversed his backward momentum from the dodge and lunged forward again, spear pointed ahead of him, nicking Liam's shoulder. Liam stumbled back to assess the damage, it wasn't a significant wound. He still had full mobility of his arm.

"You are not welcome here, Princeling," the sound of many layered voices poured from the leader's mouth as he took another expert strike towards Liam, missing his mark. "You should have stayed on your side of the border."

"We are chasing down criminals to apprehend them for crimes against the crown." Liam stared into the man's eyes, realizing they had turned a dark shade of red. This must be their magic at work.

"You chase the wrong criminals," the man said, kicking forward into Liam's thigh and knocking him back.

"Well, excuse me." Liam rolled to dodge another blow, finding himself directly behind the man. Taking advantage of the angle, he thrust the sword through the man's back, coming to a complete stand. "I can assure you, I have no intention of staying in your shithole of a kingdom."

The man laughed as blood began to gurgle deep within his throat spilling out over his stained lips. As soon as the body was lifeless, Liam kicked forward to push the body from the blade of his sword. The body of the cultist leader crumpled onto the ground before him. Liam looked around at the carnage that surrounded him, bodies lay strewn on the forest floor. To his pride and relief no more of the tribesmen remained standing, all of them slain by one of his men. Unfortunately, there were only about seven Oich guards left standing, all in various states of injury.

"Let's get the fuck out of these woods," Liam called to them, eyes glancing at the tree line yet again. "Before more of them show up."

Chapter Forty-Nine

Morrigan

Morrigan stood off to the side of the anxious crowd avoiding contact with all of the men standing there. The war chief had called everyone to an emergency meeting, so here she waited for him to start. He took his sweet time with it too, she dreaded pointless socialization more than anything. She was too old for such drivel, having done it for the better part of several long and grueling centuries. Mankind always found reasons to gather and socialize; it was in their very nature to live in groups. Morrigan had learned over the years that sometimes being alone was the safest and most efficient way to live. It kept her away from men and their dramatics, hopefully this meeting wasn't anything too ridiculous.

It had been a week or so since Catriona had managed to access her magic, so Morrigan doubted this meeting had anything to do with that. She had learned many years ago that if she chose to live with others, she needed to go along with whatever ridiculous rituals or rules they came up with no matter how ridiculous and a waste of her time they were. These warriors needed the children of old if they wanted to survive until next winter, and the children needed the support these warriors provided. It was a mutually beneficial relationship and considering how Morrigan was only here for the children of the ancients, well, she was stuck here with these men.

Catriona had finally recovered from severe burnout. With plenty of yarrow root and Bridget's healing magic the girl was back on her feet within a day. She had earned her markings that day when she gave herself over to the flames completely. There was no doubt in Morrigan's mind that Catriona came from two different bloodlines that carried magic from the Goddess of War. There was no other explanation for it.

Catriona's powers aside, Morrigan found herself utterly in shock at how that entire training session had gone and felt some guilt about how that day was managed from the very start. Had she known the girl was that broken she would not have encouraged that large of a blow out at first. Luckily, Grace was there to show Catriona those who truly loved her. That had been enough to pull the girl back from the edge. Morrigan was rarely caught off guard like she was that day, a lesson she would remember. Her inability to relate and socialize with the children of the ancients was to blame for her failure to understand her pupils. It was a failure that could have ended the girl completely. In an attempt to prevent such a failure again, Morrigan forced herself to remain in the crowd. She needed to be around people to understand them.

Since the first training session, the girls had been getting along quite well. In the mornings all four of them would meet up in the burnt clearing and spar. Each of them was taking turns training with Bridget, pushing her with varying lessons in combat. The blooded was picking techniques up rather quickly. Morrigan had just introduced her to staff fighting this morning, hoping the girl could graduate up to a spear soon enough. After they sparred for several hours, Morrigan would work with the girls on tapping into their magic. Grace needed some fine tuning with hers but otherwise she had her power mastered. Grace appeared to be distracted the last few days; she was having difficulty paying attention to their conversations. Morrigan suspected it had to do with the deep bruising she saw around the girl's throat. Grace had been wearing her spiked jacket to try and conceal the bruises; she even began to wear a higher neck tunic underneath her regular corset. Something had rattled the girl, but if she didn't want to talk about it Morrigan wasn't going to ask. The girl was capable of handling a great deal before she needed someone to come to her aid, but having turned over a new leaf, Morrigan would continue to watch over the princess to ensure she could in fact handle whatever was going on with her.

Catriona was able to control the flames now; she had been concentrating on creating smaller fires rather than infernos. It was difficult for her with all that pent up rage she had been holding inside but she was mastering it slowly. She no longer appeared to want to feed herself to the flames, another good sign indeed. Morrigan still watched her carefully, as did the others, to make sure they wouldn't almost lose her again. That emptiness no longer seemed to call to her, Morrigan hoped that Catriona would never have to feel that again, but that's not how the world worked, the girl's wounds were deep, they cut into her soul. Morrigan found herself not only sympathizing with whatever the girl hid in her past but felt the need to protect her from future harm. Morrigan recognized this emotion with Grace and Bridget as well, none of them had made it through the world up until this point unscathed.

In regards to training, Bridget was having difficulty reaching the full potential of her power. She still remained unmarked. The blooded was able to heal all sorts of wounds with minimal effort, it was impressive to see in person after all these years of having the gift of healing absent from this world, but the girl seemed to outright refuse to cause harm with her gift.

Draining life from another was the last piece she needed to fully come into her power. This irritated Morrigan, she could understand a healer not wanting to cause harm. Such was the nature of a daughter of healing, wishing to do nothing but aid others, but Bridget would have to make a choice one day, and Morrigan hoped she would choose to use it rather than get hurt.

The boy, Clyous, had come to their sparring field today to train with them. His gift of foresight made it incredibly hard for anyone to actually spar with him; he knew every move coming his way. Grace had fun toying with Clyous at first, creating illusions during the sparring match, but Clyous was a quick learner and began figuring out which illusions were real, and which weren't. The only one who seemed to have an edge on Clyous was his twin sister. They were so familiar with each other's techniques there was no need for his power. There was not much for him to work on, visions came to him when a future had been decided, or when he touched objects. There was not more she could teach him, so he stuck around to help the girls. Morrigan suspected he was there more for Bridget than himself. Young love was refreshing to watch.

They now all stood together with the other members of the group, off to the side of this camp's meeting spot. Everyone except Rama, who was undoubtedly with Flinn going over whatever details about the announcement. The boy, Danny, stood behind Catriona as they waited, his arms wrapped protectively around the girl's waist. For a fiercely independent youth it was surprising to see how comfortable Catriona was with this protective, if not possessive, touch. Morrigan supposed after years of not having that type of protection that she enjoyed this deep down. Nothing against her brothers, but they were weaker than Catriona. It's hard to feel protected by someone you outmatch.

Morrigan watched Menolayous with interest, noticing that he stood farther off to the side than even she. He still hated crowds but was forcing himself to stay. There was a kindred soul if she'd ever met one, they shared a very similar dislike of being around people. Menolayous was a man of few words, and when he did speak, she swore she could hear the touch of a Gaelach accent. He did well hiding himself from the world while simultaneously being true to himself, she supposed this was what attracted Grace the most. Morrigan watched him closely, following his eyes that were trained on Grace as she chatted away with Bridget and Catriona. Morrigan knew he had seen the bruises as well, but she suspected Grace had not told him either. That would explain why he seemed to be standing guard over her now.

Whatever she had shown him through their bond had the quiet one smitten. Morrigan did not see this as a bad thing, the two seemed to complement each other rather than be similar. He got her to work on how she talked and interacted with others, and she pushed him out of the darkness. They brought out the best in each other, a rare and beautiful thing, but they had not yet made public claims of each other. Normally, this would be fine, but Grace was attracting attention from others in ways that were not good. Morrigan had seen how the eldest brother looked at Grace. Morrigan sensed attraction from him, even lust, but also a great deal of caution. Morrigan was interested to see if he would risk upsetting his brother for the girl he now coveted, or if the quiet one would find out first. Morrigan also sensed a darkness surrounding the child of the Mountain God every time the giant looked upon Grace. It was as if he was conflicted with how he saw her, as an enemy or as a potential lover. Every time Morrigan tried to look closer at the darkness it was as if it noticed her attention and skittered away into hiding. Morrigan hadn't the faintest idea what it was, but she was concerned about Grace's safety.

The older war chief finally emerged from the newly built longhouse with Rama walking beside him. Morrigan had to admit, the war chief's way around building structures that mirrored those of his homeland was impressive. With Grace's help sketching out his designs and Clyous's craftsmanship, they were able to create efficient and intricate structures in no time. The warriors had been working from sunup until sundown for several weeks now, building a sturdy wall around Collie as well as a few of the more important structures. They had completed the wall yesterday, finally securing the outpost in a way that was more than relying on the cover of trees to protect them. It was an impressive feat to say the least, especially since they were set back a few days after that scourge attack. Morrigan watched as the warriors parted to allow the war chief and the Prince of Thieves to walk through their ranks. Flinn walked to the center of his men, a silence befell the crowd. The amount of respect this war chief commanded impressed even Morrigan, leadership like this did not happen every decade. The old man had been fighting side by side with these men for years, earning every drop of love and respect from them.

"Lads," his voice rang out. "And lasses, I've some good news for you all." Everyone was staring at him now, watching intently. "As you are all aware, in a week's time other war chiefs will be coming here to Collie for a war counsel. You lot have been working tirelessly to expand Collie, and it is for a purpose. I am pleased to inform everyone that Collie is no longer a war camp, but now a village."

Murmurs started to spread through the men like wildfire. "Collie has been altered to allow the arrival of your families. We wish to make this place a home where we can all expand our families and live our lives free from the oppressive reach of Oich. Lads, we have proven we can do just that."

Cheers rang through the men. They felt genuine excitement for this news. "Tomorrow you will report to Rama and myself for orders. This recovery process will take several weeks, and we will have to send out teams to bring your families home safely. Remember lads, in order for your families to be protected we need to get them here without drawing attention from the crown. At least not yet. Anyone impatient enough to try and leave before they are permitted, just know you could be responsible for the deaths of another family. The road is dangerous; the only safety we can guarantee is here behind the wall you all have built."

"Now, for tonight we have brought out the kegs and barrels, and we have several boars on the spit. We will celebrate Collie's future, and tomorrow we will work for it."

As if on cue, men started pulling barrels out of one of the storage huts nearby. Cheers went up as drinks started being passed around. A few of the musically inclined warriors brought out drums, fiddles, and windpipes. For a strategy to keep the men inside, this was not a bad idea. The festivities would be enough of a distraction to keep those wanting to break for their homes, at least remaining until morning.

A smile spread across Morrigan's face as she watched the children of old join in. They too deserved some entertainment after all they have been through. They had been working hard, all of them having been surviving for too long. They were all safe here, they could actually learn to love their lives if they choose to. The twins had managed to get hold of drinking horns and were now engaging in a celebratory drinking contest. Danny and Bridget stood by their partners laughing merrily at the siblings' drinking competition. The giant was helping carry out more kegs of ale. Grace found herself suddenly surrounded by suitors offering to bring her drinks, Menolayous did not look pleased.

"Care for a horn?" The old war chief had sidled up next to her holding up a drinking horn.

Morrigan smiled at him wickedly. "I am much younger than you, war chief. You really think this wise?"

361

"You may look young, but your soul is ancient. I am the closest to your age currently present." Flinn chuckled as Morrigan took the horn. "I figured I was your best chance for conversation."

"So it would seem." Morrigan threw the horn back, draining every drop. "Truth per horn?"

"Don't mind if I do." A mischievous smile spread across his weathered face before he too downed a horn. "Age before beauty."

She snorted at the comment before saying, "I have always liked redheads. Their passions run high, making them the best sleeping companions."

The war chief's face turned the same shade of red as his hair, Morrigan cackled with delight at the sight. "Your turn."

"Why do I have a feeling I just signed up to be tormented for the remainder of the evening?" Flinn laughed heartily.

"Because you did so." Morrigan smiled at him. "It is still your turn. I would like to hear stories of your homeland. It has been many years since I last visited."

Chapter Fifty

Grace

Grace was handed a cup of ale by yet another man wanting her attention. Her head was starting to spin from the spirits, all the attention she was getting, as well as the attention she was not from the man she was hoping to get it from. Instead, she took the horn with a smile, engaging in conversation with a younger man who had short brown hair. She wasn't paying attention enough to have caught his name. Normally, her sharp tongue was enough to keep suitors at bay, but with this warband in particular, the men weren't easily scared off. They were braver than the men who frequented her family's court. Another change she was noticing was that the men did not stop from approaching her just because she was a princess. This was newer territory for her, she appreciated the genuine attention she was getting, but she was a little disappointed that Menolayous was not the one spending time with her.

Menolayous, as usual, was standing off to the side being his normal quiet and brooding self. More so than ever, keeping a watchful eye over her as more and more warriors flocked in her direction. She could feel his unease from here, she was beginning to feel uneasy too, this was getting ridiculous. There were too many people for him to feel comfortable, but he stayed, nonetheless. She was pretty sure it had everything to do with the fact he had seen the bruises and was worried someone would attack her.

"You're welcome to join me," she shot down their connecting mental pathway. *"You might have fun if you actually try."*

"I'm not the biggest fan of crowds. And you, beautiful, are the center of attention right now," he grumbled back. *"Would hate to interrupt."*

"Jealous?" She laughed at something the young man said, not actually having heard it.

She could sense the irritation and jealousy flowing from him before hearing his voice, *"Regardless, I'm not fun at these things."*

"Then why are you standing here torturing yourself?"

"Are you going to tell me about your bruises?" he shot back.

Fuck, it *was* about her neck. She didn't answer him when he had first seen them, not wanting to start something between the brothers. Her silence on the matter seemed to make matters worse. She had done her best to hide them without being obvious about it, but Menolayous seemed to miss absolutely nothing when it came to her. She kind of liked that, but at the moment found it slightly irritating. She could handle herself; she had handled herself. She sent a very clear message to his brother that she was not going to allow anything like that to happen to her again. She was confident after reading his emotions that he finally understood she meant no harm, but he stood by his threat. One she could respect to a degree, but she sensed something dark within him, something that made her uneasy.

What she was not expecting was his attraction towards her knowing that his brother felt the same. Grace had made a point of staying away from the giant as best she could. He rode that dangerous line, one she was all too familiar with and had to keep herself from riding with him. Normally, Rama would have been the obvious choice for her to pursue, he was her type after all. Cocky, dominating personality, and great with conversation. He wouldn't have been a boring choice that's for sure, but she wanted something real, someone who wanted her for her, not for her crown, and not just because of her looks. Menolayous wanted her for who she was, and she very much wanted him, brooding protector as he was at the moment.

"Nope," she responded, *"but if you come over here, I'll let you kiss them and make my neck feel better."*

"I'm being serious," he growled, waves of irritation now mingled with subtle hints of arousal. *"I want to know what happened. Those look like fucking handprints."*

"Maybe I like being choked," she teased.

"Grace!" he snapped out loud, ignoring the looks from everyone around him before returning to their silent conversation. *"Nobody gets to put their hands on you like that."*

"Well, I've been trying to get you to come down here and put your hands on me for the last hour," she snapped back, effectively silencing him. *"If you're just going to hide in the shadows instead of coming down here then stop acting like a jealous lover."*

She threw another cup of spirits back, swallowing a mouthful of the spiced mead. She slammed their connection shut, effectively blocking him out. Satisfied she could no longer feel his emotions, she reengaged her conversation with the young man in front of her. She watched as the man's eyes grew wide, and the men nearby stepped away from her with some urgency. She turned, hoping to see Menolayous finally coming to her. Instead, she had to crane her neck to stare at Rama.

"What the fuck do you want?" Grace rolled her eyes at him before turning her back to the big brute.

"You looked like you needed company," Rama's words had the surrounding warriors scattering.

"I don't need anything from you, thanks." Grace crossed her arms, back still to him in obvious defiance.

She could feel Rama's large hands plant themselves on either side of her chair, spinning her around to face him. Caught off guard, she let out a tiny gasp as he lowered himself down to her level. She took him in then, all of him. For a large brute, he was certainly handsome, but right now he was using his size to try and intimidate her. She could sense an array of emotions coming from him, mostly excitement and attraction. He was flirting with her. Great, just what she needed. If it wasn't the darkness surrounding him it was this.

"You sure?" A mischievous smile spread across his face. "Looks like I did you a favor, scaring away all of your would-be suitors."

"I can handle myself, as you are well aware." She reached up, using the point of her fingernail to slice open the scab that had formed over the cut she had given him, a drop of blood forming.

Rama glanced down at her, eyes finally falling to the bruises on her throat. His smile vanished; she could practically taste the regret pouring out of him.

"Grace I—" he started.

"Not here," she warned, she had gone this far in protecting Menolayous, she wasn't about to let this idiot bring him even more concern. "Besides, you can't undo it. If you didn't mean the words, you shouldn't have said them, and I know you meant them."

"Is there a reason why you haven't told my brother?" He seemed genuinely curious, his eyes still boring into hers.

"You told me not to break his heart. Pitting two brothers against each other would do just that," she answered honestly. "I'm not into destroying families or friendships."

"You know, out of everyone here, he's the one I'm most scared of," Rama admitted, finally taking a seat next to her. "Even more than Cat."

"I don't believe that." Grace was surprised, it very well could be the alcohol. "Catriona is volatile. She could kill all of us at the drop of a hat."

"Oh, I'm not denying her power, or yours." Rama reached for a cup of ale, downing it. "None of you have seen Menolayous in action yet. Not completely. He's the most skilled warrior I've ever met. Put him on a battlefield and he could easily decimate any enemy."

"More skilled than you?" Grace taunted, also drinking another cup.

"Yes. I'm large, I've always used that to my advantage. I've always been strong. Danny is strong for his size and unpredictable, his strength has always been swordplay. Menolayous has always bested us in the ring, and on the range his aim is impeccable."

"Why don't I see him train?" Her head swooned then, the drinks finally catching up to her. "Never mind, I know the answer."

"You like my brother, don't you?" Rama smiled at her as he handed her another drink.

"Yes," she answered before taking the cup, drinking from it, then paused. "Should I be concerned that you're poisoning me? That's more believable coming from you considering our last conversation."

Quicker than she expected, Rama pulled her chair closer to his, gently pulling her face to his, stopping before their lips touched. "What about me? Do you like me?"

"No," Grace slurred, irritation at the audacity this man had to even think touching her would be acceptable. "I've fucked men like you before. Not interested in what little you have to offer me."

A smile cracked across his face at that. She was drunk, her head spinning, but she was getting angry at how comfortable he was manhandling her after their last face-to-face conversation. She was losing grip on her powers; she couldn't stop herself from trying to sense everything going on around her. There were stares, plenty of envy, and a lot of lust. A good portion of it radiating off Rama, she could also sense great violence surrounding him like a storm cloud. She tried to close down her senses before they started to influence her own. She should have stopped drinking when Rama first approached her, she should never have let her guard down this much around a man who carried that much darkness in him.

"I don't have anything little, Princess," he practically purred.

"What about keep your hands off of me, did you not understand the last time?" she hissed, pulling her face from his grasp, willing her heart rate to slow down.

Rama shrugged, still looking at her as if she were a new and interesting challenge. "I tend to do what I want, when I want, but this wasn't all about what I wanted was it? Why else would you be sitting here as long as you have with me if not to draw attention from someone else."

That asshole was pushing on her very last nerve. He was the one that put himself here, and the only way she was getting away from him would be to cause a scene. That was the last thing she wanted to do, especially with Menolayous so close by. He was probably staring at their exchange completely confused.

"But you're welcome." He smiled at her, leaning back in the chair comfortably.

"For what?" she snapped, wanting nothing more than to wipe that handsome yet cocky smile from his face with a swipe of her fingernails.

"Menolayous is coming." Rama winked at her before glancing up. "Brother."

Rama was indeed correct, Menolayous was now standing right behind her. A large hand gently resting on her shoulder, letting her know that he was in fact there. Rama scooted his chair back away from her, finally pulling his emotions back to where she could no longer sense them. If she didn't know better, and at this point it was questionable, she would think he had done all of that on purpose. Not just hitting Menolayous's jealousy but getting her to drink so she couldn't contain her power. Asshole! He definitely knew exactly what he was doing. The question was, why? She thought he wanted to keep her away from Menolayous.

"Come down to join the festivities?" Rama asked Menolayous casually, as if he hadn't intentionally drawn him out of hiding by flirting with her.

"Just came over to check on Grace," he grunted, not wanting to start up a conversation it seemed.

"I was just telling Grace about how you like to throw knives." Rama downed another drink. "Want to have a friendly competition?"

The implication was there, a test for his brother. Grace held her breath, hoping this was not about to turn ugly. Rama seemed to be wanting to toe that line, Menolayous saw it too. She had no doubts about that. Menolayous knew his brother better than she did, maybe he could see that storm cloud circling them as they all stood there.

"No," Menolayous answered. Grace felt his hand move to the back of her neck. In her head he said, *"let's go."*

The two brothers were now staring and sizing each other up. Were they checking each other's intentions or was Menolayous making a claim on her. Would Rama respect it? What was going on? Grace was too drunk and not in enough control of her powers to clearly see everything going on.

"Are you alright?" she asked, looking between the two.

"Please Grace, don't fight me on this," his voice echoed. *"I can't give you what you want here, but I would like to spend time with you away from all of them."*

"Menolayous, would you walk me home?" Grace stood, stumbling a little. *"I'm all yours."*

Menolayous smiled at their private dialogue, gently leading her away from his problematic brother. She finally relaxed as Rama remained seated, staring at them as they walked away. As the two made their way towards the edge of the festivities, the old war chief who was engaging in a drinking game with Morrigan shouted and fell backwards out of his seat when Morrigan's raven started flapping its wings in his face. Flinn's booming laugh echoed throughout the party, effectively drawing everyone's attention to him as the bird continued to squawk at him angrily.

"Can I take you to a lake I found a few years back?" he asked, gently intertwining his fingers and hers while steering her away from the crowd gently. "It's one of my favorite places to visit when I'm here and need to get away."

"Only if you make sure I don't fall on my face." She laughed, almost tripping over someone.

"Deal." He smiled back at her. "It's maybe a few hours' walk from here."

They walked to the edge of camp, slipping out one of the few hidden outlets within the town's wall. Once free of the chaos behind them, Grace found that she was able to breathe easier. The night sky acted like a blanket thrown over her head, with no moon visible that left just the stars to light up their surroundings. Relief flooded through her as they moved farther away from Rama and any other man that felt entitled to her attention. She was finally alone with Menolayous, where she had wanted to be the entire night.

They kept going for several more minutes, Grace was hardly able to see anything in the darkness now that the campfires and torches were behind them. She was game for whatever Menolayous brought her way, even if it wasn't to show her a lake. Or was he being literal? It was hard to tell with him.

"If I run into a tree I'm going to be mad at you," she said half-jokingly. "I'm too drunk for this."

Menolayous stopped then, turning to her. "Do you want to go back?"

"No, I just can't see." She laughed. "It's like I'm wearing a blindfold. I have no idea how you're able to see out here."

"If you can't see maybe we should come back to the lake at a different time," he sounded concerned, like he was overanalyzing what she had said. She was now convinced he actually meant to take her to a lake instead of out in the woods to have his way with her. Of course he was being literal, she rolled her eyes at her own ignorance.

"Is that all you wanted Menolayous?" She gently pulled him towards her, hoping to clarify what was happening. "To show me a lake? At night?"

"It's a beautiful lake," he said gruffly. "But no. I wanted you all to myself, as selfish as that is."

Grace stumbled forward slightly and Menolayous quickly wrapped her in his arms. He gently walked her back a few steps, her back now pressed softly against a tree. She welcomed the tree's stability, how it managed to keep her upright and steady as the ground seemed to be spinning out of control. Being in his arms was also very nice.

"It's not selfish if we both wanted it." It was her turn to reach out to him; she wrapped her arms around his neck gently. "Took you long enough. I was beginning to worry you were being serious about walking over an hour to see a lake."

His body stiffened at their proximity, but he did not pull away. "You're the only one who knows how difficult this is for me. I'm not experienced, Rama—"

"I really don't want you talking about your brothers right now." Grace took a steady breath. "I want you. Not them. I understand you, and I'm okay with going at your pace. I promise."

She could feel the tension in his arms slacken slightly. "Can I kiss you?"

"You don't have to ask." She could feel her cheeks heat up a bit. "And, you don't have to treat me like I will break. I promise if I don't like something I'll tell you."

369

She could still sense his hesitation. She wanted to reach out with her powers to calm him, but she knew he had to do this on his own. Besides, the world was still spinning a little too much for her to have any real control of her magic. She stood there for a moment, debating on whether she should try and kiss him or pull him closer. Both seemed like bad ideas, she was just being impatient. She still couldn't see anything, a fact that annoyed her greatly.

Apparently, Menolayous had no issues seeing in the dark, the jerk. She felt his hands in her hair at the base of her neck, gently pulling her face to his. She inhaled sharply in surprise before his lips found hers. His lips were so soft and they moved against hers so gently. Slowly she kissed him back, trying not to push her desires past what he was comfortable with. After another moment or so he broke away from their kiss, but he still held onto her.

"Are you okay?" he asked her in a whisper.

"More than okay," she answered. "You don't have to keep asking. I can take whatever you throw at me. In fact, I might even like it."

"Promise me you'll say something if I do something wrong," his voice was almost pleading. Permission was important to him she realized.

"I promise." She leaned forward, gently catching his lower lip between her teeth and sucking it before releasing it. "I want your hands on me. I want you to explore, to figure out what you like."

"What do you like?" She could feel him harden against her as he asked.

"When you're ready to find out let me know," she teased.

His lips crashed against hers, more eager this time. Instead of the same gentleness as before, this kiss was more demanding. She moaned quietly as he pressed himself against her, the sounds she made seemed to excite him. His hands began to roam down her body, hovering around her breast. With a free hand she took his hand and placed it on her breast. That was all the permission he seemed to need.

He squeezed gently before running a thumb over her thin tunic, hovering over her hardened nipple. As his thumb made circles it sent shivers of pleasure through her. It had been a while, since she'd had any sort of release involving another person. She moaned again, this time loudly as he continued to tease her nipple through the thin cloth. She gasped for breath as his lips left hers and began to kiss her neck. She wanted more, wanted him to be able to get to all of her.

370

"Can I take this off?" she asked breathlessly.

"Please," his voice seemed strained.

She reached up and began to untie her corset from the front slightly frustrated that she couldn't see. She felt him shift backwards as if angling himself for a better look. Once freed from the corset all that remained was the tunic. She reached up to start untying the knots, but he reached forward to help her. As soon as the ties were undone Menolayous pulled open her tunic, revealing her bare breasts.

"You're so fucking beautiful," he said breathlessly.

"You're welcome to them," she said in a sultry whisper.

She felt him bending down in front of her then he started kissing her breast. She took deep breaths as his tongue and teeth explored, enjoying the sensations from his mouth. She began to feel a throbbing sensation between her legs at the contact. She reveled in it, how good it felt, how relaxed she was, all of it. After several moments she heard him swear in frustration, before grabbing her by the waist and lifting her into the air effortlessly.

As he pressed her up against the tree she wrapped her legs around his waist, feeling just how hard he was between her legs. In her new position, her chest was now directly in his face, allowing him easier access to run his tongue around the hardness of her nipple. His hands now gently ran up her thighs and cupped her ass as his tongue worked. She could feel him grow harder against her. She felt the need to grind against him, to bring his cock even closer to her. It took every ounce of internal strength not to reach down and grab him with her hand, she wasn't sure how he would handle that. She was beginning to feel overwhelmed with her own arousal, she could sense he was too. They were connecting through their mental pathway, she realized. They were feeling each other's emotions, as well as each other's arousal. This was getting serious quickly, not that she minded of course, but her worry for him began to sober her slightly.

"Is it your intention to completely take me right now?" she asked, sensing him pause. "I'm okay with that by the way, but if your immediate answer isn't yes, maybe we should slow down. Wouldn't be fair to either of us if we kept going."

"Sorry…" He grunted, gently setting her down.

"Don't be," she answered. "You're better at this than I expected for being so new to it."

She could feel the conflict brewing in him, that same intense arousal she had felt in that forest weeks ago. A kernel of doubt existed within him, that flash of pain, and it began to grow inside him once again.

"You don't get to turn this negative." She grabbed him, refusing to let go of his arm as he attempted to step away.

"I'm not trying to," he answered, sounding frustrated. "I need a minute to calm down."

She wished she could see him then, to see his face, but she could feel him. He wanted to keep going, the desire burned painfully inside him, but he was nervous, too nervous. He wasn't ready yet, and that was okay.

A memory pulled at her then, from that night at camp. "You don't take care of yourself often, do you?"

It was a very personal question, she knew it, but she had her suspicions about him. Those scars on his arms were self-inflicted and old, but it concerned her that he would intentionally cause himself pain as a type of punishment. Just like when she was helping him untangle his hair weeks ago, his arousal was almost painful.

"No." To her surprise he actually answered her.

"May I?" she asked, she wanted to ask why but now was not the time. She felt it was more important to make this a positive experience for him. She would readdress the self-inflicted pain later.

"What are you trying to do?" he asked curiously, at least he wasn't pulling away.

"I want to take care of you." She gently tugged the strings on his trousers. "There are ways I can do that without going over the edge myself, if you're okay with it. Ways that won't leave you feeling so vulnerable, just yet."

"But what about you?" His voice sounded strained as she slowly began to loosen his trousers, but she could feel his arousal flare up again like a warming fire. He was curious, genuinely curious at her intentions. She did not feel hesitation or doubtfulness like she had moments ago.

"I have no problem taking care of myself." She slid her hand inside, reaching for his cock. He groaned as soon as her fingertips found him. "Maybe one day soon I'll let you watch as I do."

She grasped him then, shocked at how long and thick he was. For the tenth time tonight, she cursed the darkness and her inability to see.

Apparently, the gods felt she didn't deserve to lay her eyes on such a beautiful sight, not yet at least. As if she had any other intention than making tonight about him, meddling bastards. She pulled down his trousers enough to free him completely. Squeezing slightly, she gave him a slow pump, feeling his body jerk at the motion.

"You tell me if this is too much," she instructed him, pumping him again. She felt him shudder slightly. "Also, you don't have to be quiet. I like hearing how I make you feel."

To emphasize her point, Grace pumped him again, this time she was able to squeeze an inhale of breath from him. With a satisfied smile she lowered herself to her knees, putting his cock at about eye level. Still grasping him, she teased his tip with her tongue. She felt him jolt at the contact but he remained where he was. Slowly, she began to fit him into her mouth, tongue working around his shaft. He groaned loudly, bracing himself against the tree with one hand while the other tangled itself in her hair. His touch and the sounds he was now making at every swipe of her tongue spurred her on. She began to suck and pump him at the same time. His breathing became more and more labored as she worked, he was getting close. She took him deeper into her mouth, managing to fit him in just enough that her lips grazed the base of his shaft. She felt the veins in his cock grow suddenly, then she tasted his release.

He gently fisted her hair, moaning loudly as he emptied himself. When he was done Grace removed him from her mouth, both of them catching their breath. Menolayous reached down, helping her rise to her feet. He kissed her once very passionately before wrapping her in an embrace.

"I take it you enjoyed that?" Grace teased, nuzzling into his chest.

He laughed, kissing the top of her head. "Yes, sweetheart, very much."

Chapter Fifty-One

Clyous

Clyous was drunk, there was no doubt about that. He and his sister decided, for no intelligent reason he could currently think of, to try and outdrink each other. What they both seemed to have forgotten, or willingly overlooked, was that their alcohol threshold was the exact same. They were twins after all, dumb and reckless, but still twins. Two sides of the same coin.

Catriona was sitting across from him swaying slightly in her seat. Danny was watching her with a smile, finding her level of intoxication extremely amusing. Bridget was laughing at all three of them, being the only one whose world was not spinning. She had opted out of their little drinking game; she was not particularly fond of the after-effects. Last time she drank she was sick the entire next day. Clyous admitted he was having fun teaching the healer a thing or two about a hangover and how to treat it.

Menolayous and Grace had just returned to the festivities, drawing Rama's attention from where he sat off to the side. Clyous could not help but stare at the giant man who had been avoiding everyone for the last few days. It was strange for him, his personality usually had him in the center of all, laughing or teasing someone but since that day Catriona had discovered her powers he had been extremely distant towards everyone, especially Grace and Menolayous. A darkness had seemed to sweep over him that day, and it hadn't let go.

Clyous opened up his magic toward Rama, hoping to catch any amount of information he could about what was going on. Too many factors were working against his magic, the most obvious being his level of intoxication. The second being that without physical touch Clyous was forced to only see futures based on any decisions Rama had made, but curiosity about this darkness had Clyous trying to figure it out. The fact that it now swirled around him as Grace and Menolayous approached was strange. Visions started to flood his mind, of Rama pining after Grace, longing for what his brother now had with her. It seemed that Rama had yet to make a decision about what he wanted to do. Clyous saw many outcomes.

In one of the strongest visions he saw, Rama was ignoring his feelings for Grace and letting Menolayous have her. Another was of Rama dragging her off into the forest, claiming her as his own. The last was images of him killing her after discovering she had harmed Menolayous in some fashion. None of these visions seemed remotely like they were centered in logic, just pure emotional reactions. Clyous shook the images out of his head, the drinks made it harder for him to leave the potential futures behind. What he had seen was disturbing, but not something he could address here and now. He would talk to Bridget about this later, see what she thought.

There were sounds of chairs scraping and then a thud. Clyous whipped his head around to see that Flinn had fallen out of his chair drunk, effectively naming Morrigan the victor of their little drinking game. Morrigan laughed as she helped him sit up. The two seemed to share a friendship, something that was new to Morrigan, at least from what Clyous had seen. Flashes of the future forced their way into his mind yet again, this time of Flinn fighting on a battlefield. Flinn took a sword to the leg, dropping to one knee before thrusting his sword through the opponent's chest. Clyous shook those images out of his head too, just what he needed, seeing everyone's deaths.

"Are you okay?" Bridget asked quietly, sensing his distress at losing a grip on his magic.

He looked at her then, smiling as if to show her he was in fact alright. Images of them together flashed through his mind. They were intertwined with each other in bed sheets, making love in a feather bed, not one here in Collie. The images suddenly changed to Bridget standing before him wearing a white dress and a delicately crafted gold ring on her finger. The next images were of her with a swollen belly smiling at him and at what they had created. This is the future he saw for them, and he couldn't be happier about it.

"Yes love, the alcohol is making it hard to keep my gift under control," Clyous answered with a smile.

"Maybe you should stop drinking then," Danny said, looking at Catriona as if he were not intoxicated himself. "Maybe you both should. I don't think Flinn would appreciate you burning his village down."

"Only if you piss me off." Catriona laughed. "Rage fuels the fire."

"You don't need to be mad to use it." Bridget eyed her skeptically.

"Shh." Catriona winked, yes, she was incredibly drunk.

"No more alcohol for the two of you," Bridget agreed, removing a cup of mead from Catriona's reach.

"Heeey!" Catriona whined.

Clyous's eyes found Menolayous again, the man now sat next to them, pulling Grace down to his lap. Clyous did not miss how that simple act alone made Danny completely interested in those two. Menolayous had never allowed anyone to touch him, not for the six months he had known him, with exception of that time his sister had surprised the broody bastard with a hug. Now, he seemed completely smitten by Grace. He doubted there had been many women before, it would explain Danny's reaction to the physical displays of affection.

Pain struck him like a thunderclap, Clyous gripped the table as a vision hammered its way into his mind. Markous was riding on a horse side by side with another man. This man beside his brother was a war chief, they were traveling to attend the war counsel and talking about it. The conversation suddenly turned to him and Catriona. Who was this stranger that spoke to Markous as if he knew them already. Realization finally struck him, the man's features so familiar to his own that it should have been obvious the second the vision overtook him. The man was older than last he saw him, but those silver eyes and white-blonde hair, this was their father.

"Clyous are you okay?" Catriona's voice cut through his visions, bringing him back to reality.

Everyone was now staring at him, his tattoo glowing from the power. Their father was alive! Alive and coming for them, and he had Markous with him! Too many emotions struck him at once; it was as if he had doubled his alcohol intake in less than a second.

"Cat!" he breathed. "Our father, he's alive!"

"What?" she asked, sobering a bit at the news.

"He's alive. He's with Markous right now. They're coming here!" Clyous was starting to shake slightly, his body not sure how to process this.

"Really?" Catriona seemed to be reacting the same. "You saw him?!"

Clyous began to answer when a shift of movement caught his attention. Menolayous stared at them both, a look of guilt crossing over his face. He and Grace shared a look. Anger flashed through Clyous, did they know? Why hadn't they said anything?

Not caring that he was breaking the unspoken rule to not touch Menolayous, Clyous shot forward, grabbing the warrior's wrist in a vice-like grip. Clyous flipped backwards in the man's memories, ignoring everything until he found what he was looking for. The memory of Menolayous talking with his father, telling him not to come to them. Menolayous had known this entire time that their father was still alive. He had delivered Markous straight to him, and all these weeks they had lived together here at Collie he had never brought it up. Rage flooded through Clyous at this betrayal, these secrets.

As if no time had passed from the moment Clyous grabbed Menolayous and sifted through the warrior's memories, in the present chaos had broken loose. The warrior stood fast, tossing Grace off to the side before planting a hard kick to Clyous's chest, sending him tumbling backwards.

"You knew!" Clyous roared, rushing back up to Menolayous, swinging for him.

Menolayous dodged the strike easily enough, dancing around him. Everyone was on their feet then, Danny grabbed Catriona around the waist as she tried to jump in, hauling her away. Bridget dived out of the way. Grace also made to intervene but was picked up by Rama who had rushed over the second he saw Clyous grab hold of Menolayous.

"This is between them," Rama's voice sounded.

"I did," Menolayous confirmed, eyes bouncing between the twins.

Clyous rushed at him again, Menolayous dodged another strike before trapping one of Clyous's arms behind his back in an expert move.

"Why did you tell him not to come?" Clyous struggled against the hold, but it was no use. "Why didn't you tell us he was alive?"

"When I told him not to come it was because I didn't know how Catriona was doing. I was worried that him suddenly showing up was going to trigger her. I told him to let you and her decide when to see him." Menolayous held him firm. "I am truly sorry for not telling you both. I should have as soon as we were all back together."

Catriona was in tears now, no longer struggling against Danny's hold. "We've been back for weeks! You could have told us weeks ago!"

"I should have, you are right," Menolayous sounded sincere, glancing at her. "I'm sorry."

"Fuck you!" Clyous snapped. "You're a fucking asshole for not telling us."

"Let go of me!" Grace demanded, trying to get out of Rama's grip.

"Not happening, Princess, this is between them," Rama answered.

"You want to fight so badly, fine!" Menolayous released Clyous, pushing him forward. "Let's go blacksmith. Let's see if you can fight better than your sister."

"Clyous, stop!" Bridget shouted. "This isn't reasonable."

"Let them fight it out, lass," Flinn's voice now echoed around them. "Men are rarely reasonable. They need to get the anger out."

Clyous charged Menolayous, delivering a hard strike to the man's face. It visibly rocked the warrior, he might be used to getting hit, but Clyous was used to striking an anvil all day. Menolayous used their proximity to throw a knee into his ribs. Clyous returned the favor with another strike. For a minute or two the men tussled, throwing elbows, fists, and kicks at each other. They seemed to tire at the same rate, both of them banged up and bleeding. One thing was clear to Clyous, Menolayous never pressed an attack. All the strikes Menolayous had sustained were because Clyous continued to push forward. Clyous had a suspicion Menolayous was letting him get in strikes, he wasn't too sure that he would be able to touch the warrior on a battlefield. This fact alone enraged him further.

"What about keep your fucking hands off of me did you not understand the first time?" Grace's voice came from the sidelines.

Her comment meant nothing to him, but it caught Menolayous's attention. The warrior suddenly turned towards his brother, a dangerous look in his eye promising pain and violence. Rama simply held onto Grace who was struggling to get away from him, but a realization seemed to click for Menolayous as if he had suddenly found the answer to a question he had been harboring. He took a step towards his brother. Rama, even as large as he was, seemed to have the good sense to let go of Grace, who shot away from the giant quickly.

Too enraged and too drunk to care about whatever that was about, Clyous took advantage of the distraction. Clyous charged a final time, catching Menolayous by the waist to try to slam him down hard into the ground. Somehow while still in midair Menolayous managed to maneuver himself and Clyous before they touched the ground. Menolayous had one of Clyous's arms now trapped between his legs, pulling it straight and locking it out. Clyous laid face first in the dirt, now realizing just how quick this man was. He knew better than to try and fight at this point, he could feel it in his arm that with the right pressure Menolayous could snap his bones.

"Are you done?" Menolayous seethed.

Reluctantly, Clyous nodded yes. Menolayous released him, rolling off to the side and leaving him in the dust. Clyous sat up, looking around as he breathed heavily. Grace went for Menolayous, who was now eyeing Rama with murder on his mind. Grace put herself between them, but Menolayous moved around her. Rama did not move, standing his ground, but his face pleaded for his brother to stop. Confusion of what was going on hit the remainder of the group as Grace tried to get Menolayous to stop. He was not going to stop. Clyous was now thankful that even though they had fought, Menolayous was not coming for him like that.

"Enough!" a female voice bellowed, ripples of power shook the very ground.

Everyone stopped what they were doing to turn and look at Bridget, her green eyes blazing with a faint and eerie glow. Clyous watched as everyone seemed to naturally bow down to her command, nobody willing to directly look her in the eye. Except Morrigan, who never looked so proud as she did watching Bridget just then. This was a wolf in charge, Clyous realized. Bridget was commanding them as the dominant wolf to stop fighting. The ripples of power died away, allowing everyone in the vicinity to breathe.

"We're done fighting tonight," she commanded, glaring at all of them. "We are a family; we are one pack. We do not fight each other, save it for the enemy."

And that was that. Clyous watched as everyone began to disperse. Danny escorted Catriona away towards their home. Grace was pulling on Menolayous, still trying to get him to leave his brother. Finally, Menolayous conceded, the two of them heading away from the village towards the forest. Bridget offered Clyous a hand, which he took gratefully as he stood. The look of disappointment on her face made him feel ashamed of his outburst. Together, they headed back to their home. Clyous glanced back at Rama, who just stood there, glancing back towards the forest like he was ashamed of something. If Clyous's visions about him were accurate at all, he had a lot to be ashamed of.

Chapter Fifty-Two

Menolayous

Menolayous felt himself slowly beginning to wake. He had slept surprisingly well, deeply and with no dreams. He stretched his arms up over his head feeling the muscles in his back awaken with the movement. He was sore from last night, not too terribly, but enough he could tell. He opened his eyes, glancing around the wooden hut. Really it was a room, with a door and a window. It was originally unfurnished and made for him and Rama to share upon their arrival to Collie, but since that awful night when the Dark One had entered his mind and had possessed him, this room and who stayed in it had changed.

Rama had since moved out, taking up residency in a stone hut not too far away from the rest of them and Grace had moved in. It wasn't a conversation either of them had, it was something that had just happened. Menolayous supposed Grace was there to protect him from any recurring conflicts with the Dark One, her magic was strong enough to protect him even in sleep. It had been strange at first, sharing a room with a female, let alone having someone there to protect him. They had traveled together so that helped ease his discomfort slightly. Grace made it easier by sleeping on the opposite side of the room to give him space.

Since her arrival, a mattress and several blankets had appeared. She had made herself at home, bringing with her luxuries he would never have thought to allow himself. To her credit, she had offered to share with him to which he politely declined. After last night's events with her, and getting into a fight with Clyous, he had taken her up on that offer, being entirely too exhausted to fight against the call of that comforting looking mattress, or how much he wanted to be close to her. Now he found himself waking up on that mattress with her snuggled up next to him.

"Good morning," she greeted him sleepily, face still partially hidden under the covers.

"Morning." He found himself smiling at her, enjoying the warmth her body was giving off against the cool morning air. "You sleep well?"

"Like a rock." She yawned. "It got so hot last night I ended up stripping down to nothing."

Menolayous felt his face flush at her words, suddenly picturing those perfect breasts he had his mouth on just last night.

"Relax." She nudged him playfully as she sat up. "I'm teasing."

"You enjoy doing that," he said as his eyes followed her movements, noting she was in fact wearing a long sleeping shirt.

"It's one of my favorite things." She winked. "On a more serious note, how did you sleep? Are you okay from last night?"

He really looked at her then, she was concerned about him. She was as protective of him as he was of her. That knowledge alone gave a slight pull on his heart strings. She cared about him, truly gave a shit. Not just if he lived or died, but she cared about how he felt about what had happened between them. It wasn't coming from a judgmental place, and she wasn't babying him like he assumed she would have. Instead she wanted the truth from him to better understand, and to respect his boundaries.

"Honestly, that's the best sleep I've gotten in years." He sat up now, ready to greet the day.

"Good. So, no regrets?" she asked.

"None." He leaned forward kissing her gently. "Thank you, for... taking care of me."

"Anytime." She gave him a smile.

Menolayous rolled his eyes playfully at her before glancing over to the windowsill. Grace had parchments scattered there with some of her charcoal, she had been busy sketching new drawings. Her gaze followed his for a moment before reaching over to shuffle through the paperwork. She grabbed a large piece, handing it to him. He stared down at a beautiful sketch of a sparrowhawk with its wings open and its claws raised as if prepared to fight. As he looked closer, he could see that each one of its feathers was in fact intricate knotwork much like that from his tribe. How she had been able to design this was beyond him. She had such talent with her drawings.

"It's beautiful." He meant it, smiling at her. "This is incredible."

"It's your tattoo." She smiled back, taking the parchment.

"Really?" He was in disbelief, looking back down at the bird of prey on the parchment before him.

"Yes." Grace adjusted herself so she was facing him, reaching out to gently touch his bare chest. "I figured it would look really good here."

"I would agree." He glanced down at where her hands were touching, imagining the artwork on his body.

"I'm ready to put it on you if you are." She reached toward a satchel pulling it closer. She brought out a hide with the same design etched into the dried flesh. "I've been practicing with the needles and ink you gave me."

"I can't think of anything else I would rather do today."

"Really?" That teasing smirk now sat on her face like she had found an easy target. "You wouldn't want a repeat of last night?"

Menolayous found himself heating up at the memory of her lips wrapped around his cock and the sweet release he found from the feel of her tongue stroking him. Truthfully, he felt himself start to harden in his breeches, damn it.

"You're too easy." She laughed, pulling out her needles and ink. "We can do that after."

Menolayous watched as she tossed her hair up into a messy bun on top of her head before rolling up her sleeves. They were apparently doing this, he laughed at her as she stuck her tongue out at him, still flirting as she set out the supplies. She grabbed a second bag of what looked like medical supplies, laying out the bandages and ointments.

"Laying down will probably be the easiest way to get to your chest." She pointed for him to lay back.

He obeyed her, lying on his back for her to get access to his already bare chest. He glanced down at it and all the white and purple scars that took up most of the space on his flesh. He imagined the image there instead, cut into his skin with dark ink, concealing all the shame he had been hiding for years. This would be a welcome change, maybe instead of looking at his scars and feeling the sting of his past he could actually feel pride in her artwork. Maybe he could actually be confident enough to remove his shirt from time to time.

"This is going to hurt," Grace said, looking down at him. "If it gets to be too much just let me know and we can take a break."

"I'm accustomed to pain." Menolayous sighed at the truth of it. "But I'll let you know."

"Good." In one motion she threw a leg over him, now straddling his hips. "Because I think there are easy ways to take your mind off it."

382

Easy ways indeed, he became very aware of the pants he still wore. Her flesh was warm against him as she adjusted herself over him, her ass accidentally grinding against his length. He stifled a groan with a cough, earning a knowing look from her as she looked down upon him.

"Relax," she demanded as she dipped her tools in the ink.

Grace had embedded two needles into a small wooden handle, the other end of it being somewhat flat. Menolayous had shown her the design he remembered from his tribe when he was younger and Clyous and Bridget had helped them make it. Clyous had made several of these needles for Grace to use with the promise that one day she would tattoo him. Bridget had provided the healing supplies, caring more about preventing an infection than anything. Menolayous had briefly shown Grace the technique his people had used, having no artistic ability himself, she had figured out the rest herself.

He felt the anxiety rise to his throat as the needle neared him, wondering just how much this was going to hurt. He knew he could handle it, but it was a new experience he wanted to adjust to quickly. Grace's face grew serious as she concentrated on the drawing she had set out near his head before glancing back to his chest. She brushed her free hand over the right side of his chest before setting the needle to work. The sharpness of the needle was pressing into his skin as Grace grabbed the small wooden club, striking down on the end of the needle firmly, pushing the ink deeper into his chest. She removed the needle before coating it with more ink, repeating the process. He realized quickly that he could indeed handle this pain, and felt his anxiety lessen as she continued to work.

"Can I ask you something?" she asked, dipping her needles in ink yet again.

"I am entirely at your mercy." Menolayous winced as the fresh ink was gently hammered into his chest.

"Why don't you take care of yourself?" She remained focused on the artwork as she spoke, "Last night wasn't the first time I caught you incredibly hard with no intention of seeking release. My understanding, not having male anatomy myself, is that's incredibly painful."

"It can be... uncomfortable." Menolayous winced as the wooden club was brought down. "But as we've discussed, I'm used to functioning in pain."

"So it's your way of staying tough?" She glanced at his face for a moment before returning to her work. "Seems ridiculous."

383

"You want the truth?" He winced again as the needles pinched him.

"I always want the truth," she answered, smiling at how he shifted under her.

"I guess I associate release with great shame." He stared up at her as she paused at his words. "With everything that happened to me, everything I've seen happen to others, I can't seem to separate the two. I would rather be in physical pain than start remembering those things while taking care of myself. Sometimes release just happens, and that's not so bad, but giving myself that kind of attention, that's difficult for me."

"And what we did—?" She remained frozen above him, staring down at him with concern.

"Did not bring me shame." He gently brushed her bare legs with his hands. "Truly. My focus was entirely on you, and what we were doing. It was different, and very... well, amazing is the word that keeps coming to mind."

She smiled slightly at his words before reluctantly going back to work. "And I suppose no amount of talking will help convince you that you shouldn't feel shame about such things?"

"Probably not," Menolayous admitted, inhaling as the needle once again pierced his skin. "I've got a lot of things wrong with me. There's a lot about me that isn't... normal, and most of it comes from the same place as these scars."

"Well, I suppose it's a good thing you found me." She smiled at him before tapping the end of her needle with the wooden club. "I'm happy to show you different ways to find release, and I can try to convince you that there's nothing wrong with you in the process."

Menolayous smiled at her words before that smile faded. He knew they needed to talk before things went any further between them, they needed to clear up a few things.

"I can't share, Grace." He looked up at her, his eyes pleading for her to understand. "I want you, if that hasn't been obvious, but I can't share you with anyone else, and I wouldn't be able to handle it if you shared anything about me with anyone else."

She paused her work again, lowering herself down to him where she gave him a passionate kiss. "If it hasn't been obvious, I've been yours for a while now, and I don't want anyone else, I can't share either. Not with this. You're not just casual sex to me Menolayous, I want all of you."

Before he could respond, or even grab her for another kiss, she sat up and struck her needle into his chest once again. He released a low laugh at that, understanding she was making a point. He continued to stare up at her as she worked, his heart feeling full after her confession. That settled it then, they were in fact together. He reached his hand up farther, his fingertips touching the bare flesh of her hips. He froze then, realizing that she was completely bare underneath her shirt.

"Grace?" he growled, feeling his cock harden against her yet again.

"Yes?" She continued to remain focused on her work, but he could see a smile tugging at her lips.

"Why aren't you wearing anything under your sleeping shirt?" He couldn't stop his hands from moving back to caress her bare ass.

"I figured if you needed a distraction while I worked you might need something to play with." She winked at him again; this girl was going to be the end of him.

Menolayous was now staring down at her bare legs, thinking about how much he wanted to see what little that shirt was hiding. He wanted nothing more than to reach out and touch her, to see what she felt like between her legs. By the gods that's all he was thinking about right now, he could barely feel the sting of the needle anymore. But he had one thing holding him back, he wanted to please her, and he wasn't sure how. As much of a tease as she was, she knew exactly what she was doing and that it was helping him. Even last night as she took him into her mouth, she did that for him. He wanted to do something for her, wanted to give her release too. He wanted to know what he was doing, not stumble around like a young boy trying to figure things out.

"I gave you a truth, will you give me one now?" Menolayous decided to change the topic of conversation, willing the throbbing in his pants to slow down.

"I suppose." Grace continued to work on his chest.

"Tell me where the bruises came from." He stared into her eyes. "Was it Rama?"

She stopped moving then, glancing down at him. Her eyes shone with fear, real fear. This was so unlike her, so unnerving to see from her. Menolayous grabbed the needle from her hands, sitting up so she was still straddling him as they came face to face. She stared into his eyes as he locked her into place with his arms, she wasn't going to get away from him before she answered. Not if she was that afraid when all he did was ask the question.

"I'll show you on one condition," Grace said, her voice steady but her body trembling slightly.

"What condition?" he asked, willing to agree to anything to get that look out her eyes.

"You promise not to take off looking for blood the second I show you. You let me explain why I haven't told you, and you take time to calm down before you decide what to do about it."

"This doesn't sound good." He was now dreading what she was going to show him.

"Promise me," she demanded.

"I promise." He nodded to her as Grace raised her hands to cup his face.

Her memories of that day flooded through him as quickly as Cat's fire could spread in a field. Her fear, what had happened to her at the hands of his so-called brother. Her reaching into Rama's mind and sensing his attraction to her, his threats. Then the images changed to the threats that she made back towards him, how she had held a dagger to Rama's throat, issuing her own warning. Why she hadn't told him right away, not wanting to pit two brothers against each other. He was proud she held her own against a man Menolayous thought he could trust. Fast forward to their conversation last night before Menolayous intervened. Menolayous took a deep breath as soon as Grace took her hand away, willing his rage to slow down. He wanted to keep his promise to her, to not get up right then and there and hunt Rama down like a rabid dog.

"I know that was a lot," Grace said carefully. "But did you see what I saw?"

"I'm trying too hard not to get up and go kill him." Menolayous gripped her hard, using her body to ground himself in the present.

"I don't think that was Rama." Grace chewed on her lower lip. "That darkness I keep seeing in him, I just realized as I rewatched my memories with you."

"How can that not be Rama?" Menolayous ground out.

"I think there's someone inside his head, telling him to do these things."

Chapter Fifty-Three

Danny

The last two days have been chaotic to say the least. Flinn had been sending out teams to the farthest ends of Oich for the men to collect their families. The strategy was to start with the farthest in case the crown started to take notice. It was far easier to defend those closer. Danny did not disagree with this, but he did see how a lot of the local boys were chomping at the bit to go back to their homes. Flinn put out a curfew and a territory restriction for the time being. This helped keep everyone more controlled, albeit stir crazy. The only ones allowed outside the walls besides the teams being sent out, were the girls and the princes. Clyous fit somewhere in there, Flinn was keeping him pretty busy at the forge working on supplies for the expansion, but not today.

Danny was standing with Catriona and Clyous on the main road by the windmill which was nearly complete in its reconstruction. Clyous had seen their father and brother's arrival, so now they stood and waited. The twins were a bit of a nervous wreck ever since Clyous's first vision. They were both very young when their father had disappeared, and after all these years finding out he was alive was emotional. Catriona had been going back and forth between excited to see her father and wanting to kick his ass for abandoning them. Clyous chose to remain mostly silent after the other night. Probably a wise choice on his part, seeing as he had successfully pissed off most everyone in their group.

Danny was still processing what exactly had happened, and how he felt about it. His brother seemed to show genuine remorse over his failure to tell the twins, but that did not excuse his actions. Menolayous seemed to know this and even let Clyous get in a few blows. What Danny wasn't totally okay with was Clyous's last ditch effort to go for Menolayous when he was distracted. Unsurprisingly, Menolayous was able to control the situation, but that was a coward's move on Clyous's part. He expected better from him, from both of them really.

What also bothered Danny was what had distracted Menolayous to begin with. It was Rama holding Grace back from intervening, at first glance it seemed a normal thing to do, but something Grace had said to Danny's older brother not only caught his attention but also Menolayous's. The look on Menolayous's face was bone chilling, Danny had never seen an expression like that from Menolayous, probably ever. For a few moments Danny was legitimately concerned for Rama's safety. As brothers, they have tussled before, struck each other, yelled, things brothers did. Menolayous usually bested them if it came down to physically fighting, but he never went above and beyond to hurt them. There was little doubt in Danny's mind that Menolayous intended to seriously harm their older brother that night. What his reasoning was, Danny wasn't sure. It seemed like an extreme reaction if all it was, was possession and jealousy over a woman.

The sound of an owl came from the distant trees before Connor's voice echoed down to them. "Two riders on horseback."

Catriona and Danny shared a look before Catriona excitedly bounded down the road. Danny watched her intently, a smile spreading across his face. She was so beautiful when excited, all her tough exterior seemed to melt away for the pure joy and excitement she felt as her father and brother approached, Clyous seemed just as excited if not anxious, unable to stop pacing. Finally, the two riders appeared coming up the hill. One of them being Markous, who smiled widely at the sight of his siblings, spurring his horse faster. The other, Danny recognized as Farren, the war chief from the Harrada Pass. Danny had only met him a few times but seeing him now Danny had no doubts he was the twins' father.

The twins broke into a run toward Markous whose horse was now galloping towards them. Danny noted that Farren kept the same pace, giving the siblings space for their reunion. When Markous made it to the twins he practically jumped off his horse, wrapping both of his arms around them. Danny was glad for it, they did not part on good terms those months back. Honestly, Markous was lucky to still be alive after how he had been treating his younger siblings, but distance made the heart grow fonder, or so he'd heard. Maybe that time apart had helped Markous understand just how much of an ass he was, and maybe reuniting with his father helped kick his ass back into something that resembled empathy.

"I've missed you two shitheads." Markous laughed, kissing Catriona on the cheek before ruffling Clyous's hair. "You look better, Cat. Not so skinny."

"Thanks, jerk face." She swatted him away playfully.

"You've gotten bigger," Clyous remarked on Markous's obvious growth in arm and chest muscles.

"Father has been drilling me every day for months now." Markous smiled wildly. "Bet I could even take Cat now."

"You wish." Catriona's gaze shifted to Farren who was now climbing off his horse.

The older war chief stood there staring at his children, doing nothing but holding onto the horse's reins. Danny held his breath at the tension hanging in the air. He mentally debated with himself if he should try to stop either of the twins if they chose to go for their father with violence, choosing to release years of anger instead of a peaceful reunion. Clyous moved before Danny could make the decision. Clyous approached his father cautiously, stopping a few feet away. Farren looked upon him with sad eyes, his gaze catching the mystical markings underneath his hairline.

"Clyous," Farren greeted, voice layered with many emotions.

Clyous did not respond with words, instead Danny watched him throw his big arms around his father. The two embraced as father and son, not caring that they were both grown men. Danny's attention snapped back to his love, Catriona just stood frozen in place. Farren and his sons looked to her then, the youngest of them all, the only girl, and right then she showed it, tears streaming down her face silently as she beheld her father for the first time in years. Danny saw her knees start to buckle and he went to reach out to catch her, but Farren's magic made him faster, as fast as Catriona was when she fought. He caught his little girl in his arms, wrapping her up in an embrace. The strength in Catriona's legs seemed to give out completely, Farren now holding her in a kneeling position as she sobbed into his shoulder.

"It's okay, Cat. I'm here. I'm not leaving I promise," Farren soothed, rocking her gently. "I'm here. I'm so sorry Cat."

Clyous came up beside her, throwing one arm around his twin and one around his father. Markous stood next to them, resting a hand gently on his sister's shoulder as she cried. Danny's heart ached at the sight of her tears, at all of their tears. It had been far too long that this family had been together. But now they had a chance to be in each other's lives again Leave it to Catriona to pour everything out at once, it's one of the reasons why he loved her so much, she held nothing back.

Movement caught his attention on the pathway leading from the village. Danny spotted Menolayous standing there in the open gap between the trees, staring at him. That usually meant he wanted to talk. Glancing back at the others, Danny formed the opinion that he would not be needed for some time. He left them, walking up the path towards his brother who was watching the family reunion with sad eyes.

"It's a great thing to see." Menolayous's eyes flicked to Danny. "A family getting back together again after so many years."

"Almost would have been better if they were able to do this weeks ago," Danny shot at him.

"That is a failure I deeply regret." Menolayous bowed his head. "I hope one day they will forgive me."

"I don't know about Clyous but Catriona already has. I guess Grace told her about how your nightmares have been plaguing you." Danny sighed. "I also forgive you, by the way. You actually let Clyous get in a few good hits. That's how I knew you genuinely felt bad about what you did."

"Fucker hits like hammer," Menolayous said. "Kid's got some serious power behind him."

"I would hope so. He beats on an anvil all day." Danny smirked. "What's up? You look like you've got something on your mind."

Menolayous shifted uncomfortably before saying, "I wanted to talk to you, in private."

"Is it about how you almost killed our brother the other night?" Danny raised an eyebrow.

"Yes. Well, that's only half of it." Menolayous shifted again.

"What did Grace mean that night?" Danny braced himself for the answer, this situation was too unusual for him to make a guess. "That seems to have been what triggered you."

Menolayous sighed, "Did you notice a couple days ago that Grace had the bruises on her neck?"

"No," Danny answered, now dreading to hear the rest.

"Well, I noticed them. It looked like a fucking handprint around her throat, like someone had choked her. I tried asking her about it, but she wouldn't give me a straight answer. And the other night at the party I watched Rama interact with her. He was using his size to intimidate her, I could feel how scared she was."

"What do you mean by feel?" Danny interrupted, confused. Menolayous scratched his head nervously. "We sort of have this open mind connection. We can talk to each other in our heads, but we can also feel each other's emotions sometimes."

"That sounds incredibly personal." Danny laughed, slightly shocked at this revelation.

"It can be," Menolayous admitted, looking slightly embarrassed. "Anyway, what Grace said to Rama during the fight caught my attention. I had my suspicions of what she meant, later she confirmed it by showing me. Rama came after her, the same day Catriona came into her power. He choked her and threatened her to stop playing games with any of us."

Danny took a second to process this. "He saw her with the whip?"

"Yes, how did you know?"

"Cat told me how Grace drew her power out. It took Bridget and a good thump from Morrigan's spear to not go after her myself," Danny answered honestly a protective look on his face. "But they explained it to me. Cat was glad she did, and I trust her. So, I dropped it."

Menolayous thought for a moment before answering, "I get everyone's gut reaction to Grace using the whip on Catriona. I had a similar one when Rama met Catriona in the ring, it was tough for me to watch. So, I get that he was being protective, but I am not okay with how our brother handled that, and I am not okay with him putting his hands on her."

"I'm not okay with this either," Danny admitted. "I don't think he would have done that if he knew what she meant to you."

"What do you mean?"

"Oh, come on." Danny rolled his eyes. "You're not hiding it well. I've known you for how many years? Not once have I ever seen you comfortable letting someone touch you, let alone seen you with a girl."

Menolayous cracked a genuine smile at that.

"Look, you and Grace might be a thing, and brother, I'm very happy for you, even if she's a brat at times, but this is also your brother. You're going to have to talk to him."

"Yeah, I know." Menolayous looked grumpy again.

"Why didn't Grace tell you about Rama?" Danny asked.

"She didn't want me hating him," Menolayous answered. "The threat he gave her, she seems to understand his reasoning. She even seems to respect it to some degree. I guess she even cut him, giving her own threat. So, she feels as though they are even."

"She's not weak, that's for sure." Danny chuckled. "It's almost like you don't need to protect her."

"Will you ever stop trying to protect Catriona?" Menolayous snapped, he had him at that. "What bothers me is that he's attracted to her. I've seen it, and I've seen Grace sense it, but it's not right. There's something dark surrounding him, not just an attraction. I can't figure out what it would be."

"Again, I'm not shocked that he's attracted to her. Have you seen her? She's Rama's type." Realizing this was not helping his argument, Danny switched tactics, "But if you haven't talked to Rama about what she is to you, he's not going to completely get it. I seriously believe talking with him is the best idea. He'll probably stop acting so fucking weird, that's probably the darkness you're seeing."

"Yeah," was all Menolayous said for several minutes, clearly going over this information in his mind.

"So," Danny raised an eyebrow, "what else would you like to talk about?"

If Danny thought Menolayous looked uncomfortable before, now he looked like he was going to crawl out of his skin.

"You've been with many women," Menolayous spoke very quietly. "I wanted to ask for your advice."

A smile now spread across Danny's face. "Advice on what exactly, dear brother?"

"Never mind, this was stupid." Menolayous turned to walk away.

"Hey now." Danny got in front of him blocking his path. "No need to run away. I'm done joking I promise. This stays between us."

Menolayous looked so embarrassed Danny had to fight back a smile, it wasn't often his brother was so easily ruffled.

"I was hoping you could tell me different ways to please a woman."

"Yeah, of course." Danny was taken aback by the request, he couldn't recall ever having any conversations with Menolayous about women before. "Can I ask you something?"

"Yeah." Menolayous would no longer look him in the eye.

"How much experience do you have with women?"

After a long pause Menolayous answered, "The other day Grace and I were kissing, by the end she had her mouth around my cock."

"And that's it?" Danny watched his brother nod. "Okay. Not a big deal. There are tons of things you can do for her."

Chapter Fifty-Four

Liam

Liam made his way towards his father's private audience chambers. Having received the summons, the moment he set foot inside the castle he decided making his father wait was not in his best interest. He veered through the gardens, rubbing the exhaustion from his eyes as he went. He had just returned from putting down a few rebels they had captured at the farthest end of Oich. It was a small group of them camping off the road, guards had found and captured them. Unfortunately, these rebels did not belong to Farroway's warband, who had mysteriously disappeared into the forests of Gaelach. Liam suspected these rebels belonged to the three brothers, his long-lost rivals. Liam had gone to get what information he could out of them, but as usual they did not speak. They now hung lifeless outside of town, backs torn open for the crows to feed on.

In an attempt to banish the dark memories from his mind, he allowed himself to think of Bridget. It had been what, a month or two since he had seen her last. When he saved her from her father, and when she had told him she would not marry him. For the first few days after, Liam had been angry at Bridget for the rejection. So what if he had been violent? Hurt people? Every one of them deserved what they got, including her disgrace of a father. It was only natural that he wanted to protect her from all the evil in the world. That included himself, it's why he left, but she was wrong, she was his whether she liked it or not. She had always been his.

Over the last month he had sent Bridget various letters, asking if she was well and apologizing profusely at the overzealous way he dealt with her father. He could admit now that doing this in front of her was the problem, not so much that he had done anything wrong. She was a gentle and kind-hearted person who had spent years helping treat patients. It was not in her nature to be violent. If it was, she wouldn't have allowed her father to beat her as he did. Unfortunately, she did not respond to any of them, and having been so busy out of the city fighting against the rebels popping up in the outer villages, he hadn't had a chance to go see her. A situation he would rectify soon.

Guards stood outside his father's tower, opening the large wooden door for him as he approached. Liam took a breath and strode inside. His father stood beside his large table map of Stone Basin, inspecting it closely.

Next to him stood a single man, tall and lanky in build. The old-blooded man wore clothing made from animal skins and furs, smaller animal bones and feathers worn as decorations. The blooded tribesman wore a cape that looked to be made out of a mountain lion skin, the head of the lion acted as a hood as it lay unused on the back of the male's neck. This was one of Gaelach's cultist leaders, Liam realized.

"Father," Liam announced himself, eyes narrowing at the tribesman. It was not that long ago he had faced down a group of them, ending their lives without mercy.

"Prince Liam." The king did not look up from his map. "This is King Rion, one of the three kings of Gaelach."

"A pleasure to meet you, young Prince." Rion flashed him a smile, the man's canines were elongated and sharpened.

"My Lord." Liam bowed slightly to the "king," never taking his eyes off the cultist.

"King Rion has come to us with a most intriguing offer." Finally, his father looked up at him. "Gaelach wants to aid us in ridding the land of tainted magic."

"Really?" Liam asked suspiciously. When they used magic themselves it seemed hard to believe they shared the same opinion on the matter.

"Really," the tribesman said charmingly. "We will pay you for them. Any that you capture. We will pay their weight in gold."

"We burn them to ensure their deaths, to purify them of the tainted magic," Liam pointed out. "What will you do with them?"

"We will sacrifice them to the gods," King Rion said excitedly. "We have found the gods favor them as sacrifices."

This guy was a loon, most of the Gaelach cultists were. "Sounds like a relatively straightforward exchange."

"One I have agreed to," his father answered. "I will allow Gaelach clansmen to enter Oich and hunt for 'sacrifices' that contain magic. They will accompany our men to help them hunt. Any rebels they find along the way will be handed over to us for punishment."

"An excellent and mutually beneficial relationship," Liam agreed, eyes still not leaving the foreigner. "But I have a feeling that's not all that's being offered."

"Very good, young Prince, you understand how the game is played." Rion cackled delightfully. "There is a girl hiding somewhere in your kingdom. She's extremely dangerous, very powerful magic. My brothers and I want her alive. In exchange, we will gift you the western half of Gaelach."

"What?" Liam stammered. "Half a kingdom for some girl?"

"Sounds too good to be true," his father chimed in. "What's so special about this girl?"

"Personal reasons." Rian smiled. "My brother Oisin desires her for one of his rituals. We are willing to pay for her."

"A girl worth half a Kingdom might be worth holding onto," Liam countered.

"You could, but she would be worthless to you. The gods will favor her as a sacrifice. She'll try to burn you to the ground."

Liam's memories shifted to the white-haired girl he had beaten. The one who escaped. Was he referring to her?

"And you are willing to give up half your kingdom in exchange? What's the catch?" Liam asked in disbelief.

"There is none." Rion smiled, pacing around the table map, putting a finger to the northern end of Stone Basin. "We plan to take Airgid within the year. We want the gods to favor us before we make our move. The eastern half of Gaelach holds our temples and ritual sites, the west is useless to us. We would rather gift it to true friends in the hopes our new friends would aid us against our enemies in Airgid."

"So you're proposing an alliance. Where you will aid us in ending our little rebellions, and we give you magic users to sacrifice, and this girl will ensure we, as friends, split Stone Basin equally?" the king asked.

"I'm tired of Airgid sticking their noses in our business, aren't you?" Rion asked. This man was clever, it now made sense why he was sent and not all the brothers at once. "Yes, that is what we offer."

The king flashed a look to his son before answering, "Sounds like we are about to be good friends."

"What does this girl look like? How will we know who she is?" Liam asked, still unsure of this new alliance. In his experience, if it seemed too good to be true it usually was.

"You know her. The white-haired girl who moves as fast as any blooded. She escaped your city about six months ago," Rion stated. How he knew that Liam wasn't sure.

"We remember." King Cathal glared at his son; Liam could hardly forget the punishment he received for that failure. "How do you expect us to transport her if she's likely to burn us all alive."

Rion pulled an object from a pouch on his belt. He tossed it onto the center of the table map. Liam and the king both stared at it. It was a circlet made of thick iron. It reminded him of what was usually attached to the end of a chain to hold onto prisoners, but sharp spikes lined the inside of the circlet. The whole object was crude looking, like it had been thrown together hastily. Unsurprising, since it was coming from such a primitive kingdom.

"Iron neutralizes their magic, much like silver does for blooded," Rion explained. "The spikes drive the iron into their blood. Wearing one of these stops the most powerful users from tapping into their magic. Have your blacksmith play around with designs if you wish, but as long as the iron breaks the skin, it works."

Liam saw a sickening smile begin to spread across his father's face. This simple device changed everything. This knowledge about iron was priceless, and Rion just gave it to them freely. Liam had no doubt that after this meeting every blacksmith in the city would be tasked with making these, to see who could create the most efficient design to use. Liam's thoughts wandered to Bridget. He used to fear above anything else that his father would get his hands on her, learning what she was. Now he was concerned that these kings of Gaelach would be a worse fate for her. He had kept her at a distance to protect her from his father, because he was not prepared to challenge him. Now a decision had to be made, bringing her in would ensure her safety from these cultists. He would have to handle his father, and soon.

Chapter Fifty-Five

Rama

Rama was unloading supplies from one of the newly arrived wagons. The first batch of families had begun to arrive, bringing with them wagon loads of supplies. Rama made a point to help unpack the wagons while Flinn welcomed them. This was still Flinn's village, he had earned the role of war chief here, and truthfully, he seemed to enjoy showing off what he had created. It was well known throughout the rebellion that the three princes were aiding the process of building Collie, this of course brought them eager volunteers, but Rama truly disliked the attention, Collie was Flinn's masterpiece, he had been the architect for this city. Rama would not take that from him with his mere presence. So, Rama had opted to help the unloading process instead using his strength and size as needed.

The last of the supplies had been unloaded as the men led the horses and wagons away. A task Rama normally volunteered for and relished, his love for horses and animals was a small comfort to him, but lately he couldn't even approach a horse without the poor creature getting jumpy. Even the little foal he helped look after weeks ago would no longer approach him. This unsettled him greatly, unable to fathom why all of a sudden he was being rejected by every creature with a soul.

Rama found himself alone, everyone else had returned to their daily tasks. He grabbed an apple from one of the crates before heading over to the main gate. He might as well walk the walls, see how the construction of new homes and buildings was going from above. They had been working hard these last few months building Collie up into something grand. Only a few days more and they would have the windmill up and running. The men had dug into the ground rerouting a nearby stream to pass through the building, allowing water to be pumped into the city for all to use. It was an important staple in this endeavor. People needed access to water if they were going to increase the population's size, and by the looks of it, Collie was going to do nothing but grow. The men were happy to bring their families to a safe place free of the tyranny of Oich. It was a dream worth working towards, and Rama was thrilled to be a part of it.

Just as Rama raised the apple to take a bite, the apple was ripped from his hand. With a deep breath Rama looked towards the wooden house beside him. The apple was now stuck to the wall, a dagger embedded through the core and through the wood. Damn it, he wanted that apple. He was hungry.

Swinging his head in the direction that the dagger had come from, Rama wasn't surprised when he spotted Menolayous emerging from the shadows. His brother wore an expression that promised danger, but he did not throw another dagger. Rama knew without a doubt that if Menolayous had wanted to hit him with that throw he would have. Oddly enough that was a relief to Rama, it meant Menolayous wasn't here to kill him, but he had anticipated this confrontation at some point, after all he had deserved the dagger thrown at him. He was surprised it had taken this long for Menolayous to approach him.

"We need to talk," Menolayous growled, approaching him with an almost unnatural steadiness.

"I gathered that." Rama pulled the dagger from the side of the house, removing the apple before handing the dagger hilt first to Menolayous.

Menolayous took the dagger, eyeing him before saying, "Grace showed me."

"I gathered that too." Rama offered him the apple, Menolayous declined. "I don't know what to say other than I'm sorry. I was wrong with what I did. I flew off the handle without figuring out what was really going on."

Why do you need to apologize? You were just protecting your brother from the witch, he should be grateful. Rama fought back that intrusive thought, he was getting tired of them.

"Why were you so quick to assume she was dangerous?" Menolayous snapped. "You seriously think I would bring someone here who was dangerous, who would hurt my family?"

"Honestly, I thought you were too enamored with her and blind to what she was doing. I thought she was manipulating you." Rama was surprised by the words that came out of his mouth, he meant them and even believed them but hearing them said aloud it now seemed ridiculous.

It's not ridiculous. You don't know anything about her. She could have him under her spell even now, he wouldn't know.

"But why?" Menolayous demanded, watching him with that predatory gaze he usually reserved for picking the enemy apart.

"I guess I was basing that on how she talks to everyone, how she enjoys pissing everyone off. I mean look at how she dresses, it's like she wants the attention. Girls like that are good at playing people." He was desperate to give his brother a reason, one that made sense even to him.

"How she dresses and talks to people doesn't give you the right to choke her," Menolayous ground out.

"It doesn't," Rama agreed, shaking his head to rid himself of that intrusive presence that was now bringing itself forward for this conversation. "I misjudged her. I assumed she was like other women I've met who do the same. I didn't want her to use you."

You did not misjudge her! The slut is twisting his mind. He needs to see that you will do anything to protect him.

"Since when has it been your job to protect me?" Menolayous asked, eerily calm, observing Rama's nervous ticks. "Last time I checked, the three of us worked together. I fail to see how Grace has somehow weakened and made it so I suddenly need everyone to look out for me."

"I'm not saying you're weak," Rama pleaded, fighting against that voice in his head. *But he is weak, you know this. He is weaker than any of you, he carries his past around like he's hiding a fatal wound.*

"Then you must mean that I'm stupid or don't understand how the world works," Menolayous snapped, his eyes now boring into Rama's as if trying to peer into his soul. "Or that Catriona is also those things. Both of us let her in. If you don't trust that, what about Bridget? Have they made their men weaker simply for being present?"

"I get that now." Rama was stopping himself from starting to argue, he wanted to listen to that voice, to prove to his brother he was right. "I wasn't being logical, I admit that."

The two brothers looked at each other for a moment without saying anything. Menolayous was still fuming, but Rama could see the wheels turning.

If he isn't willing to hear your warning about how dangerous the witch is, there is no point in trying to convince him. You have to take matters into your own hands, to protect your family.

"I get that you acted out believing you were protecting our family. I can't exactly fault you for that, because deep down I believe all of us would do the same if there was a genuine threat, but you need to trust us and not go off of assumptions."

Rama nodded, allowing Menolayous to regain control of the conversation.

"You're attracted to her." It wasn't a question.

Rama nodded again, not sure what to say. "I'm not going to ask why you thought flirting with her was a good idea. You're being fucking weird about it." Menolayous shook his head.

"That I know," Rama agreed. "I honestly think it's a combination of not trusting her and not wanting to hurt you."

"That doesn't even begin to make sense."

"Again, not arguing with that." Rama wanted this conversation to be done with, he needed to make Menolayous feel at peace again. *"Menolayous hasn't felt a moment of peace in his life until he found you and your other brother. Now this woman comes in and disrupts your life, it isn't fair to him."*

After another moment Menolayous said, "Grace is my person. I am choosing her, she chose me."

"I truly am happy for you brother," Rama started, hiding the lie.

Menolayous held up a hand to stop him. "You will not touch her again. You will not hurt her again. Do you understand?"

"Yes," Rama answered, knowing full well that Menolayous would stand by his unspoken threat.

Menolayous nodded and turned as if to leave.

"Menolayous," Rama called out, Menolayous paused. "Are we good?"

It was a moment before his brother answered, Menolayous eyed him up and down seriously, examining every unspoken thought and movement Rama was sure he could see. Menolayous sighed deeply before his eyes snapped back to Rama's, Rama could see traces of sadness there. "That's up to you. I drew my line in the sand. You pick what you're going to do about it."

He left Rama standing there, alone yet again. Rama was tired of being alone, he couldn't handle the darkness that would surround him when nobody else was there.

"There is a lot you are going to do about it," the voice in Rama's head went on. *"You now know what you have to do, the boy is under her spell. You need to prepare yourself for what you must do to save your family."*

401

"What do I need to do to make this stop?" Rama asked the voice echoing in his head, feeling very sure that listening to this voice was his only chance to keep his family together.

"You will need to bring her to me."

Chapter Fifty-Six

Bridget

"We're missing a few of our men," Bridget heard Flinn tell Rama as she and Clyous stood nearby in his forge.

"How many?" Rama inquired, sounding concerned.

"Four. They were sent to the villages just below the Harrada Mountains. The other groups who went further west have returned already."

"It's possible they were found," Rama answered, running a hand nervously through the strip of short hair on his head. "We should keep an eye out, keep track of our returning families. If any more don't return we need to have a backup plan in case the crown has learned of what we're doing."

"Alright," the war chief answered. "Farroway arrived this morning. Cheeky lad has been causing absolute chaos along the coastline. Young Daniel could take a chapter out of his book by the sound of it, but it means we're all here now."

"Good. We'll call the meeting tomorrow night. We'll give everyone time to rest first and acquaint themselves with each other."

"I'll let them all know," Flinn said before taking off.

Bridget and Clyous glanced at each other before looking back at the giant man they called their friend. He seemed exhausted or incredibly stressed, it was hard to pinpoint exactly what was going on in a man's head when he spent most of his time observing everyone else. Rama smiled at them before walking over.

"You okay?" Clyous asked him.

"Yeah. Just not sleeping," Rama answered. "How are you guys?"

"Fine," Bridget answered, still watching him carefully. "Why aren't you sleeping?"

"Crazy dreams." Rama shrugged. "It's probably just all the stress from what's going on. As you heard, we've lost some people."

"You and Menolayous doing okay?" Clyous asked.

"About as well as you and he are doing," Rama said pointedly, obviously not wanting to elaborate on the situation.

"Fair enough." Clyous went back to hammering, taking the hint.

Bridget rolled her eyes at both of them. "You're all so dumb."

"Be careful Bridget. Looks like Catriona is rubbing off on you," Clyous teased.

"How's reconnecting with your father?" Rama asked him.

"Fine." Clyous began hammering again. "He's teaching Catriona more about her fire magic."

"That's a good thing," Bridget pointed out, catching the sour tone layering Clyous's voice.

"Yeah, sure is." Clyous continued with his work as if not believing a word out of his own mouth.

"Where's Markous?" Rama asked.

"Oh, he's training with Danny and Menolayous." Clyous dunked the metal into a nearby bucket of water, releasing a hiss of steam.

"Why aren't you with him?" Rama asked while watching him curiously.

"Because I needed space to think, and I doubt I'd be welcome," Clyous answered, wiping sweat from his brow. "I haven't decided how mad at my father I am for not coming for us years ago."

"If everyone else is accounted for," Rama started as nonchalantly as he could make himself sound. "Where is Grace?"

"No idea." Clyous glanced up at him suspiciously, memories of his visions a few nights ago were clearly resurfacing.

Rama shifted uncomfortably under Bridget's stern gaze; she too was picking up on something she did not approve of. The wolf inside her growled its irritation in his direction, it hadn't been comfortable being around him for days now. "It's no concern of yours. I would suggest you don't bother going and looking for her, least you cause more of a rift between you and your brother."

"Noted," Rama said. "Well, if you two need anything, I'll be helping Flinn with finding more housing for our newest arrivals. They are coming in droves; we're going to have to build a whole new section of city just to house them."

"Bye." Bridget watched him leave before turning back to Clyous. "Is there anything I can do?"

"No, sweetheart." Clyous leaned over and kissed her gently. "Thank you. I've got to catch up on these. The more people we get, the more Flinn needs supplies to build."

"Okay." She smiled at him. "I'll see you later."

Bridget left him to his work, making her way towards what was now the village center. Flinn and Clyous had made sure to build her a shop, giving her the space to work as a healer. Her powers, now that she was aware of them, had helped her significantly with treating patients, but it was not necessary for most minor injuries. So, she kept stock of as many herbs as she could have on hand. It was an art, managing herbs for treatment, something she was reluctant to give up on. She had been perfecting this skill most of her life, she couldn't imagine ever giving it up.

Bridget opened the door to her shop, stepping inside. She might as well take inventory while she was here. Bridget knew she was lacking certain herbs. She could only forage for so much. Other herbs and plants she had to be purchased in Oich. She had a large supply of rare plants as well as her medicinal journals still in her room back at her father's. Those journals were irreplaceable with the information they carried, years of her research and experience organized in one place.

"You feel frustrated," Grace said, stepping into the shop. "What's wrong?"

"Nothing really." Bridget sighed, glancing her way. "My medicinal journals are still back in my room in Oich. They could be very useful here; they're not doing any good collecting dust back at my father's house."

"What's in these journals?" Grace asked, hopping up on the table and leaning against the wall.

"Herbal combinations for different sicknesses." Bridget began to count vials. "I reference them a lot. It helps me remember what I've done in the past. What's worked and what hasn't."

"Maybe someone can grab them for you," Grace suggested.

"No, I'd have to grab them myself, where they are wouldn't make sense unless it was someone who knew where to look," she answered. "What brings you by?"

"I was wondering if you had something to help someone sleep without nightmares?" Grace asked.

"Menolayous again?" Bridget was concerned, flashbacks to the night the Dark One had entered him through his dreams crossed her mind.

"No, I can keep those away for the most part. I mean for me."

"Seems like everyone's having trouble sleeping because of nightmares lately," Bridget said thoughtfully. "Can I ask what they're about?"

Grace shifted uncomfortably. "A lot of memories. They seem to mostly be about my time captive with the Dark One. I keep reliving it. I can't get his voice out of my head, promising he's coming for me."

"That's scary." Bridget looked at her friend. "I have herbs to help you sleep more soundly, but I can't guarantee it will completely keep the nightmares away."

"I'll try it." Grace perked up.

"You'll need to make a tea out of it." Bridget began rifling through her vials, filling a wooden bowl with different dried plants. "No more than one cup a night, an hour before you go to sleep. You might wake up a little groggy."

"Thank you." Grace smiled. "What do I owe you?"

"Nothing." Bridget laughed, handing her the tea after rolling it into a cloth bundle. "How's it been with Menolayous?"

Grace smiled at her. "Great. It's nice having someone to snuggle up to at night."

Bridget smiled knowingly, thoughts drifting to Clyous for a moment. "And he's transitioning to that well? I know he's a bit standoffish with people."

"He's the one who started sleeping in my bed." Grace tried to hide a smile.

"So, are you guys—?" Bridget raised her eyebrows in question.

Grace turned red, surprising for how bold Grace was normally.

"He's surprising me, that's for sure," she admitted, still red in the cheeks. "I wasn't expecting such… enthusiasm."

"Enthusiasm isn't a bad thing." Bridget laughed.

"I guess I expected him to be more cautious about it," she divulged. "I did not expect him to know as much as he does, considering…"

Menolayous's experience with women became apparent to all the women in their group about a month or so ago. For Bridget it was when she saw all the scars, the night the Dark One had possessed him. There was something the Dark One had said to make it all click. None of them openly discussed it, but as women who have had to survive this ugly world filled with predators, they understood. The men were oblivious, of course. For Menolayous, that was probably more of a blessing than anything.

"He did grow up with Rama and Danny. He's bound to have heard things," Bridget pointed out. "Maybe even seen some things. Menolayous doesn't miss much."

"No, he doesn't." Grace smirked. "Unlike all the 'experienced' men I've been with, he seems to know just how close I am and exactly what to do to get me there."

"That's great," Bridget said. "I'm a little jealous."

"You and Clyous aren't?" Grace asked, surprised.

"No." Bridget sighed, noting the disappointment in her voice. "It's like he's waiting for something. He seems to be cautious about pushing for anything. The few times we've kissed we've been interrupted before it goes very far."

"That's frustrating," Grace pondered. "Is he nervous?"

"No, I don't get that from him," Bridget answered. "I'm worried it might be about Liam. Every now and then he starts asking questions about our relationship."

"That's unusual." Grace chewed her lip. "Is he mad at you after he asks those questions, or upset?"

"No, but I can only imagine what's going on inside his head. Liam did kill his mother, and torture Catriona. I guess I don't blame him."

"Sounds like you two need to talk," Grace offered.

"Yeah," was all Bridget said. "I like him a lot. I would like us to be more."

"Then you should probably tell him that," Grace said. "How long has it been for you?"

"Years." Bridget gave her a look. "Literally years. I'd been fine for the most part, but being so close to Clyous, it's like he woke that part of me up again."

Grace chuckled at that. "Have you tried to initiate it?"

"Well, no." It was Bridget's turn to blush.

"Why not?" Grace asked.

Bridget didn't have an answer she was willing to give Grace. The truth was that with Liam she wasn't allowed to initiate sex. It angered him, almost as if he took it as her trying to dominate him. The last thing she wanted was to irritate Clyous in such a way. She didn't think she could bear it if he were that irritated at her cravings.

"I know you wolves have your rules and what nonsense," Grace said, as if she were reading her mind, "but he's not a wolf. Don't treat him like he would be the same."

Bridget nodded, that was in fact a perspective she had not considered. She was free here, free to do what she wanted. Clyous had made it clear in the past he did not hold the same thoughts and beliefs as male wolves. Maybe he was waiting for her.

"While I'm here—" Grace looked around nervously. "Do you have any of that preventative conception tea lying around?"

Bridget cracked another smile. "Of course I do, Catriona and Danny make sure I have to remain stocked all the time."

Grace laughed at that. "Those two never take a break. I heard him trying to convince Catriona that marriage was a good idea the other day."

"Really?" Bridget asked, scooping herbs from a jar and adding them to a fresh bag. "Like he proposed?"

"Not exactly." Grace thought for a moment. "If anything, it sounds like he's trying to wear her down."

"What would he be trying to wear her down for? It's not like she would be against marrying him, would she?"

"It sounded like the idea of marriage itself is what bothers her," Grace answered.

"Maybe it has something to do with how her father abandoned her family at a young age?" Bridget sealed the bag shut. "Maybe she's afraid getting married would make Danny resent being with her?"

"That actually sounds like something Cat would think." Grace looked impressed. "Are you sure you can't get into people's minds like I can?"

"No." Bridget laughed, handing her the preventative tea. "Catriona isn't all that complicated once you get to know her. She wears her strength and independence like armor, but underneath it she's afraid everyone will see her as a weak little girl. I don't think she could handle Danny abandoning her."

"Danny never would," Grace argued. "You can just tell. He's not that sort of man."

"No, he's not, but a part of her must think she's someone who could easily be abandoned, whatever reason that may be."

"Maybe her father being here will help some of that," Grace suggested. "If he truly is the center of her self-confidence issues, he might be the one to help her unpack all of that internal baggage."

"It's always the parents, isn't it?" Bridget sighed. "If I ever have children my only goal is that my children don't have to recover from their childhood."

"That's a most excellent goal." Grace smiled knowingly. "Maybe we could all strive for that same future."

Chapter Fifty-Seven

Catriona

Catriona swung her leg up, missing the strike as he moved quickly out of her reach. Anger drove her, giving her an extra bit of power as she continued her assault. She wanted to cause pain, to hit, to hurt him. She knew this side of her was the bad side, it took over when it decided to come out. She knew deep down she needed to control her anger instead of letting it control her. Fuck it all.

Fists thrown one after another, he continued to dodge her attacks. He was faster than her, a rare feat indeed. She hadn't yet been able to make contact with him. She shouldn't be surprised at this revelation, seeing as it was her father she was trying to strike.

"You've gotten faster, Cat," Farren commented, as she dodged a strike from him. "You should be using your fire in your strikes."

"I'm fucking mad at you." Catriona breathed heavily. "I don't want to kill you."

"As glad as I am to hear that—" Farren began to circle her "—you need to try. I've failed you as a father, but I will not fail in teaching you about your magic."

"Fine!" Catriona shot flames from her hands, cradling the tiny infernos in her palms.

Farren, now at least ten feet from her, waved his hands at the ground. A wall of flames erupted around them, trapping them in a perfect circle. Catriona glanced around at his flames. A mix of oranges and reds, different than hers. Hers burned gold and white.

"My flames will keep yours from spreading to the trees." Farren shrugged as she examined them.

"How?"

"You can learn to control what your flames burn," he answered simply. "You can decide how destructive you want to be."

With that thought left in her mind, Farren punched in her direction, sending a fireball directly at her. She dived out of the way just as her father sent a ribbon of flame at her legs. As a response, she shot a column of flame in his direction. He might be faster than her physically, but her fire was unbeatable. Her flames caught his forearm as he tried to dodge it, searing his flesh.

He began laughing, almost morbidly, at the fact that she had got him. "That's my girl."

"I'm not your girl anymore." Catriona's rage fed into the fire almost as if the flame itself looked to draw it from her. "You left me!"

"I did." Farren sent a wave of orange flames in her direction. "That is my biggest regret in life. I should have come back for all of you."

"You should have!" Catriona shouted, pumping more of her white fire into their sparring circle.

Her flames began to take over what little space they had. She saw the look on her father's face as he realized just how powerful her inferno really was. Her flames scorched the earth, sucking what life the grass once held and reducing it to dust. The more she destroyed, the lighter she felt. She poured her emotions into her flames, letting them consume everything.

"If you let your fire feed off you it will take everything," Farren warned, using his flames to cocoon himself against her onslaught. "You have to choose what you feed into it."

"Fuck you!" she roared, pushing more energy into her white flames. "I've got a lot more that needs to get out."

Her father grunted, trying to fend off the power with the heat beating down his defenses. Farren was still channeling a good amount of his power into the protective ring of fire, not able to put all of his power against hers. For some reason this infuriated her more. She needed to challenge him, to fight him. If he held back, well that just wouldn't do.

Suddenly the flames disappeared, Farren pulled from his own, sending a wall of flame in her direction. She ran at it and at the same time she wrapped herself in her white flames, penetrating the wall as she went. She felt a lick of his flames on her back as she pushed through. This felt good, going after him. Channeling her rage into something more real. It was intoxicating to do, only spurring on her drive and her rage more.

"Let it all out then," Farren panted, evading another fireball just in time. "But don't think for one second I'm going to let your flames take you."

"It's not your choice anymore!" she raged on. "You gave up that right!"

"I'm still your father, I will protect you against yourself." Farren rolled away from an oncoming stream of flame.

"You failed!" Catriona moved her hands, causing the line of fire to snake its way towards Farren. "You weren't there to protect me! You left me! I was alone."

"You had your brothers, your mother, you were never alone." Farren countered as he wove a wall of flame to stop the approach of Cats magic.

"I was alone!" Catriona cried. "Do you seriously think any of them truly understood me like you did? I needed my father there! If you were there it would have never happened."

"What wouldn't have happened?" Farren was breathing heavily as he held her flames at bay.

Catriona began to cry, shaking her head frantically. "Any of it. If you were there you could have stopped it all."

"Let it out, Cat, I deserve your anger." Farren began to sweat from the exertion of it. "You are right, I failed you. Make sure I feel it!"

Catriona felt raindrops begin to strike her flesh. The first few fizzled as they touched her skin, but then the downpour hit. The rain came fast and heavy, as if a lake was being dumped on them from above. Within seconds she was soaked through, her wildfire smothered out of existence. With strands of soaking wet hair now falling into her face, Catriona glanced up at the sky, then back to her father with a scowl. She had completely forgotten they had an audience.

Morrigan stepped into their line of sight, arms crossed in frustration. "You are both imbeciles."

"Why?" Catriona shot out at the sorceress.

"Because your father is right, you are letting the flames consume you." Morrigan then glanced at Farren. "And you do not have the amount of power to save yourself from your daughter's rage. She will reduce you to ash. That will not help her, that will send her over the edge."

Catriona glanced at her father again. Morrigan was right. As mad at him as she was, she didn't want to kill him. She felt the hold on her power finally slacken, as she let the heat from her flames cool with the rain. There was something calming about the water, something that grounded her. She

412

wasn't sure if it was the presence of Morrigan's magic or that she had been forced to cut off her fire. She was glad of it then, finally able to breathe and recenter herself. The rage no longer controlled her. The rain suddenly stopped.

"Show her," Morrigan said to Farren flatly. "Show her why you made the choice."

Farren pulled up the side of his tunic revealing a nearly identical marking that Catriona earned when she learned of her power. It wasn't until he turned away that she saw the scars. Her breath caught in her throat. What appeared to be decades old scars crisscrossed across his lower back. She shared those scars. He turned back to her, showing her his palms. They too bore strange and ancient wounds, perfect circular burns enveloped his wrists and his throat.

"I've been caught before," Farren stated. "When I was about twenty years old. I was originally from one of the farms up north, near the Harrada Mountains. A few new blooded guards caught me using magic. They spiked me to a tree using iron nails, an old superstition the crown is too stupid to realize has validity. The iron neutralizes our magic when in contact with our blood, and keeps it hampered when we're surrounded by it. They beat me and tortured me, were going to let me die, but they didn't expect other slaves to take pity on me. I was freed. Made my way to the capital city where I met your mother."

Catriona looked at him, really looked at him. Realization crept in. He spent their childhoods teaching them to fight, to protect themselves. He never told them of his magic; it had been in order to protect them.

"The day I left our family I was captured again. This time by the crown. I was lucky in the fact that the king was too self-assured, too confident when I was in chains before him. In order to escape I had to burn through those chains, and they too left scars."

Farren ran his hand nervously through his white-blonde hair before continuing.

"I am ashamed to say that I waited for his son to get close. I overestimated the love he should have borne for his heir, and I underestimated a mother's instinct. I was going to take the child and use him to escape. I was prepared to kill the young prince to accomplish my task, but his mother could sense it. I took the opportunity when I had it to escape. I burned the child, and my flames aided in the death of a mother who wanted nothing more than to protect her child."

413

Shame filled his features as he spoke.

"I fled the capital for my very life. I was barely able to make it out of the city. I wanted to come back to all of you. I did, more than anything, but I'm a marked man. I knew if the crown found out about my family, he would make you suffer my debt."

Tears began to pour out of Catriona's eyes. She was so terribly sick of crying, but she understood everything. She could understand not wanting to put them at risk. She could understand that fear, but she wasn't sure she would have made the same choice.

"They found us though." Catriona went lifting up her tunic to reveal her scars. "We weren't safe there. They eventually found us."

It was Farren's turn to openly weep.

"You two are the last of an ancient and powerful line." Morrigan looked at them both. "Your wildfire is not from Stone Basin, but a land beyond. More importantly you are the last of your family. You cannot heal the wounds you carry with you overnight, but in order for your family to be whole again you need to allow yourselves to start healing."

Catriona listened, really listened to the wisdom behind the sorceress's words. It appeared that her father did as well.

"Understand each other and accept the past as it is meant to be, the past. Decide how you will move forward," Morrigan continued to lecture. "You only get one life; there will be no guaranteed chances later on. Choose to move on now."

"You're one to talk." Catriona laughed through her tears. "You keep being born into different bodies."

"That is because I am special." Morrigan cracked a smile. "You are not me."

Chapter Fifty-Eight

Danny

"We should scout the lake," Danny suggested as they all stared up at the now completed windmill, the wind catching the fan blades just enough for the behemoth to move with the wind. "See how easy it would be to dig a channel and bring water to this great beast. Then maybe we could get a working water system going and we wouldn't have to worry about well water anymore."

"You do realize that the lake is on the opposite side of Collie?" Grace asked him in disbelief. "We would have to create a channel through Collie to get it here."

"That can be done," Danny said encouragingly. "We would just have to mark the easiest path, and we can create a cover for the channel to protect it from everyday foot traffic."

"You're insane," Grace mocked, glancing down the street in the direction of the lake. "I can't see how that would work, you couldn't get enough water here to do anything worthwhile."

"That's the point of the windmill, it should pump the water through some smaller channels," Danny argued, clearly getting annoyed at Grace's continuous criticism of his plan.

"You would need two," Grace mumbled, beginning to catch on to his annoyance. "But whatever. Wouldn't want to crush a man's weird water obsession."

"Sounds like an excellent day to go on a hike." Menolayous shared a knowing smile with Grace, trying to decrease the tension. "It's already a beautifully warm day."

She rolled her eyes at him in mock irritation before saying, "Oh alright. Fine, let's go scout out this lake you can't seem to stop talking about."

"Really?" Danny raised an eyebrow at Grace. "He suggests it and you finally give that mouth of yours a break?"

"There's plenty he does that can occupy my mouth," Grace retorted. "But we wouldn't want to upstage you and sweet Catriona."

415

"There are a few things a father would prefer not to hear." Farren, Clyous, Bridget, and Markous approached them. "Anything to do with my daughter's sex life would be one of them."

Danny laughed out loud as he watched Catriona and Menolayous turn a dark shade of red. Grace, unsurprisingly, did not seem affected at the approach of the old war chef. Clyous and Markous shook their heads in mock disappointment as they stared in the direction of their little sister, earning a rude hand gesture from Cat in the process. Farren seemed to thoroughly enjoy torturing his youngest child at every opportunity, a trait that did not discriminate amongst the rest of the family. Danny was genuinely happy how the family had been enjoying their reunion this past week, after years of being apart they seemed to fit back together seamlessly. Well, as seamlessly as possible after the first few days anyway. Both of the twins had a lot of pent-up emotions about reuniting with their father which resulted in a lot of talking and Catriona nearly burning down the surrounding forest, again, but it had all worked out in the end. Even Markous seemed to have turned over a new leaf. He was no longer being the ass that Danny remembered, treating his younger siblings with significantly more respect than the last time they were all together.

Neither Farren nor Markous had attempted to assert themselves as Catriona's protectors and confront him about their relationship. Not that it would have done any good, but Danny was happy he did not have to put anyone in their place. Danny was not playing when it came to his woman, nobody was allowed to interject themselves into their relationship. Danny had a lot of respect for the older war chief, but he would go toe to toe with anyone who felt entitled enough to try and tell Catriona what to do. His love for her eclipsed any other relationship or social protocol he had ever encountered. He was glad the situation hadn't even presented itself.

"We were just talking about a day trip to the lake," Grace offered a change of subject. "To map out an efficient path to dig a trench back to Collie."

"That sounds like fun." Markous smiled at her. "Mind if I join in?"

Danny did not miss the look Menolayous was now giving Markous, who was entirely too busy eyeing Grace up and down. Grace was hardly paying attention to him, again glancing towards the windmill and the streets surrounding them, trying to calculate something no doubt.

"Only if you promise not to be an ass," Catriona responded with a raised eyebrow. "I am not opposed to trying to drown you while we're there."

416

"Ha!" Markous forced a laugh. "Like you could."

"What about you Clyous, care to join us?" Menolayous asked, eyes still on Markous as if he were assessing his threat level.

"No, I'm good," Clyous responded. "I've got a time-sensitive project I'm working on."

"Whatever." Catriona rolled her eyes at her twin. "Bridget, want to come?"

"No, thank you. I've got a few patients stopping by in an hour that I need to be there for." She smiled sweetly. "But if you wouldn't mind, could you collect a few herbs for me while you're out?"

"Of course," Grace answered, finally pulling her attention back to the group.

"Great!" Bridget said excitedly. "Let me go get you guys a bag."

Danny watched as Bridget took off at a run back in the direction of her shop, not a few blocks from where they were standing. She had gotten faster he realized, her constant training with Catriona and Grace was really paying off for the mild tempered woman. Bridget was back to wearing her usual dresses when she was not training with the others, still preferring the more gentle and feminine lifestyle. Still, she was learning how to pack a punch, literally. Danny had assisted the other day with training, challenging the girls to fight him with actual weapons. He was proud to say that all of them had been able to keep up with him if not challenge his own skills. Catriona especially, her proficiency with the two short swords he had gifted her was advancing beyond any level he had with them. Then again, he was easily distracted by her when they fought, at least that's what he told himself after she beat him.

"Father?" Catriona asked as they waited. "Do you want to come?"

Farren smiled at his daughter warmly. "I'll leave the hiking to you youngsters. Gone are the days where I considered that fun. Besides, I figured I'd spend the day with your brother, see if he needed help in the forge."

"Really?" Clyous couldn't contain the excitement in his voice.

"If you'll have me, that is." Farren smiled as he watched Bridget return, carrying a bag.

"Here." Bridget hefted the bag to Menolayous, who slung it over his back easily enough. "If you don't mind collecting yarrow root while you're hiking, my supply keeps running low."

417

"Sorry," Catriona teased. "Fire is hard to pull back sometimes."

"The way you do it, of course." Farren gave her a fatherly expression, reversing Catriona's sarcastic tone.

"We should head out now if we want any hope of making it back before nightfall," Menolayous interjected, glancing in the direction Grace was again absently staring in.

"Does this place have a problem with scourge?" Markous asked, realizing the danger behind Menolayous's warning. Scourge were drawn to larger groups easier than they were individuals.

"Not really," Catriona answered. "It's not like I can't burn them to death."

"You are over assured of yourself, you know that?" Markous complained, his hand instinctively reaching for the sword at his hip to ensure that it was in fact still there.

"Have fun kids," Farren wished them all a farewell, gently cupping Catriona's face in a fatherly way. "Markous, if you guys are attacked make sure to hide behind your sister."

The group erupted in laughter at Markous's expense, who was taking the jab from his father decently well. Catriona hugged her father goodbye; she rushed to catch up with the group as they started towards the main gate of Collie. Connor was manning the lookout post by the open gate, making sure to wave down at them as they passed through. Danny waved back at the young boy, happy to see the teenager was finally starting to show through the baby face he still carried. Connor had been encouraged by Flinn to start training with some of the warriors, so once a week Connor came to the sparring pit and trained with either Danny, Menolayous, or Rama. The boy was still very young and new to fighting, but he had a drive that rivaled them all. Danny was sure he would make a fine warrior someday.

"Lead the way." Grace stared at Danny with an amused expression on her face. "Oh master of water delivery."

Danny flipped her an obscene gesture as he walked by, taking the lead. Grace's laugh echoed behind him. Much to his surprise Grace had been working on her approach with people and had become more pleasant towards not only himself but their whole group, Danny was probably the slowest to warm to the princess, but now they seemed to have come to an understanding of sorts. Grace's insults had dulled and had become almost playful, and Danny's threats hadn't been as necessary as they once were. Their banter back and forth resembled something more like siblings than like enemies, although he doubted either of them were ready for that level of caring just yet. Danny was at least happy with the progress Grace had been making with Catriona, it was good to see them become friends. Danny was more impressed with how much Grace's presence was positively affecting Menolayous, he had never seen his brother smile so often or appear this comfortable around others before. Danny suspected Grace was the main catalyst, and based on how Menolayous couldn't keep his eyes or hands off her any given second, Danny suspected his brother had taken some of his advice.

Together, the group traveled north along the newly built walls of Collie until they were able to pass the city completely. All the while, Markous was making a point to try and talk to Grace the entire time, asking questions about Airgid and the culture there. Grace responded to him for the most part but kept her answers short, her eyes constantly searching their surroundings. Markous, the oblivious idiot, kept going with his line of questioning, thinking that her responses meant he had somewhat of a chance. It wasn't until Catriona reached over and slapped him in the back of his head before he finally gave it a rest. They continued walking, the heat from the sun beating down on them until they managed to get underneath the trees. Spring was definitely at the end of its days, with an early summer seemingly around the corner. Danny was thankful for the warmer weather and the sun. Menolayous removed a waterskin from the bag that Bridget had given him, passing the water around to everyone to make sure nobody was overheating.

It took them another hour and a half of walking through the woods before they came to the outskirts of a clearing. Danny had followed the clearest pathway from Collie to this clearing, mentally mapping out what he believed to be the most efficient line possible for them to dig a trench to start filtering the water down to the city. Finally, as he broke through the tree line, the edges of the lake appeared. Catriona came up to him, breathing heavily from the exertion and the heat as she stopped beside him, her eyes catching the beauty that was before her. He reached out to her, entwining his hand in hers as she continued to look on. A crystal-clear lake stretched out before them, further than any of their eyes were capable of seeing. The water seemed to be an almost perfect reflection of the sky above, small streams emptied themselves into the lake from various points of entry. Trees surrounded the lake, encapsulating it from the rest of the world. Large rocks and pebbles littered the shoreline in various sizes and colors.

"It's beautiful," Catriona breathed as she continued to stare at the water.

"You weren't kidding, were you?" Danny overheard Grace ask, most likely to Menolayous.

"You should see it at night," Danny heard Menolayous answer sweetly. "The stars reflect off the surface almost perfectly."

"Last one in is a lame donkey!" Markous shouted as he sprinted past them all, shedding his weapons and clothing as he went.

"That makes it significantly less romantic," Menolayous murmured.

"Hey asshole, at least keep yourself covered!" Catriona shouted at him. "I seriously will drown him."

"Come on!" Danny laughed as he too tugged off his shirt, wanting nothing more in that moment than to feel the cool of the water surrounding him. "You don't want to be a lame donkey, do you?"

"I'm not stripping naked!" Catriona laughed uncomfortably. "It's not so easy being a female, you know."

"We're all family here, basically," Danny answered, puzzled by her sudden show of modesty. "I really don't think you have anything to worry about from my brother or yours. Unless it's Grace you're being shy about?"

"Don't be a dick," Grace said as she started unlacing her corset. "You wear a chest wrap don't you?"

"Yeah," Catriona answered, her face turning red, and not from the heat.

"It's fairly common for women to just wear that and their cloth undergarments," Grace said in an encouraging way. "And I absolutely promise to smack the shit out of anyone here who makes you feel uncomfortable about wearing that. It's too hot to not jump in."

It was Menolayous's turn to step in front of Grace, shielding her from everyone as she finally shed her corset. "You don't wear a chest wrap, love."

Danny watched as Grace looked up at Menolayous, a coy smile splayed on her lips. "So?"

"Is your plan to strip completely naked in front of everyone?" Menolayous asked as kindly as possible, but Danny could tell he was struggling with keeping the intensity out of his voice.

"Is yours to hide on the shore while everyone else swims, or are you actually going to strip down to your undergarments?" Grace teased, feigning innocence. "Fine, I'll make you a deal. I'll wear your shirt and my undergarments. Your shirt is long enough to cover my ass, and your green shirt isn't as see through as my white one."

Menolayous shifted uncomfortably at this. Danny and Grace were both acutely aware of Menolayous's issue revealing his bare torso to anyone because of his scars. Danny could see his brother thinking it over and was curious to see if Grace would actually be able to convince him.

"Or I'll just strip down to nothing," Grace stated factually. "Your choice. I'm going in whether you want me to or not."

"Fine," Menolayous finally ground out, still blocking everyone from getting an eyeful of Grace as she dutifully removed the remainder of her clothes.

Danny glanced over at Catriona who had now successfully stripped down to her undergarments and chest wrap. He watched her intently, his eyes raking up and down her body hungrily. Her body had gotten stronger over the last few months; muscle packed onto her limbs and little to no fat left on her. Catriona had thickened from regular meals and constant training. She was mostly muscle at this point, with just enough meat on her to give her gorgeous curves. By the gods, he could just drop down to his knees and worship her right then and there. He wasn't the shy type, and even felt pride at her being his woman, but as he could see in the way she held herself, she was more of the shy type. Bold in personality and strong-willed, but even as she stood there amongst family and friends, she was still covering herself awkwardly.

"What's wrong?" Danny asked, quietly coming up to her and gently wrapping his arms around her in an embrace.

"I just hate showing myself this much," Catriona answered, burying her face in his bare shoulder. "When it's just us it's different. But I can't stand people looking at me, I feel…"

"Vulnerable." Menolayous finished for her as he stood still facing Grace, dozens of crisscrossed scars littering the flesh of his back. "I understand that completely, but if I can do it, you can too."

Catriona's eyes were now locked onto Menolayous's back, as were Danny's. Menolayous did understand Catriona in the fact that she hated anyone commenting on her scars. Danny knew his brother meant to be helpful and could feel Catriona start to relax in his grip. Hidden behind Menolayous's imposing figure, Danny could see Grace take Menolayous's shirt from him and slide into it. Finally, Menolayous stepped aside, allowing

Grace to be seen by everyone else. The princess stood there comfortably in a shirt that nearly made it down to her knees with her hair tied up in a bun at the top of her head, but it was Menolayous who turned to face them and it was he who attracted everyone's gaze. On his bare chest now stood a large tattoo of a bird of prey.

"When did you get that?" Danny asked incredulously.

"I did it!" Grace said, proudly showing off her artwork. "Doesn't he look so good with it?"

"That's incredible!" Catriona exclaimed, staring at the tattoo with great interest.

"Thanks," Menolayous murmured, not looking anyone in the eye.

"Seriously!" Catriona continued, "I kind of want one."

"Really?" Danny asked, surprised.

"Well not that specifically, and not on the chest." She scrunched her nose playfully at him. "But that looks incredible. It would be cool to have one."

"I would be happy to design one for you." Grace beamed at her proudly.

"You would look really good completely naked with tattoos," Danny murmured in her ear, Catriona's cheeks turned a bright red once again.

"No sex in front of us, please," Grace lectured as Menolayous began to strip down to his undergarments. "We already hear you two enough back home."

"Plug your ears," Danny grumbled, burying his face in the nape of Catriona's neck affectionately.

"Cat," Danny could hear Grace say as he continued to bury himself in his woman's hair, "I would kill to have a body like yours. Don't sell yourself short. Big breasts aren't everything, I promise."

Chapter Fifty-Nine

Clyous

"So, what is this project you're working on?" Farren asked him as Clyous finally opened up the flames to the forge.

"Do you remember the traders that used to come by once a month with precious metals and stones? And do you remember how you would buy some materials and talk about how you wanted to eventually start making fine jewelry?" Clyous asked as he shed his shirt and reached out for his smithing apron.

"Yes of course," Farren answered, rolling up his sleeves and finding a spare apron nearby. "I enjoyed making jewelry, but I never had the chance to really work on delicate or fine pieces."

"I also have an interest in learning to make elegant pieces." Clyous smiled as he pulled out a wooden box, setting it on a nearby table. Clyous opened the box and fished out a small gold ring with a small emerald set in the center. "This has been my newest project."

Farren took the ring and held it closer to his face, examining the ring closely. "A solid ring, sturdy craftsmanship."

"Thank you." Clyous took the ring back from his father, fishing out parchment paper with a design etched into it. "I want to engrave this design around it, but I have never been good at engraving small details. I was hoping maybe you could help me finish it?"

"I would love nothing more." Farren smiled at his son. "Tell me though, whose ring is this?"

Clyous beamed up at his father with pride. "I was planning on proposing to Bridget with this ring, I just haven't been able to finish it."

Farren smiled brightly. "I would be honored, son."

Clyous pulled out more tools from his wooden box, laying them out on the table as Farren sent some magical fire into the forge to get the heat going. There was a flash, and Clyous found himself lost in one of his visions. *Farren and Markous stood back to back on a battlefield, wolves surrounding them as his father's flames surrounded them in a protective barrier. A large bear and mountain lion stood at the edge of the flames looking in, their red eyes fixed on their prey.*

"Tell me about her," Farren said as he fanned the flames, pulling Clyous from his vision. "All I know is she's the village healer, and she's a blooded."

"She is the kindest person I've ever met in my life." Clyous walked the tools over to the anvil, laying them beside the forge for use. "She's the one who initially saved mother from the scourge, risked her life to try and save all of us actually. Without her, we probably would have never made it out of the city alive, at least Catriona wouldn't have."

Farren was silent as he continued to feed the flames, the heat increasing greatly. "Sounds like a strong woman."

"She is," Clyous answered. "Maybe not a warrior's strength like Cat, but more like mother. An internal strength that never stopped her good heart."

"That is a rare quality," Farren agreed. "I am beyond happy for you son. Finding your other half, well... there's nothing like it."

"No, there's not." Clyous used the metal prongs to take the ring and place it in the open flame. "How did you know our mother was the right one for you?"

"I simply couldn't live without her," Farren answered with a sad smile. "I would have done anything for her. It didn't matter in what capacity I was in her life or how long it took for love to grow between us. As long as we were together, we were happy."

"I can understand that," Clyous answered thoughtfully, "I feel the same way about Bridget."

"That's great to hear, I'm truly happy for you." Farren beamed at him with pride.

"Was our mother a fire wielder as well and we didn't know it?" Clyous asked curiously. "I mean, Cat is so strong, and I can see things. Morrigan says it's likely because both our parents were from the Goddess of War and Fate's bloodline."

"No." Farren thought for a moment. "She didn't possess the same attributes Cat and I do. Not that either of us ever spoke to each other about magic, likely for the same reason I kept it from all of you, to protect us."

424

Clyous nodded, looking to the ground as his mind whirled. "She had a knack for knowing things were about to happen."

Farren chuckled. "That's for damn sure, I guess I always attributed that to a mother's intuition when it came to you lot. But I suppose the iron bars I fastened to keep you all safe to hamper any potential magic you kids would inherit could have hindered hers as well."

"That's logical." Clyous nodded.

"You're a lot like her you know," Farren said staring at him with those steely grey eyes. "You have a peace about you, and an understanding of the world. It's nice to see that part of her lives on within you."

"Part of her will remain with all of us." Clyous took a moment to remember his mother's soft and gentle face. "It's rather humorous that Markous didn't acquire any magic."

"Yeah… well… we made most of our first time mistakes with your brother," Farren joked. "He did his best at trying to take over for me when I disappeared."

"He did," Clyous answered truthfully. "He's still an asshat."

"Would you indulge your old man and answer me a question, since we're on the topic?" Farren asked as he waved his hand over the flame, taming it down just enough to not damage the emerald.

"Of course." Clyous slowly rotated the ring allowing equal exposure to the flames.

"Has Cat found happiness?" Farren asked. "Your brother alluded to the fact that she was pretty broken after everything. She seems happy, but it's hard to tell without prying."

"She was broken for a while, but she's healing." Clyous glanced at his father, his eyes catching on the scars that completely surrounded his wrists like he was wearing bracelets. "Danny is good for her. I promise. He's the one who was able to pull her out of it."

"Good," Farren said, mostly to himself. "I know I have failed you all these last few years. It's something I will never be able to make up for, but I thank the gods every day that they have kept you all together and have at least given you the opportunity at happiness."

"We've done our best," Clyous tried to hide the irritation in his voice. "I do not give any credit to the gods for our survival; they have taken too much from us for me to forgive them."

425

Farren nodded in understanding. "I can understand your pain. Regardless of the gods and their presence, I am still thankful I have found you all again, and I wish nothing more than for your happiness and good health."

"Thanks." Clyous pulled the ring from the flames, setting it gently down on the anvil. "I am sorry. I'm still angry at the world at times."

"I completely understand." Farren donned leather gloves and picked up a small chisel. "Let's work on creating art for your beloved, shall we?"

"Yes please," Clyous agreed, crouching down for a better look.

"You still socialize with everyone outside of the forge, right?" Farren asked as he slowly began to carve. "You were pretty quick to dismiss the invitation to the lake. I can understand working on this ring, but I worry you're closing yourself off."

"Oh, no I usually go with them, but not today. They have an important task to do while they are out there that Bridget and I couldn't be a part of."

"What task is that?" Farren asked as Clyous gently rotated the ring with the prongs once again.

"They're all hunting," Clyous answered.

"Nothing too dangerous I hope, unless they want Cat to roast it alive first." Farren chuckled.

"More like something giant," Clyous answered with a laugh. "She won't be wanting to roast this prey, I promise. They'll be fine."

Chapter Sixty

Rama

He watched from the tree line, his gaze sweeping over each of them as they relaxed around the lake. He had spent the last hour standing against the heat of the day watching as they cooled themselves off. Rama couldn't think of a worse torture, he was likely to die from heat exhaustion before the one who forced him to come here made his move.

His eyes shot to Grace as she slowly emerged from the lake, dripping wet with Menolayous's shirt hugging her every curve. Rama willed his betraying eyes to look away, that was his brother's woman, he should not be staring at her like this. Unfortunately, he was no longer in control of his body, he hadn't been for some time. The Dark One had found a way to slip into his mind while he dreamed, setting up a permanent fortress inside of Rama's head. He hadn't realized the presence at first, but after enough out of character incidents and the voice inside his head that would begin to argue with him, he realized he was no longer safe in his own mind. The Dark One definitely had an infatuation with Grace, like a genuine pervert, he wanted her badly. It was why they were here; Rama was sent here to kidnap Grace and take her to him. Rama had fought against the Dark One with everything he had but was unable to free himself. The last thing he wanted to do was take Grace away from his brother, to hurt her the way the Dark One planned. Rama was willing to end his own life to stop it from happening, but the Dark One had stopped him from succeeding with that as well.

"Can you either make your move, or can we go back?" Rama shot down the connection the Dark One held over his mind. *"Unless you really want me to die before I'm able to grab your little treasure."*

"You are surprisingly defiant for someone with no control," the Dark One acknowledged him begrudgingly. *"I would normally have minimal respect for that, but my patience wears thin."*

"By all means, strike me down for my insolence," Rama taunted. *"Put yourself out of the misery I will put you in every second you stay inside my head."*

"I have no doubt you will try your best." The Dark One forced him to look around again, seeing Grace begin to wander away from the others. *"Lucky for you, now seems as good a time as any to finish this."*

Good, Rama thought to himself. If he could push just a little harder, make his body stumble and give himself away, she would see him and run. He needed her to escape from this. He might not be able to control his actions anymore, but maybe if he put all of his energy into it, he could manipulate his body just enough to make a noticeable mistake.

"You do realize that I can hear your thoughts, not just talk to you?" the Dark One sounded irritated as his many layered voices echoed throughout Rama's head. *"You will be unable to do any of that."*

Rama's body stopped moving as his eyes saw Catriona also headed the same direction as Grace, breaking off from the three men who remained distracted while swimming in the lake. Rama could feel the Dark One's focus narrow in on the two women, his perverted eyes raking up and down their bodies, assessing them. Rama felt sick to his stomach, the fact that he could feel what this freak was feeling was enough to make Rama want to rip off all his flesh just to feel remotely clean again. He wanted these women for their power, and he had two ways of getting it. The Dark One's primary plan was to breed them, in an attempt to mix blooded magic with that of an ancient bloodline. If that failed, he would devour them, literally. Devour their flesh and their magic along with it. If Rama was in charge of his body to any degree, he would be gagging right now at the disgusting plan this monster had for them.

"We will try to get both of them," the Dark One said as he made Rama move forward once again.

"I fucking hate you!" Rama shouted inside his mind. *"You pathetic piece of shit. If you were a man at all you would be the one here trying to take them on yourself, not using others. You must be one of the weakest creatures in this land if you have to stoop so low as to possess someone like me to do your dirty work."*

"I picked you, Prince, because your mind was weak enough to take over," the Dark One answered as if he were entertained. *"And feeling the turmoil, I am putting you through, that I will put you through for harming the women in your life. That's a special treat I plan to indulge in."*

"They won't let me hurt them," Rama shot back as he neared Grace, her back to him as she rifled through a bag on the ground. *"They will kill me before you get the chance."*

"You underestimate the weakness of a woman's heart." The Dark One steered them even closer, now they were feet away from an unsuspecting Grace. *"They care for you as a brother, as a friend. When they realize you are no longer in control, they will not be able to bring themselves to hurt you."*

"They will," Rama argued defiantly. *"My brothers will end me just to save their women, as they should. Even if they know it's not me, they won't let their women get taken."*

"They will choose to watch their women get hurt if it means I don't slit their throats in front of them," the Dark One said triumphantly.

Realization dawned on him, as if he had finally realized why exactly the Dark One had picked him of all people to perform this kidnapping. Rama was the only one that could walk away from this fight alive. His size and strength would allow him to get ahold of one of the women, and the vile creature was right, they wouldn't be willing to kill him to save themselves; and his brothers, they might be willing to, but the Dark One was prepared for that, he was going to make Rama hurt the girls in front of his brothers. Hold their very lives in his hands to keep them at bay. This bastard was sick enough to play this sort of twisted game, if not just to break them. He enjoyed breaking people.

"I will fucking kill you!" Rama growled as he slowly began to reach out towards Grace. *"If you hurt them, I will fucking rip you apart."*

"Not before you rip them apart," the Dark One taunted. Rama's large hands wrapped around Grace's throat and yanked her backwards.

Rama had Grace pinned face first against a nearby tree, his large hand wrapped around the front of her throat. He could feel her breath get knocked from her lungs on impact, she pushed back against him trying to find leverage but was unable to. *"What I've learned from this witch, is that she can't cast her magic without being able to fully concentrate. As long as you are actively controlling her breathing, she can't take over."*

Come on Grace! Rama fought with everything he had to try and loosen his grip around her. *Fight me!*

"Rama!" Catriona's voice shouted, alerting everyone to what was going on.

Rama pulled Grace to him, pressing her back to his chest as he unsheathed a dagger and placed it at her chest. "You cast your flames, and she dies."

"I can't believe it." Catriona took a fighting stance, eyes narrowing at him. "Grace was right. The Dark One took over."

"I see you've finally found your wildfire," the many layered voices pushed past Rama's lips. "I see how bright it shines within you. I want it."

"Let her go and come and get it," Catriona taunted.

The men were now sprinting their direction having obtained their weapons. A small seed of hope began to sprout within Rama, maybe they could kill him before anything bad actually happened. Catriona looked ready to burn him to ash. She needed to be strong, needed to survive this. *She won't*, the voices taunted. Rama ignored it, Catriona would fight him. She had to.

"You for her," the voices spoke to Catriona through his mouth. "An easy enough arrangement."

No! Rama shouted down the connection.

"Let her go!" Danny commanded, his long sword held pointed in Rama's direction ready to strike.

Menolayous was circling behind them, his axes at the ready. "Rama, if you're in there, please, let her go."

"Your brother can see and hear everything." the Dark One's gaze now tracked Menolayous as he circled them. "But he's not in charge anymore, as you are well aware."

"Let her go," Catriona demanded, taking a dagger from her brother Markous who was also circling Rama until he found a position off to the left.

"You for her," the Dark One offered once again. "Simple trade."

"No!" Danny shouted in defiance.

"Done." Catriona tossed the dagger and stepped forward.

Rama felt his body move faster than he was used to, pushing Grace into Menolayous's arms as he inched forward for an attack. Ramas' large hand wrapped around Catriona's wrist pulling her to him. She instinctively tried to pull away but had no chance against Rama's brute strength. Rama felt himself pull her against his chest, placing the knife against her throat. His eyes watched as Grace slowly recovered her breath while the others tried to take a step towards him.

"I wouldn't do that if I were you," the Dark One taunted, the blade drawing a few drops of blood from Catriona's exposed throat. "One wrong move and I will start poking holes in her. She doesn't need to be alive for me to take her magic, she's only alive because I feel like playing."

"Burn him, Cat!" Markous called out, panic lacing his every word.

"I can't!" Catriona cried. Fuck, the Dark One was right about this too.

"It's your choice," the Dark One whispered in her ear. "Rama wants you to kill him. In fact, he's begging you to because he knows what I'm going to do to you."

"Oh, I will burn you," Catriona promised, trying to pull away from the lips now pressing against her face. "I will make you regret every breath you have ever taken, every thought you have ever had."

"I don't doubt your resolve," the Dark One answered as Rama's free hand began stroking Catriona's bare leg. "But after enduring how much from me first? What's your breaking point?"

"Stop." He could hear Catriona's voice tremble underneath his touch, Rama's conscious mind began to thrash violently against the magic that held him captive. "Please."

"I want to know who." The voice now serious, less taunting, but still quiet enough that the others couldn't hear. "Who was able to traumatize you before I could? I don't like people taking away my firsts."

"Please, stop!" Rama could feel the tears falling from her eyes now as his hand slid to her exposed lower abdomen. "Rama, please stop."

Burn me! he was practically shouting inside his head. *Kill me!*

"You fucker!" Grace coughed as she was finally able to breathe.

Rama observed the lethal expressions worn by everyone present, the terror of what was about to happen finally hitting them. Rama wished more than anything that he could stop this, that he could just will himself to die. Anything to protect his family from this, but this is what the Dark One wanted. He wanted to rip them apart, to break them. At some point Catriona would kill him, he prayed to whatever gods who bothered to listen that she would just do it now and save herself from this.

A distant bird call sounded, then everything began to move. Catriona suddenly reached up grasping the hand that held the dagger to her throat. She unleashed a controlled inferno up Rama's arm, sending pain shooting not only through him but also the Dark One. The pain was just enough for Rama to gain the smallest amount of control back, just enough that he was able to force himself to loosen his grip on Catriona. Rama could feel his flesh melting as Catriona ducked forward, escaping his grasp. Rama's body turned to flee behind him, but there stood Morrigan, blocking his path. A strong sense of hatred and familiarity washed over him as the Dark One focused his attention on her.

"You again!" the voices rattled from Rama's open mouth.

431

"Me!" Morrigan answered, before clapping her hands together, sending out a shock wave of magic.

Rama felt himself get thrown backwards, crashing against a small tree and landing on his back. The magic being produced by Morrigan now held him against the hard dirt struggling to move against the powerful wind. Menolayous and Danny sprang into action, pinning Rama's arms down to the ground. Catriona and Markous returned to the fray, bringing with them a set of chains and shackles. They were secured around Rama's wrists before Morrigan put a stop to her magical gusts. As a group effort, Rama was dragged to the base of a tree where he was attached with chains. After they checked to see if he was able to break free, it was determined he was secure. Everyone took a step back, catching their breath.

"What the fuck is happening?" Markous asked, sword pointed at Rama as he looked at everyone else around him.

"You may have inadvertently joined us on a hunting mission," Grace answered him as she allowed Menolayous to examine her throat for injuries. "Sorry about that. You were very helpful."

"Are you okay?" Danny murmured, cradling a shaking Catriona in his arms as she buried her face in his chest.

"His arm," she muttered, glancing in Rama's direction. "I destroyed his arm."

"You had to," Danny responded gently. "You'll see. Rama's going to yell at you for not doing it sooner. It's okay."

"Congratulations," the voices spoke through Rama once more, proving he had not vacated just yet. "A clever trap indeed. It's not often I get outplayed."

"I've been outplaying you for centuries," Morrigan hissed, eyes remaining focused on Rama, ensuring he wasn't able to break free. "You have become predictable in your old age."

"I'll keep that in mind," the voices hissed at her. Rama's gaze now turned to Grace. "Well, get on with it girl. Kick me out of this body. Your friend has been begging on your behalf for hours and I tire of it."

Grace snarled in his direction as she took a step forward, rolling up the sleeves of Menolayous's shirt.

"I'm still trying to decide which of you is my favorite," the Dark One said, eyes bouncing between Grace, Menolayous, and Catriona. "So much potential for pain. I can't wait to see what it will take to break you."

"Fuck off already," Grace growled, her hands going to the sides of Rama's head.

Rama could feel Grace's magic now pulsing through him, pushing the Dark One out slowly. It was like bright light was filling him up inside driving back the darkness. Rama could feel his body completely shudder as the Dark One finally escaped. Rama could feel the magic fading as reality came crashing back to him. He took a deep breath and was able to control his lungs. His eyes glanced around at everyone, seeing them from his own perspective. Tears began to trickle down his face, regret and shame from allowing that bastard to control him overcame even the pain from his fried arm.

"I'm so sorry," Rama wept, still chained to the tree. "You should have killed me. You still should. I don't... I..."

"He's him?" Danny asked Grace, who nodded her head.

Danny stepped forward, unlocking the shackles that held his brother. Rama allowed his hands to drop into his lap, gasping in pain as the flesh of his arm broke open at the movement. Danny stepped back, giving him space. Catriona stood farther back than anyone, staring at him with too many emotions. Rama couldn't blame her, she probably looked at him and was still seeing the enemy, still unsure.

"I'm sorry about your arm." Catriona wiped a tear away from her eye, still keeping her distance.

"You should have killed me sooner," Rama reasoned with her. "That wasn't me, I tried to stop it. I never would hurt you, either of you."

"I know," Catriona answered with a weak smile.

"Let's return to Collie," Morrigan cut in. "Knowing him, he will be sending scourge out hunting for us. Best beat them back, and get his arm healed by our wolf girl."

433

Chapter Sixty-One

Rama

Night had come, the darkness blanketing Collie as if it were tucking the ever-growing city in for a night's rest. Rama sat by the great fire located in the center of the longhouse. It had been several days since Rama had been freed from the Dark One's grasp, the malicious creature no longer shared control over his thoughts and actions. Rama was thankful for his family, thankful that they were able to recognize the intruder in his body and were able to expel it. All that Rama carried with him from that exorcism was a large scar taking up half of his right hand and forearm. Bridget was able to heal the wound as soon as they had returned to camp. Rama still bore the shame with his scar, wishing that his body hadn't been the tool the Dark One had chosen to use to harm Catriona and Grace. Rama wished Catriona didn't feel remorse for having to burn him, he was proud that she had done what was needed to protect herself from him.

After the exorcism, because really there wasn't a better word for what needed to be done to free him, everything between him and his family had returned to normal. For the most part. He no longer shared feelings of violence or lust towards his brother's woman; he no longer felt the urge to harm those he cared about. In turn, his brothers felt comfortable around him again, no longer questioning his motives. Rama wasn't sure that was logical on their part, but he appreciated being included once again. Inclusion or not, whether his brothers were able to forgive him or not, he was unable to forgive himself.

That was truly the reason why they were all sitting here now, at this meeting. Rama's family had kept the possession of the king of the rebellion quiet from the other war chiefs and had continued to delay the meeting until Rama was sure the Dark One no longer kept a seat in his mind. It wouldn't do Stone Basin any good if the Dark One sat in on their liberation committee, as Bridget was attempting to call it now.

Beside him sat Flinn, who stared into the flames as if he were seeing something of great interest dancing there. Farren sat on Rama's other side, his focus moved between everyone else who was present. Across from them sat the war chief Farroway. He was a powerful looking man, built with the same height and stature as Danny. His dark brown hair was also curly, but shorter. Farroway's piercing green eyes glimmered of the light from the fire. Rama could tell Farroway had been spending plenty of time at sea. His once pale face was now tanned into a soft golden brown. Something had changed him from the man he knew, a rage sat behind those brilliant green eyes, a rage mimicking that rage of Catriona's. Rama could see that this man who sat before him was no longer who he had been.

The war chiefs had chosen seating that made an inner ring surrounding the fire. There was an empty space where McKinlay used to sit, a seat deliberately left as a place of honor for their fallen brother in arms. Each and every one of them mourned McKinlay and the loss of his men. Not only was it a devastating loss to the rebellion, but many of them were close friends. It was a loss that Rama wished to repay this Dark One for.

Rama looked at his brother Danny for moral support. His brothers were no less than he in the eyes of the counsel, their voice as heard as his own, but they never wanted to lead. Danny sat just behind the inner circle; arm casually draped over Catriona's shoulders. Beside them sat Clyous and Bridget, their attention continually shifting between the war chiefs. Markous sat on the end looking excited for the meeting to begin soon. Morrigan stood against the wall in the back of the longhouse, occasionally glancing over at Flinn. Her focus remained over the ones present that had magic. This woman took her role as guardian of the ancients seriously, as she had proven that day at the lake. Rama truly believed that without them here, Morrigan wouldn't have bothered aiding the rebellion. She had a knack for watching over them, almost as if they were her own children. Her pet raven began to caw, signaling the arrival of their final guests.

Two more figures entered the longhouse. Most had been patiently waiting for the royal to make her entrance, others, like Farroway and the two advisors he had brought with him, grew more frustrated by the minute. Rama suspected this tardiness was to make a point, Grace was a princess after all, from a kingdom that was well known for their games at court. Without so much as a glance in anyone's direction, Grace strode in, carrying her head high with an heir of authority he had yet to see. Menolayous followed her closely, eyeing everyone in the room. Grace seated herself in McKinlay's empty seat, a gesture that did not go unnoticed by the war chiefs. Menolayous stood behind her, a subtle smile displayed on his face. Farroway wasn't the only one who had changed recently.

"And who is this delight?" Farroway asked, eyeing Grace as if she was the most irritating thing he'd ever seen. "You must be important if it's what's kept us waiting."

"This is Grace, Crown Princess of Airgid," Rama introduced, staring at the young war chief and his boldness.

"Princess?" Farroway's eyebrows raised, voice laced with sarcasm. "What a pleasure to have you here!"

Grace stared at him, sizing the poor bastard up. The glare that she threw Farroway's direction was cold enough to freeze over water. Grace was a formidable opponent, Farroway would learn that soon.

"Can we begin now?" Farren interjected, breaking up the tension.

"Yes, shall we?" Flinn answered, looking at Rama expectantly.

Clearing his throat Rama began, "As you are all aware by now, we are one war chief missing. McKinlay and his warband are gone."

"What happened exactly?" Farren inquired. "We've only heard rumors."

It was Grace who spoke, "Your warband was set upon by the blooded tribesmen of Gaelach. They were all dragged back to a ruined temple of their Moon God. The men were sacrificed there."

Grace used her powers to project images into the space around them in the longhouse. Everyone, but Morrigan and Menolayous jumped at the sudden imagery. Grace's mark behind her ear glowed a bright purple as she focused on weaving her illusions.

Blooded tribesmen appeared around the site, covered in animal pelts and armor made of bones. The tribesmen appeared to be chanting around an altar, standing in a semi-circle. They were performing a ritual sacrifice on a human male. Sounds of the man's screams echoed through the longhouse as did the chanting.

"What in the fuck!" Farren stood and jumped back, his face filled with utter disbelief.

Flinn also stood as if expecting the illusions to come for him at any minute. Rama looked upon the sacrifice, horrified. He recognized this man, he was a warrior from McKinlay's camp. The cult leader continued to cut into the man's chest with a sharp looking obsidian dagger, opening a hole just underneath the ribcage.

"This was the last survivor from the warband," Grace said. "I was brought to the camp just before this ritual."

436

Rama saw tears streaking down Bridget's face silently as she watched. Clyous held her gently, his eyes glued to the horror before him. Catriona and Danny looked on silently. The only indication that Danny was affected was the muscles clenching in his jaw. Markous looked as if he was prepared to march of into battle against these cultists. Catriona stared at the man being ripped apart with cold, almost dead eyes, a response that was slightly concerning to Rama. This was most likely a trauma response, considering how recently she had been tortured herself. Menolayous on the other hand refused to watch, as if he had already seen this. It was likely he had; Grace must have shown him.

"Why were you brought there?" Farroway asked, still focusing on the scene before him, voice filled with anger.

"Those with magic were warned of a great evil that has risen from the shadows. It was a warning and a call for aid. Myself, and others like me were headed south to find more of us, to find your rebellion. What we didn't know until we entered Gaelach territory was that the Dark One was there and has been having the tribesmen kidnap all those in their territory and bring them to him," Grace answered.

The scenery changed again. They still remained at the ruined temple with the black banner of Gaelach waving above, three crossed swords hovering above an ancient altar. A sinister creature stood amongst the tribesmen. It wasn't a creature, Rama realized, it was a man. He was covered in dark bearskin; the head of the bear used as a hood to partially cover his hair. Black paint and dried blood stained his skin, black tattoos filling in what gaps were left. He stood as tall as Rama, but his build was tall and lanky. The man's eyes were blood red, and his teeth! His teeth were all sharp, like they belonged within the mouth of a wild animal.

The Dark One. Fear clutched at his heart as he witnessed the evil standing before him. His presence was unnerving, unnatural. It made sense why he appeared to be a creature at first. Grace looked upon her illusion with a combination of fear and anger. Everyone else in the room seemed to share a similar reaction to himself at the sight of this new enemy. Everyone but Menolayous, who remained plastered to the wall, terror filled his eyes, freezing him into place. This was the monster that invaded his dreams, stemming from a long-lost memory. Suddenly the illusion faded, and they were all back in the longhouse.

Morrigan said, "This enemy is beyond any one kingdom. He strives for total control. His end goal is the complete takeover and destruction of Stone Basin. No human, no blooded, no child of the ancients is safe. With each life he takes, his power grows. He devours the magic through the flesh and souls of his victims."

"And who are you?" Farroway's attention now swung to Morrigan.

"I am Morrigan, Guardian of the Ancients," she answered simply.

"And what the fuck does that mean?" Farroway glared.

A wicked smile appeared on the wild woman's face as she pushed off the wall. She stopped only a foot from the war chief who was now standing with his fists clenched tightly as if preparing for a fight.

"It means I am the one here you should fear, boy." Sparks of lightning began to crackle in the space around her.

"Sit down, Farroway," Rama commanded. "She's been an ally to us for several months. I would hate to have to clean you off the walls."

Farroway sat reluctantly, still glaring at the woman.

"This Dark One is the one responsible for the deaths of McKinlay and his men?" Farren asked.

"Yes," Grace answered. "Among other crimes."

Silence filled the room for several minutes. Rama glanced around the longhouse watching everyone intently.

"For the last few years, we have been doing what we can to be thorns in the side of Oich and its crown. Many of us have fallen victim to the pain and suffering that is regularly inflicted upon its citizens," Rama began. "But we were never strong enough to openly fight against them."

"We can now," Flinn spoke up, finally shaking off his stupor. "Collie is fortified well enough. The men have brought their families here and we are strong enough to keep building, to protect ourselves without hiding. Collie is ready to create an army."

"But now we seem to have a new enemy emerging from the dark." Farren stared into the flames as if looking for comfort there. "We cannot ignore this new threat."

"So we are here to decide what to do?" Farroway sighed, looking around the room. "Why are these people here? Do they command warriors? Are they to join our cause?"

"Everyone here is a leader in their own right or is a weapon at our disposal," Rama answered flatly.

"Really?" Farroway looked around. "I see a blooded. Princess of Airgid I get. You have your magical protector in the corner. I see your two brothers here."

His eyes locked onto Catriona. "What do you do gorgeous? Comfort Danny when he returns from battle? Cook his meals, tend to his wounds? Or do you bat your pretty little eyes at the warriors to give them hope before setting off for battle."

Catriona's eyes flicked to Farroway. The steely grey suddenly came to life turning a liquid silver. He held his breath knowing Farroway had just stuck his foot into a hornet's nest. Danny and Farren began to rise as if prepared to defend Catriona's honor, but she was faster. With a subtle wave of her hand, flames from the fire jumped at Farroway, catching his coat on fire. With a yelp, Farroway stood and flapped his flame engulfed arm around as if he could put out the flames. Catriona's smile grew as Farroway panicked.

"Cat," Clyous said softly.

Catriona looked at her brother before waving her hand. The flames disappeared. Farroway stood there trying to catch his breath. Interestingly, his coat and arm appeared unburned. Farren chuckled at the realization, giving his daughter a look that said he was proud. Great, the whole family was unhinged. That was where Catriona got her temper from, Clyous must be more like their mother.

"I'm the bitch you want on your side," Catriona answered. "Because I'm the one who's going to burn the crown and kingdom to the ground."

Rama looked at Farroway with a shrug. "Told you we had weapons present. Try to stop pissing them off, would you?"

Farroway glared at Catriona before Flinn said, "Sit."

"Combining our forces seems like the only guaranteed way to survive two different enemies," Farren spoke up.

"Agreed," Flinn grumbled.

"Agreed," Farroway huffed.

"Agreed," Rama concluded the vote. "Collie seems as good a place as any. We should pull everyone here in order to make centralized strategic plans. Collie should be our most defended outpost and where our men can bring their families to safety."

"We have already started with our men," Flinn interjected. "But in order to house an army and their families, we would need to expand."

"With an army we could expand in no time. Push into Gaelach territory," Danny added.

"Agreed," Farren said, the other two war chiefs nodded that they did as well.

"I am having trouble with the thought of abandoning our years-long resistance against Oich. Too much has been lost with this campaign. The king and his heir still need to pay," Farroway argued.

"Agreed." Catriona sat forward, eyes staring at Rama. "You want my help, you promised me I could be the one to kill him."

"And I will uphold my promise," Rama assured her.

"You can't just ignore the Dark One," Grace cut in.

"Unless you're going to pledge Airgid's total support in our endeavors you don't get a vote," Farroway snapped, all his niceties burned away apparently, assuming the prick had any.

"You would be a fool to ignore the darkness," Morrigan seethed.

"Did anyone say that we would abandon our pursuit of Oich?" Rama inquired. "That would never be my intention."

"We need justice for McKinlay. He was one of us," Flinn argued.

"What the fuck is the Dark One?" Farroway asked, looking at Morrigan. "Is he one of you? With magic?"

"He is the God of Death trapped within the body of a mortal," Morrigan answered. "He has somehow learned of a forgotten dark ritual that allows him to absorb one's life essence. For mere mortals it seems he can trap their voices, their memories. For children of the ancients, he takes their powers too. He possesses his hosts completely, utilizing their skills and magics to get a stronger foothold on this continent. With each recurrence and the longer he can walk in another's body, the more powerful he becomes."

"That's why he wanted me so badly," Grace said. "I come from a strong line of magic users."

"That's not all he wanted you for," Menolayous spoke from the shadows. Everyone's attention now turned to him. "He's been obsessed with trying to find or make someone who has both types of magics. He's obsessed with trying to breed a female of magical origin with one from a shifter bloodline, which he currently is inhabiting."

Only silence answered him. Rama stared at his brother, realizing now there must be a direct connection between Menolayous and the Dark One. Things were beginning to click inside his head, how the Dark One plagued Menolayous's dreams, how his brother knew this information. Shit!

"How do you know this, lad?" Flinn asked cautiously, pieces must have been coming together for him too.

Menolayous stared at them all for a moment, then took a deep breath. "I was born and raised in Gaelach. My entire family was murdered there. I escaped when I was about thirteen."

More silence from everyone. In the decade Rama, Danny, and Menolayous had been together calling themselves brothers, he had never known that. He and Danny had always assumed Menolayous was from Oich like them, but now the day of their meeting made more sense. A lost boy coming south with only the clothes on his back, acting as if he was fleeing something. He was fleeing Gaelach.

Grace reached back for him with sad eyes. "You don't have to do this."

Rama watched his brother shake his head. "I do. It's the only way to protect you, all of you."

Menolayous took her hand almost reluctantly, then the images of Menolayous's mind surrounded them. Rama observed the village of blooded tribesmen, Rama assumed Menolayous had been there, seeing exactly as they were now. Houses made from logs and stones stood erect and clustered underneath trees the size of small mountains. Tribesmen and women sat around various campfires sharing fresh meat from a hunt. Primitive as they were, they were equally violent. Fireside squabbles appeared normal as two of the tribesmen pulled daggers on each other. Off to the side away from the center of activity were several unblooded. They were tied to a tree, held there by the collars around their necks. The men and women looked thin, malnourished as they stared at the food being devoured by the tribesmen before them. Many were filthy and barely clothed.

"What none of you know about Gaelach, is that unblooded were the lowest on the food chain. Those not kept directly as slaves hid amongst the different cave systems that ran underneath the kingdoms, but occasionally one would have to leave the caves in order to gather supplies, hunt, or scavenge for food. It's when we left the caves that it was most dangerous for us. We were constantly hunted by the blooded above ground, but down below we had to fend off the scourge in order to survive. And trust me when I say,

441

being ripped to pieces by a scourge in the darkness was a preferred option if one of the tribesmen captured you. My family was captured when I was about eight years old, it was just me, my mother, and my sister. My father was killed years before by a scourge."

"Those who were not moon touched were considered inferior, even to animals. Animals still called to the Moon God, so they were treated honorably, as were horses and pigs. The blooded chose to keep those without blooded magic around for sport. When they weren't being used for slave labor or as sacrifices to the Moon God, some of the blooded would release an unblooded just to watch them run. As they attempted to escape, they would be hunted down by tribesmen in their wolf form and torn to pieces just for the fun of it. That's if they were lucky. Sometimes their deaths took longer."

Bridget seemed most affected by this revelation; however, shock reverberated through everyone present. They watched in horror as a teenage boy was dragged back to the campsite by a band of these tribesmen. The boy was suspended in the air by ropes as the monsters below took pleasure in burning him with torches or cutting open his flesh. The boy succumbed to his injuries after some time, but the mutilation of his suspended corpse went on for days. His body eventually stripped of its flesh hung there while the birds picked at the rotten meat. Markous looked like he was about to throw up.

"New blooded are outlawed in Gaelach, they believed the gods only blessed those born a wolf, and those that were created were an abomination." Menolayous went on as the images changed to one of the hunts he had just described. "If you were caught trying to escape or if you displeased a blooded you were likely beaten, tortured, and raped. If a woman got pregnant from one of those encounters, she would be killed after the birth. The child would only be allowed to live if it turned out to be moon touched. The tribesmen of Gaelach did not care about age, gender, consent, or even bothering to provide food and water to their slaves. They simply did not care enough."

The images then changed to what looked like a makeshift city surrounding ruins. Huts erected from sticks and mud surrounded a fallen temple. Blooded wandered around freely but the human slaves were huddled inside a wooden corral meant for sheep. They slept in the dirt, barely enough room for anyone to completely stretch out. The blooded would occasionally pick someone at random to pull out and torture. Some were tied to a post to be whipped or burned as the blooded stood back and enjoyed the torture. Rama caught movement from Danny as he looked away, fists clenched in anger at the sight of the whipping posts. Catriona glared at the images with an intense anger, refusing to look away as she watched a woman burn to death.

The images continued to rotate through a cycle, showing that others were strapped down to altars as knives carved into their flesh. Body parts and organs were removed as the priests chanted. More often than not men and women were pulled from the corrals to be beaten and raped. Regardless of injury, those who were left alive were tossed back into those wooden corrals. Wounds were infected from the mud and dirt; corpses were left there to rot.

"Full moons were for hunting. Equinoxes were for the gods. Tribesmen gathered at the ruins to celebrate the changing of the seasons. Mass sacrifices were the way of life during those times," Menolayous spoke slowly, as his focus was now on a young girl being held down and mounted by several blooded. Rama watched a tear slide down Menolayous's face as he watched the memory. The girl's screams echoed through the room for several moments before her throat was cut, they could hear the tribesmen laughing as her blood saturated the ground. She couldn't have been older than eighteen.

"That was the last time my sister was raped. I managed to escape a few days later."

Everyone's heads whipped to Menolayous before the images shifted again. The Dark One now stood before them. Only this was the Dark One nearly a decade younger. His eyes were not blood red but brown. His teeth were not sharpened as they were in Grace's memory, and he did not wear nearly as much body paint.

"This is Oisin, one of the three brothers who rule over Gaelach. Oisin is the oldest of them, and the most sadistic. An obsession with not being able to use magic because he was blooded is what led him down the path to becoming the Dark One. Somewhere he discovered ancient magic rituals that allowed him to change his shift."

"What do you mean change his shift?" Bridget spoke up, sounding confused.

"He isn't a wolf any longer," Menolayous clarified, not taking his eyes off the Dark One. "He shifts into a bear."

"How is this possible?" Morrigan seethed.

Images again flashed to the Dark One. This time Oisin shifted. Unlike what Rama was accustomed to seeing, the Dark One indeed shifted into a large black bear.

443

"Abomination!" Morrigan spat. "A crime against the natural order!"

"You mean to say everything else he has allowed and done isn't an abomination?" Grace snapped in Morrigan's direction. "You are older than any who has walked this continent and yet you have done nothing to save those trapped there?"

"Believe me, girl, I did not know. Magic had been lost to that kingdom for over fifty years, I never ventured there except in passing," Morrigan defended herself. "I would have acted if I had known."

"The brothers were exceptionally good at keeping their evil doings hidden from the rest of the continent," Menolayous interjected. "Nobody who isn't from Gaelach knows the truth."

"How?" Bridget asked, still wide-eyed and staring at the monstrous bear.

"I don't know how," Menolayous answered. "Some say Oisin braved the cave system and stumbled across ancient texts, but nobody knows for sure. After he learned how he taught his brothers. Rion shifts into a mountain lion but Ammon has kept his wolf form. They kept the secret amongst themselves, but it sparked their pursuit of magic. Oisin has been trying to create a blooded with magic for a decade. This devouring people and their essence is something newer. That wasn't even a consideration before I managed to escape."

Silence again. Nobody spoke as the images died away and the comforting scene of the longhouse returned. Rama watched as Grace went to Menolayous, his brother not only allowed her to embrace him, but he actually pulled her closer. Grace whispered something to Menolayous as he buried his face in the crook of her neck. Rama's conflicted heart broke at the sight. He was happy she was able to chase away the shadows appearing in his brother's eyes.

"And you survived that?" Farroway broke the silence. "You were raised in that?"

"Yes." Menolayous's gaze went to the war chief, his eyes narrowing. "I did not immediately recognize Oisin the day we rescued Grace, but he's worked his way back into my nightmares. It has triggered a lot of memories I had hoped to forget completely."

"Fuck." Farroway sat back in disbelief.

"This black magic of his allows him to enter people's minds when they sleep," Grace spoke up. "My power can barely keep him at bay, he is incredibly strong and he has set his sights on all of us."

"He will come for us at some point," Morrigan agreed. "It is the way of a parasite, they will search out a new host once they drain the old dry."

"Why is he so obsessed with finding a blooded with magic?" Bridget asked nervously. "Aside from me, it's incredibly rare. One magic typically cancels the other out."

"More power," Rama added in. "If he steals power, then he wants to keep his growing. The only two magic sources that we know of on this continent are blooded and magic from the ancient bloodlines. All other magical sources have become extinct. Giants, elves, fae, they all died out hundreds of years ago. That's all that's left."

"He is a fool then," Morrigan scoffed. "The magic of the land will never be gone completely. Unless of course he finds a way to drain that as well."

"That's a concerning thought." Catriona looked at Morrigan as her drop jawed. "Let's not give him that idea."

"I don't think we have much of a choice but to prepare for war," Danny interjected as he glanced at their brother, his voice commanding everyone's attention. "We need to defend against both. Because both will be coming."

Rama watched as everyone around the room nodded in agreement. The horrors they had all just witnessed through Menolayous's eyes humbling whatever arguments they had previously held. Suddenly, a silvery glow began emitting from Clyous's mark, his eyes going blank. Everyone's attention snapped to him. After a moment the glowing ceased, and Clyous's eyes turned to Rama. A sad truth was held within those eyes, he could see it as if looking through a window.

"I've just bore witness to a hundred different possibilities, now that the decision has been made." Clyous spoke with a sincerity that even Morrigan shifted closer to hear. "A war is coming, from both enemies. They will come for us relentlessly until we break. I have seen this war last a generation, and I have seen it last but a season. Many will die, from both sides. The outcome is determined by the decisions we make as we move forward."

"What decisions need to be made to ensure our survival?" Farren asked his son.

"I can only see the outcome after the decision has been made, but I see three that will dictate whether or not we win the war," Clyous answered back. "The only one who can lead us out of this war as the victors is Rama. If he does not command the rebellion, Stone Basin will fall. If any other takes his place, if he is lost to us, we will all die at the hands of the Dark One and his forces, destined to live our lives as playthings for his amusement."

Rama felt all eyes on him in that moment. Disbelief now flooding his system. Him? Was he the only option? They were likely to fail that many times?

"Morrigan," Clyous continued, "you need to save as many of us as you can. We need to gather all the children of the ancients we can to keep them from the Dark One's grasp. If he gains too much power, if he can get his hands on Catriona's fire or my sight we are all lost."

"This I must do," Morrigan agreed, the raven on her shoulder squawked in agreement. "This I will do."

Clyous turned to Grace and Menolayous then. "If you cannot get Airgid to join our cause many will die. You must find a way to sway your mother. If you don't, there is a possibility you will lose him to the darkness," Clyous said and gestured towards Menolayous.

Rama watched as Grace nervously clutched Menolayous's hand. Rama knew what that look was, she had resigned herself to protect him from his past, her well-being be damned. He could practically hear the words "over my dead body" screaming from her lips. The icy cool rage that now shone from behind her eyes was enough to chill any man to the bone, there was no question she would do exactly that. He could agree with her on that, he would do everything he could to keep his brother from returning to that life.

Well, there it was, their path was now laid out before them. One decision had created a million more that needed to be made still. The weight of each decision could tip the scales in either direction for how this war would play out. Nerves rattled him, his adrenaline spiking at the thought of a full-scale war. They had been playing games up until now he realized. Attacking traders and terrorizing forts. That was child's play to what was required now. Clyous was right, many were going to die. They needed a leader, Clyous had stated it had to be him, but would everyone else agree?

Rama glanced around the room. Danny and Catriona looked at each other knowingly before looking at him and bowing their heads slightly. Clyous couldn't take his eyes off of Bridget who was looking at Rama with wet eyes. She, too, nodded towards him. Menolayous and Grace were staring at him. Menolayous held his brother's gaze for a moment before also nodding his head. Farren and Flinn looked to Farroway who rolled his eyes before bowing his head to him. And just like that it was decided.

Flinn's laughter boomed. "What do we do first, King of Thieves?"

"Let's bring everyone home," Rama answered, this he knew was the right call.

Chapter Sixty-Two

Markous

Watching his little sister this past week had been the blessing that Markous truly needed. He had been guilt ridden leaving her behind those months ago. He was even more ashamed to admit the guilt had not hit him until after he had reunited with their father. No, Markous had been too consumed in his own anger and grief to think past his own chance to escape. Leaving his brother and sister behind wasn't even a forethought.

When he left, Catriona might have physically been healed, might have even forged new friendships, but she had withered away inside. That fight, that drive had completely disappeared. All that was left of her was a body that refused to eat, that shrunk away from flames. His baby sister, the one he had watched grow up into a very stubborn and hot-headed woman, the same one who had no issue throwing hands any man who irritated her was barely strong enough to touch the inferno that had been inside her all along. Markous had seen all of this but was too consumed with his own grief to help her. Truthfully, he didn't know how.

That was his baby sister. The narrative that kept replaying in his head was that he wasn't strong enough to protect their mother or the twins. When push came to shove, he was easily overpowered and forced to watch the horror that was inflicted upon the women in his family. Catriona wasn't the only one who had nightmares, who was forced to replay everything of that day. It wasn't just their mother's screams that plagued his dreams, but hers too. Anger drove him on as he remembered how all the blooded stood there and allowed it to happen. How the guards seemed to revel in it. Hatred of all blooded had become his focus for a time until his father made him train with a few blooded warriors at the Harrada Pass encampment.

This hatred of blooded had even extended to the redheaded healer that had tried to help them. For that he also felt shame. There was not a mean bone in that woman's body, she risked a lot to do what she had done for them, but in his misguided state of mind he blamed her for their mother's death. Markous could tell this started to cause a rift between him and his brother. This, paired with his hatred of blooded kept them from talking about what had happened.

Clyous had always been the most levelheaded out of all of them. He did not speak about that night and did not appear to be as affected. That alone infuriated Markous. How dare that not affect him, but also a small part of Markous believed that's how he himself should have been handling the situation. Markous had discussed this at length with their father, Clyous had a logical mind. He had always been good at separating emotion from fact. Clyous was so good at it he didn't seem to hold a grudge against all blooded. He even kept that blooded healer as his partner. At least that's what it looked like, they were living together. This angered him while they were on the road. Now, Markous could see how good the redhead was for his brother. Just as Danny was for Cat.

This home his siblings had built for themselves, this new family, they needed these attachments. They belonged here. Markous loved his siblings deeply, but he didn't belong here. Markous had felt like an outsider since day one. No, his place was side by side with their father.

"We should be back before the next full moon," Farren said to Flinn and Rama as they stood by the main gate. "It will take at least a week to get all of my men ready for a march, longer to get back to Collie."

"Try to send them out in squads," Rama suggested, the giant of a man slipping seamlessly into his new role. "It would bring less attention than an entire army marching our way."

"As you wish, My King." Farren mock bowed to Rama, soliciting a booming laugh from Flinn.

"I hate all of you," Rama muttered as the war chiefs laughed at his expense.

"I will be sending out my last group to Oich on the morrow," Flinn informed everyone. "Upon their return that will be the last of the families brought into Collie. I'll have our boys do a supply run as well, since gaining entrance to the capital unless it's under siege seems rather unlikely in the near future. Discreetly of course."

"I'll be going with them," Bridget announced, everyone turned to her in surprise. "I need to collect my medical journals from my house, and certain supplies I can only get in town."

"Is that wise?" Flinn asked her gently.

"I'm the only one who knows what to get," Bridget answered. "And my presence would be a lot less noticeable than any of yours."

Markous watched his brother's regularly controlled demeanor change to something more… protective. This was going to be interesting.

"I'll go with you," Clyous informed her.

"No, you won't." Bridget looked at him with an arched brow. "That doesn't even make sense. You're wanted in Oich. The guards would see you."

"You shouldn't go alone." Clyous looked as if he were ready to fight over this. "Besides, there are ways inside the city without being noticed. They are shockingly ill equipped when it comes to guarding their dear capital."

"She's not going alone," Grace said. "I'll be going with her."

Markous watched in amusement as Menolayous swung his head towards Grace. Unlike his brother, Menolayous seemed to know better than to try and argue with a woman who has made up her mind. That was confirmed when Grace shot him a challenging look, he shrugged it off. Farren was watching Clyous too, amusement filled his silvery eyes as he managed to keep a straight face. Young love indeed.

"She's more than capable of handling herself." Catriona put a hand on Clyous's shoulder. "She'll be fine. You, dear brother, won't be."

Clyous was visibly struggling to keep his mouth shut. Even Bridget was cracking a smile at the sight of his restraint. Clyous was not used to being the center of attention, that was usually reserved for Cat.

"As fun as it is watching you struggle with this, son, we need to hit the road." Farren chuckled, embracing his youngest. Farren moved to Catriona next, scooping his daughter into his arms. "I love you both. We'll be back in a month."

"You'd better," Catriona warned him as they broke away. "There's nowhere on this continent you'll be able to hide from me."

"Oh I have no doubt." Farren's eyes twinkled with pride before standing in front of Danny. "Try to keep her out of trouble will you."

Farren and Danny shared a short embrace. "I can only do so much, as you know." Danny laughed.

Farren made his way to Bridget, gently patting her cheek. "You be safe, keep my boy on his toes. He needs his feathers ruffled."

Bridget showered him with a warm smile. Markous felt Catriona slam into him, nearly knocking him over as she threw her arms around him.

"You had better come back on time," Catriona lectured him as he wrapped his arms around her.

"When I finally get back, I give you a week before you're sick of me." Markous laughed, wrapping one arm around Clyous.

When they finally finished their goodbyes, Markous watched as the sorceress sauntered up to the group. She carried a spear that was taller than she was and wore a thick cloak, odd for springtime. Her regularly loose flowing hair was now braided back, but she carried nothing else, no waterskin, no bed roll, nothing.

"Mind if I accompany you part of the way?" Morrigan asked with her clipped accent.

"Not at all." Farren answered.

"Are you in need of supplies?" Markous asked as a horse was brought to her.

"No," Morrigan answered simply, climbing up onto the great black beast.

Markous didn't know how to respond to that, she was probably used to living off the land. He also noticed she did not give anyone the chance to embrace her goodbye.

"Do you really need to leave today?" Bridget asked, nearing the horse.

"I must begin my new task." Morrigan gently reached down to palm the redhead's face. "I have done all I can for you four. There are more I need to save."

"And you want to do this alone?" Catriona asked, the sorceress and his sister grasped forearms in a warrior's goodbye.

"I have been alone for decades," Morrigan answered. "Being around you all has been smothering, if not a nice change of pace."

"Give them no reprieve," Grace called out, smiling at her.

Morrigan nodded to the Princess of Airgid. Flinn stepped forward to approach the sorceress then. His hand casually rested on her knee as he leaned closer to her. An action that was somewhat surprising to everyone present.

"Don't be gone for too long now." Flinn smiled up at her. "I won't have anyone to drink with."

Morrigan leaned down, kissing the old war chief on the forehead. "Try not to die of old age before I return."

Flinn's laughter boomed as Morrigan nudged her horse forward. Markous and Farren mounted their horses. As the three of them rode their horses to the front gate, Markous looked back to his family. Clyous and Catriona waved to them as the gate was opened. Farren and Morrigan spurred their horses forward. Markous waved back before spurring his horse on. Markous would accompany his father back to the Harrada Pass and help move the forces to Collie. Markous had every intention of fighting on the frontlines, just like Catriona most likely did, but they would still be together, to be whole.

Chapter Sixty-Three

Bridget

"I'll be fine, I promise." Bridget assured him as Clyous helped tighten the straps to her pack. "Your sister did a good job teaching me how to defend myself."

"I know," was all he said, his silence more frustrating than anything.

"Then I don't understand why you're being so silent." Bridget gently took his hand, staring into his eyes.

With a sigh Clyous answered, "I just don't want you that far away from me. I'm going to be lonely."

"Your sister will still be here," she answered, slightly confused at the smile now spreading across his face.

"That's not what I meant." Clyous gave her a wink, his large hands now resting on her hips.

"Oh." Bridget felt her face flush as she understood the look he was giving her.

They had yet to be intimate past a few shared kisses, something that Bridget was really hoping would have changed by now. The funny thing about Clyous was that he never pushed her, as if he was trying to be careful of something. This frustrated her because she wanted him, but she knew that she shouldn't be the one to make the first move. He probably was still wrapping his head around the whole Liam thing, something she could understand. Sleeping in the same place as him made things even more difficult for her to keep from wanting him. Most nights he behaved like a perfect gentleman, other nights she woke to find herself wrapped up in his arms as if he had reached out to her in his sleep. Or maybe she had gone to find him, she wasn't sure. It was nights like those that made it perfectly clear just how much she wanted him, how her body ached for his touch, and the look Clyous was giving her now seemed to be full of promise. But they are on the eve of war, this was her last chance to return to Oich as herself without being hunted.

"You know as well as I do this is my last chance to go back." Bridget looked up at him hoping he would understand.

"I know," Clyous answered, seeming to retreat into his regular controlled demeanor.

"Bridget, it's time to go," Grace called from the gate.

She felt Clyous's hands drop and move as if to pull away. Unwilling to let this feeling between them pass, Bridget wrapped her arms around his neck as she pressed her body against his. Before he could speak, she kissed him, tangling her fingers into his hair. He reacted just as she had hoped. His hands secured her hips against him as he gently nibbled on her lower lip. She could feel the want in him, his need for her. She felt it too but pulled away, resisting the urge to push further, she had probably already crossed a line being the one to make the first move.

"Bridget?!" Grace called again.

"Hurry home?" Clyous pleaded quietly.

"Most definitely." Bridget smiled as she pulled away.

Bridget released Clyous and reluctantly walked over to her friend. Grace stood by a group of warriors, every single one of them outfitted for travel. These men were as eager to collect their families as much as Bridget was reluctant to leave.

"I see you're taking my advice and pushing him." Grace arched an eyebrow.

Bridget smiled at her as they turned to the gate, remembering their conversation. What Grace had suggested made sense, but something deep within her was too nervous to be as brazen as someone like Grace. She did not want Clyous to look at her and not want her, to look at her as if something was wrong with her. The gate was raised by Connor, who waved to the group as they exited Collie.

"Be safe, Miss Bridget, Miss Grace." Connor smiled at them as they passed.

"Stay out of trouble, Connor." Grace waved at him kindly.

The group made its way to the main road through the trees. Collie may be expanding but they had not bothered to connect the village to the rest of the world yet. A tactful move on Flinn and Rama's part, there was no point connecting to the rest of the world before they were ready to deal with the consequences. Not that the village was well hidden anymore, the wall now expanded several miles from its original borders. If one wandered into the forest, it would only take several minutes to come across the structure.

After several minutes of traipsing through the trees they made it to the ruins of the collapsed windmill. To everyone's surprise, as soon as they rounded the corner, they spotted a lone figure waiting for them. Menolayous was casually leaning against a pile of rubble with a traveling pack at his feet. Bridget smiled at the sight of him, quickly looking at Grace who looked like she was trying to conceal a smile. For a man who hardly ever spoke and did his best to stay away from groups of people, Menolayous was unarguably smitten with Grace. Bridget was truly happy for them, they seemed to bring out the best in each other.

"Couldn't last a week without me I see," Grace said as Menolayous joined the group.

"I don't think I would survive a week without sleep," Menolayous answered matter-of-factly. "Really, this is for self-preservation."

Bridget giggled as Menolayous fell into step beside them. They were cute together; there was no doubt about that. A small part of her had wished Clyous had been there waiting with him. But she was glad he was not; it was too dangerous for him to enter Oich.

The group continued to follow the road towards the capital city, a few of them scouted ahead to make sure they wouldn't meet anyone on the road. The men set a pretty steady pace, none wanting to be the one to slow down the group. Bridget was able to keep up easily enough for the first several hours, but as they continued on without any change of speed, she began to feel the effects of the exertion. Mostly, the group chatted amongst themselves quietly, excited to see their families. This excitement showed when the men regularly refused to stop for breaks. They continued at a steady but enduring pace until the sun began to set.

Menolayous was the one who called a halt to their progression, sending men to scout for a safe place to camp off the road. A heavily wooded area was found several minutes from the main road. It provided adequate cover for them as they settled in for the night. The men had gone hunting, bringing back several rabbits. They built a fire, quickly skinning and dressing the rabbits before staking the carcasses over the flames. After the meat was cooked, all of them sat and shared dinner together. They ate quickly, talking in low voices so as not to attract attention from the road. When everyone was finished the men made sure to stomp out the fire before retiring to their bedrolls. Watches were picked before everyone had settled in, Bridget said goodnight to Grace and Menolayous who had set up their bedrolls at the edge of camp, away from most of the men. Bridget had drawn the short straw for first watch, not that she minded.

The men didn't take long to fall asleep. After such a grueling march she expected they all must have been exhausted. She felt the ache in her body as well, but her wolf kept her body very active. She was stronger and faster than the typical unblooded man, which meant her endurance was better. Regardless of that, her wolf was restless tonight. The moon was full and high in the sky, its push and pull calling to her wolf's desire to act out. She could not calm it with a walk; she could not risk leaving the men unguarded. She wasn't going to be getting any sleep anyway; they needed to rest before they completed the journey to the capital city.

Bridget quietly walked away from the men, making her way towards a small gap in the trees just ahead. She leaned up against a tree trunk, gazing up at the night sky. Through the branches she was able to glimpse the moon and stars shining brightly against the dark veil that covered the sky. With the men's breathing and snoring now in the distance, Bridget was able to breathe and let her mind wander.

Her mind wandered back to the blacksmith she had left in Collie. She enjoyed watching him when he worked in the forge, after she spent a few hours in her shop she would bring him lunch, and they would eat together. She would talk with him as he worked, but sometimes she would just sit and watch. On especially hot days Clyous would remove his tunic, showing off all those perfectly formed muscles to her. She felt herself starting to get worked up as she imagined those strong hands on her. Her wolf whined in protest as she shook the fantasy of Clyous bending her over that same anvil in her head.

She realized it had been way too long as the ache between her legs started. Being close to Clyous like she had been, even thinking about him, was becoming painful. Fighting against the feelings of arousal from her fantasy, Bridget opened up her senses in an attempt to ground herself. The cool breeze danced across her face sending subtle shivers down her body. The smell of dirt filled her nostrils, damp soil from the spring rains. She could still scent the lingering smoke from the cooking fire earlier. Her ears perked up at the sound of twigs snapping.

Bridget quietly moved in the direction of the sound. Another reason why having her on watch duty tonight was a good thing, she could hear exceptionally well. If this was an intruder trying to sneak up on them, she would be able to find out before any of the men would have.

Carefully, she stepped around the sleeping men, making her way to the opposite side of the camp. She passed two empty bedrolls as she entered the trees, thinking maybe someone had woken up to alleviate their bodily functions. She still had a duty to make sure that's what it was.

As she neared the location, she could hear breathing from what sounded like two different people. She was a decent distance away from camp now, far enough away the other men would not hear movement. She slowed down as she neared the source, taking care not to make noise herself. She shouldn't go much farther without letting someone know.

The breathing her ears had picked up quickly turned to moans of pleasure. Bridget froze in place; this had to be Menolayous and Grace. That would explain the two empty bedrolls back at camp. Bridget's nose scented something that had her wolf stirring. Unfortunately, the beast knew exactly what those two were doing. The sounds and smells of arousal now overtook Bridget's senses, rooting her to the spot. Bridget's mind knew she should turn around and leave them to their alone time, but her wolf was too curious, too affected by the state they were in to allow logic to make the decision.

Against her better judgment, Bridget inched forward peering around the wide tree trunk. Grace and Menolayous were indeed tangled up in each other's arms not thirty feet in front of her. Bridget's eyes locked onto the couple, finding it impossible to look away. Try as she might, her wolf growled at her attempts to flee, ultimately keeping her there rooted to the spot.

Menolayous had Grace's back against a tree trunk, his hands expertly removing her corseted top and tunic as they kissed. Grace shrugged the top off easily enough, her breasts now completely exposed to him. Bridget watched as Menolayous's head dipped down as he put his mouth to Grace's breast. The moan that escaped Grace's lips was enough for the familiar throbs of arousal to begin yet again between Bridget's legs. Damn the full moon and her wolf.

This was so wrong, and she knew it. These were her friends. She shouldn't be watching them. She shouldn't be turned on by watching them, but she couldn't avert her eyes, the aching feel of arousal now taking over. It wasn't as though she was particularly attracted to Menolayous, or even Grace. No, it was a desire for that activity that she craved, how she desperately wanted that to be Clyous's tongue caressing her nipple. It was this growing frustration at not having Clyous the way she wanted him.

Menolayous removed his mouth from Grace's breast leaving a subtle bite mark around the areola. Bridget watched as Menolayous's hand slipped down into the front of Grace's trousers. Grace separated her legs slightly, allowing him better access. Moments later Grace gasped, her face contorting as if she was experiencing great pleasure. Bridget watched enviously as Menolayous's hand was moving back and forth in a rhythm, certain motions had Grace closing her eyes as if she were trying to bite back making noise.

Bridget continued to watch as Menolayous dropped to his knees before Grace and began to remove her boots and trousers. Before Bridget knew it, Grace was completely naked, her leg now slung over Menolayous's shoulder, while Menolayous's mouth and fingers began to work her. Bridget could almost picture herself in Grace's position with Clyous between her legs. That thought alone intensified her desire for Clyous to be inside of her. Grace's hands now found themselves firmly grabbing his hair as he worked. Bridget's cheeks began to heat at the sounds of her pleasure, her own arousal intensifying at the sounds she was able to pick up.

"Not that I particularly care," Grace's voice echoed inside Bridget's head, *"but Menolayous is not going to be kind if he catches you watching."*

In panic and shame, Bridget hurriedly pulled herself away from where she stood, quickly and silently returning to camp. Luckily none of the other men had awoken to the love making in the forest. No, that was just Bridget's wolf meddling where it shouldn't have. Bridget returned to standing guard where she was supposed to be. That was so stupid of her. She should have just left them alone, hopefully Grace wouldn't be too mad at her. She took a deep breath trying to steady her racing heart. She really needed to get this thing with Clyous figured out before she made any other terrible judgement calls.

Chapter Sixty-Four

Grace

"Hey dumbass," Grace shouted down a mental pathway she had barely used before.

At this distance she was lucky to be able to find it, let alone shout down it. But this seemed as good a time as any.

"What do you want?" Clyous's voice echoed back, sounding irritated. *"It's the middle of the night."*

"Your girl is about to pop," Grace shot back trying to not to focus on the man in between her legs, just for another moment. She laughed to herself, wouldn't that be funny to send down the mental connection.

"What do you mean?" was the only response she got from him.

"Don't play stupid." Grace could feel her frustration building; she wanted to return to her man. *"Bridget has been suffering for weeks now. I don't know what kind of game you're playing in not fucking her, but it needs to stop."*

"I'm not playing any games, not that it's your business," he shot back at her, sounding unconvinced himself. *"What do you mean she's suffering?"*

"If you don't fuck your girl soon, I'm going to take pity on her current condition and do it myself. You know exactly what I mean, and don't think for one second I won't do it. Quit dragging your feet already!"

And with that Grace slammed the connection shut, her senses fully returning to the present. Grace was suddenly aware of the fingers embedded deep inside of her, applying pressure to that spot that had her legs starting to tremble. For never having been with a woman before her, Menolayous certainly seemed to know how to please her. Grace suspected after their first intimate encounter Menolayous must have gone to talk with his brothers. Most likely Danny, seeing the current state of his and Rama's relationship.

When she took him into her mouth that first night, she did not expect him to react that way. That night, Menolayous had insisted they sleep next to each other, it was their new sleeping arrangement to go hand in hand with their new relationship, but even with all that he hadn't sought out much more from her. She was starting to get concerned she had crossed some sort of line with him; he had gone back to his quiet secretive self. On the third night something had changed, he had either decided or got the courage to hold her when they slept. A nice change from the awkward sleeping arrangement they had before.

As if touching her had changed the dynamic completely, he acted as if he were on a mission to give her a release like she had for him. He began to dabble in whatever knowledge he had picked up, testing out different things to see how she reacted. Of course she was okay with this experiment of his. Holding her from behind had quickly turned into his hand wandering between her legs. She could tell at first he was trying to figure it out, but it honestly didn't take long once her body started to react to him. He might have been told different things to try, but his attention to her, catching the most subtle changes, that was definitely all him.

She had to admit that the night he had started to use his tongue, their entire dynamic had changed. She no longer felt like she had to stop herself from touching him. He became ravenous for her contact, almost like he gained an appetite for it. For several days it had seemed like his sole purpose was to get her off. As amazing as that type of attention was, she did what she could to make it fair, but he wouldn't let her touch him until he had made her climax at least twice. She definitely tried, but his ability to toss people around and pin them down was as arousing as it was frustrating. She was not a match for him in that regard. Truthfully, it had turned into some sort of game between them. Who could get the other off first. That's how they ended up in this situation. She had started to rub him under the blankets once everyone had started to go to bed, not thinking he was brave enough to do anything surrounded by everyone else. She was wrong. He had practically dragged her out into the forest for what he had assumed was privacy.

Now she stood before him completely naked, one leg draped over his shoulder as his tongue licked down her center and his fingers began to curl inside of her. She had never experienced a lover like him before, someone so determined to please her. Not that she was complaining, she just didn't feel as if she deserved someone like him.

With another curl of his fingers her back arched as another wave of pleasure rolled through her. Taking advantage of her movement, his teeth gently grabbed hold of her sensitive nub, flicking it with his tongue. She felt herself clenching around his fingers, soaking them as her third release for the night took over, a very audible moan now escaping from her.

He removed his fingers from inside of her, staring up at her with a mischievous smile. "I think that means I win."

460

"You don't win until I give up." Grace smirked at him, still trying to catch her breath.

"Is that so?" Menolayous underhooked the leg that bore all her weight pulling her down.

Quicker than she expected, Menolayous had managed to roll her sideways, so he was now on top of her. Gasping in surprise at the sudden change of positions, Grace was now lying on her back completely naked, with a fully clothed Menolayous between her legs. Grace wasn't sure she would ever get used to how quickly he moved. For a moment, Menolayous looked triumphant, until he realized the position they were in. Grace watched his face drop slightly. She did not take it personally. She knew for a fact he was enjoying this. She could feel his bulge pressed up against her. No, she knew this was difficult for him. This was the first time Grace had been completely naked in front of him, or even below him in such a compromising condition.

Grace remained still, allowing him the space to work out in his head what he was going to do. She might enjoy pushing his limits, making him rise up to a new challenge, but she would never push past his boundaries. It wasn't just about sex with him; she actually cared about him. So, she remained motionless, staring into his eyes as he took in the situation.

"Are you wanting more?" he asked.

"I'm game for whatever pace you want to set." She gave him a small smile. "Truly."

He seemed to take in her words and think for a moment. She watched him intently as he looked at how their bodies touched, what was around them. It was almost as if he was assessing a battlefield, like he was checking for an enemy lurking around a tree. Grace was thankful she had sent Bridget running when she did. Grace had been in her fair share of exotic entanglements and considered herself relatively open-minded. She knew her friend meant no harm, it was innocent enough on the healer's part, but Menolayous would not have appreciated someone else being nearby, especially watching.

With the lack of activity, Grace felt the cool night breeze sweep over her as she stared up at him. The space between their bodies removed her only heat source, causing her to shiver slightly. Menolayous's attention snapped to her as if a predator had finally located their prey. Pulling his tunic over his head and tossing it to the side Menolayous stared down at her with that hungry look in his eyes. She inhaled sharply at the sudden view before her; a well-muscled torso covered in various scars and now a vivid tattoo she had put there. Now she could sit back and drink up the sight of him.

He had remained mostly clothed during their intimate entanglements. This nakedness, actually showing himself to her, was a big step for him. He watched her closely, most likely trying to gauge her reaction, something he did all the time. He needed to see how she reacted to him. This was his way of gauging if he had her permission to keep going. With this realization in mind, she allowed her eyes to roam up and down his bare chest. Scars be damned, he was well cut and beautifully proportioned. Years of honing his body into the weapon it was, that had shaped him like this. She bit her lip, thinking about just how much she wanted him inside her.

His lips crashed against hers; she could feel his bare chest pressed against hers. She could feel him shudder as her hands gently roamed around his bare torso, feeling the real him for once without the layer of clothing as a buffer. She could feel one of his hands reach between them, tugging at the ties of his trousers. She reached down to help him, and after a moment or two, he now lay completely naked on top of her.

The skin-to-skin contact was enough that Grace felt that familiar ache of arousal return. She repositioned herself directly below him as he kissed her. She could feel his tip nudging her entrance, and what a tease that was. Feeling him there, having him that close, her body ached for it.

Then he pushed inside of her, not taking it slow like she had assumed he would. Menolayous, in one single motion buried himself completely inside of her. Her back arched as her body struggled to take in his size. A sound came out of him similar to hers. She looked up at him and could see the pleasure and need in his eyes.

She gave him a reassuring smile as he searched her face. Then he unleashed himself on her. Much like the first, he put a lot of power behind his thrusts. He fucked hard, almost as if his life depended on it. Him being on the thicker side only added to the harshness of his thrusts, he was stretching her without giving her much of a chance to get used to his size, but the thing about her that Menolayous had figured out relatively quickly is that Grace enjoyed a little pain with her pleasure. This was no exception.

With each demanding thrust she could feel the buildup within her. She was very close to her release. She arched her back at the next thrust, ripples of pleasure moving through her at the feel of him. He took her by the hips then, holding them up for a better angle. He pulled himself even deeper into her, coaxing her moans and gasps out with each new thrust. The buildup was so intense, at this next thrust she was pushed over, feeling her tender internal muscles clench around his thickness. He stayed buried in her, hands still gripping her hips firmly as he released inside of her with a loud moan of his own.

They stayed that way for a moment trying to catch their breath. He bent down to kiss her gently before removing himself. He rolled to the side, pulling her up and onto him. He held her close to his chest in a warm and loving embrace. She smiled as she lay her head down, listening to his steady heartbeat.

"Are you okay?" he finally asked, still holding her to him.

"What, are you worried you hurt me?" Grace couldn't help but tease him.

"Grace." She could hear the warning in his voice, if she didn't actually answer him, he would undoubtedly begin to panic.

"No, you didn't hurt me," she conceded, angling her head so she could look into his face. "It was perfect."

He began to run his fingers through her loose hair. They lay like that for another minute before he quietly said, "I love you."

Her body tensed at those words, hundreds of different emotions and memories hitting her at once. Nobody had ever said those words to her before, not even her parents. She knew they cared of course, but they never said it. Grace never had any true friends back in Airgid, only people who wanted something from her. No lover had ever told her that, not that she would have believed them.

Menolayous had seen Grace's ugliness from the beginning and instead of brushing her off he kept coming around. She had seen into his nightmares, and she showed him hers. They accepted each other. This game they had been playing was not out of boredom. She wanted him, wanted to encourage him to come out of his shell, and he genuinely wanted to make her happy. No, Menolayous was real, he meant what he said.

"I love you too," she whispered, tears pouring down her face.

At the sound of her voice he sat up, grabbing her face before she could hide it. "What's wrong?"

"Nothing's wrong." She laughed, wiping away her tears. "I just wasn't expecting that. Nobody has ever said those words to me before."

"Fuck everyone else," Menolayous growled, holding her face so she had nowhere else to look but him. "I love you. Nothing else matters. The world can burn for all I care."

"I'm just really happy that we found each other." Grace smiled, wiping away her tears. "You'll always have me. I'm hard to get rid of."

A smile spread across his face as he pulled her closer. His lips met hers in a heart meltingly gentle kiss. His arms now held her close promising not to let her go anytime soon. Yes, this was love, Grace realized. Love was its own special kind of magic, something she was never going to let go.

Chapter Sixty-Five

Bridget

The final march to the capital city was probably the most awkward situation Bridget had ever found herself in, and unfortunately, it was all her own doing. After being caught by Grace she had retreated back to the camp where she stood guard as far away from them as she could. She had heard their return about an hour later, but she was so embarrassed she didn't even turn to look their direction. She felt Grace's presence nudging on their mental connection like she had wanted to talk. Bridget was still too embarrassed, she wouldn't let her friend in. Grace had fallen asleep and Bridget remained on watch duty the rest of the night, not waking her relief up as was planned.

Now, after a hasty breakfast and an early start, the men began moving again As they neared the capital nobody spoke, the occasional warrior broke off from the group to head to their own personal home. By midday, Bridget still hadn't said a word to anyone and the only remaining warriors besides Grace and Menolayous were two men a little older than she was. Their families remained inside the city center. They would be entering the front gates just after Bridget, Menolayous, and Grace in order to seem less suspicious.

Bridget could feel Grace's presence nudging their mental pathway yet again as they neared the gates. Bridget did her best to ignore it, but the insistence of her wanting in reminded Bridget of a toddler repeatedly hitting a wooden spoon on a cooking pot

Suddenly, Grace stepped in front of Bridget and blocked her path. Bridget halted, watching as Menolayous cast them a glance but continued walking forward. Bridget's eyes went to the dirt, too afraid to meet Grace's gaze.

"We can do this the easy way or the hard way," Grace spoke, gently cupping Bridget's face and forcing her to look up. "Either way, we're talking."

Eyes following Menolayous as he glanced back at them, Bridget said in a panic, "Not here, please."

"If you let me in an hour ago, we wouldn't be having this conversation for everyone to hear." Grace raised her eyebrows at her. "And

465

no, I'm not going to force my way in. That would leave you with a headache for days."

"*Okay fine,*" Bridget said collapsing her walls. "*I'm sorry okay. That was very wrong of me to do. I'm a despicable person for it. I have no excuses for my behavior; it was uncalled for. You shouldn't even call me your friend—*"

Grace put a hand to her own head as if she were in pain. "*Maybe I'll be the one with a headache.*"

"*Sorry,*" Bridget said, looking down to the ground again.

"*Will you look at me, please?*" Grace asked, Bridget complied. "*First off, if I want to call you my friend, I will. I don't need your permission. You still are by the way.*"

Bridget let out a very small sigh of relief...

"*Secondly, what you did wasn't that big of a deal,*" Grace said. "*Honestly, you're more embarrassed about it than I am.*"

"*I just—*" Bridget didn't know what to say. "*I shouldn't have.*"

"*You're not the first wolf I've been around. I grew up in a kingdom surrounded by them. I know what a full moon can do to even an older blooded.*" Grace looked at her sympathetically. "*I'm also a woman. I know how hard it can be if it's been too long.*"

"*I still shouldn't have been watching.*" Bridget looked at her with regret. "*For that, I'm sorry. Whether it's been a while for me or not, I should have known better.*"

"*If Menolayous wasn't so private I would have asked you to join us.*" A smile appeared on Grace's face. "*Or, if he wouldn't have a problem with it, I could easily provide you a solution to your problem.*"

Bridget's face heated so fast at what Grace had implied it was almost painful. "*I can't tell if you're joking or not.*"

"*I'm not joking.*" Graces face turned very serious. "*Menolayous is an incredibly private person and he isn't one to share. It's why I'm not planning on telling him about this.*"

"*I meant about—*" Bridget was still incredibly flustered. "*I will definitely not be repeating this story to anyone either.*"

Bridget watched as Menolayous glanced their direction again, his eyes examining Grace as she stood with her back to him. He watched them for another moment before turning his gaze away from them. They were probably having a silent conversation as well, she realized.

"Come on." Grace looped her arm around Bridget's, pulling her along down the road. "We're good I promise."

Bridget finally felt herself relax at those words. She was thankful Grace was not mad at her let alone outright rejecting their friendship over this.

"I'm just happy that the sight of my bare breasts left such an impression on you," Grace teased. *"I hope you think of them often."*

Bridget's jaw dropped, was Grace able to hear her thoughts? As if answering her question Grace threw her head back and laughed, a deep genuine laugh. Bridget lowered her head to hide her red face as best she could, but Grace kept towing her along.

"So, what did you need to grab from here?" Menolayous asked as they all headed through the gate.

"I just need to grab some things from my house, some herbs and my journals," Bridget explained. "If we're doing a supply run, it wouldn't hurt to get some cloth for bandages."

"I need to go get some supplies for camp anyway, I'll pick you up some cloth," Menolayous offered. "Meet you back at your house?"

"Yes." Grace kissed him sweetly. "Maybe grab a wagon for everything?"

Menolayous nodded before veering off towards the town square. Grace watched him as he walked away, smiling before turning back to her.

"Lead the way." Grace raised her arm as if pointing in a direction. "I've never been to this city. I'm in your capable hands."

"Why did you have to make that sound dirty?" Bridget huffed, leading the way to her family's home.

"Dirty jokes will forever be your penance." Grace laughed, dodging a few blooded who weren't paying attention to where they were walking.

Together, the women wandered through the busy town square making their way through all the side streets. Grace seemed to have no issue navigating around the blooded they encountered. In fact, her provocative choice of outfit was attracting a lot of male attention, but Grace brushed past each and every one of them as if they were stray dogs. Bridget watched the irritation her friend was so good at igniting in men, they simply didn't know what to do. Bridget was giggling at Grace's antics by the time they reached her front door.

"So, this is your place?" Grace asked as they walked into the foyer. "It's nice."

"It's just a house; there hasn't been anything worth staying here for in years." Bridget looked around with a sad sigh. "I only wished I had figured that out years ago."

"No time like the present." Grace shot her a comforting smile. "Come on, let's grab your things."

Bridget led the way to the back room where she kept all her medical supplies. Picking up an empty crate she began to fill it with all of her supplies. Grace found another crate out in the hall and helped collect her things. After about an hour Bridget felt confident that they had collected anything important. At least four crates were stacked in the foyer filled with various odds and ends from her practice. Finally, Bridget found her medical journals, pulling them out of their hiding place.

"This is them?" Grace asked, looking at the bound books Bridget held.

"Yes." Bridget gently placed them in the last empty crate. "They mean a lot to me. There's a lot of good information in them, before I actually learned how to use my power I had to heal people the old-fashioned way."

"Why did you hide them?" Grace asked.

"My father was away a lot, but whenever he came home, he had a habit of trying to purge the house of anything related to healing," Bridget explained. "He didn't approve of me wanting to become a healer. He felt it was beneath a woman of my station, that it ruined my marriage value."

"Ugh, don't tell me Oich still expects its noble ladies to remain pure before marriage too." Grace crinkled her nose in distaste. "That's such an outdated tradition."

Bridget laughed at that. She had always thought the same thing. Bridget took a moment to look around, a lot of memories were inside this house. Most of them were unpleasant. Now that she had spent time away from this place, she could truly see how horrible it was. Leaving here was one of her better life choices, there was no doubt about that.

"I think that's Menolayous," Grace said, opening the front door.

Menolayous was pulling up to the house with a wagon. He smiled once he saw Grace, hopping down out of the seat to help load the crates. The three of them loaded the crates in the back of the wagon, maneuvering the cargo around the supplies Menolayous had acquired while finding the wagon. Once they were done Menolayous helped Grace up to sit beside him. Bridget suddenly realized there was no place for her.

Before the feelings of rejection and abandonment began to creep in, Grace smiled at her. "Turn around Bridget. Someone's here to see you."

Bridget turned, spotting a familiar figure leaning in the doorway. Bridget's heart skipped a beat as Clyous stood there beaming at her. How had she not sensed him nearby? She should have at least heard him approach. She glanced back at Grace who was now winking at her. Grace had made it so she didn't sense him, she had used her powers of illusion to mask him. But why?

"Remember my warning Clyous," Grace called out as Menolayous steered the horses towards the road. "I'll see you both back at home. Try to stay out of trouble."

With that, Grace and Menolayous were gone, leaving Bridget and Clyous alone. Bridget turned to look at Clyous, a million questions wanting to come out in one breath. Clyous smiled, holding the door open for her. She stepped inside the house, and Clyous shut the door behind her.

"How did you get here so fast?" she asked, turning to him.

Clyous was suddenly there, wrapping his arms around her waist and pulling her closer to him. "I borrowed a horse."

The look in his eyes was enough to make Bridget shudder. This was similar to how she had left him, but now it was more intense. She could practically taste the desire pouring out of him. She wrapped her arms around his neck, not once taking her eyes from his.

"Why?" There was no way he had ridden all night on horseback just for her.

"I needed you," was all he said before kissing her.

This kiss was unlike any that they had shared before, it was devouring. Bridget could feel that need coming from him as he pulled her closer to him. Her smaller frame was now crushed up against his as he continued to kiss her. Excitement ignited within her as she kissed him back just as passionately. Maybe it was the residual effects from last night, or maybe it was how passionate Clyous seemed, but Bridget was finding herself wanting to push for more.

With her teeth, Bridget gently bit down on his lower lip, eliciting a sudden stillness from him. She could no longer feel Clyous trying to pull her closer, his hands on her hips now felt splayed open as if afraid to move. She released his lip, panic slowly flooding through her replacing the excitement, had she been too forward? Had she crossed a line by appearing too wanting, too dominant? As she started to pull away, she found that he held her secure, not allowing it.

"Why are you pulling away?" he asked, his eyes searching hers desperately.

"I shouldn't be pushing," she stammered, almost ashamed to meet his eyes. "I'm sorry."

"Let's clear one thing up now," Clyous growled, turning her face to look up at his. "I want you to take charge of this. I want you to do what you want. I will submit to you Bridget, not the other way around."

She stared up at him, jaw dropping. He wanted to submit to her?

"And if you keep comparing me to a wolf and what you assume my expectations should be, I swear I'm going to bend you over my knee and redden that beautiful ass of yours until you decide you want to do the same to me." As if to emphasize his point he lifted her off the ground forcing her legs to wrap around his waist. "Do you understand me?"

"Yes." She gasped, not just at being lifted off her feet but his words.

"Right." He turned and started walking up the stairs. "Let's continue this in the bedroom."

She wasn't sure what it was, but she decided then that Clyous was telling the truth. She was overthinking everything, assuming he was like Liam. He most certainly was not, so why should she go back to acting like she did all those years ago. Clyous had made it clear from the beginning that he did not want to own her. She belonged to nobody; she no longer had to behave like a submissive wolf. She was in charge of herself, her own destiny, and right now what she wanted was him.

"Stop," she said as they were halfway up the stairs. She shouldn't have been surprised that he did in fact stop. He looked into her eyes, curiosity flooding them. "Turn around and sit on the stairs."

He complied with her orders, turning on his heel and lowering himself so he was now seated on the stairs. Her knees came to rest on either side of him as she now straddled his lap. A small smile spread across his face as he stared into hers. Bending low, she took his face in her hands, kissing him. Her kiss was demanding as her teeth caught his lip once again. This time instead of stilling, his hands found their way to her ass. Roughly pulling her forward. She could feel his cock pressed up against her center, their clothing acting as the only barrier. Her pulse quickened as arousal began to flood through her, overcoming all of her senses.

Before she knew it she found herself rocking back and forth, grinding herself against his erection. A moan escaped his lips as she continued to grind into him, each point of contact spurring her on even more. She could feel his hands push down on her hips, as if trying to make her grind against him even harder. His mouth broke away from hers, going to her neck. She gasped loudly as she felt his teeth gently nip her throat. Suddenly, he leaned back as far as the stairs would allow, planting his feet and arching his pelvis harder into her. She was getting tired of these stupid clothes getting in her way.

She reached for her tunic, pulling it up and over her head. As she tossed it aside, she let loose a small laugh. Clyous was now staring at her bare breasts, a hunger seeming to settle over him. He went to grab for his tunic, but she stopped him, she was enjoying this desperate look on his face. Reaching between them she now palmed the outside of his trousers, causing him to jerk suddenly in surprise. She stared into his eyes, and her fingers began to trace the outline of his erection over his trousers. With her free hand she pushed him backwards, holding him down as she continued to tease him.

Her hand crept its way to his belt line, slowly undoing the opening of his trousers. Her hand pushed its way in until her hand was grasped around him. His flesh was so soft to the touch and warm. She could feel a slight tremble from him as she took hold of him, pumping his hard length.

"By the gods, Bridget!" Clyous breathed heavily as she pumped him again.

"You want me to take charge?" she teased, pumping him again.

"Let me touch you, please," he begged, staring at her as if he were asking to devour her.

She felt herself clench at his words, her arousal becoming too great to continue teasing him like this. She nodded, allowing him to lift her up again as he stood. Quickly, he sprinted up the stairs and carried her into her room, gently depositing her on the bed. She found herself now sitting on his chest as he laid on his back, trying to pull her closer to his face.

"What are you doing?" she asked, trying to stop him from scooting her up farther.

"Can I taste you?" he asked, smiling up at her. "You're so fucking wet, I want to see if I can make you come on my tongue."

471

Her face grew hot as he wrapped his arms around her thighs, dragging her center even closer to his face. "Wait."

"What's wrong?" he asked, pausing and taking in the flush of her cheeks. "Have you never done this before?"

"No!" She gasped as one of his bare hands brushed her thigh, sending shudders down her spine.

"Oh sweetheart." He smiled brightly at her. "Then I beg you, may I be the first."

She quietly asked, "Are you trying to have me sit on your face?"

He playfully nipped at her thigh. "Yes, and while you do, I plan to use my tongue and teeth to coax the best orgasm out of you that you've ever had."

Images of last night briefly flashed through her head, how Grace seemed to like it when Menolayous did it to her. Although, she wasn't sitting on his face! She reluctantly allowed him to scoot her over his face where she hovered nervously.

"Do I do anything?" she asked nervously.

"Sit your ass down." He laughed. "And hang onto the headboard."

Before she could catch her breath, she felt his tongue swipe down her center. She grabbed onto the headboard, her immediate reaction was to arch forward, but he held her firmly in place. The sensation of his tongue grazing her delicate nerve endings was nothing like she had expected. With each swipe of that torturing and talented tongue of his, she felt as if she were seconds from jumping out of her skin. She could feel pleasure build as his teeth gently nipped her nub, her orgasm nearing like a stampede of wild horses. As soon as she felt him suck her soft flesh into his mouth, the tip of his tongue teased her into very loud and audible moans. She hung onto the headboard as her orgasm finally hit, her legs trembling.

Clyous scooted her hips down to his chest as he looked up at her with a smile on his face. "I'm going to assume that was to your satisfaction?"

She nodded, still trying to catch her breath. It only took a moment for her to recover before she decided what she wanted. Scooting all the way down so she was sitting right above his groin, she stared into his eyes before lowering herself onto his cock. She moved painfully slow as she lowered herself onto him. She needed to adjust herself around him, and by the gods was that an adjustment, she could feel him stretch her as she moved, feeling him completely fill her as she sunk herself all the way down. She loved watching the tortured look on his face as she moved slowly.

"You're so damn tight, sweetheart." He breathed heavily, staring at her. "I'm at your mercy."

She bit her lower lip nervously. "I've never been on top before. I understand the mechanics but—"

"This is all about you," he said. "Move however feels the best. I'm going to love every second of it no matter what you pick to do to me."

She began to ride him, experimenting with different angles. Each and every time she impaled herself on him, she could feel the subtle build of another orgasm. Clyous, who was still holding onto her hips, reached one hand forward and began to circle her bundle of nerves with his thumb. That touch combined with the penetration was like fire hitting her veins. She began to roll her hips, discovering happily that with him still inside her it pressed on just the right spot. She picked up the pace, sounds now coming out of her every few moments. She was never allowed to make sounds before, this was freeing, and the groans and gasps of breath coming from him were just the medicine she needed.

They seemed to hit their climax at the same time. She could feel herself clenching around him as she came down. He took a few moments longer to finish, his hips thrust upward as he emptied himself inside her, it was like her body was trying to pull every last drop from him. She collapsed on top of him, exhaustion hitting her finally. Clyous took her into his arms throwing the comforter over her as he sat there and held her.

"You're so fucking amazing," he murmured, kissing her forehead. "I should never have waited this long."

"I think we're both to blame for that." She laughed quietly, snuggling up closer to him. "But now we don't have to wait anymore."

"Give me about ten minutes, sweetheart." He laughed. "That's the only waiting I need."

"But what if that's too long?" she teased.

"We've got the rest of our lives to keep doing exactly this," she heard him say as his hand found its way to her bare breast. "But if that's too far away I can happily keep entertaining you until then."

She gasped as his thumb began circling her already sensitive nipple. "You don't have to do that."

"No, but I want to." He bent down to kiss her passionately. "I wasn't kidding. We have all night for me to worship you properly."

She was suddenly underneath him, his hands now freely roaming between her legs. With each touch of his fingers that familiar return of arousal hit her hard. She kissed him passionately, gasping as he plunged fingers inside her. She could feel just how wet she was, either that was mostly her or some of his last release. Something about that made it even more arousing as he worked. She could feel him start to harden as he worked her, every time she made a noise or arched her back to something he had done right, it spurred him on. Even though he took charge, she realized that he was still submitting to her. He was making her the priority, something she had never been before. This alone proved just how much he cared for her. She was important, he wanted her to be happy. It made her feel loved in a way she'd never felt before, it made her feel powerful. And, like he promised, they continued to make love to one another the rest of the night.

Chapter Sixty-Six

Bridget

The sun's rays reflected off of the mirror attached to her vanity straight into her eyes. Bridget woke up because of the brightness, rolling over and turning her back to the window. As she rolled, she bumped into Clyous who was fast asleep beside her. She smiled, gently draping an arm over his bare chest, memories of their activities from the night before flooding her mind. She smiled as she watched him sleep and found comfort in the steady rhythm of his breath. If there was ever a time in her life she could claim she had experienced bliss, it would be this moment. With a dull ache between her legs and a full heart, she felt truly happy and at peace. Part of her wished this moment would never end, that they could remain here in this room forever without having to worry about an impending war or their friends risking their lives daily. Not once in her life had she felt so comfortable and at peace inside this house.

She heard a gentle knocking on the front door downstairs. Who would be knocking at this hour? Must be someone looking for medical aid. Bridget reluctantly removed herself from her nice warm covers, dawning a robe, quietly making her way down the stairs. Knock. Knock. Hoping Clyous would remain asleep and upstairs she rushed to the door, he was technically a wanted man, and she did not want anyone to see him. Whoever it was could wait, she had every intention of politely reminding them what normal hours for visitors were.

Bridget reached the front door, turning the handle as she pulled it open. As soon as that door opened a crack his scent filled her nostrils, horror took over the peace she felt moments before. Panic immediately struck her like a bolt of Morrigan's lightning setting off every warning bell she had within her. He could not be here! Not now! Liam stood in her doorway, smiling at her like she was the most precious thing in the world. Fuck!

"Liam?" she asked nervously. "It's really early. Is everything alright?"

Liam smiled and answered, "I just wanted to see you. I hope I didn't wake you."

Trying to keep the door as closed as possible she wedged herself in the tiny space between the door frame. "It's really early Liam."

"I know, I'm sorry." He looked like he meant it. "I just couldn't stop thinking about you. I know last time I was here I probably crossed a line with how I reacted to your father, and even though I don't regret it I wanted you to know that you are safe with me. I wasn't trying to scare you."

"I know you weren't," she answered cautiously, mind whirling in every direction trying to find a way to end this conversation quickly and without raising his suspicions.

"I know I asked you a while ago, but you never answered. I respect your choice not to, but I just wanted to make the offer again for you to be my wife and my queen. I would make you happy and would take care of you. Nobody would ever lay their hands on you again, including your father."

"Liam." She sighed stepping out onto the porch. "I already told you no—"

She froze at the expression suddenly appearing on Liam's face. Her eyes focused on the subtle flare of his nostrils and his deep inhale of breath. His wolf had alerted him to a change in her scent. Before she could open her mouth, his eyes snapped to hers, she no longer stood with Liam but the crown prince, and he was promising violence.

"I smell another male all over you," Liam growled. "Who?"

"Liam!" she snapped, trying to draw his attention back to her. "That's none of your business!"

"Of course it's my business. You are mine!" He leaned forward, crowding her space and inhaling deeply, smelling her. "Is he still here?"

"I'm not yours!" Her wolf started growling in response to his, accepting his challenge. "What I do is none of your business."

"Move aside." The crown prince pushed the door open, sidestepping past her into her home, nose in the air trying to track down the perceived intruder.

"Liam!" she shouted, chasing after him. "Stop! You've lost your mind!"

"Where is he?" the prince snarled as he made for the stairs.

"Liam!" She reached to grab him but he was too fast. "You are not welcome in my house. Get out!"

They were at the top of the stairs now, Bridget trying to grab him or get in front of him as best she could, but Liam was too fast, too strong, too focused. Liam had made it to her bedroom door which was now mysteriously shut and locked. Good, that meant Clyous had at least heard them and was awake. The crown prince threw his shoulder into the door, shaking the house on impact. It budged slightly but did not give way. As he did it again, Bridget tried to grab his arm but was pushed off to the side. By the third time the door broke, revealing a half-naked Clyous trying to dress as quickly as possible.

Liam stood there for a moment staring at Clyous, anger rippling off him to such an extent she could almost see it. "I know you."

"Liam please—" she tried again, praying to whatever god could hear her to stop this impending violence.

"You were there that day when I flayed your twin's back open," Liam snarled. "How's she doing? Does she still dream of me?"

Clyous stood at his full height, bare chested with tunic in hand, staring down the Crown Prince of Oich and said with a smirk, "I've been too busy fucking your woman to ask."

Liam lunged for Clyous so fast, Bridget was hardly able to see Clyous swing. The blacksmith's fist connected to the prince's mouth with such a powerful impact, the blooded actually fell back and hit the ground. That was an impressive feat coming from a human. Clyous was strong for a human, hours beating an anvil had packed on muscle that had at least given him a fair chance. Bridget gasped at the sight of his arm, the bones in his hand and forearm now twisted at an odd angle from the impact. Clyous might be strong, but he essentially just punched a wall of stone. His arm was broken from that single strike.

Liam was on his feet in a flash, barreling towards the man she loved, every particle of his being promised death, but Bridget was faster than either of them. Using one of the techniques Catriona had taught her, Bridget dove for Liam's legs. Wrapping her arms around his thighs and using her momentum and body weight, she rolled forward dropping him face forward. Together, they hit the floor, Bridget rolling away from him and back onto her feet.

"Run!" she screamed at Clyous.

Clyous, realizing the severity of the situation did not argue, instead he vaulted over Liam and dashed through the door. Liam scrambled to his feet and shot after him, but Bridget stood in his way. Redirecting Liam's moving body sideways like Catriona had her drill dozens of times, she was able to throw Liam headfirst into the wall. She could feel her wolf clawing at its cage, an overwhelming desire to meet this challenge with the dominant wolf. Never had she felt so protective of anything, the desire for violence was foreign to her, but she was willing to come face to face with the man she had called her friend for so many years, she was willing to fight him, to hurt him before he would hurt one of her pack.

Being completely honest with herself, she wasn't sure she had what it took to take on a warrior like Liam, but that no longer mattered to her as she snarled his direction in warning. If he didn't stay down and submit to her wolf, she would unleash herself on him until he did. She was no longer the sad little girl who submitted to every single one of his whims, she was stronger than that girl.

"Move!" Liam warned as he stared at her in disbelief. "I don't want to hurt you."

"No!" she snarled back.

The challenge was made. Liams fangs began to elongate as he snarled at her, the usual pull of the dominant wolf no longer tugged at her as it had in the past. Instead of submitting, her wolf snarled back, ready to meet this predator head on. She did not back down. They looked at each other for maybe a second before the prince lunged. Bridget grabbed the collar of his jacket and while falling backwards she used his momentum and threw him up and over her. Liam went flying, crashing into the door across the hall.

A look of shock momentarily passed over Liam's face before he made to get up. Picking herself up she scrambled back into her room towards her open window. Mid leap she shifted, the auburn wolf crashing through the window down to the ground a story below. Her paws hit the cobblestones before the pieces of glass. Bridget spotted Clyous mounted on the horse, cradling his broken arm.

"We need to get to the forest!" Bridget commanded, letting that unfamiliar power ripple through her. *"I'll be right behind you."*

Clyous nodded, kicking his horse into motion towards the other side of town. He couldn't fight Liam like that, not unless she could somehow heal him, but she knew within a matter of moments the blooded guards would be descending upon them, then Liam would have them. Liam would rip Clyous limb from limb and force her to watch. Their best chance was to get as close to Collie as they could before they were inevitably caught. Bridget could keep pace with a horse in her wolf form, maybe even outlast the beast. As long as Clyous could get a decent enough head start, they should be able to make it.

Bridget glanced back up at the window, her eyes focusing on Liam. The crown prince stood there amidst the destruction of what was once her house, glaring down at her as if seeing her for the very first time. A dominant wolf, capable of matching his strength, and willing to challenge his authority. No, he saw her now for who she always was, who she was too afraid to show anyone. She was not the submissive wolf he and everyone else believed her to be.

"What's going on?!" Grace's voice demanded through their mental bond. *"I expected you to be enjoying yourself, not wanting to kill him."*

"It's Liam!" Bridget shot back. *"He's coming for us. Clyous is hurt!"*

"Where are you?" Grace's voice was now panicked.

"Still in the city." Bridget was still staring down Liam, who was now glancing in the direction Clyous had gone.

"Get as close to Collie as you can! We're coming for you!"

Bridget snapped her teeth and barked a warning at him before turning her back to him. Another insult, another challenge. She took off bounding down the cobblestone street catching up with Clyous effortlessly. A howl came from behind them, echoing through the buildings as they ran. The ripples of power that emitted from that sound was enough to put her fur on end. That was a command from a lead wolf, a call for aid. A chorus of howls responded from around the city.

All her senses were going haywire. Where a dominant wolf's command was used to bow her into submission, she now felt the need to rebel. Where a wolf's cry for help used to put her on the defensive, now she felt the desire to fight. Her wolf had challenged a dominant wolf, and in that short amount of time she had not only managed to throw him around but had escaped. She no longer bowed to him. She had proven them to be equals. These facts would have scared her half to death, but they only added to her need to fight.

She could sense Liam had shifted and was now pursuing Clyous. About six other blooded, guards she assumed, joined the chase. Side by side, Clyous pushed his horse through the city streets as Bridget bounded next to him. She glanced up at him, how he kept his arm pulled tight against his torso. Anger seared through her, she wanted to stop and turn around and fight, but she knew she didn't have a chance against that many, especially not with Clyous. That injury, that damned broken arm could be the defining factor if they were caught. Rage pushed her on as she maneuvered ahead of the horse, pushing a few inattentive citizens out of the way so Clyous wouldn't have to slow down.

Finally, they broke free of the city's confines, gaining speed on the open ground and making their way towards the tree line. Bridget glanced back, Liam and the guards were slowly gaining on them, but they were still some distance away. She ran, pushing herself harder than she ever had before. The very presence of her wolf kept the horse moving at a terrified pace, not wanting her to get too near. Good, maybe they could make it close enough. Their best chance was to make it into the trees, the flat ground gave the wolves the advantage over the poor horse, but the hills and dodging of trees might even out the playing field. They had to try.

Part Three

Collie: City of Hope

Chapter Sixty-Seven

Rama

"Where are you?" Grace's voice suddenly echoed through his head, causing him to drop his bow as he gripped his head in pain.

"Ow, what the fuck?" Rama shot back, rubbing his eyes as if it could get her voice out of his head quicker. *"I'm hunting by the river. What do you want?"*

"Bridget and Clyous need help!" Grace's voice now seemed anxious.

Suddenly, several other energies began to push on his mind, all felt different from the next. Grace was definitely there, her icy presence at the center of all of them.

"What do you mean?" Danny's voice came suddenly.

"Where is my brother?" Catriona's presence entered his mind, it was the exact opposite of Grace's, the burning heat from her energy seared his insides.

"The crown prince is hot on their tail. They're maybe ten miles from Collie now," Grace explained. *"Menolayous and I are closer, we need you to get here. Clyous is hurt."*

"Gladly!" Catriona shot down their communication bond.

"We're on our way from the main gate," Danny answered.

"Tell Flinn to send some men with you!" Rama looked around, he was closer to Grace than Danny was, maybe by a few miles.

"Too late, Cat took off the second you mentioned the crown prince," Danny answered as if he were running.

"That piece of shit hurt my brother!" Catriona snapped, her words literally burning into their bond. *"He's mine."*

"This is not going to end well if we're all going off half-cocked!" Rama abandoned his attempt to hunt, running in the direction Grace had said Bridget and Clyous were. *"Can we talk to them yet?"*

"I can, you're all out of their range still," Grace replied.

"We don't have a choice at this point," Menolayous cut in, *"Grace and I should buy you guys some time to get here, but please don't slow down. I'm not exactly keen on fighting off a dominant wolf on the hunt and six blooded guards."*

Rama ran south, pushing through the thick brush for a more direct route. He didn't have time to take the pathways if they were really that close. He needed to get to them, Grace and Menolayous couldn't handle that many alone. He had no idea what shape Bridget and Clyous were in. These were his people, his family, he wouldn't let them fight alone.

He kept this pace for maybe twenty minutes before he heard it, the howls of the hunt. The large crashing of bodies through the trees indicated that Menolayous and Grace had not caught up with them yet, but they had to be close. It also meant that Clyous and Bridget were still in motion, that they hadn't been caught yet. He sent a silent prayer up to whatever god was listening as he made his way towards the sounds of the chase.

Rama used the downhill momentum to make ground; he was nearing them with every step. The sound of large bodies crashing through the brush had ceased, meaning they had all stopped running. His heart dropped as he pushed himself harder, now steering himself towards the sound of a fight. He could hear them now, snarling and snapping as if they were fighting each other. Sprinting up the next hill he saw them. The large auburn wolf he recognized as Bridget was actively engaging in a three versus one fight. Her wolf, at least double the size of the others, was putting up a huge fight. A small spark of pride ignited in him as he continued to move. Clyous was nearby dealing with two guards in human form, actively engaging in sword play, but something was wrong, one of his arms was pinned tightly against him. He only had one arm to fight with.

A black wolf as large as Bridget approached the scene, issuing an unheard command. Two of the wolves were able to pin Bridget down while the third shifted, rushing in and slapping a silver pronged bracelet around Bridget's front leg. Rama watched in horror as Bridget was forced to shift, screaming in pain at the process. The silver that punctured her flesh now held her wolf at bay as the guards shifted and seized her. Blood trickling down her arm as she fought against them.

The guards grabbed Clyous too, holding the blade of a sword to his throat, warning Bridget to stop fighting against them. They forced Clyous to his knees, grabbing him by the hair and making him face the dominant wolf. The black wolf shifted last into none other than the Crown Prince of Oich who was now stalking towards Bridget.

"Stop fighting!" the prince commanded Bridget. "I didn't want to use the cuff on you, but you gave me no choice!"

"Bullshit! You brought it to use it." She still struggled against the hands that held her, "You could have at least done me the honor of fighting me wolf to wolf instead of your trickery!"

The prince actually looked at her as if he was upset. "I will never hurt you, Bridget. Him on the other hand…"

The prince turned to Clyous now, kneeling down so he came face to face with him. Rama was proud to see the expression on the young man's face, he looked so much like his sister then, defiant and fearless.

"What's your name?" The prince glared.

"Clyous," he answered. "Yours?"

The prince smirked but did not answer. Instead, the prince reached out grabbing Clyous's injured arm and twisted. Clyous to his credit did not shout out or make a sound. His body did jolt forward from the pain, but he was held firm by the guards. Clyous leveled a cold look at the prince refusing to show just how much pain that move had caused, yes, this was definitely Catriona's twin.

"Liam please," Bridget was pleading. "Leave him alone."

"I cannot allow another to take what is mine," the prince answered. "You seemed so willing to fight me until I got ahold of this boy, now you beg for me to spare him?"

"She's not yours," Clyous spoke up. "She is her own, she belongs to nobody but herself."

The prince struck him, eliciting a scream from Bridget. Rama had no other choice; there wasn't a guarantee anyone else was close enough to come to their aid. Guessing he was doing this alone, Rama began to move towards them.

"Liam please! I love him," Bridget sobbed. "Please don't!"

"You should be ashamed of yourself for having lain with someone as lowly as him, you have tainted your honor beyond repair," Liam seethed.

Rama could see the prince's body language shift then, fuck! That was not the right thing for her to say, this man was clearly unhinged.

"I would let them go if I were you." Rama called out to them, resting his axe on his shoulder. "You're in my kingdom now, Princeling, and those are my subjects."

All of the blooded looked at Rama as he approached. He was most interested in the prince and how he reacted, once the recognition of who Rama was hit, the prince began to smile wickedly. This was going to be an interesting fight to say the least.

"Your kingdom?" The prince strolled in his direction.

"Mine. Since you have such a problem understanding the concept of possession." Rama nodded, mimicking his smile. "Have you failed to realize I have stolen this from you too."

"So, you must be Rama, the Prince of Thieves." The prince stopped approaching, now eyeing Rama up and down.

"King of Thieves," Rama corrected. "I've got a higher rank than you do."

Rama was satisfied at how the prince's expression changed into something more feral. Getting under his skin would hopefully throw the blooded off enough Rama might walk out of this alive. Maybe.

"Where are your brothers?"

"Oh, they're keeping busy." Rama winked. "I've sent them to lead a siege against your city while I keep you trapped out here."

Rama could see the unease ripple through the guards, even the prince shifted uncomfortably for a moment.

"You don't have the men," the prince snorted.

"Maybe you are smarter than you look. Here's an offer for you, me for them." Rama looked down at the prince, only a few inches shorter than him.

"Not interested." The prince smirked. "I could have all three of you today."

"There you go dashing my hopes that you had any intelligence in that big head of yours." Rama acted disappointed. "You won't survive all three of us. Wolf or not you're smaller than I am, and you know what she is capable of—"

"Shut up!" the prince snarled.

This surprised Rama, was the Crown Prince of Oich protecting Bridget? He didn't want Rama to finish the sentence because the guards didn't know. If they did, he would be forced to do something about her, probably by his father. He looked at Bridget again, realizing now that all she was wearing was a thin robe. Fucking shit! The prince had caught them having sex, that's why he had pursued them all the way out here. This scenario continued to get worse by the second.

"How about this, Princeling," Rama changing tactics, "fight me. One on one. I win; you let them go. You win; do as you were planning to do. Refuse my offer, and I start talking, in detail, about everything I know about our mutual friend."

Panic flashed through the prince's eye for only a moment before answering, "Done."

A smile spread across his face as Rama readied his battle axe. Prince Liam unsheathed his sword, and without pause, lunged at him. The prince was quick, but Rama could match him. Dodging the first swipe of the sword, Rama pushed the hilt of his axe into the prince, knocking him back. As the prince recovered, Rama threw his axe up overhead and brought the blade down with both hands. The prince dodged at the last minute letting the axe hit the dirt.

Rama took a strong kick to the side that sent him rolling. He was on his feet as the prince charged him, Rama caught the prince's sword hand, pulling the man close enough to headbutt him. Rama took the sword tossing it out of the way. As a man, the prince could not match him, although it felt like he was hitting a boulder. With a laugh Rama watched as the prince shifted, apparently realizing it too.

The wolf came for him. Rama grabbed its jaws holding them back so they couldn't snap around his throat. The wolf reached forward, raking its sharp claws down Ramas's front. He could feel his skin rip open and the warmth of blood seep down him. Anger replacing the pain, Rama delivered an overpowered blow to the wolf's head.

The prince broke away from the force of the blow only to dance around the giant and reengage. Rama felt the fur brush against him moments before the teeth sank into his thigh. The teeth did not linger; they accomplished their goal. Rama looked down to see blood now gushing out of his upper leg next to his groin. The asshole just bit through his artery.

"No!" he could hear Bridget scream.

Rama watched the wolf that now paced before him. Clever fucker was now waiting, Rama figured he had only a few minutes left before he bled out.

"Come on then!" Rama challenged. He wasn't out yet.

Rama continued to stand there for a moment as the wolf watched him. He could feel the lightheadedness come on a moment later. He couldn't push the attack. Physically, he didn't think his body would make it a few more steps. He was losing a lot of blood from his two wounds. He also knew the wolf was waiting to see him weaken before reengaging. Rama was still in the fight, fuck it, he took a knee.

Just as he watched the wolf rear up to come for him, a lone figure put itself between the teeth and him. Rama recognized Menolayous immediately, his brother facing down the wolf, twin axes in hand. He watched as his brother expertly dodged the fangs, bringing up the edge of his blades and slicing into the wolf's face. The black wolf stumbled back, shaking off the blow. Blood now flowed freely down the wolf's cheek as it narrowed its eyes at this new threat.

Just as the guards began to move in their direction Rama could hear the distinct crack of a whip. From behind a tree Grace had appeared, aiming for the guard that looked as if he were going to head straight for Menolayous. The claws of the whip sliced down the guard's torso, creating several deep slashes that went through the guard's tunic. Blood appeared just as the guard looked down, eliciting an enraged growl. Rama realized then that the tendrils of her whip were barbed with silver blades. Fucking clever.

"What's the matter? Don't you want to play?" Grace teased, her whip now moving freely beside her mimicking the same movement as a snake trying to move through the leaves.

The guards snarled at her in unison, another one breaking off to join the one just injured as they prowled in her direction. She watched them carefully as they approached, never once letting her whip stop moving. The two guards circled around her, the one behind her shot out as if to grab her. Grace was faster. In one fluid motion she spun, bringing the tail of her whip down across his face, shredding his cheek with her silver blades. The other guard moved as she spun around, her whip wrapping around his throat. She shortened the whip between her hands and pushed it down, bringing the guard to the dirt from the tug. As soon as that guard hit the ground another one charged from the group that held their healer and blacksmith as prisoners. Faster than her whip, she retrieved a dagger from somewhere hidden on her, throwing it at the approaching blooded. It sank deep into his shoulder, dropping him to his knees with a cry of rage and pain.

Menolayous was now actively engaged with the prince, rolling away from the beast as it swiped at him. Rama watched his brother swing his axes at the creature's hide, narrowly missing it. Their odds of survival were certainly better than they were moments ago, but with Grace taking on three guards while Menolayous fought with the giant black wolf alone, it still wasn't looking good. Rama had to do something; he couldn't leave them to fight alone. Rama tried to stand, with everything he had, but his body couldn't bear his weight. Looking down, Rama could now see he knelt in a pool of blood, his leg still seeping. Fuck this shit. Rama felt cold, as if a winter breeze was moving around the woods specifically targeting him.

Just as the dizziness began cloud his vision, Rama heard crashing coming from behind him. Suddenly, fire erupted from the ground, snaking its way past him and working its way towards the black wolf. The prince and the guards all jumped back at the flames in shock. Menolayous disengaged from the prince, making it past the fissure of flame before it separated the black wolf from everyone else. He proceeded to engage with the three guards Grace was beating back with her whip. Bridget had taken this opportunity to break free from her captors, twisting her arm free and striking one guard in the groin. The guard doubled over as she spun on the other, taking him down.

The prince stood there watching the chaos take hold as fast as the flames had appeared. The wolf's black head swung around wildly, trying to avoid the flame which now surrounded him. As he continued to fight off the effects of blood loss, Rama couldn't help but laugh, the sound of it echoed through the forest as he watched the prince shift back into his human form. Wide eyed, the prince stared at him through the flames.

"Now you're going to die, Princeling." Rama continued to laugh. "She's found you now."

As if to answer the prince's unspoken question, another vein of wildfire separated him from his guards. The prince now found himself standing in a tunnel of fire, the only open area to escape was now being blocked.

Rama stared at his sister-in-law; it was as if he was staring at the War Goddess herself. Catriona stood blocking the path, her white hair unbraided and whipping freely in the wind and flame. Her silver eyes locked on the man she had promised to kill. She held her arms out and pointed her palms towards the ground. Flame billowed from her hands; she fed the wall of flames into something larger.

Bridget was now to him, Clyous was helping him sit down so she could get to his wounds. Rama watched as Bridget's hand touched his wounds. He saw the glow, then felt the warmth as her magic started to stitch his artery back together. Rama looked back at Catriona and the prince; this was going to be the showdown of the century, and he was there to witness it.

"So, you survived our last little encounter," the prince said with a snarl.

"Unfortunately for you." Catriona looked eerily calm, her mark glowed as her magic continued to feed her flames.

"Just my luck, both the women I've been searching for in one place." The prince looked around at his men who were still fighting with Menolayous and Grace. "And another whore to drag home with us. The barracks are going to be busy tonight."

Rama literally cringed at hearing that. This fucker was so messed up in the head it wasn't even funny. Looking at him through the flames, Rama wasn't sure if the prince was bluffing or serious. Oich was well known for having laws against rape, not from a sense of kindness but rather that the blooded didn't want to breed and taint their familial lines. Rama had heard stories of soldiers breaking these laws, and the prince executed them. But he had also seen the prince publicly torture others, had heard stories of the carnage the young prince and his men left behind them. The prince would most likely spare Bridget from the other guards, but not from himself. There seemed to be a sense of possession the prince held over her, a desire to claim her as his. How far would he go to stake that claim? It was such a sickening thought, such a disgusting promise. This was exactly why he couldn't abandon the fight against Oich and the crown. This cruelty needed to end, they needed to protect their people.

The prince moved, shifting mid stride he went straight for Catriona. As if anticipating this, Catriona had unsheathed her two short swords, holding the blades in a reverse grip. As the wolf neared, she rolled underneath him, the tips of her swords grazing his underbelly. As he recovered, so did she, and with unmatched speed she charged at him. Shifting back into human form at the right moment, the prince dodged her blow, grabbed her around the throat and slammed her into the dirt. Rama recognized this move; he had done it to her a dozen times to prepare her for this. He prayed now she could handle it.

Still gripping her throat, he mounted her before she could squirm too far away from him. "I'm really quite glad you survived our last encounter. Gives me the opportunity to really sink my teeth into you this time. I've got a few friends who have been begging to meet you."

With both hands on her throat, the prince drug Catriona down a few inches, closer, squeezing his hands together tightly. "You think you knew pain last time?"

So fast that Rama barely saw it, Catriona had thrown both of her legs over his shoulders connecting her feet behind his head. His arms were now locked and trapped. As she squeezed her legs and arched her back, his grip on her throat loosened, pushing him father away from her. She rolled, taking him with her. Rama let out a shout of triumph, pride flowing through him as much as Bridget's magic was. Their training had indeed paid off.

Danny appeared out of the tree line, rushing up to the flames as if expecting them to let him in. Instead, he was met with a sudden flare up, as if the flames were warning him to stay back. Frustrated, Danny stopped trying to advance and instead looked around. Spotting Rama nearby he was suddenly beside them, looking over Rama's wounds with worry. Rama looked at his brother for a moment, trying to figure out why he was just now appearing.

"Where the fuck have you been?" Rama winced as Bridget continued working on his leg. The blood had finally stopped.

"She's a lot faster than me, okay?" Danny glanced at the ever-evolving sparring match beyond the flame wall.

"Aren't you going to go try and help her?" Bridget asked distractedly.

Danny watched his woman for a moment through the flames before turning back to the others. "She won't let me in. She wants to take him in a fight before she burns him to death. She wants to prove to herself she can take him. Besides, she's beating his ass."

They all glanced up just as Catriona sent a wall of flames at the prince, catching his arm on fire. Panic appeared to seize the prince momentarily before realizing Catriona was coming for him again. Seemingly done fighting hand to hand with a woman who clearly was out for his head, the prince made a very rash decision. He turned and dove through the wall of flame rolling as he hit the ground on the other side. The prince's guards were to him then, having given up fighting with Menolayous and Grace. Catriona stopped and glared at them through the flames, eyeing the prince up and down as if he was a coward. The prince was singed and bleeding from his wounds but otherwise appeared to be fine. The roll had extinguished the fire that had caught his clothes.

Rama watched as his glare went from Catriona to Bridget. Bridget, with her hands still busy healing Rama, looked up and growled a warning.

Making it very clear to him that these were her people, and he needed to stay away. A sound came from behind them. Rama glanced back to see a dozen or so of his rebels charging towards them. The rebels blew on a war pipe, a long golden rod stood over them a few feet in the air. It emitted a low but loud noise, sounding the order to attack. The green flag of Collie rose above their heads as they charged, the two crossed battle axes hovered above the trees and stood brightly in the sunlight.

The prince and guards watched with wide eyes as the rebels approached, taking off back towards Oich in retreat. Once the blooded were gone, Catriona let her flames die. She was breathing heavily but looked mostly unharmed. The warband suddenly dissipated into thin air. Grace strolled towards them, the smuggest look on her face.

"Nice party trick," Catriona said to her, still standing in the same place.

"I could say the same to you." Grace winked at her approvingly. "Way to turn up the heat on the prince there."

Looking around it appeared that they had survived a forest fire. No more leaves remained on any trees and all the foliage touched by Catriona's fire had been spared. The tree trunks and dirt had been kissed by the flames and were now black and charred on the surface.

Rama whistled at the sight of the destruction, impressed. "Brings a whole new meaning to hot-headed."

"How can you still be making jokes?" Grace eyed him up and down, taking in his injuries. "Bridget, you look like you're about to pass out."

"I'm tapped out at the moment." Bridget slumped to the ground, finally removing the silver pronged cuff, blood running down her arm from the incisions it had made. "But your artery has stopped bleeding. I call that a win."

Grace stepped forward and took the cuff from her. "We need to get you all back to the village to rest and patch you up."

"Sounds like a good plan," Danny chimed in.

"Maybe for all of you, but I feel fit as a fiddle," Rama teased.

Rama looked over at Bridget who stared back with tears in her eyes. Before he could say anything, he could feel her tiny arms wrap around his neck in an embrace. His heart melted at the kindness of it. Wincing, he wrapped his uninjured arm around her returning the embrace.

"Thank you," she whispered in his ear, "for saving him."

"Don't you mean both of you?" He whispered back, she didn't answer.

After breaking apart, the group managed to get Rama to his feet and started heading towards Collie. Thankful they were all alive and well, mostly well, he replayed the events of the day in his head as they walked. The prince was cunning, but he had a weakness, Bridget. Even after seeing her with his sworn enemies, he protected her. Rama could almost take him one on one, but the prince was smart. Willing to wait. Catriona almost had him too, but he was stronger than her. Without her flames he wasn't sure who would win. He felt a strategy brewing.

Chapter Sixty-Eight

Grace

"What was his promise again?" Grace asked Catriona as all four of them stood in the alleyway, staring up at the large building beside them.

The four of them had managed to sneak into the capital city early this morning. The plan was to carve out some retribution for their friends, who had been hunted down like dogs by the crown prince himself. With the help of her powers, Grace was able to mask their presence into the city well enough. Catriona was still livid at not having been able to kill the crown prince after that, Grace herself was a little testy about all of the guards managing to escape. This was all part of Rama's grand plan, to start hitting the crown where it hurt, their capital city. The more chaos they could incite, the more they could disrupt the flow, the more attention they brought upon themselves. Which kept the attention off of the few stragglers left trying to flee to Collie from all ends of the kingdom.

"I believe he called you a whore." Danny smiled wickedly at the two women in front of him, this man lived for chaos Grace was beginning to realize, he was a perfect match for Catriona there were no doubts.

"No, right after that?" Grace contemplated for a moment.

"You're not helping, brother," Menolayous said quietly. "If you get them too riled up they might burn the whole city down."

"That's a problem?" Danny feigned innocence. "I don't see a problem."

"He promised to drag us back to the barracks so his men could stay busy all night," Catriona answered a little too cheerfully ignoring the men, pacing in the alleyway like a wildcat prepared to hunt down fleeing game.

"Well, we're here." Grace winked at Menolayous, the only one in their group who seemed to be looking out for danger instead of creating more problems. "Let's keep them busy, shall we?"

"My pleasure." Catriona smiled, lifting her hood to reveal her bright white hair, a sure-fire way to get the guards to recognize her. There was no holding back now.

Catriona stepped from the shadows and approached the entrance of the barracks, facing them head on as she would any opponent on the battlefield. Grace walked by her side, allowing her illusions to drop completely. There was no more hiding for them, they were here to fuck shit up. They wanted everyone to know who had come for them. The crown prince wasn't the only one allowed to make threats, this was theirs. The boys followed several feet behind them. They walked in through the front entrance into what looked like a dining hall. At least twenty guards sat at the long table eating a meal. There were a few servants present, still bringing out the food. The unblooded looked upon them warily, moving from the hall as quickly as possible.

"Disgusting vermin," one of the older guards was overheard talking to another. "The Moon God will not be pleased with them, having stooped so low as to try and breed with the gutter rats."

"Relax." The younger guard laughed. "They just want to get their dicks wet. I doubt she'll even make it until the end of the week."

"It's the principal of the matter," the older guard grumbled. "They soil themselves with her filth."

"You older religious nuts are boring." The younger guard took a drink from his cup. "You act all pious, but the Moon God doesn't give a shit about who sticks their dick in what."

"I think a bear trap might be a good place to stick it." Danny called from the back of the hall. "Or each other's asses."

All the guards stopped talking as the rebels approached. "Who are you?"

"Oh, just a couple of whores apparently." Grace batted her eyelashes at the man. "The prince sent us."

Grace could practically feel the eyeroll Menolayous gave at that comment. She also knew for a fact that both of the men behind them were prepared for a fight at a moment's notice. Danny was more willing to have this engagement while Menolayous was more nervous. She knew it was not because they couldn't handle themselves in a fight, she had proven that true enough. Regardless of their opponents being blooded, the girl's magic leveled out the playing field quite nicely. What she knew bothered her lover more than anything was the context of why they were here. The prince's comments had rattled him, unsurprising considering his past. Menolayous knew what men like this were capable of, and the fact Grace and Catriona had targets painted on their backs, it made him all the more nervous when dealing with their enemies. Although threats from the Crown Prince of Oich in this nature went against the very laws of Oich, it was not unheard of. The prince was beyond reasoning when dealing with them at this point, his rage took over all logic. Who knew what he would be willing to do.

"Did he now?" The guard who spoke stood to face them.

"Yes. He wanted us to keep you busy." Catriona smiled at him innocently before unleashing death upon them.

Raising both her arms in one fluid motion, fire erupted down the line of seated guards, all of them suddenly engulfed in her white flames and crumbled to ash. What servants had remained began to scream and run from the hall, just as Grace hoped they would. At the end of the day they didn't want to harm innocents. They just wanted to kill the guards and send a very strong message to the crown that this type of warfare would not be tolerated any longer. They would no longer be able to torture and crush the will of their people.

The boys moved, coming around the sides to engage with a few guards emerging from nearby rooms brandishing weapons. Grace and Catriona in unison now moved from room to room, checking for anyone who could be hiding. It appeared most of the guards at these barracks had been at the table enjoying their dinner before they were crisped to death.

Grace reached for a door handle, pushing against the solid wooden door. It wouldn't budge. She put her shoulder into it, still nothing. The door was locked from the inside. Grace whistled to Catriona, signaling her to come over. Catriona visually examined the door for a moment, inspecting the door lock. She simply grasped the door handle firmly allowing her flame to cover her hand. After a few seconds, Grace watched as the metal and wood began to bend and warp with the heat, Catriona stood there as if melting a door open was a common everyday occurrence. Catriona winked at Grace before pulling the softened metal handle completely from the wood frame. Grace wasted no time booting the door where the handle had been.

The wooden door flew open, Grace entered the room swiftly with her dagger in hand, Catriona was hot on her heels. Someone was in here, that was for sure, someone wanted to keep them out. Grace was unsure if it was a guard or an innocent servant, that was the only reason why Catriona hadn't completely engulfed the door with her flames. They didn't want to hurt innocents, but they were prepared in case they met an enemy. Grace froze a few feet inside the room, shock and disgust now taking hold of her. Grace had overestimated their entry into this place, the women were not prepared for the sight they had walked into.

The room appeared to be sleeping quarters of a few different guards. There were a few beds in the room, other than that there was no real furniture. There was nothing special about this room, save for the terrified looking guards in the back corner reaching for their swords. This was not what shook Grace, the guards meant very little to her in the grand scheme of things. No, it was the young woman who lay there on the centermost bed.

The young woman lay unmoving, seemingly motionless. It was the blood that caught Grace's attention first, then the unnatural stillness. Grace took another step inside, her dagger raised in the direction of a guard, but her eyes scanned the woman. Grace almost vomited right there. The woman lay on her back, completely naked and spread bare to the room. Her face was every shade of black and blue; Grace wasn't able to discern any particular facial features through the extent of her injuries. One of the woman's arms was broken, twisted at such an extreme angle that she could see where the bones were separated underneath her blood-flecked flesh. Bite marks, both animal and human covered her breasts and torso along with many other scratches and scrapes. Her legs were the worst of it, her legs had been forced open so violently her hips no longer seemed to be in their sockets. Blood covered every inch of her lower body, varying shades of it from different assaults, and what was left of between her legs was a gory unrecognizable mess.

Ice-cold fury came over Grace, seeing what had been done to the woman. She had been trapped here with these monsters for days by the looks of it, enduring unspeakable things. There was a slight rise and fall of the woman's chest, so slight she almost missed it. Thank the gods. Grace could feel the boiling hot rage rolling off her friend as Catriona took in the sight, narrowing her eyes on the blooded guards standing in the back of the room. Grace knew what was coming to them, like mice now caught in their trap, they had nowhere they could run.

The two women split up, approaching the guards from either side like two predators closing in on their prey. Grace held her dagger at the ready as Catriona drew one of her short swords. The guards glanced between the two of them, trying to decide the best course of action. They were looking between them, trying to figure out which one they would have an easier time taking, trying to calculate their best chances of survival. They picked Grace, raising their swords and swinging sideways with that unnatural speed gifted to all moon touched. Unlucky for them, the women were also gifted, their magic allowed them to move fast too. Grace stepped sideways bringing the edge of her dagger across one guard's forearm before driving her dagger through his eye and into his skull. Simultaneously, Catriona stepped forward slicing the other man at his groin, tearing apart clothing and flesh all the way up to the bastard's neck. The beast collapsed to the ground, bleeding profusely.

"You don't deserve a quick death." Grace spat on the dying man, stepping over him to get to the woman. "It's okay. You're safe now."

Catriona rushed over as well, taking visual stock of the woman's injuries. Grace wasn't too confident she was going to make it, there was too much blood loss, and too many bones were broken. Even if Bridget were here Grace wasn't sure she would survive. The woman stared up at them weakly, her breathing labored from what Grace guessed were broken ribs. Grace stared into her eyes, amazed that she could get them open at all with how swollen they appeared. The pupils were different sizes, one very large taking up almost all of the color while the other was so small she could barely see it. Blood and clear fluid seemed to be leaking from her ears and nose as she stared up at them, her skull on the left side appeared to be dented in slightly. No, there was nothing they could do for her now.

"Kill me." The woman's voice was barely audible, more like an exhale of breath. "Please."

Grace and Catriona shared a look, Grace did not like the idea of killing her but letting her die slowly from her injuries felt wrong. Letting the woman linger in such a state seemed cruel. By the looks of it, this poor woman had been raped by several different guards, if not all of them. She could understand not wanting to live after something like that even if she was capable of recovering from the physical wounds. She's been in Menolayous's head enough times to know that surviving wasn't the hardest part, it was living with it afterwards. Who was she to make this woman to live with something like that?

Catriona nodded to Grace, taking the woman's hand gently. Grace took a deep breath before thrusting the tip of her dagger through the soft part of her throat. The least she could do was make the poor woman's death quick. Blood trickled down the blade until Grace removed it from her flesh, whatever remained left in her body came pouring out through this new wound. Catriona let out a pained snarl, releasing the woman's hand before kicking a guard's lifeless body.

"I fucking hate all of them!" Catriona shouted, still kicking the lifeless corpse of the guard.

Grace covered the woman with a nearby blanket. "Me too."

497

Danny and Menolayous rushed in with their weapons raised, they must have heard Catriona shouting and assumed they were in danger. Danny immediately lowered his weapon, relieved that the girls were fine. Grace watched Menolayous as his eyes moved to the dead woman on the bed then to the dead guard Catriona was kicking. She could sense the darkness pulling at him, he knew exactly what had happened here.

"Cat!" Grace barked, getting her friend's attention. "Let's finish what we came here to do."

"Right." Catriona nodded, striding back out to the dining hall.

Grace gently took Menolayous's hand, pulling him from the room. Danny followed closely behind, the three of them moving towards the barracks' entrance. Grace watched as Catriona walked to the center of the dining hall, completely engulfing herself in her flames as she went. With every step she took, another small patch of fire ignited. Within moments the walls were being consumed by Catriona's distinct white flames.

Grace, Danny, and Menolayous ran from the building, stopping in the street to look back. Grace watched as the white flames began to pour out of every window and doorway, sending a column of smoke straight into the sky. A crowd was gathering now to watch the burning of the barracks, both blooded civilians and slaves alike. Catriona strode from the fire carrying the banner of Oich, a red and black flag with the emblems of downward facing sword with a crescent moon above the hilt. Catriona's casual walk from the flames caught the attention of all, surprise and fear now thickening the air at the sight of her magic. Catriona stared at them, defiantly holding up the banner and ripping it in two. This action elicited gasps from the crowd, defiling a flag was an act of treason as was burning down a building, Grace assumed, frustrated at their priorities. Catriona tossed it back into her flames.

"The crown will pay for everything they have done, for all the rapes and murders, for all the torture they've put our people through!" Catriona shouted at them. "Go ahead and spread the word, let the king and his precious son know that I'm coming for them. That King Rama of Collie is coming for them."

Distant howls went up throughout the city, and what was remaining of the capital's guards were now alerted to the fire. A little late to the party Grace figured but, now they knew. The crowd continued to watch Catriona as she walked to them, glaring at them all.

"Not so great with speeches, are you?" Grace mocked.

498

"You can do them from now on, Princess," Catriona sneered. "They got the point."

"We need to leave now," Menolayous spoke quietly. "Before the other guards get here."

"Can I burn the city down as we go?" Catriona asked Danny, who only laughed.

"No," Grace interjected. "Too many innocent people."

"Soon, I promise." Danny kissed Catriona's forehead, wearing an unsettling chaotic smile.

"You are both insane." Menolayous pulled Grace along, taking an alleyway away from the burning building and crowd.

"So?" Catriona asked, following closely behind.

They moved as a group, Grace twisting her illusions around them so they were not easily spotted in the chaos now erupting in the city streets. People were running either to the burning building to help put it out or running from it to spread the news of what had happened. Guards in their wolf form sprinted past them as well, failing to recognize them thanks to Grace's powers. Grace could overhear some of the conversations happening on the street. The talk of the white-haired witch burning down the guards' barracks was the news on everyone's lips, but everything else seemed to vary based on the allegiance of the one talking. Unsurprisingly, those loyal to the crown spoke of all the death and destruction Catriona had brought to the beloved city guards, how she must be an evil demon sent to kill them all. But mostly, Grace was hearing talk of the rebellion, and how they were finally making a stand to protect the people. This surprised Grace, even the blooded nobles spoke as if they agreed with the rebellion fighting back against the evils of the crown. Maybe they had more support than they were aware of.

Chapter Sixty-Nine

Morrigan

With frightening efficiency, Morrigan pulled back on the ice shard in her hand, using the strength of her body and magic to vault the improvised spear in the direction of the approaching tribeswoman. The ice shard flew from her grip, spiraling through the darkness before it pierced through the woman's flesh. With the ice spear now protruding through her chest, the woman collapsed before dark blood began to trickle from the wound.

Others quickly jumped over her, continuing to advance on the sorceress. With a thousand years of existence and battle-hardened experience under her belt, Morrigan stood her ground with no fear. These enemies were but flies, insignificant to her and the mission at hand; and so, she batted them away like flies.

Raising her arm in the direction of the oncoming vermin, electricity danced at her fingertips. A rather ugly looking male approached her, not ten feet away. His dark matted hair ignited as her bolt passed through him, eyes going blank as his flesh charred from the inside. He too fell to the dirt, a steaming hole now visible where her magic passed through him.

The next two were now before her, closing what distance there was between them. Morrigan thrust her spear forward with both hands, lowering her center of gravity. As the tribesman inadvertently pushed himself into the sharp point of her spear, the momentum and Morrigan's position had his body flying up and over her and landing somewhere behind her. Morrigan ripped her spear from that corpse, swinging the butt at the other approaching blooded.

The creature dodged her spear, feinting off to the side and slicing a bone blade towards her throat. Morrigan fell backwards, narrowly avoiding the sharpened bone, bringing her spear up as she drove it hard into the man's stomach. She stared into his face as blood trickled from his mouth.

Morrigan pulled her spear from his corpse as soon as he hit the ground. Breathing heavily, she glanced around the forest, no more tribesmen were near. Her eyes focused on the small group of humans cowering in the dark. A mother and father with their two children. Morrigan had come upon them as she made her way through the wilds of Gaelach, drawn by the young boy's light.

"You need not fear me, Morrigan called out to them, keeping her distance in order to not frighten the children.

"Thank you," the mother stammered, holding onto the toddler.

"Who are you?" the father asked, assessing if Morrigan was a new threat or their hero.

"I am Morrigan, Guardian of the Ancients." Morrigan rested her spear against the tree. "I have come to Gaelach to help free our people from the cultists."

"Why?" the father asked suspiciously, ignoring the shushing from his woman.

"I have failed the people of Gaelach for not acting sooner. I wish to rectify that mistake," she answered simply, staring at the boy. "You do know that your boy possesses magic?"

The parents glanced at each other nervously. "I can see the light within him." She attempted a comforting smile. "What can you do?"

The boy smiled back nervously. "I can see in the dark. Sometimes through things."

"A fine gift indeed." Morrigan turned to the parents. "He will be hunted by the rulers of this land for his light. It will draw them to him."

"We don't know where else to go," the mother pleaded.

"There is a hidden city just south of us," Morrigan explained. "The King of Thieves uses Collie as his stronghold. You will be safe there. There are more with the light."

"I've never heard of Collie," the father said suspiciously.

"It is a newer city, once a stronghold for the Oich rebels. It has since been fortified, and families have moved in to live there. It is protected well by rebels and gifted alike," Morrigan spoke to the parents in what she hoped was a compassionate voice. "It is a safe haven for all, but there are those like your son, people he can learn from to hone his gift. People who will protect you all."

Morrigan watched as the mother, still clutching her children, shared a look with her husband before she spoke, "And, will we be able to go there? Will they accept us?"

"Yes, they will." Morrigan smiled down at the boy.

"Come with us!" The boy reached for Morrigan as if seeking comfort. "Please?"

Morrigan glanced up at the parents before responding, "My job is out here, little one. I must find and protect others who travel."

"I haven't seen any new travelers for days," Storm's voice echoed inside her head, he was flying nearby scouting. *"It is likely these are the last trickling from the borders of Airgid."*

"Please," the mother asked, fear consuming her features. "We have almost been caught a few times now. I'm worried that we won't make it."

"It's true," the father spoke up, staring Morrigan in the eyes. "With two little ones we move too slow. I can't protect my family from a hunting party of any size. We chose to come south instead of north because others with the gift described a vision of a woman, who looked a lot like you. You were the beacon we were coming to find. We can't make it all the way without your help."

"You did send out that vision to all the gifted," Storm teased her from above. *"Wouldn't hurt to check in with the girls either. See how they've been fairing with all the newcomers."*

Morrigan sighed heavily before answering, "Fine, but we need to move now, before any more silverbacks catch a whiff of the carnage here."

502

Chapter Seventy

Clyous

Screams echoed throughout the night as wolves ran rampant in the streets of Collie. Clyous stood in his shop, watching as warriors battled fiercely. Men he knew, men he's lived with for months now were taking up sword and axe to defend their home. Off in the distance he could see Grace desperately fighting some tribesmen. What started off as Grace defending a small family had turned into her fighting for her life as the cultists realized who she was. His eyes swept the streets for Menolayous, knowing the warrior would not stand for this, but Menolayous was lost in battle bloodlust, fighting against an enormous bear and mountain lion.

Panic overcame him, where was Bridget? He tried to step forward but couldn't move. It was like some magical force kept him rooted to the spot. He searched for her, hoping to catch a glimpse of her fiery red curls, but she was nowhere to be seen. Rama and Danny now entered the street, fighting as a unit to defend each other from the blooded guards advancing on them. Clyous watched his friends fighting, desperate to help them. Flinn rode into battle on the back of a very large black horse with a fiery mane. Flinn jumped from horseback to enter the fray. The horse turned its head to look in Clyous's direction.

Clyous could tell something was not right with this animal as its unnatural eyes seemed to peer into his very soul. The horse's nostrils flared, steam billowing out of the dark openings. It neighed at him angrily before charging at him. Clyous glanced around, seeing only two options; a sword rested against a work bench within reach, or he could duck behind the forge to get away from the attacking beast.

Clyous was able to lunge for the sword, as he swung the weapon upward, the horse immediately halted its advance. The creature stomped its feet angrily before taking off away from him. Now able to move, Clyous exited the forge ready to fight, nearly tripping over Flinn's dead body. Clyous didn't have time to stop, Grace was quickly losing her fight as the others remained unable to break away from theirs.

Where was Catriona? Where was Bridget? Clyous still did not see either of the women as he rushed to Grace's side. Just as he got there fire erupted, igniting every building in sight. Thick smoke filled his lungs as he watched the enemy burn. Every single enemy was now completely engulfed in flames, screaming as their very existence was snuffed out.

Clyous sat bolt upright, gasping for breath as his nightmare faded off into the night. Or was it early morning? Clyous glanced outside the little window in his treetop hut, the very beginnings of sunrise appearing in the lightening sky. Glancing back down beside him, Bridget was still fast asleep. Her naked body covered by their shared blanket, breathing softly as she continued to slumber. He smiled down at her, admiring just how beautiful she was.

Everything had changed that night he had received that invasive mind-to-mind conversation with Grace. He was not entirely sure if Grace was kidding or not about pleasuring Bridget if he didn't, but when Grace started yelling at him saying Bridget was having a hard time, he made the decision to grab a horse from the stables and ride all night and day to get to the capital city.

He hadn't been pushing for a physical relationship with Bridget for one reason, he didn't want to be anything like Liam. The few conversations they had about her past experiences proved to him that she never really had much of a choice when it came to sex, she was expected to submit to Liam. The sex and the relationship were never about her. He now strived to prove to her that he was different.

Bridget stirred gently, opening up her emerald-green eyes to peer up at him. "Everything ok?"

"Yeah, just a nightmare." Clyous smiled at her. "Everything is fine."

"Want to talk about it?" Bridget asked sleepily, sitting up to get a better look at him.

"No, sweetheart, that's okay." Clyous thought for a moment before sitting up himself, reaching for the satchel beside their bed. "Actually, I have a question for you."

"What's up?" Bridget began rubbing the sleep from her eyes, opening her eyes just as Clyous held a golden ring out in front of her. "What's this?"

"I'm in love with you, Bridget," Clyous did his best to hold his nerves at bay as he spoke. "I have been for some time now. I made the mistake once, not speaking up for what I wanted. I refuse to go another year waiting to get enough courage to act."

"Is that—?" Her eyes widened as they homed in on the delicately carved emerald ring he now held with a steady hand.

"Bridget," Clyous began, "would you make me the happiest man alive, by agreeing to be my partner and light in all things? To grow old together and love one another as fiercely as we are capable? To forever be my rock in uncertain times, and allow me to be with you every step of the way as we take on the world?"

Clyous held his breath as he waited, watching the shocked expression on her face as she took in his words. For a moment, Clyous began to regret his timing. Maybe he should have planned something more romantic than proposing in the middle of the night after a nightmare? Then again, he'd probably spend months trying to plan the perfect proposal, and the gods knew how bad he was at postponing things when it came to trying to make her happy. He had already spent months trying to perfect his ring for her before his father pointed out she wasn't one for overly flashy jewelry.

"Yes," Bridget's voice finally broke him free of his self-doubt. "Yes, I'll marry you!"

"Really?" Clyous practically choked out the words, relief moistening his eyes more than he would care to admit.

"Yes, really!" Bridget threw her arms around him, tears streaming down her face as she embraced him.

Clyous winced slightly as she squeezed his recently broken but magically healed arm, it was still tender to the touch, but this moment was worth it. He began peppering her forehead with kisses until she released him, stealing an actual kiss from him amidst her joyous celebration. Clyous gently took her hand, sliding the golden band over her ring finger. They both looked at it, Clyous comparing the gold to her beautifully pale skin. Bridget held her hand up to her face to examine the details better, her eyes still leaking tears of joy.

"You made this?" Bridget asked, still admiring the work. "Clyous, this is beautiful!"

"My father helped before he left," Clyous admitted. "He showed me a new technique for the setting."

"I love it." She took his face in her hands, kissing him passionately. "I love you!"

"I-love-you-too!" he managed to say in between her kisses before they tumbled backwards into bed. "You realize you can't marry me if you suffocate me to death, right?" He laughed.

Bridget swung a leg over him, seating herself directly over his hips teasingly. "You'll survive, I'll be gentle."

"Please don't be." Clyous smiled at her.

Chapter Seventy-One

Rama

"Where have the two of you been?" Rama asked them as Bridget and Clyous decided to finally join the rest of them for dinner.

"And I thought Cat and Danny were bad," Grace teased them as they sat down at the table inside the longhouse. "You two have been going at it all day."

Catriona's face turned a light shade of pink at Grace's comment, throwing a piece of bread in the princess's direction. "You're such a nuisance."

"A speaker of fact, if you will." Grace laughed, taking a bite of her mutton.

"Sorry," Bridget said while sitting down, trying to hide a smile on her face.

Catriona glanced at her brother then, who was also hiding a smile. "What?"

"Nothing," Clyous answered, grabbing himself and Bridget bowls for dinner.

"Horse shit." Catriona eyed him up and down, suspicion taking over. "You're hiding something."

Everyone's attention now snapped to Clyous, who continued to load up the dinner bowls with heaps of mutton. Menolayous was the first to notice, cracking a silent smile before returning to his food. Moments later, Grace's head snapped in Bridget's direction, her eyes immediately dropping to the healer's hand, which now bore an elegantly carved golden ring.

Suddenly, there was a loud squeal from Grace as she launched herself at the healer, wrapping her arms around her friend in excitement. "THAT'S SO AMAZING!"

"Fuck!" Danny stood up suddenly to avoid the knocked over bowl of mutton that had narrowly missed his lap.

Catriona was the next to realize the ring's presence, she too launched herself into the group hug surrounding Bridget. The men, Menolayous excluded, stared at the scene unfolding before them with confusion. Clyous began to laugh at the sight of the girls who were still talking in high pitched and squealing voices. They were without a doubt causing a scene, drawing attention from everyone else in the longhouse.

Menolayous stood up to face Clyous, extending out a hand. "Congratulations."

Clyous reached out and shook Menolayous's offering. "Thank you."

"I still don't understand what the fuck is happening." Danny's eyes kept bouncing between Clyous and the overly excited group of girls.

"We're engaged!" Bridget was able to squeak out while still surrounded by the other two.

Rama's laughter now boomed throughout the longhouse as he stood up and wrapped Clyous in an embrace. "Congratulations!"

Danny, finally having caught on, smiled at the news as he too embraced Clyous in congratulations. The girls finally stopped their high pitch screeching, allowing everyone else a turn to congratulate the bride to be. Catriona turned and punched her brother in the shoulder, then proceeded to hug him.

"That's so exciting!" Catriona said as she ruffled her twin's hair. "You're finally giving me what I've always dreamed of having, a sister."

"Glad you found a way to make this all about you." Clyous laughed as he ducked out of her reach. "You know the standard way to congratulate someone isn't to assault them."

"It is for Cat." Bridget laughed, pulling away from everyone to entwine her hand in Clyous's. "It means she loves you."

"I wouldn't go that far," Catriona joked, still bouncing with excitement. "When's the wedding?"

"Now I see why the two of you have been fucking all day," Grace teased, sitting back down at the table.

"Grace!" Bridget turned bright red.

"We were talking about doing it soon," Clyous interjected, completely ignoring Grace's comment. "On the full moon."

"Is that for some wolfy tradition we need to know about?" Danny asked, wiping mutton off his seat before sitting down.

"Weddings on a full moon mean mating for life," Bridget answered. "But we wanted a morning ceremony."

"Father should be back by then," Catriona stated. "What happens if he's running late?"

"Then we proceed without him," Clyous answered factually. "I spoke with father at length about this before he left. He doesn't want me to put anything off just because of him. Wars are unpredictable as is, if we sit around waiting it could mean waiting forever."

"That's a wise view on it," Menolayous acknowledged.

"You realize that's in less than a week?" Catriona pointed out.

"That's completely okay." Bridget glanced at Clyous with a shy smile. "We didn't need anything grand anyway."

"Have you thought of where?" Grace asked, still excited about the wedding conversation.

"Collie obviously," Clyous answered. "But where specifically, no."

"What about the lake?" Danny suggested. "It's beautiful there."

"That's an hour or so hike from here," Bridget answered, after thinking for a moment. "I would like something a little closer. I would feel more comfortable here than being that out in the open."

"Besides, there's enough workers digging that channel right now anyway. Takes away from the scenery," Catriona added in.

"Fine, whatever." Danny took a drink from his tankard of ale. "That's where we'll get married then."

"We're not engaged!" Catriona rolled her eyes at him.

"Yet." Danny winked at her.

"There's a lovely spot by the river," Menolayous cut in. "It would take a day or two with a group to make a clearing, but it could be done."

"That sounds lovely," Bridget answered.

"Perfect!" Rama exclaimed happily. "I'll get a group together to start clearing that spot first thing in the morning. If you two don't mind coming with me to pick the exact spot that is, I promise I won't try to kidnap anyone this time."

The joke did not land the way Rama had intended it to, instead it just created momentary awkward silence.

"Yes, we'll come with you," Bridget answered with a smile that said she understood. "We wouldn't need anything big though."

"How many people?" Grace asked her. "For the ceremony."

"Probably just you guys," Clyous answered. "You're our family. We don't need anyone else."

"Aww," Rama teased. "What about the after party?"

"Why is there always an after party with you?" Menolayous stared at his brother with slight irritation.

"It's a wedding!" Rama shrugged, ignoring the stare. "Besides, having a celebration with all of our new arrivals will help boost morale."

"He has a point." Danny laughed. "We're not all allergic to social events like you, brother."

Menolayous flipped them both off before turning to Grace, who had already moved on in the conversation.

"An after party would be fine," Bridget answered. "As long as it's not too much trouble."

"None at all," Rama answered, patting Danny on the shoulder hard. "Leave that to us. We'll work on getting food and drink together."

"Brilliant." Grace turned back to Bridget. "What about a dress?"

"The new seamstress has set up a shop next to mine," Bridget said thoughtfully. "We could talk to her about making a dress for each of us."

Catriona choked on her drink before saying, "All of us?"

"Well yeah, aren't you going to stand up there with me?" Bridget asked with a slight smile.

"I don't even own a dress," Catriona sounded slightly panicked.

"Not true," Bridget insisted. "You have the red traveler's dress I gave you."

"Oh, that one," Catriona mumbled.

Danny leaned closer to her, not bothering to lower his voice. "I love that dress on you."

"She'll wear a dress," Grace answered factually. "We would love to stand up there with you!"

"Yeah," Catriona didn't sound so sure, but there was no room for argument.

"We should go first thing in the morning, after you and Clyous have scouted out your spot," Grace said excitedly. "Oh, this is going to be fun."

"Then we'll steal Clyous when you steal Bridget to get the party plans figured out," Rama boomed, mirroring Grace's excitement. "All three of us, Menolayous."

Menolayous glanced up before exclaiming, "Fine, yes."

"Woohoo!" Danny cheered excitedly.

"What's with all the celebrating over here?" Flinn approached them from across the room.

"Clyous and Bridget are getting married!" Grace announced happily.

"Is that so!" Flinn's excitement quickly grew to match the rest of the party. "That's wonderful. Congratulations!"

"Thank you!" Clyous managed to get out before he was suffocated by the war chief's embrace.

"This is cause for celebration!" Flinn's voice boomed nearly as loud as Rama's.

"That's what we said!" Danny laughed as Bridget was now caught up in one of the war chief's famous hugs.

"If I prayed to the gods, do you think they would come down and spare me from you all?" Menolayous grumbled to nobody in particular.

"Cheer up dark and broody," Grace shot at him, "nobody's asking you to stand up and make a speech."

"How can I be of assistance to you?" Flinn asked Clyous, who was looking rather overwhelmed with everyone present being so excited.

"Why don't you meet us here for breakfast, and you can come with us and figure out where the ceremony is going to be held," Rama offered. "After that we have some party planning to do."

"Perfect!" Flinn gave Rama a firm pat on the back. "I'll be waiting for you lot here first thing in the morning."

"Thank you!" Bridget called after the war chief as he departed. "He's such a kind man. Very fatherly."

"He's been like a father to all of us," Menolayous acknowledged. "Although I think Connor is the only one he has officially claimed."

"Are you okay with all of this?" Catriona asked Bridget. "We're not being too much?"

"No, this is great!" Bridget said excitedly. "I never thought I'd have such close friends this willing to help me with a wedding."

"Of course we're willing." Grace smiled. "If you don't mind being parted from your beloved for another hour or so, would you be willing to come with us to go talk with the seamstress? I see her over there across the room. Wouldn't hurt to give her a heads up we're coming."

"Of course." Bridget allowed Grace to pull her across the room, grabbing a reluctant-looking Catriona in the process.

The men stood there watching for a moment as the girls made their way over to the older woman. She was one of the newer refugees from one of the large eastern villages in Oich.

The men turned and looked at each other in an awkward silence for about a minute or so before Danny broke the silence, "So you make jewelry huh?"

"You're an idiot." Rama laughed at Danny, picking up a tankard and taking a deep swig.

"Yes." Clyous laughed, "I'm assuming that means you're interested?"

"I was going to wait until your father returned to ask for his blessing," Danny said. "But since we're on the topic of engagements..."

"Hey, if you're crazy enough to want to marry my sister I'm not dumb enough to stop you." Clyous smiled at him. "You just have to convince her to say yes."

"Oh I have a plan," Danny teased, standing up to embrace Clyous once more. "But thank you."

"Do you know what kind of ring you're thinking of?" Clyous asked him.

"Not just yet." Danny laughed. "I'll think on it, but for now let's focus on your wedding, shall we?"

"Aww," Rama teased, directing his attention to the still silent Menolayous. "Everyone's getting married. When are you going to ask Grace?"

In response, Menolayous just stared at his brothers with an irritated look on his face. After another few seconds of dead silence, Rama clapped his hands together to change the subject.

"Well then," Rama turned back to Clyous and Danny. "Knowing you, you've probably got something completely romantic you want to do for the wedding but can't figure out how to pull it off. How can we help?"

Clyous stared at him for a moment before answering, "Am I that predictable."

"Unfortunately, yes," Menolayous answered with a hint of a smile. "What can we do to help."

Chapter Seventy-Two

Liam

"Make sure those shackles are secured!" one of the soldiers shouted over the crowd as the mass of captured refugees were rounded up.

Liam looked on the scene with a transparent face, doing his best to hide his distaste for this whole ordeal. King Rion sat upon a horse beside his, staring down at the newly captured prisoners with a hunger that gave Liam a large sense of unease. These prisoners were caught fleeing from Oich towards Gaelach's border, as had many others across the territory. They all bore the curse of magic and were captured successfully by Oich soldiers with the aid of those iron cuffs and some of the cultist tribesmen. This group of ten or so were kept under guard until Liam and the cultist king were able to arrive. Now Liam watched as his citizens were shackled together like livestock and prepared to march into Gaelach territory where they would undoubtably face horrors beyond their imagination.

"A nice sized group to be sure," King Rion said, voice elated and heavy with his Gaelach accent.

"I expect the gold to be delivered to my father, the king, soon." Liam glanced Rion's direction, assessing the man carefully.

"There's a wagon already traveling the main road." Rion smirked. "It's like you don't trust me, young Prince."

"It's because I don't," Liam snapped, holding none of his fierceness back.

"Good." Rion smiled back at him, revealing his sharpened teeth. "No ruler can truly trust anyone. Least of all his allies."

"You tribesmen are a strange lot," Liam countered, watching as one of the soldiers began beating a man who was resisting being shackled to the others. "You would think an ally would want to be trusted."

"I trust your participation in our agreement to stand as long as it benefits you." Rion too stared at the beating, but with a look of fascinated interest. "It is a matter of time before you have absorbed enough of the dominant wolf's magic to be able to confront your father, to challenge him. I

514

aim to make you an ally, not just Oich. This will ensure our kingdoms have a long lasting and mutually beneficial arrangement."

"Speaking of challenging the king is considered treason." Liam watched as the man was finally forced into shackles, he felt a small amount of disappointment that he was not able to break away and escape.

"You would be a fool to not acknowledge the natural succession of a moon touched." Rion glanced between Liam and the prisoners with interest. "Our kingdoms may differ slightly in our beliefs, but we are children of the Moon God. Our very nature is the same. It is impossible to change."

"We are not the same." Liam glared at the king. "We hold ourselves to a higher standard here in Oich, we do not disgrace ourselves with raping those beneath us, we do not eat people or sacrifice them to the Moon God. Your ways are archaic; we have advanced our society to something more civilized."

"You speak with the superiority of a king." Rion seemed to approve. "But lack the self-reflection of a wise man. You speak of our savagery, but do you not burn those with the gift alive out of fear? Entering this small village I saw several men and women hung just outside the city walls, collecting crows. Some of them even appear to have been hacked apart by some of your men before death."

"It is an unfortunate consequence to those who refuse to submit," Liam ground out through clenched teeth, he couldn't believe that he felt the need to justify this to someone like him, never thought he would ever have to justify these cruel acts as if they were acceptable.

"But you see." Rion clapped his hands happily. "You too, play the game of dominance. We just go about it in different ways. Where you argue that we belittle ourselves by bedding down those who refuse to submit, I would argue you waste the possibility of life by just killing them. At least when we kill, there is something meaningful behind it. A sacrifice to the gods means more than just a public execution."

"How can you be so sure of the gods paying attention to your sacrifices?" Liam argued back.

"Those are secrets I will keep to myself." Rion smiled at him as if baiting him. "Your acts to dominate leave you with a finality of death. It's brutal and uncreative. It lacks the follow-through to completely take over someone else. My people have spent generations mastering how to break others. To break someone, by torture, rape, starvation, means you are making them submit to you at the end. There is no greater form of dominance over another than devouring them, one way or another. We do not judge you for how you choose to assert your power over your people, but do not make the mistake that you are better than us."

Liam's gaze returned to the poor group of prisoners being led off by Gaelach cultists. Liam knew deep in his heart that they would be dead soon, and there was nothing anyone would be able to do about it. These poor bastards had chosen to flee Oich for the safety of this rebel city, fleeing from the cruelties of the crown, just to be captured and handed over to a greater evil.

"You do not like the cruelty," Rion stated simply watching where Liam was focused on.

"I am not a fan of unnecessary pain," Liam answered honestly, knowing that any attempt to deny it would make him look weaker in the eyes of this king. "But I am no stranger to doing the dirty work myself. I acknowledge the necessity of it."

"Good." Rion nodded his head with approval. "You could always step up and challenge your father. Once you become king you will have the power to change things."

"You seem awfully focused on me challenging my father." Liam raised an eyebrow suspiciously. "Why?"

"I'm sure you want to hear me say something like, 'Because we think Oich would be easier to take over with you in charge than your father', that way you would have a reason to strike me dead here and now." Rion laughed at Liam's expression, knowing he had hit the mark closer than the young prince suspected possible. "No, I just believe we would work together better. Where you would look upon my brothers and I as equals, your father will never look at us as anything other than subordinates to his power."

"And what happens if I challenge him and lose?" Liam countered, curious at how this man's mind worked and his blunt honesty.

"Then I continue my alliance with him," Rion answered simply. "Until your father believes we no longer benefit him in some way, we are safe."

"You're surprisingly intelligent for a savage." Liam laughed at the king's bluntness, his father never spoke this openly, he always had an agenda hidden somewhere in the background.

"I shall take that as a compliment." Rion waved at his men as they took the shackled prisoners down the road towards the village exit. "How about we spend some quality time together, young Prince? Really get to know each other, to better our alliance."

Liam gave him an incredulous look. "The problem with two blooded males, is nobody would ever submit to being the bottom."

Rion roared with laughter, nearly falling off of his horse in the process. "Not what I meant, but I like how you think. My men tell me of a large rebel force moving from an eastern mountain pass this direction. A sum of maybe fifty warriors, new blooded, magic wielders, and slaves alike. I would like to engage this force, ambush them and collect more with the ancient bloodline. Oich could use more slaves, and new blooded to dominate."

"Where are they now?" Liam asked, intrigued at the idea.

"Three day's ride from here." Rion thought for a moment. "Give or take. They have since given up trying to conceal themselves as they marched. They have split up from an original fighting force of a few hundred."

"Sounds like an excellent opportunity to hit our mutual enemy where it hurts the most," Liam agreed, calculating in his head how many of his soldiers he could collect and how quickly. "Give me a day and I can round up enough men for the mission."

"I can meet you back at the capital by tomorrow, twenty of my own in tow." Rion smiled, excited at how easily Liam seemed to want to join him.

"I will meet you at the capital tomorrow midday. Have your men ready for travel." Liam kicked his horse into motion.

"I will be waiting for you, young Prince." Rion called after him as Liam's horse charged down the road, soldiers jumping on their own horses to follow behind him.

Chapter Seventy-Three

Bridget

"The whole point of tonight," Grace said as she stood in the doorway, blocking Bridget from being able to leave, "is to keep you and Clyous away from each other."

"I have never understood that tradition." Bridget glared at Grace. "Seems redundant to me considering we live together."

"That's why the boys are watching him." Catriona interjected, uncorking a liquor bottle and taking a seat on the feather mattress in the middle of the room. "I don't see why you're being so paranoid, it's not like he's going to suddenly change his mind. The idiot is in love with you."

"Not sure that's a helpful approach." Grace shot Catriona a look, who shrugged and took a large drink from the glass bottle. "Or the alcohol."

"I'm willing to share." Catriona smirked at her holding out the bottle.

Bridget took it from her, putting the bottle to her lips and taking several deep drinks. "It's not just that. The first night of the full moon is tomorrow. I get antsy."

"I don't know how you blooded do it." Grace declined the bottle, steering Bridget over to the bed and sitting her down next to Cat. "Three days every month where it's hard to do anything but try and control the wild animal inside, sounds like a nightmare."

"It can be." Bridget shrugged, taking another drink before handing the bottle back to Catriona. "Most the time it's manageable. I'm just... nervous as is, you know."

"Totally understand that," Catriona slurred slightly.

Grace shot her another look. "Why are you here? You're certainly not helping."

"You knew that before you told me to show up. That one's on you, Princess." Catriona toasted her before taking yet another drink. "Weddings make me uncomfortable. No offense. That by no means is a reflection on how happy I am that you're marrying my brother, because I am. And I

518

promise, he does not have the same reservations I have, so don't think he's doing the same as me."

"Why *are* you being an ass about it?" Grace asked as she strode across the room, grabbing a small leather satchel.

"I don't know." Catriona thought for a moment, clearly affected by the quarter of the bottle she had already had. "I guess I just don't feel like anyone is going to find me worthy enough to marry."

"Now I know you're drunk." Bridget took the bottle from her. "Danny won't shut up about it. You're not that dense."

"No," Catriona answered. "But how cruel would it be for me to marry him, then him finding out later that it was a mistake, that I trapped him."

"When you sober up remind me to address this topic again," Grace said, clearly irritated. She pulled ink and other items out of her bag and set them down before her. "Tonight is supposed to be fun, and about the bride to be."

"Sorry," Cat murmured, watching Grace intently. "What are you doing?"

"I brought a gift for Bridget," Grace answered as she finished emptying the contents of her bag onto a clean cloth. "I designed her a tattoo."

"Really?" Cat and Bridget asked excitedly, sitting up for a better look.

"Yes." Grace handed Bridget her sketch on a piece of parchment. "You might be swayed by the moon, but you've got the brightness of the sun behind you."

Bridget stared down at the artwork, utterly shocked at its beauty. Unlike the tattoos Grace had been doing for Menolayous which seemed mostly composed of Gaelach knotwork, hers used delicate and artistic strokes, like that from a paint brush. The drawing was an artistic portrayal of the sun, with rays extending outward like ribbons dancing in the wind. The right side of this masterpiece lacked the same sun rays and elegance, instead it was a beautiful portrayal of half the moon. Where it lacked ribbons it gained beautiful shading, looking so realistic to what she was used to seeing in the night sky.

"By the gods, Grace," Bridget said, staring at this masterpiece, "this is beautiful."

"Seriously," Catriona agreed, looking at it.

"Thank you!" Grace smiled at them both. "Where would you like it?"

"Oh, I don't know." Bridget thought for a moment. "Would you be able to put it on the back of my neck?"

"Pull your hair up and get comfortable." Grace took the bottle from Catriona, using the contents to clean her instruments.

Bridget obeyed, twisting her long curly hair up into a bun at the top of her head. Grace pointed to Bridget's blouse, indicating that it too needed to be removed. Reluctantly, Bridget began to undo the strings, facing away from the other two as she lowered her top for easy exposure to the back of her neck.

"You could probably lay face down on the bed and I can get it at that angle," Grace suggested, pulling a chair up next to the mattress. "I promise I'll stop trying to get you naked after this."

"Ha ha." Bridget smirked, climbing onto the bed with her head facing Grace. "I'll be a married woman after this; it would be inappropriate to keep up your dirty comments."

"Then I guess I've got one more night to convince you," Grace teased. "You comfortable?"

"Yes," Bridget answered after adjusting the pillows.

Grace dipped one of her needles in the ink, bringing it to Bridget's skin before tapping the end of her needle with her wooden hammer. Bridget flinched slightly as she felt the sharpness of the needle. It wasn't nearly as painful as she had suspected it would be so she released a breath.

"You excited to get married?" Catriona asked, taking a seat nearby to give the entire mattress to Bridget.

"I am," Bridget spoke through the pillow as she felt another tap from Grace. "Very much."

"You're going to look beautiful in that dress," Grace complimented her as she continued to work. "With all the riches in Airgid I've never seen such an elegantly designed dress."

"Isn't everything in Airgid dripping with jewels and finery?" Bridget asked, wincing at the next hammer tap.

"Yes, but there the jewels steal the show," Grace answered dipping her needle inside the ink. "Your dress makes *you* stand out."

"I would love to visit Airgid someday," Bridget said.

"Me too," Catriona agreed. "I've never been outside of Oich."

"I'll take you both sometime," Grace promised, continuing to carve into Bridget's flesh, slowly creating a masterpiece. "If I don't accompany you two, some rich noblemen will try to sweep you up for himself."

Catriona snorted at that; eyes focused on Grace's work. Bridget herself giggled at the joke. The one absolute thing all three of them could count on while visiting Airgid, was the fact that they would stand out like sore thumbs, and not in a good way. Knowing Catriona, she might end up lighting some poor fool on fire.

"Do you have any plans for after the ceremony?" Grace asked, trying to keep the healer distracted from the needlework.

"I mean, isn't that obvious?" Bridget squealed slightly as the needle dug into the sensitive skin just over her spine.

"I meant after everything." Grace laughed. "But sure, if you have your whole wedding night planned out don't be shy and share."

"Can we not?" Catriona started laughing.

"We don't really have a grand plan." Bridget squeezed her eyes shut as the hammer drove the needle into her flesh yet again. It might be a gentle process, but it was not a comfortable one. "We intend to stay here in Collie, to see the end of the war. Flinn has done a great job turning this place into its own city. We don't see a reason to uproot and start over, especially since we plan on having children."

"Aww," Catriona made an un-sarcastic sound. "You guys want to make me an aunt?"

"Why do you have this knack for always turning it about you?" Grace playfully scolded. "Do you have an idea of when you two wanted to start trying? I would assume you would need to stop taking the tea ahead of time."

"I haven't been taking the tea," Bridget said. "Ow!"

"You what?" Grace asked, pausing in her work.

Bridget looked up at her two friends, surprised by the look of shock on their faces. "I haven't been taking the tea, at all. Why are you looking at me like that?"

"Any particular reason why?" Grace asked, pulling herself together far quicker than Cat was able to.

"It's not a fool proof remedy," Bridget said slightly defensively. "And if the gods were to bless us with children, I personally wouldn't want to deny that gift. Neither does Clyous. We've had conversations about it. I promise I'm not blindsiding him."

"No, no," Grace began to back track. "I'm sorry. I don't think that at all. I'm just surprised to hear anyone say that."

"That's okay," Bridget tried to say comfortingly. "I understand that my beliefs aren't common with others our age."

"You do you," Catriona said, finally pulling her expression into something other than shock. "I support you with whatever your choices are."

"I don't know if I'm ready to have children," Grace said, slowly returning to her work. "I want them someday. Maybe in a year or two. After the war has calmed down, or Menolayous is ready."

"You two would make great parents," Bridget said after taking a deep breath, the needle once again digging into her flesh.

"You and Clyous too. I don't think there will be a child smarter than your guys's," Grace returned the compliment.

"I don't think I want children," Catriona said quietly, drawing both her friends' attention to her. "This world isn't safe enough for children, and the gods know how horrible of a mother I would be."

"You would be a great mother," Bridget tried to offer compassionately.

"No, but I appreciate your attempt." Catriona smiled at her kindly. "Really, the fact doesn't bother me."

"What about Danny? Doesn't he want kids?" Grace asked, surprised.

"He's got a take it or leave mentality about it," Catriona said after thinking for a moment. "I guess I lucked out in that department."

"Well..." Grace said, tapping the needle with her hammer once again. "Whatever is in store for us in the next year, it's going to be interesting that's for sure. Especially with little feet running around everywhere."

"That would be amazing!" Bridget sighed happily at the thought. "Ow!"

Chapter Seventy-Four

Clyous

"You think they'll notice?" Danny asked, holding a wet rag to his split lip.

"Are you seriously asking if the girls are going to notice when we all show up to the wedding cut up and bruised?" Menolayous asked incredulously, wrapping his wrist. "No, not at all. They don't pay attention to us."

"It is what it is at this point." Clyous laughed as he glanced around the living space at the four of them. "In hindsight, maybe we shouldn't have gone to raid traveling merchants the day before my wedding."

"What's life without a little fun?" Rama moved carefully through the newly raised house, doing his best not to bump into the freshly painted walls. "We needed to blow off some steam after spending the last few days putting this place together."

"It was needed," Menolayous agreed, leaning back in his chair. "I for one was surprised at how easily the slaves just handed over the supplies."

"It's a pity they didn't join us," Clyous said. "They actually seemed to know about the rebellion and were on our side."

"They probably had family they needed to get back to," Rama chimed in, finally finding a safe place to sit. "I don't blame them. At the very least it seems we're turning the tide as far as Oich citizens are concerned. I've been getting a lot of reports about villages pushing back."

"We can thank Catriona for that one." Menolayous nodded. "She's practically lit most of the capital city on fire. They started constructing a wall trying to keep us out, but she keeps burning that down too."

"It is becoming one of our favorite past times." Danny smiled mischievously. "We try to hit the capital every other week or so. Keep them on their toes."

"It's definitely working." Rama chuckled. "They are so busy trying to survive your onslaught they haven't been able to send out regular patrols. Most of our rebels from across the kingdom have been lucky enough to make it here without discovery."

"I wish my father was here," Clyous said. "But I've seen him on the road, so I know he and Markous are okay."

"Once he gets here, we'll be full force again," Menolayous acknowledged.

"I'll have my entire family back," Clyous added in.

"That would be good," Rama said warmly. "And maybe you can finally show everyone this house you've been secretly working on for Bridget."

Clyous looked around the living space, feeling a sense of pride with the final touches he and the guys had managed to finish this week alone. Flinn had been gracious enough to give them their own house, one he had built on the very outskirts of Collie near the border wall. It just so happened to be in one of the locations the water trenches were dug, allowing Clyous access to siphon off some water for an herb garden for Bridget. The guys had helped him with the garden's finishing touches just the other day, giving them all day yesterday to finish painting the inside. Their little raid today had provided him with some decent furnishings for their new home. Clyous really wanted to show Bridget he was there to provide for her and the family they wanted to start. Having their own little property on the outskirts of Collie provided them room and security, while also being able to remain here with their friends. In his mind it was the perfect wedding present.

"You've done an amazing job on this house," Danny acknowledged, looking around yet again. "She's going to love it."

"I hope so." Clyous smiled as he too looked around.

"Can't you look ahead and see?" Rama asked him.

"It's not always a good thing to look ahead." Clyous sighed, weighing his words carefully, "Too many outcomes, too many potential changes, it's enough to drive you mad. It's impossible to be all-knowing, and it sucks the joy out of life."

"I don't think I would want to know my future," Menolayous spoke softly.

"Speak for yourself." Danny laughed. "I would kill to be able to stay three steps ahead of your sister. That woman is absolutely wild."

"But you love it," Clyous teased him.

"Every damn minute of it." Danny smiled back at him, his eyes glancing over to Rama who was unusually quiet. "What about you, big brother? Wouldn't you like to be able to know what fate is bringing you?"

"I don't need to see what I already know is coming," Rama said with a surprising amount of seriousness.

"Probably for the best. If you knew the next girl you would wind up chasing you would put her on some unspoken pedestal, and by the time you finally found her she would probably be a goddess to you," Danny jested, attempting to get a smile out of the giant.

"No." Rama looked to the floor with shame. "There won't be any women in my future."

The sound of pain laced in his words drew everyone's attention to him, especially Menolayous's. The usually happy and jovial giant, the most social member out of their found family, suddenly seemed very alone. Danny's smile vanished as he glanced from Clyous to Menolayous as if asking what to do.

"You can't punish yourself forever," Menolayous offered. "It wasn't you. *You* didn't hurt anyone."

"But it was me." Rama looked back at his brother fiercely. "It was my body that he used to hurt them, his vividly detailed plans that were constantly playing out in my mind as I actively sought out a way to make his sick fantasies come true. I might not have been in control, but I still have to live with the fact that I did those things to them."

"They know it wasn't you," Clyous tried to comfort him with this knowledge. "Grace and Cat don't blame you."

"But they still flinch if I get too close," Rama shot at him. "Whether they admit to it or not, there are moments where they see me and immediately react as if I would hurt them again. Cat won't even look at me when she's training. Grace won't stand near me, there always has to be something between us."

"That's—" Danny started.

"Smart," Rama finished for him. "I would never expect them to trust me again after that. I am proud that they are cautious instead of foolish, but knowing what I've done, what I was going to do, seeing the fear and mistrust in their eyes... no. I don't need to see what fate has in store for me when I already know I'll never be able to find someone of my own."

Clyous heard his words, allowing them to pull at his power momentarily. Clyous looked ahead, seeing variations of Rama's future. The time frames scattered themselves like dice on a gambling table at a tavern, some possible futures involving his death on the battlefield or dying of old age in his home. Some futures Rama seemed to walk the streets of Collie, surrounded by free people who looked up to him, and sometimes he sat completely alone on the city walls. Nearly every future he saw seemed to show Rama surrounded by at least one member of their found family, if not the whole lot of them. Clyous's heart warmed at the sight of all of them together in ten years, their children running around them playing together. The rest of them stood by their respective partners watching their children play, Rama behaving as an overjoyed uncle as one of them playfully tried to take him out at the knees. Rama might not have a partner in these futures, but he would find happiness within family.

"You'll never be alone." Clyous smiled at him kindly. "You just have to make sure I survive my wedding tomorrow, okay?"

Rama smiled up at him, taking the change of topic. "I can promise you through the ceremony, the after party I won't make any promises."

"I am not excited!" Menolayous let his eyes shut and head fall back in frustration. "I don't genuinely know who is going to be worse to babysit. Grace, Cat, or Danny."

"I can almost guarantee it's going to be Cat." Clyous laughed at their friend's frustration. "I'll put money on something accidentally catching fire. No magical powers are needed to predict that."

"No, it's most definitely going to be Grace." Danny smirked at Menolayous. "I intend to keep Cat plenty occupied. You, my dear brother, are in charge of your woman. And I have no doubts she is going to make you earn it tomorrow."

"I wish you were kidding." Menolayous let loose a nervous laugh. "Fuck me."

"Oh, I have no doubts she will." Rama snickered at his expense.

Chapter Seventy-Five

Morrigan

"We are here," Morrigan said to the family, looking up at the gates of Collie from the road.

It had taken her and Storm a week to get the family here from where she had rescued them. They had moved slowly, using Storm's view from above and the boy, Garreth's powers of sight to help guide them through the safest route. Escaping Gaelach was the trickiest part. There were too many unorganized cultists wandering around patrolling the border. Once they had crossed back over into Oich it had been significantly easier to move around. The Oich patrols seemingly vanished, possibly rerouted to another village or city to deal with havoc her friends had most likely unleashed on them. A solid strategy on Rama's part, giving refugees a fighting chance. There was only one instance of coming across the pathway of three scourge. Morrigan was able to handle them easily enough, but she had to resist the draw to hunt down any other hives that were most likely dwelling in a nearby cave system. She needed to remember that was no longer her responsibility, for too long she had neglected the safety of her people to obsessively hunt those monsters. This family depended on her, she would see it through that they reached Collie.

"I didn't believe you when you first told us of this place," Egret said, arms wrapped around both her children as she stared at the size of the city walls.

"I've never heard of Collie, I expected this to be more like a rebel camp. Maybe a few protective barriers. But not... this." Jahar nodded in agreement with his wife.

"It is relatively new." Morrigan glanced around, seeing dozens of citizens outside the city gates this early in the morning.

"How can we thank you for getting us here safely?" Egret smiled at Morrigan.

"It does not require thanks." Morrigan smiled back awkwardly, her eyes darting back to all the unusual early morning activity that surrounded them. "If you stick to the main road it will lead you to a longhouse sitting at

527

the top of the hill. There you will find breakfast, and someone to greet you and begin your integration into Collie."

"Are you not coming with us?" Garreth asked, looking up at Morrigan with a worried expression.

Morrigan crouched down before the boy, offering him a smile. "No, child. I'm going to see what everyone's doing this early in the morning, but I am not leaving Collie just yet. You will have plenty of other children your age to play with now, some with powers similar to yours."

Garreth hugged Morrigan quickly, saying goodbye. His parents and younger sibling spoke their farewells and made their way inside the city gates. Morrigan glanced around again, surveying all the citizens off to the side of the road. Tables and chairs were being set up around newly formed fire pits while some of the men were carrying down barrels of ale and other spirits. A few of the women were cutting fresh fruits and vegetables at a few of the tables. They were undoubtedly getting ready for a party.

"So, I see you couldn't stay away from me for too long, could you lass?" Flinn's voice laughed from somewhere behind her.

Morrigan spun around and came face to face with her favorite war chief, a smile now spreading across her face. "I could say that to boost your ego, but that wouldn't entirely be the truth."

Flinn embraced her warmly. She had missed his company; there was no denying that. She just wasn't about to admit to it either.

"What is the celebration?" Morrigan asked as she pulled away, gesturing towards the fire pits. "Surely you didn't do this all for my return."

"In an attempt to impress you I would say yes, but you would know I would be lying." Flinn chuckled. "Looks like you made it back in time for the wedding."

"What wedding?" Morrigan asked curiously.

"Young Bridget and Clyous of course." Flinn beamed proudly. "Follow me, it's due to start soon. I'm sure you wouldn't want to miss it."

"Certainly not." Morrigan fell into step behind him, anxious to see her friends again.

Morrigan took Flinn's extended arm in hers and allowed him to escort her towards the forest. By the looks of it, a freshly manicured pathway led from the outdoor kitchen towards the river. Morrigan watched as a few Collie citizens ran up and down the path carrying bouquets of wildflowers. It wasn't until they had made it to the river's edge that Morrigan spotted a wooden archway standing at the end of the path, partially covered with those bouquets of wildflowers. Standing beside this archway attempting to fill in the gaps with the freshly picked bouquets were the three princes of the rebellion, well... two princes and one king, as well as the groom to be. All of them were dressed nicer than she had ever seen them, sporting brand new embroidered tunics and nice trousers. Clyous was wearing a blue vest over his new clothes, distinguishing him from the others. All the boys had their hair combed and pulled back out of their faces, everyone except Rama and his short center strip of hair he was easily identified with.

"Looks like you missed a spot," Morrigan called to them teasingly, Storm landing on top of the archway and squawking in agreement.

The four men glanced over their shoulders at her, their faces lighting up in recognition. Clyous was the first one to drop the flowers he was holding, rushing to her for an embrace. This warm-hearted greeting took her by surprise, but she allowed it. Even gave him a slight pat on the back.

"I hear a congratulations is in order." Morrigan smiled at the blacksmith.

"Thank you!" Clyous beamed at her. "I didn't see you coming, but I'm glad you're here."

"Glad you're back!" Rama called over from the arch, trying his best to tie more flowers to it while talking.

Danny was next to come to Morrigan, he too embracing her unexpectedly. "Glad you're not dead."

"That was a lovely greeting," Menolayous shot at his brother, he approached Morrigan with a smile but did not reach out for an embrace.

"I am glad to have made it back in time." Morrigan smiled and glanced around, focusing on the pitifully decorated arch. "Do you need help with that?"

"We did not anticipate how many flowers we would need to cover this thing," Rama said, finally able to secure the bundle he had to the wood. "I'm not sure how you can help with that."

"Stand back." Morrigan waved him away from the arch, sticking her hands in the dirt along the path.

Rama did as he was commanded, everyone was staring at her now. Morrigan allowed her powers to trickle from her fingers, soaking into the dirt below. Wildflowers suddenly began to pop up out of dirt covering the pathway in the direction of the arch. Vines and wildflowers suddenly began to climb up the archway, covering it completely with gold, purple, pink, and white flowers. Everyone in the surrounding area now stared at her and the archway in awe.

"I thought your power was related to the weather?" Danny gaped at the flowers.

"Nature and the elements," Morrigan corrected him. "I can cast lightning just as easily as I can summon flowers."

"Well then…" Rama whistled, looking at the arch. "That could have saved us hours."

"If that arch took you hours to decorate there is a bigger problem," Morrigan jested.

"They've been drinking," Menolayous offered with a shrug.

"Of course they have." Flinn laughed. "Come on, if you lads are ready it's time I went to collect the bride. Morrigan, will you join me?"

"Wouldn't miss it for the world." Morrigan smiled at her friends.

Flinn took Morrigan by the hand, gently escorting her away from the archway as the boys took their positions. A few Collie citizens looked to be taking seats at the edge of the tiny clearing, preparing what looked like musical instruments. Morrigan and Flinn made their way through the trees for a few minutes before coming across the girls.

Grace was the first to be spotted, wearing a gold embroidered green linen gown with a brown leather corset, the green made her eyes shine brightly. The dress left no room to the imagination, showing off her bosom as if the dress were made for her specifically. Grace's hair was twisted up into neat, braided spirals off her shoulders. Catriona on the other hand was wearing a beautiful maroon linen gown with gold embroidery. The dress was well shaped to her thin and athletic figure, showing off the curves of her hips and bosom. Her white hair was also twisted up in braided spirals, being held at the top of her head with what looked like an elk horn.

Both girls were busy trying to help secure a crown of white flowers to Bridget's fiery red hair, which hung loosely down her back. The girls turned to Morrigan at her approach, their smiles lit up the darkness of her heart at the sight of them. Catriona and Grace moved to the side, allowing Morrigan a good look at the bride and her dress. Bridget was wearing an elegant white linen gown, the shoulders fell off to the sides covering her pale skin with lace.

530

Golden embroidery covered her corset in unique sun patterns, fitting her body snuggly just before the skirts of her dress cascaded to the ground. Bridget did not wear a veil, and barely any jewelry. Upon her neck she wore a dainty chain necklace with a heart shaped pendant, barely enough for it to pull from the beauty of the gown. Morrigan felt tears well up in her eyes.

"Morrigan!" Bridget called out smiling, rushing forward to embrace the sorceress. "You made it! I'm so glad you're here!"

"I am happy to have made it in time." Morrigan smiled around at the girls. "You all look so beautiful."

"Thank you!" Bridget smiled, her eyes already wet with happiness.

"Are you ready, Miss Bridget?" Flinn asked, his voice was choked up like a proud father at the sight of her.

"I think so," Bridget answered, taking a deep breath.

"Here." Grace smiled at the bride, handing her a beautiful bouquet of flowers. "Cat and I will walk ahead. See you down the aisle."

Morrigan watched Grace and Catriona take off towards the ceremony. Morrigan's ears could hear instruments being tuned in the distance. Bridget was standing there awkwardly for a moment, lost in her emotions.

"Would you allow me the honor of escorting you down the aisle, lass?" Flinn asked kindly.

"And me as well," Morrigan offered, it seemed almost fitting for herself and the war chief to stand in where Bridget's parents traditionally would.

"Yes please." Bridget gave a weak smile, her nerves taking over now.

"Grab on, lass," Flinn said reassuringly, offering her his arm for an escort. "And just say the word if you change your mind. I can create the biggest distraction; nobody would notice you slipping away."

Bridget laughed heartily at Flinn's joke, taking his arm in hers, while snaking the other around to grab Morrigan's. "Thank you both, so much, for being the parent figures I never had."

Chapter Seventy-Six

Grace

Grace took her position by the archway with Catriona standing beside her. Across the now very floral aisle stood Menolayous and Danny. Rama stood in the center of the aisle with a silk ribbon in his hands, he was the one officiating the ceremony today. Per Bridget's request they had kept the wedding party small, just her found family and a few of the musicians off to the side. Bridget wanted the privacy so it did not take away from how meaningful this day was to her. A fact that Grace respected, her experience with weddings in Airgid was that they were large affairs meant to outdo the last one. Weddings in her home kingdom were more of a rite of passage than they were about the love a couple shared. Honestly, most weddings in Airgid weren't about love, they were usually arranged for political gain or very rarely were thrown together to hide a pregnancy. Love was not usually part of the equation.

Bridget and Clyous's marriage was undoubtedly about love, something that moved Grace deep down. That's why, when Morrigan and Flinn came into view, escorting an emotional and nervous Bridget between them, Grace could not help but shed a few tears of joy for them. Bridget was absolutely stunning in her dress. The seamstress, Ariona, did such an amazing job for last minute orders. She did such a great job on all of their dresses honestly, but especially the bride's. Grace made a mental note to use this seamstress from now on as a thank you for her hard work. It wouldn't hurt for Grace to have more than one outfit anyway, especially since she had no plans to leave Collie and her friends anytime soon.

"Wow," she heard Clyous say as he finally spotted his bride.

Grace glanced at the blacksmith, his eyes wide and wet as he took in the beautiful sight of his wife to be. Grace's heart melted at the sight, yes this was definitely a marriage for love. Nothing in the world had ever seemed so right. Who cares if Bridget was blooded and Clyous gifted, or the fact that he was a slave and Bridget a noble. Love should hold no boundaries. They beat the system; they chose to break the rules and follow their hearts to find happiness. Albeit Grace had to push a little bit at the end, but not because they didn't love each other, they were just nervous figuring out how to love each other. They put in the work; they had the connection.

Morrigan and Flinn escorted Bridget to the archway, stopping just a few feet from Clyous. Bridget turned to give them both a loving embrace before stepping forward to stand before her fiancé. Tears were freely flowing at this point from both the bride and the groom, and Grace, since she was choosing to be honest with herself. The musicians had stopped playing their sweet melody, allowing silence to fill the air.

Rama spoke then, not the cocky older brother he usually was, but a king filled with authority and confidence. "We are gathered here today for the most sacred of occasions, the marriage and union between two lovers into something more eternal. Before I continue with the sacred oaths, is there anyone here who would like to contest this union?"

There was a stark silence only for a moment before Rama continued. "Good, because I would have knocked their lights out."

Bridget giggled at the joke, her eyes returning to Clyous who seemed absolutely captivated by her presence. Grace glanced over at Danny, who was staring at Catriona with a similar expression. Yes, this man's heart was filled with love as well, she knew it was a matter of time before Danny actually proposed to his woman. It was clear he wanted the eternal connection Clyous and Bridget were confirming through marriage. Grace's gaze fluttered to Cat's quickly, she seemed intent on not looking in her lover's direction. It was almost as if she knew exactly what he was thinking and was afraid to meet his gaze. Grace sighed at this, her eyes returning to the ceremony as Bridget and Clyous began to exchange rings, speaking out loud the traditional Oich vows. Catriona would come around, she loves Danny. This recent interaction with the Dark One had shaken her up, something Grace understood now that her and Cat had become closer.

Menolayous shifted across the aisle from her, catching her attention. Grace was surprised to see Menolayous intently staring at her, his eyes boring into hers in a possessively sweet manner. Seeing her staring back at him, a small smile crept up the corners of his mouth.

"What?" she asked curiously, trying to appear as if she wasn't distracted from the ceremony.

"Nothing," Menolayous teased, his eyes remaining locked on her, contrary to his statement.

"Why are you staring at me like that?" she asked, her gaze returning to the ceremony as Rama began to loosely tie the ribbon around Bridget and Clyous's intertwined hands.

"You are breathtakingly beautiful," was Menolayous's answer before he finally turned his gaze back to the ceremony.

Grace found herself blushing as she did the same. Bridget was now reciting vows as her and Clyous were joined by the ceremonial ribbon. Grace glanced back at Menolayous who was focused on the bride and groom, but there was a distinct difference in how he held himself. He almost seemed... lighter. Happier maybe. Grace could not stop herself from imagining it was them up there speaking the vows of marriage. There was no doubt in her mind that they loved each other, that they were it for each other. Grace entertained the idea of marriage to Menolayous, cut away all of the politics and bullshit her people would expect from her at her station, she would be overjoyed to just be married to him. To be eternally bonded to him, and deep-down Grace knew that he felt the same. He would go through the uncomfortable group setting of a wedding if she asked him. But truthfully, she didn't want the big party either, she wouldn't want a second of that day to make the love of her life uncomfortable.

"Now that the sacred vows of marriage have been spoken to us and before the gods," Rama announced loudly, "under the rule of Collie, I hereby ordain this marriage. You may now kiss each other to end the ceremony."

Grace watched as Bridget threw her arms around Clyous's neck as he pulled her to him, they shared a loving kiss. Everyone present began to applaud them, congratulations being spoken to the newly married couple. Grace once again glanced at Menolayous who stood back to allow the bride and groom space to maneuver freely. His eyes drifted to her; a wide smile now spread across his face so uncharacteristically. Yes, she wanted to be married to this man, to have him in her life forever. She didn't give a shit what was expected of her status in Airgid, she didn't care that they were from two very different social classes or came from different kingdoms. None of that mattered to her, she only wanted him. A fact that should scare her but instead left her feeling elated and comfortable in her decision.

Chapter Seventy-Seven

Menolayous

Menolayous watched as the bride and groom walked hand in hand down the forest trail, back in the direction of Collie and the awaiting after party. He watched as Morrigan, Flinn, and Rama took off after them, giving them space and setting them apart from the group as the happy couple. Danny had whispered something in Catriona's ear, causing her to laugh out loud as she started down the trail after everyone else. Menolayous chuckled as he saw his brother reach out and pinch Catriona's rear as she walked by, getting the usually proud warrior to squeal and speed up ahead of him. Danny was happy to give chase. It was heartwarming to see that Danny was still able to bring out Catriona's feminine side, where she felt safe enough to let down her walls around everyone. She deserved that opportunity.

Menolayous caught Grace by the waist as she walked by, pulling her into him gently. She turned to face him, arms wrapping around his shoulders. She leaned forward and placed her lips against his sweetly. His heart soared at the contact, finding that he was only truly at peace with her in his arms. After their kiss broke apart, he buried his face into her bare shoulder, inhaling the rich floral scent that surrounded them.

"Hey," Grace said, her voice breathy.

"Hi," Menolayous responded, his lips finding the soft skin at the hallow of her neck.

"What's on your mind?" Grace asked with a giggle as Menolayous nipped her throat gently. "It's not all lust I'm sensing from you."

Menolayous thought for a moment before answering, "I'm just happy. Happy to be with you, happy to be with our friends, happy for those two who just got married."

"It is a good day, isn't it." Grace stared up into his eyes, a smile securely fastened on her face. "I'm happy too."

And that was the reality of it. Menolayous, arguably for the first time in his life, was perfectly happy. He had a woman he practically worshipped standing by his side, friends that would die to protect each other, a home where he felt safe. The things he had been missing his entire childhood, and he had her to thank. Grace might not have provided him with all of those things directly, but she had taught him how to observe and appreciate what he already had around him. Her presence in his life allowed him to drop his guard and live.

"Come on," Grace said, pulling him gently towards the forest trail. "We have a party to go supervise. I know you're not a big fan of parties, but this is for our friends."

"Just give me a heads up if you plan on getting completely drunk again," Menolayous pleaded, mostly in humor. "You're the only one I'm willing to babysit tonight."

"I wasn't planning on drinking much today," Grace answered. "Unless being drunk would allow me special favors from my protector."

"Special favors?" Menolayous was confused by the comment.

"Sex." Grace laughed, continuing to pull him down the trail, they were nearing the clearing back into Collie.

"Oh." Menolayous felt his face heat slightly at having missed the innuendo. "How about I promise that regardless?"

"Then you'll see me sober as a bird," Grace said as they stepped into the clearing, the party already started. "I like to enjoy it without alcohol."

Menolayous smiled at her as she dragged him towards the tables now heavily laden with food. He was so lucky to have her in his life, he wouldn't even know how to begin making it even. His thoughts wandered back to the wedding ceremony, a small mostly private event that was intended for the two lovers to profess their love to each other. Menolayous hadn't witnessed many weddings, a few smaller ceremonies as a child before they had gone into hiding underground.

Oich traditions were slightly different than his, he could only imagine the traditions Airgid had for its crown princess when she was to marry. A small part of him felt a sting of insecurity, the realization that her parents would most likely not approve of him. After all the conversations Menolayous and Grace had about them, they seemed very set on Grace marrying for political reasons. Should he care about her parents' opinion of him? He wasn't sure that he did. The only person's opinion he cared about was hers.

He was not overly concerned that Grace would reject him, he knew within his heart that she wouldn't leave him for another, but would she marry him despite what her family might expect? Or would they expect them to have a large royal wedding? At the end of the day, it didn't matter. Not to him. He was hers, and she was his. He would do whatever she asked whether it be a royal wedding or none at all. He only wanted to be with her.

"Here." Grace handed him a sweet roll. "The baker put a berry glaze on it for the party. It is positively divine."

"I love you," Menolayous said with a smile, taking the sweet roll.

"I love you too." She smiled back, her eyes seemed to pierce his as she searched through his emotions. "If all it takes is a sweet roll for you to profess your love for me, I should have started off giving you a cake rather than sucking your—"

"Hey guys!" Danny came crashing into their conversation, flagons of sweet wine in his hands as he passed them out. "They did something special with the wine. I've never tasted anything so sweet."

"You're spilling." Grace shot out of his reach, preserving her dress from a certain stain. "You're drunk already."

"It doesn't take much with this." Catriona wandered up, holding her own half-empty cup. "It's like honey and blackberries. It's delicious."

"I'll try some if you keep your man away from me with those full cups." Grace laughed, taking a cup.

"To love," Danny said, raising his drink as if making a toast. "To the happy couple, and to good days to come."

Chapter Seventy-Eight

Danny

His world was definitely spinning after a few cups of that blackberry and honey flavored wine. That stuff was dangerous; he could hardly taste the alcohol before he started to feel the effects. He took a sweet roll off of one of the food tables, savoring the flavor as he took a bite. His eyes remained trained on his friends who were enjoying the party. Clyous and Bridget seemed lost in their own world, seated side by side at a table off towards the edge of the forest. Both of them were smiling and whispering to each other as they picked at the food platters that were placed before them. Danny's heart warmed at the sight of their love, they both deserved happiness after all they had been through. Finding one's partner for life was definitely worth celebrating.

Grace and Menolayous were easily found walking towards the bride and groom, carrying their own plates full of food and taking a seat. They were greeted warmly by the happy couple, the four now engaging in merry conversation. Danny was pleased to see the closeness in which Menolayous sat next to Grace, she might grate on Danny's nerves, but she made his brother happy. There was no denying it, you could see it in the way he sat, walked, talked, and actually socialized with others. Before Grace, you wouldn't have seen Menolayous at a party like this, he would have stuck to the tree line and watched everyone from the side. It was amazing what love could do to a person.

Speaking of love, his eyes searched for Catriona, who was talking with Morrigan by the wine. Her hair now flowing freely down her back instead of up like how it was for the wedding. By the gods he loved her hair, especially when she let it down. As if sensing his eyes on her she glanced in his direction, offering him a small smile before returning to her conversation with Morrigan. His eyes wandered down the length of her body, he loved that dress on her too. It hugged her muscular body in all the right places, making it so he wanted nothing more than to rip it off of her. There was plenty of time for that later, now it was time to celebrate with their friends.

Rama was helping unload a wagon of barrels, carrying them to where the bar was being set up. Danny decided to go over to his older brother and check in on him. The truth of the matter was Rama seemed in good spirits, but he hadn't been the same since that day at the lake. If Rama's impromptu confession last night meant anything, it meant that his brother was not okay, and that the King of Collie was putting on a mask of sincerity. Danny could understand that within reason, especially since the knowledge of his possession by the Dark One was kept within their family, it wouldn't do anyone good to know their king was being controlled by the enemy, even for a short amount of time, but to wear that mask around him and Menolayous, that wasn't like him.

"Another refill?" Rama laughed as Danny approached, reaching out to take his brother's now empty cup.

"Only if you have one with me." Danny smirked at him, trying to appear less under the influence than he was.

"I'm afraid I'll have to pass this time." Rama refilled Danny's cup anyway, handing it back to him.

"You always drink." Danny took the cup but continued to stare at his brother. "Why not now?"

"I've got a lot of work to do, can't be drunk and help contain this party." Rama shrugged, grabbing another barrel and setting it up at the bar.

"That's a bullshit excuse." Danny raised his eyebrows in argument. "Why aren't you over there with our family, spending time with them?"

"You know why," Rama said with a lowered voice. "It's the same reason why I haven't had a single drink since—"

"You're being obnoxiously self-pitying you know that?" Danny stared at his brother. "We all know that wasn't you. Catriona knows that wasn't you."

"But that doesn't mean either of us are over it," Rama growled at him. "It didn't just happen to her, you know. I was trapped with him for weeks, trapped with his thoughts and sick twisted fantasies. Not just about Cat and Grace, but about our brother too. Memories and plans played out in my head as if I was being forced to live through them, as if I was the one doing them. So fuck you for expecting me to just be okay with it."

"I'm sorry." Danny was taken aback by his brother's intensity. "I didn't realize how bad that could have been for you."

"No, you didn't, and no I don't want to talk to you about it." Rama glared at him, keeping his voice low so as not to cause a scene. "You're drunk, and you're an ass when you're drunk. Go bother Catriona and leave me be."

Rama turned his back on him then, retreating back to the wagon where he continued to help the barkeep unload the supply wagons. Danny sighed, resigning to the fact his brother was probably right. Now wasn't the best time to talk to Rama, but he would soon. Rama was right, Danny didn't realize the extent to which he was being tormented by the Dark One. Rama had always been a cocky bastard, but he loved women. Not in a creepy way but in a protective way. It's why he slid easily enough into a brotherly role with Catriona and Bridget. He had a gentle heart when it came to women, children, and animals. What he was forced to do, the things he was forced to remember or plan from the Dark One's twisted mind would be Rama's worst nightmare. Danny owed him an apology but now would not be the time.

Danny made his way over to where Catriona and Morrigan were talking, wrapping an arm around her waist gently, needing the reassurance of her presence. He felt guilty about how he handled his brother, and she brought him comfort. Even if they didn't talk about it. She seemed to know he needed comfort, her free arm wrapping around the one he had around her. She did not end her conversation, but her acknowledgment made his heart flutter with appreciation. By the gods, he loved her so damn much, he couldn't imagine not being in her life.

"I'll leave you two." Morrigan chuckled, stepping away and towards where Flinn sat, the war chief's eyes tracking the sorceress's every movement. "I believe I am being challenged to yet another drinking game."

"Knock him dead." Catriona chuckled, fully turning to embrace him now. "What's wrong?"

"I'm an ass when I'm drunk." Danny sighed, placing his full cup on a nearby table to free both of his arms, wrapping them around her. "I was a dick to Rama."

Catriona kissed him on the cheek gently. "You can apologize tomorrow, but maybe you should stop drinking for now."

"I think that's a good idea," Danny mumbled, burying his face in her hair.

"More people are coming down from the city," Catriona observed, nudging him to look in the direction of the gates.

Danny turned and looked in the direction of the main gate, Cat was right, dozens of people were coming down from the city towards the party. Some citizens were bearing plates of food or barrels of whatever drink they possessed. A group of men were carrying a boar tied upside down to a spit, headed for the fires. A small group of citizens carried with them a variety of musical instruments, some that Danny did not recognize. He suspected these could be Gaelach refugees, instruments they did not use on Oich. A group of teenage girls approached Bridget and Clyous's table bearing armfuls of gifts, setting them on the table before the married couple. At first the two seemed surprised at the sudden appearance of the Gaelach refugees, but after Menolayous greeted the refugees warmly in what Danny assumed was the native tongue of his countrymen, he relayed the information to the couple. Bridget broke out in a smile, warmly embracing the girls in appreciation.

"That's sweet," Danny heard Cat say as she too looked on the scene unfolding before them. "Seems the different kingdoms have no issues mingling now that we all live here in Collie."

"Good." Danny smiled at the slowly increasing party goers. "There should be no reason why anyone wouldn't get along."

Music began to play as the party goers began to line up for what appeared to be a dance. There was a sharp distinction between Oich refugees and Gaelach refugees. For starters, those from Oich tended to wear long skirts or trousers and tunics. They were in varying degrees of quality, which Danny knew to be the distinction between villages and cities they came from, and most everyone from Oich had long hair, men and women included. Those that had managed to escape from Gaelach had more of a wild appearance. Some of them wore cotton and linen similar to that of their Oich counter parts, but a good majority of them had animal skins somehow added to their wardrobe. You could tell that these individuals were transitioning to the more comfortable and easier to create fashion from Oich, but they all bore various tattoos and piercings that Oich citizens did not share. The other very distinct feature that Danny noticed was that those from Gaelach wore their hair significantly shorter than those from Oich. Men and women alike had hair that that maybe came down past their jaw line, and if there was enough hair their the Gaelach people incorporated elegant braids.

"That looks like a lot of fun," Catriona remarked, her eyes still focused on the dancers.

Danny glanced at where she was looking, watching as people came together, twirling to the beat of the drums. Some formed lines where they danced in what seemed like very specific routines while others found a partner and followed their own motions. A few of the Gaelach citizens watched as the Oich citizens admired them from the sidelines, they reached out and snagged the arms of those standing off to the side, pulling them into the dance. Those that were pulled into the dance were twirled around and lead by those who knew the dance. Laughter and shouts of excitement came from dance floor as the music began to pick up its pace.

A green blur suddenly moved past them, drawing both Cat and Danny's attention to it. Menolayous of all people was dragging Grace towards the dancing, surprising all of them. Grace was smiling ear to ear, laughing as Menolayous spun her onto the dance floor. It was times like this when Danny remembered that his brother came from a completely different culture than he and Rama had. It had been over ten years since Menolayous had even visited his homeland, until recently that is, but he appeared to remember their customs well enough. Danny was impressed with his brother, seeing him smile and enjoy himself with the woman he loved was a sight to see.

Clyous and Bridget were now on the move headed for the music. Catriona laughed as she watched her brother be dragged in the direction of the festivities. As they made their way by, Clyous reached out and snagged Cat's arm, dragging her along with him. Instead of resisting she grabbed hold of Danny, pulling him along as well. Once they reached the crowd, Danny took the lead, spinning Cat into the crowd of dancers. He wasn't sure if he was doing it right, still drunk but quickly sobering, but it did not matter, everyone was there to have fun.

Catriona laughed excitedly as Danny continued to spin her through the crowd, savoring every minute of joy he had to offer. They continued to dance to the beat of the music, which seemed to have changed tempo at least five times. Bridget and Clyous removed themselves for a break, headed for refreshments as Danny and Cat continued to dance. It wasn't a bad idea; he was parched as probably was Cat. He took the next opening in the crowd and snuck them through, finally breaking the trance the music had held them in. Catriona went to grab a table, securing one where they were lucky enough to just be themselves. Danny poured both cups full of water, smiling at her as he took his drink.

"I haven't had this much fun in years." Catriona gasped, smiled at him, her face lit up and full of life. "Thank you, for dancing with me."

"Anytime." Danny took another drink from his cup, refilling it with the pitcher stationed at the table. "Thank you for coming with me."

Catriona leaned forward, kissing him passionately. "Always."

"Cat," Danny said seriously, looking into her eyes intently.

"What's wrong?" Catriona asked, her smile fading slightly at the sight of his intensity.

"Nothing is wrong," Danny said, putting his cup down and grabbing her hands up in his. "But I've been wondering something."

"Oh no." She made to stand up, panic now blossoming in her eyes.

"Oh yes." Danny gave her a mischievous grin. "Catriona, will you do me the honor of at least considering that you might marry me someday?"

Cat burst out laughing at his words. "That is probably the least amount of commitment I've heard in a proposal."

"Yeah, well I'm trying not to scare you off." Danny pulled her hands to his chest, staring into her storm-grey eyes. "But I mean it. I want to marry you. I want to be your husband, for the rest of our lives. That doesn't have any other strings attached. We could travel the world, start a family, open a knitting shop, or burn down all of Oich for all I care. The only thing that matters to me is marrying you, all the other commitments mean little to me in comparison."

He could see the tears start to flow as she stared back at him, at least she was no longer trying to pull away. "I would be trapping you for eternity. If you haven't been able to tell yet, I'm all sorts of fucked up."

"Yeah, but you're my kind of fucked up," Danny said reassuringly. "I promise, you have never done anything that has made me question my love for you. Not even for a second."

Catriona bit her lip, thinking hard on his words. "You realize if you leave me, I'll probably burn you alive for the insult."

"Baby." Danny kissed at the tears flowing down her cheeks. "I would feel absolutely insulted if you didn't."

Catriona thought for a moment before a small smile appeared. "Okay. I'll marry you."

"Really?" Danny asked excitedly.

Catriona nodded her head just before Danny lunged forward, wrapping her up in his embrace. He kissed her passionately, deeply, in a way that he hoped would convey the message to her that he was hers. She kissed him back; he could feel her hands grazing his sides as his went straight into her loose flowing hair. He could tell by the way her back began to arch into him that she was more than a little aroused. He nipped her lower lip with his, eliciting a small gasp from her as he did. Oh, he was definitely going to fuck her tonight, so well she would be feeling it for the next week. By the gods he was happy to have her in his arms. He definitely felt like celebrating by burying himself deep inside of her. Now he needed a way to get them away from the party.

Chapter Seventy-Nine

Catriona

Catriona yawned as she turned over, her body bumping into Danny's as he lay fast asleep beside her. She opened one eye to take in the view, his mostly naked body exposed to the early morning air as his more private areas were covered by a thick blanket. Catriona admired the sight of him, feeling the tenderness of her body after many hours of intense love making. She had no regrets; she was completely satisfied with how the night had turned out.

Yesterday, the wedding ceremony itself was in the early morning hours, but the party had raged on throughout the night. Cat and Danny had snuck off several times throughout the event, needing privacy to properly satiate one another. She had never had sex that much before, but she had honestly lost count how many times they had snuck off. By the second or third time Danny had managed to secure a few blankets and a more private spot for them to continue to return to. By the time night had fallen and the party had begun to slow down, Danny and Cat had snuck off for one final time, retreating to their hidden spot within a hollowed-out tree where Danny had proceeded to tease and torture her for hours, not allowing her a release until it was almost painful. It wasn't until she threatened to burn him that he finally made good on his promise, giving her the most intense orgasm of her life.

Afterward, they had fallen asleep out here, not a care in the world. It was arguably a stupid idea, staying out beyond the walls of Collie where any scourge could come upon them, but they were not thinking about that, they were entirely focused on each other and with living in the moment. Catriona glanced around through the opening of the tree, the first beams of daylight working their way through the forest. A few birds had awoken from their slumber as well, filling the forest with their unique chorus.

"Someone is here!" Morrigan's voice echoed through her head at such a volume that she jumped.

Apparently, it had done the same with Danny, sending him to his feet from a deep sleep as he reached for his sword.

"Little early for your good morning greeting!" Clyous's voice was also heard grumbling through their connected pathway.

545

"Shut up!" Grace snapped. *"I sense them too! In the forest near the gates."*

"There's plenty of people still in the forest by the gate," Rama complained, *"myself included. People stayed out all night partying. I don't see anything amiss."*

"It's him." Morrigan's voice shook Catriona to the core, she knew which him she meant. *"He's looking for one of us in a borrowed body."*

"I'm going after him," came Rama's gruff voice.

"Wait for one of us," Menolayous lectured. *"We're not far from the gate."*

"Neither are we," Catriona shot down the bond, locating her dress and pulling it over her head.

"We'll come up behind them," Danny agreed, dressing quickly. *"We're in the forest."*

"That was dumb," Bridget lectured. *"We're coming too."*

"No!" Grace, Catriona, Rama, and Morrigan all snapped at her.

"Stay hidden, he has not figured out about you yet," Grace said softly. *"Send your husband, we might need him to see."*

"Fine." Catriona heard Bridget sigh. *"Just be careful please, all of you."*

Catriona and Danny shot into the forest, moving in the direction of an energy that seemed to pulse at them. Grace must have marked the man somehow, alerting everyone to his proximity. A clever trick to be sure. Catriona was only armed with a dagger, as was Danny. They had not thought to pack all their weapons this far out after the party, but Catriona still had control over her flames, so they were not completely defenseless.

As they neared the main road, Catriona could see a Gaelach cultist now standing in the roadway facing the main gates of Collie, not one hundred feet from the threshold. The once slumbering party goers were now awake, running to the safety of Collie's walls as Rama and a few other warriors made a line of defense, separating the tribesman from the people. Clyous, Menolayous, and Grace were now at the front gates, coming up alongside Rama as he held the defensive position. Morrigan stood at the top of Collie's walls, peering down over the now empty clearing as her raven circled the field below, most likely looking to spot additional enemies. Danny and Catriona slowly separated, taking position behind the tribesman as his attention was solely on the group in front of him.

"What do you want?" Rama's voice boomed over the early morning clearing.

The tribesman cocked his head to the side, eyeing Rama with interest. When the tribesman opened his mouth, foreign words came forth. Catriona recognized the dialect as traditional Gaelach, unfortunately she didn't know how to speak it. Menolayous took a step forward, speaking to the tribesman in his native tongue. For a moment the two spoke back and forth before Menolayous glanced at Grace and retreated a step back into the defensive line.

"He says he is here on behalf of Oisin, his king." Menolayous announced loud enough for everyone to hear him. "He says he has a gift for the groom, specifically the twin brother of his newest plaything."

Catriona felt her magic flame up at the words, but she willed it back down. Danny began to move silently off to the side, circling the tribesman for a better angle in case he wanted to push the attack. And everyone claimed she was the hot head, yet here her fiancé was planning the best way to cut the blooded's head off.

"What is this gift?" Clyous asked and Menolayous translated it.

The tribesman removed a large pouch from his belt, tossing it on the ground in front of Clyous. A small cloud escaped the opening. Before anyone could move the tribesman spoke again.

"He says that you are the head of the family now, and he is willing to offer more riches than you have ever seen to sell your sister to him," Menolayous ground out the words.

"Tell him to fuck himself in the ass," Clyous snapped, stepping forward to grab the pouch.

"What does he mean you're head of the family now?" Bridget's voice echoed down their shared connection; she was watching through someone's eyes undoubtedly.

"Be careful grabbing that!" Morrigan snapped, but it was too late.

The second Clyous touched the leather of the pouch, the markings along his spine and head lit up. Catriona started, wanting to run to him but resisted. Clyous was lost within his power, staring into the past at whatever was within the pouch. He was lost in the trance for only a minute before his power subsided. A fact that should have relieved Catriona, except the look on her twin brother's face was worse than the sudden use of his power.

"What did you see?" Catriona called, staring at the broken look on Clyous's face.

Clyous would not look in her direction, but she could see his body start to tremble. Grace took a step forward, grasping Clyous by the shoulder. She gasped loudly, as if touching him had caused her severe pain. Menolayous moved in her direction, but she shook her head, communicating something silently. Menolayous began to circle the tribesman, making his way closer to Danny.

"Clyous, what's wrong?" Catriona called, trying to decide if she should rush to her brother or attack the blooded beast that caused whatever was happening to him.

Tears were now streaming down her brother's face, as he looked up at her finally. "Cat! I'm so sorry."

"What is going on?!" she shouted, staring as her friends all seemed to be sharing a silent conversation. "Will someone fucking tell me!"

The tribesman turned towards her; a sickening grin plastered across his face. Menolayous was to Danny then, his axe sheathed at his side as he grasped Danny firmly. Rama leaned back to the warriors that stood behind him, they nodded and began to retreat back into the city.

"Cat," Grace choked out, glancing to her with tears streaming down her face.

"Control your powers girl!" Morrigan shouted down the bond at Catriona.

"What the fuck is happening?" Catriona began to glance around, trying to determine if she was missing anything vital.

"It's father," Clyous cried out, sinking to his knees. "He and Markous— they're gone."

"What do you mean, gone?" Catriona snarled, no longer caring about the tribesman standing feet from her.

Danny was refusing to be led away; in fact, he had begun to fight against Menolayous in an attempt to get back to her. Rama charged forward to assist Menolayous in dragging Danny back to safety, he was fighting tooth and nail to get back to her. Catriona watched this in shock, watched them all in utter disbelief. The way they were acting, it was like they were expecting her to explode. Which meant the words that had just come out of her brother's mouth, were real. Catriona began to shake as her rage flared to life, she could feel the fire stirring underneath her skin.

"What do you mean, gone?" Catriona shouted again, the energy from her magic shaking the ground slightly beneath her power.

"Control them!" Morrigan ordered, Catriona ignored her.

"Grace, don't!" Bridget shouted down the bond.

"It's now or waiting until she finds out. It's safer for everyone if she's out here," Grace retorted.

"Show me!" she screamed, tears of rage now pouring down her face.

Grace closed her eyes, sending the images down their shared bond. These must have been the visions Clyous had seen when touching the pouch, which Catriona now understood to be ash. The images of a battlefield suddenly took over in her mind. Bodies of warriors lay all around, blood and guts, and smoky piles of ash. Distant cries of men who lay dying filled the air as the victors moved about the well-used battlefield. Catriona focused in on those who moved freely, she recognized Oich soldiers who had apparently teamed up with a few dozen Gaelach tribesmen. She immediately recognized the Crown Prince of Oich standing amidst the dead, his armor and longsword covered in blood and grime. A tribesman she had never seen before, tall and lean and wearing a mountain lion skin as a cloak, stood beside the prince with a smile across his face.

"We have done well!" the tribesman declared, smiling at the carnage.

"What did you expect?" Liam laughed, taking deep breaths.

"Your Majesties." An Oich soldier came running up to them, bowing between his words. "We have caught the man. He currently stands surrounded at the base of that hill."

"Lead us!" Liam demanded.

Catriona watched as the soldiers led Liam and the tribesman to a hill, where they looked down to see a dozen or so soldiers surrounding the body of a dead man, and one who remained upright and ready to fight. Catriona gasped as she recognized the two rebels who were surrounded. Lying dead on the ground was her brother Markous, his throat having been ripped out by a wolf's fangs. Catriona felt tears pour down her face as she looked into her older brother's dead eyes, his last expression in this world seemed to be filled with immense pain.

Catriona's eyes flew to her father, the only survivor still standing and willing to fight. His weapons lay in the mud, freeing up his hands to use his magic. It was his only chance at survival she realized, to take them all out at once, but she saw the flames in his eyes, they were slowly flickering out. He was exhausted, he didn't have much left in him.

Movement from the trees had Catriona reluctantly looking away from her father to see the commotion. A very large black bear was now stomping across the battlefield in the direction of her father. The Oich soldiers and tribesmen made room for the massive beast as it stalked forward, bowing their heads in respect and submission. The only two blooded that did not bow at the bear's approach were Prince Liam, who looked uncomfortable in its presence, and the tribesman that stood next to him.

"Brother." The tribesman smiled at the bear, who began to shift into a man.

Catriona's heart began to beat faster at the sight of him. Tall and lean, black tattoos covered his body, his face was painted like a black skull. The man smiled back, revealing two rows of sharpened teeth and glistening red eyes. The man turned his attention to Liam, sizing him up like his next meal. Catriona recognized this man from images Grace had shared. This was the Dark One.

"King Oisin," Liam acknowledged with a nod of his head, "glad to have you join us."

"I heard you captured prey I have been hunting for some years now," the Dark One spoke with many layered voices at once. "But I understand this prey is also yours, Princeling."

"He murdered my mother," Liam snarled, refusing to submit to the power emanating from the Dark One. "I have agreed to give you the girls, but this one is mine."

"Rion." The Dark One looked at his brother.

The other tribesman, King Rion, turned to Liam then. "Do as you want with him. Torture him if you will, kill him if you must, but we would like to claim his body afterwards."

Liam had the good sense of looking disgusted. "What for?"

"We wish to devour him," the Dark One replied, "so I might take on his power."

"Never!" Farren shouted as streams of fire escaped his fingertips. "I will burn you fuckers to ash."

"No, you won't." Rion laughed. "You are fading fast. You took injury while protecting your weak son. Pretty soon this negotiation won't even matter, and we will take what is yours anyway."

Catriona cried openly now, seeing the gash across her father's back. Blood was dripping down into the mud in a steady stream, indicating that he was slowly bleeding to death. Catriona felt the fire and rage of her magic rushing to meet her father's, even though she knew this was a memory. She glared at the Dark One and his brother, she stared at Liam, daring him to turn and acknowledge her. This piece of shit, this monster had taken her mother from her, her brother now too. He was going to burn for it; she wouldn't rest until he felt every ounce of pain she has had to endure by his hand.

"If you surrender now," Rion called down to her father, "we will stop pursuing your daughter."

She could see how the tribesman's words froze her father in place. "You are hunting my daughter? You are the ones who continue to send your men after her?"

"We want her fire," Rion answered. "But, if you surrender your flames to us, we have no more need of her. You have our word, she would become... unnecessary to our plans."

"You would leave my children alone?" She could see the fight in her father fading, how she wanted to call out to him, tell him to keep going.

"You have our word," Rion called out to him.

Catriona watched as her father glanced down at Markous's lifeless body and lowered his hands. Rion and Oisin shared a look with each other before glancing at Liam.

"He is yours, Princeling," Oisin spoke with that unnerving power, "but I want his body."

"You can do whatever it is you sick bastards want to do after I've killed him," Liam snarled, she could see the excitement in his eyes.

The three of them made their way through the circle of blooded, stalking closer to her father. He had dropped to his knees, grabbing onto Markous's corpse as he rocked back in fourth as tears flowed freely. Liam slowly crept in his direction, believing that Farren was fading quickly from the injury. Catriona began to scream at her father to stand up, to fight. She pleaded with the memory as if she were actually there, begging him not to allow this. She sank to her knees beside the image of her father as she stared down at her dead brother. She knew this wasn't real, or at least happening at present, but she would be with him until the end. It was the least she could do, whether it made a difference or not she would be here until the final blow took her last parent from her.

"Do you remember me?" Liam asked her father. The point of his sword digging into Farren's chest.

Farren looked up slowly into Liam's eyes. "You are the young prince I burned all those years ago."

"Very good," Liam snarled back. "You took my mother from me that day, old man, but I got my revenge sure enough. I am the one who killed your wife and scarred your precious daughter. She might have gotten away from me, but I was the one who broke her."

Farren looked up at Liam, Catriona could see a small spark of his fire still remaining in his molten eyes as he threw his head back and laughed. "You did not break my daughter. She's going to break you."

Liam stuck his sword tip into Farrens' shoulder, drawing blood through his already ruined tunic. Instead of reeling back in pain, Farren remained kneeling where he was, laughing like a mad man.

"You want to know how I know?" Farren asked, finally ceasing his laughter. "Because, after all of these years, you're still too stupid to realize when you've stepped into a trap."

"Oisin!" Rion called, jumping in front of his brother as if to shield him.

Oisin slammed his foot down into the ground creating a solid wall of ice that surrounded the two tribesmen and Liam. Just as the Dark One's foot hit the soil, a white and blue flame erupted from Farren, pushing flames outward at least fifty feet from the center. Liam dove for cover behind the ice, narrowly missing the flames as they continued to spread. Catriona wailed as she took in the sight, her father's last act on this earth was to try and take out the enemy. She screamed as she watched the flames die out and witnessed the carnage that lay before her. Dozens of enemy soldiers lay dead, burnt beyond recognition as the ice wall the Dark One had been actively feeding his magic was mostly melted away. But at the center of the inferno was a pile of ash.

Where Farren had kneeled before his dead son was nothing. Her father had ensured that the enemy would not be able to take his power by burning himself and Markous into nothing. Her father had done the very thing he had been trying to teach Catriona not to do, he had given himself over to the flames completely. He had fought until the end and had almost successfully taken out their enemies, he sacrificed himself. His last act in this world was an attempt to protect her and Clyous, to deny pure evil what it craved the most.

The images faded then, her consciousness returning to the present. She remained kneeling in the dirt, only instead of on a battlefield she was kneeling on the road leading to Collie, and instead of her father's flames surrounding her, it was her own distinct white flame. She let loose another wail, throwing her head back and unleashing her power further up into the sky. Only the release of her flames made the sharpness of her father's and brother's deaths lessen.

Her hair whipped around her as the flames began to turn the grass and trees surrounding her to ash, even her clothing was not safe in this inferno. She had no desire to pull her powers back, in fact she wanted her flames to devour. The enemy wanted something to devour, did she ever have the perfect gift for them. The tribesman that once stood feet from her now lay burning on the ground, Catriona glared at the body, pushing more energy into her flames. She watched as his corpse began to turn to ash as the fire licked his charred flesh.

So, they wanted to hunt her? To devour her power? Oh, she planned to give them exactly what they wanted. She would force feed them her flames, and relish in their deaths as they burned at her feet. The Dark One's pathetic ice wall was no match for her power, she would break through his magic in seconds. There wasn't a place on this continent where they would be able to hide from her. Liam! She would go for him first; she would burn the entire continent down to get to him.

"Cat!" a voice called from a distance, barely loud enough for her to hear.

The flames coming from her had grown so large, the weather surrounding her had begun to change. The wind was picking up, taking her flames even farther, enveloping the surrounding area. The smoke began to act like dark clouds, surrounding the growing inferno like bad weather being brought in. Catriona could see what remained of a wall, pieces of it still engulfed in white flames while other parts had crumbled leaving charred holes. This place was supposed to mean something, but she couldn't remember what. The only reality she could remember was the reality of her father's and brother's deaths, and the men she held responsible.

Catriona felt the ground shift beneath her feet, suddenly she sunk into it, a hole forming underneath her. Her concentration broke for an instant, stopping the flames from pouring out of her. As she made to climb from the hole, the walls around her closed in, trapping her arms and legs so she couldn't move. Panic and rage set in as she struggled to free herself, she could feel her blood heat up once again calling out to this new challenger. Suddenly, rain began to pour from the sky, drenching the remaining flames surrounding the forest and city around her.

Catriona coughed as she struggled against her cage, the pressure from the soil squeezing her ribs together tighter. Two familiar bodies approached her, however she could not remember who they were, if they were friendly or foe.

The black-haired woman held her hands before her, magic dripping from her fingertips into the earth surrounding Catriona. Silver markings flamed to life as this sorceress worked her magic, creeping up the woman's bare arms to show her markings. This woman was no friend if she was responsible for trapping her here. The other woman, a brunette, approach her cautiously with outstretched hands. A purple mark behind her ear and down her neck burned bright as she too began to pump magic in Catriona's direction.

"I'm so sorry Cat," the woman said almost convincingly.

"Don't you fucking touch me!" Catriona shrieked, struggling against the ground as it held her tightly.

The woman gently lay her hand on Catriona's face, releasing her magic into her. Catriona struggled for a moment before she began to slow, the woman's magic sapping her energy piece by piece. Within moments Catriona had stopped struggling against her captors, recognition slowly coming back to her. These were her friends, but why were they trapping her here. Catriona looked around sluggishly, as if she were so drunk she could barely function. Her eyes trained on the destruction around them, the surrounding field burnt to ash, leaving only charred dirt behind. The outer gate and wall to Collie was burned, the flames extinguished by those who could wield water. The windmill, Flinn's pride and joy, was destroyed, lying just outside the outer wall in pieces. She had done this. Catriona wailed in agony at the realization she was responsible, at the knowledge that her father and brother were dead. Grace's magic continued to flow through her, slowing her down even harder. Catriona found it impossible to keep her eyes open anymore, so she relented, succumbing to the deep sleep necessary to stop her destruction.

Chapter Eighty

Clyous

It had been one week, seven days since his wedding. You'd think he would be happier, but he wasn't. Through no fault of his bride's, Clyous had learned of his father's and older brother's deaths the morning after their nuptials. The bag of their ashes being hand delivered to him was an especially vile strategy, the Dark One knowing all too well that all Clyous had to do was touch the pouch and he would see the dark end his family had met. It was an especially clever strategy, especially knowing that he wouldn't be able to hide this from Catriona after having the vision in front of her. He wished it could have been different, wished he could have had more time to pull himself together and tell her in a way that could have eased her into the information, but she knew him too well, they were two sides to the same coin. Catriona wasn't capable of letting something go, not something that serious. The Dark One had counted on her inability to control her rage. Lucky for them, he hadn't counted on the fact that Catriona was outside the city walls when he planned his little ambush.

Grace was right to show her while Catriona was still outside of the city. The second Grace had discovered what Clyous's vision was, they had all immediately went into action to try and contain Catriona's blow out. She knew something was wrong, she could tell they were all talking without her. Thinking back on it that might have been a poor choice, but they were all concerned about getting Danny away from her. Clyous knew that she would lose herself to her rage, and harming Danny would be something she would never come back from. What made it worse was the fact that the love-struck fool fought with them, trying to get back to her as if he could have somehow shielded her from the pain. He was in complete disregard for his own safety at that point. It took both Rama and Menolayous to drag him back behind the safety of the walls before Catriona's power erupted.

They all made it just in time before Catriona was completely sucked into the vision Grace had shown her. Clyous could hear his sister wailing as he ran for cover, wanting nothing more than to run towards her, to share in this grief with her. He could hear her yelling at the ghost of their father, telling him to get up and fight. Promising she wouldn't leave him. It's when she fell silent, he knew she had gotten to the part where their father sacrificed himself.

It was deathly calm then, the air around them so still Clyous couldn't hear any birds chirping not even a breeze moving through the leaves in the trees. It was as still as death itself; Catriona's power then hit like a thunderclap.

Waves of heated wind rushed past the walls of Collie, making the structure sway from the impact before the flames hit. They were lucky enough to have gotten the front gate closed as the white flames rocked against the wooden beams, climbing their way up and over like an enemy scaling the walls. Everyone near the gate scattered, taking cover further into the city. All that remained were their friends, moving off to the side but staying as close to the walls as they dared. Morrigan began feeding into her powers, using what elements she could to try and contain the flames to what they had already burned. Danny was still fighting with his brothers, trying to get back to Cat. Clyous could still hear Cat's wails over the sound of the flames. Every second that went by the flames seemed to grow, getting larger and burning hotter.

Clyous knew his sister had power, it was no secret to anyone that she outmatched their father when it came to raw flames, but nobody, not Morrigan, not Grace, not himself, expected this much to come pouring out of her. Her wielding today made that day out in the field look like child's play, there was no reasonable explanation for how her flames were able to reach inside Collie this far from where she was on the road. If they had known, maybe they would have done it differently. That was on him, he told Grace to show her. He believed there was a wisdom to it, but maybe there weren't any good choices to have been made.

Catriona was nearing burnout, he could feel it as could the others, but her power had raged on, so intensely that heat from the flames had begun to affect the weather around them. At first Clyous had thought it was Morrigan trying to summon a rain cloud, but the look of shock on Morrigan's face proved that was not the case. It wasn't until some of the refugees came running, those with the blood of the ancients rose up to help protect their new home. The variety of powers he watched be used to contain the flames was incredible, he had never seen so many magic users in one spot before. He counted twenty of them, every single one of them taking up a line of defense within the walls and wielding their powers together. They were able to beat the flames back enough to allow Morrigan and Grace to get through. They made it to Cat and were able to subdue her and put her into a deep sleep, ending the inferno.

Clyous had thought a year ago he had faced the worst possible day of his life, watching as his sister was strung up and beaten while his mother was burned alive. He believed they were all to die that day, he was man enough to admit how scared he was. That was nothing in comparison to what he had witnessed outside of Collie. He was forced into a vision where he had to watch his brother and father die, then stand by as his twin sister nearly destroyed herself and everyone they cared about in her own inferno. Knowing his wife could also be caught up in the flames, his friends and found family, that was the scariest day of his life.

Catriona had remained in bed for days recovering from her burnout. Bridget had run out of yarrow root several times trying to keep her riding at surface level, sending Danny out to collect more. Danny, aside from collecting the yarrow root, refused to leave Cat's side. Everyone had made a point in dropping by at least once to see how she was recovering, but her burnout had quickly turned to grief, keeping her bedridden for an entirely different reason. Her grief lasted maybe a day or so before she was up and moving. Like him, she had to work through her grief, so she joined in the repairs for the wall, working from sunup until sunset trying to right the wrong that she had committed. Not that any of them blamed her, they all knew she hadn't intended to lose control like that, but the citizens of Collie were now scared of her, most reluctant to get close to her as she worked. Clyous knew that was a hard transition for her, but she was bearing it with as much grace as she could, her guilt overriding her self-pity.

Clyous had jumped headfirst back into the forge. Now that a portion of the wall needed repairing, he was working double-time to repair or create more tools and spikes for the job. Keeping his hands busy was the only thing holding him together, well... that and Bridget. His grief was nearly overpowering, he felt like crawling into bed and staying there for the next few months. He knew this wasn't an option, he couldn't succumb to that. Bridget wouldn't let him anyway.

Bridget strolled into the forge carrying a basket. He could tell by the smell of it that she had brought him lunch knowing he hadn't bothered with breakfast and left their home headed straight to the forge. He found a place to stop working, setting aside his tools and removing his gloves to go greet her. He had given up trying to argue that he didn't need to eat, she was persistent. So, he walked up to her and gave her a kiss before sitting down at the shop's table. Bridget took pride in removing the food and setting it in front of him. He glanced up at her, appreciating her devotion to ensuring he ate. It's what kept him from spiraling into the darkness, she was his light.

"The ladies at the longhouse gave me an extra roll to make sure you are eating enough." Bridget smiled at him as she removed a glass bottle from the basket. "And one of them made this cider from apples."

"Thank you." Clyous gave her a half smile, staring at the food as he prepared himself for the challenge of eating it.

Bridget's attention immediately moved to a figure approaching them from the street. Clyous glanced up, his breath caught at the sight of his sister. Her face and clothing covered in dirt from working on the wall. By the look in her eyes, she had either been up working for hours, or she hadn't been sleeping. Both were possible. Catriona approached them cautiously, eyes downcast as she neared, hiding the shame she had been carrying around from them as best she could.

"Hi," she said as she entered the shop, waiting by the entrance as if expecting them to turn her away.

"Hi," Clyous responded, staring at her intently, trying to discern if she had been eating.

Apparently, Bridget was of the same mindset. "Have you eaten lunch yet?"

"I wasn't hungry," Catriona answered quietly, revealing that she had slipped back into her old habits once again.

"Sit," Bridget commanded her, pulling out a chair. "You will eat. Clyous, share."

"Yes ma'am." Clyous smiled at his wife knowingly, her dominating side was almost motherly at times.

Catriona knew better than to argue and took a seat across from him. Clyous handed her the extra roll from his lunch basket as Bridget dug up an extra plate and cup from deep within the shop. She set it before Catriona, then took the time to portion the food out evenly. Catriona glanced up at Bridget, who stood by with her arms crossed as she waited. Catriona dared not roll her eyes as she forced herself to take a bite of the bread.

Seemingly satisfied, Bridget uncrossed her arms, leaned over and gave Clyous a quick kiss on the cheek. "I'll leave you to it. Make sure she eats everything before she leaves."

"Yes sweetheart," Clyous said affectionately, laughing at the expression on his sister's face. "You won't win with her; you might as well eat. I will be reporting back to her."

"Whatever," Catriona said as she took another bite, the expression on her face was like she was chewing on dirt.

"What brings you here?" Clyous asked as he too began to dig into his plate. "I know for a fact it wasn't for a lunch break."

"I was wondering if you could make something for me," Catriona said, taking another bite.

"What tool did you break now?" Clyous groaned, he was repairing hammers left and right from this new reconstruction job.

"Not a tool." Catriona glanced at him nervously. "A bracelet."

"Come again?" Clyous nearly choked on his cider. "You want jewelry?"

"I want an iron bracelet," she retorted, he could hear frustration laced in her words.

"Why in the fuck would you want jewelry made of iron?" Clyous was confused at the request as well as her defensiveness. "You know iron… stops your magic. Why in the fuck would you want to get rid of your magic?"

"I don't want to get rid of it, I want to control it." She tried hard to keep the anger out of her voice, she was failing. "A bracelet is something I can take off, but I need something to help me keep a lid on it so next time—"

"There might not be a next time." Clyous was angry now, why, exactly he wasn't sure, but an iron bracelet seemed like an easy out to him. "You're still new to your powers, just like me. You'll get control over them."

"When?" her voice cracked as she sat up straighter. "After I've burned the world down? After I've accidentally killed the only family I have left, all because I can't control my emotions?"

"You'll get there." Clyous felt his voice starting to rise, "None of us blame you for what happened. The Dark One set us all up!"

"Maybe you should blame me!" she shouted, standing from her chair. "That bastard wouldn't have been able to set us up if I wasn't so predictable. My lack of control is no longer just that, I am a liability to everyone I'm around."

"You're not a liability!" Clyous was on his feet now, shouting back at her.

"Really?" Catriona grimaced. "What if I had hurt Bridget? Would you still be saying the same thing?"

"But you didn't!" Clyous tried to say without yelling, he failed.

"You were all prepared for it though. You had to drag Danny back behind the walls to protect him from me." Tears were beginning to form, but Catriona beat them back. "Nobody was prepared for the amount of destruction I caused, if I had lost myself while in the city—"

"But you didn't," Clyous managed to say with an even voice. "Last week wasn't something that is likely to be repeated again. You already survived the odds for that being used against you a second time."

"I still have you!" she shouted. "You seriously want to sit here and tell me that it can't happen again while I have you in my life? Are you able to use your power to look ahead and assure me that it won't happen?"

"I can't," Clyous admitted, his eyes downcast. "I haven't been able to look forward since."

"Then you can't tell me that for certain." Catriona had finally stopped shouting, he could sense she wanted to comfort him but wasn't sure how. "I need help, Clyous. Please! Be my brother and help me protect the ones we love, help me protect myself from feeding myself to the flames. Give me a fighting chance."

After a few moments of silence between them, Cat sighed and turned to leave, looking positively defeated. Deep down Clyous could understand why she wanted the bracelet; he could see the sense in it. Who was he to deny her a fighting chance, give her something that at the bare minimum brought her peace of mind. Her power wasn't like his, where his was rooted in control and logic, hers was fueled by emotions. Looking at her request as an easy way out was foolish on his part. They were not the same and she had a point, whether he agreed with it or not, she had been through so much. She would never be whole again, she was cracked on the surface, her emotions always ready to spill out at a moment's notice.

"Fine!" he called after her. "But take your lunch or I'll tell Bridget you started a fight just so you didn't have to eat."

Catriona shot him a look over her shoulder as she walked out of the shop. He didn't miss the middle finger she threw in his direction before snagging her lunch plate and walking off. She would eat it; she wasn't that far gone at the moment. If he knew his sister, as soon as the wall was rebuilt, she would begin training doubly as hard. She had a target in mind; her sights set avidly on the Crown Prince of Oich. She would begin to obsess over it, losing herself to her mission of revenge, but that was better than letting herself fade away into nothing. Revenge motivated her to keep going, it was the preferred option as far as he was concerned. At least they could do something before

560

she lost herself totally, all because she hadn't given up. He supposed he should start working on that bracelet, maybe it really could provide her with a sense of security.

Chapter Eighty-One

Morrigan

"The time has come for you to seek out your mother's assistance," Morrigan stated to Grace, knowing the princess was not happy about the topic. "We desperately need the reinforcements after the loss of our Harrada Pass battalion."

"You do realize that me going and asking my mother for help does not mean she will help," Grace said, exasperated. "She is not a fan of agreeing to anything she is not in control of."

"Your mother is a wise woman and will see the necessity of aiding us," Morrigan countered, stroking Storms feathers as he sat on her shoulder.

"You assume too much." Grace rolled her eyes. "But at least I can say I tried. Just don't expect much from her."

"I expect most people to lean towards self-preservation," Morrigan chided, not necessarily at Grace. "Unlike our fire bird of course, she chooses to destroy everything around her."

"That's not fair." Grace turned to her, narrowing her eyes at the sorceress. "That was a complete set up. The Dark One knew what hand to play with her; he set it up so she would lose control."

"She shouldn't be so predictable that her enemies can use her powers against her," Morrigan shot back.

It was no secret that the Dark One had intentionally set Catriona up for such a large power release, he was smart enough to play her heartstrings, knowing that the girl's emotions and powers were connected. The more power one of her bloodline possessed, the less in control they were of themselves. It was nature's way of counterbalancing the magic. Just as Grace could only project images or enter people's mind through touch, she could not manifest anything physical. Morrigan was limited as well, given the gift of the elements and nature, that variety proved her to be powerful, but her limits for each power were limited compared to others with individual gifts. Clyous could see past and present but would constantly battle the edges of reality and his visions, never fully able to predict the outcome due to the world's ever-changing nature. Bridget had the worst of it, her power was naturally geared towards healing which gave her an aversion to violence and harming others. Her inability to use her power to drain another of their life force had kept her as the only child of the ancients who hasn't received her mark. Morrigan knew of this balance, knew of Catriona's unpredictability, but she could not help but be angered at the incident. Catriona should have had more control over herself than she has proven to have, she should not be so easily used against her friends.

"It's kind of hard to be unpredictable when your enemy enters your mind while you sleep and uses his spies to watch you." Grace's defense of her friend was admirable, as well as genuine, a stark difference in the princess that Morrigan had met nearly a year ago.

"Catriona will eventually lose herself to the flames," Morrigan warned. "She has shown that with her lack of control, it is inevitable. Defense of your friend is an admirable quality, but do not let yourself get caught up in her firestorm when she decides she is done."

"Fuck you," Grace snapped, turning on her heel and walking away. "Seriously, fuck you."

Morrigan watched the princess stomp away, she could practically feel anger radiating off of her. She glanced over at Menolayous who was staring after his woman before turning his predatory gaze to the sorceress. Morrigan stared back at him for a moment, acknowledging how a lesser woman would quiver in fear from his gaze. He was a powerful warrior, for a human without the gift of magic he was as formidable as if he was. He came from the same people Morrigan's current body had, channeling years of a warrior spirit and hard lifestyle. The man had survived things most would not, making his gaze and its promise of death all the more intimidating.

"I would expect you to find something more colorful to say than that." Morrigan once again stroked the feathers of her raven as she stared at the warrior before her.

"It's always bothered me," Menolayous started slowly, sizing her up as he spoke, "how we are from the same people and that you have stood by for the last decade allowing our countrymen to be tortured and terrorized by someone you claim to be mortal enemies with."

Morrigan sighed at the truth of his words. "I was too focused on another task, believing that at the time the world was better without me directly in it. An error, as I have admitted."

"All those years hunting down scourge, for whatever your obsessive reasoning is it kept you from looking at those around you. You missed the big picture," Menolayous said. "Have you ever stopped to think you're still too busy going for the enemy to see what you're doing?"

"I am fighting the enemy." Morrigan narrowed her eyes at the warrior. "I am doing what I am supposed to."

"You are abandoning your people all over again!" Menolayous snapped. "You claim to be the Guardian of the Ancients, but instead of trying to help the one who needs you most, you're condemning her. You and I both have seen the limits people can be pushed to, you and I both know more than anyone how dangerously close she is to jumping off that cliff. I am trying to pull her back, while all you're doing is telling her it's a matter of time before she jumps. You don't know how to be a friend, let alone a guardian of anyone. You're just a spear thirsty for blood."

His words stung as they hit her, he was right. Morrigan was not thinking about Catriona and how to help her, she was more focused on the fight ahead. Menolayous turned on his heel, taking off after Grace, leaving Morrigan standing there to sift through his words. Maybe he was right, maybe Morrigan had forgotten how to be anything other than a tool for vengeance. In that regard, it meant she was the older version of Catriona, if the girl managed to survive that long. Morrigan felt the unfamiliar pangs of guilt as she thought harder, unraveling her past actions into something more realistic to understand. There was a good chance Catriona would die in this war, a fact that Morrigan looked at as an inevitability, but maybe she shouldn't be bracing for it, maybe she should be doing what Menolayous suggested and be a friend. If Catriona gave herself over to her flames, it wouldn't just be her failure to choose life. It would be Morrigan's failure at not doing everything she could to help her.

Chapter Eighty-Two

Catriona

Morrigan glared at her from across their training ring, her irritation with Catriona's attitude obvious to everyone. Catriona glared back at her but kept her mouth shut. Morrigan was not the one she wanted to pick a fight with. The old hag had become insufferable since Grace left for Airgid. Morrigan was acting as if Catriona was going to have another explosion at any moment, not that she could blame her. Catriona was responsible for a rather large hole in the southernmost wall of Collie.

Morrigan's newest criticism was how Catriona was interacting with the new gifted warriors. Morrigan had brought back quite a few gifted individuals, they joined the girls every morning just outside the city walls. Catriona had attempted to help train the younger ones in hand-to-hand combat, but Morrigan was concerned she might get set off and burn someone by mistake. Hence Catriona's attitude problem.

She wasn't particularly thrilled about being treated this way, she didn't need people tiptoeing around her or thinking she wasn't in control. Morrigan had also started to try and talk to Catriona about controlling her emotions. Those were fun conversations, always reminding her how little control she had. Cat took it as patronizing, whether that was the old sorceress's intention or not. It was no secret to anyone in Collie just how dangerous she was, and she was treated accordingly by the citizens. Some were brave enough to come around her while others avoided her completely. Both responses broke what was left of her heart.

Morrigan guided the group of newer recruits back in the direction of Collie, steering them away from Catriona. Catriona felt the heat begin to radiate from her palms, but she was unable to call her flames to her hands. What nobody knew, or had realized, was that Catriona now wore an iron bracelet on each wrist. Clyous had crafted them for her a few days ago, plating the iron with silver so as not to be overly obvious to those who understood the meaning. He had given them a simple design, knotwork similar to the design painted on the inside of their family home. It was enough to keep her flames at bay, but not enough to cut her off from her magic completely.

Catriona could still feel the heat of her flames beneath the surface but was unable to touch them when wearing both of the bracelets.

"I think she's just worried about you," Bridget said while watching her, compassion filling her eyes. "I don't believe she's trying to be cruel."

"Doesn't matter does it?" Catriona snapped. "She's not wrong. Better to keep everyone safe from the unpredictable freak."

Bridget audibly sighed before saying, "You're taking things out of context. I understand you're emotional right now, anyone would be, but your magic is controlled by your emotions."

"Hence the unpredictable," Catriona snapped.

Bridget glanced around them, eyes scanning the forest beyond before settling back to her. "Yes, you're unpredictable right now. That doesn't mean we love you any less. It is what it is, we're working with the situation that was handed to us."

Catriona picked up a rock, throwing it into the trees. "I know," was all she said.

"Losing anyone you love can be absolutely devastating." Bridget's gaze softened. "I get it. I really do. And I'm sorry, what happened to your brother and father was horrible."

"I'm not sure I can handle losing anyone else." Catriona felt the tears begin to creep up on her with this confession. "I don't know how to deal with this much loss."

"I don't know either," Bridget said softly. "But you still have me, you still have Clyous and Danny and everyone else."

Catriona shot her a small smile. "Thank you."

"Morrigan could be handling it better," Bridget confessed, staring in the direction of the forest again like she had seen something. "I don't believe all those years of solitude have helped her people skills any."

"I swear she's nicer hunting down scourge." Catriona faked a laugh, trying to lessen the tension. "You're not wearing your ring?"

Bridget looked down at her bare hand before returning her gaze to Cat. "I really don't want to ruin it during training, so I left it at home."

"That's smart." Catriona could see the logic in it.

"I see you're wearing new jewelry?" Bridget asked with a raised eyebrow. "Are they helping?"

Of course her twin brother would consult with his wife about her request, it should have been obvious. Catriona shifted uncomfortably, ashamed that she felt she had to stoop so low she had to wear iron to keep herself from losing control.

"They seem to keep the flames back." Catriona looked to the ground, avoiding her eyes. "But they don't cut me off from them completely."

"I understand why," Bridget said soothingly. "Really, I do. Clyous only told me because I caught him working on them. You shouldn't feel shame for something that gives you peace."

"I feel shame for needing them to feel peace." Catriona looked up at her friend finally, her sister-in-law. "I should never have gotten to a point where I needed them."

Bridget's attention suddenly turned from Catriona to the tree line. Her head cocked to the side as her eyes searched, as if the wolf inside was seeing or hearing something they could not. Catriona glanced in the same direction, not seeing anything. A low growl emitted from Bridget's throat as her head snapped back to Catriona.

"Run!" Bridget snarled. "Now!"

Before Catriona even had time to react, several large wolves burst from the trees running straight at them. Bridget shifted just as Catriona rushed to remove the bracelets, sending a wall of flame in the direction of the oncoming enemy. Her flames were weaker than she expected, clearly the iron took a while to get out of her system. The wolves veered away from the flames, separating into different directions to find a way around the wall of flame. Bridget turned and charged behind them at more wolves who were coming from behind.

Catriona turned to send more flames their direction but stopped herself. Bridget was there, and she was right, Catriona was too unpredictable right now. She wouldn't risk harming her friend with her flames. Instead, she unsheathed her short swords and ran out at one of the wolves now approaching from the side.

With a downward slash, Catriona sliced through the first wolf before spinning into the next, dodging a vicious bite. Three more came for her, she blasted small amounts of fire their direction to keep them back. Out of the corner of her eye she watched as Bridget's auburn wolf fought off two others.

There was maybe a total of fifteen wolves surrounding them. At first it seemed that the wolves were coming for her. Strategically that made sense, she was arguably the bigger threat with her fire magic, but now the majority seemed to be going towards Bridget. Catriona ran to her friend, angry not only at them starting to target her but that she couldn't use her magic to stop them.

Catriona was about twenty feet from Bridget, who was doing her best to fend off three wolves at once. Catriona watched as a wolf in the background shifted back into human form, approaching the distracted auburn wolf. Something wasn't right, Catriona realized, he carried a shackle with him.

"Look out!" Catriona screamed, running even harder.

Several wolves now took to placing themselves between the girls, snarling a warning. Catriona charged, swinging the swords wildly. She could hear the yell of pain as the auburn wolf was finally pinned down by its throat. The man ran up securing the shackle to a paw. Catriona watched in disbelief as Bridget was forced to shift, screaming at the application of this strange new device.

The wolves all began to shift then, angry guards now stood at the ready pulling free their weapons. With a roar Catriona engaged with the group, bouncing between enemies as she slashed. She called upon her magic then, if she could keep the fire concentrated on her, she could get to Bridget.

"Stop!" one of the men ordered. "Or I'll slit her throat."

Catriona paused long enough to see the guard now holding Bridget by her hair, knife to her throat. Catriona stopped moving, lowering her blade only slightly. She glanced into Bridget's eyes, fear filled them. Catriona was sure her eyes reflected the same.

"That's a good girl," the soldier practically purred. "Now drop your blades."

"Don't do it." Bridget's voice echoed in her mind. *"They won't kill me, Liam won't allow it."*

"I'm not sure they're here for you," Catriona answered, glancing around. *"Can you reach Morrigan?"*

"I'll try."

"Let her go and I'll drop them," Catriona bartered.

"Ladies first," the soldier snarled, digging the blade into Bridget's neck, a drop of blood appearing.

"They don't know who you are," Catriona announced. *"They're here for me."*

"Morrigan is on the way." Bridget's voice sounded terrified as it rang through her head.

Catriona dropped her sword, glaring at the guard who held her friend hostage. Two guards shot forward and grabbed her, forcing her to her knees. Another swooped in securing a similar cuff to Bridget's on her wrist. Catriona cried out in surprise as sharp barbs punctured her flesh, blood now trickling down her arm. At a quick glance Catriona realized the cuff was made of iron. A more savage rendition of what Clyous had made for her, and one she could not remove.

Catriona desperately grasped for even an ember of her power, but she couldn't reach it. It felt as if a pocket of cold water had drenched her, causing her flames to die out. The disconnection was not only a shock, but it was painful. Like a piece of her was missing.

"What the fuck did you do?" Catriona spat trying to pull from her captors.

"Iron neutralizes magic." The guard laughed. "Just like silver tames the wolf."

"What do you want from us?" Bridget asked carefully as two guards took her from the captain, binding her hands.

"From you, beautiful," the soldier gently stroked the side of her face, "nothing really. We came for the cunt that's been burning holes in our city. You were a happy accident."

"Fine. You have me then," Catriona bit out. "Let her go."

"No!" Bridget snarled, pulling away as the captain reached out to touch her again.

Reaching out, Catriona realized the iron kept her from speaking into Bridget's mind, hopefully Morrigan would get here in time. There was only one option Catriona could see that could buy them time, or at the very least get their perverted attention off her friend.

Catriona made her move, throwing herself sideways, her body crashed into one of the soldier's legs, knocking him to the ground. As he fell his grip on her arm loosened. Catriona launched herself onto the other guard who still held onto her, also knocking him flat. The other guards began

569

shouting as she crawled her way onto him, drawing a dagger from her boot and thrusting it between his ribs.

"Grab her!" she heard the captain shout. "Do not kill her, the king wants her alive!"

Catriona managed to plunge the dagger into the man several more times before they got to her. She felt a body crash into her, knocking her off her victim with such force she wasn't able to react. Before she hit the ground, she felt several hands on her, grabbing hold of her arms and legs. She was forced on her back while one guard sat on her hips as two more pinned down her arms.

Catriona could faintly hear Bridget screaming her name as a large fist came crashing down on her face. The impact was jarring, her vision blacking out for a moment. Another strike knocked her head back, grinding her skull into the ground painfully. It was as if she was getting hit from two different directions with each impact. Blood flowed freely from her mouth and nose down her chin as the strikes kept coming. She couldn't hold the darkness back any longer, she lost consciousness.

Catriona awoke sometime later, her head pounding. It felt like she was lying in the back of a wagon, the hard planks of wood pressing against her back. Opening her eyes, she found herself staring up into the nights sky. How long had she been unconscious? She did a quick head-to-toe assessment, feeling pain and soreness in her extremities and her head.

The cart must have run over a tree root or rock because it jolted the wagon violently. Catriona gasped at the pain of her shoulder crashing into the wood as the wagon jolted. Movement caught her attention; there was a body sitting up by her head.

"Cat?" she heard Bridget's voice whisper. "Are you awake?"

"Yeah." Catriona whispered back, trying to fight off the extreme dizziness as she sat up. "What's happened, where are we?"

Bridget's figure became clearer; Catriona visually inspected her friend. There were no visual signs of injury save for the small cut on her throat from the dagger earlier, and from the cuff still locked onto her wrist, so that was a small relief. Her clothes seemed intact, another good sign, they hadn't raped her... yet. Hopefully the warped morals of Oich would keep them from it, but Catriona doubted these particular guards concerned themselves with that ancient mindset. What was concerning was that her hands and ankles were bound with rope, as were Catriona's, she realized.

570

"We're on the road headed to the capital." Bridget shuffled forward. "After they knocked you senseless, they tied us both up and dragged us away from Collie to a hidden wagon. Morrigan wasn't able to get to us."

"But she knows?" Catriona fought off the dizziness and panic.

"Yes," Bridget whispered, eyes glancing up to where one of the guards sat.

"Good." Catriona breathed easier, laying back to center herself in the world again, her head was spinning as if she'd had too much to drink.

"Why did you do that?" Bridget was tearing up now. "Why would you fight knowing that they would eventually stop you? They beat the shit out of you. I'm pretty sure you have a concussion."

"I'm pretty sure I do too." Catriona raised her bound hands to gently touch her swollen face. "Because I know what's going to happen to us. I was trying to buy Morrigan more time, but I also wanted that captain to stop focusing on you."

"I don't understand."

"They came here for me, Bridget. They don't know who you are other than the fact you're a blooded who picked the wrong side. That makes you an easy target," Catriona explained. "If you are able to escape they won't care much, but they are most likely going to rape and kill you. Without the prince's protection they will do what they want with you."

The look of shock on Bridget's face drove Catriona on. "For whatever reason they want me, they have to wait until they bring me back. Where I will most likely be raped, tortured, and possibly killed. I'm not going to be able to escape my fate unless our family comes for me in time, but that doesn't mean you have to suffer too."

"We're in this together," Bridget growled. "Sacrificing yourself will not guarantee they won't touch me."

"No, but I've got to try." Catriona let a tear slide down her cheek. "I've survived this before, I will again. If I can save you from that I will."

"I've been beaten before. I'm not so breakable you need to ruin yourself to protect me."

"I'm already ruined," Catriona whispered, the darkness of her confession saturating their breathing space. "I've never told anyone before; I've always felt that speaking about it gave it life."

"Cat, I—" Bridget stammered, unsure of what to say or do.

"When I was sixteen, the boys were with mother across the city purchasing supplies. They left me in charge of the shop while they were out. A patrol of three blooded guards came by and took advantage of the easy target I was then. Two of them held me down while their captain raped me. They shoved my face down into the dirt so I couldn't scream. When he was done, they just left me there. I hid it from my family because I was ashamed."

Silent tears were pouring down both of their faces now.

"That's why you started training again?" Bridget asked. "Clyous said you started up again as a teenager."

"Yes," Catriona choked out. "It's why I knew what happened to Menolayous before everyone else. I saw myself in him. Grace found out when she searched my memories, but she kept it between us. I haven't even told Danny."

"And why you took on those rich pricks that followed me into the forest that day." Realization of all these many events finally dawning on her. "And why you hate ground fighting."

"A lot has changed during our last year together." Catriona smiled halfheartedly. "But just like that day in the forest, I need you to listen to me when I say run. Not fight. Do this for me."

"I won't leave you." Bridget ground her teeth. "I don't run anymore."

Catriona remained silent for a moment, weighing her words carefully. "If you get the chance to run, you need to take it. They don't know about your magic, so you can still talk to our family. You getting away might be the only way to save my life."

Bridget was crying now, staring into her eyes as if this was the last time they would see each other. "I hadn't healed you because I didn't want them to see."

"Good." Catriona gently touched her bound hands. "That was the smart choice. I can handle a concussion for now."

"I love you."

"I love you too." And Catriona meant it.

Bridget had so much to look forward to, a real life with her brother. Catriona knew she had a death date hanging over her head, she knew the risks of choosing to fight in this war. When push came to shove, Catriona would do whatever it took to protect her sister. Even if it meant reliving her worst nightmares, even if it meant her death. The second she could give Bridget a fighting chance, she was going to take it. She just hoped that Bridget would listen to her and run.

Chapter Eighty-Three

Danny

All he could hear were shouts from the guards on duty, and citizens of Collie running to their homes. They weren't under attack, that was for certain, but something was wrong. Danny made his way quickly towards the newly reconstructed gate, looking for anyone who might have the answer. Connor was running in his direction, his face pale.

"What's happened?" Danny asked, catching the youth by the arm and forcing him to halt.

"Wolves, fighting outside the walls." Connor pulled away from Danny and continued to run towards the alarm bell.

Danny glanced at the walls, a realization hitting him. The only people out there were the children of the ancients, practicing where their magic couldn't harm anyone. The wolves of Oich attacking them was an expected move, but Collie had no blooded of their own, except... FUCK!

"What's going on?" Rama asked as he approached, battle axe in hand.

"Wolves," Danny repeated as he made towards the gate, "fighting outside the gate."

"We don't have any—" Rama kept pace with him. "Bridget. Fuck!"

"What the fuck is happening?" Clyous came running towards the gate from the center of the city, wielding his smithing hammer looking for blood. "Where is my wife?!"

Rama signaled for the gate to rise, allowing them passage through as the alarm bells began ringing. More citizens scattered inward towards the city center as Collie warriors began to mobilize. The three men shot out of the open gate in the direction of the training arena, only to be stopped short by Morrigan who was headed their direction. Danny took one look at the sorceress and was able to tell something terrible had happened.

"They are gone," Morrigan said, her face pale.

"What do you mean they're gone?" Clyous seethed, staring over her shoulder as if expecting to see who she was talking about. "Where's my wife?"

Morrigan looked at him with sad eyes. "Taken, by the crown."

"What about Cat?!" Danny's heart dropped, he already knew the answer. His woman, his wonderfully wild and violent woman would have fought for her friend.

"Gone." Morrigan swallowed, looking sickened. "There was evidence of a fight. Blood everywhere. Three wolves killed by her twin blades. I believe they cuffed her with iron, probably using Bridget to subdue her long enough to apply it. It's the only logical way they were able to be taken so easily. Otherwise, she would have burned them to ash."

"Why didn't we hear her?" Rama asked as he looked to Clyous, who had lost all color in his face. "We should have heard her yell for help!"

"Grace is the connector, without her nearby you without magic cannot communicate," Morrigan tried to explain.

"Fuck that!" Danny turned on his heel, moving with purpose back into the city. "We have to go after them!"

"Right behind you!" Clyous was hot on his heels as they aimed towards the stables.

"You will not survive against that many blooded without help!" Morrigan caught up to them. "I am coming with you."

"We're all going!" Rama agreed, his long legs putting him before the others.

"No!" Morrigan said to the giant. "Gather troops, send out a squad after us. Prepare for battle. If we cannot get to them in time, we will need our forces to infiltrate the city."

Danny could see the hesitation in his brother's face before Rama relented. "Fine, but ride now, ride hard! I'll send warriors after you."

Danny pulled himself up on a black horse, ensuring his longsword was now strapped to his back for quicker access. He didn't care who was coming after him or who was even coming with him. He was going to find his woman and kill all of those blooded bastards who had hurt her. A quick glance at Clyous said he was of the same mindset.

"Storm," Morrigan called to her raven after she had mounted her horse. "Fly ahead, find them."

The raven took off, soaring into the sky so high that Danny could barely see it anymore. That mattered little to him, he kicked his horse into a run, followed closely by Clyous and Morrigan. He knew Clyous was feeling the same fear and anger he was. He knew Cat. She would fight until the bitter end. She would be protective of Bridget, who would fight back as well. She wouldn't stop until she was made to stop. That either meant her freedom in some off chance she was successful, or her death if she failed. Danny prayed to whatever god was listening to protect them as their horses began sprinting down the road towards the capital city of Oich.

Chapter Eighty-Four

Bridget

It was early morning when the wagon was driven through the city gates. Bridget caught sight of the walls being constructed, apparently the crown was getting tired of all the escapes that kept occurring. The soldiers who had captured them now walked with the wagon, keeping anyone who dared to approach at a distance. It had taken them longer than it should have to arrive at the city, the men had taken several detours in an attempt to thwart any rescue missions. After several minutes of traveling on one of the main streets through the capital, they passed the skeletal charred remains of what was left of the guards' barracks, a memory of a recent mission clicked in her head.

"Your handiwork?" Bridget glanced at Catriona, who shrugged innocently.

Damn that girl could do a lot of damage, Bridget had forgotten just how powerful Catriona really was when she was unleashed. Even with the recent incident at Collie, it was hard to fathom how one person could have that much power inside them. Bridget eyed the iron cuff cutting into Catriona's arm, it was amazing how that small device kept that amount of power at bay. She glanced at her own silver cuff, amazed at how this metal was capable of controlling her wolf so effectively.

Her anxiety began to get the best of her as the wagon approached the castle. Their fate would be decided soon. Catriona looked unnervingly calm, not in submission and acceptance, but like she was waiting for the inevitable. Cat had been looking for an opportunity on the road to attempt to escape, but the guards had been exceptionally good at leaving no openings. Bridget knew without much doubt that what Cat had warned her would happen was accurate. Time and time again her eyes had been opened to the ways of these corrupt men, how the very morals and beliefs she was raised with that should have protected her, were a gilded cage meant to contain her. It did not matter at the end of the day who she was to them; they would take what they wanted because they felt entitled to do so.

It was obvious to Bridget that the guards were in fact after Catriona. The guard captain had used her to disarm Catriona and did not realize who she was. Arguably, that was a blessing, if Liam had sent them, he would have

577

ordered iron to be placed around her wrist too. She was thankful at least Morrigan knew what had happened. There would be a rescue attempt soon, she just hoped that it came in time. The wagon pulled up to one of the side entrances into the castle. They would be brought before the crown; the only question was which one waited for them.

"You two," the captain ordered, "grab the bitch and follow me."

"What about the other one?" one of the nearby guards asked.

"Fuck her for all I care. She's of no further use to me now that we're back in the capital." The captain waved a hand dismissively.

Firm hands gripped her ankles, hauling her bound body from the wagon and dropping her hard on the cobblestones. The wind was knocked from her lungs on impact; she struggled to catch her breath as several pairs of legs moved around her. She could hear Cat fighting them, throwing herself around the back of the wagon and kicking out at them.

"Get your hands off her!" Catriona's voice struggled as she too was dragged out of the wagon. "Or the crown prince will rip your throat out."

"No!" Bridget managed, why was she telling them about Liam.

"What do you mean?" The guard captain yanked on Catriona's hair hard.

"Don't you recognize her?" Catriona mocked him. "That is Prince Liam's beloved."

The captain's gaze shot to Bridget then, eyes narrowing on her hair. She growled at his gaze in warning. Realization seemed to dawn on him then, Catriona laughed wickedly.

"You know for a fact anyone who touches her will die at the hands of your crown prince," Catriona sneered. "If you're dumb enough to risk it."

"Bring her too," the captain decided, releasing his grip on Catriona. "Just to be sure."

That's why Cat brought it up. She did it to keep them together, to keep Bridget safe just a little while longer. The guards stood them both up, cutting the bindings that restrained their legs. "Try to run or kick at us, and we'll break your legs."

With two guards on each side of them, the girls were marched through the side entrance of the castle. Bridget was slightly familiar with this entrance, having spent so much time here in her youth. Unfortunately, she realized very quickly where they were being taken. These hallways didn't lead to the dungeons, or to Liam's quarters. No, they were being escorted to the king's private chambers, possibly the worst possible outcome.

Bridget began to tremble slightly as they neared the king's chambers. For years, Liam, who was a monster in his own right, kept her hidden from his father. The king even scared him. She did not know what exactly would happen, she did not know how the king viewed her relationship with his son, but if anyone in this kingdom was capable of finding out about her magic it was him, he hunted magic users for sport.

They were finally brought to the king's chambers; two guards opened the large wooden door, granting them access. The girls found themselves standing in a large audience chamber. Books lined the shelves against the walls as a large map table stood in the center of the room. Aside from their escorts, at least three more guards piled into the room behind them. The group as a whole seemed nervous to enter the room much farther than they already had.

After a minute or two of awkward silence, a large and imposing figure emerged from a connecting room. The king strode before them, glaring at the guards for the intrusion. Bridget was suddenly forced to her knees before the king, gasping at the sudden violence. She could hear Cat swearing as she too was forced to her knees. The king eyed them for a moment before turning his attention to the guard captain.

"Is this her?" The king gestured to Catriona, who was staring at him as if wanting to burn him alive.

"Yes, Your Majesty." The captain bowed. "This is the girl with fire magic. She killed a few of my men before we were able to subdue her."

"And how did you manage that without being fed to her flames?" The king was curious, she realized.

"We used this blooded traitor to encourage her compliance," the captain said rather smugly. "She now wears a cuff of iron to keep her magic tampered."

"But you haven't managed to tamper the rest of her." The king visually examined the injuries to her face. "You'll need to finish breaking her before she tries something stupid."

"Any particular way, Your Majesty?" There was an unsettling gleam in the captain's eye now.

"I don't particularly care. Be as creative as you want but let her keep all her limbs. The Gaelach bastards wanted her alive, I didn't ask if that meant in one piece, best not to test it." The king bared his fangs at Catriona as she began to struggle against the hands that held her. "Send someone to find King Rion, he's somewhere around here. Let him know we've brought him his prize."

"Fuck you!" Catriona roared as she launched herself sideways, kicking out at the nearest guard.

Bridget watched with tears in her eyes as her friend fought her hardest against them. Bridget launched herself at them, knowing that their efforts ultimately wouldn't stop what was going to happen, but she had to try, Catriona had to try. It was in their nature to fight back, to resist. If they could injure just one of them, it would be worth it.

But with their hands bound and six blooded guards between them, the girls could only do so much before they were effectively contained. Four of the six guards had managed to drag Cat out of the king's private chambers and down the hall while the other two pinned Bridget to the ground.

"Enough!" the king ordered, power rippling through the room. "Let go of her and go wait outside."

Bridget stared at the king in shock as the guards released their hold on her and exited the chambers. The king studied her for a moment before approaching. Bridget did her best to stand steady, hoping she could control her facial expression enough to at least appear unafraid.

Quicker than Bridget thought possible, the king pulled a dagger from his belt and sliced at the rope at her wrists. As the ropes fell to the floor the king sheathed his blade, stepping away from her.

"You seem smart enough to realize trying to run would be pointless." The king sat down in a cushioned chair facing her. "As would attacking me. Have a seat."

Bridget remained frozen in place, eyeing the king suspiciously. She knew he spoke the truth. There was only one door in and out of the king's chambers. There were at least four blooded guards out there, not to mention a powerful dominant wolf sitting not ten feet from her. If she tried to escape, or even fight him she would be put down in less than a minute, and what good would that do her or Catriona? Maybe she could take advantage of the king's good humor, or Liams, to save them.

"My patience wears thin, as do my niceties." The king's eyes blazed.

Reluctantly, Bridget peeled herself from the wall, taking the seat across from the king. She observed him then, a seasoned warrior who made it a point to see what was around him. What flesh was exposed bore various scars, from what looked like a combination of blades and claws. As far as living as a blooded, you wouldn't have been able to climb the pack hierarchy without facing many challenges, and the fact that he wore a crown was proof enough of his victories. Similar to Liam, he had black hair but he had thick greying streaks. He was about the same height as Liam, arguably broader in the shoulders, but it was his face that gave away their relation, the king looked like an older battle worn Liam. Unlike his son, there was no warmth or kindness, there was darkness behind them.

"So, you're the runt my son has been so infatuated with over the years." His steely eyes raked over her. "You don't seem like a runt to me. The fact that they had to cuff you with silver indicates you no longer lack control of your shift. When did that change?"

"About a year ago, when I finally found something worth fighting for." Bridget said flatly.

"Tell me, was that when you joined the rebellion, or was that when you found her?"

"I found a new pack," Bridget said defiantly.

The king smiled at her. "And what about a new lover? Doesn't seem like you give my son any amount of consideration anymore."

"That's his own doing, not mine." Bridget glared. "Ruthless bastard isn't an attractive quality."

"Further proof that my son was a cunt-struck fool." The king glared at her. "He disillusioned himself into believing he needed to make you love him when he should have just claimed you."

"I am nobody's to claim," she growled in warning.

"I see you are from a strong bloodline," the king acknowledged. "You are young, beautiful, and you're a fighter at heart. The prince should have claimed you years ago, but instead he was too worried about keeping you away from me."

"Where is Liam?" Bridget stared back, unnerved by the expression King Cathal wore.

"Away." His head cocked to the side, a predator watching his prey. "Would you submit now, to being claimed?"

"I submit to no one." Her muscles tensed as she watched the king lean forward slightly.

"You would breed strong heirs." It was an odd statement, one that didn't quite fit the look he was giving her. "Since my son failed to claim you, I guess I'll have to. Wouldn't want your bloodline to be watered down with weakness or tainted by one of those with magic. You will submit to me, even if I have to beat you within an inch from death. I made the mistake of failing to be heavy handed with my last wife, one I will not make again. I wouldn't want you to believe you were remotely close to being my equal. It might give you false hope that you stand a chance if you were to challenge me."

"You are right." Bridget took a deep breath, eyes fixed on the king in the best Catriona glare she could muster. "I'm not you're equal, I'm better."

And before she knew it, he was on her.

Chapter Eighty-Five

Liam

Liam lowered himself from his horse, stretching his legs out after the long ride. He had returned a day early from patrolling the northernmost villages. He had been helping some of the tribesmen hunt down those with magic. This alliance was important for the progression of Oich, but working together had done nothing to sweeten the bitter taste in his mouth that came with working with those savages.

They had successfully trapped and captured at least three magic users, handing them over to the clansmen to be taken back to Gaelach. He thought Oich guards were ruthless and cruel, but their actions paled in comparison to the clansmen. Those poor bastards who had been caught endured far more primitive and sadistic punishments from the cultists, being burned alive seemed like a mercy.

The only good part about this mission was the death of an old enemy. That white-haired bastard that was responsible for his mother's death was caught marching a squad of soldiers south from the Harrada Pass. The clansmen and Oich guards had attacked, slaughtering all but two. By the time Liam had gotten there the man's son had been slain. Liam watched as the older man collapsed to his knees wailing in agony as he held his son's corpse. It reminded Liam of how he had held his mother. Unfortunately, before Liam could engage and claim his revenge, the sorcerer had surrounded himself in flames. There was barely anything left of them, just ash and bones. He had incinerated himself and his son's body while killing a few clansmen in the process. Liam was disappointed he was not the one to kill his old enemy, but he was satisfied he witnessed the man's death. It provided some closure, at least.

"Your Majesty." One of the guards approached. "The king has sent you a message."

"And?" Liam rubbed his temples, it was too early for a summons. He would like to at least wash up before being given his next task.

"The fire bitch has been captured."

Liam froze, eyes locking on the guard. "Where is she?"

"The east tower," he answered with a hint of a smile. "King Rion is already there."

The east tower was typically where they kept important prisoners, or prisoners that needed to be broken. Considering how much of a wildcat that girl was he had no doubt the guards were putting her through the gauntlet trying to get her to submit. Liam took off in the direction of the east tower. The bitch was infuriating, it would be a great thing to see her broken, but he hardened his resolve at the thought of Rion already there, what abhorrent punishment he was applying to the girl to try and break her spirit.

Sure enough, as he approached the base of the tower, they could hear a woman's screams, followed by a string of profanities even Liam had never heard. That was definitely her, still fighting, he was unsurprised. He felt a small pang of pity for her, he wished King Rion on nobody.

Liam entered the tower and climbed the stairs up to the third floor where he was met by several clansmen. Across the wooden landing two guards stood watch over an entryway. Looking through the open space, Liam could see the bars of the cell just inside. He could hear the girl inside, shouting and swearing at her assailant. It sounded like they were actually fighting with her. Rion looked to him with a smile as he leaned against the doorway, watching the scene unfolding as if it were great entertainment.

"I see you finally have your prize," Liam said with distaste. "Didn't your mother ever teach you not to play with your food?"

Rion threw his head back and laughed, welcoming Liam's approach. "My mother was the one who taught me these games. Besides, I already took a bite. It didn't break her like it would most of them, it ignited more fire, so my men will need to tire her out before I have another taste."

Liam's eyes swung back to the girl, re-examining her. Her face was bruised and bleeding from the beatings she had taken. They had apparently cut her loose, either by design or mistake. Regardless, the girl was on her feet actively swinging at one of the three men trying to grab her. The men laughed as she fought, goading her into tiring out faster. She was slower than she normally was, either due to injuries or being cut off from her magic. Liam noted her right hand was twisted and bent out of shape, most likely broken. The most obvious change to her appearance was her hair, her usual long white hair was kept in a tight braid, however now it hung loosely to her shoulder as if it had been cut off with a knife. Her clothes were askew, ripped open in sections and barely hanging onto her as she tried to fight, Liam could see claw and teeth marks raking her upper torso through the loosened fabric. His eyes caught hold of how loosely her trousers were fitting on her, how they were obviously ripped and manipulated, how blood seemed to be forming between her legs through the fabric. His heart dropped at the realization, he may hate the bitch but this was too far.

"Alright, pretty girl," Rion righted himself off the doorframe taking a step into the room. "I think I'm ready to go again."

One of the guards towards the back shifted, leaping up and grabbing her forearm. Teeth punctured flesh, drawing blood as the wolf violently shook, ripping even more flesh. She screamed just as another guard whipped forward to grab her other arm. They dragged her towards a wooden table. The guard took the girl's free hand, forcing it flat on the table while another walked up holding large iron nails and a hammer.

"Let go of me you sack of shit!" Catriona shouted, trying to pull away, panic had set in.

"Help me hold her!" the guard with her hand called out.

The two guards who had been standing in the background rushed forward to help hold her in place. one of the large iron nails was placed on the surface of her hand as the guard lifted the hammer. He brought it down swiftly, striking true. The nail pierced her hand, forcing out a shriek of pain from the girl. The guard struck the nail three more times before it went through the other end of the wooden table. She was shaking now as they forced her other hand up to do the same. Liam stepped forward as soon as her second hand had been successfully secured to the table. Her blood now pooling on the tabletop, her body shaking.

"May I ask the point of this?" Liam asked, trying to conceal the shock he was feeling as he witnessed this occurring in front of him.

"That's right." Rion circled her around the table, eyes glancing up at him. "You don't rape here. Well, dear boy, since we are such good friends and all, I feel like educating you. There are two good reasons to rape your enemy. One we have already covered, to assert my dominance over them. To break them. This pretty little thing is refusing to break, so the beatings will continue until she does. The second reason is simply because I want to. I want to see if I can breed that fire out of her, and I'm not opposed to keep trying until she starts reproducing."

Liam swallowed hard, his eyes locking with hers as she lay there staring up at him. "You do realize it's unlikely for a blooded and a magic user to breed offspring with both traits. It's literally unheard of."

"If she is unable to produce the offspring I want, Oisin has other ways to trap her magic." Rion positioned himself right behind her, adjusting himself underneath the loin cloth. "Until then, we've got plenty of time to play around and see what fate has in store for us."

"Ask them how they caught me." She was breathing heavily but still stared at him defiantly. "I can guarantee you won't feel so satisfied when they tell you how they managed to catch me."

His heart hurt at her accusation; he was not satisfied with this. Watching this unfold in front of him had him seriously considering finding a way to stop it. It's not that he had compassion for the girl, it was the principle. This was beyond torture, this was... words could not express how horrible this was. And he was expected to just stand there and let it happen, to watch it, and enjoy it. This went against everything he's ever believed, how his mother had raised him to be. Not that he had done a particularly good job sticking to those lessons over the years, but he had never lost himself to the darkness this deep. He couldn't just stand there.

"What if I changed my mind?" Liam said to Rion. "What if I wanted to keep her for myself?"

"Fuck you!" she screamed.

Rion smiled at him, nodding to the guards. They stepped forward, a guard seizing her shirt and ripping it off her. Another ran to grab a whip from a chest nearby as the other guards fought to remove the rest of her clothing.

"Too late," Rion mocked as he began aligning himself behind her. "If you don't want to watch, I would leave. You would be a fool to try and back out of our deal now."

Liam felt his anger rising with the need to challenge this man and get him away from her. But he knew he was outnumbered; he knew that his father would not back his decision. If he were to intervene, it would be him against not only Rion and his clansmen, but also the Oich guards as soon as his father commanded it. If he could get her out of the tower and on a horse, he just might be able to get her out of the city before anyone was the wiser.

"How did you catch her?" he quietly asked the guard captain, averting his eyes as Rion began his awful task, calculating just how many of them he might be able to take down before they were able to call for help.

"There was a redhead with her. We used the blooded traitor as a shield until we could get the iron on her." The guard captain was also averting his eyes from the scene unfolding before them, raising his voice to be heard over her screams.

"Where is the redhead?" Liam asked, panic seizing him, there was only one redhead he cared about, only one who would have been with this girl when she was caught.

"She was left with your father, Your Grace." The guard looked at him questioningly.

Another cry of pain before the girl began to laugh, a laugh that stilled his heart and turned everyone's attention to her. "Run little prince, before the evil you do to me, happens to her."

He looked at her again, this woman splayed out nailed to the table, her blood pooled beneath her as it ran down her legs from the two open gashes on her back. Her face seeping blood as she raised it towards him, chin held high in defiance. He could see hatred in her eyes, hatred for him and his men. But he could also see fear there, not from what was happening to her, but fear for Bridget. He might be her enemy, but she knew he was Bridget's only chance of survival. She had just warned him to save her, unknowingly giving herself over so Liam could rescue Bridget instead of her.

He spun on his heel and bolted from the cell, taking off down the tower steps, heading in the direction of his father's chambers. He could hear someone behind him; with a quick glance he was able to tell it was Rion. Why had this monster given up his torment of the girl to follow him? He had no idea, but there was some solace that the girl would at least have a moment's peace before his return. If she was lucky she would bleed out first, but that was unlikely based on the injuries he had observed.

Liam did not wait for the guards to open the doors to his father's chambers. In fact, he did not wait for them to greet him. To his surprise the guards appeared to step in his way as if to stop him, but Rion shot forward burying a bone knife in the ribs of one before tackling the other. Liam did not ask why this savage king helped him, his senses now overwrought with her scent.

Throwing open the door, Liam launched himself into the audience chamber which was now littered with strewn about furniture and papers. After a quick scan his eyes locked onto two bodies. Bridget was being pressed face first into the wall, her small body nearly engulfed by his father's larger form. His father had a grip on her hair as he pushed her into that wall, his head snapped in Liam's direction as he entered the room, his nose crooked and a healthy stream of blood now flowing from the nostrils. Claw marks

587

raked across his father's face and neck, blood dripping steadily onto the carpet where his bent crown now lay. A tiny sliver of pride flared to life at the fact that his girl had been the one to inflict that, but the rest of him was pure rage.

"Let her go!" Power rippled through the room at his command.

The king raised his eyebrows in disbelief. "You think you can order me around?"

"Let go of her, or I'll kill you," Liam promised, unsheathing his sword.

With a hard shove, his father pushed Bridget to the floor as he turned to face his son. Rion stepped within the chambers, shutting the door behind him. The savage king made no move to aid either man, seemingly content with just watching. Liam ignored him, focusing all his attention on the King of Oich.

"Was that a challenge?" The king stared, pulling free a small throwing axe from one of the selves.

Liam growled, baring his fangs at the older wolf. It was a challenge. Nobody was allowed to touch Bridget, to hurt her. Liam should have challenged his father months ago, years ago really. He wasn't ready then, but he was now.

"You will pay for everything you've done to her," Liam said glancing at Bridget. "And my mother."

"I have clearly failed as your sire," King Cathal snarled. "Looks like I couldn't beat the bitch out of you or your mother. It appears that it would be prudent of me to focus on creating new heirs rather than allowing her line to continue."

He knew one day this challenge would come. It was the natural order of any wolf pack. The one who won, the one who proved to be most dominant, they would inherit the power. None of that mattered to Liam. He wanted revenge for his mother, for all the years of cruelty, and to protect the woman he loved. Rion was right, he alone had the power to change things.

"I never wanted to be king anyway," Liam pointed the tip of his sword in the direction of his father. "I wanted to be a knight."

Liam moved first, swinging the sword in an upward arc aiming for his father's gut but the old wolf dodged it, feinting to the side and angling the axe at Liam's thigh. Liam rolled to the side, dodging a second blow by ducking behind a cushioned chair.

Liam threw his arm back, his elbow connecting with his father's jaw. The old king launched himself forward, striking at him from nearly every angle. Liam continued to block the onslaught, surprised at just how fast and strong his father actually was. He was forced to take a few steps backwards as his sword absorbed most of the strikes. Finally, the king drove his axe down, Liam thrust his blade directly overhead to catch it. With the blades still connected, his father used his weight to push down, forcing Liam to take a knee so he didn't lose his grip.

"Submit or die," the king hissed at his son.

"You'll have to kill me," Liam grunted from the strain.

Liam heard movement behind him. It sounded like someone running towards them. He saw his father's eyes shift just above Liam's shoulder, seeing something that startled him. Then Liam saw Bridget's slender hand grabbing the king around his throat. A bright golden light appeared where her hand grasped, the king suddenly looked afraid. His father's face suddenly paled then drastically lost all color before the darkness in his eyes lost all traces of life.

The King of Oich dropped to the floor like a wet rag; his body crumbled upon itself. Liam stared in shock at his dead body. Bridget had done that; Bridget had used her magic to kill the king! His eyes now flicked to hers; she stared back at him, her breathing hard. Her hair was loose and free, dirt covered her trousers and tunic. She appeared relatively unharmed, but a golden light now emanated from between her breasts. She pulled her shirt down slightly to see the source of this magical light. Sitting in the center of her chest was a golden star.

"Thank you," she breathed, her eyes snapping back to his, "for challenging him to save me."

"You killed him with magic." Liam looked back at the corpse on the ground in disbelief. "And saved my life."

"I'm proud of you, Liam. This is the first time I've seen the real you in years, I wasn't about to lose you to that man again." She caught her breath. "Where is she?"

Liam looked at her stunned, he couldn't believe the words that had just come out of her mouth, a glowing golden aura now surrounding her. "East tower."

Bridget nodded again before starting towards the door. Rion stood there, jaw dropped completely open. Fuck! King Rion, hunter of magic users, had just witnessed Bridget wield magic. By all laws, Bridget had just been promoted upon the death of the king. Rion was not only staring at a witch, but a queen by her own right.

Bridget bared her teeth in warning as Rion's shocked expression turned into something more feral. His stance changed as his hands slowly moved towards his belt. Liam made to move, but the door to the king's chambers was thrown open, knocking the savage king over. Several bodies poured in; weapons raised to attack.

Chapter Eighty-Six

Grace

As soon as Menolayous kicked the door open Grace and two other warriors piled inside the king's chambers. Grace was first in; dagger now pointed towards the prince. Quickly glancing around the room, she spotted Bridget standing right in front of her, relief swam across her face. Behind her lie a corpse, upon further inspection it appeared to be the King of Oich. A fresh marking now glowed between her breasts above her heart. Grace then knew exactly how the king had died and how Bridget had earned her mark.

"Grace!" Bridget flung herself into Grace's arms, tears flowing down her cheeks.

Menolayous and the two other warriors pointed their weapons at the prince and what looked like a clansman. Grace ended the embrace quickly, shoving the healer behind her protectively.

"Are you alright?" Grace asked, glaring at the prince who was on his knees, hands raised.

"I'm fine," Bridget choked out, eyes locked on Liam. "Leave him, we have to get to Cat."

"Where is she?" Menolayous asked.

"East tower, I know the way, follow me." Bridget pulled Grace towards the door.

"It's been a long time, Menolayous," the clansman said with a smile.

Grace's eyes immediately flew to Menolayous, who went completely rigid at the sound of the man's voice. They knew each other she realized, and not in a good way.

"We have to go!" Bridget cried. "They're hurting her."

"Menolayous!" Grace snapped, breaking whatever trance Menolayous was in.

"I will tell Oisin and Ammon you said hello." The man smiled wickedly.

591

As a group, the warriors exited the king's chambers, following Bridget through the courtyard. Bridget glanced around nervously, probably expecting to see guards. Lightning suddenly cracked across the sky, distant screams now echoing around them.

"Morrigan is here. She and the gifted are leading the charge through the city," Grace explained as they ran.

Bridget turned eastward as they ran, a loud boom sounded in the distance followed by what sounded like a building crumbling. "You're attacking the city?"

"We don't leave any member of our family behind," was all Grace had to say about it.

"How did you guys get back from Airgid so fast?"

"We never made it. My mother sent troops through Gaelach to aid us a few weeks ago. We met up with them on the road."

"Airgid has joined us?" Bridget took another turn, a three-story stone tower now looming before them.

"They're the ones who got us in the castle walls, them and Connor. Rama's men are protecting the children of the ancients as they push the attack."

"Clyous and Danny?" Bridget asked, looking worried.

"We made the executive decision that they shouldn't be the ones to come find you," Grace answered honestly. "Just in case."

"Rama is keeping them planted at the city's edge," Menolayous added.

Bridget made it to the tower door, forcing it open as she threw her body against it. As they entered, Menolayous shot ahead of them, taking two stairs at a time. Finally, when they reached the top, two guards drew swords as they alerted others of their presence.

The two Collie warriors with them moved forward to engage with the guards. Three more exited the room to fight them. Menolayous fought with such a cold fury it chilled Grace to the bone. Something about that man in the other room set him off, now he exuded death. Grace and Bridget fought past the melee, forcing their way into the cell.

Bridget's audible cry broke Grace's focus. She bolted into the cell expecting... well... not expecting that. Catriona was the sole occupant of the room. At first glance it looked as if Catriona was lying face down, draped over the table, but the sight and smell of the blood made it obvious that it wasn't that simple.

Catriona's hands were nailed down to the wooden tabletop, blood still pouring from her open wounds. Her face, oh gods her face, deep gashes now cut into her flesh down past her cheekbones. Several open gashes from claws and teeth covered her, adding to the already sickening amount of blood covering her naked body. But none of that was the worst of her injuries.

"Go find us a wagon, and some clothes," Grace overheard Menolayous order the two warriors.

They must have finished off the guards then. Bridget rushed for Cat, checking to see if she was breathing. Grace glanced at Menolayous, all the color had gone out of his face. Grace felt as if she were going to throw up.

"She's breathing." Bridge looked to them. "She's in shock. Help me get her off this thing."

Menolayous moved forward, gripping the head of one of the nails and pulling the first free of wood and flesh. Catriona's body remained motionless, which Grace found very concerning. Menolayous moved to the last nail, ripping that one free as well. Grace and Bridget moved to catch Catriona before she collapsed to the floor. Grace's eyes visually measured the iron nail Menolayous had dropped to the ground, the torturous thing was nearly as thick as her thumb.

She fought back the urge to vomit as she looked upon her friend's scarred face. It was as if time stopped, like they had been cut off from the rest of the world. Her once long hair now cut to her shoulders, an uneven job most likely done by a blade. This couldn't be real, this couldn't be. Grace watched Bridget grasp Catriona's hands, using her magic to close the wounds. Menolayous stood behind her, handing over a blanket he had found.

"We need to get her out of here," he said. "It will be better if we can get her out of here before she wakes up."

"Just let me stop the bleeding." Bridget was focusing hard on Cat's hands, the holes slowly beginning to close.

"Let's get those fucking bracelets off you," Grace said, reaching for the one on Cat's arms.

"We should leave it for now," Menolayous stated, voice empty of any emotion. "We can't risk her burning anyone while trying to flee enemy territory."

Grace looked at the wickedly designed cuff, her anger directed at that device. That iron contraption was the only way they were able to catch her, the only way they could hurt her. Allowing it to stay on her, even for another moment, felt as if they were allowing her to be hurt again. This wasn't true of course, but everything felt wrong. Menolayous of all people knew better than anyone what Cat had gone through, what she would have to live with. She would follow his lead on this, even if it didn't make much sense.

Instead, Grace reached for the silver one on Bridget, separating the pin that held together the locking mechanism. It clattered to the floor as the healer's hands moved to touch the wounds on Catriona's back. Menolayous turned from them, granting as much privacy as the situation would allow. The sounds of battle drew closer, swords hitting shields, shouts from soldiers, they needed to move faster. Where were the two warriors with that wagon?

"Almost done." Bridget breathed. "I just need to see exactly how bad it is down there."

Time suddenly seemed to speed up, Grace wasn't able to track what happened in real time. Grace held onto an unconscious Cat, holding her up for Bridget to heal her. What Grace did not expect was Bridget to put her hands on Cat's thighs as she tried to heal those wounds. Cat's body jerked awake, now launching itself at the healer. Grace could not hold her, her own blood and gods knew what else making her slip through Grace's fingers, Catriona wrapped her bloody hands around Bridget's throat.

Bridget and Catriona went down; Catriona was trying to squeeze the life out of her best friend. Grace launched herself at the two women, earning a sharp elbow to the face from Catriona. Menolayous was there, breaking the grip Cat had on Bridget, who was starting to turn purple. Menolayous had her arms in a death grip, rolling Catriona off their friend and pinning her to him. Catriona clawed at him, screaming as she raged. Grace shot forward, cupping her friend's face with her hand. The person she saw before her held no resemblance to Cat, instead there was a wild animal fighting as if it were backed into a corner. Grace focused her power, entering the woman's mind. Waves of pain, such physical and emotional pain Grace wasn't sure how she was enduring it. Grace pushed a tidal wave of calmness into Cat, willing with all her might for her friend to stop fighting. After a few moments Catriona stopped thrashing. Menolayous released his grip, removing himself from her stilled naked body.

"Are you okay?" Grace asked Bridget, watching Catriona lay there, eyes open but eerily empty.

"Yes." Bridget inhaled deeply, rubbing her throat.

594

"That was fucking stupid!" Menolayous barked at her. "Everyone's the enemy to her right now! You can't just go and touch someone like that after what she's just been through. Unconscious or not she's still ready to fight to the death."

"I was trying to stop the bleeding." Bridget wasn't arguing exactly, pain laced her features. Not pain from Cat's hands, but at not being able to help.

"She doesn't know!" Grace snapped at him, matching his rage. That man in the king's chambers really affected him. "I need you to collect yourself, we need you here, not back in Gaelach."

"Fine," Menolayous snapped, still pacing. "Sorry, just, try not to touch her anywhere private. That's going to trigger her."

"It's fine. I wasn't thinking about that. I was too focused on healing her wounds." Bridget met his gaze, her strength showing as much as her humility.

"You can't fix everything," Grace explained as the two warriors arrived carrying clothes. "Help me dress her. Slowly. Let's avoid her lower half if we can."

Bridget nodded as the two women took great care in dressing Catriona in an oversized tunic that thankfully fell past her knees. Grace decided that trying to wrestle breeches on her wasn't going to be beneficial for anyone. They needed to get going.

Catriona appeared awake now, her eyes open but unseeing. She had made no effort to assist them when they dressed her, but she didn't fight them either. Bridget was right, she was in shock. That violent outburst must have simply been a defensive reaction.

Menolayous crouched down beside her, staring into her face as he gently said, "We need to leave. I'm going to need to carry you to the wagon."

There was no reaction, no movement from her, just that empty presence.

Menolayous said softly, "They're all gone. We killed them. It's just us now, me and Grace and Bridget. I'm going to pick you up now, nobody's going to hurt you anymore."

There it was. Catriona's eyes flicked up to meet his. They held for a moment before flicking to the other two. Grace noticed no other bodily movement from her; it was as if she was frozen in place. A single tear slid down her cheek before her eyes went blank, staring off at the wall.

Menolayous slowly reached one arm underneath Cat's legs and back, lifting her to his chest as he stood. Luckily, she made no move to fight him. Grace nodded to the warriors who took point, leading the way out of the tower. Grace and Bridget stayed next to Menolayous and Cat as they made their way from the tower. A horse drawn wagon waiting for them just outside the tower's entrance. The horses were being minded by Connor whose oversized armor was covered in blood and dirt.

"Thank you, Connor," Grace said, taking the reins as Menolayous gently handed Cat to Bridget in the back of the wagon.

"Is Miss Catriona alive?" The teenager's face now contorting with grief at the sight of all the blood covering her.

"Yes." Grace tried to give him a reassuring smile. "They both are thanks to you. We might not have gotten here in time if you hadn't shown us the way into the castle before the attack."

Raw emotion took over his features as he stared at the two women. It was true what Grace had said, Connor's knowledge of the city is what led them to finding Bridget so fast. Grace could sense them, but the cuffs they had been wearing made it extremely hard to locate them precisely.

"Help us get out of here?" Bridget asked him, wanting to pull him away from the ongoing battle, he needn't die today.

"As you wish, Miss Bridget." Connor hopped up into the driver's seat next to Menolayous.

Menolayous handed the young man the reins, unsheathing his axes in case they needed them. Grace hopped into the back of the wagon, helping Bridget wrap Catriona with blankets. The wagon jolted, pitching them forward at a fast trot. The two warriors that had accompanied them ran alongside the wagon, weapons drawn.

"We've got them!" Grace shouted out into her mental connections.

"Good," Morrigan's voice echoed back. *"I will take out the west wall. Make your way to me. We shall clear a path."*

"Go to the western wall," Menolayous instructed Connor.

The horses changed course and headed to the western side of the city. Now outside the castle grounds, they suddenly found themselves surrounded by an ongoing battle as blooded guards in Oich's red colors fought against heavily armored blue knights from Airgid. Grace recognized her countrymen's blue and silver as they clashed with the red and black of Oich. The Airgid banner was being carried through the city streets by her men, silver crested mountains surrounded by a golden sun.

"How many?" Bridget asked as they rode through.

"My mother sent me a hundred soldiers," Grace said, watching as the wagon moved through the battle with increasing speed. "She is engaging Gaelach from the north. That prick Farroway has been shuttling my troops down to Oich. She's leading the charge with Rama."

"Thank the gods." Bridget breathed a sigh of relief.

As if on cue, Rama's voice boomed down the mental pathways. *"How are they?"*

"I'm okay," Bridget answered nervously.

"Where's Cat!" Danny's voice came out panicked. *"I can't feel her. She's not answering me."*

"She's alive," was all Bridget said.

"Danny, where are you?" Menolayous asked, glancing back at Cat, who was still gazing off into nothing.

"How is she? Why can't I feel her?" Danny barked.

"He's next to me." Rama echoed. *"Clyous too. Tell us."*

Bridget appeared to be having her own private conversation with her lover. Undoubtedly, they were prepared for the worst. Grace had her suspicions that Rama and Clyous were prepared to grab ahold of Danny who could do something stupid.

"You can't hear her because she still has an iron cuff on. It's stunting her magic," Grace explained.

"Then take it off her!" Danny snapped.

"We can't risk it. Not until we get out of the city," Menolayous explained.

"Tell me what happened!" Danny was shouting now. *"Tell me why it's necessary to keep that fucking thing on her!"*

"She's in bad shape brother," Menolayous pushed out. *"She isn't able to discern us from the enemy right now. She tried to kill Bridget just for touching her."*

"*She's been raped,*" Grace said, saying the words everyone was dreading to hear. "*I don't know how many times. She's also been tortured. We found her nailed to a table.*"

There was silence for a few moments, all they could hear was the battle they were passing through. Sorrow and rage radiated down every mental connection Grace was open to. Tears streaked down Bridget's face as she stared down at Catriona, who still hadn't broken free from her trance.

"*She's still in shock,*" Bridget said into the silence. "*I've healed what I can. We're getting her out.*"

Another moment of silence passed before Morrigan spoke, her words were heavy with grief, "*Get her out of that wretched city. I am clearing the way now.*"

The sound of a man's broken wail echoed through them all. Grace could feel Danny's anguish down the bond, it was absolutely soul shattering to hear.

"*We've got him, just get here,*" Clyous finally said, his voice cracking with heartbreak.

"*We'll meet you outside the city walls,*" Menolayous said.

Chapter Eighty-Seven

Morrigan

"They are coming." Garreth spoke with a voice older than his age, the little boy stood on the wagon looking out into the city through the crumbled walls. "They're in a wagon. One of them looks really hurt."

Morrigan peered in the direction the boy was looking; she could only see city buildings and soldiers. "Very good, Garreth. Thank you. Run along back to your father."

The little boy nodded, hopping down from the seat and into his father's arms. Morrigan turned her attention back to the city, calculating the best possible way to bring her friends out. She raised her hand in signal, five volunteers who bore the blood of the ancients stepped forward.

"On your command," Queen Valeria said, stepping up to stand beside Morrigan. "Guardian."

The Queen of Airgid stood ready to fight, standing side by side with those who also shared the gift. The woman wore plate armor; the chest piece engraved with gemstones designed into it. Her long light-brown hair was braided in an intricate style, that fell down past her shoulder blades. She wore an elegantly designed sword on her hip, showcasing the money and privilege she brought with her from Airgid. The woman radiated power, an unmoving display that even Morrigan found herself respecting. It was no wonder Grace was as strong as she was with a mother like this, she had to be to survive. The woman looked like Grace, their faces nearly identical if it wasn't for the years between them. Grey streaks brushed the queen's temples and were woven into the braids she wore. Unlike her daughter, the Queen stood with a slender frame and possibly a foot taller in height.

"Make a gap for the wagon to come through," Morrigan commanded. "I shall be covering their escape."

"You heard her!" Valeria shouted the order, calling her troops to attention. "Make a gap. Send these inbred fleabags to the Abyss!"

A small squad of soldiers dressed in Airgid blue stepped through the wall with their weapons unsheathed, prepared to block out any who tried to follow the wagon through. Five magic wielders also stepped forward, the queen included, making sure to have a clear shot of the oncoming carriage. Morrigan herself crawled up onto part of the demolished wall, placing herself high enough over the others that she wouldn't hit them with her magic. The scene before her was a mesh of swords and axes beating against the Oich blooded, the Collie warriors and the Airgid soldiers working together to create enough chaos for this rescue mission to be possible.

Morrigan could sense her friends approaching just beyond the last remaining building. Morrigan stretched her hands out into the sky, reaching out with her magic to where she could feel the electricity humming in the air and start to swirl around her. Storm flew past her, landing somewhere behind her and out of her range. Morrigan pushed her energy into the sky, lightning erupted so thunderously it shook the very cobblestones that lay on the ground beneath them.

Valeria moved next, stretching her ungloved hands out before her, violet swirls of magic escaping her fingertips and shooting out towards the enemy. Morrigan watched in fascination as the queen's magic bounced between enemies, seeming to cocoon them before moving on to the next. Enemy soldiers left and right began to scream, dropping the ground as they faced their worst nightmares. For that was the queen's power, as a daughter of chaos she was able to break into their minds and show them what they feared most. This tactic enabled her to affect fifteen or so at a time, allowing allying forces to swoop in and finish them off. The air around them suddenly filled with the sounds of men screaming and of wolves whimpering.

The remaining children of the ancients took the opportunity to send out their magic. One woman, clearly a daughter of the mountain who was gifted with magic rather than size, betrayed by the type of magic she possessed, drove her fist through the ground beneath her, creating an opening fissure that moved off to the side, cutting off a small squad of wolves that were headed their direction. Another woman drew back her bow string, weaving her magic into the bolt before letting it fly. Once in the air the arrow seemed to have a mind of its own, swerving up and down and maneuvering through the battlefield as it pierced through several enemies before moving on to another. A young man began to wave his hands in a circular motion, his magic infused in the air to create a whirlwind which he pushed towards the buildings. This funnel grew so large it now towered over the buildings, eating itself a pathway through the battlefield just as the wagon rounded the corner.

Morrigan put her lightning to work, focusing on the wagon as it appeared young Connor spurred the horses on through the chaos. Any enemy that came within ten feet of the wagon, Morrigan struck them down with her magic from above. The wagon moved wildly, veering away from clusters of battles surging around them. Connor was steering the beasts while Menolayous guarded from any potential assailants. Morrigan watched as the wagon neared and the young man drove the horses through the Airgid ranks, maneuvering the hefty wagon through the debris of the collapsed wall. A few of the Oich guards came bounding in the wagon's direction, the wolves picking up the pace as if trying to beat them to the perimeter. The queen sent another tendril of her magic their direction, cracking like a whip across their hides, the wolves collapsed in convulsions of fear as Morrigan finished them off with bolts of lightning.

Morrigan could feel her power begin to drain her, burnout approaching at the sheer amount of magic she was channeling. The wagon flew by her, finally making it to the border wall unharmed. Morrigan was able to glance down at its occupants. Grace and Bridget were in the back of the wagon, looking slightly ruffled in appearance but otherwise unharmed. It was the figure that lay between them that stopped Morrigan's heart. Catriona lie unmoving underneath scraps of a horse blanket, her hair significantly shorter and caked in dried blood. Morrigan caught a glimpse of the healer working her magic, a golden light radiating from her hands and chest as she worked to fix the wounds on her sister. There was so much blood, so many wounds healing as the carriage moved, Morrigan nearly lost all concentration on her magic at the sight of it.

Chapter Eighty-Eight

Rama

Rama watched as his brother paced back and forth like a caged animal waiting for the wagon to arrive. Clyous was the opposite, he stood there unmoving with his eyes focused on the city. Clyous was so still Rama had to keep checking on him to make sure he was breathing. Rama couldn't blame either of them, he was anxious too. Menolayous's warning of how bad of shape Catriona was what set everyone on edge.

The sounds of the distant battle called to him; Rama wasn't used to being sidelined during the action. Truthfully, his anxiety could use an outlet, a violent one. But his place was here beside his family, supporting his brothers and sisters and ensuring their escape. It was already hard enough watching Danny completely shatter before him, that was the first time in his life he had heard his brother cry before, he never would have imagined the impact his brother's heartbreak would have on him.

"There!" Clyous called out, suddenly springing to life as he spotted a wagon approaching.

Rama looked at the wagon, young Connor drove the rickety thing like a bird with its tail feathers on fire. Menolayous sat next to him on the driver's bench hanging on for dear life. Danny began running towards the wagon which was now ten feet away. Rama took a few long strides in order to catch up to him, Menolayous shaking his head at their approach. Fuck, it must be absolutely terrible if Menolayous was trying to tell him no.

"Where is she?" Danny shouted as he continued to advance towards the wagon.

"Danny..." Menolayous started to speak but their brother heard none of it.

The wagon came to a complete stop in front of them, showing a morbidly gruesome scene in the back. Clyous practically flew over the edge of the wagon, wrapping his arms around his wife as he pulled her from the back, checking her over for injuries frantically. Bridget was covered in blood and appeared disheveled, but it didn't take long to realize that it wasn't her blood. Bridget assured him she was fine and kept insisting on going back to

602

Catriona. That was when Rama's eyes drifted to the bloody mess covered by scraps of blanket. Catriona lay there practically lifeless, the only indicator that she was still alive was the rise and fall of her chest, and even that wasn't in a normal rhythm. Fresh wounds and mostly healed wounds now covered her arms and what he could see of her bare legs, wounds made by wolves' claws and teeth. It appeared that she had been mauled by a pack of dogs. Her hands were both wrapped tightly with bloody cloth, Rama wasn't sure what injuries lie beneath but considering the bleeding hadn't stopped he assumed it was bad.

"Cat!" Danny lunged for her, trying to make his way around Rama.

"You shouldn't touch her!" Grace barked as she tried to place herself between them.

Rama reacted to the urgency in Grace's voice, snagging Danny up once again in an iron embrace to keep him from launching himself into the wagon. "Hold on a moment, she's safe now. Just stop."

"Cat!" Danny shouted, his eyes wild and showing how little control he had of himself.

Menolayous was there now, putting himself between Danny and Catriona. "Listen to me, brother. She's alive, alright! She's breathing. Bridget has been mending the wounds, but she's tapped out at the moment. I need you to stop trying to fight us to get to her. The last thing you need to do is startle her; she can't discern friend from foe at the moment."

"Let-me-go!" Danny continued to struggle against Rama's grip.

"Not until you settle down!" Rama commanded, squeezing tighter for emphasis.

"She tried to kill Bridget," Grace said from the back of the wagon. "She didn't even recognize her. You can't just rush in here and start grabbing at her. That's what they did."

At those words Rama could feel Danny's muscles slacken in his grip, realization finally hitting him at what his woman had endured. Menolayous stared into Danny's eyes for a moment before nodding. Grace began to talk quietly to Catriona as she gently pulled back the blanket, trying to sit the girl up slowly. There was an audible gasp from Clyous as he looked at his sister, all the color draining from his face. Clyous released Bridget to take a few steps away where he began to empty the contents of his stomach. Rama felt inclined to do the same, but he needed to maintain his hold on Danny. Her bare legs were covered in deep slashes and bite marks, different from the wounds made

603

by the wolves. It was as if she had been attacked by a mountain lion or something more feline. There was blood soaking through the tunic from between her legs, though luckily not enough that it could be considered life threatening. Rama didn't need to see a wound to know exactly what had happened to her, he had seen it played out in his mind dozens of times. He had prayed to the gods that it would never become a reality.

He hadn't hesitated to start gathering men for a rescue although he had wished he had been quicker. The Oich guards had taken an alternative route to throw them off once they gave chase. Even Morrigan's raven wasn't able to find the wagon until they were too far away.

Danny collapsed in Rama's arms, a wail of anguish breaking free from his lips as his body lost its strength. Tears were flowing freely from everyone present, even Connor who did his best to avert his eyes from the back of the wagon. Rama finally released his brother, setting him down on the ground gently to work through his pain. Rama was no longer worried Danny would be rushing in, the weight of what had happened to her finally hit everyone.

"We figured we'd keep the cuff on until we could find some sort of replacement that didn't cut into her skin," Grace suggested. "Her magic will be too unstable right now. At least until she comes back to us."

"Who did this?!" Danny demanded, his mourning now mixing with rage. "Who the fuck did this to her?!"

"I've caught glimpses of a clansman," Grace said with her eyes closed, hand gentle on Catriona's forehead. "They call him King Rion. Apparently, this was his plan for her all along. He wants to breed a shifter with magic."

"Show me!" Danny stood up, grabbing for his weapon at his side. "Show me his face."

"Not right now!" Menolayous shouted, launching forward to grab Danny's hand as it went for the hilt of his sword. "Revenge later. We need to get Catriona back to Collie. We need your help to do that. She'll need you when she comes back to us."

Danny was seething, his eyes darting between Menolayous and the capital city. Catriona's body jerked suddenly, catching everyone's attention. Danny's eyes fell back on her, his decision made. He would not abandon her now. He removed his hand from his sword.

"When we get back—" his watery eyes turned to Grace. "I want to know who I'm hunting."

"When we get back and get her settled—" Grace stared at him with equal intensity "—I'll go with you."

Chapter Eighty-Nine

Grace

Grace took a deep inhale of the night air, gulping down the cool summer breeze as she stood on the walkway outside her tree home. The house to the right was lit up with candles on the inside, it was where Catriona continued to lay catatonic with Danny sitting beside her. The house was filled to the ceiling with grief. Every single one of them had gone over to sit with her, to try and talk to her, to see if anyone could get a spark of life from her. Every single one of them had failed.

It had been three days since they had rescued Catriona from Oich, three days where Bridget worked tirelessly, edging close to burnout most of the time to heal what she could. The flesh wounds were an easy fix, once those had been mended, Bridget had made the unfortunate discovery that Catriona had several broken ribs, a broken wrist, and a pretty severe concussion. Her bones had been reset and now mended. It was safe to say that all that was left as a wound was what had happened to her.

There had been several instances like tonight where Grace could hear Cat screaming. She never said words, and the screams suddenly came on in her sleep. But that's all it was, Catriona would finally fall asleep just to relive her worst nightmares. The first few times everyone had come running, but it was quickly realized that adding people into that small home during one of her night terrors only made it worse. Catriona had come to accept Danny's presence, not that she spoke to him, but he had a way of comforting her once her nightmares took over.

"*You really should be getting some sleep,*" her mother's voice echoed down their mental connection.

Grace sighed, of course her mother was up at this hour. "*It's kind of hard to do nowadays. Why are you awake?*"

"*Similar reasons as you,*" her mother's voice said matter-of-factly. "*The weight of the crown and knowing you have the power to help those in need can weigh heavily on you. Especially when helping others means putting your own people at risk.*"

"*It's a bit late for a lecture, don't you think?*" Grace rolled her eyes regardless of the fact that her mother wasn't there to see it.

"You will be queen one day, it's never too late for a lecture," her mother corrected in that commanding voice of hers. *"I brought my troops down here, marched them through enemy territory to make sure you were alright. I put hundreds of lives on the line, if not the entire kingdom, all to protect my daughter."*

"How surprisingly maternal of you," Grace mocked.

"One day when you have children of your own," Grace could hear the tone in her mother's voice that meant she was swimming into dangerous waters, *"you will understand the sacrifices you are willing to make for them."*

"You've always picked the kingdom over me," Grace snapped back, not caring about her mother's mood. *"Time and time again I came to you for help and you always picked them."*

"I picked teaching you how to think for yourself, how to navigate our world to best keep you safe." The tone in her mother's voice changed to something softer, *"I never picked them over you."*

As easily as it was for Grace to be mad at her mother, the change of tone proved to her that her mother wasn't lying. Her resolve softened as she took in another deep breath, there was literally no point in arguing with her. The past was the past, for whatever her mother's reasons were. They could only move on from here, it was better than living in the past.

"Thank you," Grace said, *"for coming to help me."*

"Always," Grace could hear the sarcasm in her mother's voice. *"I wouldn't have had to if you hadn't run away with one of our bravest soldiers and our kitchen's hunter."*

"Yeah well—" Grace spared a moment to remember Darragh and Ingrid. *"I appreciate it nonetheless."*

"I see you have made yourself a home here." Her mother changed the subject, undoubtedly feeling the pain of Grace's loss. *"You have true friends, a rare treasure indeed."*

"Something that unfortunately I never would have found back home." Grace did not mean that harshly, just factually. *"They don't care about my rank and privilege. They only care about honesty."*

"That much I was able to discern. Each one of them is unapologetically themselves, no wonder you fit in so well."

"Thanks." Grace cracked a small smile.

"You find yourself surrounded by good people. Take some advice from your mother, keep them around."

"I wasn't planning on letting any of them go." Grace wasn't sure how to take her mother's comment.

"And some advice from your queen," Grace's mother continued, *"you find yourself surrounded by the next generation of Stone Basin's rulers, assuming your friends win this rebellion. Strengthen your bonds with them. Help them learn how to assume their roles as leaders."*

"That's very strategic advice," Grace teased.

"You will one day inherit my throne. It would be prudent of you to make allies now before that time comes."

"Does that mean you will continue to support me while I'm here?" Grace was slightly shocked at this sudden revelation.

"I will leave my troops with you to better fortify this city while you call it your home. They will only answer to you," Grace's mother answered reluctantly. *"If you disappear again, or if you meet an unfortunate end, they will return home. Until then, they are yours, use them to strengthen these relationships you have been tending to."*

"Thank you, Mother." Grace felt a wave of emotion at her mother's kindness, as politically centered as it was.

"Tell me about this man you have been staying with," she said as an order, not as a request.

"I'm surprised you didn't take the opportunity to degrade him by calling him boy or something else insulting." Grace's defenses were back up at the mention of Menolayous.

"With the others, you used to frolic in front of me to get a reaction, those were boys," Grace's mother countered. *"This one is a man. Older in the head than the years he's walked on this continent. And unlike the others, it's obvious you both care a great deal about each other."*

"We do," Grace answered simply. *"Menolayous is mine, and I'm his. There's not much else to say."*

"And how does he feel about you eventually ruling over Airgid?" Grace's mother asked not to be spiteful but to face a harsh reality. *"He doesn't seem to enjoy being around people as much as he would have to while living alongside a queen."*

"That's a conversation to be had," Grace answered flatly.

"I genuinely encourage you to have it," her mother responded. *"You seem good for each other. Best not set yourself up for failure and work out what needs to be worked out now."*

"Thanks, Mother, I'll get right on that." Grace rolled her eyes again, making sure to shoot an image of her doing so down the bond.

Her mother chuckled in response. *"I'll be taking off at first light, I've been away from our home for too long. Your father will undoubtedly be trying to hang half of my advisors by now."*

"They deserve it." Grace cracked a smile at the thought of her no-nonsense father doing just that. *"Want me to come say goodbye?"*

"No," her mother answered. *"You know we're both not good at that. Just make sure it's not the last time I see you."*

"Deal," Grace didn't argue, she and her mother were not that comfortable being affectionate.

"And Grace," her mother started, *"I hope your friend will be okay. I hope she's strong enough to pull through."*

New waves of emotions hit Grace at the reminder of how broken Catriona really was, how it wasn't her physical wounds that could lead to her death anymore. How she was important, how all of her new family was important to her, how she cared for each and every one of them in their own way.

Grace decided to say the words that had been missing from their relationship for years. *"Thanks, Mother. I love you."*

It took a moment before her mother responded to her, clearly surprised at her daughter's confession. *"Love you too. Give them more chaos than you ever gave me."* And with that, Grace could feel the mental connection between them close.

A tear slid down Grace's cheek at the sudden absence of her mother. Not that she would ever admit it to the old warhorse, but Grace did hold some affection for her deep within. Her mother's sudden appearance and support with her troops, and her approval of Grace's choice to remain here and fight were overwhelmingly emotional. It wasn't often, if ever that Grace felt as if her mother approved of her actions. The fact that she didn't dismiss Menolayous meant something to her, even if her disapproval wouldn't have changed anything.

"Are you okay?" Menolayous asked, his voice shocking her back to reality.

"Yes," Grace answered, giving him a small smile. "I was just talking to my mother. She's leaving first thing in the morning, but she's leaving me troops."

"That's great." Menolayous came to stand beside her, his shoulder gently brushing hers as he looked on into the neighboring house.

"She likes you," Grace admitted, glancing into his face. "She doesn't like anyone."

"She loves you." Menolayous shrugged. "Perhaps your mother recognizes that I love you too."

"She does, but she reminded me that we have a potentially hard conversation we need to have." Grace glanced down over the balcony, eyes straining to see the darkened forest floor below.

"And that is?" Menolayous asked, voice surprisingly calm.

"What we're going to do when I become queen." Grace was afraid to look at him, too nervous the facts she was about to present to him would scare him away from her. "I would be in charge of a kingdom, I would be constantly surrounded by advisors and politicians. I wouldn't be able to take off into the woods whenever I wanted, I wouldn't be able to hide from everyone. You would be surrounded by people you wouldn't trust—"

"I can see why you think all of that would matter to me," Menolayous said, giving her a half smile, "but it doesn't."

"But it does," Grace argued. "It matters to you. I don't want you to stick around with me and then be blindsided when I finally take over the throne."

"It almost sounds like you're trying to end things between us," Menolayous countered, raising an eyebrow.

"Gods no." Grace laughed nervously. "Ugh… I'm not good at conversations like this."

"Like what?"

"Mixing what I want with what is expected of me. The two things always seem to be at odds." Grace reached out and took his hand in hers. "I want to be with you. More than anything. But someday, I'll have no choice but to ascend the throne. I just don't want you to think I'm tricking you into anything. I wouldn't want to force you into a marriage or expect you to just accept court life. I don't even accept court life. I don't want you to feel trapped there."

Menolayous looked at her for a moment before throwing his head back and laughing. This took Grace completely by surprise, unsure what was so funny. Menolayous gently grabbed her, pulled her close, and kissed her more passionately than he ever had before. Grace's heart fluttered at the sudden affection, lost for a moment in the feel of his lips on hers.

"Believe me when I tell you that I'm willing to fight my way to the underlands and back if it means being able to stay by your side." Menolayous placed his forehead against hers. "My version just might very well be the royal court of Airgid, but I don't care. You are what matters to me most, and as long as you'll have me, I intend to be by your side every step of the way."

"I literally want nobody else but you," Grace whispered, her eyes watering, "ever."

"Perfect." He smiled at her. "Let's get married before you become queen, so we can avoid the royal wedding altogether."

Grace laughed, blinking away her tears of joy. "I would love nothing more, but even a small ceremony here, after everything seems wrong."

"My people don't do ceremonies," Menolayous offered. "Our marriages are much more simplistic."

"How so?" Grace was curious now.

"Well for starters the only people who need to be present are the bride and groom. Nobody else need be there as a witness. They speak their vows over a particular ceremony, and it is solidified by the gods." Menolayous was holding her closely as he spoke.

"What's the ceremony?"

"Typically, my people will tattoo each other, marking them as a married couple for everyone to see." Menolayous shrugged. "Takes the whole wedding rings thing out of the picture. I can understand if something like that isn't appealing to you, it's very basic."

"No." Grace gently reached out and touched his face. "I love that, just the two of us."

"Really?" Menolayous released a tense breath, the one and only indicator that he was nervous about this conversation.

"Really," Grace answered. "But that means you would have to tattoo me, and no offense but you're not the resident artist."

"Good news is I've been practicing." He smiled at her.

"Really?" It was her turn to be shocked.

"I've been practicing your tattoo since you agreed to be mine," he admitted, cheeks turning a slight shade of pink.

"I want to see it!" she said excitedly.

"You can only see it during the ceremony." Menolayous shrugged his shoulders slightly. "Brings bad luck otherwise."

"Then I guess we're doing it tonight." Grace kissed him fiercely. "Because I cannot wait another minute."

Chapter Ninety

Danny

Danny watched as Bridget busied herself around the room. The healer's visits were no longer revolved around trying to mend a physical wound on Catriona but centered around trying to get her to eat. Catriona hadn't eaten anything since her rescue, even when Bridget tried to pour food in her mouth. That ended in a disaster with Bridget being thrown across the room by Cat's knee jerk reaction to being touched. Bridget meant well enough, but her desire to try and help Catriona had become obsessive. Danny couldn't blame her; he wanted to do anything he could to help Catriona. He just wasn't sure there was anything to be done.

Danny hadn't left their home since arriving back in Collie, refusing to leave her side for even a moment. He sat in a chair by the window day in and day out, giving her the space she needed. The first few days he had tried to talk with her, tried saying just about anything to let her know that he was here. The only reaction he was able to get from her was from her eyes, a small trace of life still in them as they shifted to look at him. But that was it. The rest of the time she was like a statue, unmoving and not making a sound. He watched each day as Bridget brought her food just for the food to just sit there uneaten. The color on Catriona's face seemed to grow paler by the day. She occasionally accepted a drink of water, usually drinking from the cup by the bed when he had fallen asleep.

Danny was barely holding it together staying in that room. He did not know how to process what had happened to her let alone how to take how she was dealing with it. He had asked Menolayous what he should do, knowing his brother understood this more than anyone. His only advice was for Danny to be whatever Catriona needed; she would tell him when the time was right. During her night terrors Danny saw the most movement out of her, she would momentarily go back to fighting for her life. The look of terror on her face, the sound of her screams equally shook him to his core as well as ignite a fire inside him that called for revenge.

Grace had searched Catriona's mind that first night, every single one of them agreeing that in case Catriona did not pull through this, they wanted to know who they needed to kill. Grace would not share with anyone else the extent of what happened, claiming that Catriona had the right to tell them on her own time, but she was able to project the man's image for them all to see. The unfortunate part was that this man had apparently escaped death, having come face to face with several of them after violating Catriona. Menolayous, the most remorseful for not having gutted the pig then and there, identified him as one of the three Kings of Gaelach. Rion, the middle brother, the one who had changed his shift from a wolf into a mountain lion. Suddenly some of the wounds on Catriona began to make sense.

It was clear that Catriona had been savagely beaten and tortured by several Gaelach cultists. They didn't do enough damage to kill her, just subdue her. Danny had no doubt in his mind that she hadn't stopped fighting, even for a second. Her injuries would not have been so severe if she had just submitted. His woman would never submit, never stop fighting them. He just wished that some of that fight was still left in her. When he looked into her face he couldn't see anything left in her eyes.

There had been talk amongst their family that Catriona, although healed physically, might choose to stop living. This was intended to harden Danny for one despicable possibility, but all it did was enrage him. Although, as each day turned to night, he couldn't help but wonder to himself if that was destined to be what happened. Every day she didn't eat, didn't respond to anyone, it was another day he felt the grave reaching out to try and take her from him. He knew deep down in his heart that there was nothing he could do to convince her to stay if that was the choice she made. But he was here ready to fight for her, anything he could do, he would do it. Whether by her request or by her demise, he was prepared to march into the heart of Gaelach territory and gut this bastard king. Oh, he had plans for this monster, plans that would make even one as sick as him turn pale at the thought.

"Still nothing?" Bridget asked as she set a plate of food down in front of Danny signaling it was time for him to eat supper.

"Nothing new," Danny said, grabbing the bread off his plate.

Bridget glanced back at Catriona, her hand gently grasping her own stomach as her face contorted in pain. "I see the weight coming off her."

"Her color is fading more every day," Danny confirmed. "I've tried everything I can to get her to eat. I'm barely getting her eyes to look at me."

"There's nothing we can do." Bridget looked as if she was about to be sick. "I wish there was, but even if we all came in and held her down to force her to eat, I'm afraid that would only make matters worse."

"Do you think Grace might be able to get inside her head, trick her into eating?" Danny asked as the thought came to him.

"I can ask her." Bridget thought for a moment. "We would need to consider putting an iron cuff back on her for that though. I'm not sure exactly how Grace's magic works but I would be afraid it might trigger Cat's fire."

"Maybe the fire would be a good thing. A change to this… state she's in." Danny stared up at Bridget, she really looked like she was about to be sick. Catriona hadn't shrunk that much, so he wondered what the issue was.

"Maybe." Bridget nodded. "I'll ask her tonight, if you don't need anything I'm going to go. I'm not feeling well."

"I understand." Danny touched her arm compassionately. "We're good. Thank you and feel better."

Bridget nodded and made towards the door, closing it softly behind her. Danny listened to her footsteps as she descended the wooden staircase back to the forest floor. His attention turned back to the window he sat by, staring at the sky as the sun began to set. So ended the seventh day of this slow and agonizing wait. Danny had lost faith in the gods the moment they allowed Catriona to be taken from him, but he still hoped and prayed that they would both make it through one more night, and if they were feeling generous maybe Catriona would take a turn for the better. Maybe she would speak, or look at him, or even eat something. Danny felt a fool to hope, but at the moment it was all he had. Reality was too dark and foreboding. All he knew for a fact was that Catriona wouldn't be able to last like this much longer. Something needed to change. Maybe Grace poking around in Cat's head would do something.

Chapter Ninety-One

Grace

Menolayous sat between her legs, shirtless, and unfortunately facing away from her. As fun as it would be to have his mouth on her as he was between her legs, what they were doing was far more intimate. Both of them had freshly bathed, and she was preparing to braid his hair for him. This was a ritual they had started months ago, it was something that they both seemed to enjoy. Ever since the very first time she had helped him with his hair she had made a point of offering to help him from then on. There was something about the closeness of it that seemed to comfort Menolayous, a rare feeling for him. This had become sort of a safe space for him, showing her just how much trust he actually put in her. She valued that trust, that love, more than anything else in the world. So, as he sat there, she did her best to not mindlessly chatter, to not to tease him, to not to do anything but provide that calm atmosphere that allowed him to let down all of his walls.

Meanwhile, her hair was a sopping mess she had tied up into a bun that rested at the top of her head, she would get to that later. She slowly pulled the comb through his damp hair, freeing any knots from the wet strands. She hummed as her fingers worked, setting the comb down, she took several pieces between her fingers, interlacing them into a tight fishtail braid. Every so often she paused, grabbing a silver bead from his hand, and weaving it into her design. She enjoyed doing this for him. Grace tied off that braid with some twine before grabbing another section. Instead of his normal single plait she wanted to do several fishtails. He could still tie them off in the back, but this style had some sophistication to it. She thought it made him look more fierce, like one of those berserker warriors Flinn told stories about from his homeland. Out of everyone she had ever met, Menolayous's skill in battle, his bloodlust on the battlefield, mimicked those stories almost too well. Part of Grace wondered if he remembered those stories from his teenage years, if he had idolized them as Flinn did while teaching him the art of the warrior.

"You stopped humming," he said gently, his freshly tattooed hand grazing hers, a symbol of their undying love and marital vows for each other.

"My mind began to wander to some of Flinn's stories." She tied off the last braided strand. "There."

He ran his hands gently over his scalp, feeling how the four separate braids curved around his scalp where they met at the back. Grace batted his hands away so she could wrap the last piece of twine, connecting the braids so they fell down the back of his head.

"Thank you," Menolayous said, turning to her with a smile.

"Of course." She kissed him as his arms wrapped around her waist in an embrace.

"Would you let me braid your hair?" he asked, peering up at her.

"I don't usually braid my hair." She gently touched the knotted mess on top of her head. "But if that's something you really want to do, I accept."

"I do," he said as he lifted her off the bed with ease.

She laughed as he set her on the ground, taking her place on the bed. With surprising tenderness he untied the unruly ball of hair, letting the still wet locks fall to her shoulders. As she reached for the comb, he gently smacked her hand. Grabbing the comb, he began to untangle the nightmare that was her hair. He was surprisingly gentle about it, she could barely feel him tug free some of the knots she knew were there.

"I'll compromise with you," Menolayous said playfully, "I won't braid all of it."

"Whatever you want, my love." She closed her eyes, enjoying the feel of his fingers running through her hair.

"Did you know that wearing braids in your hair shows that you're ready for battle?" he asked her as he worked.

"No." Her eyes were still closed. "Is that a Gaelach tradition?"

"Yes. One of the few I still follow," his voice answered her. "Only the warriors wore their hair in braids. It was an honor to be able to wear your hair in braids and there was no greater act of love and loyalty than having someone else braid your hair."

She smiled up at him. "Is that why you were so odd about it that first night?"

He smiled back before turning her head back to facing away from him. "Yes. I knew that you were unaware of its meaning, but it was still a comforting gesture on your part."

"And you only offer to braid my hair now?" she teased.

"You are particular with how you dress and how you present yourself," he answered as his fingers worked. "But it's about time you wore your status more openly."

"I'm not crazy about flaunting being a princess," she said dryly, irritated at her royal heritage and the expectations that it came with.

"That's not the status that I meant." He tugged on a strand playfully. "It's not even the one that matters. I'm talking about your status as a warrior, and my wife."

"So, this is you publicly claiming me now?" she teased. "The tattoos weren't enough?"

She felt his hand then, gripping the hair by the base of her head he pulled her back forcefully. She smiled as she stared up at him, his eyes narrowed at hers as if he were staring down an enemy.

"If you haven't figured out by now that you are mine and nobody else's…" he growled.

"No need to play dirty." She winked up at him as she arched her back to make her breasts stick out more prominently. "There's nobody else, love. There won't be anyone else."

"I'm not the one playing dirty," Menolayous mumbled, forcing her head back to its original position.

She laughed at his annoyance. "So, if braids mean something special, does short hair mean something too?"

"Short hair is meant for slaves," Menolayous said as he went back to braiding.

"Is that why Rion cut Catriona's hair off?" Grace asked before she could talk herself out of the question.

"Yes," he answered. "He was publicly claiming her as his property."

Grace's heart sank deeper into her chest at that answer. Cat had stood no chance against them.

"Rion, Ammon, and Oisin kept my hair short," Menolayous said. "They would pass me around between the three of them, I was their favorite for a while. Anytime my hair got long enough to run my fingers through it they would shave it off down to the scalp. I have scars on my head from their knives when I started to fight back."

She tried to turn to face him, to look at him during this admission, but he held onto her firmly, choosing to keep her from staring at him as he spoke.

"That's when they started making me watch as they hurt my sister. They thought it would break me, that I would stop fighting them and just submit to their will. But she was a fighter too, she made them kill her, she was smart enough she forced their hand. She gave me a gift by doing that, she made it so I no longer felt the need to stay there. She set me free that day, gave me the courage to run. So I did. They didn't think I would be so bold, they were not prepared for my escape. I haven't cut my hair since. In honor of my sister's sacrifice. A promise to keep fighting, no matter what."

Grace sat there for a moment, allowing the silence to settle before she spoke, "You should be proud to wear those braids. I am proud of you and what you have become."

"Have you gone to see Cat?" he asked, his voice was somber.

"Not today," she answered somewhat guiltily. "As of last night, she still hasn't eaten and is barely speaking to anyone. Poor Danny is beside himself. None of us are sure whether we're helping or making it worse by being around her. Bridget still seems determined to get her to eat something. She thinks I can get into her head and trick her into eating. I'm not so sure I can."

"Catriona is going to have to figure out how to deal with what's happened, there's nothing anyone can do to help now. She has to make that choice, to find that strength," he said as he began to twist strands of hair. "Bridget pushing could make it a lot worse."

"Bridget feels responsible," Grace brought up as she thought. "I think she's looking at this as a wound she can heal."

"You can't heal from something like that," Menolayous said. "Not fully. The darkness of it leaves scars on your soul. No matter how hard she works at it, it could even be years down the road after she's felt fine and functional, the darkness will still be there. It won't ever go away. The best we can hope for is her finding a reason to keep fighting it."

"But she's survived this before. She's overcome so much already." Grace sounded hopeful, prayed to the gods there was some truth to it. "She's strong. She can fight it."

"Unfortunately..." Menolayous sighed. "The more you survive it sometimes makes it easier to succumb to that darkness. She's been through a lot. Nearly as much as me. The difference between us is the will to live. Where I fought tooth and nail to survive, just to spite the darkness, she sinks into it. We almost lost her once when she stopped eating. It took everything out of Danny just to get her to eat again, to want to fight."

"She still has Danny," Grace countered.

"You don't always choose to keep living for someone else," Menolayous answered gently. "Others can be fickle. Their loyalties can change. Their reasons could be selfish. And they can die."

"I think it'll destroy Danny if she chooses darkness, knowing that their love wasn't strong enough to keep her going."

"Their love wasn't strong enough to keep her safe." Menolayous tied off a braid. "She's got to love herself enough to keep going."

"I don't know if she can," Grace said sadly. "Bridget brought her a tea to help rid her of any possible unwanted pregnancy. She hasn't touched it. She just stares at it like there's no point to it. Like there won't be a future for her where she would need it."

"That doesn't bode well." Menolayous began braiding another section of hair. "I'm not saying any of this because I don't want Cat to make it. I want her to be okay; I want her to fight. I love her like a little sister. I'm just trying to be as realistic as I can be. Since I first laid eyes on her I knew she'd been hurt. I've seen others in similar situations; I've been through it. She probably can't see any kind of a future she's willing to get to."

"The world shouldn't be like this." Tears began to form in her eyes. "It shouldn't be normal for people to be victimized in such a way. We should be protecting our children better than this, we shouldn't be relying on those who have survived to point these things out to us, to be the ones to protect us from similar trauma."

"I became protective of others because there was nobody to protect me. I know what it's like to have nobody in your corner. Until I found you." He gently wiped a tear that had made a run for it down her cheek. "But if we had met on a similar timeline as Cat and Danny, before I had decided to fight against the darkness, I can't say for sure that we would be how we are now."

"I hate all of this." Grace laid a hand on his forearm, fingers brushing across old scars. "I hate that you have to carry these. That the darkness has still got a hold over you."

"I did these to myself." Menolayous extended his arms so she could see. "Most of these anyway. When the nightmares blended with reality and I couldn't tell the difference anymore, or when the dark whispered to me telling me to kill myself, I would cut myself. It was a form of grounding. The physical pain took my attention from the pain I was feeling on the inside. There's no need to feel bad about these scars, each one of them was a victory of sorts."

"I don't know what to say." Grace leaned up and kissed him. "Just that I love you. And I hope you never have to ground yourself like that again."

Sounds of screaming came from outside, sending both of them vaulting off the floor and reaching for their gear. Menolayous didn't bother with a shirt, he focused on pulling his boots on quickly before grabbing two battle axes. Grace was right behind him after slipping into some pants and boots. Quickly wrapping her bladed whip around her loose flowing tunic, she sheathed her dagger, grabbed a short sword and barreled out the door after him. Without her leather corset there to protect her flesh from her blades, she was careful how she chose to move as they ran, she wished they had more time.

As they descended the staircase, they observed absolute chaos flooding in from the walls. Oich and Gaelach soldiers were pouring over the far south wall, spilling out into Collie like water emptying into a dry damn. The few rebels that were in fact on watch duty were quickly overrun, fighting their hardest against the intruders. The rebels that were not trying to shuttle away the women and children to safety were rushing towards the attackers.

The clash of steel and silver rang out as the two forces collided. Collie was caught off guard, she realized. There weren't enough warriors on this side of the city to defend the walls. They should not have been this badly prepared, especially after leading an attack against Oich itself not but a week ago. Oich striking back should have been expected. The Collie and Airgid warriors were currently outnumbered three to one, and by blooded no less.

Menolayous looked at her then. "We need Catriona if we're to survive this."

She nodded reluctantly at this wisdom. As much as she hated to admit it, he was right. The only way to even the odds was to get their friend out on the battlefield. To give Catriona free rein to kill as she pleased. Grace was terrified at the thought, this very well could be the chance to get Catriona up and fighting again. But at what cost to her soul? Would Catriona be able to differentiate between friend and foe? It was a risk worth taking, Grace realized, as she watched several blooded shift and start tearing through the streets.

She kissed him quickly. "I love you."

621

"I love you too." And with that, he spun around and bolted down the stairs.

Grace watched for a moment as he charged the line, battle axes flying in a cold-calculated assault. Grace watched in awe at how well he moved, nearly as fast as Catriona, but no magic fueled him. What she was witnessing was years of honed skill.

Tearing her eyes from the man she loved, her husband, she watched as some of the blooded began to shift. She turned on her heel, sprinting back up the stairs and across the rope bridge until she found herself in front of Catriona and Danny's home. Before she reached the door Danny flung it open, wild eyes met with hers.

"What's happened?" Danny demanded.

Grace could see Catriona still sitting at the windowsill that she had been for days, but she turned, her eyes locking with Grace's, curiosity shone through the dark. There was still life in her eyes, thank the gods. Grace swallowed air, calculating her next words carefully. Her words could mean the difference between Catriona actually responding to someone and breaking free from the darkness. She had to try, for her friend, for all of them.

"Collie is overrun," Grace breathed, looking at Catriona. "Blooded outnumber us three to one."

Danny looked like he made to move, to run towards the stairs, but he stopped himself. Grace watched as he glanced back at Catriona, who had set her feet on the floor, fists clenched. *That's the most she's moved in days.* Danny realized it, and stopped to watch, to hope.

"Cat, we need you," Grace called from the doorway. "If you don't fight, Collie will be overrun."

Danny was watching her carefully before asking, "Who?"

"Soldiers from Gaelach and Oich," Grace answered, reaching out with her power to touch all of her loved ones, ensuring her new family was still alive and well. She felt a dark presence approaching from the south wall. Two dark life forces accompanied the bitter presence she was beginning to know too well. "The Dark One and his brother have arrived; they brought Prince Liam with them."

Grace watched as Catriona stood. The movement was slow, calculated, testing. Danny watched her as unreadable emotions passed over his face. Grace felt it too, the energy now surrounding them. This reaction, her responding to them at all, was a surprising change. Grace watched

Catriona stroll over to her gear. Catriona stripped off her oversized tunic, not seeming to care about her nakedness, before pulling on a pair of trousers and boots. Grace and Danny watched her scarred and bruised body move as she wrapped her breasts, tightening them down to her chest. Her once long hair now barely touched her shoulders, staying out of the way of her current movement. She did not bother with a tunic before going to her weapons. Grace's body tensed as Catriona picked up one of her short swords, staring at it like a long-lost friend. She could sense Danny tensing as well, unsurprising considering how worried everyone was about her trying to kill herself. With one swift motion she sheathed the swords on her belt, starting for the door.

Danny partially blocked her exit, his voice pleading, "Cat?"

She looked into his eyes then, focusing on the man standing before her. "I'm sorry, for everything."

"You have nothing to be sorry for," his voice barely a whisper, not bothering to fight back the tears. "I love you. I want to help you. Tell me how, please."

"Let me do this." The fire now reached her eyes; Grace could sense the burning hatred flowing through her friend. "Let me kill the men who hurt me."

A wave of relief poured from Danny before he said, "I'm with you, until the end. Always."

Catriona's fire dimmed for only a moment. "I love you too."

Grace stepped aside as the two passed her. The sheer amount of rage and power radiating off Catriona was like standing next to an open forge. Danny was hot on her heels, relief acting as a barrier protecting him from her intensity. Grace was frozen, unable to tell her emotions from theirs. She watched as they went. Should she be happy Catriona was responding to them, that she was gearing up and ready for battle? Seeing what was coming, without Catriona's power and skill, this would be the end of them all. But Grace sensed something unsettling within her, like there was a different type of darkness driving her.

"She's coming," Grace sent down the web of mental pathways. *"Catriona is coming to fight."*

"Gods have mercy," Morrigan echoed back.

"For them," Rama cheered.

"For all of us," Morrigan clarified. *"Best to stay out of her way if you can. That girl will bring down upon her enemies the power of a thousand suns. Wildfire has no allies."*

Chapter Ninety-Two

Morrigan

"Inside!" Morrigan bellowed, sending a spear of ice through the chest of a Gaelach tribesman.

Morrigan stood at the entrance of the longhouse, guarding it from the invaders as their people made it inside. Two children of the ancients stood with her, having been trained in combat. The rest of them were scattered throughout Collie, doing what they could.

Morrigan could feel their lights as they danced around the city. Those that were able chose to engage with the enemy, using their gods given powers to drive back the bloodthirsty wolven. Those who could not fight were helping others make it to safety. One of those safe spots was this longhouse.

Morrigan watched as the petite woman, Yara, ducked underneath a tribesman's sword, slicing at the tendons behind his ankles. The tribesman collapsed with a short-lived snarl before Yara's dagger sliced his windpipe. Seeing more tribesmen rush at her, Yara placed her hands on the dead man's chest. As if life had suddenly returned to him, the dead tribesman clumsily got to his feet, launching himself at his approaching comrades. With Yara still maintaining a physical connection to his back, her undead human shield attacked. Morrigan watched, fascinated at how the young woman could manipulate the dead like a child could manipulate a doll.

"More are coming up from the gate!" Yara shouted as swords pierced her body shield, forcing her to jump back and break that vital connection.

"I've got it," a middle-aged man named Lief said while stepping forward.

Morrigan pierced the chest of a charging tribesman with her spear, digging the blunt end into the ground so the beast's momentum tossed it up and over her. Leif dropped his axe, pushing his palms out in the direction of a dozen or so blooded. Suddenly and without warning the blooded began to stumble. A few of them began to shift back and forth uncontrollably while those who remained in human form were blinded.

"Yara!" Morrigan ordered, turning her own powers to the group. "While they're blinded!"

Yara charged forward with her daggers, dancing between the unseeing enemy, dealing death blows as she moved. Morrigan sent streaks of lightning through those that were still wolven, the smell of cooked meat mingling with the metallic scent of blood.

With only five blooded enemies remaining, an arrow whizzed through the air striking Leif in the upper thigh. His hands dropped their hold, releasing the enemy from his blinding touch. Yara found herself surrounded, quickly touching a corpse she'd felled, using its body to block the attacks now directed towards her. Morrigan stayed her hand, worried she would hit Yara with lightning.

"Oh no you don't, you blooded bastards." The war chief's voice boomed around them.

Flinn and six of his warriors including young Connor charged from one of the city's streets. Swords and axes clashed as the two opposing forces met with violence. Some of the rebels released a war cry as they fought, working in teams of two to take on a single blooded. Morrigan shared a quick look with Flinn, he smiled at her before swiping a large battle axe at a grey wolf.

Seeing a group of oncoming soldiers thoroughly handled, Morrigan rushed to Leif's side. "Hold still."

Without warning, Morrigan grasped the shaft of the arrow, pulling it free. Leif yelped in pain, grabbing at the bleeding wound.

"I can't feel my powers," he said through gritted teeth.

Morrigan looked hard at the arrow tip. "It is of iron."

"Fucking bastards," Leif growled as he began wrapping his leg with a shred of tunic he ripped from himself.

"Your power will return to you soon, no need to worry," Morrigan said as she broke the arrow in half.

"I'm more worried about the hole in my leg," Leif grumbled.

"You will live," Morrigan answered sternly.

Flinn and Connor made their way to her, letting the others take over guarding the longhouse. Flinn smiled as he extended a hand, helping Morrigan to her feet. Yara ran up, crouching down to examine Leif's leg.

"Ah, nothing like an early morning battle to get the old bones moving," Flinn teased.

"Just what I need, any bone of yours to wake up." Morrigan winked.

Flinn let out a hearty, booming laugh.

"Should I go see if any more women and children need escorting to the longhouse?" Connor asked, glancing around like an excited wolf pup on the hunt.

"Easy, lad." Flinn chuckled. "Your sword will have its fill of blood by the end of the day. We're needed here to defend the families inside."

"Yara, get Leif inside. Get some able bodies to assist you. Bridget will need space to work on the injured."

Yara nodded, helping Leif limp into the longhouse. Flinn's warriors fanned out, taking defensive positions around the longhouse entrance. Morrigan glanced around as the battle still raged, the clashing of bodies and steel had at least moved farther away from them.

"The kings of Gaelach and King Liam of Oich seem to have joined forces. They led a three-point attack on our southern and eastern walls. They've set on us with at least four hundred blooded soldiers. We have maybe three hundred, one hundred of them are left over from Airgid. About eighty children of the ancients."

"Only thirty of them are capable of combat and those are scattered amongst the battle. The rest are too untrained or too young," Morrigan answered sorrowfully. "We are outnumbered, and they have a surprise attack to their advantage. It is a full moon tonight, so it will call to them as they fight."

"What of our firebird?" Flinn asked just as a plume of fire erupted into the air not half a mile away.

"She has joined the fray." Morrigan stared at the flare, shaking her head at the lack of control.

"Good, we need her," Flinn said seeing her frustration. "I can always rebuild the city. I can't raise the dead."

"Yes," Morrigan mumbled as she gripped her spear tightly. "Homes can be rebuilt from the ashes. We should let the dead lie in peace. There will be plenty of them by sunset."

Chapter Ninety-Three

Rama

"I've got you." Rama held the child in one arm and his battle axe in the other. "Just keep your eyes closed for me."

Rama carried the little girl through the house, careful to step over the dead bodies that littered the floor. He had seen the enemy soldiers force themselves into the family's home. It didn't matter to him that he was alone, he would defend his people. Luckily, he had made it in time to save the girl from what soldiers remained. Unfortunately, the rest of her family did not make it. Rama made quick work of the two soldiers left alive, doing his best to minimize the gore in front of the child. He was unable to save her from seeing whatever had killed the other soldiers before he got there. They looked as if they had been thrown against the wooden beams repeatedly until their spines snapped. One of the girl's parents must have had powerful magic, not enough to save themselves, but enough to at least keep their daughter alive until he got to her.

"What's your name?" Rama asked as he made it through the front door, the girl was probably about four years old.

"Kyra," her muffled voice answered, her face still buried in his shoulder.

"Okay, Kyra." Rama glanced down the alleyway, trying to decide the safest route. "Do you have any other family here in Collie?"

"No," the tiny voice cried, her little hands clinging to his vest as her body trembled.

"It's okay, Kyra. Everything's going to be okay," Rama said trying to make his voice as soothing as he could. "I'm going to take you somewhere safe."

His heart broke for the child losing her family at such a young age. Rama took off down one of the city streets, making his way carefully to avoid any of the enemy soldiers. Normally, he would like nothing more than to have the opportunity to crack skulls, but not with Kyra in tow. An intense protectiveness had swept over him the moment he had picked up the child. He couldn't risk her safety for the thrill of the fight. He needed to get her to safety. Rama assumed there would be defenses around the longhouse, that's where people were most likely fleeing to.

Rama stalked down the street with the girl still clutching to him for dear life. He could hear the sounds of fighting all around him, it came from too many directions for him to accurately determine how close he was to the individual skirmishes. Careful to step over the shredded bodies of fallen warriors, Rama made his way towards the longhouse.

Rama froze in place as a rather large black wolf emerged from an alleyway onto the road in front of him. The wolf looked directly at him, as if recognizing him. Rama raised his axe, taking a defensive stance as he maneuvered Kyra out of sight the best he could. Rama recognized the wolf immediately, the crown prince, now king he supposed, bared his fangs in warning. Rama could feel his heart beating nearly out of his chest. If this turned into a fight, Rama feared for Kyra's safety. Knowing that prick, he would use Rama trying to shield the child to his advantage.

The wolf's eyes shifted to the small human, his fangs suddenly disappearing. The wolf snorted air in their direction, as if to show he would not attack first. Rama glanced around, not trusting another blooded to not be lying in wait nearby. He saw no one. Liam was too cunning, too blood thirsty to not take advantage of an opportunity to take out the rebel king, it would be the strategic move to make.

The wolf raised its large head, sniffing the air. After a moment its head snapped forward as if it had scented what it was looking for. Without bothering to glance their way again, Liam bounded away to track down whatever he was looking for. Rama was frozen in place, not from fear but amazement. Had Liam really not taken advantage of this opportunity? Why? Rama looked at Kyra, thinking, maybe he drew the line at children. Maybe there was hope for the bastard yet.

"Liam is here!" Rama shouted down the web of metal connections, hoping someone could hear him amongst the chaos.

"Where?" Catriona's voice seethed, surprising him with its intensity.

"Headed towards the market," Rama responded. *"I found a little girl, I need help getting her to safety."*

Nothing. He heard nothing. Maybe Catriona was in the middle of fighting? That would seem likely. Rama assumed at this point everyone was actively engaged in combat or about to be. He was hoping someone would help him get Kyra to safety.

"If you can make it to the longhouse," Morrigan grunted from exertion, *"there are enough of us here to protect the child."*

"I'm on my way." Rama started moving again. *"Where is everyone?"*

"Myself and the war chief guard the innocents at the longhouse." Morrigan's words were clipped, she must be fighting. *"I do not see the others. Everything is too chaotic to focus completely. I sense two very dark figures have entered Collie. I can sense Catriona's rage. That is all I can see from this distance."*

"Makes sense." Rama turned onto a street where several warriors surrounded a wolf, trying to get past the teeth and claws to land a killing blow.

Kyra began to scream as they neared the fighting, trying to crawl up Rama's arm even more as if to escape the beast. Rama danced around the warriors, putting his distance between them when a new group of Oich soldiers poured into the street. Rama now stood between the Oich soldiers and the Collie warriors.

With a shrill battle cry, Catriona launched herself from a nearby roof, bringing her two short swords down and piercing through the chest of one of the soldiers. Catriona, blood soaked and wild, kicked herself up and away from the soldier she had impaled, taking her blades with her. She rolled as she hit the ground, swiping at the legs of two more soldiers as she moved. She rolled up into a standing position, able to throw up her blades to block an incoming strike from an Oich soldier.

"For the brotherhood!" The Collie warriors charged into the melee. "For the white flame!"

Rama threw himself and Kyra off to the side, making room for the sudden rush of soldiers running past him. Rama hugged a crying Kyra, doing his best to shield the child's eyes from the violence. After several minutes, with the help of a bloodlust driven Cat, the Oich soldiers were slain. The Collie warriors let loose a cheer before taking off down the pathway towards another group of foes.

Rama watched as Catriona stood there, staring down at the bloody and mangled corpses, kicking the head of one of the dead bodies so hard he could hear the neck snap. Her chest rose and fell deeply from the exertion of the fight; her eyes were feral. Rama stared at her, examining every aspect of the woman who had been practically lifeless the last week from the trauma she had endured. Just days ago, he had been afraid she would take her own life, forcing him to bury a sister and watch his brother's world completely shatter. Before him now stood vengeance itself, there was barely anything of Catriona left.

With blood streaked across her scarred face, her liquid silver eyes shone brightly in contrast with the gore she wore. He observed her dress then, tightly fitted pants and boots, her chest was wrapped tightly with cloth, it was what women typically wore underneath clothing. Her short white hair was caked in blood and dirt. Catriona was dressed for one thing and one thing only, to kill efficiently. There was nothing that would restrict her movements, allowing her full range of her abilities, but she also wore nothing that protected herself from injury. She did not care if she lived or died, she only cared to kill as many of her enemies as she could.

"Cat?" Rama took a step forward, stopping dead in his tracks as her eyes shifted to his with a look that promised death.

Kyra cried out, shifting in his arms as she glanced at Catriona. Suddenly seeing the small human's presence, she took a step back. Catriona glanced down at herself after seeing the terrified look on the child's face. Vengeance was gone for a moment, and Catriona stood before them.

"I'm sorry." Cat took another step away, looking around as if suddenly realizing where she was. "I'm scaring her."

"You're scaring me," Rama barked. "What the fuck, Cat? Why aren't you wearing armor?"

"Restricts my movements," was all she said, taking another step away from the crying child.

"Gets you killed more like." Rama found that he was angry at her for her lack of caution. "Where's Danny?"

Shaken by his question, Catriona turned on her heel to flee. Rama shot forward, grabbing her shoulder before he thought better of it. Catriona turned on him then, startled by the contact, and lashed out like a wild animal. Rama made to move, jumping away from her reach, but Catriona's strike never connected. Catriona barely raised her arm before freezing in place. There was a momentary look of horror that passed over Catriona's face as she stared at her raised arm, seeming to be confused as to why she had stopped, but her silvery eyes met Kyra's hazel ones, the child's fearless stare cutting through her soul.

"I'm sorry," was all Catriona said before taking off.

"I'm not sure which one of you should be more feared," Rama said softly to Kyra, who kept her eyes on Catriona as she fled. "Not many men are willing to face death so fiercely."

Rama took off again, steering them towards the longhouse. He could see the trail of bodies leading up to the entrance. Oich soldiers, tribesmen, even wolven bodies littered the ground, their blood seeping into the earth. The bodies of the enemy greatly outnumbered those of the collie warriors. Looking ahead, Rama realized why.

True to her title, Morrigan, Guardian of the Ancients, stood at the front of the defense line sending storm clouds over the city bringing bolts of lightning down on distant figures. Rama could never not be in awe of the sorceress's power; her command of the elements was a feat of old tales.

Flinn commanded small squadrons of warriors, directing groups to either circle the perimeter or to rally in preparation of a counterattack. Rama whispered comforting words to Kyra as he approached his allies, warriors moving aside to let him pass.

Flinn spotted his approach, voice booming over them all, "Ready to join the melee, Your Highness?"

"I'm not sure where you've been, old man." Rama laughed. "I've been out in the thick of it."

"What have you there?" Flinn spotted Kyra in his arms.

"This is Kyra." Rama hoisted the young girl up a few inches to show her the old war chief. "Kyra, this is my good friend Flinn."

Kyra peered at the old man shyly before hiding her face in his shoulder. Rama could accept this, this small sign of normalcy amidst the violence that surrounded them. Flinn did his best to wave and appear non-threatening, but considering he appeared battle torn it was not going well. Morrigan approached them then, leaving the warriors to continue their defense, her eyes locked onto the child.

"You carry a bright light," Morrigan said as she visually inspected the child.

"Can you try to use words that make sense to others." Rama stared at her incredulously. "It's too early in the morning for you."

Morrigan scowled at him. "This is a child of the ancient ones, the light of her magic is bright, nearly as bright as Catriona's."

"What?" Rama asked, looking down at the girl, her hazel eyes stared back at him.

"May I?" Morrigan reached forward as if to take the child from him.

"No!" Kyra shrieked, throwing a hand out at Morrigan while trying to hang onto Rama with the other.

To everyone's surprise, Morrigan was knocked backwards by an invisible force. All eyes turned to the child, who was still trying to burrow into Rama's shoulder. Morrigan threw her head back and laughed, a sound Rama rarely heard from the woman.

"She is a strong one indeed." Morrigan smiled as she got to her feet, dusting herself off. "It seems she is quite fond of you, young King."

"Kyra," Rama tried to sound soothing as he held onto the child, "Nobody here is going to hurt you. You're safe. I'm going to leave you here—"

"No!" Kyra glared at him defiantly.

"Good luck with that, lad." Flinn chuckled. "You can take your spot with me; we need a plan. Our warriors need orders."

Rama resigned to carrying the ferocious four year old, conceding with the fact that he was needed here. They needed to regroup and make a counter assault. As king, that was his duty. His days of fighting in the trenches were over.

"Any word on my brothers?" Rama readjusted the small child as he glanced around.

"You can track our firebird from here." Flinn pointed down the hill at the buildings. Sure enough, Rama could see a line of flames progressing north towards the city market. "My best guess is she's tracking Prince Liam, and I would bet a cask that Danny is tracking her."

"Sounds right." Rama watched the city below, most of the blooded had grouped together at the eastern wall. "Menolayous?"

"There." Morrigan pointed just to the east of them, below the hill.

They were close enough to his brother that Rama was able to pick him and Grace out from the enemy soldiers they were fighting. Menolayous danced through their enemies dual-wielding battle axes, bare chested, and covered in his enemies' blood. Rama had seen his brother cut loose on a battlefield before, but it had been nothing like this. Rama noticed he had taken to Catriona's approach about wardrobe and restrictive movement. Rama ground his teeth at the lack of armor his brother wore, how unprotected he was, but unlike Catriona, Rama knew Menolayous cared about surviving this battle, his reason fought beside him.

Grace kept up with him, cutting through soldiers as she followed Menolayous's lead. They worked together as they fought, delivering distracting strikes so the other one could deal a final blow before they moved on. Pride filled his heart as he watched them, they were so in tune to each other he had no words for it. It looked to him like Menolayous was moving somewhere with a purpose. After a moment of searching, Rama finally found his brother's target. An enormous black bear and a large black and grey mountain lion ran side by side to the marketplace. Menolayous was hunting down two kings of Gaelach who seemed dead set on the direction they were moving. It was the same direction Catriona moved, tendrils of her wildfire marking where she had been. Cat was probably hunting down another king, Liam. Why everyone was converging on the marketplace was beyond him.

Until he suddenly realized why. "Where the fuck is Bridget?!"

Chapter Ninety-Four

Clyous

These images, these events were so similar that Clyous was having trouble differentiating what was real and what was part of his vision. He had dreamed this exact scene a few weeks ago, this attack on Collie, these soldiers, this death and destruction. He understood now why his sister and Bridget were missing from this dream, this vision. Their capture was the catalyst that set this pathway of fate into motion. He did not see them because they were not supposed to be here, they were destined to remain captives, but their fate had changed when Grace had decided to accept her mother's help and bring her countrymen back to Collie. Without that decision, they would not have been able to attack the capital city and rescue the girls. They would have been lost to them forever, enduring god knows what type of torment.

As Clyous racked his brain to remember important details from this vision in hopes of turning the tide, he held onto Bridget's in a tight grip as he pulled her through the chaos. With a war hammer in hand he took the lead, keeping her as close to him as possible. He knew she was angry, angry at him for taking a decision away from her. He was not thrilled about the situation they were in, so she would have to stay angry for the time being. He wasn't dragging her along because he believed her to be weak, that was far from the truth, her skill as a warrior had improved significantly since his sister's training regimen. No, the issue was Bridget kept trying to stop and help everyone they passed. Clyous didn't have time to explain to her she needed to save herself from burnout, she would be desperately needed after the battle. He also couldn't explain the gut feeling he had that the enemy was here for her. So, his current plan was to get her to the longhouse. There she would be protected, and there she could help those who were hurt. Bridget was a determining factor for everyone's survival; he felt it deep in his bones.

"I can keep up with you," Bridget grunted in frustration as Clyous sharply turned down another street, dragging her along behind him.

"Well aware." Clyous released her hand as they came upon three enemy soldiers.

Clyous swung his hammer low before bringing it in a nearly perfect arc, connecting the hammer into the soldier's chest. Caught completely by surprise, the blooded did not block the powerful blow. His chest caved in on the impact, crumbling the young blooded to the ground. Bridget descended upon the next blooded soldier, dagger in a reverse grip she made a well-placed slice across the soldier's neck, severing the windpipe before advancing on the next. Clyous swung his hammer at the soldier's legs, the blooded effortlessly avoided. What the cocky bastard did not expect was Bridget to slip the tip of her blade through the back of his ear and into his skull. The movement was so quick, so calculated, it required very minimal effort on her part. Her knowledge of human anatomy was terrifying.

"I've seen this before," Clyous tried to explain as he grabbed her again. "Weeks ago, in one of my dreams. I need you to get to the longhouse."

"You've seen this?" Bridget no longer pulled away from him. "And the outcome?"

"Not good," Clyous answered, veering away from a nearby skirmish

"And you need to get me to the longhouse because you saw me die?" He could hear the change in her voice, the fear sinking in.

"I couldn't see you or Cat," Clyous answered. "But I saw the Dark One come and kill. I have a gut feeling he's here for you and my sister, since they couldn't keep you the last time."

"Then we need to get to Catriona." Bridget pulled from his grip, halting their progression. "We can't let them hurt her, not again."

"Look around," Clyous snapped, his frustration bubbling over. "You see how everything on the other side of the city is on fire? That's my sister. She knows they're here, and I'll bet my life she's hunting them down right now. I wouldn't be worried about her; I would pray for anyone getting in her way. It wouldn't be safe going to her now, she wouldn't be able to keep her powers from hurting us."

"He's right," a male voice called from an alleyway.

Clyous turned suddenly, lifting his war hammer in preparation for an attack. Bridget emitted a low growl as she did the same with her dagger. Liam stepped from the shadows; his eyes were fixed on Bridget. His gaze held a sense of confusion as he stared at her, nostrils flaring as if scenting the air. But to Clyous's surprise, Liam not only stopped advancing but showed absolutely no amount of hostility towards them. In fact, he seemed meek as he stood there. Something wasn't right. Clyous glanced around to see if another enemy lay in wait nearby.

"King Oisin and King Rion are leading the attack on your rebel city in the hopes of capturing you and any other magic users they can." Liam was completely ignoring Clyous's presence, an interesting change from trying to kill him on sight. "Unfortunately, Rion has high hopes that he'll be able to breed your little friend. He wants to recapture her before she has the chance to get rid of any offspring."

"He will never lay a hand on her again!" Bridget snarled protectively. "Neither will you."

"What was done to your friend was—" shame, actual shame contorted his features "—despicable."

"Don't you dare pretend to have a shred of honor after what you did. Even if you didn't do it yourself you allowed it to happen."

"I haven't pretended to have honor for some years now. I might be a monster, but there's lines even I won't cross." Liam stared at Bridget for a moment before saying, "She picked you, you know. I was in the process of forming a plan to get her out of the city when she warned me about you, knowing I would abandon her to save you. Not that she was fully aware of my plans if at all, but I wanted you to know that I'm still Liam. I wasn't going to let that happen to her."

"So, you'll burn and torture women, peeling the flesh from them as you whip them to death, but you draw the line at rape?" Bridget huffed an exasperated laugh. "I've watched you cross lines for years now. I've seen the aftermath of you asserting your control. I've heard the stories about you and your men beating and raping women in the town squares just to show them you were the ones in charge."

Liam looked as if she had struck him but quickly tried to change his expression to something more controlled. "I won't deny I have committed heinous crimes against my people. I have done evil things acting as the crown prince. I've killed, I've tortured, I've beaten men and women. I have so much innocent blood on my hands I'll never be able to wash it off, but I have never hurt a child, I would never allow a child to be hurt. Nor pregnant women, and I've never, ever, raped anyone."

"I don't believe you," Bridget spat at him.

Liam responded quietly. "Don't for one second think I'm defending my actions or trying to claim I wouldn't have hurt her. Because I would have, I would have whipped her to death or tortured her. I was supposed to hand her off to the kings of Gaelach, a trade for more land. I hated her so much I very easily could have killed her instead of handing her over. I wouldn't be able to truthfully tell you which path I would have taken, but I wouldn't have raped her, I wouldn't have let my men either. And believe me, if I knew what

637

Rion's plan for her actually was, I would have killed her so he wouldn't have been able to."

Clyous studied the man before him, staring into his eyes. Bridget was doing the same, determining if they could trust a word out of his mouth. Clyous glanced around them again ensuring no other enemy was sneaking in closer to them for a killing blow. This situation was too bizarre.

"Why would you have spared her from that if you hate her so much?" Bridget asked, her voice had less of an edge to it. "Why do you hate her so much?"

"Because," Liam choked on his words slightly, "she reminds me of me. She is what I should have been. She fought against the odds to protect her mother, it didn't matter to her if she lived or died. She risked everything to protect her family. She didn't let fear stop her. I should have fought harder to save my mother. Every time I look at her, I feel ashamed, weak in comparison, and I hate that more than anything."

There was silence between the three of them for a moment before Bridget said softly, "You were just a child, Liam."

"And she was just a woman." Liam's eyes were wet with unshed tears. "I recognized her that day as the daughter of the magic user who burned me, the one who escaped the night my mother was killed. I remember him vividly. She looks just like him, has his powers. I see her and I feel shame for my failures to protect my mother, and I blame her for her father's actions. I know it's not fair or logical, but I hate her for all of it."

"Why are you here?" Clyous demanded, not sure if he should be trusting a single word from this man.

"I came to warn you that they were coming for you." Liam continued to stare at Bridget, ignoring Clyous. "A small part of me hoped I could convince you to come with me, to get you out of here, but I see now that you wouldn't leave, especially in your condition. You won't leave your pack; your maternal instincts won't allow it."

There was sadness in Liam's eyes as he looked at Bridget, a unique form of submission. Clyous saw him bow his head, it was as if years of fighting for dominance were lifted off his shoulders. Bridget, however, appeared to be growing increasingly feral at his stare, energy radiating off of her in ripples. He was submitting to her, Clyous realized. Liam was accepting himself as the lower wolf, and Bridget was showing her dominance over him.

Clyous felt the sudden tug of consciousness as his powers pulled him into a vision:

Clyous stood in a small room beside a birthing bed. Bridget lay there wrapped up in blankets, her face was covered in sweat and her hair a mess from a strenuous labor. In her arms rested a freshly swaddled infant, eyes closed and breathing softly as if it was held by its mother. A small patch of red hair rest atop the crown of its head.

Catriona and Danny were there too. Catriona was covered in a large black cloak; she too held an infant child. This infant, however, was awake and cooing up at Cat. Tears flooded down his sister's cheeks as she handed him the babe. Danny gave Cat a reassuring squeeze on her shoulder as Clyous brought the babe to Bridget. Bridget smiled at the child as she took the babe in her arms, pulling its tiny mouth to her swollen breast. The babe latched on instantly, calming as it suckled. Relief swept over everyone in the room at the latching. Clyous felt his heart swell at the sight of his wife breastfeeding the two infants.

"You're pregnant," Clyous stated as he was drawn back to reality, "with twins."

Bridget looked him in the eye, sparks of joy shown in her emerald eyes. She knew he realized now that she was with child. She must have been hiding it for some time. He couldn't recall her last monthly cycle, for at least two months now. She must have been pregnant when they took her and Catriona. Did she know then?

"They will want your babies." Liam broke apart their tender moment with his warning. "I didn't scent it when you were in the castle, Rion didn't either, but you reek of it now, you won't be able to hide your condition from any shifter. You'll need to flee."

"Your soldiers are here too. Why can't you have them protect her?" Panic now flooding through him.

"They're not mine anymore. When Bridget killed my father, she inherited the crown and became the Queen of Oich. She is the pack leader now. They don't follow me. The soldiers that are here bonded with Rion, they refused to submit to a woman, broke the bonds with their pack and joined another."

"What do you mean I inherited the crown?" Bridget glanced at him incredulously.

"You challenged my father Bridget, and you won." Liam stared at her in disbelief. "You know how the magic works. Oich is yours."

Chapter Ninety-Five

Bridget

"Mine?" she said in disbelief.

She never really considered her altercation with the dead king as an official challenge, but all the components were there. By right, she supposed she had succeeded Liam. The blooded of Oich knew it, and they waited for her.

She looked at Liam, sizing him up. She had never feared him before, but now he seemed rather subdued, submissive. Any dominance he had possessed as a wolf was gone. He was within his rights to challenge her for the crown, but it was obvious he was not here to do that. Bridget was not sure why, was it because he could sense her pregnancy, was it because he was finally free of his father? Liam's sudden reappearance was surprising, especially after his confessions. Today, kneeling before her, she saw more of the true Liam, the boy she had grown up with. She did not see the evil prince.

"Not for long," a cocky voice drew her attention to several figures approaching them. "Making a dominant wolf submit is another way to win a kingdom."

"I'm not too sure, brother," an array of perfectly in sync voices echoed in response. "A mother wolf will fight more fiercely than most."

Bridget watched in horror as the two Gaelach tribesmen approached with weapons in hand. Oisin smiled at her wickedly, revealing his blood-red eyes and sharpened teeth. His unnatural presence shifted the energy around them, darkening the shadows as he moved. Rion remained in step with his brother even though his presence did not pull the same attention. Bridget growled at the man responsible for raping and torturing her friend. A lack of dark magic did not minimize the evil that lurked beneath his skin.

"She is not yours." Liam stepped between them, his sword drawn.

"Little Liam," Oisin chided. "You can't be foolish enough to think you would win this fight, especially when you couldn't even handle your own father."

Bridget lowered herself slightly into a more defensive stance as Rion started to circle around Liam. Liam's sole focus was on Oisin. The brothers were right about two things. Liam wouldn't be able to take them on alone, but she knew he would try, she could sense his resignation. Liam was prepared to die today, as was Clyous apparently. Bridget's eyes tracked her husband as he stepped up to Rion, war hammer at the ready. Maybe all three of them had a chance if they could keep the brothers from shifting. They were right in assuming Bridget wouldn't submit and allow her babies to be harmed. She would fight to the death to keep her babies out of their clutches, as would their father.

"Now, now, girl." Rion smiled at her. "You can make this easier on yourself, or harder on them. Either way we'll have you and your baby."

"Don't take another step." Clyous's voice came out raised in warning.

"You look familiar." Rion stared at him as if actually seeing him for the first time. "Have I fucked you?"

"What?"

Rion stared at him for a moment like he was working out a puzzle. "Ah, that's what it is. I fucked your sister. Your twin I'm guessing."

Clyous glanced at her, pointing at Rion. "Him?"

He was asking if this was the man who had hurt Cat. She nodded. Clyous launched himself at the shifter, catching the man off guard as he buried the war hammer into Rion's rib cage. There was a sickening crunch. Bridget knew Clyous was strong for a human, ribs were definitely broken with that impact. As soon as realization sank into everyone's minds, they moved. Rion fell back shifting into a sleek looking black and grey mountain lion. The beast hissed, throwing itself to the side as Clyous went to attack again. Oisin moved towards Clyous as if to protect his now injured brother. Before Bridget could move, Liam was there, blocking a strike from Oisin that was aimed at Clyous's throat.

"Run!" Liam shot back at her as he swung his sword at the approaching mountain lion. "I've got him! Run!"

Oisin swiped at Liam again, his attack blocked easily enough by her old friend. Clyous dodged a swipe of Rion's claws, kicking the lion directly in the head with his powerful legs. Bridget made to advance forward and slash at the beast, but Clyous shoved her backwards, placing himself between her and their enemies.

"Go!" Clyous yelled before swinging his war hammer at the beast. "Protect our babies."

Frustrated that the two men before her would not allow her to help, she suddenly realized this was no longer just about her, her children were most important. Clyous was acting as any father should, fighting to protect his offspring. Liam also fought, protecting her and her family. The Crown Prince of Oich died that day with his father, before her fought her childhood friend. The boy who stood up for those in need. A defender of the weak. A knight.

Bridget decided to listen and was about to turn and flee when two familiar figures exploded from the shadows. Menolayous fell upon Oisin with such deadly speed and accuracy that Bridget's blooded eyes could barely track his movements. Carrying twin battle axes, Menolayous spun into the fight like a hurricane, blades slashing at any inch of skin Oisin had showing.

Instead of backing away, Liam advanced using any opportunity Menolayous provided to strike at the Dark One. Quickly losing ground, Oisin began to cast various magics in their direction. Shards of ice sprang from the ground, nearly impaling Menolayous, but the warrior was too quick. Liam, not so much. An ice shard pierced through his calf, forcing him down to a knee.

Grace had managed to ensnare Rion with her whip. The woven leather wrapped around the lion's neck forcing the silver blades to dig into his flesh. Rion was forced to shift back into human form due to the piercing blades, the silver reaching his blood stream.

"Fucking cunt!" Rion roared, reaching for a bone dagger strapped to his hip.

Grace moved quickly, coming up behind Rion and placing a palm on his temple. Rion froze as Grace's mark behind her ear began to glow. Bridget knew she had entered the man's mind, that she was digging inside that black hole for something to use against him. She did not pity the monster, what Grace was planning on unleashing would be well deserved.

"So, you like to rape anyone weaker than you, huh?" Grace seethed as her power flared. "I can see it in your mind. Doesn't matter to you if it's a child, man, or woman. You'll fuck anything if it makes you feel stronger, more powerful than them."

"Get-out-of-my-head-bitch." Rion was locked into place by Grace's magic, but she could tell that he was desperate to resist her.

"I see your fear." Grace smirked. "Now live it."

Grace stepped back, releasing her grip on Rion. Bridget watched in morbid fascination as Rion was no longer held by Grace's power. As if Rion saw something approaching him, his eyes grew wide in horror. With a shout of fear, Rion slashed his bone dagger at the empty air in front of him. Grace tugged on her whip, which still dug into the shifter's throat, knocking him on his back. Rion shouted as he slashed at the air again, as if he was fighting off an invisible foe.

"Brother, stop!" Rion shouted. "It's me! Stop!"

"I'm here, brother!" Oisin shouted as he continued to battle Menolayous and an injured Liam. "Fight against her hold."

Rion shrieked in pain as he plunged his own dagger into his thigh. As if he was unable to recognize that he himself had caused that injury, Rion continued to stab at the air, occasionally sticking himself with the blade. Blood began to flow freely down the tribesman's bare thighs as he slashed and stabbed. With each wound the shifter shrieked in pain and fear but he kept going. Whatever nightmare Grace had concocted was expertly woven.

"You see how easy it was for your brother to turn on you?" Grace taunted as she circled the man who continued to injure himself. "Your brothers do not love you. You're only good to them as long as you remain useful."

"Rion!" Oisin shouted, sending a gust of wind at Liam, knocking him down.

Rion plunged the tip of his bone dagger into his groin. Bridget watched in disgust as Rion twisted the dagger and slashed upwards. Blood began to run down his legs freely as a chunk of meat fell from beneath his loincloth. Bridget stared at what was once Rion's manhood, now severed and bleeding into the dirt.

"You'll never rape again." Grace kicked the dagger from Rion's hands, releasing him from her vision. She pulled Rion by his braid, grabbing the bone dagger and sawing through the fibers of his hair. "That's for Menolayous and Catriona, you worthless piece of shit."

Oisin managed to break past Menolayous and Liam to get to his brother. Grace had made the mistake of solely focusing on Rion, she was unprepared when Oisin got to her. Oisin slashed upwards, his sharpened blade slicing through her tunic and flesh. Bridget watched as blood began to pour from Grace's side.

Menolayous roared, launching himself at the Dark One and pushing the shifter back away from Grace. Clyous joined the fray, the two men working in tandem. Grace stumbled backwards away from Rion and into Liam's arms. Liam caught her, dragging her farther away from the injured shifter who thankfully was just lying there bleeding.

Bridget was at Grace's side, lifting the blood-soaked tunic to see the deep gash. Grace's face contorted in pain but it changed to fear as soon as she realized who was holding her.

"Get the fuck off me!" Grace tried to scramble away from Liam, bleeding even more from the drastic movement.

"Relax," Liam held onto her tightly. "I've switched sides."

"You can't switch sides," Grace said, seething. "You're literally the bad guy."

"Let me heal you." Bridget looked between her two companions, neither bore a fatal wound, but Grace was bleeding more.

"Her first," was all Liam had time to say before a wall of fire sprung forward.

The flames snaked their way between the shifters and her friends, effectively ending the fight between Oisin and Menolayous. Bridget watched as Oisin scooped up his unconscious brother before taking off down a side street. Menolayous, realizing that he could no longer pursue the Dark One, ran to Grace's side, startled at Liam's presence. Clyous joined them, glancing around, his eyes searching. There, emerging from the wall of flame strode Catriona, soaked in blood and gore from the battle. Her eyes were hard, unforgiving molten silver, and they were focused on Liam.

Chapter Ninety-Six

Catriona

Rage was all she felt. It was what fueled her very existence. Without her rage, she was nothing but a hollowed-out shell. There wasn't much left to her anymore. Her soul had been shredded for the final time. She couldn't remember how she had survived the first assault, but she had. She must have buried her soul deep enough that they couldn't quite reach it. Losing her mother was enough to break her. She hadn't had time to hide herself, to harden before she learned of her father and brother falling on the battlefield. It all happened just when she started to feel alive again, when she started to be happy, completely happy.

Then there wasn't enough recovery time before her capture. She was unprepared, caught off guard by the surprise attack. The worst part of it was she could have escaped, could have spared herself everything that had happened to her, but she had made a choice in order to save Bridget. Innocent and naive Bridget, who had successfully beat back the darkness from infecting her soul, she would not have survived. Catriona had already survived so much, was already tainted, it made no real difference if it happened to her again. At least that was what she had told herself. She had never been more wrong.

This last week had been like living in a fog. Anytime she felt anything, it came with such intense pain she wasn't sure she would survive it. Her mind couldn't stop wandering back to that night, to all of the other nights, reliving that pain and those experiences. The emotional pull was so strong she couldn't tell the difference between her memory and reality, and when she finally grounded herself from the memories, the physical pain was still there.

Bridget did what she could for her by healing the wounds to her body, but they were still painful to the touch. Every time she moved, she was reminded by the painful strain of her muscles and flesh, and even though you couldn't see her wounds on the surface, they were still there. Bridget had to touch the wounds to heal them, something Catriona could barely handle. Being touched. But it needed to be done. As necessary as it was, Catriona could not allow Bridget to heal her down there. It wasn't an option, even the

645

thought of it was too triggering. So, the cuts and tears were healing with time as best they could.

No, the only way Catriona had survived this long was to dissociate. Mentally checking out was the only way to keep her from going back to that tower, facing those men, feeling that pain and humiliation. It was not foolproof, she found herself back in that tower a few times a day, but it beat being there every waking moment. Things like eating, drinking, bathing, or simply talking to someone pulled her out of her stupor, sending her straight back to that tower. So, she avoided all of those things as a form of self-preservation. Menolayous understood where she was at, what she was doing to survive. He did his best to explain to the others; they just couldn't see it the way it truly was. What they saw was the assault, every time they looked at her that's what they saw. It's why she never told anyone the first time; she didn't want that to be who she was. They saw her as broken, which she was. But her friends, her family, they were putting themselves into her position trying to understand her, but they couldn't because they'd never been through it. Except Menolayous.

Her heart broke for Danny. She could see the pain, the anger, and him not knowing what to do every time he looked at her. She couldn't blame him; she knew her disassociation scared him. Everyone was worried she would try to end it all. It had crossed her mind. The idea of not having to feel any more pain when she was overflowing with it was alluring, but planning something like that out, performing any action at all, brought her out of the fog enough to feel. And it was still too painful. She wished she could be more for them, wished she could comfort Danny enough to stop hurting.

But she couldn't. She didn't have that much left in her. Grace coming into her home was the first time Catriona had been present in reality without the darkness consuming her. The fear of imminent battle centered her as her friend spoke. She had come for Catriona, asking her to fight. They would all die, that's the only reason her friend had come to her knowing what she was.

However, once Grace mentioned that the Dark One and his brother were on the battlefield, that Liam was within reach, something in her snapped into place. Rage flooded in, removing everything else. Catriona found herself not only anchored into reality, but that she craved to be here. The fog was gone, and she no longer felt pulled back to the assault. Instead, Catriona found herself moving to her weapons, donning her clothes. The pain of movement was no longer intensified; she moved with a purpose. Her sole focus was to get to those three men, those who owed her a debt. A debt of flesh and blood, one she would be glad, elated even, to call in.

As Catriona dressed, she made sure to have movement. All sense of modesty had left her. Everyone had seen her wounds, what was a naked body compared to that? She didn't bother donning armor; it would limit her movement. In truth, she did not care for the protection. While she had found her purpose, she still couldn't find it within herself to care what happened to her. If she died, she died. A small part of her wished that it would be the outcome, it just had to wait until after she exacted her revenge. Dying would bring her a sense of peace she could never have while she still breathed.

She caught a glimpse of herself in the window; an ugly scar ran down her forehead to her cheek just missing her eye. A souvenir from that day, forever marking her as their victim. Her short hair was next to be seen; she had Rion to thank for that. The sight of her marred beauty began to tug at her grip on reality. She found herself moving, craving that deadly focus to recenter herself.

Danny was suddenly there, giving her something new to ground herself with. His eyes mirrored her pain; inner hope shined behind them at her sudden responsiveness. She raised her hand as if to reach out and touch him, but she saw the scars. They had nailed her to a table. She felt that tug but buried it. She apologized to him, for everything she had put him through, for not being strong enough to stop it. He asked how to help her, what would help her. She gave him the only answer she had, let her kill them all, and he stepped aside so she could.

She flew out of their home, down the stairs and towards the promise of vengeance. She moved quickly, faster than her broken and starved body should move. She felt her familiar fire coursing through her veins, her magic filling any void her body had and driving her on. She saw them, the soldiers of Oich and the blooded tribesmen of Gaelach were working together as an invading force. Their supernatural abilities gave them an edge over the defending rebel warriors; they were faster and stronger than their human foes. But Catriona could see the difference Danny's training had made for their warriors now that a battle raged on.

Catriona fell upon her first group of victims, three Gaelach tribesmen too busy engaging with rebels in swordplay to even notice her. Catriona came up behind the first one, shoving her short sword through his back, the tip breaking through his flesh at the chest. Hot blood trickled over the hilt of her sword, coating her hand and forearm. She heard his guttural scream as her blade entered him. She felt a sickening satisfaction at the feel of his blood, the sound of his pain. It delighted her knowing she had gotten to him before he could do that to her.

Only a second had passed during her glorious revelation. The tribesman's companions were now aware of her presence and turning to engage with her. Catriona ripped her sword free as she twirled towards the next. Her blade connected to the next man at his hip. She dug the side of the blade into his armor and flesh as she swiftly traced her blade in an upwards motion across his torso. A deep slash opened up following her blade, spilling the man's blood and innards onto the dirt before the remaining tribesman was now facing her and bringing a club up to strike at her. With his blooded abilities he moved fast, but her fire made her faster. Before he could even fully raise his club for an attack she drew her blade across the soft flesh of his throat. A deep cut appeared as blood sprayed from the opening wound, coating her face and chest with warm droplets. She watched as the man sank to the ground, a gurgling sound came from his open mouth as he drowned in his own blood.

The rebel warriors cheered as she stood over the dying and mutilated bodies of her enemies. The warriors moved back into battle leaving her standing there. She looked down at the dying men, savoring the sound of pain and death emitting from their final moments. To her surprise, the sight of them did not tug on her reality like she thought they would. She had assumed they resembled Rion too much. Instead, she found that she was strongly rooted in the present. She also felt something she hadn't felt since that day, it was power.

She had done that to them, she sliced up their flesh, spilled their blood, ended them before they could hurt her. Their deaths pleased her, they empowered her. She realized then the more she killed, the safer she was from another capture. If she could get to them first, kill them before they hurt her, then she was safe. Everyone she loved was safe.

Catriona returned to the battle, dancing between her enemies and allowing her blades to sing as they sliced and stabbed past the blooded tribesmen's defenses. Every gasp of pain and shriek of failure brought a smile to her face. Feeling the warm spray of blood on her as she hurt them brought her such satisfaction. They would endure their suffering the few remaining moments they had left in this land. She delighted in being the cause of it. They thought they could break her, that they could ruin her. They were dead wrong.

Catriona slashed and sliced, another body dropped to the ground, bleeding and lifeless. She stabbed another, her twin blades slicing through his flesh like butter. She finally came upon an Oich soldier, unlike their allies they wore more armor and their weapons more sophisticated. But the results were the same, she still killed them. She had lost count of how many she had killed today. It wasn't enough.

She came upon a small pack of wolves. About six or so blooded had shifted to hunt more efficiently. The pack circled two Collie warriors, trying to find an opening. The wolves growled and snapped their fangs at the warriors to distract them, another wolf sneaking up behind and sinking their teeth into one of the warrior's calves. The warrior went down, allowing an opening of such magnitude that each limb now found itself in the mouth of a different wolf. The second warrior slashed his blade at anything with fur. He too went down, leaving his defenses open. Catriona watched as the pack began to tear the two apart, she felt reality begin to tug at her. She had been prey to a pack not that long ago. She flung herself into the fray, slashing her blades wildly at the beasts, but she was too late. The two warriors lay dead before her; bodies covered in blood. She felt a sharp pain on her wrist. Looking down she saw a brave blooded had sunk its fangs into her flesh. An intense rage flared inside of her, how dare they touch her, how dare they make her bleed. She grabbed hold of her internal flame, pushing it outward so suddenly the approaching pack had no time to react. Her white flames engulfed them all for several seconds, burning so hot she was turning the color of them her signature white. When the sharp pain of the fangs ceased, she pulled her power back to survey the damage. Her fire had caught a nearby building on fire, but it had dealt with the wolves. Six charred corpses lay surrounding her, the meat and fur had burned off leaving the blackened bones of the wolves.

Catriona took a moment to center herself, catching her breath from all the exertion. She quickly evaluated her body, it was still holding strong. She felt a couple small wounds like the bite as well as some soreness, but her energy was still high. Her magic was not even close to burning out. She felt strong. If anything, she wanted to push even harder, to let loose, but she wanted to cut loose on two specific blooded males.

With a new deadly focus, Catriona went on the hunt. Every enemy she encountered she killed. Every Collie warrior cheered on her success, doing their best to stay out of her way. She moved through the city leaving destruction in her wake. She spotted a large black wolf stalking through the streets. She sprinted in his direction, killing with fire so she wouldn't slow. Liam was hers; she would not let him get away. The thrill of the hunt began to take over with her target so close. She lost sight of him but continued to race to the last place she saw him. She skidded onto the street, weapons raised as she was prepared to confront the prince, but he wasn't there.

No! No, No, No, No! Where the fuck did he go? She glanced around desperately; there was no sign of him. Fuck! She moved to a nearby home, pulling herself on top of it. Maybe she would see him from up here. Once on the roof her eyes searched the battle below. There was no sign of Liam. She cursed out loud, angry at losing him, her eyes caught another large figure moving down a street. Excitement flared up again, had she found him?

Rama came into view, his large hulking figure moved through a battle ridden street. Catriona expected to see her friend charge into the fray and engage with the enemy as he always did. Instead, he slowed, staying away from the fighting. This was not normal for him. Catriona's eyes narrowed in on him, assessing. She was completely shocked when she spotted that he carried a child with him. Movement caught her eye, their enemies had spotted Rama and the child.

Catriona flung herself from the rooftop, thrusting her downward facing blades through a soldier's torso. She kicked off, pulling her blades free of him and rolling as she hit the ground. Careful not to unleash her power in the direction of her friend and the child, she enjoyed cutting the enemy down. When the dust began to settle Catriona remained rooted to the spot, catching up on her breath.

Rama approached her cautiously, child in hand, observing her closely. Relief that he and the child were unharmed was a momentary emotion before she was taken aback by Rama's anger. She wasn't sure what he was saying exactly but he was mad at her lack of armor. She mumbled an answer, slightly ashamed that he was accusing her of wanting to die. He wasn't wrong exactly, of course he would see through her. She mumbled an apology, she meant it of course. She never wanted to be such a burden to everyone. She didn't want to hurt them.

She turned to flee from him, wanting to hide from his knowing gaze. She felt a large hand grip her shoulder, yanking her backwards to face him. But it wasn't Rama who had grabbed her, it was Rion. Rion stood before her smirking down at her. She moved to strike him, her panic completely taking over. An invisible force caught her arm, freezing her in place.

She pushed against it trying to make the strike connect, but it was like pushing against a wall. Suddenly, reality rushed in on her, revealing it was in fact Rama before her. The little girl in Rama's arms glared at her, her tiny hazel eyes shining brightly as she stared down Catriona. This child was magical, Cat realized, and she had protected Rama from her.

Shame flooded Catriona once again, how she had nearly struck her friend. Her lack of control was unacceptable. With a final apology Cat turned and fled, away from her loved one whom she had nearly hurt, and away from the child who did not deserve to see the nightmare she had become.

650

Catriona ran through the city, allowing her flames to whip out at any enemy soldiers she saw. She continued to slash at enemies with her twin swords if they got close enough or burned them if they were at a distance. A nightmare she had become indeed, especially with how much she reveled in the destruction. She continued to hack her way through the city, searching for any sign of her targets.

She felt herself start to tire, her energy was draining. She had killed a lot of men today, dozens if she had cared enough to count. Anyone would be crippled from exhaustion by now, but her magic had helped drive her. If she couldn't find either of her prey soon, she might not have enough left in her to face them.

"Get the fuck off me!" she heard Grace's voice ring out.

Catriona froze, letting her ears search for her friend. Off to her right and a few streets over she heard the clashing of steel and screams. Catriona rushed in the direction of the fight, they would not take Grace. They would never take anyone again, she would burn them all to ash.

Catriona came upon the scene, assessing as quickly as she could. She saw Menolayous fighting with a tribesman. She spotted her brother and Bridget, they looked fine and unharmed. Then her eyes fell to Grace, she was bleeding from a severe wound to her side and being held down by none other than Liam.

Fire erupted from her hands, fanning out and pushing the tribesmen away from them. She let loose a battle cry and charged at the crown prince, knocking him backwards and away from her family. Liam rolled to his feet, favoring a leg. She noted the injury there.

"Stop," Liam demanded, holding his hands in front of him. "Wait a second! You just let them get away!"

Catriona's response was to send a wave of fire in his direction. Liam rolled out of the way, the flame missing him by inches. Catriona rushed at him, swords arcing downwards before he could stand. Liam caught her by the wrists, disarming one of her short swords before tossing her back away from him.

"Cat!" Bridget called to her from the wall of flames.

Catriona charged at Liam again with her remaining sword, she held the pommel with a reverse grip, slicing upwards at Liam's torso. He caught her a second time, twisting her wrist until she was forced to drop her sword.

She sent a knee into his ribs instead. Liam pulled her to him before lifting her up and tossing her back.

She hit the ground and rolled, snarling at him. She was angry at how sloppy she was being. He shouldn't be able to catch her let alone disarm her. She could still feel the impressions from his hands, she felt the strings of reality begin to tug on her. No! Not now!

"I'm not here to hurt any of you," Liam tried again, hands raised in a type of surrender.

"Liar!" she spat at him, in truth he had yet to press an attack.

"You look like shit," Liam assessed her. "Is that your blood? Bridget should look at you."

"Don't pretend like you suddenly give a shit," Catriona snapped.

"I don't, really," Liam answered. "But Bridget cares about you. You should let her tend to your wounds. You've been through enough—"

"Because of what you put me through!" she shrieked in rage. She sounded crazy, she could hear it in her own voice.

She watched his expression change to something she's sure he intended to look like regret. "You didn't deserve that. I'm-I'm sorry for what happened to you."

"You watched it happen!" Angry tears flowed freely now, she wished she had more of a grip on her emotions, but realistically that had never been her strong suit. "You gave me to him!"

"I didn't know that's what he wanted you for." His voice was quiet, infuriatingly quiet. "Nobody deserves that."

"You tried to take me too!" she snarled, reaching for the depth of her powers which were becoming increasingly depleted.

"I tried to save you," Liam argued. "Until you gave me something more important to save."

She pushed out a hand sending white hot flames his direction. Liam rolled out of the way just in time to miss her fire, but he wasn't quick enough to dodge her fist to his face. She wished she was strong enough to have caved in his cheekbone or at least snapped his head backwards from the impact. But a week of not eating, how close to burnout she was, and not being physically stronger than a blooded male all tipped the scales unfavorably. The strike to his face momentarily surprised him and drew some blood from his nose.

"Seriously," Liam said, pinching the bridge of his nose once he was able to make distance between them. "I'm not your enemy anymore."

"You'll always be my enemy." Catriona seethed, shooting another stream of flames his direction.

Liam once again was able to roll out of the way of her flames, only infuriating her even more. Liam put his hands up again as if he were surrendering. She caught a glimpse of Menolayous pacing around the edges of her fire, like a predator looking for a way in. Her eyes quickly darted to Grace, who sat next to Bridget as she was working her healing magic on Grace's side. Clyous stood next to Bridget with his war hammer in hand, his eyes darting between Catriona and his wife, seemingly unsure of who needed his attention more. Not a single one of them seemed to want to stop her, not that it would have mattered much. Liam's body language continued to baffle her as if he truly did not want to fight her. She didn't care. He was not walking away from this encounter alive.

"Look, I get it. I have been in your shoes; I would try to kill me too." Liam shuffled to the side. "Arguably I deserve it, but I'm not going to just roll over and die. I would be of more help to you alive. I can help you hunt down the kings of Gaelach. I will swear my allegiance to my queen; I can help protect her. She needs to be protected from them; her child needs to be protected from them. You need the help."

Catriona's gaze shot back at Bridget who looked at her through the flames. They locked eyes for a moment before Catriona caught a brief nod from her sister-in-law, verifying that Liam's words were in fact true. Bridget was pregnant. Grace and Menolayous looked to the healer then, coming to the same conclusion Catriona had. Clyous was unphased, meaning he already knew. Catriona suddenly found it hard to move, hard to think, as those strings of reality began to tug at her once again. *She's pregnant. She was pregnant when they were taken, they were taken because of Cat. She could have lost her baby.*

Catriona shook her head as she tried to keep those memories from invading her senses. A distorted laugh left her lips as she tried desperately to ground herself back in the present. She could feel their hands on her once again, she jerked her arms forward to free herself from them. There was nobody there, but she could still feel their claws and teeth start to dig into her flesh. She shook violently, launching herself to the side away from her invisible enemy. Their laughter began to echo through her mind so loudly it was almost deafening.

"Cat!" Menolayous shouted from the other side of her flames. "It's not real. We're real, we're right here with you. Come back to us!"

Catriona felt her power rearing its ugly head up again, reigniting within her a need to protect herself. She let loose a scream, breathing fire from her mouth in the direction her assailants should have been standing. Liam jumped backwards, fear contorting his face as he watched her. Clyous grabbed hold of Bridget and began to drag her back away from Catriona's ring of fire, Grace and Menolayous following closely behind him.

"Let go of me!" Bridget snapped, pulling from Clyous's arms. "We can't leave her like this!"

"Are you fire resistant? Are our children?" Clyous grabbed her once again trying to pull her farther away. "She's lost it. Can't you see that? She's fighting with memories. She's about to lose control."

"We can talk to her!" Bridget argued but allowed herself to be pulled back even further.

"I don't think you can," Liam called from inside the ring of fire.

"We need to ground her back into reality," Menolayous said, staring at Catriona as she continued to scream and pull away from an invisible enemy.

"How do you usually do that?" Liam asked, pacing the edge of the flames looking for an out.

"I usually project an illusion of you," Grace snapped at him. "And she tries to kill it."

"Lovely." Liam sighed. "How bad are her explosions?"

"Did you see that big ass hole in the wall when you came in?" It was Clyous's turn to snap at the prince.

"Fuck me." Liam let his head fall back in exasperation. "Fine."

"Liam, what are you doing?" Bridget asked, watching as the prince shed his coat, freeing the movement of his arms.

"Looks like I'm trying to die a hero," Liam called back without glancing at her, his eyes focused solely on an increasingly erratic Catriona. "Get her out of here, blacksmith."

"She's going to kill you!" Bridget shouted as Clyous resumed his effort to pull Bridget away.

"I honestly don't think any of you are going to be too sad if she succeeds." Liam looked to Bridget one final time. "My death was sealed the second she found me. Our fates are tied. One of us has to die for the other to live. If this is the end of me, at least you'll have time to get away before her flames engulf everything."

"I for one won't feel sad," Grace said, her words laced with distaste. "I hope your death brings her some peace."

"Would you believe me if I said I do too?" Liam asked, rolling up his sleeves.

"Nope." Grace glared at him. "See you in the underlands, Prince."

Liam raised his middle finger at her as the group fled, earning a smirk from Grace as she went. Menolayous lingered a moment longer, staring at Liam as if picking him apart.

"If you survive this, and she doesn't—" Menolayous started. "I'll skin you alive and feed you to the crows."

Liam watched as Catriona rampaged nearby, her focus on her memories. "Catriona."

Catriona heard his voice, snapping her attention in his direction. Her eyes focused on him and as they did, she could no longer feel the fangs and claws digging into her flesh. Her world focused again, revolving around the Crown Prince of Oich as he stood there, trapped within her ring of fire. Like trapped prey, he looked at her with wide and terrified eyes, but he had determination written all over his face.

"Would you stop fighting your demons for one moment and focus on me," Liam snapped, lowering himself slightly as if prepared to dodge another stream of white flames. "I'm right here. You want to fight someone, fight me."

She could fight him; she would fight him. She inhaled deeply, drawing back some of her power from the flames surrounding him. The prince was here; she could finally kill him. Revenge for her mother and father were within her grasp. All she had to do was...

"Cat!" a familiar voice called, rushing her direction but stopping at the outer ring of her flames.

Catriona glanced towards his voice, she saw Danny standing there staring at her. He was trapped on the outside and looking for a way in. She would not allow him in. She needed to do this alone. She needed to kill the man who took her family from her, the same man that gave her to those monsters.

"I have to do this." Catriona shouted to him. "Win or lose. I won't be a victim any longer. I won't let them get away with hurting me."

"I expect nothing less," Danny called over the flames, tossing something in her direction. "You'll need these."

Catriona looked at the two objects that hit the ground not a few feet away from her. Her two short swords, Danny must have found them just outside the fire ring. She kept her eyes focused on Liam as she bent to snatch them up.

Catriona moved, taking advantage of Liam's broken concentration. She held both swords and twirled, slashing at him like a hurricane coming in from the ocean. Liam managed to dodge the first several strikes before the tip of one of her swords caught him in the chest, carving out a long slash in his flesh. Liam grunted at the impact, looking down at his blood-soaked tunic. Upon an exhale of breath, the crown prince changed tactics, charging at her and catching her around the waist.

Catriona's back hit the ground; she felt his weight on top of her. Panic began to flood through her as Liam pinned one of her arms down, knocking one of her swords from her grip. *No! She would not let this happen again!* She screamed and flames burst through her lips and surrounded the crown prince's torso. The flames lasted as long as her breath did, Liam's body falling backwards from the blast. Catriona scrambled backwards away from him. His flesh was black and burned, parts of his face so charred it looked as if his skin were about to fall from his face like raindrops falling off a branch. He was still alive she realized, still breathing.

She grasped the sword tightly as she launched herself forward, piercing him through his torso and digging her blade into the ground beneath him. Before he even had chance to react, she shot to her feet and threw her hands forward unleashing every last drop of her power in his direction. She could hear his screams as her flames engulfed his entire body, charring it and turning it to ash. She relished his terror; it was so deafening it easily blocked out the memories of her own screams. Catriona threw her head back and laughed as she emptied what remained of her power into incinerating his corpse. Tears began to stream down her face as her power faded, his screams no longer existed, yet she could still hear them.

She had done it! Liam was finally dead! She looked at his charred remains, utterly fascinated at the fact that moments ago in that same spot lie her oldest enemy. She swayed slightly as she stood there, the emptiness of her magic taking its toll. She took a second to breathe deeply, inhaling the residue of her smoke. *She had won, finally destroying the monster who had taken her family. He wouldn't be able to hurt her or anyone else ever again.*

"Cat?" Danny's voice came from a distance as he slowly approached her.

She glanced at him, a slow smile beginning to spread across her face. Danny froze in place, staring at her as if trying to assess if she was alright. All of her flames had died out, proving no danger to him as he approached. She would never hurt Danny, not intentionally. He was staring at her strangely, as if seeing her for the first time. He didn't seem scared, a blessing she realized. Any rational person should be running from her at this point. Instead, he looked at her with an expression of understanding and hope. She saw him through the tears running down her face, happy to share in this victory with him.

Chapter Ninety-Seven

Danny

There were no words to describe the events that had taken place today. Danny was still trying to grasp everything that had happened, his heartstrings had been stretched over the battlefield, straining him to his maximum capacity. Not only had his unresponsive lover finally come back to reality, but he had to watch her fling herself headfirst into battle. It was something he didn't like doing when all he wanted was to protect her. Menolayous had told him she would tell him what she needed from him, and she did, so he watched and followed her path of bloody destruction through Collie.

He had seen bloodlust in his fellow warriors before, but nothing this extreme. Catriona made war look like a child's game. Her inhuman abilities shone as she cut through enemy after enemy as if she were channeling the Goddess of War and Fate herself. Catriona was responsible for slaying dozens of enemies with her blades alone, reveling in each kill as if it gave her a tiny piece of the vengeance she so desperately sought. Danny would have been convinced she was the goddess reincarnated if it wasn't for the morbid brutality. Catriona did not go for clean kills. Instead, she seemed to enjoy hacking her enemies to pieces. She was precise in how she carved up their bodies and enjoyed watching each and every one of them suffer before burning them. It was exceptionally hard for Danny to watch the woman he loved behave so... darkly, but he figured she needed this to feel safe, she needed to do this to regain the power that had been taken from her. He did not try to stop her.

At the very end of the battle, he had finally managed to find Catriona, this time facing off with Crown Prince Liam. Her flames had prevented him from coming to her aid, not that she needed it. He was able to toss her the blades she had lost earlier, solidifying the crown prince's demise. He expected it to be brutal up until the end, but he had not expected that. She cooked him alive, once his body had disintegrated into the burnt ground, she sat back afterwards and laughed. Laughed. And cried. And screamed. He supposed there would be some sort of emotional release for her after killing the man that took her family away from her. Having that kind of release was normal, but he was not expecting something that extreme and in such variety. It was almost as if she had lost control of herself and her emotions.

Now the battle was over. Collie had won; no small thanks owed to a slightly unhinged Catriona. What was left of enemy forces had fled once the Dark One had, the fighting coming to a nearly complete stop. Danny now stood at the outside entrance of Collie, staring off into the forest as the remaining enemy disappeared into the trees. His friends had found him there, all of them converging at the front gate.

"Glad to see you made it," Menolayous said walking up to stand by Danny.

"You too," Danny murmured, glancing around at their group.

Grace was lowering herself to the ground in obvious exhaustion, Menolayous rushed to her side to help her. There was a large gash in her tunic that was soaked in blood. There was no injury there, Bridget must have healed it. Rama was approaching, carrying a small child with him. Danny stared at his brother in surprise, as did everyone else.

"So, this is Kyra," Rama introduced the little girl who was burying her face into his arm. "Since I know you're all wondering."

"Where are her parents?" Grace asked, staring up at the odd pair.

"D-E-A-D," Rama spelled, shooting Grace a lecturing look. "Kyra is a little nervous right now. She won't let me put her down. Kyra, this is my family, my brothers and sisters. They're all very nice, I promise. Well... except Grace."

"Hey!" Grace rolled her eyes at the giant. "Don't turn her against me right out of the gate."

"Hi," Kyra's little voice squeaked before she buried her face in Rama's arm once again.

"What are you going to do with her?" Bridget asked, eyes focusing on the little girl with compassion.

"I don't think I'm getting much say in the matter," Rama answered, patting Kyra on the back gently. "She literally won't let me leave her, so..."

"Fatherhood looks good on you," Menolayous said to Rama then turned his attention to Clyous. "Both of you."

"Wait, wait, wait," Danny interjected, looking between Clyous and Bridget. "Are you telling me the first we're hearing about you being pregnant is after a battle?"

"There's been a lot going on," Bridget answered somberly, her eyes catching on Catriona who was now approaching the front gate, dragging a corpse behind her. "Is that Liam?"

Everyone looked at Catriona now, who nodded in their direction before stopping just beside the gate. They all watched in shock and varying stages of horror as Catriona lifted the corpse against the wall and began to hammer nails into its outstretched hands. Rama was quick to shield Kyra's eyes from the appalling sight before them.

"No." Danny looked away from the gruesome scene. "There's hardly anything left of him to worry about."

"Why is she doing that?" Bridget looked as if she were about to be sick.

"Fuck if I know." Clyous's eyes were transfixed on his sister who was now working on the other hand of the corpse she had propped up against the wall.

"I'm scared to know what she did to Liam." Rama was also watching her intently, although his gaze was trying to evaluate her sanity rather than being shocked by her actions. "I caught a glimpse of her in battle; I almost regret that we unleashed her on our enemy."

"They deserved whatever she threw at them," Grace said defensively.

"Not saying they didn't." Rama began to rock a quiet Kyra in his arms, trying to soothe her into a sleep. "But she was scary to watch. She tried to come after me, but little miss here used her magic to stop her and she ended up knocking Morrigan on her ass sometime later. According to our mutual friend she's supposed to be pretty powerful. She made Cat back off."

"Cat sounds like she's lost it," Clyous said, still not taking his eyes off his sister, who was now working on a second corpse and nailing it to the front gate. "She looks like she's fucking lost it."

"Everyone works out the darkness in their own way." Menolayous looked at the scene somberly. "She hasn't come for us, Rama excluded, I think it's safe to say she's still in there somewhere. I personally would rather her be nailing the enemy to our front gates than back in the room and being unresponsive."

"Agreed," Danny said, launching himself sideways as Bridget began to heave her stomach contents onto the ground next to him. "You, okay?"

"I don't know," Bridget answered after her vomiting slowed. "I can't tell if this is pregnancy, Cat's art project, or the fact that I've reached burnout."

"You shouldn't be pushing yourself to burnout in your condition," Grace lectured gently, helping hold Bridget's hair back.

"She was too busy trying to heal everyone on the way over." Clyous shot his wife a knowing look. "Good luck convincing her to stop doing that."

"Looks like you need a good dose of yarrow root tea," Grace said. "And you have plenty of people to heal the old fashion way."

"Morrigan and Flinn have been protecting the longhouse. Most of our citizens were able to flee and seek shelter there, our wounded are being brought there as we speak," Rama verified.

"We should probably check in with our friends," Grace said. *"You guys alive up there?"*

After a few moments of silence passed everyone glanced around at each other, they had all heard Grace down the bond. Even Catriona, who had finished with her corpse and sauntered over, not saying a word but listening down the bond intently.

"Morrigan?" Grace tried again, concern blossoming in her chest.

Another moment of silence passed before the older woman's voice radiated down the bond, her voice strained with emotion, *"Bring me the healer! Now!"*

"Fuck!" Rama gripped Kyra tightly and took off through the gate in the direction of the longhouse.

Everyone else followed him, trying to keep up with his giant gait and the exhaustion from the battle. Catriona followed everyone from behind, still not speaking but sticking close to Danny as the group moved. He noticed how her eyes continued to roam over all of the destruction surrounding them as if she were still searching for the enemy. He accepted that this might be her default from now on, always expecting to see them lurking in a dark corner. At least until she killed them all.

The group of them neared the longhouse, Danny noted just how many bodies littered the ground surrounding the perimeter of the building. Wolves, men, women, soldiers from Airgid, warriors from Collie, nobody had been spared in this onslaught. It had been apparent to the enemy that attacking the longhouse meant attacking civilians. What they weren't expecting was for the civilians to fight back. For what it was worth, the longhouse appeared to be untouched. He supposed this should count as a victory for Collie, but it was hard to count today as a victory with so many of their people lying dead in the street.

"Over there!" Grace pointed towards Morrigan who was sitting on the ground with her back facing them.

As they approached, Danny could see a small crowd gathering around her. Fearing her harmed, he was quick to realize she sat with two other figures. Young Connor sat beside her, covered in blood and dirt from the battle, a fresh wound on his forearm. But Connor's wound was not fatal, not serious enough to warrant such a tone in Morrigan's voice. No, the reason for the sorceress's panic lay with the man whose head rested in her lap.

"Flinn!" Danny shouted, sprinting to the old war chief.

"Don't trouble yourself, young Daniel." The old man laughed, blood trickling from the corners of his mouth. "It's not like I'm going anywhere."

"By the gods!" Bridget breathed as she dropped to her knees, examining the foot-long gash on Flinn's abdomen, his intestines peeking out of the gushing wound. "Hold on."

"I've got nothing better to do, my dear." Flinn laughed again, spraying blood with his exhale. "Sorry about that, lass."

"Can you do anything?" Morrigan asked Bridget, tears welling in her eyes.

"I'm burnt out," Bridget cried, looking around frantically as if a solution would present itself.

"I wouldn't worry your pretty head." Flinn coughed once again, more blood spraying from his lips. "I've made my peace."

"You shouldn't have done that!" Connor openly wept, staring down at the only father he had ever known. "You should have left me to die. Then you wouldn't—"

"I've lived my life, son." Flinn reached out, gently placing his hand on the boy's arm. "You have yet to live yours. I regret nothing."

Danny stared down at this heartbreaking scene with tears in his eyes. Flinn had been a father figure to so many of them. He had taken Rama, Menolayous, and Danny in when they were teenagers; adopted them into his warband, taught them how to fight, and how to be men. Flinn had saved them, whether he had known what he was doing at the time or not. That was

662

who Flinn was, a loving and caring person who would give you the shirt off his back if you needed it. With Connor it was different, Flinn had taken him in with the understanding that this was his son. He had saved Connor from a slave's life in the city, and Connor had saved his by being the son he had always wanted. Watching this fierce warrior, this big-hearted man, lay dying in front of them all… it was too much.

"You stick with the king," Flinn said, still looking at Connor. "Rama will take care of you, raise you right. You hear me?"

"Yes," Connor said, his voice barely audible.

"Good." Flinn smiled, his teeth now coated in blood. "You live your life, boy. Do that for me, won't you? Find a way to be happy, after all of this. That is my dying wish from you."

"I will," Connor sobbed, grasping his father's hand tightly.

Flinn looked at Rama then, pointedly. "You have two children to care for after today. Try to keep them out of trouble. Raise my boy to be a man, like I did for you and your brothers."

"I will," Rama promised as he held onto Kyra, tears silently trickling down his face.

"And if you let my beautiful city fall." Flinn coughed again. "I will come back as a scourge and rip you a new asshole."

Rama choked on a tear-soaked laugh. "Wouldn't want to see your ugly decayed face anyway. You have my word."

"Good." Flinn coughed, turning his attention back to Morrigan. "One last truth before I go? Sorry to be lacking any decent drink at the moment."

Morrigan nodded, swallowing back her tears. "You, Flinn, the old bear of a war chief, have been the first man I've cared about in a long time, and I am furious at how slow you were to dodge that sword."

Flinn chuckled, blood gurgling in his throat. "We all slow down one day, but I am happy to have met you before I met that sword."

Morrigan laughed at that, her hand clasping his bloody one. She watched him for a moment and how his eyes seemed to be growing heavy. The color of his face now a pale white in stark contrast against the dark red of his blood. Everyone around them stood by watching the scene, tears streaming down their faces. Clyous held onto Bridget as she sobbed into his shoulder. Menolayous knelt down beside the old war chief, placing his old, bearded axe in his now lifeless hands, a Gaelach burial tradition Danny thought to himself. Grace rested a tattooed hand on his shoulder gently. Rama held onto the little girl in his arms, bobbing up and down in an attempt to comfort them both. Danny looked at Cat then, she stood on the outskirts of the small crowd looking in, her face blank and emotionless. If it wasn't for a single tear falling from the corner of her eye, Danny would have feared she had gone comatose yet again.

Morrigan reached out, gently lowering the old war chief's eyelids before kissing his forehead gently. "Have a safe journey through the underlands, my friend."

"He shouldn't have saved me," Connor wept, not speaking to anyone specific.

"He did what any father would do to protect his child." Morrigan glanced at the young boy. "Do not tarnish his memory and sacrifice."

"His sacrifice was for nothing." Connor thrust out his injured arm, revealing the injury to have been made from the mouth of a blooded wolf. "I'm going to turn. I'm going to be forced back to Oich, to live under those evil people. I won't have a choice."

"New blooded bond to the nearest pack leader, the nearest and most dominant wolf," Menolayous said calmly.

"Yes, exactly!" Connor cried. "I don't want to go back there, not after everything they've done to us."

"Connor," Bridget said as she wiped away her tears, crouching down in front of him. "You won't ever have to go back there if you don't want to."

"But I have to bond, don't I?" Connor looked up at her unashamed at his tears. "New blooded have to."

"Then you will bond to me," Bridget said compassionately.

"And that will work?" Connor dared to look hopeful.

"It will work." Bridget nodded. "I'm sorry I don't have the magic right now to free you from this curse, but I can promise to bond to you, so you never have to go back to that city again. Is that acceptable to you Connor?"

Connor nodded, wiping away the tears on his face. "Yes, Miss Bridget."

"Good," she said.

Rama looked at her then, realization slowly dawning on him. "Can you really bond to new blooded?"

"You doubt me?" Bridget gave him a look that could freeze over water.

"Never." Rama smiled at the intensity of it. "How many can you bond?"

"An infinite amount, if they accept it." Bridget raised an eyebrow. "Why?"

Rama sighed deeply, glancing around at the battlefield surrounding them. "I have a feeling we're going to have a lot more new blooded emerging at the next full moon."

"That's in two days," Danny said, glancing up at the sky.

"It's an unfortunate circumstance," Rama agreed, "but one we can turn to our advantage. We have a new-blooded fighting force, something that would give us an edge in this war, and every single one of them will answer to the new Queen of Oich."

"I would need them all in one place," Bridget spoke as her mind reeled.

"Head into the longhouse," Rama said. "The rest of us will start picking through the carnage. We'll send any injured your way. Do your healer thing but find those who are likely to turn and talk with them. Whatever you need, Connor and Clyous will help you get it."

Connor looked from Rama to Bridget. "I'm here for you, Miss Bridget."

"Come on." Clyous gently helped Bridget to her feet. "Let's get you up there and see how bad the damage is. Get you off your feet and to some yarrow root."

"Do not overwork yourself," Grace warned her sharply. "Do not think I won't put you to sleep if you start to exhaust yourself. If you think Clyous is being a controlling ass you haven't seen me yet."

"Thanks, Mother," Bridget joked, starting in the direction of the longhouse. "Connor, can you run to my shop and bring back all the bandages and liquid bottles you can find. Its going to be a long day."

"Yes, Ma'am." Connor took off in the direction of the city square, where her shop was located.

"I need to start organizing the warriors," Rama said, looking around. "Will the rest of you please start sorting through the carnage. Our priority should be wounded first. After they're all taken to the longhouse we should start collecting the dead."

"Sounds easy enough," Catriona spoke finally. "I get to handle the enemies."

"Cat," Rama's voice was stern, catching everyone's attention. "Our wounded come first. Kill the surviving enemies for all I care, but can you wait to start nailing bodies to the wall until after our men are taken care of?"

Catriona narrowed her eyes at him for a moment before relenting, "Fine."

"Why are you nailing bodies to the wall?" Grace dared to ask.

"Why not?" Catriona responded, flexing her hands to reveal visible scars, a deranged look in her eye.

"Alright, can we just stop," Rama put his foot down. "Dissect her mental health later. I for one am happy she's talking and not trying to *kill* me. But we have a job to do."

"I think we should hash this out," Grace responded. "I need to know if working side by side with her is going to result in me getting burned or watching her burn herself."

"I'm not going to burn you," Cat snapped with that wild expression still in her eyes. "And I don't plan on killing myself just yet. Rion escaped. After we're done here, I'm going after him."

"Yet?" Menolayous repeated, but his words washed out with everyone else's.

"The fuck you are!" Danny spoke up, his voice filled with rage he did not expect to come from himself. "I just got you back and now you want to take off?"

"Going after them right now is suicide," Grace countered.

"Don't care," Catriona stated simply.

"You haven't eaten in a week. You're running to near burnout." Danny made to reach for her, but she stepped outside his reach. "Please Cat, don't disappear on me."

There was a moment of silence between them as Cat's expression seemed to soften ever so slightly. "I won't just disappear, but I am going after them as soon as I've rested. We can end this war if we catch up to them, not taking advantage of their retreat is a strategic mistake."

"The girl is right." Morrigan stood, wiping her eyes. "To end this war quickly, it would be prudent to begin our search for the Dark One and his brother before they can amass more to their cause."

"It might be a while until they're back up to fighting strength," Grace chimed in. "I made Rion cut his own dick off. It's going to take some time for him to recover, and they are going to move slowly."

Catriona stared at Grace, a smile slowly spreading across her face. "And you guys are thinking I've lost my mind because I'm nailing bodies to the wall."

"It's a fucking weird thing to do," Grace countered.

"Bridget will need us for the full moon," Morrigan cut them both off. "She will need all of us. After that, Firebird, I will go with you to hunt them down."

"Deal." Catriona nodded to the sorceress.

"Can we at least talk about this?" Danny started to say.

"Talk about it later," Rama's voice was starting to rise. "There are injured people still out there while all of you are bickering. Apparently, a siege wasn't enough to take the fight out of you."

"Sorry," everyone chimed in.

"Go out and find survivors!" Rama started in the direction of the warriors grouping up just outside the longhouse. "Now!"

Chapter Ninety-Eight

Grace

Grace stood at the edge of the gulch looking around at all of the other children of the ancients. There were about twenty of them who were able and willing to stand guard throughout the night. That's why they were here after all, to ensure that none of the new blooded that would be transforming during this full moon were able to escape and harm anyone else. Grace glanced through the trees as the sun's finals rays sunk below the horizon, washing out what was left of their light source.

"I still don't understand the plan." Catriona stood next to her, fidgeting with all the surrounding bodies within reach of her. "There are far too many people here."

"You will need to contain us," Bridget explained calmly, looking down into the gulch below. "The first time a new blooded shifts is... chaotic. Until they come under the influence of a pack leader they are wild and out of control. You need to keep your flames burning until sunrise to ensure none of them are able to escape and turn any other Collie citizens. Everyone else is here as a precaution."

"In case I lose control," Catriona finished for her.

"In case they get past your flames," Bridget corrected. "Grace is here in case you get out of control."

Catriona shot her friend a look, there was no humor in it. "Lovely."

Grace blew her a kiss.

"They will not get past us," Morrigan said factually.

Bridget nodded as she glanced up at the sky. "I'd better get down there. Remember, it's going to sound like were ripping each other to pieces down there. It's important to hold the line, not to come try and help."

Grace caught the sudden change in Catriona's demeanor at the mention of wolves ripping each other apart. Catriona was covered nearly head to toe, a stark contrast to how she was dressed for battle, but the scars on her forearms, neck, and face shone like silver shining in the moonlight. If Bridget hadn't been there to heal her, Grace was sure Catriona would have bled out.

668

Bridget's abilities had made her continued existence in this world possible, without the fear of becoming new blooded herself. Although, from what Grace could sense radiating off of Catriona now she wished that wasn't the case, every waking moment of her existence was painful enough she didn't want to be there.

"Good luck," Grace called to Bridget as the healer turned on her heel, stalking down the gulch.

"If you need us, we will be there," Morrigan promised, her accent thicker than usual.

"Thank you," Bridget called back to them, aiming for the tree line where the new blooded waited.

"You know, if I didn't give you shit about how weird you're acting you would just be pissed at me for babying you," Grace said, glancing back to Catriona.

Catriona brushed her short hair out of her face, glancing back at Grace. "I know."

Grace chewed on her lower lip as she watched Bridget disappear into the trees, just as the final rays of the sun disappeared. "You ever want to talk—"

Catriona gave her a look so intense that it made Grace internally flinch. "Don't!"

"I mean it," Grace shot back just as viciously, treating her like a delicate little flower wasn't going to do Catriona any good. "When this is all said and done, I'll go with you to hunt the fuckers down, and after that if you ever feel like talking, or even letting me tattoo over those scars, I'll be there for you. Just don't expect me to hold back on calling you on your shit."

A small smile teased the edges of Catriona's mouth at that. "I wouldn't want you to."

"Good." Grace smiled, satisfied at Catriona's answer.

"Be still now," Morrigan warned, signaling to the others to circle around. "It is time."

"I'm scared," Catriona whispered just loud enough that only Grace and Morrigan could hear. "I don't want to lose control and hurt anyone down there."

"We won't let you," Grace promised. "I'll be in your head the whole time, monitoring you."

"I'm not sure that's a place you want to be." Catriona glanced at her looking distressed. "I don't want to be there."

"It is time," Morrigan said, the raven sitting in the branches above squawking in approval.

"Light it up," Grace said, bracing herself to enter Catriona's mind.

Catriona bent down low to the ground, placing her palms gently on the dirt below. Grace watched her friend inhale deeply, and on the exhale, flames shot from her hands, fanning out into two perfect strings. Grace watched as the flames spread around the edges of the gulch, disappearing as the rock formations blocked the view, only to reappear directly across from them on the other side. Catriona's flames connected, then fed off each other and grew into larger flames. Grace monitored Catriona's mood and her stress levels, and so far, she was stable. Catriona took in another deep breath, breathing more of her white flame into the already existing wall. The flames grew to the height of a man, the thin line expanding to several feet of thickness. Standing before them was a near impenetrable wall of white flame.

"Try to maintain this without expending all your power," Morrigan coached. "We cannot afford burnout."

"Got it." Catriona grimaced as she concentrated.

The sounds of howls began to echo through the trees, the flames barely doing anything to stifle the sounds. Grace shuddered at the intensity of the wolves, a new howl joining the chorus as each new blooded shifted for the first time. The howls and whines had no discernable pattern, it was a chorus of chaos as more shifted. After several minutes, a loud growl reverberated through the trees, silencing the chorus. Grace knew from her experience with the blooded in Airgid that this was Bridget announcing herself as the pack leader. A moment of silence followed as the wolves took a moment to decide if this was acceptable. Several other growls came from inside, significantly less than those who had participated in the pack howl. These were the few that felt they were able to challenge her, those wolves who felt like submitting wasn't an ideal option.

Suddenly the growls turned into barks and whimpers, sounds of the wolves coming head-to-head in a physical clash overwhelmed the surrounding area. Grace could hear what sounded like the gnashing of teeth and flesh being torn as the wolves fought over position of the leader. Grace stilled her own racing heart at the sound, knowing this was normal wolf behavior. Bridget would be fine, she knew what she was doing. She couldn't sense anything unnerving from her friend down there, but she did sense pain from a few of her challengers. A wave of panic flooded over her, Grace whipped her head to the side as she watched Catriona squeeze her eyes shut, shaking her head as if trying to shake away the memories.

Grace stepped closer, prepared to grab hold of her friend if needed. She knew that Catriona would not react kindly to being touched, so she held back until it was necessary. She watched intently as Catriona fought to remain in the present, she could feel Catriona resisting the pull into the darkness. It was an intense twisting of her very soul, her will struggling against her pain. If Grace wasn't so invested in making sure Catriona won that particular battle, she would be impressed with the sheer intensity of it.

"We are with you, Firebird," Morrigan remarked, crouching down so she was at Catriona's height. "We will not let you fall."

Grace could sense how Morrigan's words had affected her friend. Instead of just brushing them off, Grace could sense some comfort coming from them.

"You are not alone," Morrigan continued, her eyes piercing into Catriona's soul. "You are flame, you are from the direct bloodline of our battle goddess, you are fight incarnate. You are not fated to fall to the darkness, do not allow it to win over you."

Morrigan began to sing, what sounded like a battle hymn in the Gaelach language. Grace wished she knew the words, making a mental note to having Menolayous teach her Gaelach at some point. The hymn grew louder as Morrigan crouched there, allowing her words to carry over the crackling of flames and the distant snaps and growls from the wolves. A woman who stood not ten feet from them seemed to recognize the hymn, her short hair and animal skin clothing betrayed her origin. The woman joined Morrigan, her foreign words matching pace and rhythm. The man behind her snapped his attention to them, he too jumped in at the start of a new verse. Shortly after, all of the Gaelach children of old were singing this battle hymn in unison, their attentions focused on the fiery wall before them. Grace, like a few others, stood within the circle completely entranced by what was happening.

Grace could feel an energy building as they continued to sing, like they were weaving an ancient spell. Grace reached out to feel those around her, it was like the words were invigorating them. Catriona felt stronger and more stable as the darkness began to recede. These words were magic, she realized, she just didn't recognize it.

"It's an old spell," Menolayous's voice echoed through their connection. *"An old chant used before heading into battle. It's meant to banish your enemies and empower you to carry on."*

"Your people weave such spells?" Grace asked, genuinely curious as she watched magic begin to fly around them.

"We still worship the way the forgotten ones had taught us. Our battle hymns are one such tradition that has remained true."

"Forgotten ones? You mean the fairies?" Grace asked. *"I thought those were just stories."*

"They are not just stories," Morrigan butted in. *"I have lived amongst the fae, fought against the sirens, walked amongst the giants, followed the wisps to forgotten realms, worshipped the gods. There was a time when magic was within the land, the forgotten ones lived amongst us as neighbors."*

"When this is over, I would like to take you back to my home. Before we were forced to hide within the caves," Menolayous said. *"Some of the forgotten ones were not lost to us, you just have to know where to seek them out."*

"Truly?" Grace asked, failing to keep the excitement out of her voice.

"Yes, Wife." She could feel Menolayous smile against their bond. *"I want to show you even more traditions from my people. I want to show you a natural magic, not just what flows through your veins. And prove to you that your first assessment of me was wrong, I have lived with magic my whole life."*

"I would love nothing more." Grace found herself smiling, the sounds of the hymn invigorating her.

Grace glanced back at Catriona who was now standing and facing her flames as she stared down into the gulch. Her eyes were like liquid silver; her short hair moved with the slight breeze emulating the movement of dancing flames. Grace tried to reach out and feel her, but found Catriona had surrounded herself with a mental shield created from the flames that burned within her. The wolves continued to fight and squabble down below, their whines and pitchy howls echoing around them were nearly drowned out by the song the people from Gaelach continued to sing. Catriona stood tall and proud, not one emotion visibly taking over. For a moment, Grace felt in awe of her, of the sheer power that radiated from her friend. It felt as if the Goddess of War and Fate was standing there instead, looking into the flames to see the future. For a moment, Catriona seemed at peace, but Grace knew in her heart this was the calm before the storm. Soon, Cat would unleash such

672

an inferno upon their enemies she would practically wipe them from existence.

Chapter Ninety-Nine

Clyous

Clyous paced back and forth at the base of the hill, glancing up at the fiery wall that surrounded his wife, trapping her amongst dozens of new blooded. Clyous had been pacing all night, the sounds of the wolf pack tearing into each other had him on edge. He knew the last several days he had been an overbearing and protective jackass towards his wife, but he wished it wasn't so. Between struggling to remain centered in reality instead of being sucked in by one of his visions, and finding out that Bridget was pregnant, most of his good sense was lost.

His most recent vision was reoccurring, all of them in various positions on an unknown battlefield. A ruined temple off in the distance with four eyed ravens surrounding the fallen stones. The events of the vision remained inconsistent. He watched time and time again as a different member of his family died a horrible and gruesome death. Danny fell to the sharpened end of a spear, Rama perished with an axe embedded deep within his skull, Morrigan bled out alone surrounded by darkness. Every single one of them died a hundred different ways, it was jarring to keep reliving. It was as if Clyous was watching his worst fears come to life, his pregnant wife being dragged away by the enemy and his sister wandering through the corpses not knowing who or what she was. It was an absolute nightmare, one that Clyous could see during his waking hours.

What wasn't helping him maintain control over his sanity was watching his twin sister completely lose grip on hers. Watching how far she had fallen was downright painful if not unsettling. As a child she had been prone to outbursts and was easily angered, but this behavior, this was something else entirely. He wished he could be more compassionate about it, truly he wanted to be, but he was scared of her, scared of what she represented. If she could fall into insanity, so could he, and right now he was trusting his mentally disturbed sister to guard his wife and child with the flames she could barely control, just weeks after they had both been taken from him.

"The sun is almost up," Menolayous said as he leaned against a tree, his patient eyes tracking Clyous's every movement. "She's fine. Grace would have sensed it if she wasn't."

"I know," Clyous said, still pacing. "I can't help it."

"You doing, okay?" Danny asked, his head tilting slightly as he too watched Clyous. "You've been acting weird the last few days."

"I wonder why?" Clyous retorted in genuine Catriona fashion. Sighing, he changed his tone. "No, my visions are shuffling through my head like a never-ending deck of cards. I can't grasp one in particular, they just keep moving around and it's hard to keep one foot in reality."

"Doesn't help that reality the last few days has been an absolute nightmare," Rama said, his arms filled with a sleeping Kyra. The poor child was exhausted but had thrown a fit whenever Rama tried to leave her behind with one of the women.

"No, it doesn't," Clyous agreed, choosing his words carefully. Danny was overly sensitive and would react out of anger if it was brought up by anyone that Catriona was losing her mind.

The day's first light began to peak over a nearby hill, breaking through the trees. Clyous took a deep breath, allowing his anxiety to slowly dissipate as the beams of light brushed against his skin. The sound of his sister's flames disappeared as it was replaced by the rising sun. Clyous stopped pacing, staring up the hill in the direction he wanted to run. He restrained himself; Bridget had specifically instructed them to stay back. Not only to keep from mixing them with new blooded which would undoubtedly send them into a frenzy due to their uncontrollable nature, but to not diminish the authority she had spent all night solidifying. She had noticed the change in him as well, he was thankful that she understood it. Not that she would allow him to continue.

Clyous's eyes tracked movement coming down from the hill. His eyes locked with his sister's silvery ones, her short hair a stark reminder that she was no longer the same. She seemed relatively calm if not tired. Grace and Morrigan followed, they too looked exhausted. The dozen or so other children of the ancients close behind, leaving their perimeter around the gulch. Once they reached them, they turned their gazes back to where the wolves waited. Anxiety began to creep back into Clyous's heart as he waited, wanting nothing more than to lay his eyes on his wife, to be able to tell his racing heart that she was in fact fine.

"Have more faith in her," Catriona said quietly as she glanced at him. "She's stronger than anyone has given her credit for. I think she would have proven that to you already."

"I know she's strong," Clyous said through gritted teeth, irritated that his sister of all people would need to remind him just how neurotic he was behaving. "But you and I both know strength does not always save someone."

She glared at him then but chose to remain silent. He knew it was a low blow, but he really didn't feel like being lectured at the moment.

"Here they come," Morrigan said, catching everyone's attention.

Clyous's eyes returned to the hill. He could see several figures moving down together, their grey and brown fur visible in the sunlight. Clyous clenched his fists to conceal his anxiety. Shouldn't Bridget have come first? A small group of wolves followed. All of them moving together as one pack. The first five wolves stopped just feet away from where Clyous and the others waited, they took a defensive formation as they looked upon the unblooded, fangs bared in warning. Catriona tensed beside him, small flames igniting in her palms as she bared her teeth at them in response. Clyous braced himself for the wolves to take her posture as a challenge, they had grown up in the capital city of Oich, she should know better than to challenge a wolf. One of the larger wolved snapped its jaws, taking a single step forward.

A single howl filled the air, echoing off the trees, causing all the wolves around them to cower down in submission. An auburn wolf stepped from the trees, stalking forward slowly. Bridget was double the size of the others, and she carried herself with the confidence and power only the pack leader could possess. As her wolf wandered closer to them, she made sure to snap her jaws at the wolf in passing, the one that dared to snap its fangs at his sister. The grey beast lowered itself to the ground in submission as Bridget's power rippled through the pack. Behind her followed the rest of the pack, some thirty or more new-blooded wolves.

Bridget shifted mid step, her auburn fur transforming into her curly red hair. Clyous breathed a sigh of relief as he saw her, she looked covered in dirt and tired, but strong and unharmed. She stepped towards him then, her eyes fixed on his, a small smile coming across her face. As she approached, Morrigan dropped to her knee in a bow of submission, the Gaelach children of the ancients following suit. Bridget stopped walking as her gaze fell over the sorceress.

"My Queen," Morrigan acknowledged. "The living embodiment of the Goddess of Healing and the Moon God. I see you."

Rama mimicked Morrigan's movements, as did everyone else. Clyous dropped to both knees before his wife in awe at her beauty and the golden aura surrounding her. Relief and pride washed over him as she smiled down at him. Out of the corner of his eye he spotted his sister shifting to the edge of everyone, trying not to draw attention to herself. She was the only one who remained standing, but it wasn't in a defiant way. Clyous knew his sister would bow to no one, but her trying to remain in the background proved to him that she meant it as no insult.

"What now, Your Majesty?" He could hear the playfulness in Rama's voice without even looking his direction.

Bridget looked at her pack before answering, "I bring with me a new-blooded army. Let's get to work."

A chorus of howls erupted behind her in agreement. It was time to end this war once and for all.

Chapter One Hundred

Menolayous

Menolayous and Danny moved through the low-lying fog, careful not to stir up any sounds. The men that followed them were expert hunters and trackers, hand selected by the brothers to travel freely through Gaelach territory unnoticed. They were currently moving through the southwestern border of Gaelach, having followed the bloody trail from Collie into the cultists' kingdom. They had been tracking the Dark One's tracks for days now, hoping to locate the bastard and his coward of a brother soon. They had found evidence of their stay in a cave not a day's march away, bloody bandages partially burned in a dead fire, and archaic drawings etched into the ground nearby. Menolayous had to hand it to his wife, she too was fierce when motivated. Her injury to Rion had slowed their escape just enough that Menolayous could follow their trail.

The warning sound of an owl came from ahead; it was one of their scouts signaling that enemies were up ahead. Danny slowly drew his sword as not to make noise and signaled with one hand to the men behind him to spread out to the sides. Menolayous lowered himself closer to the ground as he inched towards the brush a few feet ahead of him, Danny by his side was mimicking his movements. Menolayous carefully moved up to the brush, peering through the branches. Ahead of him, he could see a small campfire surrounded by five of the Dark One's cultist tribesmen. Off to the side and shackled to a tree stump were at least eight men and women, all of them looking as if they hadn't eaten for days and had been enduring regular beatings.

Menolayous narrowed his eyes as he observed the tribesmen, they were arguing over what was left of the night's dinner. The two largest of them were standing chest to chest as they bared their teeth at each other. Their false sense of security presented Menolayous and Danny a unique opportunity to attack before they even realized they were there. Menolayous signaled to his men to prepare for the attack as Danny began to move to the left, searching for an easy way to move through the brush. Menolayous moved to the right searching for the same. After a minute of silently searching he found an opening and waited. His ears perked up at the sound of a night lark signaling to him that Danny was ready.

Menolayous gripped his battle axes, taking a deep breath, he stood and pushed through the opening in the brush. The tribesmen turned to look his direction, completely missing Danny sneaking up behind them. One of the tribesmen rushed forward to Menolayous as Danny drove his silver-edged sword through another one's chest. Chaos erupted as their men came crashing through the brush, weapons flying as they engaged the blooded. Three of the four shifted into wolves as they engaged with the oncoming warriors.

The one charging for Menolayous remained in his human form, swinging his mace down towards Menolayous's head. Menolayous danced around the attack, slashing the edge of his battle axe against the blooded's abdomen. The cultist barely slowed at the injury, coming back with his elbow and connecting with the side of Menolayous's face. Menolayous was fast, but the average blooded was faster. He spun with the momentum from the blow, angling his axe towards the tribesman's leg, severing the muscles of the thigh.

The man snarled as he was forced to take a knee, attempting to raise his mace once again, but Menolayous was already in motion, the blade of his axe coming down, severing a hand from the wrist. Before the tribesman could scream Menolayous knocked him backwards, pinning him to the ground with a blade pressed against his neck. The man snarled up at Menolayous but otherwise stopped resisting. Glancing around, Menolayous was able to discern that his men had finished off the remaining cultists with minimal injuries. For humans, they were getting good at killing blooded.

"Where are your kings?" Menolayous asked, turning his attention back to his prisoner.

In response, the cultist spat off to the side, answering in ancient Gaelach.

"What did he say?" Danny asked, coming up beside Menolayous, pointing the tip of his sword at the man with clear distaste.

"He said to go fuck yourself," Menolayous answered, pressing the blade of his axe into the flesh of the tribesman's throat, cutting through the flesh and drawing a river of blood. "He wasn't going to tell us."

"Maybe they can help." Danny nodded over to the prisoners who were actively being freed by their men.

Menolayous stood, shaking the blood from his axe before walking over to the fearful looking men and women. He spoke to them in his language, noting the shock on their faces once they realized he was one of them. A few of the women began to weep with joy, grabbing his hands as a gesture of thanks. One of the men began to speak back and forth with him for a minute before turning to the woman beside him, his wife.

"He said that an injured mountain lion and a large bear came through the other day. He wasn't aware they were any kings, but the others seemed to fear them. He said they went west, away from the Airgid border," Menolayous translated to Danny. "They have been overhearing talk about gatherings at an old temple built to worship the God of Death. He suspects that's where they were headed. These cultists had changed their plans after their visit to head that direction as well."

"There are temples dedicated to the God of Death?" Danny asked.

"It's in ruins now," Menolayous answered, "but Gaelach has temples all over for every god. Before these brothers had taken over, this kingdom was very spiritual."

"I didn't know that," Danny said, surprised. "I don't know a lot about your homeland."

"Not a lot of people do." Menolayous removed a waterskin from his belt, taking a deep drink. "We're a people who don't like to be disturbed, or in more recent years, seen."

"And you used to be like them?" Danny asked, his eyes returning to the freed prisoners.

"Yes," Menolayous answered simply. "My family and I were captured when I was very young. I spent the first few years of my life living in and out of cave systems. I think it's why I can see so well in the dark, and why I'm better at being quiet than all of you. I had to be in order to survive."

"That's—" Danny paused "—I have no words for that."

Menolayous shrugged. "It is what it is."

"Now I think I understand why you never told us." Danny looked at his brother, really looked at him. "How could you have explained all this to two teenage boys."

"I couldn't even explain it to two fully grown men," Menolayous replied. "You had to see things to even begin to understand."

"Yeah," Danny said sadly. "Comparatively speaking, it's not the same but I feel like I've seen too much."

"It's why I've been fighting all these years. Hoping one day nobody will have to live like this again, never have to see the horrors done here." Menolayous offered Danny the waterskin, which he declined.

"I feel like a terrible brother, not having been there for you when I knew you were hurting," Danny admitted. "I feel like a terrible man, I don't even know how to help my woman."

"You're not meant to help," Menolayous answered simply. "There's nothing you can do that's going to make it all better. Just… keep being there, and if you can't handle it then have the strength to walk away."

"I could never walk away. Even if she could never be with me again. I could never not be there for her."

"I know." Menolayous gently grasped his brother's shoulder, the physical contact he had avoided for so many years still had him flinching, but the reaction was less than it ever had been. "It's why you're not terrible. You don't need to try and understand what happened to her, or what she's feeling. Be the one normal thing in her life she can look at, the one thing that won't change. Treat her like Catriona, not a victim."

"I think I can do that." Danny sniffed, sucking up the emotions that threatened to spill over.

"Good. Now we'll need to decide what to do next. I know the temple they are talking about, it's on the peninsula northwest of us. Maybe a few more days on foot."

"How do we get word back?" Danny asked.

"The bird has already overheard us." Menolayous pointed straight up at a raven circling above them, Morrigan's raven. "Tell them we are moving forward. They are going to be traveling the tunnel systems leading to the temple's underground chamber. Send Catriona and Morrigan through there, maybe she can smoke them out, and tell Rama we'll need his men surrounding the temple for whenever they do finally pop out."

The raven cawed as if approving the message, turning back south and flying off. Menolayous and Danny watched as the bird continued on its path towards Collie.

"That thing freaks me out," Danny admitted. "I've heard Morrigan talking to it but I thought it was because she's a crazy old sorceress."

"There's a lot about natural magic you don't know, brother." Menolayous smiled. "You'll get there."

"So, onward to the temple?" Danny asked.

"Let's see what kind of trap we can lay for them," Menolayous answered.

Chapter One Hundred One

Catriona

"They are moving to lay a trap!" Morrigan shouted as she shoved her way through the wooden doors of the longhouse, making everyone jump. "Our boys are headed to the western peninsula, to the ruined temple of the Death God. They believe that is where the two cowardly kings are going, they are hiding within the cave systems."

"They found them?" Catriona straightened, stilling the dagger in her hand.

"They found their trail," Morrigan corrected. "They have requested that warriors surround the temple, and for me and the firebird to enter the tunnels."

A malicious smile began to spread across Catriona's mouth, her eyes wild and crazed. "Let's go."

"Not so fast." Rama pointed directly at Catriona to halt her movements. "Morrigan, show me on the map."

All of them circled around the map that had been laid out on the table, the longhouse since converted into their own personal leadership sanctuary after the last of the wounded had returned home. Bridget and Clyous stood side by side, hands intertwined as they looked upon the map. Morrigan pointed to a peninsula just north of Collie, and according to the parchment there wasn't anything on it.

"Here." She plucked the dagger from Catriona's hand and thrust it through the wood, marking her place. "There is an old, ruined temple connected to several tunnel systems. It has been abandoned for years, forgotten by most. With no fear from enemies approaching them from three sides, it is the perfect strong hold to hole up in."

"But it allows no escape." Rama studied the map. "If they were overrun, they couldn't flee anywhere but to the cliffs."

"Their path of retreat would be the tunnels," Morrigan explained. "They connect underneath the temple itself and lead all throughout Gaelach."

"You've been there?" Catriona asked, eyeing the old sorceress.

"Many centuries ago," she answered.

"Enough that you're comfortable with maneuvering the tunnels?" Rama asked.

"Yes," Morrigan answered simply.

"Show me the plan then." Rama handed her a dagger off his belt.

Morrigan took it, stabbing into the wood again a few inches away from the other. "This is where the firebird and I will enter. Once we do, we will work through the maze to get underneath the temple. We will push them to the upper levels, where your men will be waiting for them."

"What if they're in the tunnels?" Bridget asked. "Just the two of you might not be enough if the remainder of their forces are hidden there."

"Two is plenty." Morrigan looked upon Catriona appreciatively. "We will smoke them out, like rats from a field."

Catriona smiled wickedly once more. "I'm more than ready."

"What about my warriors?" Bridget asked, studying the map. "Where is the best place for my new blooded to be?"

Rama pointed just north of the temple. "How about here? They can be our safety net, standing by to catch any that manage to escape."

"Won't you need us at the front?" Bridget glared at the giant. "We are stronger and faster than humans."

"But they are untested in battle as far as their shifts go. It's too risky to overly rely on them for this. They would be best helping to catch a few stragglers," Rama answered simply.

"You have Airgid soldiers fighting with the Collie warriors," Grace pointed out. "And as many with ancient blood as volunteers. I wouldn't worry that the humans won't be a match for the cultists. Especially if Catriona is hot on their trail burning them out of their hiding spots. The entire battle will be chaotic."

"They can handle it," Bridget argued. "I will be there to keep them in line."

"No-the-fuck-you are not!" Rama stared at her in disbelief. "Not in your condition you won't."

"And what makes you think you're going to stop me?" Bridget growled, baring her teeth at him. "You are not my king, you are my brother, so stop acting like it. All of you need to stop treating me like I've suddenly turned to glass."

"Woah, woah, woah." Grace threw her hands up. "Can we simmer down before her baby hormones convince her to eat you alive?"

"This might be fun." Rama smiled at Bridget's show of hostility.

"We do not have time for this!" Morrigan snapped. "We must move."

"Sweetheart," Clyous said softly.

"Don't you 'sweetheart' me!" Bridget redirected her snarl at him. "I'm not throwing myself into battle, what I'm saying is I need to be there. If anything, to keep a grip on my wolves."

"She has a point," Catriona said simply. "We're wasting time arguing. Nobody here is going to stop her, so just accept the inevitable and give her a plan that keeps her out of the thick of it."

"Thank you." Bridget nodded towards Catriona.

"Here." Rama pointed to the map reluctantly. "Keep your pack back behind this line. Catch any strays coming your way. If we need the backup, I'll call for you."

Bridget nodded her agreement.

"Connor," Rama called to the young man who was playing with Kyra quietly in the corner.

"Yes!" Connor shot up, standing straight and waiting for orders like the overeager teenager he was.

"Do you have a weapon?" Rama asked him, smiling as Kyra waddled over to Connor and started tugging at his hand impatiently.

"Yes," Connor answered.

"Good. Go gear up, and spread the word, all able-bodied warriors are to be prepared for a march. We leave at dawn." Rama dismissed the young man, who took off at a sprint, leaving an upset looking Kyra standing there staring after him. "Come here, little one." Rama scooped her up, tickling her sides, getting her to laugh. "I will need to find you a babysitter for a few days, won't I?"

"Good luck with that." Grace scoffed as the child looked up at him, her eyebrows furrowing. "You're going to have to sneak off when she's asleep."

"Shhh," Rama said, trying to make Kyra laugh once again, the child was no longer amused. "You're giving away my strategy. See, I told you Grace was mean."

"Let us go, Firebird," Morrigan said to Catriona, "We're going hunting. We leave in an hour."

"I'm already packed." Catriona gripped her dagger which was still lodged in the table, pulling it free.

"Good. As am I?" Morrigan smiled, revealing a hint of her wild side.

"If you're leaving now, how will we know when you're springing the trap?" Rama asked.

"The princess can sense us when you are close enough," Morrigan answered. "It will take us extra time to navigate the tunnels. You will not be far behind."

"Be safe, will you?" Bridget reached for Catriona but stopped herself, her eyes filled with emotion.

Catriona nodded, glancing around at everyone before turning towards the wooden doors. Morrigan was hot on her heels, the two of them eager to start their mission. Catriona only needed to stop at her tree home before she was ready to leave, she needed her traveling pack and twin swords. Truthfully, the thought of food turned her stomach. Still, if she truly wanted to take on her last surviving enemy and win, she needed to be at full strength. There was nothing at that moment that she wanted more than to get her hands on Rion and his brother. The pain she planned on inflicting upon him, the gods would cringe at it. Catriona was traveling with the one person she never had to worry about letting her unleash her full potential near, Morrigan was equally obsessed with ending the Dark One as she was Rion. Morrigan wouldn't care how twisted Catriona would be, how dark she went, as long as they ended the brothers once and for all. So, the two women collected their things, and within the hour found themselves exiting the gates of Collie, ready to track down their prey.

Chapter One Hundred Two

Morrigan

Drip. Drip. Drip. The only sound Morrigan could hear as they silently moved through the tunnels was the slight dripping of water. Morrigan had spent years hunting scourge through tunnels like these, decades if not centuries honing her ability to hide and conceal her presence. She was impressed that Catriona, the hot-headed mess the young woman was, she was able to match her stealth.

The two of them had entered the tunnel system a day ago, or what Morrigan would assume was a day ago. It was hard to keep track when underground. They had found evidence of the brothers from the beginning, trails of blood and discarded bandages. But as they progressed through the tunnels it seemed Rion was beginning to heal, and the blood lessened. There was a window of a few hours where they were lost, unable to figure out which tunnel the brothers had taken. The two women had accidentally come across a small hive of scourge before picking up the brothers' trail yet again. Evidence that they had met up with other cultists became more and more present. Ritualistic drawings were found on the tunnel walls, along with extinguished torches and collapsed altars. There were even a few intact skeletons found laid out on the altars, further proving their near proximity to the temple of death.

"I wish we had the ability to sense energies like Grace," Catriona complained, stepping over a pile of bones.

"That would only be helpful right now if scourge had energies to read," Morrigan answered, trying to reach out with her magic to map the tunnel walls ahead.

"They don't have energies?" Catriona asked, surprised. *"Why?"*

"Energies are for living things. These creatures are brought back to our world by the Death God, therefore they lack any embers of life. They are driven by darkness from the abyss, that is why the only way to ensure they are defeated is to burn them completely."

"How were they made?"

"Centuries ago, when the God of Death entered the first person to create the Dark One, he also created the first scourge. Through an unholy ritual, the Dark One was able to reanimate a recently deceased corpse. But, like all magic, it came with a balance. The person they tried to resurrect did not come back as who they were, instead it was a dark

creature driven by hunger, driven by death. It is why any dark one is able to control them, they come from the abyss, made from the same darkness."

"How do you know so much?" Catriona asked, glancing at her with interest. "It's not just because you're old."

"I helped resurrect the corpse." Morrigan turned to face Catriona, staring her in the eyes. "Before I became the Morrigan, my lover was obsessed with attaining magic for himself, unsatisfied with being a mere mortal amongst the children of gods and the forgotten ones. He studied an ancient and dark set of magic hoping to become powerful. There was an accident where one of our friends died. He believed he could bring him back, I was heartbroken and naive enough to think it would work. We brought our friend back alright, but my lover inadvertently allowed the Death God to take over his body. I was chosen to become the protector of the bloodlines because of my involvement; it was my penance."

Catriona stopped walking, her jaw dropped as she stared at Morrigan after her confession. "So, your obsession with killing scourge—"

"—was me hoping that if I could end them completely, maybe I could finally end my reincarnation cycle," Morrigan clarified. "I am so tired of dying, it is an exhausting process, Firebird."

"So everything that has happened, with the Dark One and his culty attempts at trying to breed the different bloodlines, or devour those with ancient blood in order to take on their power, that's all your fault?" Catriona just stood there, staring at her incredulously. "Everything that they did to me, was because of choices you made centuries ago? I lost my mother because of a creature you helped create?"

"Yes," Morrigan answered, just before Catriona's hand shot out and slapped her across the face, the sound reverberating off the stone walls.

"Fuck you!" Catriona seethed, visibly trying to hold back her magic.

"You are not the only one my mistakes have harmed." Morrigan gently touched her swollen lip, easing the sting. "I have become more and more reclusive with each rebirth, hiding from my mistakes as best I can. It would be a lie to say that my absence has not only allowed atrocities to happen within our continent but has allowed the Dark One to work in the shadows, learning these new rituals. I am sorry for everything I have done that has affected your life for the worse. I know that my actions over the last few centuries do not erase the darkness I am responsible for, but please, Firebird, take some advice from an old woman, do not hide from your problems as I have. Do not shut out the people in your life. The consequences can be irreparable."

"I don't want to be lectured by you anymore," Catriona spat, not bothering to conceal the menace in her words. "You have lost that right."

"Then hear this—" Morrigan took a step forward, mustering what strength she still possessed "—you might never forgive me, which is something I would never blame you for, but you will hear me. For the first time in over three centuries, we have the ability to permanently banish the God of Death back into the abyss, trapping him there so he cannot return to this land."

"And how exactly do you plan to accomplish that?" Catriona did not back away from Morrigan's powerful energy.

"Your flames, Firebird," Morrigan answered. "Your flames are special, different from any other wildfire I have seen. You are not only a descendant of the goddess, but you have been blessed by her. You and your brother hold the future of this land and its people in your hand. If you can burn the Dark One, let him perish in the fire once he fully possesses the body he is in, we have a chance!"

"And this is why you have been relentless in me learning about my power?" Catriona asked, glaring at the older woman.

"No," Morrigan confessed. "I wasn't sure until you had blown a hole in the city wall. I knew you were powerful, but the magnitude you possess hasn't seen a likeness since the goddess herself last walked the continent."

"Then what are we waiting for?" Catriona grimaced, turning on her heel and heading down the tunnel. "The quicker I burn the fucker the sooner I can get the fuck away from you."

Menolayous had been right that day, she had lost touch with her side of humanity. Morrigan knew she would never be able to fix the mistakes she was responsible for, that she could never expect to be forgiven, but if she could help this woman even the score, help her find some peace within her, that would be enough. Morrigan rushed to catch up, matching Catriona's pace as they moved through the tunnels. There was no point in concealing their sounds now, if the enemy was close by, they had surely heard their echoes.

They turned a corner only to come to an immediate halt, standing not ten feet from them were a dozen or so tribesmen, having been equally surprised at the women's appearance as the women were to them. Morrigan slowly began to raise her spear as dozens of blades and clubs were pointed at her. Slight movement caught her eye, a man with a limp was moving in the center. Her eyes locked onto King Rion, who glanced between her and Catriona, his face paled at the realization.

"They might have prisoners," Morrigan warned, watching as Rion began to glance around for an escape.

"Don't care!" Catriona stepped forward, shooting her hands out in front of her as she allowed her flames to pour from her palms.

The roar from the flames was deafening as Morrigan threw herself off to the side, the heat from the exposure singing her hair. She could hear the tribesmen shouting and cursing as they began to scatter, trying desperately to avoid the flames. Through the bright white of Catriona's magic, she was able to see Rion duck underneath one of the columns and flee in the opposite direction.

"He runs!" Morrigan bellowed over the sound of the screams.

"Let's see if he can outrun a wildfire!" Catriona pushed more of her flames outward, a crazed look in her eye.

Morrigan watched in utter disbelief at the magnitude of flames that poured from this girl, how she put all of her life's energy into feeding this hungry beast, and a hungry beast it was. The flames crawled their way through the tunnels, devouring everything as they went, chasing after the many tribesmen who fled from the magic. Morrigan was now standing feet behind Catriona, shielding her face from the heat coming from it all, the brightness nearly impossible to see through as the flames continued to move through the tunnels. Morrigan knew unleashing her upon them would be a force of nature, but she was still surprised at it all. She had come to end the Dark One once and for all, but to also help the girl find peace. There was no fathomable way Rion would be able to make it out alive now that Catriona had found him, but as Morrigan now looked upon all the rage and hatred the woman poured into her magic she questioned if ending the bastard would bring her peace after all.

Chapter One Hundred Three

Bridget

The sounds, Bridget had never heard anything like it. She had been in battle, heard scourge ripping families apart, watched bones snap and flesh get shredded, she'd watched Catriona's flames destroy everything around it, heard the flesh drip from bone and bones turn to ash. Bridget had believed she had heard the most unsettling noises she would ever hear, she was wrong. Bridget crouched on top of a boulder, letting her wolven senses expand outward to better grasp the situation as it was unfolding. Her men and women, her new-blooded warriors, they stood behind her silently letting their newly acquired senses reach out.

Bridget knew Catriona and Morrigan had found the Dark One and his brother, she could hear the chaos from tiny fissures in the ground. It wasn't just the two blooded down there that her family was confronting, by the sound of it there were dozens of other blooded as well as scourge. But those weren't the sounds that made her want to retch the contents of her stomach up. The two women moved throughout the tunnel system, every sound they made echoed back to her, similar to the sounds inside a castle's ballroom like coughing or footsteps, these weren't just footsteps and coughs from a nobleman. These were the dying screams of men and woman who knew there was no hope for escape, the roar of the fire as it overtook them, and the crackling of the flames as it devoured them like a hungry animal.

"Miss Bridget," Connor said, getting her attention, then pointing over to a small plume of smoke rising from the ground.

"The smoke has to go somewhere," Bridget explained. "It's sought out small fissures to escape."

"Sounds like the smoke is the only thing able to escape," Connor grimaced, he too could hear exactly what Bridget could.

"War is a nasty business." Bridget stood, facing Connor. "Death is ugly. It's why I've never fallen captive to the glorification of it."

"You've always been the one to patch us up, I can see why it's never been appealing to you," Connor surmised, wincing as another loud shriek pierced the air from below. "I might be inclined to agree with you. Catriona scares me, truthfully."

"She scares everyone," Bridget admitted. "But she's on our side, and without her, it's possible this war would have gone on for many more years. I am thankful it will be over soon. I like to believe this way will save many more lives. Remember, those poor souls down there are the ones that like to torture and mutilate others in the name of their god. All of Stone Basin will be safer without their existence."

"Yes, Miss Bridget." Connor agreed, jumping off to the side as pressurized smoke suddenly blew from the ground beside him, a small amount of flame feeding into the air as if it were starving.

"Everyone, keep your ears and eyes open," Bridget ordered. "Pay attention to the ground. You don't want to get caught in one of those vents."

There was a murmur from her soldiers as they all began to stare at the ground and shift uneasily. Bridget had seen what Catriona was capable of above ground, she could only imagine what havoc it brought below.

"Have you guys ever heard of a volcano?" Grace's voice echoed down their bond, connecting all of them.

"No, what is that?" Rama's inquiring voice echoed.

"Apparently, it's a mountain that holds liquid fire, occasionally the mountain purges this fire, destroying everything around it," Grace responded, *"so I've heard anyway."*

"Sounds nightmarish," Bridget commented.

"These plumes of smoke remind me of volcanos," Grace said. They must be experiencing similar ventilation issues to what Bridget was.

"I was going to compare this to the stories I've heard of the fire lizards," Rama chimed in. *"What were they called? Dragons? The amount of smoke and flame pouring out of this cave opening is absolutely crazy."*

"Don't tell Cat about these dragons, she might want to go find them and bring one home," Danny cut in.

"Relax, they're a myth," Rama exclaimed.

"Dragons are very real," Morrigan's voice echoed down the bond. *"I just haven't seen one in hundreds of years."*

"Great..." Clyous chimed in. *"Just what we need."*

"I'd rather be a volcano than be a lizard," Catriona huffed, a jet of flame erupting from a fissure off in the distance.

"We can see that," Clyous snapped. *"We're still up here, can you not?"*

There was a moment of silence, Catriona did not answer. Instead, another flame erupted from a soft spot in the ground, sending up large plumes of smoke. Bridget did not see where the flames had emerged, but judging by the distance and location she would guess they were close to where Clyous was positioned.

"Fuck off!" Clyous snapped down the bond.

"Children, please—" Rama's voice interrupted *"—can we focus on the impending battle? Fight later."*

"We approach the temple entrance," Morrigan called.

"Archers are in position around the outside entrance," Menolayous finally spoke.

"Good, everybody hold the line until my order," Rama commanded, no room for games now that the edge of battle was so close.

"Be ready," Bridget commanded her warriors, standing and drawing her sword. "Connor, you stay with me."

Her warriors fanned out taking their positions. Their goal was to intercept any who tried to flee, her new-blooded warriors were the only thing standing between the cultists and their freedom. Bridget would not allow a single one of those evil creatures to escape, she could not allow it. She chose to look at them like a disease and Catriona's flames as the treatment. If they failed to treat the disease, undoubtably it would resurface in the future. It was best they cut away all that they could.

Connor stepped up beside her, Flinn's old battle axe in his hand. "I can fight, Miss Bridget."

"I know you can," Bridget said as compassionately as possible. "That's why I need you by my side. I need the extra protection, my babies need the extra protection. Will you protect me, Connor?"

The youth nodded his head, looking older than he was in years. "I can do that, Miss Bridget."

"Good." Bridget turned back in the direction of the temple, unable to see the ruins from where they stood. "Because here they come."

Chapter One Hundred Four

Catriona

Catriona barreled down the tunnel, focusing solely on Rion who was fleeing ahead of her. If she could get close enough, she could send her flames in a concentrated wave at him, engulfing him completely before he could escape his confinement. Part of her felt that it was too quick of a death for him. No, she ran him down like the beast he was, he would perish by her blade. He would suffer, just as he had made her. He would feel as many sticks from a blade as she felt teeth rip into her flesh. She would make him scream louder than she had, make him beg like she refused to do. Grace had taken away the very thing Catriona wanted to peel off of him, but there was plenty of flesh left for her to work with. Starting with his fucking hands.

Catriona's flames had cleared out most of the tunnels, charring the stone as they moved their way through the maze. Burnt corpses lay littering the tunnel floor, signaling to Catriona that she had indeed ended what trap they had laid out for them. Now she remained focused, arguably too focused on her fleeing prey. Morrigan was right behind her, the old woman was surprisingly fast.

"They're nearing the end," Morrigan huffed, continuing their pursuit. "Storm tells me we near the temple."

"Who?" Catriona shot back, not taking her eyes off the tunnel before her.

"The bird," Morrigan answered.

"The bird has a name?"

"No, I've been calling it bird for centuries," Morrigan's voice laced with sarcasm.

"Centuries?" Catriona rounded a corner, a dark room coming into focus just ahead. "Another one of your cursed friends?"

"Yes, actually," she replied.

Morrigan's comment was lost as soon as Catriona's boots touched the cobblestone floor. Just as she realized she had entered the bottom of the temple, half a dozen tribesmen stood at the ready facing them with their bows

694

notched and pointed their direction. Catriona caught herself, twisting just enough to seize Morrigan before the old woman made it completely into the room. Arrows flew in their direction, Morrigan threw up one hand and sent

out an energy field, knocking most of the arrows back. But not all of them. One of the arrows found itself lodged in Catriona's shoulder. Before the pain hit, Catriona watched in utter disbelief as Morrigan reached down and grasped the shaft of the arrow, ripping it from her flesh. Then Catriona felt the pain and let out a stream of curses.

"Iron tipped." Morrigan glanced at the arrow, tossing it to the side. "Your magic will be gone for a few minutes. "Hopefully I pulled it out fast enough."

"Fucking awesome," Catriona said through gritted teeth, getting to her feet.

Morrigan stepped forward before the tribesmen could notch another arrow, lightning ripping from her fingertips as each bolt struck a cultist dead. Catriona looked on, impressed as the bodies hit the cold stone floor, their flesh sizzling from the wounds created by the lightning.

"I'm not sure which one of us would win in a fight." Catriona laughed, glancing back to the wound in her shoulder.

"It would be me," Morrigan said assuredly. "Come. Rion still flees. Our friends have engaged in battle above ground."

The two women were on the move again, this time running through the underbelly of the temple of death. Catriona didn't waste time looking around, but what she saw as she ran past was enough. Statues woven together with wicker branches stood twice her height, they were positioned everywhere throughout the temple. Altars covered in bones, ritualistic runes and symbols drawn on the floor and walls with blood, it was disturbing enough that Catriona was thankful to not have time to let her eyes wander. Great evil was present here; she was desperate to get away from it.

Catriona took the steps to ground level two at a time, desperate to gain ground on her fleeing prey. The walls of the temple were collapsed around her, as was its roof. Where she expected to find more of the enemy waiting for her, she saw a battle being waged. Collie warriors sporting their double axe banner and green tunics were engaging with the tribesmen, the blue banner of Airgid lay askew in the mud as its knights in blue and silver armor went toe to toe with wolves that measured up to their chest. A large grey and white wolf, larger than even Bridget or Liam bounded through the bodies, taking controlled swipes of its claws at Collie and Airgid warriors as it passed by. This must be the third brother, the third cultist king, Ammon.

"Watch out!" Morrigan grabbed Catriona by her injured shoulder, dragging her to the ground just as a spear sailed through the air where Catriona had been standing.

"Thanks." Catriona moved into a crouching position, glancing around at the chaos.

There! She could see a mountain lion moving through the battlefield, trying desperately to avoid engaging in any fighting. Catriona started off after him, slower now that her magic wasn't fueling her speed. Morrigan was on her heels as they pushed through the warriors, avoiding blades and arrows from every angle. They pursued Rion for ten minutes as they ducked and weaved, the mountain lion moved closer to the edge of the peninsula rather than trying to escape back into the continent. The battle was thinning, that was how far they had made it before the mountain lion began to slow. Finally, Rion had stopped running, turning to face Catriona and Morrigan who had skidded to a halt, not more than fifteen feet stood between them.

Rion shifted back into his form as a man; a cocky smile splayed across his pale and sickly-looking lips. "We meet again."

"Have we met?" Catriona shrugged. "Couldn't tell."

Rion snorted, turning his attention to Morrigan. "He's been waiting for you."

As if on cue, a monstrous black bear stalked out of the woods towards them. Shifting mid step, Oisin and his darkly painted body emerged from the fur, his sharpened teeth and red eyes the only bright thing about him. Morrigan trained the tip of her spear on him, following precisely with every movement.

"We meet once again," the multi-layered voice poured from Oisin, sending chills down Catriona's spine.

"I see you have finally taken over his corpse," Morrigan said cooly as she lowered herself in a defensive stance. "Do the brothers know yet or are they still convinced Oisin is in there somewhere?"

"Know what?" Rion asked, glancing at his brother. "Oisin?"

A sickening laugh came from the mouth of the Dark One, his sharpened fangs shining in the sunlight. "We have been doing this dance a long time Morrigan, are you not sick of it yet?"

"Sick of it enough to kill you and be done already," she snarled.

"We both know we will never be rid of each other; we are fated to remain on the same reincarnation cycle." Oisin paced around them in a half circle. "Just join me, together let us break the cycle. Let us fight against the very gods that have chosen to torture us for centuries."

"I shall pass." Morrigan waited for the Dark One to step within range, before tossing a glass orb at his feet.

Oisin hissed as dust rose up from shattered glass, enveloping both the Dark One and Rion. As the two reeled back from the cloud, they coughed hard enough it appeared they could no longer breathe. That is when Morrigan chose to strike. With a battle cry the sorceress launched herself forward, striking straight and true with her spear directly at the Dark One's chest. He darted off to the side, the tip of her spear grazing his ribs, drawing a dark and unnatural looking blood. The Dark One did not pull any weapons, instead he chose to engage with Morrigan with just his hands. Dodging and ducking her many strikes, the woman pelted him relentlessly with attacks.

Catriona glanced at Rion, shooting her hand out to send flames his direction. She felt nothing, no traces of her magic that she could reach. She felt as if her magic was trapped under the surface of a lake, waiting to burst forth at any moment. Catriona unsheathed her two short swords, not terribly unhappy that this was her current and only option. Rion's eyes widened as he watched her approach, he took a step back and his whole body visibly clenched. He froze then, looking down at his legs, his eyes widening in shock.

"Silver dust from our forge," Catriona said, positively overjoyed. "Courtesy of our queen, who's smarter than you and your brothers combined."

Rion glared at her then, realizing the loss of his shift. "Clever."

"She wanted to pay you back for the silver cuffs." Catriona took a fighting stance. "Now it's my turn to pay you back."

"You can try." Rion glanced behind her; a smile slowly spread across his face. "My friends would disagree."

Catriona glanced behind her, the sun disappearing behind a thick fog bank that seemed to be coming from the ruined temple. The sounds of screams mixed with the unnatural clicks and screeches of scourge began to echo in the distance. Rion bolted for the fog bank; Catriona was quick on his heels. It took a matter of seconds for the fog to reach them; Rion disappeared into it. Catriona froze, anxious to follow him. Scourge had joined the battle;

she could hear it in the fog. The fog bank now feet from her and closing in fast, she could make out the sounds of at least a dozen of those demonic creatures. She tested her fire again, nothing. Fuck!

She heard Morrigan shout, glancing back at the one-on-one battle behind her. Morrigan was attempting to engage the Dark One in close combat, but he kept producing stolen magic to keep her at a distance. Morrigan dodged ice shards as she continued to advance, jumping over a deep fissure that opened up in the ground before her. Catriona swore, as much as she wanted to chase after Rion, she knew it would be her guaranteed death, not his. Morrigan had successfully gained enough distance to thrust her spear towards the Dark One yet again, her movement wild and powerful. Lightning crackled around her with each advance; each strike a distraction from her spear.

Catriona was impressed by the sorceress's form and was starting to believe that in a fight between the two, Morrigan would win, not herself. But the older woman made a mistake, her front foot got too close to the Dark One as she thrust forward with her next strike. The Dark One was able to grab Morrigan's spear at the same time he tossed her off to the side. Morrigan went down hard, meeting the rocky ground with a sickening thud. Before Morrigan could recover, the Dark One who had kept control of the spear, turned it on the old woman, thrusting the tip through her ribs, and into her chest.

"NO!" Catriona bellowed.

Rage fueled her on as she closed the distance between herself and her opponent. Oisin looked up at her with a fierce smile as her blades swung. Catriona delivered as many blows as her body could manage without the aid of her magic, pushing him back and away from Morrigan's body. Oisin continued to dodge each strike, eventually grabbing one of her blades, the edge not appearing to do hardly any damage to his flesh, as he dragged her closer to him. With his free hand he grasped her other wrist, locking her into place and preventing her from continuing to attack.

Those beady red eyes locked on hers, as the monster leaned forward to take a long inhale of breath inches from her. "So... Rion has succeeded in his endeavors."

Catriona screamed in frustration, kicking both her feet to his chest, and pushing off of him. Oisin let her go, watching as she fell back and made her distance. Oisin cocked his head as he stared at her, his sharpened teeth forming a sickening smile.

"Go now, girl, leave this battleground." Oisin pointed to Morrigan, who was able to shift to her side. "Let the adults work out their differences."

Catriona opened her mouth to speak but instead charged at him again. Swords flying, she slashed at him, going for his legs. Oisin kicked out at her, his large foot connecting with her chest and knocking her backwards. Catriona fell, glancing up at the monster who was surprisingly not pushing to attack.

"Go!" Oisin shouted at her. "Do not be foolish to think that I will spare you if you keep this up. I do not go easy on you for sentimental reasons, it's out of a morbid curiosity for the future."

What in the fuck was he talking about? Catriona rolled to her feet, grabbing for her fallen swords, she stared at the Dark One, evaluating him. She was outmatched in skill, that was frustratingly obvious. If he hadn't decided not to kill her, she would most likely have been gravely injured by now. No opponent she had come up against had been this quick, this skilled at deflection. She supposed this meant that Oisin was gone, and that this body was fully possessed by the Death God.

"You are not skilled enough to face a god," Morrigan spoke through their bond, her voice sounding weak.

"Worked that out for myself, thanks." Catriona didn't bother glancing in the sorceress's direction. *"You going to make it?"*

"No," the answer was short and to the point, very typical for Morrigan.

Catriona felt a familiar pang of sorrow. Yet again, another friend of hers would die today, maybe even more than one. Catriona was not sure how the others fared against the scourge. Her heart felt heavy, but her rage felt... hot.

"Your magic has returned to you," Morrigan's voice came. *"Use it! Do not let him devour my body, for it would give him access to the power of the gods and would end me."*

"I can't kill you!" Catriona watched as Oisin began to walk towards Morrigan slowly.

"I'm already dead," Morrigan answered. *"We will meet again, Firebird, you will only be granted a break from me."*

"You're a pain in my ass, you know that?" Catriona stabbed her swords into the ground, standing and facing Oisin whose attention turned back to her.

"Do not do this, young one," the Darks One's layered voice warned. "I am giving you an escape, for now. However, my patience grows thin. I do not care what you carry inside you, if you continue to push me, I will destroy you."

"Add your magic to mine," Morrigan called, sitting up to face her, blood streaming from her mouth as she began to drown in her own blood. *"My final act on this plane of existence will be to help destroy him, that is as good a death as any. Do it!"*

"OKAY!" Catriona bellowed, pouring her energy into a controlled blast in Oisin's direction.

Oisin dodged the initial plume by rolling out of the way. Catriona watched as her flame was caught up by the wind, twisting off to the side. She watched in utter disbelief as her fire was absorbed into a windstorm, created by Morrigan, with Oisin trapped in the center. Catriona let loose a hysteric laugh, he could not cross her flames. Morrigan used her magic to trap the Dark One in a funnel. He could not escape as long as they both worked together. Catriona pushed more of her energy into the flames, watching as the windstorm grew in height, doubling the size of its base as the fire fed it. Catriona watched and laughed as the Dark One's fur cloak was whipped around his body, unable to move one direction or the other. She watched as it grew harder for him to stand, the power of the wind and flame knocking him from side to side, making him unstable.

Catriona fed the flames; she poured into it all the rage and sorrow she had in her. She felt lighter every second she fed her flames, allowing them to take everything from her to keep growing. She knew this wasn't what anyone else would want, how her father had told her not to give herself completely over to them. But how could she not after everything, how could she not want to put everything she had into ending this mother fucker once and for all. She could feel the heat of her fire from where she stood, the wind Morrigan commanded whipping her short hair around her face. Catriona watched as the base of the firestorm began to expand, inching closer to Morrigan's slumped over body.

"Morrigan?" Catriona called, her focus now on the fading body of her friend.

"I do not have much left in me. I will pour what I have left into the firestorm. You should do the same. Let the flames go, burn us both," Morrigan's voice was barely audible.

"I hate you." Catriona felt the tears begin to pour down her face. *"Until next time?"*

"You will never be rid of me, I promise." Morrigan almost sounded like she was smiling. *"Keep strong, Firebird. Do not give up. Burn them all back into the abyss."*

Catriona felt a shift in the winds, her eyes returning to the firestorm before her. The base expanded suddenly, but the height collapsed. Catriona felt her friend fade from this world, her last bit of life force used to cocoon the Dark One between their magics. Now! She had to do this now. With a wail of anguish, and a roar of rage, Catriona allowed the last of her restraints to snap. She fed the flames with her very essence, pouring into it every thought, memory, and feeling she'd ever had. The heat of the flames that burned around the Dark One was far greater than what she burned that day at Collie, but she kept the explosion condensed inside the dome of air. She watched with a sickening smile as Oisin collapsed to his knees, suffocating on the flames as they enveloped his body. Catriona watched in satisfaction as his body began to turn to ash before her. After a few moments, the Dark One's body had completely turned to ash, only to be lost in the wind.

Catriona chanced a glance at Morrigan, her body was now gone and disintegrated as well. Sorrow began to creep into Catriona's heart, dampening her flames. Catriona squeezed her eyes shut, fighting back the tears, she needed to stay in control. Morrigan tasked her with finishing this, and she would. She had some choice words for the sorceress in her next reincarnation, maybe even a few good punches to the face for all the woman had put her through, but Catriona was comforted in the knowledge that they would meet again.

Catriona threw her hands out straight to the sides, redirecting her flames back towards the battle now completely engulfed in fog. She was tired of these monsters lurking in the dark, tired of these creatures that called themselves men who preyed on those weaker than them. Catriona was just tired, and it was time to be rid of them all. Catriona sent her flames through the battlefield, letting it seek out all that was dark and evil. Her fire snaked through the skirmishes, engulfing all those with black hearts or no souls. She protected those who had a light, they were not worth consuming after all. They were what was good in the world, some burning brighter than others. Her friends, her loved ones, her family. They needed to survive, what was left of them needed to survive, or this was all for nothing.

Catriona felt the first waves of exhaustion hit as she pushed herself past her limits, it wasn't time to give up yet. Her fire had almost reached the edge of the battlefield. She was almost there, the darkness almost extinguished. She felt her own darkness creeping up on her as she emptied herself into her magic, the pain she had been carrying around with her finally disappearing along with any energy she had remaining. For only a moment, she felt something she never would have dreamed of feeling ever again. It was momentary, flickering in and out of her life like a twinkling star, the brightness of it in stark contrast to her never-ending darkness. Catriona found herself sinking into it now that her task was done, her mission finally fulfilled. Catriona collapsed, falling face first into the dirt, unable to move, hardly able to breathe. A large black raven flew overhead, circling Catriona as it cawed, as if it were searching for something. With a feather light heart, Catriona gave herself over to this one thing, happily embracing it like an old friend, afraid of it leaving her at any moment. Catriona laid there, giving herself over to the most powerful feeling she had ever felt, peace.

Chapter One Hundred Five

Clyous

A dozen or so black crows circled over the battlefield, each bearing four red eyes that scoured the fresh corpses, looking for a meal. Their black wings beating with force as they circled above the dead. Despite the black feathers they almost looked reptilian. The unnatural creatures were familiar to him; he had seen them before in a vision. They must be creatures that belonged to the Death God. Or he was seeing things, he wasn't sure anymore. Too many images flashed through his mind; he had a hard time grounding himself in reality anymore.

Smoke still escaped from the embers, sending a column skyward and signaling to the world that the deed was done. The Dark One was no more, cast back into the dark abyss where he crawled from. Clyous stood at the top of the hill surveying the destruction below. A multitude of bodies lie scattered on the charred land; none having been able to escape his sister's wrath. Her flames had flared out to such a degree it had leveled the forest completely. Small fires still ignited in what remained of the forest beyond, but the epicenter of her destruction spanned at least a hundred feet from her.

Clyous had watched her from this hill, one of Morrigan's last acts before succumbing to the flames, was to warn everyone to stay back. The sorceress needed his sister's flames to finally put an end to the Dark One, and then she sacrificed herself in the process. Most were saying Morrigan's choice was noble, but Clyous knew the impact her death had on his sister. Especially since it was Catriona's flames that ended the messenger of the gods.

Catriona's wail had reverberated through the battlefield as her flames wept across them all. As if the flames had a mind of their own, they sought out and destroyed every single one of their enemies, leaving their allies whole and intact. Clyous had believed them all to be done for as soon as the fog bank allowed the scourge to pour out from the tunnels, but his sister had managed to protect them all. His sister's wail broke his heart, unfortunately it had become a familiar sound over these past months, but her cries seemed to fuel her flames.

After the flames had died, he and the others had ventured into the ash to find Catriona unconscious, at the point of ignition. Catriona had mourned the death of her friend, mourned the losses she has experienced over the last two years, mourned for herself.

Danny was the only one brave enough to step into the ring of embers and embrace her, Bridget bringing her back from the brink of death. It took about an hour or two for Catriona to recover enough to sit up on her own, and for the tears to stop. Once Catriona was calm enough to be moved, Danny had carried her to the top of this hill where they all stood now. A council of burnt out and bloody warriors ready to determine what was to happen next with the rule of Stone Basin, just as his dreams had predicted. Against all odds, they had achieved the unbelievable, somehow his found family had managed to claw their way into the best possible outcome his visions were able to predict. He was hopeful that now he would find some peace, no longer being plagued by the constant shuffling of outcomes.

"The sooner we start, the sooner we can rest," Rama's sage advice brought Clyous back to the present.

"The Dark One is dead. As is Morrigan." Grace spoke with the authority of the heir to Airgid. "I can no longer feel either of their energies."

"That is some comfort," Bridget spoke factually. "Morrigan will return. She'll be born into the next generation as she always is, her loss is only temporary."

"Hopefully," Catriona's voice was shaky. "If my flames were enough to banish the God of Death back into the abyss, maybe it sent her there too."

"Unlikely," Rama said as sympathetically as he could. "Your flames are what created her rebirth cycle to begin with. The Goddess of War herself blessed Morrigan, your ancestor. She will rise from the ashes again. You did not end that stubborn woman, I promise."

Catriona gave him a shaky nod, appearing to accept his logic.

"But once again, Rion and his brother Ammon managed to escape," Menolayous spoke from the shadows.

"The Dark One is dead, he can no longer influence their actions like he used to," Bridget explained.

"They were all monsters before Oisin became the Dark One." Grace ground out. "If they are not brought to justice, they will continue to leave pain and suffering in their wake."

"Agreed," the group spoke in unison

"We need to track them down and end this, once and for all," Menolayous seethed.

"We will, My Love," Grace spoke quietly to him.

"A more pressing matter is the kingdoms," Bridget pointed out. "The monarchies, aside from Airgid, are in a state of ruin. They need to be dealt with before an ill-prepared opportunist tries to take advantage, or we'll wind up having yet another crown to bury."

"From my understanding, Your Majesty, you now own Oich." Rama raised his eyebrows at her playfully. "You're now top dog."

"Technically, but that was never my intention when I killed him," Bridget answered thoughtfully. "As you saw during the assault on Collie, I'm not well received amongst all of the blooded."

"You'll need to put them in their place," Grace spoke up. "Establish your dominance right out of the gate."

"And we'll be there to help you," Rama stated. "It's important we establish quickly. We haven't spent the last few years fighting this rebellion just for fun. Collie warriors will escort you there and remain until you can establish the new hierarchy."

"What about Collie?" Danny asked, finally taking his eyes off Catriona.

"We will rebuild as soon as Bridget and Clyous are established as the new rulers," Rama answered. "Collie will be the new capital of Gaelach."

"And Grace is to inherit Airgid someday soon," Danny spoke up. "A new dawn is rising over Stone Basin, with new rulers at the head of each kingdom. It's what we've been fighting for."

"A more peaceful era." Bridget nodded. "We can make a change, an actual change in our cultures. We can finally end the corruption and brutality towards each other. We can finally live in a safe world."

"You might be getting a little ahead of yourself, wife." Clyous smiled at her politely. "It's going to take years to change the ways of Oich. The blooded are set in their ways, they won't take kindly to their slaves being elevated to equal status. There will be unrest. It won't be an easy overnight transition."

"It's worth doing," Bridget answered.

"That's not what my brother is saying," Catriona spoke finally, her voice slightly shaky. "He's trying to politely tell you that as the queen of blooded who only respect power and dominance, you are going to have to deal with your citizens firmly. You will have to end those who stand against you, quickly and harshly."

Bridget stared at Catriona, pursing her lips as she heard the words. After a moment Bridget sighed, giving a slight nod. "I will do what needs to be done if it liberates those who have been abused for so long."

Catriona looked her sister-in-law up and down, sizing her up. "I hope that's true. You can't show weakness. Especially in your condition. They will rip you to pieces, they will target your baby—"

"Can we not?" Clyous interjected, placing a comforting hand on his wife's lower back. "I don't want to hear it."

"But you need to." Catriona's silvery eyes flicked to her brother's. "You step into that city unprepared, and they will make what they did to me look like a fucking picnic compared to what they are going to do to her. Do not make the mistake of looking at this like an easy and righteous transition. That's how you lose."

"She's right," Bridget said quietly. "There's no point in pretending. We won this war because we fought harder than they did, it would be a mistake to think the fighting is simply over and that peace would be automatic."

"I had more of an issue with her descriptions," Clyous murmured.

"You won't be alone," Rama promised. "You have us as allies. Just because we're separate kingdoms doesn't mean we aren't still friends. Collie will never abandon you."

"Neither will Airgid," Grace promised. "The only way we can truly bring about change is if we continue to work together. No kingdom is perfect, but maybe with each other's support we can get close to it."

Catriona scoffed at their words, earning a few glances from those surrounding her. "What?"

"You're being a bitch," Grace warned her.

"She's being realistic," Danny defended her.

"You're all being idealistic." Catriona shot back. "There's been too much death, too much loss for this happy paradise you all are conjuring up in your minds. The Dark One might be dead, but how long until he tries to

706

come back? How long will it take for you to get the kingdoms the way you want them? In the meantime, it doesn't erase the scars left behind."

"It gives people a chance to heal," Grace countered. "Hopefully, if he decides to try to come back, the people will be in a better position to fight back."

"Will these heal?" Catriona shouted, lifting up the bottom of her tunic to reveal the deep scars that covered her abdomen. "Will time make these disappear? What future does someone like me have?"

Everyone went silent as tears began to run down Catriona's face. Rama averted his eyes, preferring to look at the ground rather than Catriona's beaten and scarred body. Grace bit her lip to keep from speaking while Menolayous looked at her as if he understood. Bridget's faced flushed with shame, not having forgiven herself for their capture. Clyous felt pangs of remorse for his sister, as much as he hated her words he recognized the truth of them. Danny was the only one to stare, his eyes tracing over each and every scar that was shown, rage and sorrow mirrored behind his ocean-blue eyes.

"Pretending that you are the fix-all solution for every single citizen will only create a divide," Menolayous interjected. "There are some that feel the same way Cat does, and your overzealous planning without that as a consideration will only fuel discontent. You will need to acknowledge and weigh the consequences the last decade has had on everyone, how this has permanently affected people. But..." Menolayous cast a glance at Catriona. "Make sure you can create a place where there is a future for those broken souls. They need genuine hope, not ideological promises."

"There's wisdom to your argument," Rama said, glancing between Menolayous and Catriona. "The restructuring process will take a lot of thought and a lot of work, but for now we need to get ourselves into Oich so we can have those hard conversations."

"We should start by taking the capital city," Danny spoke, taking his eyes off Cat. "We can work on the outer villages and farmlands afterwards, but we need to establish a stronghold, that is the best place to do it."

"We have no idea what is waiting for us there," Clyous pointed out. "We don't know how many are left that would oppose Bridget's rule. We don't know how many supporters she has. We would be walking in blind. One wrong move and we could accidentally turn our supporters into the enemy."

"I get that you were raised in the city," Grace started, "but you truly have no idea how the blooded hierarchy works, do you?"

"We won't have to enter the city to find out what we're up against," Bridget explained.

"Why's that?" Rama asked even though Bridget wasn't speaking to him.

"They're going to meet us at the front gate." Bridget shrugged.

"And any challenger will present themselves." Grace nodded. "Which means Bridget has to face them, alone, king-consort. Are you prepared to let your pregnant wife be a queen?"

Chapter One Hundred Six

Grace

"I don't like this," Clyous said as they neared the front gates of the capital city, his eyes fixed on the wolves now lining up outside their walls. "They look ready for a fight."

"Anyone like fried wolf?" Catriona offered, glaring at the city with a hatred that burned hotter than the fire she could wield.

"We don't know that they're here to fight," Bridget argued, dismounting from her horse.

"One can hope," Catriona cut in, earning a disappointed glance from both Bridget and Grace. "What?"

"We don't need you to start a battle if one doesn't need to be had," Bridget lectured. "These are my people."

"Your people have been wicked." Catriona flipped her dagger in her hand. "I hate this fucking city."

"I'm at least happy Cat's with us in case this goes south," Clyous said nervously.

"Aww..." Cat said in a mocking voice. "That's the nicest thing you've said about me in weeks."

"If you want to level the entire city," Rama responded to Clyous's comment, staring at Cat with a worried expression, "it's why we brought my army. Not the destroyer of nations."

"I kind of like the sound of that." Catriona smirked, catching the edge of her blade with her fingertips.

"What are you doing?" Clyous asked as Bridget shed her traveling cloak and began to walk towards the gate.

"Meeting my greeting party," she answered simply. "Stay here."

"I don't think—" Clyous began to argue.

"Don't start undermining her now," Grace snarled at him. "This first impression is everything."

"She's pregnant." Clyous turned at Grace, holding back his rage. "What if something happens—"

"Then I'll be making a bunch of new fur cloaks," Catriona assured her brother, which seemed to do the exact opposite.

"She'll be fine," Grace promised, watching as Bridget shifted, bounding her way towards the wolves. "This is normal for wolves when a new leader comes to take over. She has to assert herself as dominant, or they'll never follow her."

"What if they challenge her," Clyous pleads, his eyes locked on his wife.

"We'll be here," Menolayous assured him.

They all watched as Bridget's wolf approached the ones guarding the gate. As she approached them, a dark grey and white wolf stepped forward from the others, walking slowly and deliberately towards Bridget's auburn one. Everyone tensed as they watched the grey wolf circle the auburn one, sniffing with every step. Bridget's wolf stood there allowing it, but her eyes remained focused on the grey wolf. Bridget's wolf suddenly lurched forward, snapping her fangs at the other wolf as she pushed the other wolf over. To everyone's relief the other wolf rolled onto its back, submitting to Bridget as she held her fangs dangerously close to the grey wolf's throat.

After another minute of growls and vicious snapping, Bridget's wolf removed itself from on top of the other, allowing it to move freely. Instead of getting up the wolf shifted into a woman, who continued to lay there on her back while Bridget shifted back herself. After another moment where the two women seemed to be speaking to one another, Bridget extended a hand to help the other woman up.

"Come on," Grace said, gently kicking her horse into motion. "It's done."

They approached Bridget as a group while she was still speaking with the woman. Rama ordered the warriors to hang back while they advanced forward. Clyous rode up beside Bridget, dismounting to stand beside her, the rest of their group followed suit.

"Hello," the woman greeted them cautiously.

"I'm surprised they let a woman lead the greeting party," Catriona blurted out, eyes narrowing at the other wolves who were shifting into their mortal form, all of them women.

"*They* no longer exist." The woman gave Catriona an interesting look before bowing her head to Bridget. "Most of those who contested your rule went with Prince Liam to attack your rebel city. It allowed the rest of us to take over, overpowering those left who still believed in a male dominated society."

"Where are those traitors now?" Catriona asked, earning glares from the surrounding wolves and a few snarls.

"Catriona is one of my war chiefs," Bridget interjected. "She speaks with the authority I have given her. I suggest you show her the respect she is owed, she may not be blooded but her magic could burn the city down at the drop of her hand."

"This is the white flame?" The woman asked, showing a new appreciation for the blonde woman still riding a horse.

"Wanna find out?" Cat asked through bared teeth, a direct challenge.

"We hold about fifty prisoners in the tower." The woman turned back to Bridget, bowing her head slightly. "A few of them managed to escape as we were subduing the ones we captured. They are long gone by now having fled the city."

"Good." Bridget nodded. "Take me to my throne. I wish to publicly claim it alongside my husband."

The woman looked to Clyous then, eyeing him suspiciously as she sniffed the air. "You have taken an unblooded husband? And you bear his human child?"

Clyous stepped forward so he was standing inches away from the woman, looking down at her. Suddenly, the mark that covered his skull began to glow as his eyes rolled back inside his head, this open display of magic had the woman jump back in fright. The wolves behind her began to whimper as well, earning a maniacal laugh from Catriona.

Clyous's mark faded in the sunlight as his eyes returned to normal. "You will be loyal to my wife, your queen, Humaria. Your future holds much promise, as long as you stay by her side."

"A seer?!" Humaria bowed her head. "Forgive me, I spoke from the old ways."

"To start with," Bridget spoke with an authority that brought everyone's attention to her, "magic is no longer outlawed in my kingdom. Humans and blooded will be considered equals from here on out.

Furthermore, marriages will not be used to strengthen family bloodlines or for political advantages. Marriages are for two equal partners who love each other. No man or woman will be above the other. Is that understood?"

"Yes, My Queen," Humaria answered.

"Take me to my throne," Bridget said again.

Chapter One Hundred Seven

Rama

Rama pulled on the horse's reins, encouraging the great beast to slow as he neared the gates of Collie. Kyra sat on the saddle in front of him, fast asleep from the ride from the capital city of Oich. Rama had made a point to trade lumber for some decent Oich horses while there, finding himself a grey steed that would actually allow his large build ride it. Connor pulled up beside him, glancing up at Rama with a faint smile before his gaze returned to the city gates. They were finally home after a week of remaining in Oich to ensure an easy transition for Bridget to take the throne. If he were being honest, he would have expected that to have been harder.

The citizens of that city seemed happy to accept Bridget as their queen, most of those who disagreed had been involved with the assault on Collie a month prior. What surprised everyone the most was the fact that the women were taking the lead in welcoming their new monarch. News of how Bridget had defeated the former king had spread, apparently influencing the blooded women to stand up to their oppressive husbands and fathers, tired of the patriarchal lifestyle they were forced to live. The human slaves had joined the blooded woman, taking on the males that remained within the city and overthrowing them. When Bridget had said she wanted to restructure Oich's culture, nobody expected that to happen before she even sat on the throne.

Now they were back home, a combination of Collie warriors, children of the ancients, and a few blooded citizens. All with the intent of making Collie the new capital of Gaelach. The guards that stood by the gate announced his arrival, opening the heavy wooden doors for Rama and his people to file inside. They were greeted warmly by the few warriors that had remained in Collie to protect the Gaelach refugees. Rama glanced at Connor beside him, a young man blooming into a warrior in his own right. Flinn had asked Rama to finish raising him, to turn him into a man, something Rama would do without hesitation. Kyra stirred on his lap, stretching in her sleep. A year ago, Rama would never have believed he would become a father overnight, let alone to two children. Well, one child and one teenager. He had a sneaking suspicion that the war was going to feel like nothing compared to raising these two strong-willed little people, but it was a challenge he was happy to take on.

"It feels weird being back here," Connor said as their horses lead the column of warriors through the gates.

"Is it weird because of Flinn?" Rama asked, steering his grey horse towards the stables.

"Yes," Connor admitted. "And not having everyone else here anymore."

"They're not far away," Rama promised. After leaving Bridget and Clyous in Oich, the other four had taken off to begin their hunt for Rion and his brother. "Neither is Flinn. That old war horse is undoubtedly watching us from the underlands, critiquing how we're not utilizing space in how we continue to build Collie."

Connor laughed at that. "Will we be able to keep building?"

"I promised Flinn to take care of you and Collie, seems only fitting that both of you keep growing, doesn't it?" Rama laughed. "Besides, we'll need to make a place suitable for Kyra to grow up in, won't we?"

Connor glanced at the sleeping child with a smile. "A child deserves the best."

"Good man." Rama nodded his approval. "I have a feeling your new sister is going to give us both a run for our money."

"Sister?" Connor smiled as he played with the word. "I think I would like being an older brother."

"I'm happy to hear that." Rama glanced at the young man, then back down at Kyra. "Because I'm going to need as many allies as possible once she gets older."

Connor laughed loudly as they approached the stables. Rama handed his reigns over to the stable master, balancing a sleeping Kyra in one arm as he dismounted. Connor dismounted as well, standing beside him. Rama looked out at the citizens of Collie, eagerly greeting the returning warriors. This place had been made a city by the kindest and most imaginative man he had ever known. A man that had been like a father to him, like he was to so many others. Flinn had requested with his dying breath that Rama continue his legacy, a promise Rama had every intention of keeping. This city started out as a few hidden huts in the forest. This city would now become the capital of Gaelach with Rama leading its people into a safer and more productive era.

No more would its people have to hide in caves and tunnels to avoid capture, no longer would they be starving and treated as slaves. Rama and Bridget were both determined to have their kingdoms work together, Grace was paving the way for Airgid to join the alliance. Stone Basin would know peace for the first time in over a century; Rama would make sure of it.

Chapter One Hundred Eight

Menolayous

Menolayous watched everyone as they sat around the fire, a pot of rabbit stew was boiling over the open flames. Danny was in charge of stirring while Grace chopped up some herbs to add to it, claiming that Danny's recipe had no flavor. The two of them had been arguing for over an hour now about what constituted a soup versus a stew. Not that any of it was relevant to their situation. They had what they had; there wasn't much room for alterations. For what it was worth, Menolayous was enjoying watching two of the most stubborn people in his life go back and forth over something so trivial. After the last year each of them had had, it was oddly comforting that their biggest complaint at the moment was the thickness of their meal.

"Whatever," Grace huffed, dumping the remaining herbs in her small bowl into the pot. "It's done. We can move on from arguing about our food to deciding our next move."

"Fine with me, Princess," Danny snapped, still stirring the contents of their cooking pot. "Map's in my bag. Unless that's too much of an effort for your royalness."

"You're annoyingly stupid." Grace rolled her eyes, but rifled through Danny's bag, nonetheless. "Here we go."

Grace laid the map out so all four of them could see it in the light of the fire. Menolayous scooted closer for a better look, noting that Catriona remained seated where she was, only glancing in the direction of the parchment. She had been eerily quiet most of the night, fiddling with the iron bracelets around her wrists. Menolayous did not expect Catriona to engage with them as she had in the past, he still expected her to be distant, but the last few weeks had taken their toll on her, no… this last year. She had lost both of her parents, her older brother, and many close friends. Her flames had been the cause of Morrigan's death, although the sorceress had demanded it from her, it was not an easy thing for Cat to do. Not to mention the torture she had personally endured. Even now, in the firelight, Menolayous could see the scars covering the skin of her arms, he knew more existed hidden beneath what showed.

"We are just north of the Temple of the Death God, along these cliffs here." Danny pointed at the map with the dry end of the spoon. "My best guess is the idiots disappeared into the tunnel system here."

"Where does the tunnel exit out at?" Grace asked, studying the map where Danny pointed.

"That's the problem." Danny shrugged. "We don't know."

"The tunnel systems in Gaelach are part of a larger network, you never know where one will lead you to. Some of them are manmade, where humans hid trying to escape the persecution of the cultists. Others conceal hives of scourge, collecting dozens of them in one place. There is no existing map of the tunnels and cave systems, it would be dangerous chasing them farther into them, when they are more familiar than we are."

"So… what's the plan?" Grace asked, looking up into Menolayous's eyes.

"Try to figure out where they are headed when they come out again," Menolayous suggested. "We can talk to some of the tribes as we pass through, see if they've caught wind of the two fleeing brothers."

"That's about all we can do." Danny grunted as he pulled the pot off the fire. "Soup's done. Best eat up."

Grace began to spoon the pot's contents into everyone's bowls, passing them all out to everyone present. Danny rifled through his bag once again, grabbing what was left of their bread. Menolayous leaned forward with Catriona's bowl outstretched in his hand. Catriona looked at it, then at him, her eyes calculating his stare. She reluctantly leaned forward and took it, resting it in her lap. The other two were too busy digging into their food to pay her much attention, but Menolayous noted how she was not immediately eating her food. After a moment of realizing he was watching her, Catriona reluctantly spooned a mouthful of soup into her mouth.

"I think we should continue north along these cliffs," Danny said in between bites. "Until we hit Airgid's border. Then we should keep to the border and head east."

"I agree," Grace said, helping herself to seconds. "Airgid's borders are well guarded, if they enter my kingdom, they will be captured. Our blooded patrol the borders, they are well trained in tracking. They won't make it far."

"It's more likely they'll remain in Gaelach, somewhere they are familiar with but not somewhere easy for outsiders to get through."

Menolayous emptied his bowl for the second time, his stomach finally satisfied. "They will travel within the tunnel systems as far as they can, only coming out to hunt or if they need to find another tunnel nearby."

"So, we just need to keep our eyes and ears open as we make our way east." Danny nodded, scraping out what was left at the bottom of the pot and dishing it into his bowl. "As long as they're not hiding in a cave nearby."

"I can sense them," Grace countered. "If we get close enough to them, I'll be able to tell."

"Good, at least you're useful for something other than being a pain in the ass," Danny mocked.

"Fuck off." Grace extended her hand, showing him a rude hand gesture.

"Oh, I'll get right on that." Danny laughed, making his way over to Catriona. "I'm turning in for the night."

"Okay," she said, glancing up at him, allowing him to gently kiss her on the lips, it was about as much physical contact she would allow. "Love you."

Danny gave her a half smile, knowing that meant she would once again be sleeping at the opposite end of camp from everyone else instead of by his side. "Love you too. Good night."

"Night, ass face," Grace shot at him as she too curled up in her bedroll. "Night, Cat."

"Good night," Catriona said, her position on the rock remained unchanged as she stared into the fire.

Normally they would be sleeping in shifts, picking who went in what order to better protect each other as they slept in enemy territory. But Catriona barely slept anymore, so picking an order was almost redundant. Catriona would wake someone when she was finally able to go to sleep, but that was usually an hour or two before sunrise. Someone was usually stirring by then, making her choice an easy one. This pattern had been going on since they had taken to their hunting mission, the poor woman was only getting about four hours of sleep a night. Menolayous understood why yet again, exhaustion was better than the nightmares that visited her at night.

Menolayous lay his head down on a rolled-up blanket, Grace curling up next to him. It wasn't long before he could hear the change in her breathing, signaling that his wife had finally fallen asleep. Danny was softly snoring not that far away. Rabbit soup and a full belly had a way of putting these two out quickly. After a few minutes Menolayous began to shut his eyes, allowing the thick blanket of sleep to slowly cover him. Until he heard twigs breaking, and the fluttering of wings.

Menolayous resisted the urge to sit up quickly, knowing that if this was an attack Catriona would have alerted them by now. He counted to ten before turning his head in the direction of the sound, opening his eyes he saw Catriona disappearing around the rocky formation they were camping behind. A large black raven sat perched on a branch just above where Catriona had disappeared. The creature was staring at Menolayous as if expecting him to do something. Gently, so not to wake the others, Menolayous slid out from his bedroll, following her trail quietly. Curiosity was what spurred him on, where she would be going in the dead of night was beyond him. She had been acting distant all day, withdrawn from them. Now she was sneaking off to gods knew where.

Catriona was out of sight, but Menolayous could still hear her quiet foot falls as she continued on her path. The distant roar of the ocean grew louder with each step, telling him Catriona was headed to the cliff. Worry began to blossom, those cliffs were a mile or so high above the ocean. In this darkness he would be worried about anyone accidentally stepping wrong and tumbling down. He could see better than most out in the dark, maybe Catriona could too? He's never asked.

After a few more minutes of following as silently as he could, he no longer had to be silent. The noise from the crashing waves down below did well to mask even Catriona's footsteps. Menolayous sped up, worried he might lose her. Finally, he cleared the tree line. Before him the trees opened up into the perfect picture, the ocean spanning beyond what the naked eye could see was before him. Menolayous glanced to either side, trying to catch sight of his friend. There were rocks to his right, large enough to conceal her easily enough if she knew he was following. The large raven had been following him apparently, it began to circle above a rock formation, cawing at him as if to tell him to look this way. His eyes caught a glimpse of metal shining in the moonlight. As he approached it he identified Catriona's two short swords propped up against the edge of the rocks, next to them were her iron bracelets.

Panic struck him like lightning then as he rounded the corner, desperate to find her. He stopped as soon as his eyes locked onto her. Catriona stood at the edge of the cliff facing out into the sea beyond. Menolayous was able to see that she was so close to the edge the toes of her boots touched the last piece of rock before the sharp decent down.

"What are you doing?" Menolayous asked gently, calculating the distance to her, trying to determine if he would be fast enough to try and grab her if needed.

Catriona turned to look at him, he could see tears streaming down her face, shining in the moonlight. Reality finally set in, not that he was particularly surprised. Catriona was here for one purpose and one purpose only; she had every intention of throwing herself off of the cliff and into the sea below. Menolayous glanced down at the edge of the cliff quickly, unable to see the bottom in the dark. That fall would be a guaranteed way to end her life and end it quickly.

"You know what I'm doing here," she answered softly, breathing through the tears. "Go away, Menolayous."

"That's not going to happen," he said, taking a single step forward, his hands raised in a way to show her that was all he was doing.

"I think we both know that you can try to tell me it's going to get better all you want, it's not going to stop me." She looked at him, with a pained expression he had never seen before.

All the hope and fire he had come to know and see within her was now extinguished. Even in her days when she lived in shock, where she barely ate, where she felt helpless, there was something to her then. Now, all he could see was pain and darkness. She had been battling against it this entire year, one thing after another, she had been able to beat that darkness back. But the woman standing before him, toeing the edge of a cliff, she had lost that battle completely.

"I'm not going to lie to you and pretend that there is a way to fix everything, because there's not," Menolayous admitted. "But I am living proof that it gets better. It never disappears completely, it's something that you'll have to live with for the rest of your life, but you don't have to let everything that has happened to you define who you are."

"Living is letting it define me." Catriona laughed, a disturbing sound considering what was happening. "Every single day for the rest of my life I'm always going to be that girl who was raped, who was tortured and ripped to pieces by my enemy. You can't look at me and not see that. I'm scarred, from head to fucking toe. Theres not an inch of me that doesn't bear a reminder of what happened to me. So don't you fucking tell me I'm letting it define me. That right was taken away from me, like my family and everything else good in my life."

"Not everything was taken from you," Menolayous countered, sliding another inch forward when she glanced back out to the ocean. "You still have us; you still have Danny. We all love you, would do anything for you."

"I am nobody's priority," Catriona cried. "You all have your lives to keep living, your duties to fulfill. I don't fit into any of it."

"That's a bullshit 'feel sorry for me' excuse if I've ever heard one," Menolayous snapped at her. "You fit into all of our lives, you are important to all of us regardless of our duties and roles. What about Danny, huh? He chose to remain without duty, without any titles so he could be with you. He made you his priority."

"For how long? How long can a man want to stand beside me when I can't even let him touch me?!" Catriona shouted, an inkling of her flame had returned to her eyes.

"That takes time," Menolayous pleaded. "That's not all Danny cares about and you know it. He won't leave you, even after years—"

"Maybe he should." She stared at Menolayous's feet as he attempted another step, halting him mid-motion. "He deserves better than me."

"I think you should let him decide what he deserves," Menolayous continued to argue, not the usual tactic he would pick in a situation like this, but he needed her to fight.

"And what do I deserve, Menolayous?" Catriona asked angrily. "I deserve to stop feeling all of this pain. I deserve to be able to sleep without reliving my worst memories. I deserve to wake up and not be in pain every waking moment of my existence."

"You do deserve that. I want that for you more than anything," Menolayous pleaded. "After we kill Rion, things will change again with how you feel. Knowing he's dead will bring you a small sense of peace."

"We're never going to find him!" Catriona shouted at him. "You, yourself, explained how complicated the tunnel systems are. The likelihood of me finding him is as likely as me getting over all of this."

"You don't know that for sure," Menolayous snapped, returning to communicating in a more aggressive manor, since she seemed to respond to that better. "You don't know what the future holds for you."

That did it, his words broke something within her. Catriona began to outright sob, her hands wrapping around her stomach as she dropped to her knees. Menolayous was able to breathe when he realized she wasn't launching herself over the edge, but her posture, her reaction to his words, her behavior the last few weeks suddenly started to replay in his mind. There was a correlation between everything.

"I know what my future holds," she sobbed, refusing to look at him. "Whether I throw myself off this cliff or not, I'm condemning more than just myself to this darkness."

"Fuck," Menolayous swore, realization finally taking hold of him as he watched her continue to hold her stomach. "You're pregnant."

Catriona didn't answer him; she didn't need to. Her sobs became more audible as she stared out to sea, fully allowing her grief to wash over her. It all made sense now. A comment Grace had made back in Collie, how Catriona was refusing all food and water while still in shock, including an anti-conception tea. How she had been picky with her food, sick at times. Everyone had just associated it with how she dealt with trauma.

"There's no way it could be Danny's," she sobbed. "How could he want to be around a child that's not his? How can a child with the parents that it has, grow up to be good and decent?"

"Rion isn't going to raise the child," Menolayous stammered, the shock of the direction this conversation had turned was tying his tongue.

"It's father is evil," Catriona shot at him. "And its mother has lost her mind. The child has no chance to live even a remotely normal life."

Menolayous continued to stare at the woman before him, tears streaming down her face as she knelt inches away from the cliff's edge. His mind struggling to catch up on what exactly was happening, trying desperately to look at it from every angle to see what he could use to stop her. He knew deep down this day would come, and that ultimately it would be her decision. But if he could stop it, get her to choose life instead, he would. He felt the wind coming in from the ocean, dark clouds slowly moving to cover up the moon, darkening the night even more. A child added into this chaos changed things; it wasn't just Catriona's life he was trying to save. She had valid points, how could a child from Rion's twisted bloodline line come into the world and expect to live a normal life? Catriona *was* broken, wounded in the head, hopefully with time she would heal, but what effect did that have on a child in the womb?

"You are talking about making a permanent decision that you can't come back from." Menolayous flinched as lightning and thunder cracked across the sky. "Not just for yourself, you're making a decision for Danny, not even giving him the respect to choose for himself. You're making a decision for that child before it's even been given the chance to take its first breath. You're making decisions for all of us, expecting us to be okay with living in a world without you! You do realize that don't you? That you are taking away everyone else's choice in the matter, and how much that will kill each and every one of us. How selfish that decision is?"

"Selfish?! You want to talk about selfish!?" Catriona seethed, her short hair whipping around in the wind as she shouted above the cracks of thunder. "It's selfish for all of you to expect me to just deal with this, to be okay with everything that has happened to me."

"I do expect that from you, Cat!" Menolayous shouted back. "You're a fighter! You've always been a fighter. You throwing yourself over this cliff is letting them win! Letting the darkness win! You have never been one to bow down to a challenge, this is you giving up!"

"Fuck you!" she screamed over more thunder.

"You don't know what the future holds. Please Cat, don't do this," Menolayous pleaded with her. "Please! I don't want to watch you fall to your death. I don't want to lose you. You're the sister I never expected to have, especially after losing mine. I love you, please don't do this."

Catriona shut her mouth then; tears once again began to stream down her face. She seemed lost for words at Menolayous's confession. He meant every word. He loved her like a sister; they had grown so close over this last year. They were the only two in their found family who really truly understood each other's darkness. Losing her after everything they had all been through would destroy him inside. It would destroy all of them.

The wind seemed to increase its intensity as he stood there, his clothes being whipped around his body violently. Lightning continued to flash across the sky, lighting up Catriona's features with every strike above the ocean. This storm was so sudden, so abnormal for this time of year, it felt magical in nature. A familiar pang thundered in his chest at remembering Morrigan. This felt like she could be reaching out from the underlands, screaming her opinion on the matter the only way she knew how.

"Morrigan did not sacrifice herself for you to do this, nor your father," Menolayous said loudly over the thunder.

Catriona looked into his eyes then; he could see the darkness beginning to fade. She was hearing him, thank the gods. Her eyes suddenly shifted to behind him, she jumped to her feet then, backing away from the edge. Menolayous launched forward, grabbing hold of her and turning to see what was behind him. With Catriona now trapped in his arms, surprisingly not struggling against him, he saw a very large black horse walking up to them, its eyes fixed on Catriona.

"This fucking thing again!" Catriona swore, her eyes still wet but fixed on the horse.

"You know this horse?" Menolayous asked, refusing to loosen his grip around her in case she had a sudden change of mind.

Lightning flashed once more, revealing something Menolayous never thought he would see in his lifetime. With a flash of lightning, the horse shifted into a ferocious looking woman. Clad in ancient looking armor and carrying with her an ornate spear, the woman looked upon Catriona curiously. She was covered head to toe with her mark, tattoos illuminated magic with a mix of silver and gold, the intricate designs spiraling up her arms and down her legs. Her hair was long and tied back in uniquely styled braids, a style Menolayous knew to be that of a seasoned warrior. It was white, just like Catriona's but not white from age. The feature that stood out the most was her eyes, they were a molten silver, like Catriona's were when she was channeling her magic.

"Rama said the old stories spoke of this horse, that it was a messenger from the Goddess of War and Fate," Catriona whispered, her eyes transfixed on the woman. "I see it everywhere."

"That looks more like the Goddess than a horse," Menolayous whispered back.

The woman's eyes flicked to Menolayous, silencing him. Catriona pulled against Menolayous suddenly, but he refused to release her. He wasn't convinced she wasn't going to hurl herself over just yet, despite the sudden appearance of this goddess standing before them. The woman's eyes returned to Catriona who stopped struggling as soon as those silvery eyes landed on her. The goddess took a step forward; her eyes locked onto Catriona. The woman extended a hand slowly, a silvery glow emanating from her fingertips like small flames from a candle. The goddess's hand hovered over Catriona's stomach for a moment, before moving up to her forehead. Menolayous remained frozen, observing what was happening. After a moment, the goddess lowered her hand once again. Her eyes turned to Menolayous for a moment, giving him the slightest of nods. She stepped back from them and in the next flash of lightning, she was gone. Catriona and Menolayous stood there staring at the empty spot where the goddess had been standing, no evidence that what they had seen had been real. What the fuck had just happened?

"You can let go of me now," Catriona spoke up after several minutes. "I'm not going to jump."

Menolayous reluctantly released her, watching her as she pulled away. Catriona stumbled forward, righting herself before glancing back out over the ocean. The dark clouds had disappeared, the moon reemerging, no signs of thunder or lightning remained. Catriona and Menolayous shared a mutual look of utter disbelief.

"Are you okay?" Menolayous asked cautiously. "What did she do?"

"She made it hurt less." Catriona wiped her face of spent tears, staring at him, her eyes no longer held darkness within. "She told me I wasn't fated to die today, that the child's future wasn't doomed because of me or his father."

"Him?" Menolayous asked.

She nodded, her shoulders slumping in defeat. "I'm tired."

Menolayous nodded, grabbing her outstretched arm and slowly guiding her back in the direction of camp. Even yesterday this much physical contact with Catriona would have been too much for her to handle, but now he could feel her leaning into him like her strength had been drained. Whatever the goddess had done to her, it seemed to exhaust Cat past the point of reason. Menolayous was nearly carrying her by the time they made it back, their fire just embers at this point. He helped Catriona lower herself onto her bedroll, falling asleep as soon as her head hit the blanket.

Menolayous stood, staring at her for a moment. He took a moment to process everything, and it was a lot. He came to the conclusion he wouldn't find any answers tonight, but he for sure wasn't going to go to sleep. So, he made his way back over to where Grace slept, sitting up on his bedroll as he continued to watch over Catriona from where she slept.

"Want to tell me what that was all about?" Grace spoke through their mental connection, looking at her, you wouldn't be able to tell she was awake.

"I don't think I even understand what just happened myself," he responded honestly. *"But it's not my story to tell."*

There was a moment of silence before Grace's voice echoed through his mind once again, *"Whatever it was, that's probably the first time I've been able to sense her sleeping so deeply in months."*

"I think it's safe to say we're not leaving at dawn." Menolayous sighed. *"We should let her sleep as long as she needs. She's got weeks to make up for."*

"Good, means I can sleep in too," Grace answered softly. *"Whatever you did, I hope it helps her."*

Menolayous thought for a moment, reaching his hand out to gently stroke Grace's hair. *"I think she'll be okay, eventually. For now, I'll settle for her sleeping. I'm curious to see what her future holds."*

"Aren't we all?" Grace scooted back to where her shoulders were touching his leg. *"I love you."*

"I love you too, get some sleep," Menolayous said, continuing to stroke Grace's hair.

Menolayous continued to study everyone around him. Based on the change of Grace's breathing, she had fallen back asleep. Danny seemed to not have woken at all, the lucky bastard. Catriona lay sound asleep on the other side of camp, looking more at peace than she had in months. Whatever the goddess did was at least helping with that. Hopefully Cat would catch up on much needed sleep and not be plagued by her memories for once. Menolayous was hopeful, more hopeful for her than he should be considering he has just watched her contemplate jumping off a cliff. If what Catriona had said was true, and everything was hurting less, maybe the goddess had given her the only gift Catriona needed, peace enough to allow herself to heal. Time would tell. Catriona would always have to beat back the darkness, a dance he was all too familiar with.

For the first time in weeks Menolayous was hopeful. Hopeful for her future, hopeful that all of his found family stood a chance of staying together, not to be torn apart by yet another tragedy. His brothers and sisters, and his wife, taking over the hierarchies around Stone Basin would change everything. A new era would rise with the sun this morning, the people he cared about stood a chance. Not just for survival, but to actually live their lives the way they wanted to. They would change the laws and culture of Stone Basin, they would stop all the hurt and the pain the people inflicted on each other. For the first time in decades, there was hope that the world would become a better and safer place for everyone. With Catriona and Bridget both pregnant, there was even hope that a new generation would grow up in a safer world, and that was worth all the pain and suffering, it was a reason to keep fighting. Menolayous smiled to himself, glancing down at the peaceful figure of his wife fast asleep beside him. The snapping of branches again caught his attention, the raven had returned, taking its position in the branches above as if prepared to take over sentry duty. Menolayous smiled, this must be Morrigan's bird. Her very presence tonight only proved to him that the gods were on their side. Tomorrow would be a new day, a new era, one he was thankful to have the opportunity to help defend.

Fin

Airgid: Kingdom of a New Dawn

About The Author

Brittany was born and raised in rural Northern California. She spent a good portion of her childhood wandering the outdoors with a backdrop of redwood trees and rocky coastal beaches. She began reading and writing at a young age, picturing herself amongst fantastical creatures. As an adult, Brittany has spent nearly a decade in law enforcement. Having witnessed and survived the trauma that a career of that nature comes with as well as a childhood full of adversities, she finds herself familiar with empowering and advocating for others who have survived traumatic experiences. Over the years, she has forged bonds with her found family, loving husband, and fellow first responders. She has discovered that having a good safety net is often the most important factor to keep someone from sinking into mental health crises. Brittany's heart is that of a fantasy writer, but her villains are often portrayals of true evil. And evil preys upon humanity in fiction and nonfiction. Her hope is that her readers never forget the importance of a good support system when dealing with any level of trauma. She writes for the survivors, wanting them to know that they are never alone and that they should never stop fighting.

www.ingramcontent.com/pod-product-compliance
Lightning Source LLC
Chambersburg PA
CBHW050837030726
47503CB00007BA/2202